I0651976

The Crimson Z

A Paranormal Anthology

Robert Cloud
Lee Rush
Richard Savage
Abby Blythe
Kara Elsberry

ISBN 0-9774682-8-3

Published 2006 Republished 2015

Published by Black Velvet Seductions Publishing

Published 2015
Printed by Black Velvet Seductions Publishing
A division of Savage Publications

Visit us at:
www.blackvelvetseductions.com

The Crimson Z
The Harbinger
Robert Cloud

Standing atop of a ladder that was perched precariously against the outside awning of the old, brick building Zachariah's hands struggled with the last knot of the banner that proudly announced that the Grand Opening of *The Crimson Z* would be on October 31st. The arthritis in his gnarled and tired knuckles made it the most difficult knot to tie. His hands already ached from the work they had done in getting ready for the opening of the new location of his jewelry shop.

It had been a tradition for generations that whenever the shop moved that the new opening would occur on Halloween. He did not intend to change that tradition even if his tired aching bones were screaming from exertion they were not used to. At his age he should be home enjoying his retirement years but the life and craft of a jeweler was all he knew and was all he had. He knew if he stopped working he would waste away to nothing.

Halloween was still a week away and if he was going to be ready to open the doors on that day there was still a lot for his old body to accomplish in those seven days. He would be done in time but only barely. How he wished for the days when his body was younger and did not hurt all the time. Hell, he was so old that even he did not know his age. At his last visit to the doctor's office the doctor had said he was in great health for a man approaching a hundred. Was he a hundred years old? It seemed like he was much older than that. He could remember things that would be impossible for him to remember if he were only one hundred, but maybe they were the memories of his own father or grandfather that had crawled into his mind and took residence as if they were his own.

He looked down the rungs of the ladder. His knees trembled as he began to lift his foot to step down. He tightened his grip upon the rung for he was not certain that the aching joints in his knees would allow him to climb down again. With pain flaring in his arthritic hands he held tight as he raised his foot to take that first step. Just then a sudden shadow loomed down and passed over him. It was larger than a bus yet looked like a giant bird. He wiped his eyes with the back of his hand, they had to have played tricks on him for its neck had extended forward of its body much farther than any bird he had ever seen and its tail looked more like the tail of a serpent but the tail ended in a barbed spike. Its wings were so wide that the tips were hidden by the shadows of the buildings upon each side of the street.

He watched as it disappeared and then closed his eyes thinking it had to have been his imagination. When he opened them he saw the shadow returning toward him and as it passed over him the wings of the shadow came together as if to lift the great beast into the sky. A sudden downdraft of wind hit the old man hard and he had to fight to keep from being knocked off the ladder. His eyes watched the shadow as it began to get smaller. Quickly the old man turned his head sending a sudden blinding streak of pain into his neck but his gaze caught nothing in the sky that could have made such a shadow. There was but one lone plane and it was too high in the sky and to the wrong side of the sun to have cast any shadow at all. Even if it had been in the right location to cast the shadow it would not have explained the sudden gust of wind.

The old man shook uncontrollably for a moment as his hand rubbed the aching hump at the base of his neck. Slowly he righted himself and tried to think rationally. He was not a child. What did he think he had seen? A dragon?

A memory returned to him of a long time past when he and some of his friends would be taken by such flights of fancy. They would dash off into the fields of their fathers and protect the flocks of sheep from dragons and other monsters. They would wave branches about like swords to ward off the predators of the skies. No dragons, giants or other beasts would lay one hand or claw upon any of the wooly flock of their fathers, but that was when he was a child of seven or eight. He rubbed his temples and then his forehead as he tried to remember, how long ago was that? He could not recall.

Once again he looked down the rungs of the ladder and with his knees still trembling both from his age and from the rush of adrenalin caused by nearly falling he began to descend yet he had only taken two steps down when again he was interrupted. Age had taken many things from him but one thing that it had left him was his hearing. That sense was startlingly acute even for a young man. Not one sound got past the old man's ears. He even knew exactly how many mice had taken up residence in his apartment above the store and he left them little crumbs of food as they were his only friends.

He heard the sound of wheels skating upon the rough concrete of the sidewalk. He looked up to see a young child of maybe seven streaking along upon a pair of those things that he thought he had heard a young man call roller blades. The skater was pretty good for someone so young. The long hair streaming from beneath the child's helmet led him to believe the skater was a girl but he had been fooled more than once, yet the grace of the skater reinforced his conviction that the child was indeed a girl.

In this small village of Hudson Falls there were not many people on the sidewalk at this time of day and the skater skirted around the few that were there like it was more a dance for her than a mode of transportation. The old man's eyes grew wide as he saw the door of the Rexall Drug Store open. The skater was too busy skating around the cluster of people standing in front of the used furniture store and did not see the glass door. It was directly in her path and the old man started to call out to warn her but his aged lungs could no longer hold the breath of his more robust years and his voice did not carry loud enough for her to hear. At the last moment the skater made a sudden and quick move to dart around the door. The skates screamed as they flew out from under her and the girl's face slammed into the open door as her knees and hands scraped against the rough concrete like cheese on a grater.

He continued to descend the ladder carefully. He wanted to rush faster so he could aid the little girl but he worried if he tried to move too fast that it would be himself in need of an ambulance therefore he went slowly. Still his eyes never left the girl or the door.

He watched as the person whose arm had been holding the door when the child had hit it darted out and knelt beside the crying child. The young lady, who could not yet be out of her teens, set her packages down and began rummaging through her purse. She pulled out a handkerchief and what looked like a wet wipe of some kind. By the time he was again standing on firm ground he could see that the young lady had the situation well under control. The young woman helped the girl to her feet and wiped the last of the tears away with another of her wet wipes and then the girl began to skate away. As she neared the only scratches his eyes caught upon her were a couple of small ones upon her lower shins. They were nothing that would mar what turned out to be a lovely little girl. He smiled at her as she neared but she did not see him instead she turned and waved to the young woman that had helped her and then darted past him with the grace of a dancer. He had been nothing in her life but an insignificant obstacle upon her journey.

The resiliency of the young had always amazed him. She had rebounded so quickly it was as if nothing had happened and he could hear the chiming of her laughter as she rounded the corner just beyond him.

His ancient bones creaked and complained as he turned back to look at the young lady who had caused the accident. Of the two she was the one that seemed to have had the worst of it though he could see no sign of any physical injury.

It amazed him that even from a distance of nearly half a block he could make out the wet trails that the tears had left on her cheeks. Her green eyes glistened with more tears that were readying to fall as she paused and placed her face into her hands and wept in silence. He queried himself, how was it possible to see the color of her eyes from that distance, hell he could even read the small lettering on the packages that lay on the ground at her feet. Surely someone his age should be almost blind. Instead he could see things he should only be able to see if he were looking through binoculars or a telescope.

The young woman knelt to pick up her two small bags. While she gathered her items she stopped and continued to cry a moment longer, holding her handkerchief to her eyes to hide the tears. Two older boys walked by her one pushed at the other laughing and nearly knocking his buddy into her, yet neither of them seemed to even notice she was there. He grumbled under his breath at the disrespect that young people of this era had. In his day a gentleman helped a lady in distress even if only for a moment or two. He just could not fathom the indifference of young men. It was not even a matter of being a gentleman anymore but just common courtesy, and it definitely was not that the young lady was unattractive. She did not dress to show off the beauty that lay within her but he could feel the stirrings within him that made him wish he was young again.

Slowly she stood and began walking in his direction, her right hand darting up and trying to wipe the tears away from her eyes. As she neared him he was struck at how much she reminded him of someone but he could not place who. Yet his heart began to pick up its pace and suddenly shyness overcame him. He felt as if he were a young lad about to ask the most beautiful girl in town for a date. His heart leapt into his throat as he thought she was going to pass him by but suddenly she paused. He began to dance back and forth upon his feet like an anxious young child desperate to see Santa. He could not understand what was wrong with him. He hadn't felt like this about anyone since the passing of his wife many years ago and this was only a little girl. Why was he acting as if this was the most important moment in his entire life?

Slowly she turned her eyes upward and she looked up at his sign and then back to him and said, "Mister, your sign is up backwards."

He gazed up, stared at the sign a moment, then laughed, and while still looking at the sign said, "Well my bones can't handle another trip up that ladder today. I will have to fix it tomorrow."

"I don't mind fixing it for you, Sir," the young lady said in such a sweet voice that he could feel his heart melting.

"But… but… you are wearing a dress?"

"Not a problem," she said. She sat her packages down and unhooked the strap from her purse. She took one end of the strap and attached it to her belt behind her back and passed it between her legs and then fastened it to her belt in the front. The belt pulled the hem of her dress up and closed the opening making a type of pants.

He watched her ingenuity stunned. She must have seen the look upon his face for she quickly explained, "I always wear dresses and at school I often help decorate so I have learned a few tricks to keep the boys from looking up my skirts."

He did not have time to say a word before she darted up the ladder and within no time she had the sign righted and was back down and had her purse reassembled. He smiled at her and thanked her profusely.

A gust of wind caught her hair and tossed it across her face. She flipped her head to get the hair out of her eyes. The wind however carried with it the still lingering scent of her tears as well as a light dusting of perfume. The fingers of the past wrapped around him reminding him of something from his childhood, a scent that his mother wore, a flower, but he could not place it. He suddenly felt an even stronger need to at least talk to this young lady for a little while. At the rate his heart was responding to her there was little doubt in his mind that if she wanted it he would offer her any piece of jewelry in his store for just a few moments to stare at her lovely smile. His late wife would have called him a foolish old man but he still felt like a young man in his old body.

She smiled at him and though she seemed to be happy he could sense that there was an incredible sadness within her that was far deeper than what could be explained by what had happened down the street. Again he was not certain how he knew that, but there was no doubt in his mind that this young woman was troubled. She lifted her hand as if to wave and he could sense she was about to say she had better get going.

The thoughts that went through his head then passed within a flash. He knew that she was a very special young lady. The very fact that he could feel her inner emotions without her saying a single word told him that there was something within her that was calling out to him. Then the shadow of the old drake passing overhead loomed in his mind and another memory of his past shot out of the darkness. The harbinger of an omen. Maybe it was more than his imagination. He felt deeply that he had to help this young lady in some way, he was not yet certain what she needed or how he would help but he knew he had no choice.

Before she had the chance to say anything he spoke, "Would you care to come inside and sit for a bit? I saw what happened down the street and you seem to be quite shaken by it. Besides, I at least owe you a drink for helping me with the sign."

She nodded and he opened the door as a gentleman should and allowed her to precede him into the establishment. The young woman stepped inside and paused just inside the door. As he stepped in behind her he could see her looking about at all the display cases. They were empty and the place looked barren but the old building had a charm of its own.

He flipped the light switch just inside the door and the overhead lights illuminated the place casting out the shadows and then the tension in the young woman seemed to evaporate. He suddenly realized that she was the first person, other than himself, to enter *The Crimson Z* since he had decided to relocate there, "Welcome to *The Crimson Z*," he announced.

The young woman laughed and said, "For all there is to it."

Then she added, "Will you be ready to open in time for your Grand Opening?"

"I am old but I believe I can make it in time," he said, as he walked toward the back of the store to go to the little kitchen area. "Would you like a soda, or something else?" He hollered back and asked.

"Do you have any bottled water?" she asked.

"Yes, I have some from Saratoga Springs. I kind of like it, it has a sweet taste."

"That is good, I prefer things without additives," she responded.

He brought back out two of the bottles. As he passed by a mirror on the wall it began to rattle and he whispered to it, "Not now Lilith, it is not time."

"Excuse me, Sir. What did you say?" she asked.

"I just said to myself 'Be still, Silly it is not your time.' It was nothing"

The girl looked at him quizzically so he tried to come up with a reasonable explanation. He hated to lie, he always had but he did not know how to explain the rattling mirror and Lilith to the young woman. Maybe he would in time if she stuck around, but if he tried now she would be out that door and running down the street in a matter of seconds. "You are such an attractive young lady and my heart was racing just thinking of being alone in this dark store with you. But as you see I am an arthritic old man and you are in no danger."

He felt ashamed for he had actually told her two lies. Outside he had felt old and arthritic but once he had stepped through the doors and into the realm of *The Crimson Z* it was as if half his years had melted away from him. He no longer hurt and his hands and bones were in nearly perfect shape again.

The young girl giggled and smiled brightly as she blushed, "Thank you, I am not so pretty, but I already knew I was safe with you. I could see it in your eyes. I get feelings about people, and you have a very good heart."

He handed the young woman her bottle of water and then opened his own. He laughed to himself thinking when bottled water had first come out he had sworn he would never spend even a single penny on the stuff and now it was about the only thing he drank. He did have a couple cans of soda in the refrigerator for guests but he never touched it. The young woman began to lean over the counter and look for something. "Is there something I can help you with?"

"I was looking for a trash can for this wet wipe. I could not throw it on the street. I just do not like to litter, besides, people are funny about things covered with blood."

He held out his hand, "Hand it to me, the main trash can is in the back. I am still setting up shop so do not have anything really ready yet. Other than the treasures display case over against that wall nothing has been set up."

She dropped the wet wipe in his hand and then turned her gaze in the direction he had pointed. She could feel her eyes growing big as she looked upon the deep red of the rich mahogany case. She was not a good judge of height but it nearly reached to the ceiling so she guessed it stood nearly eight feet tall and was at least six feet wide. The front was divided into three panels. The lower one foot stretched the full width of the cabinet and then the upper portion was divided into what looked like two doors. Across the top was a decorative scrolling that had the phases of the moon carved into the scroll work.

However the most striking feature was a deep intricate carving across the faces of the two doors. It appeared to be a tree, but one that was bent to form a very stylistic shape that resembled the letter *Z*. The roots were twisted and gnarled from the right across the bottom to the left and became the base of the trunk of the tree but they were more than that for they also looked like they were the feet of a startlingly beautiful but completely naked woman. She leaned to the right, her legs crossed slightly, she was naked and it actually caused the young woman to feel herself blush as she looked at how sensual the woman was, yet she was still the trunk of a tree.

One of the tree woman's arms crooked above her head and it and her hair became the branches which intertwined across the two doors. Down at the base one of the tap roots descended and connected to a circle that surrounded the entire work. Connected to the circle at twelve equidistant points were characters that she recognized from the Hebrew alphabet.

The young woman had never imagined anything like this in her life. The entire cabinet was the most strikingly beautiful piece of furniture she had ever seen. She could not even begin to imagine what kind of treasures it might hold within that he would defer to them and not to the cabinet itself as so valuable.

The old man turned and left the room as she began to walk over to the case. When she got closer she noticed that the engraving that formed the pattern was more than simply a deeply carved line. There were raised portions within the lines so she inspected them even closer. In the poor light it was hard to tell but it looked like there were some strange characters carved within the lines.

"Yes, the case is a beauty." She nearly jumped out of her skin as she had not heard the old man approach and he was less than a foot behind her. She turned and stepped away a bit, smiling at him. She did not feel frightened of him it was just that she was not used to having people get that close to her without her noticing them. He continued, "It is a copy of the original that was made when the original store was open."

The old man laughed and placed a key into a hidden spot at the bottom of the doors, "Don't go asking me how long ago that was because I have no idea. It has been in my family for many generations." Then he sighed, a deep, heavy sigh and added, "It looks like it will pass into the hands of my great-great nephew though for I have no son to pass my trade on to."

With a twist of the key the two great doors swung open almost magically. The backs of both doors and the interior behind them were lined with red velvet. Sliding glass doors further divided the case and protected the pieces of jewelry within.

She stared in awe at the hundreds of pieces adorning the shelves. There were rings, bracelets, necklaces, pendants, cameos, and many more items and each one looked as if it were crafted with a care and artistry beyond anything she had ever seen or even imagined. She had seen exceptional jewelry before. Her mother wore very expensive pieces but what was in this cabinet was far beyond anything she had seen even in museums. The craftsmen that had made these pieces of jewelry were true masters and she had no doubt that she was looking at the finest works that had ever been created.

Her gaze was caught by an exquisite golden ring, like two coiled serpents, that held the very first place within the cabinet. Her eyes were drawn down to a pendent that looked so delicate that she was sure it would crumble beneath the touch of a feather. All the upper shelves were mostly full but once in a while there would be a blank space as if a piece was missing from the collection. She continued with amazement through the various pieces, a set of pendants all alike except for a size variance, a bracelet of gold and lapis which were one of her favorite gemstones. All the pieces were of gold, some had silver in them some had gemstones others did not.

Finally her gaze lit upon the bottom shelves and she noticed that they were empty like they were waiting for new pieces that had yet to be made.

She started to turn wanting to ask him about the blank places in the collection but before she said a word he was answering as if he had read her mind. "The blank places are for pieces that have been sold. In time it seems that all the pieces that are marked with the jeweler's mark of *The Crimson Z* find their way back to this shop so it has been a tradition to leave the spots open."

She could feel her own eyes widen at the thought that somehow the pieces always returned. Could that mean that they were somehow magical? She imagined them being woven with some special enchantment that enveloped the person that bought them and then when the person was no longer in need of the magic the piece would mysteriously find its way back into the hands of the owner of *The Crimson Z.* She turned and looked at the empty places amongst the jewelry and wondered what wonders those pieces were weaving in the lives of the people that possessed them.

Her gaze drifted amongst the variety of rings, chains, charms, earrings, and other jewels that had every size and type of gemstone imaginable. Slowly she turned towards him and smiled broadly. "Did you make all of these?"

He laughed, "Sometimes I feel like I did. They mean so much to me. But that ring of coiled serpents up in that corner is several hundred years old. Do you think I could have made it?" He smiled at her and raised an eyebrow, "Surely you do not think I am that old?"

She smiled, "Well, I guess not. You are old, but not quite that old." She smiled teasingly and added, "At least I do not think so."

The old man wiggled his eyebrows and she realized he had seen through her tease. She giggled. There was something about the old man that made her feel very warm and safe. If she had had a grandfather she would have hoped he would have been a man like this man. She held out her hand, "My name is Melanie it is nice to meet you." Then as an afterthought, something she thought a gentleman of his era might like, she curtsied.

The old man's face brightened, "My, that is something I have not seen in a very long time. I did not know anyone even knew how to do that anymore."

Melanie laughed and said, "I saw it in an old movie once. I thought it was sweet so I practiced it. I never thought I would do it. Yet, you seemed like someone that would appreciate it, and it felt right."

He took her hand, kissed it and then bowed to her, "Why thank you, Miss Melanie, it was indeed a pleasure."

She giggled shyly, the kiss was a little more than she had anticipated and her heart raced. Why would an old man kissing her hand cause her heart to race? And make her feel giddy?

The old man added, "Most people call me Zach. My last name is Zachariah and it is where the *Z* in *The Crimson Z* comes from."

Melanie giggled again, everything seemed so formal. Yet she felt it was somehow more. Her own heart was telling her she needed it to be more. She did not know why, but she felt comfortable around this man. It frightened her a little, that it was the first time she had ever met him and she was having such deep emotions but all her life she'd had feelings about things and they had never steered her wrong. She knew that she would be safe with this man and she knew that he was going to play a major role in her life.

She smiled at him and said, "It has been a true pleasure to meet you, Zach... um, Mr. Zachariah." She lowered her gaze to the floor and thought. It did not feel right calling him by the name Zach as everyone else did. That just did not show him enough respect and yet calling him Mr. Zachariah seemed too formal, almost like it was distancing him from her and she did not want that.

There were no adults in her life that she was close to other than a couple of teachers, and even more disturbing to her was that there were no male figures in her life at all. She did not hang around the boys her age because she could tell all they wanted from her was to get under her dress. They did not care that she had a mind and a heart. They were too worried about their own hormones, and what conquests they could brag about to the other boys.

Something about this man told her she would be safe. Even if he saw her as a sexual being he would not pursue it. She raised her head and looked at him, she could tell from the look on his face that the look on her own face had caused him to worry, "Excuse me, Sir. It just does not seem right me calling you Zach, and I know it is proper to call you Mr. Zachariah however I am worried that that would send you a message that I want to be distant from you, and I do not.

"I would like to be your friend. I would like to come and visit and talk with you more. Would it be alright if I call you Papa Zach? That is how I would refer to a grandfather if I had one and it would mean a great deal to me to be allowed to show you that respect."

"I do not know what I did to earn the respect, but I would be honored. You certainly may call me Papa Zach."

She smiled brightly and said, "Papa Zach, you said you were not done unpacking. Could you use some help? Your sign says you will be opening next Friday, and tomorrow is Saturday. I could come and help you."

The melody of her voice as she said the word 'Papa' catapulted Zachariah's mind back to a moment in the past, to a happy time when his mother had called his father 'Papa' and it warmed his heart to hear the lovely young lady call him by that name. His gaze had also drifted to the floor while his memories of his loving parents and the love they shared filled his head. He suddenly realized that it had gone quiet in the shop except for the girl's exuberant breath. He looked up at her. For a moment he had forgotten the question she had asked him. He quickly replayed her last words through his mind and then it returned, she had asked if he could use some help, and he could see from the bright look in her eyes that he would have a bit of an argument with her if he were to say no. Yet there were things about this girl he already felt that told him he wanted her near. He could feel her emotions coming off of her like radiant heat from an old wood burning stove. He could see occasional flashes of light dance around her, little bits of energy that clued him in that she was more than just a special girl in her polite and sweet nature. This girl had a gift that was something he needed to be close to. It made him feel alive and even younger than the magic of his shop. His heart felt youthful for the first time since the death of his wife.

Yes this girl was far more special than any of the other clients that had come into his shop but most importantly she had given him the first of the elements of the commission. She had given him a gift of blood of an innocent child. Now he had to wait for her to commission a piece of jewelry. It was imperative that she be around as much as possible and even though that was part of the requirements which he had to fulfill, it was something his heart was more than pleased to follow. He hoped that what she would ask for would be something very special so that he could put all of his heart and soul into its design. He wanted to create for her something that would help her feel how beautiful she truly was.

He smiled, "I guess I have made you dance long enough for your answer. Melanie, you are welcome to help but I do not have any cash on hand. I have not sold a piece in quite some time and all my money is either tied up or has gone to paying the rent on this place and buying back one of the treasures."

"Oh no! No, Papa Zach. I don't want to be paid. Well, if you want to pay me you can tell me some stories about the treasures. I get the feeling from the way you say they return to you that each of them has a special story, almost magical and my curiosity about them is piqued. Besides I love to listen to stories from older people about the past. People my age just do not respect the generations of the past and there is so much rich history in their tales and legends." She looked at him. He could see the anticipation building to where she was almost dancing before he finally gave his answer.

"Yes." He smiled for to hear the respect in her voice about history was just one more thing that made this young girl so special to him. She truly was a treasure. He already knew she was more valuable than all the treasures in that cabinet combined for she was a living, breathing jewel.

"Yay!" She jumped up and down and kissed his cheek. Then she walked backwards toward the door, he watched as she turned her head every once in a while as if she were trying to make certain she didn't bump into something as she headed for the door, but she kept looking back to him to make eye contact as she spoke to him. "Papa Zach, I am sorry I cannot stay longer but dinner will be on the table soon and I do not want my mother to worry. I will tell her about you and this place and she may stop in to check it out to make certain it is what I say it is. I will be here bright and early tomorrow. Just tell me when?"

"It is Saturday get here when you feel like it. I am usually up before the sun."

She ran to the door then stopped ran back and kissed his cheek again, "Thank you, thank you," she said then ran out the door. The last thing he heard was her singing happily, as she was nearly halfway up the block.

As the sound of her voice faded, the mirror on the wall began to rattle. Zach got up and walked over to it. "Quiet, Lilith. Do not be jealous. I know she is young and sweet but I still love you my wife. I have loved you since the day I laid eyes on you and I will always love you." Softly he stroked the glass of the mirror and slowly it settled down. Zachariah felt a cold tingling at the front of his skull, he could remember a time when it was warm and pleasant but that had ceased long ago and now it felt more like icy fingers reaching into the frontal lobe of his brain.

Zachariah, the blood of this child that she brought you, I can tell it is truly an innocent this time. Zachariah could feel a quivering of those cold tendrils as he felt her excitement.

"What has happened? Why has it taken so long? I do not remember ever getting this old before."

It has not been that long, my love. Living in New York and Boston finding innocent children was hard to do. When the blood of a non-innocent is used you do not regenerate as much. The last time you only gained back ten years. That was only thirty years ago. Your body is the same as a man who is one hundred and ten.

"It is not that the magic is getting old?"

No my love. He remembered one of the things that had always been a strong hatred for Lilith was to see a child harmed or abused. It was one of the few times he could recall while they were married that she had actually gotten violent with someone. *Innocence is harder to find. These are days of child molestation, and parents teaching their children to hate others because of race, or religion. Even small children steal, lie, cheat and not just little innocent things of growing up but things of a malicious nature so they are not innocent. Their blood is not as strong.*

"Oh yes. Now I remember. Back in the 1920's wasn't there one time when the blood actually caused me to age?"

Yes, the little monster was killing cats and dogs when he was only three and four years old. He killed his sister when he was six and his parents when he was seven. We happened to get his blood when he was eight. We were both weak because it had been sixty years since the last time we'd had an innocent and I could not tell his blood was tainted. It nearly killed you my love. A sudden memory a fiery flash in her eyes surfaced, eerie almost supernatural, he could not recall when it happened but he remembered the feeling that it was not right. That night when I became corporeal all I could do was hold you in my arms. We were lucky that another innocent came only a couple of days later or you might have died and I would have been forever trapped in this mirror.

"Well, Melanie has to commission a piece for me to work on for the blood to work. I do not know how to get her to get the courage to do that. Maybe just bide my time."

The mirror began rattling again, Melanie, is it! This had better just be business Zachary or when I get my body back you will wish it had been.

Zach smiled then his heart grew cold as he suddenly remembered the cruel temper Lilith had shown when she had been even the slightest bit jealous. Though there had been no reason for her to be jealous her hatred would boil within her until she exploded and hell's fury would be unleashed upon the object of her jealousy.

"There is nothing to be jealous of Lilith. Look at me I am an old man, she is still a child she could not possibly see anything in me. You know I would be a fool to care for anyone but you." He prayed with all his heart that that would ease her temper but there had been times that nothing he would say would douse the flames once they had been lit.

We will see Zachariah, and you had better not be lying to me. He could almost feel her smile wickedly at him. It was a strange sensation to know what her spirit was doing even though she had no form. *Why did you not tell me Zaven had appeared?*

"Zaven?"

I can see him in your mind, you old fool! Have you lost your memory of him already?

The image of the shadow was pulled into his memory by the icy tendrils, forced there for him to see again and relive. His heart raced wildly, he had not known she could force him to recall memories and see things from his recent past. He wondered if she could only see things he had seen or if she could see and feel all his thoughts, if it was the latter he was a dead man.

He tried to build a barrier in his mind to protect those other thoughts just in case and as he did he began to distract her by discussing what she wanted to hear, "It had been so long since Zaven had been a harbinger that I had not even recognized his sign. The shadow nearly scared the wits out of me."

Yes, my Love, Zaven has searched long and hard this time, we could not afford to have the child be another monster. Someone like that would surely kill you this time, it could have last time.

Zach leaned forward and kissed the mirror, "You will see Lily it is only you I love and I am looking forward to holding you in my arms again, even if it is only for a night. Now I need to bid you a good night, I suspect the girl will be here before I normally get up in the morning so I am going to set my clock an hour earlier.

Good night, my love.

***

The bell at the door chimed before his coffee had even finished percolating. Quickly he walked to the door but just before he got there he remembered that once he opened that door he would appear to be every bit the old bent arthritic man she had seen outside the day before so he slowed and bent over and shuffled the last few steps to the door so that the change would not be so dramatic and sudden that she might notice a shift in his appearance. It was difficult for him to maintain the posture though for he was excited about her arrival, feeling more like a boy opening the door for his girlfriend than an old man opening one for his assistant.

Slowly he opened the door and Melanie smiled up at him, "Good morning, Papa Zach," she almost sang then she stepped around him and nearly danced into the shop.

He watched her as she walked about looking at everything. There was a bounce in her step like she was filled with exuberance. He wondered if it was the joy of having someone to talk to, for he had felt that emptiness and sadness in her the day before. Perhaps it was from how excited she had seemed about the idea of him telling her the stories. Could it be that all her happiness could be wrapped around the thought that when she had finished her tasks for the day she would get to listen to one or more of the tales of the treasures?

Whatever it was it was filling his heart to see her in a much happier state of mind than she had been in the day before. Still there was a barrier within her that he could feel that was holding her back from releasing her true joy. Something deep inside her that was dark and sad kept her from truly knowing what happiness really was.

"Melanie," he said, "why would you rather be here helping an old man on a Saturday morning than out with your friends." Zachariah was afraid he already knew the answer but he had to hear it for himself.

The young girl found a rag and some cleaner and had already begun cleaning the glass display cases. She looked up and said, "I really like to be of use to someone."

"Oh, sweetheart, I know young girls like you have lots of friends and you usually go places and talk about boys and shop on Saturdays. Why are you here and not with them?"

She looked at him and smiled, "Oh, I am your sweetheart am I, you dirty old man." Then she laughed but the laughter slowly faded and he could see tears begin to form in the corner of her eyes so he walked over to her.

"Listen, Melanie, you can tell me. I do not know anyone else to tell, so I will be your confidant, and your friend."

She walked around the cabinet and wrapped her arms around him, he had not expected that and it shocked him, yet somehow it seemed right too. He knew she could trust him, maybe somehow she knew it too. She looked up to him and said, "I don't have any friends. They make fun of me because I don't wear jeans and gym shoes but dress up all the time except for when I had classes that required me to wear other kinds of clothes.

"I just want to dress this way. No one makes me. I prefer to dress like a woman and not be sleazy and slinky. I don't like the types of tight fitting clothing that the girls wear that show off their bodies. I want to be attractive, but refined, like a southern belle, or a princess not a teenage vamp trying to lure her boyfriend.

"So they all make fun of me and don't want anything to do with me. I eat lunch alone in the library. I study alone." She laid her head against his chest and added, "You are the first person in ages that has tried to be a friend to me that did not try to lift my dress."

Then she stepped back and wiped her eyes and said, "So, Papa Zach, I am with my friend. I am here and I am helping him get ready for a very important day for him." Then she turned and went back to scrubbing the glass without another word. Zachariah almost felt like a heel for having pushed that confession out of her but at the same time he felt warm inside for it was true he did like the girl and would be her friend, her true friend.

For hours she worked hard at scrubbing the glass of the cases. Every so often she would look up at him and see him going over some of the drawers of the jewelry that would stock the outer display cases, his eyepiece examining each piece meticulously. It was odd how close she had come to feel to him in such a short period but she already felt like she had known him for a very long time. There was something about him that touched her deeply and made her feel warm and comfortable, almost loved. It was a feeling she had never felt before. Melanie could not understand the reason she felt like this but it was wonderful, and she wanted more of it. She wanted to be with Papa Zach as much as she could because the time with him seemed to make all the pain and loneliness of her life disappear. She had not lied to him about truly being alone. Even her own mother did not love her. She made no qualms about telling her every day that she did not.

Melanie could feel the tears come to her eyes again but as she did, she looked up at Papa Zach and she no longer felt the need to cry. Instead, she felt the need to run over and jump in his arms and hug him like she had never hugged anyone in her life. She smiled to herself, what were these feelings within her. He was an old man and she would be eighteen soon. Their ages were too far apart, why would she feel this way toward him and in such a short time? Yet there was no doubt that her heart beat a little stronger every time she looked at him.

It also had to be her imagination but when he was inside his shop he did not appear to be as old as he had when she had first seen him. He appeared to be much younger, sturdier, stronger, but that was impossible. It was like he was two different men.

There was only one other thing that held as much fascination for her as did Papa Zach and that was the mysterious cabinet. Though she did not look at it nearly half as often as she did him, she still looked at it quite a bit. She glanced up as she finished cleaning the glass of the last case and it was just past six. She decided to let her curiosity have a little freedom.

She got a can of spray wax and some clean cloths and walked over to the cabinet, but as she looked at it she realized that it did not need waxing. Papa Zach had given her the key to it earlier so that she could clean the glass inside it as well, so she slid the key in the lock and as she twisted it she heard a slight click and like magic the two doors began to open slowly on their own. Her eyes again grew large as she became transfixed by the startling beauty of the masterpieces that aligned the shelves within. She reached toward the glass but her hand paused short of it, fear filled her. She just did not feel right.

The jewelry inside was worthy of being in the Smithsonian or the Louvre but not touched by someone as plain and unattractive as she was. Somehow she felt if she were to clean them she would taint them and they would lose their value. Slowly she lowered her head feeling as worthless as her mother had always told her she was.

She knew he was standing behind her long before he spoke. It was unusual that anyone could get so close to her without her noticing but there was just something so unique about the old man that not only made her comfortable about him but made her know she was safe. She had no need to have her guards up when he was around. It was as if he and she had been friends since time had begun and she trusted him like she trusted no other.

"So, I guess you are ready for your first payment?" He spoke, his voice not the quivering voice of a man that had to be past a hundred but the voice of a strong young man. His voice alone sent shivers down her spine making her feel as if it entered her soul and caressed her heart. If there was not such a huge age difference she felt that a man like Papa

Zach would be a man she could live with forever. He continued with his soothing tone, "I promised you a story about these pieces, is there one that draws your attention and summons you to hear its story more than any of the others?

Melanie looked at all the pieces and immediately knew what piece she wanted to hear about. There was something about it that drew her more than the others. Though it was exceptionally crafted it looked like it may have been the first piece that the master worked on before he had perfected his talent.

"Go ahead," Zachariah urged her, "pick one out."

She turned to him and tears were in her eyes as she said, "Papa Zach, they are so beautiful, I am afraid to touch them. I am just a plain girl I do not compare to these at all."

Zachariah took her by the shoulders, looked into her eyes, and said, "Of all the jewels in the world there are two that sparkle brighter than any gemstone and those are your eyes. Of all the treasures in the world there is one that is more finely crafted than any craftsman could ever dream of making and that is your soul. You have no reason to doubt your value you are the greatest jewel in this room. So slide open the doors and choose a piece of jewelry for me to tell you a story about."

Melanie could feel her heart melting; no man had ever spoken to her like that. No one had ever placed such a value on her. Suddenly she felt very beautiful at least in the eyes of Papa Zach. She turned and pushed the doors aside and reached toward the very first piece in the collection, a ring that was made of a pair of entwined serpents. Before her fingers touched it she heard a gasp from behind her and turned to look at Papa Zach. He had gone white, even whiter than his frail translucent skin was in its normalcy. "Is something wrong, Papa Zach?"

"Sweet girl, I promise I will tell you the ring's story, but I ask you let it not be today? I need time to get used to the idea of that one. There are some personal feelings that lie deep within my family's memory on that piece."

Melanie nodded and then said, "Well then, you mentioned some pieces of legendary proportions. A story perhaps that is filled with a magic that is unbelievable?"

Papa Zach's color returned quickly and he smiled. Slowly he reached for a pendant that dangled from a chain of gold so delicate it looked like it was spun from the silken web of a spider. The pendant was that of finely etched foil leaves of gold wrapped about one another to forever capture the beauty of a real rose in the soft metal. It was lightly etched with a webbing of gold lace about the rose. To Melanie it looked like if you were to even touch it within the gentlest of grasps that it would be crushed beyond repair.

"The story behind this piece is one of those of myth and legend. It encompasses creatures long forgotten and others greatly misunderstood. It's about love between two of these that cursed them beyond the end of their days. Yet it is a story of such profound beauty and love that it touches the heart like few others. Oddly the story is a story told by yet another creature of legend. It is told from the heart of the son of one of the two accursed lovers as he tells it to one he loves but knows he is doomed to never be able to truly love." A tear slid down Zach's heavily wrinkled cheek and got lost in one of the canyons of his age. Melanie felt her heart tug and she wanted to reach out to him but saw him straighten his shoulders as he began to unfold the tale before her.

Love of a Pendant's Heart
Lee Rush

Chapter One

The purple hues of dusk were darkening as he stepped under the willow tree, edging forward silently. He knew she was there… he could tell by her scent on the breeze that wafted through the willow branches. He peeked around the trunk of the huge tree and smiled down at her, not surprised that she was asleep. She had been asleep the first time he came upon her in this very place. Adrian had been as touched by her beauty then as he was now but that first time… well, that was different. Then he had needed to feed; now he just longed to see his love.

Over the time he had known her, his feelings had grown and his heart ached for her when they were apart. Her human life and his Anthro life seemed to conspire to keep them apart but he came to her as often as he could.

That first time he had introduced her to the dark pleasure that paved the way for future feedings, his only intent had been to have her available when he needed her blood. The way she responded to him and the way that response made him feel had begun to change his future plans for her as well as his attitude toward her. At first, he fought the feelings, tried to keep her in place as simply something he *used* from time to time but that didn't last long. She touched his heart with her innocence and then her love for him and his picture of her as *dinner* quickly faded.

Although he had not been able to give her any sort of commitment, she had remained available to him and even desired him, engendering a type of love he had never wanted to feel again. Too many times he had loved and lost because of who and what he was. Too many times he had grieved and been forced to go on again. He wasn't going to do it again… but she had changed that and he wasn't sure if it was a change for the better.

At least he hadn't been sure… he was now. He loved her with all his heart and knew as he slid his hand into his pocket and fingered the small metal piece there, that this day would bring changes. Changes he hoped she could accept.

He watched her for a few more minutes, then stepped back and composed himself. Putting most sad thoughts aside, he stepped toward her as he normally would, brushing the hanging branches back without trying to be quiet.

She shifted, trying to ease back into the pleasant realm of dreams. Even though she had been dozing, the soft susurration of the moving leaves was enough to disturb her in this place of quietude. She had come to her favorite place in the world to relax and read her newest acquisition of poetry in the late afternoon. Apparently she had dozed off as the warmth of the afternoon turned into the cooler shading of dusk, and then the buzz of the evening insects lulled her.

She opened her eyes slowly at the rustling sound and smiled softly. Dangling in front of her face was a pendant of spun gold, slowly swinging from side to side on a delicate chain. The barely risen moon shone through the leaves and highlighted the details of the pendant… a rose of gold surrounded by webs of the finest spun threads of gold. Tiny leaves with all the intricacies of real rose leaves and the delicate petals made her gasp softly as she reached up with one slender finger and pushed the pendant to widen the arc of its swing.

She cleared the sleep from her throat and spoke. All things, even her voice seemed soft in this special place at this special time of day where the heat of the day had been banished by the darkening skies and the scents of the night blooming flowers filled the air.

"I wonder… who would be showing me this beauty?"

Turning first her head to catch a glimpse of his fur covered hand, then turning her upper body to gaze up at the creature that teased her with the necklace. Her heart leapt as she caught sight of his face, his strange eyes looking down at her. No, not strange… his. Eyes like none she had ever seen before… blue with spikes of green around the irises. Once upon a time, his eyes had seemed strange to her but no longer. She knew him now, knew his moods, knew his eyes as they changed color when he was excited, and she knew his touch as well. She delighted in the knowing of him. There had been times she had despaired of ever seeing him again because of the things he was required to do in his different half-life but he came back again and again and each time he returned, her heart was filled with more love for him.

"Hello, Adrian."

That's all it took to bring all the feelings for him back in full force. Some might say she was daft for being here with him, daft for a young woman to be with such a creature at all, but they didn't know him. He was a special creature whose history was buried in the days of old when such as anthrofoxes were the norm in these parts. She had known him for a few years now and he was always the same... always the soft auburn fur covering his body, always the almost human visage that smiled at her, gallant and polite beyond belief.

"Good evening, my dear Crys," he murmured as he moved around to stand in front of her. He smiled as he saw the light in her eyes that always shone forth when they were together.

He let the delicate chain slip between his fingers until it dropped into her hand. As she closed her hand around the pendant and chain, trapping the exquisite pendant in her palm, he leaned down and kissed the back of her hand causing her to shiver with pleasure. He peeked up over her hand as he kissed it and smiled that sexy smile that seemed to light up his expressive face.

"It's lovely, Adrian," she whispered, her voice reduced to even greater softness as the twinkle in his eyes caused her heart to beat faster.

"And a bit more permanent than the red roses I usually bring. I hope it pleases you, my sweet Crys."

"It more than pleases me, Adrian. Where ever did you find such a lovely creation?"

He sat beside her on the blanket and leaned back against the tree trunk before he answered her. A shadow crossed his face, but was it from a cloud across the moon? Or a sadness in his expression? Her heart skipped a beat at the thought that she may have caused him sadness when all she ever wanted to do was see him smile.

He was shaking his head as he slid his arm around her shoulder. She sighed happily at the closeness she had missed for so long and nestled against him as he pulled her close. The warmth of his fur against her skin tickled her flesh and delighted her as his tail wrapped up around her legs.

His breath ruffled her hair as she snuggled against his neck. The colors of his fur against her flesh blended in the early evening dark and it was as if they were both human… or both anthrofoxes instead of one of each.

"My father said it belonged to my mother, Crys and therein lies a sad tale."

"You've never spoken much about your family, Adrian. She almost held her breath at this revelation, anxious to hear more and perhaps learn something of the past that had put sadness in his eyes each time he left her.

"My family is long gone, sweet Crys, so there isn't much to talk about. As for my mother, well, her story is a sad one as I said… and not one I like to tell very often."

There was a slight catch in his voice as he spoke of his mother and it clenched at her heart.

"I didn't mean to…"

"No, of course you didn't and you should know the story if you are to wear her necklace."

She smiled in the darkness and leaned into his embrace a bit more, now anxious to hear the tale.

Chapter Two

William rode into the village just as he did every other month. It was the way he kept in touch with the people in his kingdom. A few days spent here and there brought problems to his attention and kept the gentry happy. If they were happy, *he* was happy because it made his rule that much easier to accomplish. As he rode into the center of the village, his eye was caught by a quick flash of bright red billowing in the breeze. He drew closer to the central well of the village and spotted what was under the billowing red. She was quite comely… buxom, fair of face and small waisted. Just the sort he usually found pleasing to his senses. Unbidden, a picture of her face gazing up at him, hair spread out on a pillow flashed into his mind and he felt a twitch in his groin as a broad smile split his face.

He stopped at the well to water his horse and was surrounded by the villagers greeting him and begging his attention as he dismounted. While he answered their questions and listened to their minor complaints, he turned from side to side to address each villager in turn but he could always see the redheaded woman from the corner of his eye. He was glad that he had worn a loose doublet for riding today and that none were aware of the twitching of his breeches under it whenever she came fully into his view.

He kept his hand on the horse's bridle to keep him calm and had to lean to the side now and then to look around the horse just to see the woman again. He wasn't sure later what he had promised the villagers when they spoke with him; he had been too involved in keeping his eye on the woman.

There she was, always at the back of the small crowd, just watching him with a soft smile on her face. The smile seemed at times to hold an innocence and at other times perhaps a bit of lasciviousness… directed at him! Even in her homespun clothing she was a vision of loveliness, and that he would have remembered if he had seen her before.

Finally, when the other villagers had spoken with him and gone about their various businesses... she was the only one left. He swept off his hat and swung it across his body as he bowed at her approach. When he stood up again, he smiled broadly.

"And what, lovely lady, did you want to ask of me?"

As he spoke, he reached out and took hold of her elbow, directing her to the wall surrounding the well so she could sit comfortably while they talked. He put his booted foot on the wall beside her and leaned forward to hear her better. The scent of flowers that emanated from her filled his senses.

"I bid you good day, Sir. I have but a small favor to ask."

"Speak then and let me grant your wish."

"I would not so readily agree were I you, Sir... until you have heard me out."

"Such a lovely lady as yourself... What could I possibly have to fear from granting a request?"

She smiled slowly, her voice dropping to almost a whisper as she gave him her request.

"'Tis been told to me, my lord that a wedding would be the future here and I would ask that it be sooner rather than later."

He was taken aback at the audacity of such a statement, and his head jerked up and away from her. When he saw the expression on her face, he chuckled softly. She was serious but there was a twinkle in her eye. This close to her he could see the light sprinkling of freckles across her face and he longed to reach out and trace a pattern between them. Then he shook his head... what was this? He had seen beautiful women before... why was this one so special? He couldn't put his finger on the reason he was so attracted to her, but his shaft certainly had no problem discerning her charms.

"A wedding, is it? Between..."

"Why... between you and I, my lord. It has been foretold, I assure you."

He laughed aloud at her words, never thinking of such a thing himself. A wedding, indeed!! He had bed many a lass as comely as this one and had never been wed. What made her think it would be different now? And there was the proposed wedding with Princess Elena to bring two realms together... this woman was beautiful but obviously a bit daft.

Cara jumped to her feet when he laughed at her, anger coloring her features.

"Do you not find me comely enough to wed?"

"Aye… you *are* that, lass. It's just that you have caught me completely unawares. I had no such thought when I first saw you."

He smiled, trying to back up a bit, surprised at her anger and a bit chagrined that he had let himself react in such a manner. When she saw the expression on his face, it was her turn to laugh, her anger forgotten. She turned around, swirling her skirts saucily and laughed heartily. Head thrown back, the deep throated heartiness in the laugh gave her an earthy appearance more than her clothing.

"No… I would guess not, my lord. But… you *did* think something else, did you not? Something to do with pleasure and passion? I could see it in your eyes, my lord. There is no sense in denying it."

A sharp shard of annoyance shot through him at the nerve of the wench and brought color to his face. Telling him what he should and shouldn't deny? Who did she think she was?

"I do not deny it, woman… I have no need to deny it. I am the lord of this kingdom and what is here… is mine for the taking."

"Taking? But surely it would be much more pleasant if it were freely given, my lord?"

She had stepped closer to him and lowered her voice as she spoke and he again felt that twitching in his loins. He *could* take her… who would stop him? He could have what he wanted and who was to tell him nay? His father, long gone, had never bid him to deny his wants and his mother had died at his birth…there was no one to deny him, least of all this wench before him. In truth, it would be better… more pleasant if she came willingly to his bed, but deny him?

He couldn't hold in the laughter as he heard her speak.

"A cheeky wench, aren't you?"

"I think you like cheeky, my lord. I see that wicked twinkle in your eye," she said as she stepped even closer to him, her breasts just barely brushing against him as she winked up at him, a devilish twinkle evident in her eyes.

He was aware of her firm breasts against him, aware of the heat of her flesh through his shirt when she stepped back, another innocent look on her face. Teasing him with her body, the saucy wench was teasing him! But Gods, the way those pert breasts felt against him! Even through the thin material of her dress and his shirt, he could feel the hardness of her nipples and he wanted more.

He stood there grinning from ear to ear and looking her over from the top of her head to the tips of her sandaled toes. Then he reached out a hand and before he could grab her wrist and pull her close, she was already in his arms, standing on tiptoes to kiss him.

His arms were around her though he did not remember making that move. Soft lips pressed against his, gently at first and then with more pressure. His tongue flicked out and tasted strawberries and something else. A momentary flash of memory shot through his mind before he realized what it was. As he savored the taste of strawberries, he also inhaled the scent of her and it was as if he were in a field of freshly cut grass. Again, her breasts were pressed against him but more urgently this time. He was becoming even more aroused by the girl who wanted to claim his heart and future and indecision taunted him. As much as he knew in his head that it was wrong to want her, that his future should lie with the alliance with Elena's father, his loins betrayed him. She was pressed tightly against him and it was not possible for her to be unaware of his desire.

He was surprised at the audacity of the wench and delighted as well. Most women these days were quite a bit different from this one. Most were staid and stuffy… not admitting to feelings such as this. But this one… it was obvious that she enjoyed the fruits of lust as well as he did. She drew her mouth back from the kiss, licked across his lips sensually and chuckled softly. Even after she leaned back from the kiss, the taste of her lingered and was as arousing as her actions.

"I think that you have seen that twinkle in my eye, my lord."

Was she bewitching him? If so… he was a willing subject. With difficulty, he looked beyond her hair, slowly taking in the surroundings. Was anybody watching them? Could any of them see the lord of the realm quaking in his boots at the closeness of this woman? There were others there, but they didn't seem to see them and that was odd as the two were enjoying their lustiness in the middle of the square, lolling against the well in the center of the village. A fog of lust surrounding him he didn't understand why no one was looking at them… what they were doing was simply *not done* in public.

"Are you a witch," he gasped out.

"No my lord… only one who has seen herself in your arms."

He was gasping for breath as she wiggled against him; his arms were tight as they clutched her to his chest. Her full breasts pressed against him, her nipples hard as pebbles rubbing across his chest. Her soft belly was tight against his hardness. The throbbing need in his loins was growing, becoming more insistent and his voice was raspy with desire when next he spoke.

"What is it you want, wench?"

"Only you, my lord... forever as mine."

"Yours?"

"Aye, my lord... mine and only mine. I am foretold to bear your sons and I would begin now."

This wench? The mother of his sons? The wife he would take? Somehow that didn't seem quite right but he knew he wouldn't be able to resist her. His loins were aching with desire for her.

"Name, woman. What is your name," the words were gasped as he sought breath.

"Cara, my lord. Surely you have seen me in your dreams? Dreamt of my touch and my kisses? You have... haven't you?"

Before he could think to deny it, her visage in his dreams was foremost in his mind, though he had not realized it before this moment. He was almost panting for breath as the freshly mown grass scent filled his senses, his loins pulsing as the heat of her body pressed against him.

She leaned back in his arms and gazed into his eyes and he felt as though he were drowning in a pool of blue water, deep and unfathomable. Her smile warmed his heart as the rest of her warmed his body.

"What is this, wench? What are you doing to me?"

"I? I do nothing, my lord, except offer myself as the prophecy foretold. It is said that I will bear you many sons, though only one of them will become renowned, the others will carry on your name and your heritage, my lord."

He moved his hands to her shoulders to push her back as he heard her words. He *wanted* to push her back, but his fingers closed on her shoulders and simply held her there. He gazed down at her, indignation flashing in his eyes.

"You take much for granted, woman."

"Nay, sir... I speak only the truth as is foretold. I will be the one to share your life and times. Can you not feel that truth?"

As she spoke, her hips pressed harder against him, swaying sensuously from side to side, causing his shaft to twitch under his clothes.

"Gods, you incense me, woman."

Her smile was sweet and wicked at the same time and she stepped back, her body no longer pressing against him. His body ached at the absence of warmth and he almost grabbed her and pulled her tight again.

He seemed to fall further into that pool of blue as he fought to regain his senses. His hand reached out and grasped at her plain gown to pull her closer, but she danced out of his reach.

"What say you, my lord? Do you believe the prophecy as I have told it? Or do you think me merely a slut who would have her way with you?"

The certainty of her words speared into his heart and mind. Was it possible? Did she speak the truth?

"Who has foretold these things, woman? Who has made you so sure in your mind that I should consider this 'marriage'?"

"The Witch of Wolstad has said it, my lord and she is never wrong. She has cast the bones and read the leaves and each time it is told the same. I am to bear your sons and continue your blood into the future."

"A witch, is it? Of Wolstad, you say? I've heard of the witch but never that she did fortunes of future happenstance. You're sure of this? Sure enough to wage your future on her words?"

The red hair fluttered in the breeze as she nodded her head, a serious expression on her face.

"Aye, 'tis true, my lord. I am the one."

He laughed heartily and caught her wrist, pulling her back against him. He leaned down and nuzzled against her neck, inhaling her scent again, getting dizzy again with the swirling aromas...berries, newly cut hay and overshadowing it all... her arousal.

"Come to the castle, wench and we shall see what we shall see."

"I come for a wedding, my lord... naught else."

"You'll come for whatever I say, woman. I make the laws here. I make the decisions, not some witch from the outer reaches and not some village wench either... even if she is as comely as you."

Surging desires squelched his sense of decorum and propriety, though he had use for neither in his position. He was the lord of the realm and what he wanted... he took and enjoyed. Yet... this one... this woman was something he had not encountered before. His loins were enflamed with need and his soul was singing as it never had before. He was breathing faster and harder as her scents filled him. His shaft was throbbing and he groaned aloud as she stepped back from him again.

"A wedding, my lord?"

He could only nod his acquiescence for she had stolen his breath as well as his senses. He had to have her and consequences be damned. He pulled her close again and tightened his grip on her, holding her as he kissed her deeply and passionately. He groaned in the kiss as his shaft throbbed against her.

Almost thrusting her from him, he remounted his horse and then pulled her up to sit behind him. The warmth of her pressed against his back and her arms around his waist seared his skin with heat.

The ride back to the castle was interminable and difficult beyond belief. All he wanted was to leap from the horse, take her into the fields and ravish her over and over again. Her nipples were hard as little buttons pressing into his back, the fullness of her breasts squashed against him, teasing him to greater heights of need. It was all he could do to actually ride to the castle and dismount his horse in the courtyard. He was sure all could see the rampant shaft beneath his clothes, but none appeared to take notice. Before his feet hit the ground he was bellowing for the priest to be summoned and a feast to be prepared.

He lifted the woman from the horse and stared into her eyes, trying to determine if she had indeed bewitched him.

"Say it, woman. Tell me you have bewitched me so I can understand this need."

"I cannot, my lord for I have not bewitched you. I have simply spoken the truth as it has been told to me."

"Now, woman. Get to my rooms now."

"Nay, my lord… not until the wedding is done."

He stood there before her in his courtyard, shaking with desire. His legs were weak and trembling, his heart was pounding in his chest and he had no breath to speak. He roughly shoved her away and rasped his commands.

"Prepare yourself then… the wedding shall begin as soon as the priest arrives."

He could barely walk as he turned away and entered the castle, waving at his aides to assist the woman in what she needed.

In his rooms, surrounded by advisors, he was in a daze… his shaft was pulsing and hard although apparently invisible to his advisors.

"My lord, you cannot…"

"I will."

"But my lord… who is this woman? Why would you…"

"Silence!!"

"My lord, the constraints you put upon me make it necessary for me to point out that…"

"I said silence!!"

He stalked his quarters, pacing like a deranged lion in his den.

"I will have this woman."

"Aye, my lord, but as a wife? As the mother of your sons? You know nothing of this peasant and your plans to wed the Princess Elena? What of your plans to meld the two realms?"

"Damn the two realms."

"My lord!!"

Faster than a cobra striking, his hand was enveloped in the ruffles around the aide's throat.

"*Enough!!* Bring the priest and the woman to me. *Now!*"

Moments later, the peasant woman was standing before him, dressed in a gown of silk that he recognized from his mother's closet. The color of the material brought out the deep blue of her eyes… eyes that sparkled with trust and lust as she gazed at him. Her creamy breasts overfilled the bodice of the dress and taunted him. His hands twitched with the need to rip the bodice from her and fondle her breasts. His breath was coming faster again and just as he reached for her, the priest rushed in… breathless from his hurried journey from the nearby abbey.

He barely heard the words the priest spoke as he blessed the union of the lord of the realm and his new found bride. As soon as the final words were spoken, he spread his arms, gathering the witnesses in a loose grasp and hurried them from the room. When he turned back to his bride, he smiled and moved toward her quickly, pulling her into his arms and gazing down into her eyes.

"I'm not sure I believe you when you say you aren't a witch, for you surely have bewitched me."

"I swear to you, my lord… I am no witch."

She stood on her tiptoes and kissed him softly… but the kiss turned from gentle to passionate as she pressed her tongue to his lips and then between them. He suckled her tongue, holding her tight, then slipped his arms under her and lifted her. In only a moment he had her next to the bed, unfastening the back of the gown she wore and then letting it fall to the floor. Under it, she had been dressed with a tight corset and pantaloons; he grumbled under his breath as he undid the laces of the corset.

"Never again, woman… you will never wear one of these again."

Then the corset was around her ankles, his hands fumbling with the pantaloons and then ripping the top of them in his haste to see her naked. She gasped as he pulled them, the material digging into her tender flesh, but she stood there, smiling up at him and reveling in his obvious yearning for her body. Then she reached up and caressed his cheek lovingly.

"My lord… we have all the time in the world now. Your haste is unnecessary. I am here and yours for all our days. It has been foretold."

She winked up at him as she said the last and leaned against him, her fingers sliding up his chest and unfastening his shirt. He pulled the shirt over his head and threw it down, grabbing at the top of his pants, pulling the tie until it came loose and then pushing them down. His eyes were locked to hers as she stepped back to give him room to move. He was almost naked and then he tugged at his britches to loosen them and let them fall to the floor. He kicked off his shoes and shoved the chausses down until he could kick them off as well. When the pants fell, his shaft stood out from his body, dark pink and suffused with the blood of his lust.

Saucy though she was, yet she was a virgin and gasped at the sight of him, throbbing and bobbing before her.

"Woman, you enflame my very soul. On the bed with ya. I'll wait no longer."

She trembled as she climbed up onto the high bed and lay back, watching every move he made. She wanted him, needed him…and feared him as she had no other. He would take what she had kept all her life and though she gave it willingly, she knew the pain it would cause… she had heard from her friends.

He almost fell on top of her in his haste to take her, not thinking of her virginity or her pleasure… only his own need. Without as much as a kiss, he thrust himself into her and plunged deep, ignoring her cry of pain.

She turned her head as he thrust into her, pressing her mouth against his arm as she screamed. She had heard of the pain, but was quite unprepared for this onslaught. Her teeth were buried in her lower lip and a tiny droplet of blood seeped from her sharp tooth, the metallic taste of blood filling her mouth. She lay there under him, suffering and telling herself it would be different next time… he would be gentle next time.

Looking up into his face, she could see that his eyes were closed tightly as he concentrated on his pleasure. Five thrusts… six… seven… and then a loud groan as he tensed over her, spilling the seed of his loins into her virgin belly. She was weeping under him as he collapsed on top of her, gasping for breath as his shaft continued to empty itself into her.

He lay atop her for several minutes as he regained his senses, feeling her treasure twitching around him and feeling something else… something strange. He lifted his head, opened his eyes to gaze down at her.

"Bloody Hell!!!"

Cara looked up at him, tears still streaming down her face and was stricken with fear as she saw the look on his face as he leaped from the bed.

"Explain yourself!! Witch!! You ARE a witch!! Naught else could explain this!"

"I don't understand my lord. Explain what? What's wrong?"

She lifted her hand to him questioningly and then she saw her hand and screamed, fainting dead away.

He stood there in shock.

There was a sudden pounding at the door.

"What? Who dares to knock upon this door in such a manner?"

He jerked the door open and stood towering over an old woman dressed in black from head to toe, completely unfazed by his angry shout. Her body was slight and leaned forward, half supported by a walking stick. Her face was a mass of wrinkles. What hair he could see peeked out from under the shawl that completed her black covering. It was stringy and gray and there was a smirk on her face as she stared at him. Her eyes moved from his face down his body and she chuckled softly as he stood there naked with his shaft limp and damp. Then she seemed to gather herself and glared up at him before she spoke. Her voice was a mixture of rasping and the croaking of an old frog as she made her pronouncement.

"'Tis the Witch of Wolstad and if ye don't want me here, I'll go and be damned with yer questions!"

She turned slowly and began to walk away. She didn't get very far before he grabbed hold of her arm and pulled her into the room, almost jerking her off her feet. Once the door was closed again, he put her down quite unceremoniously. He was seething with anger at what he viewed as a huge joke… and at his expense! Who would dare to embarrass him like this?

"You surly pup! Dare ye not to lay hand on me again, else ye repent in sorrow."

He stood back and looked at her, his mouth fairly hanging open.

"Sorrow? I already have the sorrow, crone! Look at my wife!"

Sense stolen from him by his shock, his hand shaking, he pointed at the bed.

The old woman turned slowly, for it was the only way she could move, and gazed at the bed. She began to laugh aloud, finally holding her belly and braying like a donkey.

"You!! 'Tis you the great one fooled! Aye, this will be a good story around a campfire on a cold night."

William's hand snaked out to grab the old woman again. Before his fingers could close around her skinny arm, he felt a force slam against him and found himself flat on his ass, sprawled across the floor, the noise of his bare ass slapping the wood as intense as the pain it produced.

"Warned ye... dinna touch me again."

"What the hell IS that? Where is the woman I married?"

She stepped closer to the huge bed, looking down at the creature laying there in a faint.

"That is your wife? Aye, 'twould be, wouldn't it?"

"I said it was, dammit! Now what the hell is wrong with her? Do something, you witch!"

He felt as if everything he had ever believed was falling in ruins around him. This was *not* something that was supposed to happen! Especially not to him! He was the lord of the realm, dammit and these things did *not* happen to the lord of the realm! He wanted his wife back and he would have her!

She stepped closer to the bed as he got to his feet again, his hands twitching to throttle the answers from her. The witch looked as though she were muttering the words of a curse as she leaned over the creature on the bed to see better. She was nodding her head and there was a crooked set to her mouth as she turned to speak.

"Well... you've run afoul of the dragon from North Pambleton. 'Tis a shame, it is. I read the leaves for this one and it was truly foretold that she would bear you many sons. P'raps at the time of the reading she had not yet been cursed."

"Cursed? Bloody hell, woman... undo the curse then!"

She craned her neck to look up at him as he stepped closer to her, careful not to touch her again. She looked at him as though he were a dolt and needed everything explained to him.

"Can't be undone except by him who put it there. Not a likely thing to happen, Lord William. He wanted her for himself and when he couldn't have her... he cursed her."

It was more than he could bear and he turned from her, pacing a few steps away and then back, his fists clenched tightly at his sides.

"What the hell are you talking about? Who wanted her? Who cursed her like this? What is she supposed to be, any way!!??"

"'Tis what they call an anthrofox, me lord. Looks kinda human, don't she?"

William looked at the bed again, this time with a different eye. Still shocked at what had happened, he now began to see the fox like features that had replaced the freckled sunlit face he had kissed repeatedly. Her face was almost human but her skin was now covered by a fine pelt of reddish fur. Her ears were the most fox like thing about her... pointed and tipped with black. Her body still looked human, though smaller than it had but it too was covered with that pelt of fur. Then he spotted her tail... tail?? Before he even realized it, his hand was pressed to his forehead as if to stave off pain and he was shaking his head. His wife had a tail... his wife... a tail.

"I heard tell the curse would begin when ye spurted yer seed inta her. And I can see from the disarray that the deed has been done. Foxy she is and foxy she will stay. 'Tis naught to be done.

"As for who it was... I said it oncet, didn't ya hear me? 'Twas the dragon from North Pambleton what done it. Fancies himself a ladies' man, that one."

Not able to believe the words from the witch's mouth, William stumbled back a few steps and fell awkwardly into a chair set against the wall, oblivious to his nakedness.

"A dragon? A dragon put a curse on her? Because he wanted her for himself? What kind of thing have I wed?"

"'Twas not her fault, me lord... she believed the leaves and came to ye."

"Mmmmmm."

The flabbergasted lord and the wizened old witch turned to the bed just as her eyes fluttered open.

She raised her hand and looked at it, hoping that what she had seen before was an illusion of some sort, then her gaze fell lower and she saw the rest of her body.

"No... what is this? What has happened?"

She gasped loudly and gripped the bedcovers tight to steady herself with a bit of reality. Her eyes were wide open as she turned her gaze to him.

"My lord, what have you done to me? Why would you do this to me on our wedding day?"

"I?" he roared. "I had naught to do with it, wench. Yon witch says 'twas a dragon that did it."

Cara stood up beside the bed on shaky legs and looked at herself in the large mirror across from the bed. She wasn't as tall as she was before. There was a fine layer of red fur covering her skin. Quite a pretty creature... *if*... it hadn't been her looking into the mirror. Her ears were pointed where they poked out from her long hair, the black tips twitching from side to side. She turned, watching in the mirror, hoping that it was an illusion and when she realized it was not, she crumpled to the floor in tears.

"My lord... I don't understand. The dragon did this? But... why? I have done naught to the dragon."

Despair and confusion filled her mind as she wept for what had happened. Cara was crumpled into a weeping ball of fur on the floor and felt his heavy tread in the boards under her. She peeked up to see him towering over her, glaring his anger at the diminutive witch.

"Do something, witch! Fix this! Make her my woman again instead of this quivering ball of fur!"

The witch craned her neck and looked up at him.

"Did ye not understand me words? I can do nothing. 'Tis the dragon that must remove the spell. 'Tis the dragon that must give ye back your woman and I doubt it will happen in this lifetime. What he wants... he takes, by hook or by crook."

William stood there with clenched fists, glaring at the witch, then at her and back again. His gaze burned into her as she sensed his anger building. She trembled as she watched his face turning redder by the moment.

"Call the physician then. Perhaps he can..."

"He can do naught. 'Tis the dragon only can remove it."

His arm swept across the top of a nearby table, sweeping aside the vase of fresh flowers brought for the wedding and a tray laden with spirits and goblets. Broken glass spun upwards as it hit the floor, almost striking her and making her cry out.

"I'll have my woman back!"

"Nay, Lord William... you will not. He will not permit it and there is naught you can do to change that."

Terrified at what he might do next, Cara gained her feet and backed away from her angry husband as tears streaked down her furry face. Her heart longed for his arms around her to soothe away her fears but the look of disgust mingled with anger on his face kept her from leaping into his arms.

His great stature seemed to melt away before her eyes as he understood. She would not be his woman again… but would stay as this… creature that stood trembling before him. She sobbed as he shook his head, not wanting to accept the facts.

"Get out, woman. Seek out this dragon and find out what he will take to return my woman to me."

"Stubborn man. Are your ears filled with beans, then? He will *not* release her. He wants her for his own."

The despair showed on his face as he gazed at Cara. The look of great sadness that took the place of the anger almost broke her heart. Fresh tears streaked down her face as she saw the disbelief in his eyes… the betrayal as tears filled his eyes.

"This cannot be," he whispered.

"My lord… can we not continue? Would it be so difficult for you to have me thus?"

Her voice held a pleading note as she gazed up him, drawing closer to him in her desire to somehow make this work… to somehow make him accept her as she now was. The foretold future was not the only thing that had brought her to him in the village square. She had often admired him from afar and been drawn to him, relishing the strength she had seen in everything he did.

He stood taller and snorted at her suggestion.

"I am a lord of the realm, woman. Would you have me shamed before the king?"

A stab if pain shot through her heart as if he had struck her. Cara stumbled backward, only catching her balance as she was pressed against the side of the great bed… the one she had hoped to always share with him. *Shamed? She would shame him?* All she had wanted to do since the first time she saw him was be with him, the fortune she had been told was only an added bonus and now he was throwing away everything that could have been. The children she had hoped to bear him would be lost. The love she felt in her heart was dying more with each of his actions and with each word of betrayal. As she stared at him in shock, her dignity was assailed and she reached for the clothes piled at her feet. Grasping the heavy dress, she pulled it up and held it against her furry breast.

"A shame for you? I would be a shame?"

She was shaking from head to toe as the meaning of his words sunk into her. She pulled the ill-fitting dress around her as best she could, covering herself from his gaze.

"I would not *think* to shame you. Would that I could undo what has been done and also undo the pain in my heart."

She stepped closer to him and she saw him wrinkle his nose, as though he had smelled something bad. Then she stepped even closer and leaned into him.

"You don't seem to like the scent of me now, William. You couldn't get enough of it this morning at the well."

She smirked at the look on his face... at least he had the decency to appear abashed at his actions. He stood his ground and at least didn't step back from her, though his nose *did* stay wrinkled in distaste.

"You know, William... there are other magical creatures to be found in this kingdom and I daresay they have not been shunned as you have shunned me. *Your* ears have a bit of a point at the tips, William... have you never noticed that? Perhaps there is even some magical creature in *your* past. But then again... if there were, mayhap you wouldn't be so upset about my appearance now."

His nose twitched again and he stepped back, giving her further cause for anger.

"I did not cause this, *my lord.* Nor did I choose it, but I *do* choose *this.* "

The anger and betrayal were evident in her voice as she spat the words at him.

"Your line dies here, my lord. You will live your life alone and it will die here, for you are sending away the truest love of your life."

She gathered what was left of her dignity and walked to the door, opening it slowly, facing the courtiers waiting in the hall. Amidst the gasps of surprise, she pushed her way through them and walked away.

William was aghast at the way things had happened and he could only stand there and watch her leave. Then he glared at the courtiers in the hallway and slammed the door as they gaped at him.

His footsteps were heavy as he stamped back and forth across his rooms. He had been so taken with her at the well... so desirous of her that he had changed all his future plans for the kingdom, just to take her to his bed. If there was anything he could do to change her back! If only there were magic spells that could be cast to bring her back to him the way she had been! He stared down at the witch as he came to a stop in front of her… he was so angry at the turn of events that he found it difficult to speak.

"There is nothing to be done? Nothing that can bring back the woman that stole my heart with her sauciness?"

"I've told ye true, my lord. There is naught to be done lest the dragon do it and he will not. He wants her fer himself and 'tis all it will be. His magic is more potent than any these old eyes have seen afore."

"Witch… I would almost give the kingdom for that to be done. Would he not take the kingdom and give her back?"

Hope at the thought caught his breath in his throat and then dashed it again as she shook her head.

"He wouldn't take it all? I would give it gladly to have that silky skin against me again. She enflamed me body and soul and naught will be the same again for me. I want her back!"

Heart pounding in his chest, he turned away from her and stepped to the window. Looking out, he saw the furry little creature walking through the courtyard with her head held high. She still held the large dress against her, leaving a wide trail through the dust as it dragged behind her. When she reached the gate, she stopped suddenly and turned back to the castle, looking up. The rapid beating of his heart skipped as he saw her face and the glint of tears as the sunlight kissed her once again. He closed his eyes and took a deep breath to staunch the tears that suddenly filled his eyes. When they opened again, dry as befitted the lord of the kingdom… she was gone and the dress lay in a pile in the dirt.

"Gods!! Why? What have I done that this should come to pass?!

The witch's voice was soft behind him and he turned to look down at her again. His body was trembling with anger and despair as she spoke.

"Methinks your line lives on, Lord William, but it will never be quite the same again."

The words penetrated his muddled senses and he fell back against the window sill, eyes closed as he contemplated her meaning.

"What are you saying, woman? She is gone… how can there be…"

The words were barely out of his mouth, his questions still forming and the witch was gone. She didn't walk through the door or down the hall… she was just… gone.

Chapter Three

"Adrian? What happened to them? Don't stop now. You have to tell me what happened next."

He smiled softly down at her and hugged her to him again. He took the hand that held the pendant and drew it to his lips, kissing each finger as it curled around the delicate chain.

"My mother told me very little of the next few months of her life, Crys. Only that it was a difficult time for her. She had so many adjustments to make in her life and the way she lived it. I think there were days that she simply cried from dawn to dusk. She was heartbroken at the way William had treated her and I think she held to the hope that he would change his mind and come for her."

"But… but Adrian… surely she told you more. You wouldn't have begun this story without an ending. You wouldn't do that to me. Would you?"

The look on her face as she gazed up at him touched him as only she could. So trusting in everything he did and said to her, she was almost childlike in her love for him. The love that she had gifted him filled his heart with joy… and clutched at it with a bit of sorrow as well.

He chuckled softly and hugged her to him as he kissed her forehead.

"You know me better than that, sweet woman. I would never think to disappoint you."

***

Cara heard the crackle of a broken branch outside her little cave and she hurried to the entrance, with a smile on her face. She was expecting the Witch of Wolstad. The witch had shown herself to be a good friend.

When she looked outside the entrance to her new home, there was no one there. She frowned and turned to go back inside, her foot bumping against something that hadn't been there before. As long as she had been in the little cave, she had come to know the area surrounding the entrance, quite well. She had labored there often enough, planting and tending the tiny flowers from the woods. As she knelt down to pick up the package, she smiled at the tiny white bells that hung from the glossy pointed leaves and gathered some to scent her pillows.

As she entered the cave, she dropped the package on the table and proceeded to her bed, scattering the little bells amongst the fragrant pine boughs. A soft smile curled her lips as the mingled scents wafted up. Unable to help herself, she drew her hands to her nose and inhaled deeply. The white bells had always been her favorite flower and she loved bringing them in where she could smell them all day.

When she had sniffed to her delight, she rose and went back to the entrance, looking for the witch. Then she remembered the package and turned to the table. The paper was decorative and appeared to be well made with a silky feel to it. Her heart skipped a beat as she realized the cost of something as fine as this paper. William! He had sent her this package! Perhaps he had changed his mind at last!

She laughed as she ripped open the shiny paper and found a piece of folded parchment inside. As she unfolded it, something slipped out and fell to the ground. Before picking it up, she read the words inscribed on the parchment.

'Please wear this always, to know your true love.'

It was signed... 'One who has always loved you'.

It *was* from William! She clutched the parchment to her chest and danced around the cave, a sudden song on her lips. She laughed and danced for several moments before she remembered that something had fallen from the parchment. She hurried back to the table and dropped to her knees to search for it.

It sparkled in the light from the cave entrance and when she held it up to examine it, she gasped with delight. It was a pendant dangling on a fine golden chain. She blew on it gently to banish the dust and watched it sway in her fingers. She smiled at the rose pendant, admiring the delicate cuts that gave it the appearance of a real rose. There was even a tiny drop of dew on one of the petals...and a *Z* cut into one of the leaves that swirled around the rose. The entire pendant was wrapped lightly in threadlike strands of gold... almost like a golden spider web.

Cara smiled softly and slipped the chain over her head, her fingers clasped over the pendant as it fell between her little furry breasts.

"What is it ye have there, lass? A pretty?"

She looked up and there stood the Witch, smiling down at her, a large tote bag at her feet.

"Aye, it is, it must be from William. Who else could have left it here? But he didn't sign the note that came with it."

The Witch stepped forward, leaned to look closer at the pendant and smiled.

"Aye... 'Tis a pretty indeed. One that cost a ransom as well, I'll wager."

"I *knew* it was from William. He has had a change of heart then? Have you seen him? Or spoken to him? When will he be coming for me?"

She was so excited, her face almost ached from the broad smile and her heart was leaping in her chest. She clasped the witch's hands in hers and tried to pull her into another dance around the cave, but she was puzzled when the witch didn't join in her joy.

The Witch was shaking her head, a sad expression on her face.

"I know 'tis what you would wish, lass, but I dinna think it's from the lord."

Cara felt the tears stinging her eyes as the witch's words sank in. She was right, of course... William didn't even know where she was living. She sank slowly onto the chair at the side of the table as the tears slipped down her face.

"I... I guess you're right. How would he find me here? But if it wasn't William, then who could have left it here? Who would give *me* such a thing of beauty?"

"I know not what to say to ye, lass. 'Tis a lovely thing indeed and ye deserve such loveliness but as to who left it... I've no words for ye about that."

Lifting the heavy bag and looking closely at Cara, the Witch ran her hand across the girl's forehead.

"Sick are ye, lass? Yer a mite pale this day."

"Well, the stomach has been giving me a bit of a problem this morning, but I feel fine other than that. And now, my head is aching as well. Must be from the upset about William and his stubbornness."

"Aye, must be then."

Days passed and the Witch's visits were frequent, but there came a time when she needed to travel away from the area and Cara fell into the despair of loneliness. Leaving her little cave, she wandered through the woods, just to be out and about…just to feel the sun on her furry little body. Stepping into a clearing near her favorite pool, she came up short, gasping her surprise.

There in the wood was a man… tall; handsome beyond belief, naked and dripping with water as though he had just stepped from the pool. He turned toward her at the sound of her gasp and looked surprised for a moment. Then a bright smile lit up his face and he bowed toward her.

"Good morning, little fox. I hope your travels are happy ones."

"Good morning, kind sir. Thank you. I didn't mean to intrude."

She stepped back into the bushes, intending to leave but wanting to stay. Something about this man drew her attention as no other had done, but she didn't know him and…

"Nay, please wait."

He reached down, turned his back to her and pulled his pants on. When he was done with the pants, he turned back to her. She had watched every movement he made and it brought a heat to her face she hadn't felt in quite a long time. The grace in the way he moved… the smile on his face… something about him drew her attention and stayed her feet.

"Now… a more proper visage for you, my lady."

She chuckled softly and stood her ground.

"I thank you Sir… but 'twas not necessary for my benefit. I saw nothing wrong with your appearance."

She couldn't believe she was saying such things to a complete stranger, but there was something about him that she hadn't felt before… even with William.

"Are you new to the area, Sir?"

"Well, not really. I've been hereabouts a time or two over the last few years. And you, lass? Are you new here?"

"I used to live in the village downstream, Sir, but…"

Her words faltered as she thought of her transformation and her reason for being in the woods. She felt the heat in her face again and her head dropped. She wasn't ashamed of what she had become but it was difficult for her to voice the explanation.

"But? It sounds as though there's a story to be told, lass. Sit and tell me while we eat." He nodded towards the base of a tall willow tree and she saw a picnic lunch spread out on the thick grass.

She smiled at the thought of dining with this handsome man, forgetting for a moment that she would have to share her tale of woe.

"Thank you, kind sir. It would be my pleasure."

She crossed to the base of the tree while he dressed and settled herself to her knees, then noticed a bit of discomfort in her back and resettled herself. When she looked up again, he was taking a seat beside her and reaching for a loaf of bread.

"Then tell me your tale, lovely lass. You lived in the village and now you don't?"

He watched her as she sighed heavily and her head drooped as she began to speak, softly, hesitantly.

"The Witch of Wolstad read my fortune, Sir and it was foretold that I would wed the lord of this realm and bear him many sons. So, if truth be told, I threw myself at him as if I were a hussy. I teased him unmercifully and he took me to the castle, wed me and then bed me. When he was done and I opened my eyes again, all I saw was a shock of surprise on his face. Then he jumped from the bed and backed away from me."

When she paused to catch her breath, it was like she was coming up for air. She had hurried through the words so quickly that it took him a moment to understand them. A wave of regret moved through him as the words sank in and he saw the tears in her eyes. She might look different but she had deep feelings of loss and was one of the most delicate creatures he had ever encountered. To think that a *lord* would behave in such a manner was an affront to his sensibilities.

He searched the pockets on his doublet, found a handkerchief and held it out to her as her story continued. Her little hand took the proffered cloth and swiped at her cheeks.

"When the Witch came, she told the tale. There is a dragon here, Sir and she said he cursed me. When the seed of the lord filled my body, I was changed to this. He was afraid and shocked and... and disgusted. He bade me leave and never return."

"Ah, lovely lass... 'Tis a sad tale indeed. A lord of the realm acting in such a manner against such a sweet thing as you is a dishonor to his position and name."

Her voice broke on the last words and she was shaking as deep sobs wracked her body. When her voice first faltered on the word disgusted, he leaned closer but when she broke down completely, he scooted over and slid his arm around her shoulders, pulling her close.

"Then he was a fool, little fox and you are well rid of him. A lovelier creature I doubt I have ever seen or ever will see again."

His scent filled her head and his gentle touches of comfort filled the hole left by the lord's absence.

"Truly, Sir? I'm not something to run from? Or be disgusted by?"

"Aye, it's most definitely true. What is your name, little fox? Although I don't mind calling you little fox, I would dearly love to know your name."

"My name is Cara. I have no last name other than the lord's and I doubt he would want me to use it now."

"It doesn't matter, little one. Cara is enough and it's a lovely name. I am called Zaven and I am pleased to have met you."

He took up the kerchief from her lap and wiped the tears from her face, smiling softly as he did.

"No more tears, Cara. Now take this and eat. You look pale and sweet fruit is always good no matter if it is for fur or skin."

He chuckled and leaned toward her, kissing her forehead as gently as possible.

She gasped at the tiny shock from the kiss and then smiled up at him, feeling the pleasure she had dreamed of feeling with William.

They passed the remainder of the day with food and talk, each telling tales of remembered times, though he had many more tales to tell than she did. The food dishes always seemed to be filled at least half way, the wine flagon was never empty but she was so wrapped up in listening to him tell of his exploits that she didn't pay attention to those details. When she yawned, he laughed out loud.

"Poor Cara... I've kept you all this day with nattering about stories of old and you are so tired you can barely keep your eyes open. Rest now. Close your eyes and rest while I pack up the lunch and then I will take you home."

"I don't know why I'm so tired all of a sudden. Surely you must believe it was not the company, Sir."

"Sir? Is it now Sir again?"

"No, Zaven. It is Zaven, for sure. It must be the tiredness taking my senses."

He chuckled and stood up to clear the lunch as she closed her eyes and leaned back against the tree. The soft sounds of his movements added to her sense of relaxation and she peeked up at him for a moment before sighing deeply and closing her eyes again.

It seemed only a moment had passed when she felt herself being scooped up and held against his chest. She was almost giddy from the closeness and was of two minds. She wanted to snuggle against him but what sense of propriety she had left dictated otherwise.

"Zaven! I can walk, you know. It's not far."

"But you are light as a feather, dear Cara and there is no reason for you to walk when I can carry you quite easily. Now… which way do we go?"

Cara gave up the argument and snuggled against him. The scent of him as she nestled under his chin filled her again and she could only point the way to her little cave, not quite trusting herself to speak. Then she was asleep again, smiling in his arms. The next thing she knew, he was leaning over her, putting her in her little bed.

"Mmmm, Zaven. How can I thank you? You gave me such a wonderful day."

"There is no need for thanks, little one, other than to let me see you again for more delightful conversation."

She stifled another yawn as she nodded up at him.

"What is this, Cara?" His fingers caressed the golden rose hanging from her neck.

"Isn't it lovely? It was left outside the cave as a gift to me, but I know not who sent it."

"It is quite beautiful. Whoever sent it to you must love you very much. Perhaps I should simply leave you be… I wouldn't want to anger your lover."

"But Zaven… I don't know who sent it."

"Well… whoever he is, maybe he won't mind a bit of conversation and a little food and drink between friends."

"If he shows himself, Zaven… I will tell him that I choose my friends and will talk and dine with them as I choose."

He laughed loudly, leaned down and kissed her forehead again and then stood up beside the bed.

"Take care, sweet little fox. I will be back to see you again."

Chapter Four

Adrian looked down just as Crys looked up, pouting at his pause. He smiled down at her and ran the tip of his finger across her pouting lower lip, the barely exposed claw teasing the pout into a smile. Once again, simply her presence touched his heart that she gave of her heart and love so deeply. He had met her and thought it was just another conquest when it started, but she had found a place in his heart that would never cease to amaze him. The love for her had grown faster and more deeply than any he had experienced in his long life and he had experienced love many times in his past. Then he leaned down and kissed her softly, nibbling teasingly at her lower lip.

"Only a momentary break, sweet Crys. I just couldn't bear another moment without kissing you."

He felt the immediate increase in warmth in her skin and knew he had caused her to blush yet again. He loved the way she responded to him… to his touch and words. It was a part of him now, his love for her. He was so very tired of his long existence. Living for such a long time might be the fantasy of some, but they had never lived it. Too often he had come to care for someone, only to lose them as they aged and he did not. Too many times the pain was deep and almost crippling as he tried to go on with his existence. This time he was determined to keep what he loved.

His clawed fingers traced lightly down her throat and he leaned to kiss the pulse point, his tongue flicking across the heat of it.

"Do you hunger, Adrian?"

"Of course, my love. I always hunger for a taste of you, but not yet… first the story and then a sweet taste. A reward for a story well told."

She chuckled softly and leaned her head back, exposing her throat completely, teasing him and offering the promise once again. She shivered against him and moaned softly as his tongue whipped against her neck again. Then he tightened his arm around her a bit more and continued in the soft, deep voice that was so sexy it thrilled her to the very core of her being.

***

Cara squatted by her little hearth, stirring the stew she had made when she heard a scraping noise outside her cave entrance and turned to find Zaven standing there, apparently trying to figure out how to knock at a door that didn't exist. Her heart pounded in excitement and happiness. She giggled as she rose to her feet, then gasped and put a hand to her back. She sighed inwardly, thinking that the dampness of living in the cave must be having an effect on her.

"Good day, Zaven. Please come in."

She watched as he ducked down so he didn't bump his head on the entrance. He was smiling broadly and carrying a small package with him.

"It's lovely to see you again, little one. I hope you are feeling rested."

She felt a momentary heat in her face at the pleasing words and ducked her head a bit to hide it before raising her head again, a bright smile on her face.

"Aye, that I am. Please sit down. Have you eaten? It isn't much but I have a stew cooking and you are welcome to join me."

"It smells delicious, little Cara and I would enjoy that. It will go well with what I have brought."

He smiled broadly as he handed her the package. When she opened it, she found a bottle of fine wine and a small cake from the local baker's shop.

"You didn't have to do this, Zaven. I don't expect you to bring gifts and I do have a few things from the village here. The Witch brings me things that I need."

"I know I don't need to bring gifts, but it pleases me to do so. You wouldn't deprive me of my happiness, would you Cara?"

She smiled up at him and shook her head.

"I wouldn't think of it, Zaven."

He chuckled softly, and stood there for a moment, glancing around.

"There is one thing I would like to bring here, Cara. If you wouldn't mind that is. If it wouldn't cause problems with your lover."

"Zaven… I've told you. There *is* no lover. Truly, I don't know who sent the necklace."

"Well, Cara… it's just that… with my size… well, I don't *mind* sitting on the floor to spend time with you, but…"

Cara looked around her little cave and realized he was right. There was a place for her and one for the Witch, who was also small of stature, but nothing for anyone as large as Zaven.

Her embarrassment was evident as she spoke again.

"My apologies, Zaven… I simply did not realize."

"'Tis nothing, little one… nothing of consequence. If you don't mind, though, I will bring a chair for me to use when I visit."

He took a seat on the floor beside her little fire and they began the exchange of stories again. Laughter and good feelings filled the afternoon as they shared her little pot of stew, filling their plates frequently. Zaven stayed until twilight and kissed her hand lightly when he took his leave of her.

She prepared herself for bed, humming softly as she slid into her bed and then caught herself. Humming? Then she chuckled to herself, surprised but happy that she had met this wonderful man. She was smiling softly as sleep claimed her.

Next day, he appeared with a large carved chair at her cave entrance. When she saw the size of the chair, she wondered at how he could possibly have gotten it there without help… at least a cart, but there was none in evidence. And then… it was inside the cave and in place near her fire pit. She didn't recall how it got inside, didn't recall how he carried it in… none of that seemed to matter. It only mattered that he was there and comfortable as they shared food and lively discussion.

As the days passed, Cara became more and more comfortable with the large man in her little cave. He was intelligent, charming, and handsome and seemed interested in every little thing she did. More and more, thoughts of her husband drifted further and further into the deep recesses of her mind.

One day he appeared at her cave without his usual smile. When he was seated in his large chair, he held out his hand to her, beckoning her closer.

"I have brought news, Cara, and I fear it will make you sad again."

Cara had been smiling when he came to the cave but her face had fallen into one of puzzlement and confusion as he sat down. She took his hand and he pulled her into a hug before he spoke again.

"I bring word of a proclamation in the realm, sweet little fox. It has been posted in each village for all to see."

"What is it, Zaven? I confess you are scaring me a bit now."

He pulled her from the gentle hug onto his lap and held her against him as he began the sorrowful tale.

"This is how it was stated it in the proclamation - Your husband, your darling William, has posted notice of 'a divorce from the woman known as Cara.' It has been signed by him and by the bishop of the church for all to see. Your disappearance has been cited as the reason and it would seem that all are in agreement with this. There is much talk in the villages as well."

He had been cuddling her against him and he felt her trembling in his arms. When she leaned back and looked up into his face, he saw the tears and then a flash of anger as the lie penetrated her sorrow.

"It wasn't my fault, Zaven. I didn't ask the dragon to change me. I only wanted to love William and give him the sons the Witch foretold."

"I know that, Cara. I really do not know this dragon, but perhaps he did it because he loves you. It must mean something that he would go to such an extent to have you for himself."

Cara stiffened in his arms and looked up again.

"Love me? Zaven, I barely know him. How could he love me?"

"Stranger things have happened, sweet little fox. Perhaps he saw you from afar and you captured his heart with your lovely smile and winning ways."

Then he pulled her close again and cuddled her, tears stinging his eyes at her obvious pain and confusion. He rocked her gently in his arms as she wept against his broad chest.

Soon he was speaking softly, beginning another of his tales of adventure, hoping to use it to bring an end to her tears and sorrow.

Then came the day when the Witch returned to visit and was surprised to find the large man there. She had just entered, her eyes adjusting to the dusky light that was the norm for the cave, when she gasped slightly at his sudden rise from the chair.

"Who are you that you are in this place? Where is Cara?"

"I am called Zaven and am a friend of the little Cara. She has gone to bring back some flowers she found. And you are?"

"I am the Witch of Wolstad. Do I... know ye?"

The Witch peered at him closely. Something about him... something seemed familiar. Was it the way he carried himself? Even simply rising from the chair there was a grace about him, an attitude that said he was more than he seemed. And he was so big!

"I don't believe we have met before."

Still, something was familiar about him. She cocked her head as she studied him.

"Aye, I'll take ye at yer word, but… it seems to this old head of mine that we have crossed paths before. It will come to me anon."

His eyes were darting between her and the entrance, as if he were thinking of escape from a foe and that made her even surer that she knew him. She wracked her brain, going through a series of faces in her head to try and match him with one she had met before.

What is it about him? What is he hiding behind that smile, she wondered. If he hurts the lass, he will find out about the wrath of the Witch of Wolstad, she thought.

Then a wide, bright smile lit up his face and she knew without turning that Cara had returned. It was obvious that he cared for the little fox, so perhaps she should let it be… for now. But the emotions flitting across his face wouldn't dispel her search for his name and face in her vast store of knowledge. When she turned to greet Cara, she almost gasped at the change in her.

When last she had seen the little fox, Cara had appeared pale and washed out; her fur was scruffy and patchy. Now she appeared to glow, had gained weight and her fur was silky and soft as the Witch hugged her. The Witch held her back and looked her over from head to toe.

"Well, I see yer in a better frame, little Cara. Stomach all better now?"

"Aye, it is. It must be the company I've been keeping."

She smiled up at Zaven as he took the flowers and found a small vase while she hugged the Witch. It seemed that he made quite a show of stepping back from the two females, thereby distancing himself a bit from their greeting.

Cara whispered to the Witch as she held her close.

"He's such a good friend. He tells me stories and keeps me busy during the day thinking of stories to tell him in return."

"I'm glad to see yer well, child."

She watched Zaven as he moved comfortably in the little home, a soft smile on her face. The Witch watched too… sure she knew the man but not able to place him. Not yet any way.

She watched Cara as well. The young woman seemed to be taken with the tall man… a good thing, in its way, to keep her thoughts from

William and his treatment of her. Her heart beat with gladness that the little creature seemed happy again, and then her eyes flashed with anger at the actions of the 'lord of the realm'.

They dined together, chatted about her travels and as they did, she became more comfortable with the stranger. Still, the sense lingered that she knew him.

The Witch took her leave of them, and looked back just before she left the cave. The two were so engrossed in their discussion that they barely noticed her departure, but something had flickered at the edge of her vision. What? What was he doing here? Was he using magic on the child? She tarried another moment watching them and then went on her way, planning to read the leaves when she reached her home. Something was amiss here and she was determined to find out what it was.

Chapter Five

Cara sat in the small pool of water, rinsing the soap root from her hair when she heard a crashing behind her. Her body jerked at the noise and she turned to face it. What she saw made her gasp in surprise and seethe with anger. A towering presence had pushed its way between the trees and was grinning down at her.

Very pointedly, Cara turned her back to the dragon and finished rinsing her hair. She was trembling as she squeezed the water out of her hair.

"What do you want? Why have you come here to torment me?"

His large head dropped down a bit at the scorn in her voice. The sunlight filtering down through the leaves turned his iridescent scales to shards of scintillating color as he moved. When he spoke again, each movement of his head and body caused more colors to bounce around the glen. He was fairly small for a dragon, the scales covering him rippled with the thick musculature under them. His wings were tucked against his sides but she could see them quivering as if he was anxious to take flight. His clawed hand reached down and plucked the delicate chain from where it lay on the little pile of clothes on the bank of the pool.

"Were I you, lovely Cara… I wouldn't lay such a pretty bauble on the ground where it might be lost."

"It wasn't on the ground. It was with my shift… until you bothered it."

The dragon towered over her, shaking his head.

"Sure you won't change your mind and come with me, pretty Cara? Everything you ever thought of could be yours, even more baubles like this one."

She stepped from the water, walked toward him and took the necklace from his claw. She put it with her little shift, reached for a towel and stared up at him as she dried herself.

"You ruined my life, dragon… and you think I would willingly go with you? I thought dragons were supposed to be wise and knowing. If you think that, then you are lacking."

"Ruined your life?"

"Yes! You cursed me… caused me to look like this! You took me from the love of my life!"

"Nay, little one… you may not see it now but I am truly the love of your life."

"You love the power you have over others and that is all you love. Not me, not anything else. Only the power."

Cara's words were bitten off in anger and bitterness at what he had caused for her.

"Now go away and leave me alone. Being in your presence tasks my patience."

By this time, she was dry and had pulled her little shift over her head. When she reached for the necklace and raised up to put the chain over her head, she saw that the dragon was gone. She smiled at that idea and let the delicate chain fall, the pendant dropping down between her furry little breasts.

"Is the little fox decent in the dell?"

She started at the soft words, and then smiled broadly when she called her response.

"Aye, she is decent, my friend. Would that you had been here a bit earlier. That dragon was here."

Zaven pushed the bushes aside and strode into the shadowed glen, looking around as he heard her words.

"Dragon? I've seen none such, my sweet Cara, but I would have protected you from him if I had. After all… I could do nothing less for my friend."

His brave words touched her heart and she marveled at the way he showed no fear of the thought of meeting a dragon face to face. The words weren't new, he had said them before, and yet… something was different this time. She stepped closer to him, her eyes never leaving his and when she was close enough, she reached up and caressed his cheek, her furry fingers sliding over the bronzed skin of his face. At her touch, he leaned down and briefly brushed his lips across hers.

Cara gasped softly, but it was difficult to tell if it was with surprise or pleasure. She pressed closer to him and slid her arms around his chest, feeling his heart beating faster as she leaned against him. Her heart speeded up to match his as she clung to him. Her breath was caught in her throat as she breathed in his scent and her words were soft.

"You have been a good friend, Zaven. It has meant a great deal to me."

He tilted her head up with a finger under her chin and smiled down at her.

"If truth be told, little Cara… I think it's more than friends I want to be."

She felt as though a bubble of fear and sadness burst inside her at his words. Her heart was pounding now and tears of joy filled her eyes. After the bad time with William, she had thought never to feel like this again… wanted… cared about. That was the feeling that had been growing inside her… that was the happiness that had been building. He *was* more than a friend now and she was finally realizing it. He had touched her heart as even William had not done.

"I think, Zaven my friend… that is something I would like as well."

He laughed with her and grabbed her, swinging her up to sit on his shoulder as he turned from the glade. In only moments they were at her little cave and he ducked inside carrying her. Once in the little home she had made, he lifted her down and held her in front of him, her feet barely touching the ground. As he looked into her eyes, he leaned down and kissed her again, softly, tentatively, then with a bit of added pressure as he pulled her small body against his.

He heard no gasp this time, but a soft moan escaped into the kiss. Cara's nipples hardened against his chest as he held her. When their lips parted, she gazed up at him and smiled a soft smile. His heart leapt with the thought that she had voiced the same wishes he had. To finally be able to hold her as more than a friend… to actually show her his love was more than he had hoped for.

Cara clung to him as she gazed up. The idea that she wanted more from him than mere friendship hadn't crossed her mind until he said it in the glen and then it was as though that had always been the way of it. His closeness, the tender way he held her was something she had not felt with William who had only expressed his lust with her. She snuggled against him and felt a dampness start between her furry thighs.

She hadn't felt like this since that day with William… no, not even then. Zaven made her feel so much more than William had that day. The softness of the lips pressed against hers… the quickened beating of his heart as he held her against him… She opened her eyes slowly and gazed up into his. Her eyes opened wider as she saw a flash in his eyes… a kaleidoscope of color she had never noticed before. Then she felt his lips again and all thoughts of the strangeness of his eyes were gone.

His mouth was so sweet to her as his tongue slipped across her lips. When he pressed his tongue into her mouth, she suckled it gently, wiggling in his arms to get even closer. Wonder surged through her mind…she was feeling things she had never felt before. She had gone to William because it was ordained, told in the tea leaves but she hadn't felt a love for him. This though… this *must* be love. This quivering in her heart as her body trembled. This surge of joy that moved through her at his simple kiss.

He broke the kiss then and gazed down into her eyes.

"Little Cara… tell me now if you wish this to stop for if it continues, I'll not swear I'll be able to stop."

Cara looked up at him, a soft smile on her lips, and a gleam in her eye and she shook her head. Was he mad? Couldn't he tell from the way she trembled how much she wanted him?

"No, Zaven… don't stop. I don't think I want you to ever stop."

A broad grin split his face as he hugged her against him.

"My little lady… it will be my utmost pleasure to grant your wish."

He held her up higher against him so he didn't need to bend down to reach her and pressed a deep, intense kiss against the sweetness of her lips. With one large hand, he held her against him while the other slipped through her fur, caressing every part of her body he could reach. When his fingers grazed her sex, she gasped in the kiss and wiggled against his fingers. Then it was her turn to break the kiss and she leaned her head back and gazed up at him.

"You take my breath away, Zaven. And you torment me with your touches. Is this your intent, sir? To tease me to insensibility?"

He chuckled softly as he gazed down at her and then kissed her quickly.

"To tease you? Perhaps to some extent my little furry lady, but only to some extent for I want to bring you pleasure, Cara. I want you to feel the pleasure that only seeing you brings me."

His words were so unexpected that her heart leapt in her chest. Her hands went to the sides of his face and she lifted her head, pressing her lips to his again. Breathless, almost senseless, she felt him carry her to her little bed at the back of the cave and then she was on her back looking up at him. She watched every movement of his hands as he undressed, her tongue gliding across lips suddenly dry from her quickened breathing. She had been a virgin when she went to William and had only seen him naked and had not enjoyed their one coupling. As Zaven's trousers dropped to the floor of the cave, she gasped at the size of him, standing out from his body, hard and throbbing, twitching as she watched.

Because her bed was of a size for her, he nudged her to the side, sat down with his back to the cave wall, smiled and lifted her up, holding her in the air facing him. She marveled at his strength and grinned broadly, trembling in his grasp. With his eyes locked to hers, he began to lower her body over his rampant shaft.

"Guide me, sweet Cara. Guide me to your treasure and let me please you beyond your wildest dreams and I will be careful of you, be assured of that."

She reached down between her outspread thighs, closed her fingers around his shaft and pulled it until it rested against the outer lips of her heat. Moving it gently back and forth, she felt it slide between the outer lips and gasped as it pressed against her clit. A shock of lightning surged through her body and her eyes opened even wider. There was a gleam of delight in his eyes as he saw her response. Her hand moved another fraction and then he was at the entrance to her treasure. His hips moved up just as his hands moved down and she felt the tip of his shaft begin to penetrate her.

A long, low, soft moan escaped her lips as she felt him stretching her heat. This was the feeling she had wanted with William… this gentleness, but it was something she hadn't experienced with him and never would.

Zaven held her tenderly, lowering her slowly on his shaft, filling her completely as he gazed into her eyes. Then she was leaning her face against his neck, inhaling the scent of him, her enjoyment at each touch showing in the way she squirmed over him. She trembled and sighed happily against his neck, her lips moving over his throat and shoulder. The muscles of her back quivered under the fine fur as his hands moved down, finally cupping her ass, one cheek in each hand. Her hips were moving with a graceful undulation.

Her eyes were closed with pleasure as she leaned against him. Her legs were spread around him as he sat there with his back against the wall. Her furry bottom rested on his thighs as she rocked on his shaft. Her clit pressed against him with each forward motion. She raised her head to his and kissed him gently. He was gasping for breath just as she was and he could feel his heart pounding as she leaned against him... the erratic beats almost matching hers.

Suddenly, she yipped as a fox would and nipped at his shoulder harder than she had before. Such wonderful sensations were building in her body. Her body was tingling, jumping with little shocks like lightning; her sex was dripping down over his thighs and balls as she rocked back and forth, side to side, up and down, always causing more pressure to tease her clit. Her muscles were clenching around him, then relaxing only to clench tight again. Her body was responding to him in ways she never thought about, as if it had a mind of its own. She rocked, shuddered, gasped and clung to him as the pleasure mounted and grew. All of a sudden, her head jerked up, her eyes wide as she looked into his eyes again.

"Zaven?"

She had no breath for anything else. She was trembling over him, her body shaking uncontrollably. And he smiled.

"Aye, Cara... let it go, lass, let it go my sweet furry lady. Enjoy the pleasure."

And it was as if the world exploded around her. Lights flashed behind her eyelids, her body quivered and she felt as though she were soaring into the sky and dropping into the deepest abyss at the same time. Her little hands clutched at his shoulders as the pleasure surged through her. Her body rocked harder, his large hands holding her down on his shaft as he twitched inside her. Together they reached the apex of delight and then slowly slid down the other side, clinging to each other, each breathing the hot exhaled breath of the other, moaning together as they kissed again and again.

"Ohh, Zaven... I never felt anything like that before. What did you do to me?"

He looked down at her with a surprised expression on his face.

"You never... what are you saying Cara? You were wed to the lord of the realm and you're... I don't understand, little one. How is it you never..."

She was snuggled against him, her trembling body slowly becoming calmer when she replied in a whisper.

"William only bed me once, Zaven and it wasn't the most pleasant thing I've ever experienced. I had heard of this pleasure, of course, but... never felt it and after this change in me, I never thought I would."

He kissed the top of her head and squeezed her.

"Sweet Cara… you are well rid of him. He is obviously an uncaring boor to treat you in such a manner. And to just bid you leave? I find that to be totally unacceptable. What you became is not your fault, but sweet Cara… what you became is a lovely little creature that is unique in all this world."

She snuggled against him, sighing happily. It was a few moments before she remembered something he said and looked up at him

"You said you would be careful, Zaven. What did you mean? Careful of what?"

He looked down at her and shook his head wonderingly.

"Cara, are you not aware of it? How can that be, sweet creature?"

"Aware of what, Zaven? I don't understand."

He laughed loudly and hugged her against him.

"Cara… surely you know you are pregnant."

"Pregnant? Why Zaven… why would you say such a thing?"

He put his large hand over her belly and rubbed a bit.

"Cara, I have seen the change. How could you not know?"

She had a shocked look on her face as she caught his meaning.

"I… it never crossed my mind, Zaven. I thought it was just that I was feeling better after the upset with William. You must be wrong, Zaven. How could that be? Between William and me? I'm so different from him now, it just couldn't be possible."

"Maybe you are different now, sweet Cara, but you weren't when the seed was planted as they say. Talk to the Witch if you doubt it, I'm sure she will tell you true."

All she could do was stare up at him, shaking her head, not sure she wanted to believe him. As she lay in his arms, she thought about the time since William had sent her away. She remembered the nausea, some vomiting… losing weight and then seeming to gain it back even though she ate no more than usual. Her hand slipped down and covered his as it rested on her belly.

"Truly, Zaven? You don't tease me?"

He chuckled softly, moving his hand from her belly and sliding it around her back to hold her closer.

"Truly, my sweet little Cara. Speak with the Witch, for it cannot be too many more months before there is another little furry bundle here."

Then his finger was under her chin, turning her face up until he was gazing into here eyes.

"If you allow it, my furry little darling, I would care for the child as I care for you."

"Zaven? You would take the child as your own? Is that what you are saying?"

His strong arms almost crushed the breath from her body as he laughed and held her tightly.

"Cara, I would take a whole herd of the lord's get, if it meant I could have you for mine."

His words melted her heart and she smiled against his neck. She leaned into his embrace and sighed happily. She reached up and caressed his face as he held her.

"What would I have done if I had never met you, Zaven?"

He leaned down to kiss her softly and whispered.

"I don't know sweet Cara, but I'm glad we don't have to find out."

The next days were spent thusly, loving and learning each other more intimately as each day passed. Cara came to know that she loved him deeply, in the way she had hoped to love William and she became acutely aware of the growth inside her belly. She had never considered what the gaining of weight could be... never thought in any way that she might carry the lord's son in her small body. She knew it was a son, for the leaves and bones had told of her future, even though the lord had cast her away. She would bear his son and be damned with him and his arrogant ways.

The Witch was a frequent visitor to the little cave and oftentimes spent the days with the couple, watching them together, watching the developing love affair. It wasn't long before she arrived at the little cave and found him alone again.

"Cara has gone to the pool to bathe. She will return shortly and I know she will be happy to see you."

"Aye, 'tis sure I am of that, but will you be happy when I speak my piece?"

Zaven looked at the witch, suspicion on his face as an invisible hand clutched at his guts. He stood up, took a deep breath, exhaled slowly and spoke between gritted teeth.

"Speak your piece then, Witch and we shall see."

"Ye fooled me for quite a while, but the truth has finally dawned on this old witch. I know ye now for whom and what ye are. So what will ye do? Strike me down? Strike me dumb so I may not speak the truth?"

Zaven stood there staring at her, shaking his head, a sad expression on his face.

"Nay, Witch. I will do naught but ask you to keep the secret for a while longer. The little one has come to love me, I think and I would not want to change that now."

"The curse was bad enough but now ye intend to fool her the rest of her days?"

He recoiled at her words, stricken to his core. He stumbled back and sat down heavily in the large chair, shaking his head as he held it in his hands.

"Nay, Witch. I only wanted to…"

"Ye only wanted to make her love ye."

The Witch sighed and shook her head as Zaven's true form became apparent to her. He was not a large dragon, but a majestic one nevertheless. His scales shone with an iridescence that did not need the sun's light to glow. His voice was soft and the sadness in his eyes was unmistakable.

"Yes, that's all I wanted… for her to love me."

"How is it that ye bewitched her? What did ye do to conceal yerself from her sharp little eyes?"

He sighed heavily as he moved from the large chair.

"'Twas the little bauble left outside the cave. It was bewitched and holds the influence of the maker and his wife within it. The maker was a true believer in love if my sources of information were correct and his spirit imbued the bauble with more powers than I have at my disposal. It was given to Cara to show her the truest love in her life and I think she has grown to know that is true.

"I *do* love her, Witch. More than that beast of a lord ever could."

"Aye, I've seen that with me own eyes."

"Then keep the secret for a while longer, I beg you. When the child is delivered and she knows I take it as well as her for my own, perhaps then she wouldn't be so against the idea of being the mate of a dragon."

"I must admit she is happy with ye. She has blossomed in her time with ye. She smiles now as never before and her heart is light even as her condition grows to a close."

Zaven was pacing the interior of the cave as he talked to the Witch and became silent as the Witch considered his request.

"Aye, all right then. Not a word will I say to the girl. But dragon… if ye hurt her, I'll find the most potent spell I can find and…"

"Have no fear of that. I love her and will do naught to harm her. This I swear."

Cara returned to the cave and found them deep in a discussion that ended abruptly when she stepped into the coolness of the cave.

"Ahh, my two favorite people in all the world. What secrets are you sharing that you have stopped so suddenly?"

She stepped to Zaven and leaned into his embrace as he looked over her head and nodded at the Witch.

"Simply plans for your little bundle to come, my love. Plans for his future happiness, of course."

She leaned her head back and gazed up into his eyes.

"Zaven, you do me honor by loving me and claiming the child as your own."

"Nay, little Cara. You do *me* honor by accepting my love and letting me love you. It is little enough that I can do for you and your child... our child."

She snuggled against him and turned her face to the Witch to speak.

"There is stew aplenty, my friend if you would join us. It would be a pleasure to share it with you."

The witch took a seat at the little table, smiling broadly as she noted the growth of Cara's little body.

"Come, child, let me feel."

Cara obediently left Zaven's embrace and walked to the Witch's side. Her gnarled hand came to rest on the furry little belly and her eyes closed as she felt the life stirring within.

"Aye, won't be long now, child. But I suppose I shouldn't call ye child any longer."

Cara giggled softly as she felt the child within squirming under the touch of the witch.

The old woman watched as the dragon reclaimed the furry little creature in his arms, able to see him now for what he was. The tenderness he showed her was beyond the Witch's comprehension. Dragons were supposed to be fierce, dangerous creatures but this one was taken over by a love she had not thought possible for a dragon to feel. She watched, smiling and nodding as the two together prepared for their little meal.

The three of them sat together, enjoying the food and drink, chatting amiably about things that passed in the village, around the realm and gossiped of stories from beyond the realm. When they had finished, Cara stood up to clear the dishes and immediately grabbed onto the edge of the table. Her face had gone pale and she gasped and winced in pain as she felt a flood of water cover her legs. She looked down as Zaven jumped to his feet and saw a pool of liquid around her little feet.

"Zaven?"

He towered over her and the Witch, concern etched into the planes of his handsome face. The witch saw shock on the dragon's face and maybe a touch of fear as well, as he gathered Cara into his arms.

"Aye, lass, it would appear that the time is ripe for a new life in this cave."

Tears slid down her face as she gazed up at Zaven. She was trembling in his arms as she leaned against him, her legs shaky and weak as another pain shot through her little body. Her belly was hard as the pain moved over it and she grimaced, her little claws now digging into his arms. He lifted her carefully and carried her to her little bed, glancing back over his shoulder at the Witch.

"I'm hoping you know what to do for her Witch, because I surely do not."

The old woman chuckled as she reached down into her ever present bag and pulled out four small packets of herbs.

"Aye, I know what to do. Fetch me some water to mix these herbs to ease her pain and get out of the way."

Zaven hurried to get the water then moved to sit at Cara's head, holding her hand in his. Long fingertips brushed the hair back from her sweaty face and soft words of comfort and encouragement fell from his lips.

"Not long, my love. Not long before your babe is here and the pain is gone. Keep that thought in your mind and keep hold of my hand. I'm here for you and always will be, my furry little darling."

Cara smiled up at him and saw the concern in his face. She squeezed his hand tightly as another pain shot through her body and she gasped loudly. Before another pain wracked her body, the witch was there and Zaven was raising her up to drink the potion the witch had prepared. Before the drink was finished, the pain etching her face had eased and her body relaxed as the pain disappeared.

"Aye, lass, it will come easier now for ye. Just relax and let yer body do the work for ye, there is naught else to be done for it."

Zaven stayed beside her, resting his hand on her belly and feeling the contractions move across it. He kept glancing at the witch with a fearful expression on his face but did not express his concern in words that might frighten Cara.

"She will be fine as a fiddle, Zaven… there is no worry to that."

Cara looked back and forth between them, a dreamy look on her face. One hand rested on Zaven's as it caressed her swollen belly and the other lay at her side. There was no pain now, thanks to the witch's herbs but she felt a sudden urge to raise her knees and brace her feet on the bed. She looked up at the witch just as the witch peeked under the bottom of her little shift, now raised above her upraised legs, and saw the witch smiling widely.

"That's it little fellow… keep coming now. Come on ye furry darlin', just a wee bit more."

"'Tis a boy, then, my friend?"

"Aye, of course, lass. Were ye not told ye would deliver the lord's sons?"

"Aye, I remember your words well, but thought that mayhap because of the change in me it might be different."

"Ah… and there he is. Such a beauty he is too."

The witch reached for a knife and cut the cord after tying it with a bit of string from her bag. She lifted the furry bundle up and showed it to the two of them.

"Now, ain't this a beauty? Lord, these old eyes have never seen such as this but it was well worth the wait. 'Tis the prettiest little one I've ever seen."

Before Cara could lift her arms to the witch, to take the child, Zaven had it in his large hand and brought it close to Cara's face.

"He is without doubt, the most beautiful thing I have seen, other than his mother, of course. What will you name him, Cara?"

Her face suffused with love for this tiny creature and the large man at her side, Cara turned her head a bit as if in thought and then spoke softly as she kissed her son for the first time.

"His name shall be Adrian, after my father. Though poor of pocket, he was wise and kind and I hope his name brings forth the same in our son."

"And with a mother such as you and a name of kindness and wisdom, our son could do no better, my love."

"Aye and with a father such as ye, the child could do much worse, Zaven," the witch said.

His head turned to the witch, a surprised look on his face, Zaven was held speechless for a moment.

"Thank you, Witch. You have no idea what that means to me."

"Aye, in fact, mayhap I do, Zaven. What has been seen by these old eyes today was never expected and has brought me joy with the seeing of it.

"'Tis in truth, a fine match between the two of yer and one I'm glad to see. And the lovely wee one makes it perfect."

Cara looked down into the face of her son and saw some of her own reflection from the pool in the woods. The child had a fine covering of pale red fur, slightly pointed ears, a handsome face like his father and startling green eyes with spikes of blue around the irises.

"He is beautiful, isn't he Zaven?'

Zaven gathered them both into his arms and cuddled them close to his chest.

"Just as beautiful as his mother, my love."

The Witch of Wolstad stood to the side and watched as the dragon cuddled the two furry creatures in his arms and chuckled softly as the babe found his mother's nipple for the first time and began to suckle. The look on the girl's face was priceless. She gathered up her herbs, put them in the bag and moved toward the entrance to the cave.

"Be well on this joyous day, little family. The gods have smiled on ye this day and may they continue to do so."

So engrossed in each other and the new babe, they didn't even look up as she walked out the door, but she turned back again and saw a sparkle next to the child's face. The pendant... the magic it had held was holding still. She knew sooner or later the truth would out but didn't believe it would matter by the time it was known. The love was apparent between these two and would no doubt grow even stronger.

Humming softly to herself, the Witch of Wolstad headed toward her little cottage near the village, smiling as she walked along.

Chapter Six

When the tale was done, Crys looked up at Adrian, tears slipping down her cheeks.

"Of course, the witch was right. He did come to tell her the truth and it didn't matter a whit to Cara when she found out. She had come to love the heart and soul within and it mattered not whether it was a man or dragon. They lived a long and happy life and had several more children. William of course, found out about the boy and tried to take him but the dragon stopped that before it could truly start.

"The boy did learn of his true father and eventually traveled between the two families. Adrian learned from both families, learned of the world and the wood, good and evil and rejoiced in his learning.

"One day, however, in returning from the castle to the cottage Zaven had made for them in the woods, he was attacked by a wolf and almost killed."

"Oh my god, Adrian! What happened to him? Did he live?"

Adrian smiled down at her and brushed her hair back from her face.

"He sits before you, Crys. Though many generations have passed and many children have been born and died, I am still here."

Her eyes went wide as she looked up at him. She had heard that vampires were immortal but it had really never crossed her mind that he was as ancient as his words implied. Then she smiled again and leaned into his embrace, not caring about his age or his past, only caring that he was here and with her again.

"Thank you, Adrian. That was a wonderful story. Thank you for sharing it with me."

"Thank you, sweet Crys, for being here to share it with me. And now, my sweet, it is time for us to share something else."

With a gleam in his eye, he smiled down at her, gathered her even closer and brushed his lips across her ear, whispering soft words.

"I have loved thee, Crys, for some time now. You have brought me much happiness in the times we have been able to be together. My only regret is that we have not had more times such as these. I have lived a long time, and loved a few in that time, but I swear, I have loved none more than I love you. I would give you a gift, my love. One that will last longer than simple roses."

She looked up at him, a soft smile on her face at the tenderness of his words.

"Adrian, you don't need to give me a gift. Being with you is gift enough. I need nothing else."

"Ah, but this is a special gift, my sweet love."

He ran his clawed fingers through her silken hair.

"It is a gift for only us to share. Say you will take the gift from me and I will make it so."

"I will take a gift from you, Adrian. But only on the condition that is from your love and not a sense of obligation to me."

"But I am obligated to you, in a sense, Crys. You have shown me a deeper love than I have ever known. Unquestioning, unconditional love and that is more important to me than you can know. But it is not the reason I want to give this gift. It's because I love you more than my existence itself."

Crys smiled up at him, lifting her hand and slipping it down the soft fur of his cheek, lost in the dark pools of his eyes.

"And I love you, Adrian. More than I thought it was possible to love anyone.

His tongue slipped out and slid around the shell of her ear as he listened to her love for him expressed almost breathlessly. He lowered his head and nibbled at her neck, letting his fangs brush against the tender, silky skin of her throat. She gasped against him and her body tensed as she anticipated the dark pleasure of his fangs again.

As his fangs slipped into her flesh, a surge of pleasure she had only known with this one, filled her with an ecstatic joy. Her body was trembling against him as he drank from her and he held her tight. She clung to him, breathing hard, and tears of joy at his love slipping down her face. When he had appeased his thirst, he withdrew his fangs and licked over the puncture marks to close them.

In a trice, he was on his feet, unfastening his pants, then kneeling beside her again, holding her against him as she labored for the breath his ecstasy had stolen from her. He leaned to kiss her softly, his furred hand slipping beneath the hem of her dress and moving slowly up the inside of her thigh. As it moved up, her legs parted almost automatically, her breath quickening again at this touch.

Her hand moved to the back of his head, caressing, ruffling the fur at the back of his neck. She heard the catch in his breath against her neck as he moved his hand up to the apex of her heat and began to tease her clit. It always pleased her that he was as excited to touch her as she was to be touched by him. Her bottom rose off the soft grass and sought to press upward even more to his hand to feel his touch more. She had been so long without him this time that all she craved was him... his touch... his kiss. She smiled softly up at him as she lifted her face to his, those last inches such a barrier to her desire for him that she couldn't bear it any longer. His lips pressed to hers and she gasped with pleasure. His tongue flicked out against her lips, then slipped between them to tease hers... his taste so sweet to her once again.

Then he moved over her and was between her legs and she was trembling with need and desire. Her arms went around his neck and pulled him into a deeper kiss just as she felt his shaft pressing against her enflamed heat. A little flick of her hips and the head of his cock entered her and she moaned softly in the kiss. Her muscles clenched around his shaft and pulled him deeper and he filled her completely. His breath caught in the kiss as she clenched around him.

She delighted in her heart that she could give him such pleasure in return. Then he stopped all movement, broke his lips from the kiss and seemed to glance up for a moment. Then he turned back to her and spoke softly again.

"My darling Crys... this gift I give you will change your life, my love. For the better, I hope. Cherish it as I cherish you and your love for me."

Her eyes opened wide and she peripherally noticed the lightening of the sky above them. She put her hands on his chest and spoke quietly, but with fear in her voice.

"Adrian, the sun."

"Never fear, my love. Everything is as planned."

He moved his hips over her and thrust his shaft into her. Before she could protest again, she was lost in the passion and moved to meet each thrust of his shaft. Deep inside she wondered at the risk he was taking but he assured her it was all right and she needed him as much as he needed her. Her body responded to each movement, the pleasure growing with each thrust. She could feel him twitching inside her and could see the morning coming closer.

"Adrian... please, love... the sun."

"Ssshhh... I love you, Crys."

And then it was too much, the pleasure had reached that height and she was lost in his love. She tripped over into the soaring joy that he always gave her and felt him pulsing deep inside her.

"My love... he will not be as I am."

"Adrian... Adrian."

She gasped his name as she clung to him, her body shuddering under him as the throes of passion and love filled her senses. Then he tensed again and she opened her eyes to gaze up at him.

"Adrian!"

He was fading over her, disappearing into nothingness still holding her close, his shaft still spurting inside her.

"I love you, Crys," a last whispered expression before he fell into ashes.

Her scream of anguish filled the little glade as her body registered the absence of him, as her mind registered that he was gone from her... forever.

"Why, Adrian? Why have you done this?"

The words screamed out in pain, sorrow and despair echoed in the glade. She was wracked by sobs, shaken by his disappearance, bereft that he would leave her like this. She couldn't understand why he had done it. He knew the sun would mean the end of him and if he *had* loved her as much as he had said... how could he leave her like this? A gift? Of a child? And he left her alone to face that without him? How could she do it... bear his child without him to help her?

She was sobbing, her heart broken at the loss of her love and as she turned on her side and curled into a ball, she saw a sparkle in the grass where he had lain beside her. One hand reached out to touch the sparkle and she found the pendant he had shown her when he had first come into the glade.

Her fingers closed around it and she brought it to her lips, kissing it as she had kissed him. Broken hearted, sobbing for her lost love, holding the pendant against her chest, her other hand came to rest on her belly. He had said the gift would change her life and that 'he will not be as I am'.

His long life had been filled with sadness he said and now hers would be just as sad without him. She longed for him, to feel his arms around her and to know that he would return as he always had… to love her and hold her again. A breeze came up then and scattered the delicate ashes into the glade where he had last made love to her.

She clutched the pendant tighter to her breast and wished on it as you would wish upon a falling star. If wishes did come true, she would see him again… somehow, she would see him again. She sat up slowly and thought she heard the murmur of his voice as the breeze moved the willow branches around her.

"I will always be with you, my love."

She closed her eyes and leaned back against the tree, more tears sliding down her face, but softer tears now… softer in the knowledge that he loved her enough to leave her a son.

The tears faded as she came to know that he would always be with her, would always smile at her in the old way, through the son he had sired this day.

Her arms wrapped around her belly then and squeezed gently. Though he was lost to her as a lover now… he would always be loved and would always love her. She slipped the delicate chain over her head and held the pendant between her breasts as Cara had held it so long ago. Maybe… just maybe, if the pendant still held the magic of old, maybe she would see him again.

***

Five months later, Crys returned to the little glade. She hadn't been there since her last fateful day with Adrian. As she maneuvered her awkward body down onto the blanket, she felt a twinge in her back and soothingly patted her belly.

"Sshh… my little one. It's a lovely day, the sun is shining, the breeze is cool and I feel your father's presence here."

She leaned back against the tree trunk, a soft smile on her face as she thought of Adrian and the times they had spent together in this place. The willow branches seemed even thicker than the last time she was here and they swayed softly in the breeze. She closed her eyes and could almost feel Adrian's fingers caressing her face. Her hand came up and touched the rose pendant suspended from the fine chain and laying between her growing breasts.

Suddenly her eyes popped open as she heard the sound of a broken branch close by. She sat up straighter, grimacing at the discomfort from the sudden move and turned toward the noise. Just as she was about to speak, a man pushed his way between the hanging branches.

"Oh! Sorry, I didn't know anybody was here."

Crys was startled by his sudden appearance in her secret place and before she had a chance to think of words to say, she gasped as she caught sight of his eyes. They were blue with spikes of green around the irises. At the same time she saw his eyes; she felt a shock between her breasts and looked down to see the pendant glowing against her skin. As the pendant glowed, the baby kicked harder than he ever had before.

She smiled up at the stranger who seemed so familiar to her.

"It's not a problem. You haven't interrupted anything here but a bit of rest."

Her breasts began to ache as she gazed into his eyes, even though he had made no overtures to her. Her breath was coming faster and the child was kicking hard enough to make her grimace again.

Her smile was genuinely welcoming to him and he felt himself smiling in return. Even though she was very obviously pregnant, he was caught by her beauty and the sudden pain in her eyes.

"Are you all right, Miss?"

She smiled again as she looked up at him, lost in those familiar eyes.

"Forgive me, Miss but… have we met before? Though this is my first time in this part of the woods… there is something about you that is very familiar to me."

She raised her hand to him, saw it trembling only a little bit and watched as he took her hand in his. The shock surged through her body at his touch and she saw the startled look on his face as he almost pulled his hand back. Then he smiled down at her and pulled her gently to her feet.

He was standing close as she gained her feet and she inhaled his scent. A dizzy sensation left her weak in the knees as she looked up at him and she leaned against him for just a moment, her eyes closed as she felt his body so strong against her.

The pendant was still warm against her skin as she answered him.

"Oh yes… I'm fine, just fine."

The Commission
Robert Cloud

Zachariah paused to wipe a tear from his eye. He looked to Melanie who had sat on the floor at his feet as he was telling the tale and saw the tears in her eyes as well. The room had grown dark even with the overhead lights on for night had come. He smiled to her and reached out a hand to help her to her feet. As she stood he added, "It is a story that is hard to tell though I have told it many times. It is like I knew those involved and the love they felt for each other.

"There is another tale behind this one that is difficult for me as well for it involves my own family. My ancestor Zakarias had lost his wife before the making of the pendant, but there was magic when someone asked for one of these pieces to be made. The magic reunited him with his wife for a short time. On the very night that he was reunited with his wife from the magic of the commission of another piece was when Zavon came to commission the pendant."

Tears ran down Zachariah's face as he recalled the memories of the time. "Something strange had happened since a commission occurred during the magic of another's piece being completed. His wife had been able to stay with him longer than she normally could. She even helped with the piece when it was time to choose and set the gemstone."

"This pendant was only the third item created by Zakarias and it was created jointly by the love of him and his wife whom he'd been able to share not one night with but an entire month." Zachariah lowered his head and wiped away more tears as they fell down his cheeks. "Their talent together was beyond anything you could imagine and she had a touch of magic about her as Zaven had said. Some who have heard the story say it is Zakarias' tears of blood over the loss of his wife that make the most magical of the pieces have that crimson hue."

Again he paused as he took a deep breath and then looked at Melanie, "I am sorry sweetheart. It is just when I think of my ancestor it is almost as if I was there and it was I that had lost my wife and was getting that second chance to be with her again.

"After all, I did lose my wife very early in our marriage, so I feel so close to my ancestor. Almost like he and I are one and the same sometimes." He smiled to her and then lowered his head a moment as he gathered his thoughts again.

"Now, back to the tale, others that have heard the tale say that it was the blood that Adrian had shed for his one true love and that somehow it had connected with my family.

"There is little doubt from the story that the wolf that attacked him was a vampire in its wolfen form and it had doomed him to many years of loss. When he met Crystal he could not bear to loose yet another." Zach wiped away another tear and Melanie turned and looked about, seeing a box of Kleenex she brought one of the tissues to him. He thanked her and continued his tale. Melanie took several of the tissues out to wipe away her own tears as she listened.

"According to the legend though, that was not the end of the story. Lilith had extracted a price from Zaven to weave such a precise spell upon the piece. When Zaven parted this world a piece of him was forever trapped within the pendant. He became a harbinger to those who held the pendant. It was for this reason that when Crystal's son inherited the piece he brought it back to my ancestor. Whenever something important was about to happen in his life a shadow of a huge dragon would pass overhead. More than once it had scared him and it had nearly frightened his wife to death the one time she had seen it. Crystal's son told my ancestor the story of the pendant and he put the rest together. My ancestor paid him a small fortune for the pendant and the man left happy. He and his family would be well financed for many generations."

Papa Zach stopped his story and rested a moment before Melanie asked a question that had bothered her from early in the story, "Papa Zach, an Anthrofox? I have never heard of that. They are not like werewolves, but always caught in that half human half fox form?"

He smiled up, how bright she was. It would not have been likely she would have heard of such a thing. "You are quite right. The legends of such are quite old, much older than the time frame of the story. Anthro-creatures date back to the time of the ancient Greeks and even before.

The oldest known civilizations that I recall were the Sumerians and the Babylonians; they also exist in the Asian legends. But those old legends are often hard to understand even if properly translated so maybe one of my ancestors updated it to a more modern time. Feudal England, when they still believed in Dragons seems a logical time.

"My own ancestors believe that Dragons were dark creatures that God did not allow upon the ark and that were therefore destroyed in the flood. Only a very few survived beyond the flood. The strongest ones that could stay aloft for all the time the waters were upon the Earth. So that would make the story even older yet."

Melanie smiled and reached out quickly kissing his cheek, "Thank you, Papa Zach for such an amazing story. I have one more glass case in the back corner to clean and then I should call it a day. My mother will be expecting me home for dinner at the normal time." As she turned to run to clean the display case Zachariah's hand rose to his cheek as if to hold the moisture of her kiss upon his cheek as long as he could.

He looked up, with his hand still lingering over the kiss, fondly pressing its memory into his mind, "Speaking of your mother, did you not say she would probably drop by?"

"Yes, I am certain she will. I am surprised she has not been here yet."

"Well, maybe she will come tomorrow."

"Maybe," Melanie said though Zachariah could see there was doubt in her eyes.

Then almost like magic the clouds in her eyes vanished as her mind grasped another thought. He could tell that anytime she was not thinking of her mother was a relief to her and he wondered why that was.

Suddenly Melanie announced, "Oh, I will be a little late tomorrow. I will be here right after Church and will work all that much harder."

"Sweetie," Zach smiled at her. "You are doing a good job; do not worry about an extra effort."

"But I want to." Melanie said, with a little pout.

Zach smiled and laughed, his hand touched her cheek and the pout melted away, "Then you work as hard as you wish."

Melanie jumped up and down and clapped her hands like a little child hearing the news of a summer field trip to the zoo. She stood on her tip toes and kissed his cheek again before turning and heading to the back room to get one of the boxes of watches to sort out. Zach watched her with a feeling of pride as if he were watching the grandchild he had never had.

He turned and looked at the ground, feeling full of shame. He hated to lie, no matter how great or small that lie was, but how would she ever understand that there had been no ancestor of his to work on the pieces of jewelry. All of them had been made by his hands except for that once piece that his wife had helped with when Zavon had come calling. He really liked Melanie and if he were to tell her that she would think he was insane and never return.

She smiled as she worked filled with satisfaction at being such a help to him, it was as if the little bit of work she was able to offer him was more rewarding to her than anything else in the entire world. She could not understand why it was so difficult for everyone in her school to understand her. She really enjoyed taking the home economics classes, learning to cook, clean, and sew with the idea of being a traditional housewife if the opportunity ever came along.

She doubted it would. Truth was she knew that she was going to have to look for work very soon. Even though her parents had money she was aware that they were not going to put anything aside for her to have a higher education. It would have been nice. She liked the idea of being a teacher but that was a dream that would not happen.

She turned and looked at Papa Zach. He was busy looking at more gemstones and jewelry. She wondered if he knew that he bit his lower lip when he was studying the stones. She could already tell when he saw one he liked because his chin would begin to quiver and then suddenly he would raise up with a smile and set it aside in a special pile with others he liked. It was funny to her that she was noticing little things about him and here it was only the second day she had spent any real time with him. His eyes sparkled when they looked at her like he wished he were so much younger. She wished he was too, but she was beginning to wonder if age really mattered if you were really in love. When she looked at him she could feel her heart fluttering like it was a flock of butterflies within her chest and she knew she had never felt that way about anyone her own age. She wondered why age should matter.

Suddenly he looked up at her and caught her staring at him, she could feel the blush rise to her cheeks as she turned her attention back to sorting items out of the boxes. She was wiping the dust that had gathered off the boxes of the watches that would go into the display case closest to the front window. Papa Zach said put something that would attract the customers but not something that would attract thieves. She had laughed and responded that there were not that many major thieves in Hudson Falls. Still he felt better to be safe than sorry and she agreed.

As she wiped the dust away from the boxes the memory of the warmth in his eyes and how she could almost feel it radiating from him soothed her. She took a little risk and glanced his way again and was pleased to see him busy with his work. There was something about Papa Zach that reached into her and made her feel completely at peace, like nothing in the world could happen to her when she was in his presence.

That blush on her face was so adorable and she had tried to hide it by burying herself again in her work. He wondered what thoughts were drifting in her mind that could bring such sweet blushes to her cheeks.

He could feel warmth coming off of her whenever she was near and that made him feel young and alive. Maybe, he thought, when he had rejuvenated and came back as his great nephew he would offer her a regular part time job after school and on weekends so she could stay on. Something told him that he would do more than just miss her if she left, he would feel empty without her there.

Then a momentary frown crossed his face. No matter how badly he would feel, keeping her around could be dangerous; she might come to suspect something after a time. The mannerisms, the movements, they may give away the secret that had been his and Lilith's for many, many years.

"Why such the long face, Papa Zach?" Zach turned his eyes to see the sparkling joy in the face of the girl beside him.

"Just an old memory from my youth, young one, it is nothing to trouble yourself about."

"Well then, smile." She giggled and leaned in kissing his cheek again, "I am done and need to be heading out but I will be back as early as I can tomorrow."

"Okay. Be careful and be safe."

"Oh, Papa Zach, I am always careful. In this small town there is nothing dangerous. No one notices me. It is as if I am almost invisible. Except for the few pranks at school from time to time there is no one that would want to hurt me."

Zach reached up and touched her cheek before she turned, "Little one, you are far lovelier than you let yourself be, and even in the safest of places dangers lurk in the shadows, so please just be safe on your journey."

She smiled at him and held his hand to her cheek. "I will Papa Zach, but no one sees me the way you seem to see me, but for you I will be safe. I will see you tomorrow."

"Yes, little one, I will see you too."

Zach could almost feel the happiness radiating off of Melanie as she stepped out the door. He closed and locked it behind her and watched as she skipped down the street. He smiled. Sometimes she did not seem like a girl her age but someone a little younger. Her spirit was so youthful and full of life.

As he turned the mirror in the back rattled wildly against the wall. "I am coming, Lilith. Settle down or you will shatter yourself."

Zach quickly walked back to the mirror hanging on the wall. Even before he got there he could hear her screams, you get your filthy mind off that young slut, Zachariah. You are a married man and your wife is here watching your every move.

"It is not like that, Lilith. She does remind me of you. In many ways she looks like you and all it is doing is making me more anxious for her to commission her piece so you and I can be together again, even if it is only for one night." Within him he could feel the muscles of his neck and shoulders tense. In many ways he dreaded that night.

Zachariah, you had better not be lying to me. If you are when I am corporeal again I will tear her throat out.

"Lilith, in all the years together I have never lied to you. Why would I start now?"

Sigh… You are right my love, I am sorry. I just tend to get jealous that you can touch others and I cannot feel your hands. I know you stroke the pane of the mirror but to me it is like your fingers are on the other side of an icy wall.

"Love, I am sorry. I wish we could be together always, but the magic only lasts for one night and only when the piece has been commissioned by someone that has brought us innocent blood does it work right."

I hunger to lay in your arms again my love. To feel your loins pressing into mine, like upon our wedding night. I feel she will commission the piece tomorrow after your next story, and commissioning it on the first day is a powerful omen. Maybe if the Lord is merciful he will give us two days this time.

"We can only pray, my love, we can only pray."

As he walked to the stairs he began to pray. There were many things he had to pray for forgiveness for this night.

***

As she ran down main street tears clouded her eyes and she wiped them away. She had promised Papa Zach that she would be there shortly after noon. It hurt her almost as bad that she had broken her promise as what had happened after church. It was nearly one when she arrived outside the door to his shop and she stopped to straighten her dress and tried to dry her eyes, but when the door opened and she saw the worried look on his face as he stood in the door she ran inside and into his arms pulling the door closed behind them.

Melanie reached over and pulled the blinds down and then buried her face against his chest and let her tears flow. She wept bitterly, and when she felt his arms encircle her, the tears came even more freely. Even she thought she was crying like a mother bereft of her child.

Papa Zach just held her in silence, stroking her hair and cooing softly to her. He let her cry as long as she needed to and as she finally began to gain control of her tears he guided her over to a chair and had her sit down.

He smiled at her and said, "Sweetheart, even with red blotched cheeks and swollen eyes I do not think I have ever seen anyone more beautiful."

That brought a small laugh from Melanie, "Papa Zach, in your eyes I know I am beautiful. It is the rest of the world that sees me as plain and ugly."

"Then they need glasses."

Even through her tears that brought another small laugh.

"Now tell me sweet child, what is wrong? What could have brought such pain into your life?"

Fresh tears threatened to fall, but a soft touch of his hand upon her cheek and her hand holding his hand to her face helped her hold back the tears. "Papa Zach, people can be so cruel sometimes."

"Yes, they can." Zachariah remembered a time in his own youth when he was the object of the cruelty of his peers, "Go on, tell me what happened."

"Papa Zach, my High School's Homecoming Dance is Thursday Night, and the game is Saturday with a Parade just before the game. It is my senior year and I have never been to a dance at my school. One of the football players that goes to my church invited me to go with him just before church began. I was so excited all through services that I could not even listen to the pastor's sermon."

She looked up at the man she had grown to respect and even love and for a moment almost felt as if she had betrayed him by accepting a date. "After the sermon I always help with cleaning up the little things that people leave behind and I was by a window and I saw him talking to some people and I could not help but hear what they were saying."

New tears began to slide down her cheek, "I wish I had never accepted his invitation.

"I heard him tell the girl he had said he had broken up with that he had asked me out like she had told him to and that once he had gotten me inside the dance he would abandon me and find her." She lowered her head, "They were going to put up a big sign above the door saying 'Housewife of the Year seeks Marriage' so everyone would laugh at me.

Melanie could not hold back her tears any longer and she began to cry again, "Papa Zach, he never liked me; it was all just a mean joke."

He stroked her cheek and smiled at her, "Then sweet girl we will make him regret his cruelty and his joke."

She sat up straight and with a look that bordered on pride and which showed the strength that he sensed lay within her she said, "When I heard them I opened the window and told them exactly what I thought of them. How dare they? They tricked me, and in church. What kind of respect is that?"

"They looked at me like I was nuts and laughed but I did not care. I knew I was right and he knew I would not be going to the dance with him.

"But Papa Zach, I so want to go to the dance, even if I have to go alone."

He held her by both her shoulders and smiled at her saying, "Then by all means you shall go. I have dresses galore from many eras and since it is just before Halloween I bet a little bit of a costume will be appropriate. They need not even know it is you. In one of the chests in my back room I have a mask of a Harlequin that would look lovely and there are many other things we can do."

"Really?" Melanie smiled brightly. "But, umm... Papa Zach?" He saw a funny look on Melanie's face as she quirked an eyebrow at him, "Why do you have so many dresses? Do you have something you want to tell me about yourself?" She smiled; he could tell she was trying to hold back a laugh.

He could not resist. He flicked a limp wrist and looked at her, "Oh, darling, I thought you knew. Vaudeville and I are good friends." Then he too laughed.

"No, Melanie. Relatives, family, I am the last of my family so I got them all, and since I did and many of them are grand dresses and well preserved we might as well make you the queen of the dance."

Melanie giggled at that. "Years ago they changed the way they voted for Homecoming Queen. Each person who comes to the dance gets a number; the ladies have a Q in front of their number and the guys a K, then during the dance each person gets to vote once for someone at the dance. Still it is always the most popular girl in the school that wins but it would be something if I actually won."

She laughed, "That is not likely though. They will all vote for Rebecca Straine, she is a cheerleader and the most popular girl. I am certain she will not wear a mask to hide her face so everyone will know who she is."

"Don't worry about her, Melanie. For now we are just going to make you a princess for the night. If you win the queen, then that will be something else." Zach smiled. "But the costume will need something else."

Melanie clapped her hands, "Papa Zach, I have some money, and I can work for you to pay off the rest. Could I buy one of your pieces to wear on the dress?"

"Oh, sweetie, I don't think just any piece would do. You need something special. However if you want to commission something and you will finish helping me get ready for the Grand Opening then maybe I can design a new piece for you that will be something just for you."

She nearly leapt into his arms, "Thank you, Papa Zach, yes, yes, that would be great. I will work for you until it is paid for."

"Hun, your presence and your smiles have been more than enough to pay for the treasure I will make for you. Maybe that old magic will return and I can make you one of my special treasures, with some magic in it." He smiled at the girl in his arms.

"Now you got here late and we spent a lot of time with this. If I am going to have the piece done by Thursday and you are going to have everything ready for the Grand Opening on Friday you will need to get busy." There was a sternness in his voice but also a gentleness that warmed Melanie's heart.

As she pulled away from him Zach could not help but notice that her torrent of tears had drenched her white blouse and her thin bra beneath. Her young nipple was pert and hard where it had pressed against him. He could feel that old arousal, especially as he saw so much of Lilith's beauty in her, but none of her bad traits. He felt like a dirty old fool and yet there was something different about this girl, something he just could not quite see. Her scent filled him with such joy and strength that he knew the magic would come even if he did not follow the normal procedures. Yet he would make certain everything was done in proper order.

Melanie ran to the back of the store to grab another box of inventory to stock the shelves. As she did her skirt swished seductively about her knees making Zach smile as that fire in him ignited even deeper. He was glad that soon he would be able to hold his beloved Lilith in his arms again and quench those flames.

He remembered that Melanie said that she had always worn dresses but he had thought that she meant to school and in public. He really did not realize that she had meant all the time, everywhere. He had expected that she might come to help him work at least once in jeans and a tee shirt, but it had been dresses or skirts and blouses every time he had seen her, and the hem of the skirt or dress had always been below her knee. He knew from her attitude and the way she had handled his telling of the first story that it had nothing to do with her religious beliefs. Perhaps it was her mother's wishes, or maybe it was something else.

As he watched her cleaning and unloading boxes he began to realize even more why she had said she had no friends. She was a bit out of step with the modern world in her ideas of how a girl should be. She wore an apron while she was working, and she seemed to be truly happiest when she was doing something like cleaning and taking care of fixing a meal for him while he was working. Melanie was more like the traditional woman of the 40's and 50's than like those of the modern era and that just made things harder on her when she had to face her peers.

Now Zach understood why part of the deep sadness lay within her. She was not exaggerating when she had said she had no friends. She had no friends because there was no one that understood what she was like. He imagined it was another reason she had attached herself to him so quickly. He was fond of a woman with those values and she had sensed that and felt at home with him. It pleased Zach's heart to know that there were still women that loved the idea that their man was their protector and guardian and that they could be a graceful feminine beauty, delicate and refined and pleasing in all ways.

He heard Melanie coming back up the stairs, and knew that if he did not get his mind off of her he would never get to the business he needed to be thinking about. She had commissioned a piece of jewelry from him and now he had to begin its design and creation and he had less than a week for the magic to perfect the creation. Even within the confines of *The Crimson Z* Zachariah's hands showed small traces of the arthritis that outside made his hands look like eagle's talons. However the rest of his body showed none of the disease. Outside the door of the shop his knees would betray the wobbliness of a man well over a hundred years old. Inside he was sturdy yet he had to act a little wobbly for Melanie's sake so that she would not become too suspicious that something was strange about him and the Z. However as he quickly wrote a note telling her that he had gone to get some supplies and would be back shortly his hands showed no trace of arthritis at all, and when he walked swiftly across the floor to the large cabinet of treasures his back, knees and legs were those of a man of only twenty. He reached under a hidden panel upon the front of the cabinet and pushed a button. Slowly the whole cabinet rotated outward and revealed a hidden doorway. He laid the note on the counter beside the cabinet and then stepped through the doorway. It immediately closed behind him.

Then before she came through the door from the basement he entered his work area and the cabinet closed behind the door hiding him and his work away from the world.

A shelf that was just a little above waist height began just inside the door on one side and lined all four walls around the room to end at the other side of the door. Upon the shelf, spaced exactly twelve inches from one to the next were white candles that began to light one after the other in a clockwise direction as soon as Zachariah entered the room.

He paused until each candle had been lit and then continued into the room. Upon the wall directly above the door was an old clock with a swinging pendulum and Roman Numerals at the hours. The wall to the left of that in the center held a Star of David crafted of gold, it had been made upon the table and was the only item that was not in the cabinet. Zachariah would never speak its tale to anyone for he had sworn he would not.

The next wall held a mirror, Zach did not know why he placed a mirror on that wall but he had somehow always felt that there was a lie that Lilith was telling him and one day that mirror would be the final proof he needed. Upon the last wall hung a pad of paper with a pencil, it was what he used when the ideas came to him as they would be doing tonight. He walked to the pad and lifted it from the wall.

There were three other items in the room. Two wooden chairs, which he never understood because no one ever entered the room but himself, and a large item that was covered with a white cloth. The cloth was covered in gold writings that were obviously blessings in Kabalistic Rituals. With a swift pull he tugged the cloth off and revealed a stone table that was over six feet in diameter and almost six inches thick. Upon the table was carved the exact same image that was upon the cabinet but slightly smaller. It was about four feet in diameter. A channel ran from the base of the image like a tap root to within four inches of the rim and then circled the stone.

Just like the image on the cabinet the twelve characters were equally placed but here the characters were larger than on the cabinet. More prominent for they were a reminder of twelve words that he would have to utter in his incantation twelve times each.

There were two other things in the room that were not visible until the cloth had been removed; the first was a basin beneath the table that held rain water that Zachariah collected only during the new and full moons. He took a cup from the basin and poured water into the carving not filling it full for he had more to add in a little while but still making certain that water covered the entire carving so that when he added his new water it would mix and touch all the parts of the carving. The other was a small chest of drawers that he used to store the items he might need from time to time during his rituals.

He looked to the mirror for he could feel the presence of Lilith with him watching to make sure he made no mistakes. Though she was not able to speak to him through this mirror he would know if she needed to speak to him.

Zach smiled. It had been easy to hide the setting up of this room from the villagers when he had moved into the shop. Using a fictitious realty company he had purchased the entire building which housed a drug store, a beauty parlor, and a few other businesses. Above it were several apartments. Behind most of the stores were other businesses like car repair shops that were small family businesses. The one behind *The Crimson Z* had been closed and he'd had a construction crew seal it off so it would look like it was being added as part of the apartment above. Since the apartment above was his, no one knew what was in the room but him. Even the Chamber of Commerce of the village of Hudson Falls,

New York had no clue that he was the new owner of the entire block in the center of the town, which was exactly the way it had to be for him to maintain the cover he needed when the magic rejuvenated him and he became young once again. He could even do a couple of special commissions as long as he did not age too much between them and no one would be the wiser.

Now he reached into a drawer and pulled out a jar that held the Kleenex with the little girl's blood upon it. It had been soaking in rain water awaiting the moment that Melanie would commission a piece.

Opening the jar, Zach fished out the Kleenex as it was no longer needed; it was the blood that was important. Reaching out to hold the jar over the center of the symbol Zach began to mutter some words in a tongue that was as ancient as time itself but was not spoken the way it had once been spoken. The people that spoke the tongue now had over time perverted it slightly. Though they were unaware of their mispronunciations, Zach was aware of them for he had learned them long ago.

Slowly the water dripped from the jar and began filling the channels of the design and adding to the water already covering each of the hidden Hebrew Kabalistic symbols within the channels of the design. Once it had filled the design it flowed down the channel to the base and then circled the entire stone. Zach stopped chanting and drank the last of the water making certain that not one drop of it was wasted.

Zachariah watched as the image carved within the table began to glow and the water and blood slowly began to be absorbed into the stone of the table. Then a flash of light rose above the table and circled there for a moment before speeding toward him. It forked into two bolts like lightning and struck the pupils of his eyes.

The golden rays entered his mind and the image of what he would draw formed in every detail, but he knew it would not last long. He had to get it onto paper. That was always a part of the ritual.

He returned the bottle to the drawer and then replaced the cloth cover over the table. He pulled a chair over to the table and from another drawer pulled out a one foot square drawing board, a piece of paper and a pencil. He laid the board on top of the cloth so that he could draw and not have to worry about the engraving beneath the cloth. Now he had to design the piece. Closing his eyes he let his hand begin to work its magic. Time passed. In his mind he drifted to the days when he and Lilith had been together and the joy they had had together. Then his mind shifted to the time he had first seen her and how his heart had raced for he had thought he had come upon a tragedy.

***

The sun had not yet risen, yet he had gotten up early and gone to the river to get water for his father. The yoke across his neck was heavy with the two large 15 gallon buckets filled to near the rim. He came over a rise in the road when he saw something dark sticking out into the road. At first he thought it was just a branch from a nearby tree that had fallen free but as he closed the distance he realized that it was the slender arm and hand of a woman sticking out of the tall brush along the side of the road.

He set the buckets down carefully, even in this moment of haste. He knew if those buckets came back less than full his father would give him hell.

He approached the woman cautiously. He was on a poorly traveled cart road, that's only traffic was between his village and the river and it was well before the time that anyone in his village would be awake. There was no one else to call for help. He was the only help this woman had.

His heart beat like thunder in his chest. He was afraid she had been the victim of vandals or a band of brigands. He was afraid she might be dead. Yet from the appearance of her body she seemed unharmed. He could not see any blood but she was not moving. He moved closer and carefully rolled her onto her back. Her eyes were closed, and for a moment he was certain she was dead then he saw her chest lift with her breath and he thanked God she was alive.

Then in the light of the moon he caught a look at her face. Her features were not like those of the women of his village, they were sharper, more heart shaped, less round. Her mouth was fuller and her nose smaller. Though her eyes were closed he could tell that they were bigger than those of the women of his village. Her long black hair was filled with leaves and twigs like she had been living in the wild for a long time. She was remarkably beautiful and in the single moment he was captivated by her.

He looked down at her body and suddenly felt heat rise to his face for the clothing she wore was tattered and almost nonexistent. He had never seen an adult female this naked before and the effect it had upon him was overpowering. He took off his tunic leaving only his loincloth on and covered her body with the tunic. Then as he looked at her his heart reached out to her and he knew that if she were not already the wife of some other man that he would someday have her as his own for from the first sight of her he loved her.

The hammering beat of his heart pushed his mind into action. Quickly he realized he had to get the woman to a healer and the only healer around for miles was his mother. If anyone could help the unconscious woman it was her.

Carefully Zach lifted her to his shoulder and then went back to the yoke. He struggled only briefly with balance but not the weight as he lifted the yoke up onto the other shoulder. The sun was rising as he entered the village and the others his age stared at him in disbelief for to carry the yoke was a task alone. To carry a yoke and a woman was a feat of strength none of them had seen. Yet Zach's heart was so filled with love that to him his strength had grown tenfold that day.

***

His hand had stopped moving so he opened his eyes and looked down upon the piece of paper. Slowly a smile lifted the corner of his lips. Well, he had said that every girl deserved to be a queen once in her life. Upon the paper before him was one of the most beautiful designs for a tiara he had ever seen. Of all the pieces he had ever made this one would be the one that brought him the most joy for to place it upon Melanie's head would truly be a pleasure. It would bring out that hidden beauty that she tried so desperately to keep hidden.

He also now knew that the sample of blood required from Melanie would be more than normal, something of this magnitude would need flesh and hair as well. This was the part he did not like but he had the tool. He brought out a device designed to help measure a person's skull for ornamentation such as this and laid it upon the glass next to the drawing.

Looking up at the clock he noticed he had been in his trance for over two hours so it would be easy to explain that he had stopped to get coffee when the inspiration for the piece came to him. That way there would be no questions from Melanie about how he had come up with the design. Walking to the mirror he looked into it and felt for Lilith's presence. Yes, she was there and he could feel that it was safe for him to leave the room. Melanie was not in the area where she would see the cabinet move.

He rolled the paper into a tube and grabbed the measuring tool, then walked to the door. However, before he touched the door he turned back to the mirror and whispered. Lilith, I know this is something we both need, but I really hate hurting this girl. Promise me you will not harm her when you come back. I know you have had to feed the last few times you have returned and I know your jealousy over this girl is great. Yet, you have no reason to be jealous; she is just a young girl with a long life ahead. I do not want you to harm her.

Zach could feel the jealousy boiling from the mirror but he could also feel Lilith acquiesce to his request. He then turned the knob on the door and heard the click. As he opened the door the cabinet had already finished its silent swing. Quickly he stepped through and swung the cabinet back into its closed position. It was less than a minute before he heard the foot falls of Melanie ascending the stairs from the basement.

"Oh, you're back, Papa Zach." She ran over to him and kissed his cheek. "I missed your company today but I think I also finished the last of the inventory. Everything is stocked and ready for the Grand Opening, now the next few nights after school I can focus on cleaning and decorating for your big day."

Zach smiled at her, his hand brushing the sweet moisture where her lips had touched his cheek. "Well, I will be busy getting ready for your big day too.

"Sorry it took so long, but I stopped for a coffee at Arthur's," the dagger twisted in his heart as again he had to tell her another lie, but how would he explain to her the truth. He hated lying, and he would not have had to if she was not around all the time but he could not bear the thought of her missing from his life, "and was suddenly struck with an inspiration of what I wanted to make you for your dance." Slowly he unrolled the paper and then revealed it to her. Her eyes opened wide and glistened with tears.

"Oh, Papa Zach, there is no way I can afford to pay for that. That piece must cost a small fortune."

"Melanie, sweet girl, you have brought a treasure into my life these last few days and befriended me, let me make it for you and then after the dance you can return it. It will be a loan, and I will pay you for the work you have done."

She jumped up and kissed him on the lips. "No, Papa Zach, you do not need to pay me, but yes it can be a loaner." Then she wrapped her arms around him tightly, "Thank you so much for making me feel special. No one has ever done that for me."

"Surely that is not true?"

Melanie stepped back and with a sad look said, "I am sorry to say, it is true. I feel unwanted, but here I feel wanted."

"Well, you have been a big help and you most certainly are wanted here anytime you wish to visit. Mayhap when my nephew comes to take over for me I can talk to him about hiring you on part-time."

Melanie almost glowed she was so happy; "You would do that?"

"Most certainly."

She kissed his lips like a girl would kiss her grandfather, but to Zach it reached deeply into his heart. He started to wonder if maybe there was a reason for Lilith to feel jealous.

Well he had to do one more thing, he had to get the sample or there would be no magic done anyway.

"Melanie, there is one thing I need to do." He held up the c-shaped tool, "I need to take a measurement so that the tiara is not too far off from the size of your head. You do not want to reshape the gold too much or you might loosen the settings."

"Okay, what do I need to do?"

Zach pulled out a chair, "Just sit here."

She did so and he slid the gauge around her scalp, forming it and shaping it. Then he said, "There, all done," but as he lifted it he tapped the back edge. A scoop in the back took a small gouge out of Melanie's scalp. It would leave a small scar but it would be hidden by her hair. She screamed out as the shock of pain hit her.

"Oh I am sorry, sweetie. These damned old tools. This one is my father's that is how old it is." Quickly Zach grabbed a cloth and covered the wound. It bled for a moment before stopping.

Melanie's eyes were filled with tears as she turned back and looked up at him, "It is okay Papa Zach, I know you would not intentionally hurt me."

Zachariah felt her words dig into his heart for he had done just that. It was not that he had done it with an evil intent, in fact with all his heart he believed it was with the will of God and for a good intent that he had taken the tissue and blood. He just hated that it had to be done without her knowledge and it hurt him deeply that he had indeed caused her pain. It felt like he had done a selfish deed and he could feel the cold blade of a steel knife slicing through his ribs seeking his heart.

He lowered his gaze to the case as a lone tear dropped upon the glass. What was done was done, and there was no turning back. Truth was there was no turning back the moment he had put the blood from the innocent child upon the table. At that moment the wheels had been set in motion and he could not stop them, any attempt to do so would have been more harmful to him and Melanie than what he had done.

The one time he had tried to stop a commission had been disastrous. He had been living in Rome and after the piece had been commissioned he had decided he just could not carry out the magic. The man who wanted the piece was a truly evil man who thought there was nothing wrong about killing a man for no reason at all. So Zachariah had packed up with the stone and the mirror, for something told him not to leave them behind, and left the city. It had taken him many days to move south to the city of Pompeii and after nearly a year had passed he thought he had finally found a way to break the magic of the commission.

He had been wrong. He had barely escaped with his life, and he had regretted surviving for the guilt that weighed upon his soul. So many others died.

One day he had gotten word that the man who had commissioned the piece from him was looking for him. He had started to pack his things to move again with plans to begin the next day. Shortly after lunch he had gotten tired and laid down for a nap. When he had awakened he was on a vessel bound to Rome. Several Centurions had taken everything in his shop including the stone and all his belongings and were taking him back. As he looked back to Pompeii he saw a billowing tower of smoke rising. No one on the ship knew what it was. He did not hear the news of Pompeii for several days, but he had no doubt that had he stayed in Rome Pompeii would have been spared.

When he had returned to Rome, the Centurions returned him to his shop and his customer showed up three days later to ask about his commissioned piece. Zachariah had been very careful in taking the last element needed to complete the magic for with the Centurions outside the door he did not know what might happen.

Six months after the piece had been delivered Zachariah learned that it had been partly responsible for the death of the Emperor of Rome but unfortunately not until after he'd had thousands killed.

He gathered the bloody cloths and the tool that had several strands of hair and a small piece of flesh hidden within. Later he would add those to the ritual and begin the making of the tiara. Placing them upon a tray he lifted the tray and then slid it under the counter and turned to look at Melanie. She had gotten up and gone to the kitchen to get a wet cloth to wipe the blood out of her hair. Once again he felt that dagger and this time it twisted between his ribs.

Zachariah turned his gaze to the clock and realized it was getting late. Soon Melanie would have to go home. He did not really want her to leave, especially after just hurting her. He wanted to spend a little quiet time with her and enjoy the last of their day together and he had enjoyed telling her the first story. He smiled for she was promised another one for her work tonight, "Well sweetie, if you want to hear a story tonight we had better let you choose what piece you want to hear about."

Using a wet cloth Melanie wiped the last of the blood out of her hair and then turned and smiled at him, "Papa Zach, you are going to be putting so much effort in on the tiara, and I know you are only going to let me borrow it for one night but that alone will be payment enough for what I am doing for you. You do not have to tell me any more stories."

She saw a smile brighten his face as he looked at her and his eyes gleamed then her heart filled with joy as he spoke, "No sweetheart, I want to tell you the stories. I enjoy having you here for one. I also found I really did enjoy telling you that story last night, especially when we got to a few of the more vivid scenes that made your face turn redder than the rubies in that cabinet."

Melanie giggled. She could feel her heart fluttering. She had truly not known how to handle those scenes when he had told them for she had not thought very much about sex at all. Until last night she had never pictured a sexual act at all and then to have one explained to her in such detail that it was impossible not to picture it was unbelievable. She looked at him and said, "Well Papa Zach, I turn eighteen at midnight on Halloween, so I do not see anything wrong with you telling me those kinds of stories. Besides in New York the legal age of consent is seventeen so if I can legally have sex at seventeen I should be able to hear stories about it." She could feel her face turning more brightly red than it had the night before. She turned to try to hide her face as for just a moment she had pictured herself in the arms of Papa Zach and as those images had caressed her mind she had realized it was someplace she really wanted to be.

Thankfully it was Papa Zach's question that pulled her mind from those thoughts and brought her back to the moment helping her to recover from the blush she'd hoped he had not seen, "Did you say eighteen at midnight?"

"Yup!" She smiled, "I was born at the stroke of midnight."

"That is interesting, and on All Hallow's Eve"

"That is right. My first breath was taken on November 1st."

Zach smiled. "Well you are a special little girl then aren't you? Perhaps I should call you my lil golem?"

Melanie laughed and hugged him, "Papa Zach, you may call me anything you wish, but ummm… What's a golem?"

Zachariah laughed for a moment and rubbed her hair, then said, "A golem was a creature formed from mud or clay that a Sorcerer breathed life into. He was supposed to do it at the stroke of midnight and they were very special creatures.

"You could not tell them from real humans, or whatever other creature they were made to represent once life was breathed into them. They were guardians, protectors of their maker, or they were their maker's companion and friend."

Melanie giggled and smiled at him. "Nah! I am not a golem. I am more the Sorceress," Melanie said then she wiggled her fingers and acted like she was casting a spell upon him just before bursting into laughter so hard she had to hold her stomach. Zachariah joined her laughter. As Melanie watched his face fill with a smile there was also some kind of shadow that hid behind his eyes.

It was like her little joke had hit a spot in him that was too close to home. She did not really believe the jewelry was magical, yet the stories were nice. Still, something told her that there was more to all of this than just stories, that somewhere there lay a lot of truth to what Papa Zach was telling her and behind that was a darkness that was eating away at his soul. She did not know if she could help but her feelings for him were growing stronger and she desperately wanted to try to free him from whatever it was that was tormenting him.

Slowly he caught his breath and smiled to her, though his eyes still held that shadow. He laughed a little and then asked her, "Do you want that story?" then he pointed to the cabinet.

Melanie did not want to let him know that she suspected anything at all was wrong, and besides she truly was excited about hearing another one of his amazing stories. She felt like she was floating on air as she bounded over to the cabinet and opened the doors. She scanned over the pieces and then saw something that caught her eyes. Most of the pieces were singular, just one item, but in one slot there were five pieces that were almost identical. Two large pendants of two toned gold, a yellow gold, and then upon it and slightly raised a rose hued gold that formed a stylistic P. There were three smaller pendants that matched the larger pieces perfectly.

"Papa Zach, will you tell me about those five pieces."

He looked where she was pointing and could feel a flush cross his own face. Melanie giggled and said, "Now look who is blushing."

Laughing loudly he said, "Then so be it, Melanie, I will tell you their tale, the tale of Peter and Evelyn."

The Anniversary

Richard Savage

Chapter One

The brilliant white headlights from Evelyn's Jaguar cut through the darkness as she drove through the night. Her only companion on this cold night was a single red rose, which sat on the passenger seat. Her knuckles were tight, as her nervous fingers gripped the leather-covered steering wheel.

Her sumptuous, silk stockinged, thighs rubbed together pleasingly as she changed gears. Wearing silk stockings had always aroused her. The tightness of the darker band at the top of her thigh and the way it hugged her securely made her legs feel lovingly restrained, making her whole body pulse and tingle with excitement.

It had been twelve months to the day since she had last met with her clandestine lover. The tension that was coiled within her was beginning to show as she neared her destination. She checked her clothing for the thousandth time, since getting dressed that afternoon.

Peter's instructions had been precise, what to wear, and when to change into it. This had done nothing to help her nervousness and anticipation of their meeting.

Peter was a stickler for detail, and she found it easy to comply with his dress code. Her crisp white, linen blouse and smart black A-line skirt did not look out of place from her normal office attire. For many years now, she had worn stockings and garter belt, so that was not unusual either. Late in the afternoon, she had changed into the final items. These she only wore on this day of the year now. Their touch on her skin felt unusual now, yet strangely comforting.

She squirmed against the Jaguar's leather seat, as the chain caressed her intimately. She looked at the amber lighted digital clock. She looked at the mileage counter willing it to speed up. Time passed incredibly slowly making her feel like a small child on her way to the seaside; constantly asking are we there yet?

Her mind drifted back over the challenging day she had spent at the office and the assortment of problems she had tackled. She contemplated the duality of her nature, her assertiveness in the office and the passivity when she was with Peter. She drew similar parallels between Peter and James, the two men she loved, but who were so different.

This early evening meeting had been her main focus for the past week and she had hardly been able to think of anything else. As the amber digits ticked relentlessly by, and she neared her destination the tension she felt rose to a crescendo.

As she drove, Evelyn went through her mental checklist. Had she dressed correctly? Was she fully prepared? God she hoped so. Peter had always been a stickler for detail and would notice a hair out of place. Yet again, as she went through her cerebral preparations, she felt a moistness, a liquid glow, like her very core was melting and with these feelings of desire, came a gut wrenching pang of guilt.

Suddenly a cold rush, swept over her. How could she betray her husband? How could she be unfaithful to such a good man, for this one night of passion? With a lump in her throat, she thought of James, and their three-year marriage and the vows she was breaking. Yet tonight, as she had done for the past four years, she would give herself totally to Peter and nothing on earth could or would stop her from making that rendezvous.

She loved James dearly. Their three-year marriage was a happy one. James was a good man, a loving and caring partner. He was a very straightforward man, uncomplicated. He was the type that if he said something, you knew he meant it. If he promised to do something, he would do it. She loved James for all that he was, yet there was one thing he was not, and could never be. He was not her Master. She had only ever had one Master. Peter.

Her love for Peter was not the same as her love for James. She loved James with her heart but Peter she loved with her very soul.

The one thing that had united her two lovers was their love for her, but the two men in her life were entirely different in nature and temperament. There was a hard edge to Peter, something uncompromising. He had a natural authority about him. He was and always had been every inch the man in control.

The flash of a rabbit darting across the road brought her back to the here and now. The rumble of the tires on asphalt lulled her back to her thoughts.

Evelyn had been married to Peter when she had met James. She had known James for years before she had married him and until then had always thought of him as a good friend. Their three-year marriage had only deepened her feelings for James.

James was altogether softer and a much more tender person, a man that loved her unconditionally just as she was. In return, she loved him. She knew he loved every inch of her soft rounded body, by the attention he lavished upon her. Yet, he was not a demanding man. He always put her needs first, which was very nice, though slightly irritating at times, as she much preferred assertive men.

Her mother had described him once as "low maintenance" He was a man that despite her flaws would always be there for her. Making love to James, was soft and tender, he never neglected any morsel of her. His tastes though were pure vanilla, missionary with the occasional oral gratification, which he was happy to reciprocate.

They first met at work. James worked in the same office block as she did, though not for the same firm, and their lunch hours had coincided. She soon came to think of him, as the big brother she had never had. Their shared lunches had been a pleasant thing to look forward to each day. They laughed freely over a coffee and sandwiches for years. That had been a happy time, which she always looked back on with fondness.

Then there was a time when they no longer met for lunch. Dark Clouds had descended in her life. It had been a bleak and stormy time, and Evelyn had retreated to a place deep within herself. It had been a time when there was no light in the day, a time when she had wanted to die. A time when she had been a soulless shell. It was in this that depth of despair that James had found her. He had breathed life into her again, bringing her back from the edge. He had brought her back into the light, helping her to see the joy of the new day and helping her to laugh again. That was four years ago now.

The engine growled and Evelyn changed to a lower gear, as the road became more winding. She knew she was close to her destination now and she felt the pang of hunger in her stomach and the all too familiar ache between her thighs. She could not wait to be with Peter.

Peter, had been and still was, her passion. Evelyn had known him for what had seemed like forever. She had known him for years before she had ever met James. Theirs had been a whirlwind romance, flowers, candle light dinners, moon light trysts. As their relationship deepened Peter's nature and his strength came to the fore. Evelyn swallowed, as she heard the words in her head *"Love, honor, and obey."*

Evelyn had been brought up to believe in sexual equality, and she did believe, but there had been something missing in her life when she met Peter. From the very start, there was a power with Peter, not a menacing power to be sure, but an authority. This was not a simple macho manifestation, but a deep-rooted natural power, a light that drew Evelyn like a moth to a flame.

It had started easily enough at an electronics trade show, she was there as the personal assistant for a corporate buyer. The meetings that she had attended had finished and she was free to browse around the exhibition. She looked around curiously although in truth electronic gadgets left her a bit cold. Across the room, she saw Peter. Their eyes met and there was an instant connection. There was a delicious flirtation as they played from across the room. Eventually Evelyn made her way to the stand where Peter was giving a demonstration of a highly complicated piece of equipment. The customer moved on, Peter stepped up to Evelyn and introduced himself. His smile that day would be burned into her memory for all eternity.

Evelyn's partners before Peter had been few. In those days of stick thin models, not everyone appreciated her fuller figure. Those who had, had left her feeling unfulfilled and that sex was overrated. The early dates and dinners with Peter were much like those she'd had in the past, with the exception that Peter had not pounced on her at the end of the first date. A simple tender kiss had sufficed at the end of the date. In fact, after the third date she had begun to worry that Peter was not as attracted to her as she was to him and it had been Evelyn that made the first move.

After dinner, she had invited him back for coffee. He browsed her CD collection as she rattled coffee cups in the kitchen. She asked him how he liked his coffee; he replied strong, black and no sugar.

Evelyn returned with a tray, with cups and a café tire. They sipped coffee for a while. Peter looked totally at ease as he sat on the couch. Evelyn, by contrast was nervous and fidgeting. What was he waiting for?

Surly he could see she wanted him, yet there he sat, pleasantly smiling and making small talk. She flirted with him, trying to add suggestive snippets like, "I have always been into bedroom design, it allows you to express yourself," into the conversation. She had expected a response like "I would be interested to see how you have decorated yours." However, no such response had been forthcoming.

It was obvious to her that Peter was interested, yet he took none of the opportunities to follow up with a suggestive comment of his own. The attraction was obvious yet he did not make a move.

They finished the coffee and she felt it was now or never. She wanted Peter and she knew that Peter wanted her. With a tremble in her voice, she said, "I would like you to stay."

"I would like that very much," he answered, his tone warm, yet authoritative. His tone made her tingle.

"Shall I slip into something more comfortable?" There was a noticeable quaver in her voice.

"I think you are fine as you are." There was something in Peter's voice that put him firmly in control. "I would like you to stand." The politeness in his request did not hide the fact that it was an instruction.

She smiled and stood, a little shakily. She had always been a little self-conscious about her body. Her teenage years had done nothing for her self-esteem. Back then, she had dreaded going to the swimming pool, even though she loved the water and loved to swim. In a swimsuit, she had felt so exposed, vulnerable, and very aware that her body was not the type found in the glossy teen magazines. As a teenager thoughts of communal showers with the other girls, had made her feel physically sick. Many nights she had cried herself to sleep, dreaming of the sylph like body she would never have. The cruel jibes made her frustrated and angry.

This was before therapy. During the many hours of therapy, she had come to realize her size 18 dress size was not at all abnormal and her Monroe like curves were not bad although they simply did not comply to the stereotypical pencil thin models in Vogue.

Yet even with her new layer of confidence, there was a tingle of apprehension that climbed up her spine, as the fear of being judged reasserted itself.

She looked at Peter, who was passively, yet happily, looking at her. Her confidence grew again, as she contemplated her own figure. She was well proportioned, her figure resembling an hourglass. She had always been proud of her trim well-turned ankles and shapely calves.

She loved the curve of her hips and the swell of her bottom that had attracted more than one wolf whistle from construction sites. It was her ample breasts that seemed to attract most men though. She had no need of silicone, her breasts were totally natural and they were still firm at 30. Sure, there were things she would change if she had a magic wand. She would wish away an inch or so from her upper thighs, maybe tighten and tone in the odd area, but there would be no going under the surgeon's knife for her.

As Evelyn stood before Peter, she assessed her own looks, more critically than any partner would. She looked at Peter, trying to read his mind. What was he thinking? She felt more than a little self-conscious. It was like stripping away the therapy sessions and going back to her days at school. She felt the weight of her nerves once more. Confidence ebbed and flowed, like breakers on the shore.

She looked to Peter for reassurance. As she looked more deeply into Peter's eyes, she bathed in the warmth of his smile. She could plainly see now, that far from judging her, he looked more like he was about to eat her up. She wondered if he knew that she could see a flick of tongue as he licked his lips. He looked as if he planned to devourer her, and she hoped to God that he was going to do it soon.

She became less self-aware as she turned her attentions to him. She felt drawn to his handsomely rugged features. He looked impressively strong and she wondered how his body would feel pressed hard against her.

Evelyn was hungry and she wanted Peter. The wait was making her feel impatient. The anticipation was torture, the tension building, making her want to scream, if only inside.

Her eyes had been fixed on his intense gaze, and suddenly her attention switched back to herself. She was standing there like a schoolgirl. She found herself fidgeting, smoothing her skirt to remove the creases that didn't exist; she looked at herself fiddling with the buttons on her cuffs, then played with her hair nervously and smiled at him. Yet now, in a strange way, she was beginning to enjoy this feeling of unease. In fact, she found this to be a big part of this brand new experience.

Her reflection was interrupted by Peter, "I like things a certain way, I hope you don't mind." Peter was calm and sat still, totally relaxed with the situation, a smile playing across his lips, "I have a feeling that you and I are very compatible."

"I hope so." Evelyn felt the blood rush to her cheeks as her heart pumped madly. She looked into the eyes of this tall handsome man, trying to see into his mind. She was nervous, yet more excited by this, than she had ever been with any man before. She felt her nipples dilate and was sure Peter could see just how excited she was. Her eyes flickered for a moment to his trousers; there was no mistaking the bulge. She was pleased to have this effect on him.

His eyes fixed on hers, "I hope so too." Peter's lips curled into a natural smile. There was a flash of white teeth and the soft edge of affection in his voice. He leaned back in the chair and crossed his legs. "I would like you to do something for me, but it must be done freely." His eyes never broke contact with hers as he spoke.

She shifted her weight slightly from one foot to the other and said, "What would you like me to do?" The tremble in her voice was half in fear of the answer and half in anticipation. Right here and now she would do anything. Her eyes were locked to his. She was drawn like a moth to the flame.

Peter uncrossed his legs and leaned forward, "Firstly, I would like you to take off your blouse."

Evelyn was not used to men being this direct with her, she felt a second rush of blood to her cheeks, but it excited her beyond belief and she felt herself moisten. Was it wrong of her to do as he asked, she wondered. Yet, it felt so right, how could she not comply?

Her heart beat faster as her nervous fingers fumbled with difficult buttons. Her mind flicked to a time in school changing rooms and other girls laughing at her developing body. She had been the first in her class to develop breasts and had been teased endlessly for it. As she loosened the blouse from her skirt, she relived every negative comment she had ever heard. Was Peter going to judge her? How much easier sex would be with the lights off.

She shook as the garment slipped from her shoulders and fell to the floor. She was revealed. Her mind raced. Where was this going? She knew it would end in sex, but this was so different from the usual courtship ritual. Would the sex be that much different too?

In contrast to Evelyn, Peter looked and sounded contented and relaxed. "And now your skirt please." His voice was calm and measured, his face placid. Evelyn found her gaze slipping from his eyes to the prominent bulge in his trousers. She felt flustered, and she contemplated sinking to her knees there and then and releasing the captive. However, the instruction had not been given and she was not brave enough to deviate from Peter's word.

She wondered what her friends would say, if she told them, a man had told her to do this and she had complied. Indeed, could she ever tell anyone how much it excited her to give this control to a man? Nice girls didn't do such things. Did they?

She had undressed in front of men before, but usually the man would be busy removing his clothes at the same time. This felt more personal. She was under the spotlight; it was her performing for him. Trembling fingers grappled with the belligerent fastening of the skirt, she quietly muttered under her breath as the clasp surrendered and the skirt puddled at her feet. Evelyn looked closely at Peter looking for any reaction negative or otherwise, as her thighs were now revealed. To her relief, Peter's gaze traced admiringly up her legs and the swell in his trousers confirmed, in a most honest way, he liked what he saw. Again, her nerves twitched and she wished this first time had been beneath the cover of a darkened room.

She looked at Peter and his eyes were still fixed on her. It was obvious that he was amused by the struggle with the skirt's clasp, yet he only kept a slight smile, not wanting to break the sensuality of the moment. "Your shoes please."

Evelyn looked down at her shoes. A part of her wanted to resist. This was wrong, wasn't it? It was wrong for a man to issue instructions for her to strip, wasn't it? She was not a whore, to do as she was told, a plaything, a life-size, queen-sized, Barbie doll. Yet this was compulsive. Peter was no monster, quite the opposite. He had a charming way about him. He was a gentleman. She felt like she was being charmed out of her clothes, but there was something compelling in the way he talked. Something in the matter-of-fact way, he asked her to remove each garment that made it impossible to refuse. She felt his glance alter from warm to steely, the longer she delayed, though in truth from request to action it was a fraction of a second. Peter was almost motionless, yet the glint in his eye and the power of his voice made each request overwhelming.

She was confused why the removal of the shoes was so symbolic, was it the reduction of height? Or her feeling of helplessness? Evelyn took a deep breath and steadied her nerve. She slipped into the abyss, as the shoes were gently slid off and she stood before him in bra, panties and pantyhose. Now resigned to her fate, she felt the sooner she was naked the better, then at least there would be the love making. Evelyn went to remove her bra, but Peter stopped her.

"Not until I am ready, please. You may remove it, but only when I ask you," he continued with cool measured voice.

Evelyn was confused, he didn't want to see her naked? "I don't understand, Peter."

Peter leaned forward, "This will happen all in good time, but it will happen in my time. I would like you to do as I ask." There was no anger in his voice, just the opposite; it was a calm response, which Evelyn found comforting rather than upsetting. "I want to savor you, as I would a gourmet meal. Which is better filet mignon or hamburger?" Peter clasped his hands together and studiously steepled his fingers "Which would you like me to consider you? Filet or burger?"

Evelyn needed no time to think "Filet." She had been regarded as a burger, too many times in the past.

Peter leaned back in the seat again. "Are you ready to continue?"

"Yes Peter." She looked directly at her lover.

Peter returned her smile and said, "I have a request. I have certain tastes and it would please me, very much, if you would address me as Sir. It is a simple word that shows respect. It is a word that shows me you are ready and willing to serve. The choice to serve is for you to make, and this is a choice you must make freely. It will feel a bit strange at first, but it is a way some people live their lives. It is a way I live mine.

"I have a profound feeling that you would take to this lifestyle. I feel deep down, that you have a need to serve. I know you have a need to please me. Do you feel you are you ready to take this first step? Do you feel you are ready to do as I ask? To please me?"

Though she was unsure in her mind of the implications of what it meant to serve, without hesitation she replied, "Yes Sir." The sir came out of her lips naturally, as an involuntary reaction to his authority and she liked the way it sounded, respectful and comforting. She was aware again of the moistness in her panties and she knew there would be no hiding it from Peter.

"Good girl," Peter said, with a flash of white teeth. Then his lips set to a warm smile.

"May I ask a question?"

"Of course, you may ask anything."

"What does it mean to serve? What is it I have to do?"

Without hesitation Peter replied, "To serve me well, requires you to do as I ask, when I ask you to do it. This requires you to trust me. I wish you to follow my requests carefully, without question, because you know it is what I wish. In serving me, it also fulfills a side of you that has not yet been fulfilled. This is very much a two way street. You must want to serve. You must want to trust. In return, our love for each other will blossom."

Reassured by his words, but still a little apprehensive she asked, "What if I fail? What if I can't live up to all you expect?"

Peter took her hand and kissed it his warm lips grazed her flesh, "I want this as much for you, as I do for myself. It is not an audition to be passed. You need to want to do this. You need to feel in your heart that this is right for you. In return, I will support you, nurture you, guide you, and hold you.

"I feel that you have been repressing these feelings of submission, a little like a caged bird. I want you to be the person that I know you have locked away deep inside you. I want you to be that person for you.

"It will seem a little strange at first, giving me that power over you. In time, and with trust, it will become second nature for you. With trust, you will focus on your service to me. I in turn will devote my life to cherishing you. Trust is needed because you have to know instinctively that what I ask you to do will not harm you. You will find a deep sense of wellbeing in your service. But it is your service to give freely."

Peter paused for a moment, to let the depth of his words sink in. With a kind warm tone in his voice he continued, "I ask you again, freely and happily would you choose to serve me?"

Evelyn searched her mind. Yes, she wanted him. Yes, she was burning with desire, but more than that, much more, she knew within her very soul that the only truth that mattered was, she loved Peter more profoundly than she had ever loved before. "Yes Sir I am willing to serve. I will do all you ask of me and I will try to serve you as well as I can."

"I can ask nothing more from you than that. This makes me very happy Evelyn, very happy indeed."

"Sir, what would you ask of me?"

Peter paused for a moment, "I am not fond of pantyhose, I would be happier if you never wore them again. Stockings are fine, but I just don't like pantyhose. I would be disappointed to find you wearing them." His words were friendly, yet Evelyn was in no doubt that his likes and dislikes must be taken seriously. There was an undeniable throbbing at her center. Her clit ached to be touched.

The suspense from what was happening was incredible. Never before in her life had she been so turned on, so very aware of her body and her needs. Right there and then she would give anything to have Peter rip off her remaining clothes and fuck her. Yet she knew she would have to wait for his instruction.

"I wish you to remove your pantyhose, please." Peter spoke as if he was at the dinner table asking her to pass the salt, yet as much as it sounded a request; there was no getting away from the power of his tone.

Evelyn looked down, as she hooked her thumbs under the elastic of the hose. She tried to make the removal as elegant as she could for Peter. Boyfriends in the past had never paused at this stage; they were so intent to getting at what was inside. There was such an awkwardness about getting them off that she vowed never to wear them again. Having removed the garment she stood head lowered, looking at her body.

She wished at that moment that she was a size 10, but the fact remained that she wasn't and with Peter looking at her with the *I am going to eat you for breakfast* look in his eye she realized, maybe for the first time in her life, she really didn't give a shit. This man lusted after her as she was, and she wanted him inside her. Size was irrelevant. She was hungry.

She was so excited she was about to explode. Her nipples were painfully hard where they pressed against the flimsy fabric of her bra. Peter would be able to see how hard they were. A glance down showed her panties were every bit as embarrassingly wet as she feared they would be. Peter would be able to see that too. Calmly she waited for his next instruction.

"Please look up," again in his tone was friendly.

She happily obeyed and their eyes met again. She looked closely at him, his face showed its 35 years. Though clean shaven, at this stage in the evening a light shadow was on his chin. His hair, a chestnut brown was neatly trimmed but slightly mussed from where he had run his fingers through it during the course of the evening. Evelyn saw warmth and kindness on his face. She returned his gaze and licked her lips in anticipation. This wait was a tantalizing game of tease and denial that was delicious.

Without her power suit, she felt more vulnerable, but the way Peter looked at her made her feel strong again and she minded less that he could see her like this. She switched her gaze from herself to Peter's face and then to his groin. He made no effort to try to hide his erection, which strained against the fabric of his trousers. Here was a man at home with his body.

She felt Peter's savoring of her body... She felt his eyes linger on her ample breasts and the fact that he could see her erect nipples and the damp patch on the front of her matching pretty pink lace bra and panties, somehow empowered her. The bulge in Peter's trousers showed that he was every bit as excited as she was. He wanted her and that made everything all right.

She became calmer and she felt her breathing grow less strained as she felt a little of the tension ease from her neck and shoulders. She began to feel comfortable, yet still excited, as she waited for his next instruction.

"How are you feeling?" Peter sat back, his thumb stroking his trousers, lightly just beyond the end of his penis.

"I feel fine, Sir." His words reassured her and she straightened her back.

"Good," Peter paused, "are you excited?"

The answer to the question was obvious in the wet stain on the front of her panties and the erect peaks of her nipples showing through her bra. He could see how excited she was but she hesitated to voice how excited she was.

"I would like you to tell me how excited you are. I know you find it difficult to verbalize this... But I want you to try."

"Yes Sir," her voice trembled and her face flushed. "I am very excited, Sir." Why should this be so hard to say out loud? She didn't understand why, but it was and she felt a little embarrassed to say it.

"Good girl. I am very pleased with you."

Pleased with her? Did he think of her as a pet? She should have been angry, yet she wasn't. She was quite the opposite. She was proud that he was pleased with her. She was proud of being strong enough to do what he had asked and she replied with a simple, "Thank you, Sir."

Peter continued to stroke his leg, his thumb now catching the tip of his member on each stroke. "Your bra now, please." The tone in his voice had not altered; he was totally calm, totally in control.

She shrugged one of the shoulder straps down and unclasped the hooks and her soft firm breasts swung free. The cool air caressed her firm orbs and erect nipples. She felt calm and relaxed, showing Peter her charms.

Her eyes flicked over her pale breasts crowned with erect pink gumdrop nipples. His smiling face and hard cock told her all she needed to know. She wanted this man.

The instruction to remove her last garment could not be far away yet it seemed an age before he said, "And now Evelyn, your panties please." She had been expecting that, and shimmied out of the lacy material. What she hadn't expected was his next request. "Would you be so kind as to hand them to me?" Again, the power of this simple request hit her and she handed him the damp swatch of fabric.

Naked and vulnerable now, she looked down at her own body, her erect nipples and damp pubic hair, and the moistness on her thigh. She felt so exposed that she wanted to hide. Her natural instincts made her attempt to cover her body with her hands.

Peter with an almost inaudible "No" stopped her. "You have nothing to worry about you have a lovely body. Let me feast my eyes upon it."

She stood still as she watched him looking at her, then she saw him switch his attention to her panties. As he fingered the cloth, she could almost feel his hands on her. She watched him scrutinize this most intimate piece of clothing. She felt a little embarrassed as he lifted the cloth to his nose and inhaled her scent. She hoped she smelled sweet. His facial expression reassured her. He obviously liked her musk.

Peter's attention moved from her to her panties and back again. When he looked at her she could see he looked at her naked body approvingly. Peter had a look in his eye that said he could and would devour her and she liked that.

"You have never given yourself to a man this way before," he held her panties to his face and inhaled again, "and it troubles you a little… yet it excites you too?" Peter's voice was calm as if he was talking about the weather.

"Yes Sir… very much," her voice was trembling and husky. She could not disguise the fact she wanted him. As she stood, her legs parted a little and she gave a little sigh as a cool wisp of air whispered across her labia. She was hungry.

Peter looked directly into her eyes. "I want you." He stood and moved to her.

Evelyn dropped her gaze but Peter lifted her chin. His hand was warm and smooth. He looked her directly in the eyes again, and stroked her cheek.

With her face in his hands Peter whispered, "I want you to give yourself to me. I want you to do it totally. I want you to do it willingly and without reservation. Do you give yourself to me?"

She felt her face melt into his hands, she felt her knees tremble. There and then, she would do *anything* he asked. "Oh, God yes." she gasped. "Yes Sir, whatever you wish of me."

"Without reservation?" Peter stroked her cheek and looked her in the eyes, never breaking eye contact.

Evelyn blurted out, "Yes Sir. I will do anything." Her words left her lips without the full implication of what *anything* could mean. There was nothing this man could ask her to do that she would not do for him. She was his. Her body shook.

"Thank you. I would like you to turn around for me."

Slowly she turned for him and though she could not see his face, the small grunts he gave, reassured her that he appreciated her back view every bit as much as he had the front.

"Truly exquisite," whispered Peter. His words were reverent, as if describing a work of art.

Peter held her from behind and whispered in her ear. "You are beautiful, truly beautiful. I wish to prepare you, *to make you even more perfect*. Please show me the way to your bathroom."

His words reassured her. It was as if her every nerve was attuned and alert. Evelyn caught the smell of his subtle citrus aftershave, as she led him to the bathroom. She felt the carpet beneath her naked toes, as she crossed the living room. She felt the blood pounding in her veins. A million questions went through her mind. Whatever would this preparation entail? Were they to shower? Was he to wash her? She knew better than to ask, yet her mind and heart raced.

They walked through her bedroom to get to the bathroom. She was proud of her bedroom's décor. It had an air of elegance, as did her bathroom. In the bathroom, she looked around trying to imagine what Peter would think. It was a large opulent room with cool marble tiled floor and walls, sophisticated antique mirrors, and art deco light fittings. Matching pink towels and floor mats and gold plated fittings crowned the appearance. She could see Peter looking around and hoped he was impressed.

He nodded approvingly and turned her to face him. "Very nice, I like it." He kept eye contact with her and continued, "Do you have a new razor?" Peter's voice was still calm.

Evelyn did not know why she trusted him, but she did, yet the request for a razor presented a new level of trust. Never had she had such an experience. Every fiber in her being, said this is not how couples made out, she should resist, yet in the same breath it felt so right to submit to this man's will. She felt like she was on a rollercoaster ride, nervous, yet at the same time excited beyond words.

Evelyn handed the razor to Peter.

He smiled reassuringly, "You don't need to look so worried." He kissed her on her lips, "I am not going to hurt you." He held her by the waist and kissed her tenderly again.

She melted into his kiss. She felt relieved at the normality of this one simple natural act.

It was Peter that broke the kiss. He looked deeply into her eyes and said, "You really are a very special lady." She bubbled over with emotions. Tears welled in her eyes. All she wanted right then was to be with Peter, to do anything he wanted her to do, regardless of what it might be. Anything!

With a last kiss, Peter knelt before her. He had lathered a bar of scented soap and was massaging the foam into her pubis. She felt his hands, strong yet gentle, pressing on her delicate flesh. She felt cherished and pampered. She exulted in her desire. He was her Master. Her body was his to do with as he wanted and it was as she accepted that her body was in Peter's control that he began to shave off her already closely trimmed pubic hair.

She looked down intently, relaxed yet fascinated as she watched his nimble fingers part her petals, opening her to the blade. His hands were steady and deftly every hair was removed, as he shaved her smooth.

Peter moved back to admire his work and smiled. "I much prefer your treasure in the open rather than hiding in the shadows. I wish you to keep yourself smooth from now on."

"Yes Sir."

She stood looking down helplessly, as Peter leaned forward and kissed her clit, holding her morsel between his lips. Holding her hips, he feasted with lips and tongue, teasing her pearl from the shell. The feeling was so intense, the contact so immediate she could do nothing but cum under his ministrations. She screamed and convulsed, as the spasms tore through her. Every nerve ending was alive. The release so complete, she would have collapsed if he had not been holding her. She felt spent, totally drained and totally relaxed. Peter swept her up in his arms and carried her to the adjoining bedroom. He let Evelyn rest as he removed his own clothes. As his speech, he did not hurry to remove his clothes. He was precise, and after removing each item, it was folded and put neatly on the back of a bedroom chair. Evelyn was captivated by this tall handsome man, so measured in his actions. She watched him strip and all the time he looked at her.

He thumbed down his last garment and his erect penis sprang out. Evelyn observed that he was a full seven inches long and was more than average in girth. She also noticed immediately that although he had a downy covering of hair on his chest, his groin was shaved smooth. She could not take her eyes of his magnificent erect phallus. She wondered what it would feel like inside her, wondered at the taste of his semen.

Peter crossed to her. "I think you are recovered enough," he smiled, as he looked down at her.

"May I ask a question, Sir?" her eyes were fixed to his firm body.

"Of course."

"I thought I was to serve you?" her eyes were warm and there was a glow still on her cheeks.

"You will serve me, and you will serve me all the better now that your lust has been sated." His hand idly toyed with his erect penis. "You were burning with lust my pet. Now you will serve me with your full attention on my needs." He walked to where she sat on the edge of the bed. "And you will start by paying homage to my cock." He offered the head to her lips and she opened to receive him.

Peter was large but not uncomfortably so. Evelyn ran the tip of her tongue over his satin dome. She licked and sucked his member taking it, little by little, deeper into her mouth. She wanted to give Peter as much pleasure as he had given her; she wanted to give him more. She understood then, the logic of Peter's earlier action. Her head rose and sunk on his shaft. She made her lips tight for him covering her teeth, so as not to nip him.

Up to this point, Peter had let her set the pace, but now she felt his needs taking over. She felt his big firm hands cradling the back of her head and felt him began to rock back and forth. It was not unpleasant and she held her mouth still as he fucked her. She heard him moan as he took his pleasure. His rhythm and depth of stroke increased. She could feel the thrust of his length travel within her mouth, suddenly the strokes changed to short sharp thrusts and she knew he was drawing close. One deep thrust and he remained still. Evelyn could feel him pulse, as she received his liquid gift.

They cuddled for a while naked on the bed, in the spoons position, his cock between the cheeks of her bottom, his arms wrapped around her. She felt warm, safe and loved. As they drifted off to sleep, Evelyn reviewed the evening's events.

She had agreed without reservation, she had surprised herself with this. Normally she was assertive, but she felt great comfort in submitting to Peter. It felt like she had discovered her true nature in the submission, and she felt stronger knowing that Peter was there. This was their first time together as lovers and yet she felt like she had known him forever, felt like she would do anything for him. She felt like she was his and only his. In an instant, she thought of her previous lovers and realized no one had ever made her feel this way. She knew at that point, that Peter was the one for her.

Over the coming months, Evelyn gave more and more of herself to Peter. His control was like a drug; the more she had the more she wanted. Peter provided the focus to her daily life. Even when they were parted, it was like he was with her in spirit. She loved the way that he would choose her clothing for the day. He would decide what they would eat. Some people would find it troubling or oppressive to have someone decide. Evelyn found her day a brighter place knowing that she served Peter. She found a profound sense of comfort and shelter in Peter's love.

The internet showed a world of those who lead and those who follow, gladly and willingly. People in the know called it *the scene* and it was a world filled with dominants and submissives.

She had been terrified, the first time Peter took her to a dominance and submission club, but once there she saw it as just a place where like-minded people came to hang out. Evelyn spent more time in the company of other submissives. Listening to their stories made her feel more at home with this new lifestyle that she heard them refer to as *the scene*. The easy matter-of-fact way they described their own service made her more comfortable with this way of life than she had ever been in the vanilla world.

As her experience and confidence grew, she found her love for Peter growing. She found herself stopping during the course of the day thinking of what he might be up to. Her life seemed focused around his wants and needs. She began to anticipate things that he might like. As he lay out the clothes he wished her to wear, she made sure he was well turned out, taking a delight in polishing his shoes, even ironing shirts was no longer a chore, for it was for her Master. Listening to the other subs, she found new ways to verbalize their relationship and she learned to speak of their love. She heard other subs call their Doms *Master*, and she liked the term. To her ears, it sounded loving and respectful and she wanted to please her master so much. She would never forget the way Peter's face lit up the first time she had called him *Master*. She loved the way it sounded and it was a title she called him gladly. She could not conceive of her life without her Master in complete control. This was no abusive slave relationship. The power he had she gave him freely.

They shared, what they came to refer to as training sessions, where Peter would introduce her to new things like nipple clamps and toys and plugs. Together they would sit and trawl the internet and Peter would explain the significance of the lifestyle in their daily lives. Each new experience brought them closer together physically and spiritually.

It took a year with the help of books, videos, and the internet, for Peter to help her come to grips with the complexity of the scene. They talked passionately for hours long into the night. Evelyn loved the way he taught her. It was done with love and affection. Each session was slow and unhurried. It was consensual, he had always insisted on that.

She remembered a time when he wished her to go through the next stage and meet other Doms and subs in the flesh. She was terrified.

He had spent hours preparing her, dressing her to the nines, in stockings and a tight leather corset. Yet, despite all the preparations, he had asked her if she wanted to go in. It was her free choice. And she loved him for that.

It was with that love, she gathered her courage and went into the gathering, that she later found out they call a *munch*. She and Peter became regulars for a while and she observed close hand all manner of things that were new to her, the art of Japanese bondage, suspension, piercing, scarification, all manner of different forms of corporal punishment and secretly she wished it were she that felt the taste of the whip and crop.

Every aspect of her life Peter made his masterly presence felt. Evelyn remembered the day a bouquet of roses had been delivered to her private office. The delivery boy entered and presented her the bouquet of a dozen roses. Her heart had leapt for joy, a present from her master, a token of his love for her. She sniffed the rose. The fragrance matched its beauty. She turned her attention to the card and smiled when she read; *For you my darling, you serve me so beautifully well, now as a token of your service to me, I wish you to remove your panties and give them to the delivery boy*. Without a doubt, the boy had read the card, if the smirk on his face was anything to go by. How could she do anything but comply? As embarrassed as she was and with as much dignity as she could muster, she wiggled out of her panties and handed them to the young man. He thanked her and left and she was left to think about it for the rest of her working day.

These games were more than a little embarrassing, yet they were a fun part of their relationship and she loved them. She loved the comfort she found in his control and the shelter within his power. The more he asked of her, the more she wanted to give. Peter was experienced in this way of life, although only two years older, at thirty-five he had the self-confidence to know what he wanted. Evelyn felt secure; it was as if she had waited her life for him.

After the visits to the *munches*, Peter introduced her to the kaleidoscope of things she has seen demonstrated in the club. These would challenge her perceptions of what was right and wrong in relationships. At this time, there were so many firsts, the night she had submitted to bondage, her first spanking, the bite of nipple clamps, and the myriad of toys, whips and floggers, all for their mutual pleasure. Evelyn learned not to tease Peter, as that would surely not work out as she had planned.

Occasionally she had tried to get the upper hand but try as she might she never did. She remembered teasing him one day, keeping him in a state of excitement, and then informing him that sadly it was the wrong time of the month. It had been her way of trying to turn the tables on her Master, but Peter did not flinch. He took a coin from his pocket and flipped it. "Now we will see. Heads or Tails" and with the tails side of the coin showing, another first, was added to her list. Sodomy. It was new to her, but she trusted her Master completely and submitted freely to this new act.

Day by day, week by week and as month followed month, Peter took Evelyn to her very limits, and she went there willingly. She was his and wanted nothing else.

Over dinner one night Peter had said, "My pet, this is my nature, and I believe this is in your nature too, although as people we are free and equal, our nature leads us to a different reality. I believe you feel the same and instinctively know what I am saying. It is my belief you wish to serve me, as much as I wish you to serve."

Peter opened a small black velvet box. Inside was a short gold chain, in the middle of which was a small amulet inscribed with an ornately inscribed letter *P*. "My pet, this is for you, I would like to marry you, but it is fair for you to know, truly know, my heart's desire. With this chain, you will serve me, as I will cherish, protect, and nurture you. In the marriage service, they use the words love, honor and obey. In the world, I want us to live in; I want those words to be very literal. I wish you to honor and obey me, and with that, I pledge myself only to you. Will you take this chain? Will you serve me and only me, will you marry me?"

Then as now, a tear trickled down her cheek and she said aloud, as she had done then, "I will." Plain and simple, yet profound. She wanted nothing more. With his proposal and her acceptance, her life was complete.

There seemed no end to this golden time. Yet, like all golden times, it had to end and when it did, it crushed her.

The thought buzzed through her mind and a tear rolled down her cheek. A golden time, but that had been four years ago. And here she was now, driving through the night.

The lights cut through the night, lighting trees and flickering across the houses, which were scattered sparsely throughout this part of the countryside. The hotel had been built in the middle of nowhere and the remoteness had been the reason they had picked it for their honeymoon, all those years ago.

She knew she was drawing close to her destination, although time had taken its toll on the landscape. The road lacked the quaintness it once had and the small shrines situated on sharp bends, gave testimony to how much more dangerous the roads had become over the years. There was the old mailbox once a bright red, now faded to a drab grey. An old oak tree who's once majestic lower branches, were now loped off. There were more than a dozen markers she used to navigate this journey and though the landmarks were older and shabbier, they were still unmistakable. She had never been great at navigation, especially out of town but although remote, she had never had any difficulty finding *Woodside Manor*.

There was a small crest to a hill before the approach to the Manor. Evelyn caught her breath as the lights played across the building, lighting the two majestic towers that flanked either side of the castellated top of the main building.

Woodside manor had once been an exclusive country club, owned by an oil tycoon. No expense had been spared on its original construction. It had enjoyed a second life as a luxury hotel, but successive owners, had let it fall into disrepair.

Evelyn's sleek, burgundy-colored Jaguar turned off the main road and up the long, winding, tree lined driveway, which led to the hotel. As she approached, her lights swung across the faded façade that had once been a gleaming white. There was a fountain in the middle of a large doughnut shaped parking area. It was once lit and the jets of water then had been bathed in colored light. Now it was dark and the water danced no more. The water was green and stagnant and the ornamental statue in the center of the pond was covered with a thick moss concealing that it had once been an attractive lady holding a Greek urn.

From the first time she had visited the manor she had loved the place. The opulence of the frontage had always reminded her of the set in the film *Gone with the Wind.* The building seemed steeped in southern colonial elegance. She felt a little saddened to see this grand building, now so down at heel. The gardens too, what she could see of them, were a faded reminder of what had once been.

Woodside Manor was no longer the prestigious venue for millionaires and playboys; it had faded, as all things fade in time.

The tires crunched to a halt and Evelyn sat in the car, with the engine still running. She touched the amulet at her throat. The chain was short enough to draw comment. A close friend had once said that the medallion on such a short collar resembles a dog's collar. The comment had made Evelyn smile and she drew her own comparison with the ownership of her as the beloved pet. Of course, a vanilla world could not see what it was, it simply made them curious. She fingered the decorative rose gold *P* and she thought of her service and what the collar represented.

She turned the key and the car's quiet hum fell silent. Evelyn sat still in the car, aware of the gifts she wore in honor of Peter. Conflict swirled in her mind. In the dark, her fingers fiddled with the car door latch. It clicked and swung open, but as she left the car, she went cold, as she thought of her husband James. Another wave of guilt tore through her. After all James had done for her, how could she do this to him? How could she betray him like this? Yet her passion for her Master was strong.

Her mind turned over the argument; she felt a strong commitment to both men. In a way, she had betrayed Peter in marrying James. Peter had been her Master for many years before she had known James. Her loyalties ran deep with both men. She loved them both. She would do anything for James, except this one thing, this one day of the year she must honor the vows she had made to her Master. How she wanted Peter. This was beyond animal lust, though in truth she felt that too, this was a bond. She had a commitment to Peter that no mortal could break. She knew no matter what, Peter loved her as deeply as she loved him.

She sat in the car gathering her thoughts for a brief moment, pondering her next move, although the choice had already been made. The choice had been made the day she said, *"I do"* to Peter.

The time of doubt was over. There was a way of getting out of the Jaguar that was more graceful than others. She had become quite expert at doing it. Keeping her knees together, she swung her legs around so she still sat on the seat, but now with her feet on the graveled car park. Then she stood. The alternative method of getting out of a low sports car, especially wearing a short skirt, was far too revealing.

Locking the car, she took the opportunity to take a closer look around the car park. Evelyn caught her breath, as she saw Peter's black sports car, with an ominous dent in the front driver's side wing. She walked over to the car and felt the contours of the indentation. She realized, as she ran her hand along the distorted shape of the depression, that the sleek paintwork had not even been broken. Her feelings turned to warmth, as she smiled, thinking back to that happy day when Peter first showed her the car. It was gleaming new, with just the showroom miles on the clock. He was like a small boy with a new toy, eager to show the trivial gadgets that please men so much in their toys. With a last stroke of the paintwork, she turned to the hotel.

Her black stiletto heels crunched, as she crossed the fine pea shingle to the still impressive, yet faded, front door. The closer Evelyn got to him, the more she realized how much she still needed him. She wanted him more now than ever. She moistened at the thought of him using her body. She was so ready; she wondered how he would have her. Would his mood today be rough or smooth?

In her mind's eye, she pictured herself tied, naked and helpless. She pictured his strong hands running over her body. She thought of the pinch of clamps on her tender parts, the smack of paddle, the bee sting of riding crop. A year had been a long time since she had felt Master's firm discipline and she longed to succumb to his will.

She wondered if Peter's features had changed over the last year. Would he look different? Any older? She had scrutinized her facial lines while she was preparing herself for this visit. Her bathroom at home had a shelf dedicated to creams and lotions, making claims to rejuvenate the skin, yet the lines crept in. Were it not for her weekly visit to the hairdresser, she knew that grey whips would streak her hair. But she did not do grey.

Would Peter's hair have aged? He would never be vain enough to use a color. Would his nice physique sport a curve of tummy as age took its toll? All the time she daydreamed, thinking of the changes she might see, she hoped that this evening, would be exactly as if it had been when they lived as man and wife. A pang of desire drove her on.

She wanted Peter alone in the privacy of their bedroom. She wanted to submit to her Master in whatever way he wanted her. Deep down, she never wanted this evening to end.

Once in the lobby the man at the reception desk didn't look up from the sports section in his newspaper, as she crossed the threadbare carpet on the way to the elevator. The interior was faded yet still clues to its former splendor were there. The art deco light fittings, antique mirrors, ornate plasterwork ceilings, and once plush couches at the edges of the large foyer all spoke of a more opulent time yet there was a grubby feel now. Unkempt plants sat on scarred wood tables and a stale musty smell filled the air.

Evelyn entered the elevator and selected the fourth floor. She found herself trembling slightly, as she approached the door to their room. Butterflies danced in her stomach. It had been a whole year since she had last seen Peter.

A flood of emotions hit her and she stayed motionless for a moment. In one breath, she knew that Peter meant everything to her, yet the trembled like a sophomore on her first date.

A shiver passed over Evelyn and suddenly she went as cold as the grave. Peter, James, her life, her loves, her heart, like a near death experience, she saw herself from above. Her life flashed before her eyes. The conflicts and emotions whirled around her head and in one instant there was a part of her that just wanted to run, run back to the arms of James. She was torn between the safety and security of home and the call of her Master.

It had been four years since she had served him full time, yet the power of his voice rang loud and clear in her ears. How she wanted the touch of his hand. She needed Peter. All the time there was Peter, always Peter and she knew as surely as night followed day that she would take these last few steps and knock on the door.

It was the same room where they had made love for more years than she could recall. The same room where she had spent her honeymoon, the room where her lover waited silently for her now.

Her eyes lingered on the tarnished brass numbers 422. There on the door below the number was their sign, a rose, now slightly wilted, yet nevertheless a symbol of their love. A fingertip stroked a slightly wilting petal and with a deep breath and a trembling hand Evelyn's knuckle lightly rapped on the door. With a sigh, her full breasts swelled against her starched linen blouse and suddenly she was fully aware of herself again, aware of the very personal way Peter has asked her to dress for his pleasure. She felt the intimacy and closeness of the chain, as she waited for a response. The metal stroked tender flesh. She could sense, just how wet she was in anticipation of this meeting. A nervous hand fiddled with the hem of her skirt.

For what seemed like an age, she waited outside the door, then the solid click of the lock and there stood Peter, crisp white shirt, and his charcoal business suit. Gold cufflinks and tiepin and the shine on his shoes. He was just the same as he ever was, he had not changed, not one wrinkle, not one additional grey hair. Tears welled up in her eyes as the love for her master overwhelmed her She caught her breath and stifled a sob, as she saw the fire red tie with the tiny white dots she had bought him so many years ago. She looked him full in the face. Yes, he was just the same. The broad, open smile and the glint in his eye, took her back to the electronics trade show where they had met, all those years ago.

She had always loved his enthusiasm, no matter what he did, he always did it keenly. How she loved him. Evelyn stepped to her Master and melted into his waiting arms as if she had never been parted from him.

She felt Peter give the door a gentle push, with a solid click, the door closed, and they were alone.

Their embrace lasted an age, and even then only broke reluctantly.

It was Peter who stepped back, to admire his beautiful lady. She had dressed according to his requests and he appreciated her attention to detail. Her full creamy breasts thrust against her crisp white blouse, her black skirt hugged her rounded hips. His gaze traveled down to her gorgeous stockinged legs and stylish Italian high heels and then back up where the whole image was crowned by the broad gold chain that hung high around her neck, resembling a collar. Affixed to the chain was an amulet, a yellow gold disk with his initial *P* inlaid in rose gold. On the flipside the maker's mark, which as a smaller yet no less impressive *Z*. The amulet matched the pendent that hung around his own neck, only the inscription on the front was an elaborate *E*.

Chapter Two

He had met the maker, Zachariah, by chance. He had been browsing an old quarter of the city, for months. Peter had been looking for a collar for Evelyn, yet he had not seen anything he liked enough to buy it. It had been a fruitless search until coming to an old shop, tucked away in a side ally.

The shop was called *The Crimson Z*. Pondering the name, he was not sure if that was a good omen or not. The window displayed some beautiful craftsmanship and a small faded sign, 'Guild of Goldsmiths, jewelry made to order.' Waiting outside the shop Peter watched a child playing on a bicycle. His gaze was captivated, and then suddenly the child slipped.

Peter rushed over to help the small boy. "Are you ok?"

"Yes Sir. I think so Sir."

The boy had sustained nothing more than a scratch and Peter cleaned it up with a Kleenex, which he put back into his pocket.

"There you are," he'd said after cleaning the scratch. "I would head straight home now if I were you."

The boy smiled, "Thank you Sir." The boy seemed happy and went on his way.

Peter's attention turned back to the shop. He was still not sure about going into the small shop. It always embarrassed him if he couldn't find what he wanted or if it was too expensive. He took a deep breath and entered. The shop was dimly lit and looked like something out of a Dickens' novel. Around the room were glass display cases in which were an array of pretty trinkets on miniature stands or on small velvet cushions. There was something very quaint about the displays, very much something from a by-gone age. The rough wooden floorboards creaked beneath his feet. The shop appeared empty, so Peter looked around at the displays. On the front counter, there was a stunning gold necklace not very long, but generous thick links. The work was lovely and he moved closer to admire the workmanship.

He was just about to touch the precious metal when, "Can I be of service, Sir?" came from a strongly accented voice, from somewhere behind him.

Peter was taken aback at the interjection and then the sight of a well-built, bearded man, who had seemed to have come from nowhere. He composed himself and replied, "Yes, I am looking for a special gift."

"For a lady, Sir?"

"Yes."

The old man walked slowly round to the other side of the counter. Although quite an age, he moved confidently and with grace, for his years. Peter looked into the large man's eyes. They still had a spark of youth, though his age showed in his body and more especially in his slightly gnarled hands. He was tall. Peter guessed a little less than six feet and wore a black suit in the Hasidic tradition. No tie but a white shirt with the top button done up. His long beard was grey as was his long hair. There were the odd traces of dark, which made Peter wonder what he would have looked like as a young man. Even now, he was well built in a way that gave the appearance of strength. Peter thought of him as a young man and was struck by his presence.

"I have been working on this piece," he said, looking frankly at Peter, "it was started a little while ago, though I had no purpose for it at the time, but I can see it has caught your eye. Please have a closer look, feel the weight of the gold."

Peter picked up the chain and said, "Thank you," as he examined it closely. It was exquisite work indeed. "Perfect," he whispered under his breath barely audibly.

"Thank you Sir that is most kind." The large man paused, and then continued, "Please let me introduce myself, my name is Zachariah. You may call me Zach." The goldsmith offered his hand in friendship and with without reservation Peter shook it.

Peter, wondered how the jeweler heard him. He also pondered that he didn't know why he trusted this man, but knew that he did. The handshake was strong and honest. He was a little dazed but happy, when he replied, "My name is Peter."

"It is good to meet you Peter." The goldsmith smiled and looking at the work in Peter's hand continued, "You know? I think this piece, when it is finished, and with the addition of a pendent will suit your need."

"It looks perfect." Peter paused to look again at the chain. "What kind of pendent did you have in mind?"

The old man smiled warmly, "I suspect the gift is to be one that is intended to show your dedication to each other?"

"Yes but…" How could he know? Peter was confused that a stranger could know so much.

"I know a great many things Peter, I can feel things that most other people cannot."

"Now Peter, the pendent, I see it as a disk, with your initial engraved upon it, maybe a little filigree work to decorate it?"

"I like the sound of that. Yes," replied Peter.

Zachariah put his hand into his jacket pocket and produced a small note pad and a pencil, "While I am drawing can I offer you something to drink?"

It had been a hot day so Peter accepted the offer, "A glass of water would be nice."

Zach went out to the back of the shop and returned with a whiskey tumbler filled with ice water. Peter took it and thanked him.

As Peter watched, the jeweler began to draw the pendent in intricate detail. The drawing was superbly detailed, the amulet, complete as he described with an elaborate *P* inscribed on the face side.

Peter felt a sting on his lower lip. He cursed under his breath. Zach smiled at the profanity. Peter used the Kleenex to wipe away the small trace of blood.

"I am sorry about the glass, are you alright?"

Peter smiled. "It's nothing really."

"Allow me to take the Kleenex; you may have a clean handkerchief."

Peter thanked him, traded the soiled tissue for the fresh linen handkerchief, and thought no more about the incident. Peter looked admiringly at the picture, "This is wonderful, exactly what I have been looking for it's per…"

Zachariah interrupted his last word, "Perfect. I hoped you would like it.

"There is still a little work to do on the chain and you will want a similar pendant for yourself, to complete the connection. It will take about a week to complete. I will see you one week from today," the goldsmith said.

"Don't you at least want a deposit," asked Peter reaching for his wallet.

"No I don't think so; I believe you will be here next week."

In the week that followed, Peter felt like he was waiting for Christmas to come. He had been tempted to pop in and see how work was progressing, but had resisted the urge. A week to the day he returned. True to his word, the goldsmith produced a satin lined box with the two chains and the two elaborate pendants, the first Evelyn's with the *P* emblazoned on it in rose gold and the second, this one his, with an elaborate *E* also in rose gold. Zachariah had used his skill well. In the case of both amulets, the portion inlaid in rose gold and stood out from the rest of the design. Peter beamed like a schoolboy who had just been given a toy. "This is wonderful, exactly what I have been looking for. It's per…"

Zachariah interrupted his last word again, "Perfect… yes, just so…" pride in his voice.

"I just don't understand how you could know… that this was exactly what I had in mind."

"Believe me when I say, I just have a feel for these things. I can't tell you how I knew you were coming to me and what you would want, I simply knew. You don't have to try to understand, you just have to accept. There is a connection between these two amulets," he paused to let his words sink in. "There are a few things you should know." The big man straightened to his full height. "The pendants have strong properties, when you both wear the amulets you are bound together, in a very profound way. And as long as you are true to each other you will be inseparable."

Peter listened to his words, connection? Inseparable? He didn't understand, but he didn't want to ask either. The friendly look in Zachariah's eyes reassured Peter. He could see no malice in the man's eyes, only warmth. He felt comfortable that this man was doing what needed to be done.

The jeweler went on, "While there is love in both your hearts the pendants will stay warm all the time."

Peter didn't realize the significance of his words then, but he accepted it.

The goldsmith smiled, "I will be seeing you again next year I expect. I have a feeling that you will want some more of my work. More than money has been exchanged today."

"Yes it has. I am sure I will be back too," and with a shake of hands he settled his account with Zachariah and left the shop.

Chapter Three

Peter's gaze never left his lady. He had always been attracted to ladies with a fuller figure. He had always admired the full roundness of her breasts, the swell of her hip. In a skirt, he loved the way it clung to her thighs and in jeans the roundness of the pubic curve. Every element of her gave him joy. Evelyn was every bit as lovely and he wanted her as much as he had that first day he had spied her from across the room. In all these years, she had changed very little, maybe a little more silver in with her long golden hair, there were maybe a few more lines, but he loved those laughter lines. Evelyn had always told him, of her conscious efforts to keep her weight in check, though in truth he had always felt it would be more to hold, more to love. When they had first met, she had been working out on a regular basis. It was true that she was not as firm as she had been, but to Peter it was the last thing on earth that mattered, Evelyn was his and that's all that truly mattered to him.

He knew then that he had to have her. These years of lust and passion had nourished him. His desire had given him a reason to exist. He looked his lady in the eyes, how he loved her with all that he was.

He lived now, for these annual meetings and if he could he would make these times together last forever. His mind took him back to when they had first met. There had been something about her that had lit the room for him. She had looked stunning in her sharp business suit. There had been an immediate connection and he had known he had to get to know her. Their courtship, though conventional to start with, had always shown promise for more. There had always been something that had made him convinced she would submit to him.

He remembered too well, the night she had first submitted to him. She had been so unsure. She had looked like a fawn, frightened and on edge, not sure if she should stand or run. He remembered shaving her and how beautiful she had looked after, the silkiness of her skin, her sweet scent and her willingness to come to heel. He had known by the look in her eye that she was submissive and he delighted in the fact that she was willing for him to bring that out and to allow him to possess her.

He remembered the joyous months of training, introducing new toys, all kinds of exotic people, various types of bondage and new rituals. He had always liked the rituals; the element he loved above all was giving a structure to Evelyn's day.

By and large he liked to keep to this daily routine all year round regardless of vacations or other things happening. The day would start with Evelyn kissing her Master's phallus, as an alarm call.

It would vary as to whether he wished to climax in her mouth or not. It might progress into lovemaking or not but it would start with the kiss. After she had provided coffee and breakfast, he would choose her clothing. Unless there were visitors or another reason, he liked her to remain naked for his pleasure until he sorted out her clothes. Peter had his preference, he liked her in stockings, but would let her go bare legged in high summer. He would choose clothing that suited her sense of style. He enjoyed the power of choosing her clothes and she enjoyed it too. She had told him she thrilled at the fact even her panties had been touched and selected by him.

Mid-morning at 11am sharp every day he had told her to go to a quiet place, usually the ladies' rest room. There she was to stimulate her clitoris to erection and hold it there for five minutes, contemplating her master, counting her blessings, and contemplating how best to serve him. Yet in all this time, he had not allowed her to climax, unless he had expressly given her permission to do so. He could feel the strain in her voice some days when he phoned after she had completed her homage.

He might phone unexpectedly in the afternoon and might suggest additional elements, like having her insert a butt plug for her car ride home. This was guaranteed to make her feel every bump in the road home. It would have the additional benefit of having her ready if he wanted to use her that way later in the evening.

The daily ritual continued at home in the evening with her cooking his evening meal. She had always said how much she loved to cook for him. In return, he was very appreciative of the care he was given, often bringing her little tokens of affection. He remembered one particular occasion when he had brought home a rose, Evelyn was over the moon and she had served him his evening meal wearing only a smile.

Regardless of the sex they'd had that night, and sex was always on the cards, Peter always insisted that her last duty of the day was to kiss his penis goodnight.

He had always got the impression from her response she loved the rituals too; this was borne out by her increased enthusiasm for the tasks.

One day he asked her and she had said she took as much pleasure in her submission, as he did. He was delighted every time she told him that. She also told him that the routine showed that he cared about her seven days a week twenty-four hours a day. He smiled when she told him that, because with all his heart, he did.

It had been the proudest moments in his life when she had accepted his collar. He remembered his fingers trembling as he buckled the clasp. It always brought a smile to his lips to remember, that after the collar had fastened tight, she had taken his member between her lips. In that climax, he knew he had found the one.

The collaring ceremony had been the culmination of years Peter had spent looking for the right lady. It had been like looking for a needle in a haystack and in finding Evelyn; he felt he had found his own personal holy grail. As he thought back, he remembered her gasps of pleasure as he teased her body, stimulating but withholding release. He remembered that she had been nervous at first, especially with the introduction of corporal punishment, but once she freely gave her control to him, he felt that she had taken to it like a duck to water.

It was clear that she was enjoying the discovery and he in turn delighted at leading her down the path of enlightenment. A path that lead to a different way of loving. A deeper way of loving.

Each step brought them closer together. The rose and trellis, the two entwined and inseparable. Peter as the trellis providing the framework that the rose of Evelyn could climb and thrive.

Evelyn shifted drawing his mind back to the present, "It has been a long time my pet."

Evelyn wiped a tear of joy and replied, "Yes, my Master, it has. I have missed you."

Stroking her hair, Peter smiled and said, "I have missed you too, oh so very much."

They embraced, holding each other tightly as they kissed passionately again.

Evelyn drew back and looked into Peter's eyes. She smiled and whispered, "I know," acknowledging that she knew he wanted more tender time too. They were both aware that time was pressing and as much as they both wanted to linger in the moment, time was not a luxury they could afford.

"Are you ready to serve my pet?" Peter stroked her cheek.

"I am Sir. I live to serve." Her smile showed the genuine warmth of her love for him.

"Thank you my pet." Peter took a step back and continued, "If you would be so good my dear, as to reveal to me the clothes with which you honor me."

All his words were so familiar the years folded back, as she remembered her training. She remembered his kindness and patience as he showed her how he liked her to dress. The way he shopped with her, guiding her in the shops. She remembered being slightly embarrassed as he asked the shopping assistant details about the clothing. Men were not supposed to be that confident, especially about women's clothing. They were not supposed to be that into shopping either.

She remembered the shopping assistant was embarrassed too when he lifted the hem of Evelyn's skirt and asked the assistant if she had four more pairs of identical panties. The assistant blushed and went to get the panties. Evelyn smiled at the memory of the incident too. It had not been the fact that Peter had exposed her panties that had embarrassed her, but the fact that her clit hood had been freshly pierced. As Peter had said this had been its first outing.

She reveled in the distance she had come since the first time she had submitted to him, in no greater way than in her own confidence in body. She remembered the first time she had stood naked in front of him. She had been blind with terror, scared to death of being judged by a new lover. It was the very fact that he had never judged her body, but had accepted her just as she was that allowed her to stand here now. Confident and ready to serve in whatever way Peter wanted.

"Yes Sir," she said confidently, as she undid the tiny pearl buttons of her blouse to reveal her naked breasts and their adorning jewelry.

Peter was delighted to see her naked and proud. He felt that her strength and confidence were the greatest gift he had ever given her.

Once more, he remembered when he'd had her pierced as a present for their first wedding anniversary. The piercings had been discussed for a while before doing them. It had rained all week, but this Saturday, the day the deed would be done was bright and sunny, it was like a message from above, a celestial approval.

The car journey was quiet. He could feel how nervous she was by her quietness. She was usually not that quiet. He patted her thigh reassuringly and they shared a smile. Yet, there was the tension of anticipation.

In the piercing parlor, it all looked clinical, very much like a doctor's examination room, with all the sterilized instruments on hand. When they had booked the appointment, they had booked for both breasts. The gold rings were there, just waiting to be fitted. Peter eyed the man that was to do the piercing with suspicion. He was heavily tattooed and looked to have more in common with a coven of Hell's Angels than the world of clinical practitioners. Yet, he seemed friendly and certainly seemed to know his business. He asked for Evelyn's breasts to be exposed and he marked the spots on each side of both nipples making sure that the piercings would be both straight and level. He remembered that Evelyn didn't say a word. She had looked at him with pleading puppy eyes. It had been a joint decision to have this done. He knew it was just last minute nerves.

He looked down at Evelyn as she sat in the chair. He held her hand.

"Are you going to give her a local anesthetic?" Peter asked.

"We don't as standard," replied the piercing specialist. "Do you really feel you want one?"

There was something in his voice that would have made Peter feel like a coward if he has said yes, so he simply said "No... We will be fine doing it like this." He had half a twinge of guilt as Evelyn was not going to get a vote on this.

He remembered how Evelyn had sat patiently waiting and how he had felt her grip his hand as the piercing needles had penetrated the flesh of her nipples. He remembered that he had carried her fingernail marks in his hand for the best part of the following week though she had not made one sound through the ordeal.

He smiled. She had worn the gold rings in her nipples ever since. Even now, here in the hotel room he was proud of her. Peter stood and admired the gold chain that joined the two rings. This had been a present on their second anniversary.

He remembered the nail marks in his hand when he had her pierced for the third time the following year. That time her nails had drawn blood.

He had nothing but love and pride in his lady. He had never felt so deeply for another. In the years that followed, he had visited the jeweler again and had the additional three smaller amulets made. These were identical in design to the pendants that hung at their necks. Peter's intention for the three new medallions was to adorn both nipple rings and her clitoral ring. There was another aspect to the design of the three new amulets; each had a tiny clasp so each could be detached. The reason for this was so Peter could decide where and when the amulets were worn.

Peter watched intently, as she put the blouse on the back of a chair. He was pleased when she paused and slowly turned for him, so he could see her better. He praised her with a simple, "Good girl."

When she had turned full circle, she stood quietly awaiting his next command. All Peter had to do was nod and Evelyn promptly undid and shimmied from her skirt, which in turn was neatly folded on top of the blouse. He was pleased again, when she stood still and then slowly turned for his pleasure.

Peter was aware of his erection straining against his pants; there was that familiar distraction of it being slightly out of place, his hand flicked momentarily to his groin to reposition his phallus. Touching his penis, even momentarily through his clothing, connected him to his more base instincts. The cave man in him wanted to throw her to the floor and simply pin her down and fuck her. However, he knew how unfulfilling such a brief explosion of desire could be. He had waited all year for this. This would be a meal he would take his time over. Yet tethered, the animal inside remained.

As he looked at her body, he began to visualize all the things he wanted to do with her and to her. Lurid mental images of rope and lash, the kaleidoscope included sounds and smells, a heady mix of carnal desires. As he looked, the tip of his tongue moistened his lips in anticipation. He felt his palms sweat and he wiped them on his suit trousers. He wrestled mentally the conflict between base desire and control. There really was no contest; years of self-discipline would win without a doubt.

Control had structured his life, from a very early age. It went back to his father, who had been a man of sometimes brutal army discipline. As a child, Peter had hated the rigid confines, but as an adult, he had come to see the beauty of control and order. His life was based on those very principles so that everything he did was considered and measured. Restraint had been the key to all he did. Yet again, his thoughts turned to the beast and hard mental images of brutal, passionate sex, washed over his mind. The control was there, always there. Despite his hunger, he would make love to his girl slowly, totally consuming her, as he always had done.

Despite her confidence she trembled, nervously awaiting his reaction. She stood vulnerable, wearing only her jewelry, stockings, garter belt and heels for her Master to see. Evelyn took a deep breath and drew her shoulders back pushing her breasts forward. Proudly displaying the chain about her waist, which was made with slightly thicker links than the chain that joined her two nipple rings. It had been the last gift he had bought her. The waist chain fastened at the front with a gold padlock that had her Master's initial *P* on one side and the maker's *Z* on the reverse. It was more than a simple belt it had a second element to it. From a larger forged ring at the back of the belt hung a second piece of chain, which was intended to pass between her buttocks, divide her labia and rejoin the belt at the golden padlock at the front.

Evelyn loved this piece of jewelry. When she wore it, she felt secure and safe in the knowledge she was held by her Master. It was also a very erotic item to wear, as the chain rubbed her clitoris and the action of walking kept her in a state of permanent arousal, as was evident by the nectar moistening her inner thigh.

Peter sat back in an armchair. Evelyn stood before him, her shoulders back, her long blonde hair trailing down her back, her skin perfect. She stood tall and straight, proud to be his. For Peter's part, he was as proud as ever, to call her his property, to care for and to nurture.

"My pet, please come to me."

"Yes Sir," Evelyn stepped towards her seated Master.

Peter made himself comfortable, as he stroked the amulet that hung from her clit ring.

He contented himself that this gave his pet pleasure, as Evelyn slowly let out a succession of sighs. He felt totally in power. It was a feeling he truly lived for, and it was nectar to die for. To have that control over another, the power to give or withhold was intoxicating.

He knew she would cum, there and then, if he was to give her the word of permission. He could see in her face the look of contentment. He continued to toy with the pendent and stimulate her fully erect clitoris. Peter looked up at Evelyn; her eyes were now closed in concentration, trying to control her body's reaction to the stimulation. She knew she was not allowed to cum until she was given permission. He could see her teeth gripping her lower lip, concentration on her face.

This aroused him even more and he felt his penis whispering its own demands, as he softly stroked it. He admired her control. She seemed to have shifted to a higher plane, where she could be in command of her own body's impulses.

Quite deliberately, he increased the level of stimulation and delighted at the changes he saw, her breath now coming in short gasps. He found himself somehow mirroring her breathing. Empathizing with her body, feeling his own body respond. His own loins feeling the same excruciating tension. Picturing how this exquisite torture would feel if it were applied to him. A little more pressure and a lower moan passed her lips. Peter moistened his own lips again, as he imagined how the pressure would feel. In turn, he could see Evelyn's reactions and the tension on her face showed her need.

He watched her as her head started to draw back, pushing her breasts further forward. Peter also noticed the muscles in her legs and buttocks clenching, controlling, and holding back the climax. Peter was proud of his lady's restraint. His own excitement was undeniable, his erection strained against his pants. His own needs made their demands, yet he would be every bit as controlled as Evelyn.

Peter felt it was now time to consume the cake so long waited for. It would be consumed slowly and completely.

Peter smiled and released the pendent and said, "The time has come to serve my physical needs. Stand straight for me now my pet, I wish to look at you."

Evelyn stood proudly before her Master.

Peter admired Evelyn's body. He could see her pride as she showed her body, a marked contrast to the woman he had first met many years ago. He loved the full roundness of her breasts, the curve of her hip, the swell of her bottom, her glorious legs and beautiful ankles. His love went beyond the physical. He loved the beautiful lady she was, her personality, her willingness to serve. She was all that he could ever want in a woman and he knew that there would never be another in his life that meant so much to him. All that he was now, lived for this annual meeting. Without it and his contact with the lady he loved, there would be no point in his existence.

Peter stood and led Evelyn to the bed by the amulets that adorned her clit ring. They knew each other so well her movements anticipated his and she moved smoothly to the bed. He removed the little chain that went around her waist and between her legs. There was no need of it now, the token chastity belt would only hinder the session that was about to follow.

He released his light hold on the jewel, "I wish you to sit."

Without a word she did.

Peter looked at Evelyn, as she sat on the edge of the bed. She looked calm and relaxed. He softly stroked her hair, "I wish to use you now my pet."

He smiled and looked down lovingly into her eyes, "You know the words I need to hear."

"Yes Sir." Joyously she returned his smile and kept full eye contact. She felt exultant, as she spoke the words which marked the commencement of service. The words she had said so many times before, "My Master, I love and trust you, all that I am, is for you to command. I freely give you my body for your pleasure. You may use me in any way you see fit; in any way that gives you pleasure." Her words came easily. She loved these rituals; they gave structure and order to her life. By following the rituals she could feel Peter's love and care. She had come to depend on these structures; they were to her like air and water.

Peter ran his fingers through her hair, "Thank you my pet, I have missed you serving me."

With the grace of a dancer, he removed his clothing. It was something he had always enjoyed since Evelyn had said how much it turned her on to watch him strip.

First his tie, then he removed the jacket of his suit. He looked down as she sat on the bed. Her erect nipples showed him the tease of the strip was having the desired effect. Shoes and socks were removed. He smiled to himself, nothing more ridiculous than a man naked except for his socks. The shirt next, carefully unbuttoned and the cufflinks removed. He saw her lick her lips in anticipation and her legs began to part immodestly. Each item was carefully removed and laid out on the dresser as if laid out as an exhibit in a museum. The pace of this strip tease was marked, no hurry, yet he didn't want to waste precious time. The trousers and underpants followed. It was an elegant procedure and now completed, Peter stood before his minion, his body muscular and taught, his penis erect. He walked slowly to where she sat. She needed no further instruction. Evelyn lifted her head and took the dome of his phallus into her warm receptive mouth.

There they stayed momentarily. He felt as if the warmth of her mouth was nourishing his very soul. Many years ago, he had taught her how to take the whole of his penis into her mouth and as he inched forward he filled her again. He could feel her breath on his shaved pubis, as she breathed through her nose. His balls rested on her chin as he stroked her hair. He felt her head push back responding to the strokes, like a small kitten, thanking her owner for affection. The small sighs also showed her contentment and told him how right it all was.

As he looked down, he looked into her eyes. She looked back adoringly. He could see in her eyes the bond they still shared.

Peter's word fell like cool summer rain, "my pet, I want you to feel the size and shape of my penis." He looked into her eyes. He felt her mouth contract on his member as if she were mapping his shaft with her lips and tongue. "I want you remember my cock as it fills your mouth, so when I fuck your pussy you will visualize its length and thickness." He stroked her soft blond hair as he told her, "I want you to remember how it feels in your mouth now, so when I possess your anus you will know just how deep you have been penetrated."

As he looked down, he could see she was smiling as best she could, and he knew she understood his intentions. He wanted her to focus on the details to enrich both their experiences, building the tension with words, as well as actions.

"Tonight my pet, I will have every inch of you. Tonight you will be totally mine again, body and soul."

Slowly he withdrew his phallus from her mouth. He looked down on his glistening member and then at his beloved Evelyn. She sat quiet and composed awaiting his instruction. Her body had a trace of perspiration; her whole body seemed to have a glow. He could see her eager to please and for his part he wanted her, needed her urgently. His eyes flicked along her body to her parted legs, her most lips told him she was ripe for the taking. His hunger was biting. Peter laid her back on the bed, the scene ahead firmly in his mind. He'd had a year to plan and he knew every bit of it by heart.

Evelyn allowed herself to be moved into the position he desired. Her years with Peter had brought with it total trust and confidence. She lay flaccid, his to do with as he pleased. She loved the freedom to just let go, to submit to his will. Giving the power to him freely was an aphrodisiac. She loved the feel of his strong arms on her body, molding her. She knew that he had her best interests in mind and in submitting to him completely, the pleasure he would give her would take her close to heaven.

He lifted her arms above her head and tied them together with a black silk scarf. The end of the scarf was attached at a central point at the head of the bed. She loved the feeling of constraint and the silk felt sensual against her flesh. A second scarf covered her eyes. She loved sight depravation too. It allowed her to surrender not only to her Master but also to all her senses. She had always felt once she could no longer see, the senses of smell, touch, and taste became more acute as if to compensate for the loss of the visual.

She could feel the warmth of his hands on her body and she loved the feel of him. She was aware of his aftershave and could smell him as he wafted around her. His hands were on her legs, she could feel him stroke her skin. Once his hands had left her momentarily she moved her legs, to discover they were left untethered, she supposed for greater access. Without the aid of sight, she could only wonder what would be next. The suspense was delicious.

She felt the nectar of love seep from her, moistening her thighs. Her body tingled with anticipation. She had waited a whole year for this meeting and she embraced the constriction, in the way a thirsty man drinks cool water. Her bonds made her feel held by her lover and so very wanted. She was hungry for whatever experience Peter wished her to have, as she knew this would be for their pleasure.

Evelyn retreated to her inner space, when she could no longer sense where he was in the room. All her senses were acutely awake. She could smell him, she felt the luxuriance of the silken fabric on her face, and wrists, the fresh sent of clean linen sheets, and even her own scent. Though few people would admit it, even to themselves, she was excited by her own scents and tastes.

Abruptly, she was brought back to the outside world. She felt the firm masculine hardness of his hands, as they traced the lines of her body. She felt his hands holding her ample breast, cupping her, while tender lips grazed a painfully hardened nipple. She loved him, and the way he effortlessly made her senses sing. He never hurried in the bedroom and she knew that she would be totally consumed. She longed for the conflagration of climax.

He treated her body as if it was a temple and she was the high priestess. In her mind's eye she pictured him paying homage to her temple of Venus.

She bit her lip, as the tender dance of tease and denial was played on her skin. It felt like electricity running through her body. She could feel his lips and tongue on her nipple. The tender lips became more insistent and from them she felt the soft grip of teeth. She slowly sucked in breath over her teeth as the pressure was applied. She craved the grip and longed for that mild discomfort. The heady mix of pleasure and discomfort. Then all too soon, she felt the nipple released and all that remained was an ache as it began to throb just a little. She lay, breathing deep, anticipating what was to come.

Peter stepped back to look at his lady, he loved the sound she made when he put her under pressure, a sound he would hear many times before the evening was out. Having teased her nipple hot it was time for a contrast. He had spent many hours in preparation for this night, as his minion would discover.

Evelyn relaxed in delicious anticipation, the waiting painfully exquisite. She had always felt the anticipation was an essential part of any love making session and had come to realize she could never predict what Peter would do next. In all the time they had been together, they had never fallen into the trap of the regular predictable sex her vanilla friends complained about.

She was brought back to reality abruptly by an intense sensation. So intense in fact that she was not sure at first whether it was hot or cold.

A moment to become accustomed and she felt the wetness and cold ache of ice. She felt it first on her nipple, a stark contrast to her Master's hot lips. She felt the trickle of the water on hot skin. She could not contain a shiver, as the ice was moved from nipple to nipple. She caught her breath, as she felt the water puddling between her breasts and then running in a rivulet to her neck. The ice was traced between her breasts again then southward coming to rest in her bellybutton. She felt no pressure so she assumed it had been abandoned there to melt. This was confirmed by a new piece of ice and its cold touch on her nipple. This too eventually made its way to her navel and a third icy finger touched her skin.

This time it started at her tummy and headed south, she said nothing, but the contrast in temperature between her hot pubis and the ice made her draw her breath slowly over pursed lips. She loved being Peter's plaything. She loved that he was in total control. It gave her permission to abandon thought in favor of sensation and she reveled in that sensory overload.

The ice played across her pubis, the melting water trickling down into the delta. She felt her legs being parted and the ice being guided along her inner lips. The cold on hot flesh, made her tingle. Against her hot excited skin the ice didn't last long. She felt the last sliver of the cube disappearing into her vagina before the next was introduced to her pubis. She could feel the ice trace every inch of the delta, between her legs and around her lips. This time a much larger piece of ice slipped inside her pussy. Peter's hands left her briefly, and for that moment, she felt alone, left to feel the melting water seeping from her pussy, the rivulet trickling across the hot rose bud of her anus. She lay, tied and helpless. The moment Peter was away felt a lifetime. The next thing she felt was his hot lips on her clit. She felt him lick and suck teasing the little corner of flesh. She felt her engorged morsel throb, aching for release, as his lips and tongue coaxed her ripe clitoris. She knew from old, he would not let her surrender to her first orgasm so easily.

Her teeth nipped her lip with frustration. She must have broken the skin, as she was aware of the coppery taste of her own blood. She didn't care. She felt that ache deep inside her wanting her to let go and surrender to her body's instinct. She felt her emotions torn between her Master's will and her own gratification. Evelyn moaned and sweat dripped off her brow. She knew how close it was, it took every ounce of self-control to hold back her climax. She clenched her fists, as she felt herself on the very brink, hoping and praying that Master would give her the permission, to let her over the edge, yet without that consent she knew she would be punished.

She involuntarily let out a low moan, as she felt him working on her dilated clit. A sigh passed her lips, followed by a gasp, as his hot mouth was replaced by ice. The flames of passion were lowered momentarily. The ice circled on her clit then traveled down her slit. For a moment she thought it was going to enter her pussy, but it went lower and stroked her perineum. It lingered there a while, before passing around the tight flesh of her anus. She knew to relax, but even so caught her breath as she felt him apply a light pressure to the cube and it slipped easily inside her tight orifice.

Her Master's reassuring words, "Savor the cool my pet; I will be warming you up there later."

The game of hot and cold continued as his hot lips returned to her clit and he played with her clit ring with his tongue. Every nerve ending in her body was alive. She was aware of every part of her being. Her clit felt huge, wild imagery flooded her mind, her clit the size of a penis and Peter fellating it. The ice in her rectum was a second phallus; two of Peter's digits in her vagina were yet another hard rampant cock, stretching her, fucking her.

A cascade of sensory overload. It was all too much. Moaning, gritting her teeth and clenching her fists, she surrendered to a shuddering climax. The waves washed over her, uncontrollably. She was lost in time and space. Her body tensed rigid as sparks of electricity arced everywhere throughout her body. Trembling, she was totally lost to sensation. Somewhere deep in the back of her mind she knew there would be a price to pay, but right here and now, she truly did not give a shit. She gushed and the world went quiet. All she could feel were the echoing ripples of her orgasm.

When the world returned to her and she was calm once more, she heard his voice. "My pet?"

"Yes Sir… I am sorry Sir… I wanted you… needed you so much."

"I know my pet." His words were soft as summer rain. "I understand… and yet you know the rule."

"Yes Sir… I know I am not to come without your permission." She had transgressed and she was calm. She knew there would need to be a payment made. She simply didn't know which form it would take. "I am ready to accept any correction you wish, Sir."

"Thank you my pet."

In their many years together, he had disciplined her in many ways and she was used to his methods. She felt his warm hand on her pubis, still cool and damp from the ice. As soon as his hand lifted, she knew what to expect. Hands clenched and she sucked in air and braced herself. No time to be scared. No time to think.

Crack! The hand slapped down; through gritted teeth she hissed more from surprise than pain. The sound of hand on skin echoed around the room, followed swiftly by a second. She loved this bittersweet sensation, the mild discomfort was more than compensated for by the pleasure it gave her. In past pubic spankings, she had even achieved orgasm. A third and a fourth. With the sixth strike still ringing in her ears she was close to coming. Her pubis burnt and all was silent for a few minutes. Her pubis throbbed and the next sensation she felt was her Master's lips bathing the area with tender kisses. She was so proud that, beyond the light gasp as each blow struck, she had remained silent. She was grateful to him for his correction. She felt nothing but warmth and affection for her Master.

"Thank you, Sir for my correction... I feel stronger for it." Her words were a not rehearsed speech. The genuine tone of her voice showed him that she truly meant it.

"My pet, I am proud of you," his words were as sweet as nectar. She felt more connected to him now than ever and she loved him with all her heart.

"That was correction. This will be for my pleasure and hopefully yours."

"What pleases you, Sir pleases me." Although she could not see what he was about to do, her words were sincere. She truly wanted nothing more than to please her Master.

Evelyn lay there tied and quiet while she listened to the sounds of Peter moving about. She heard muffled footsteps on the carpet, the rattle of what she guessed were toys being taken from a wooden box. Each sound prompted a question, what was that?

Evelyn knew the suspense was a big element of the game. Each delay felt like an eternity and she was yearning to know what was in his mind.

She was much more curious than worried. She trusted Peter implicitly. She could smell leather, faintly at first, but it became more distinct. She felt a tap on the nose. She smiled as she recognized the toy, the end of a riding crop. She felt the end of the crop slide from her nose onto her upper lip and down onto her chin. She felt him trail the leather end of the crop across her chest and onto her breasts. She felt it slide lower along her tummy and onto her pubis. It lingered there for a moment before descending to the moistness of her sex. She felt the crop probe, before being withdrawn. There was silence and she waited in quiet anticipation. The leather smell again accompanied this time by her own familiar smell.

"Kiss the crop please my pet," he said as the crop grazed her lips.

She could taste herself now on the crop as she first kissed the leather then took it into her mouth, she knew, from past sessions with the crop that Peter liked the leather wet. The crop slid from her lips.

Peter looked at the glistening wet leather. It pleased him to know that they were still exactly in tune with each other.

"Speak again the words my pet." He had always made her repeat her statement of submission and compliance. The statement reassured him of her consent and filled him with the knowledge that whatever happened

Evelyn freely entered into it. He knew that Evelyn was more confident in the scene because she was given the option to opt out, though in all these years she had never used it.

"My Master, I love and trust you, all that I am is for you to command. I freely give you my body for your pleasure. You may use me in any way you see fit; in any way that gives you pleasure."

"Thank you my pet. These bee stings will renew our bonds to each other. It will not last long but it will give you something physical to comfort you over the next week."

"Thank you, Sir." Her voice was steady.

Peter swished the crop through the air, allowing himself the feel of the tool. A few quick slices through the air and he was ready. He knew this preparation built tension. He felt exhilarated. The power of pain and pleasure was indeed intoxicating. He had developed his skills with crops, paddles, and whips over the years. He considered himself experienced at administering corporal punishment. He took a pride in his ability.

He heard Evelyn gasp loudly as with a crack, the crop stung her lower belly. He had harbored reservations in the early days of his discovery of the BDSM lifestyle. He had worried about inflicting pain. The question haunted him. Was it right to hurt the one you love? However, as he traveled the path, he became aware that the recipient craved the discomfort, asked for the discomfort, and needed it. He in return craved the power and aphrodisiac qualities that inflicting the discomfort gave him. It had been he that had introduced Evelyn to the bittersweet delights of the crop, the cane, the paddle and the whip. She had needed no persuading to try any of them and she responded warmly to all the toys. It was more than just wanting to please him. Peter had the feeling that she craved the very physical nature of corporal punishment.

He loved the sound of her light moans, as he quite deliberately landed the crop on her pubis. He arranged the strikes to form a cross, the last of the strikes just above her clit.

"Only four more to go my pet."

"Thank you Sir, I am here for your pleasure."

"Thank you pet," he said respectfully.

Evelyn sucked in air as the last four stings struck her breasts on either side of the nipple rings that held the amulets.

"I am very proud of you my pet."

He could see her warm smile as she replied, "Thank you Sir. I am proud to serve you."

Peter removed her blindfold to allow her the chance to see her darkening welts and to allow him the chance to see her sparkling blue eyes.

"Now for pleasure my pet," Peter's voice was low and gravelly and the way he said it, Evelyn could tell there was nothing but love and lust on his mind. "How are you feeling?"

"I feel fine, Sir," though in truth her arms ached a bit and the spanking and crop had made her sore. However, it was a wonderful feeling to be this used again after the long year, and she wasn't going to be weak enough as to complain before her Master.

Evelyn allowed Peter to move her into a new position. Without untying her, he turned her over so she was face down. The sheets felt cool against her hot skin. She was very aware of the stings that had been laid on her flesh as they came in contact with the smooth sheets. Each had its own little fire, each called out, in its own way.

She felt his warm firm hands lift her hips and position a pillow beneath her, to raise her bottom a little higher. She moaned as he slipped a finger into her hungry pussy, its presence was so very welcome. She was oh so very ready. A second finger entered her channel of Venus, and she pushed back to take it deeper.

She felt a smart smack on her bottom and Peter's playful rebuke, "At my pace my pet. The pleasure is mine to give, not yours to take."

"Yes Sir. Sorry Sir"

In her position, she could see very little, but she felt oh so very much. She felt his fingers continuing to explore. A new sensation of fingers from his other hand toying with her labia and along her slit. She felt his fingers playing with the ring and medallion, which hung from it. All the while, the two digits inside her pussy explored her. She could feel the pressure on the front wall of her vagina, massaging her G-spot. After he had played there for a while, he pushed back and she could feel the whole of her love passage being stimulated. She yearned to be fucked. Hard. She knew of old, that was not Peter's way, not yet. First the tease.

His stimulation held out the carrot of release, yet it was just out of reach. She felt the tension grow within her. That long nagging ache started from deep within her loins. It started low and built to a mighty crescendo.

She was not to orgasm without permission, yet she yearned to. Her breath came in short hot gasps. The howl of nature's call filled her mind. Again, her hands gripped tight trying to fight the urge to cum.

He removed his fingers and moved back. Peter's voice rasped with emotion, "Onto your knees my pet."

Evelyn's only reply was to move into position for him, giving him better access to her. She was rewarded with the soft caress of his tongue. He was skilled in his oral ministrations. He ran the tip of his tongue along her slit to her vaginal opening and then slowly back to her engorged clit. He licked and nuzzled at the extended flesh before licking his way further south where he played and teased along her extended labia lips. He was not in any hurry, the time spent teasing here he regarded as one of the most essential parts of lovemaking. Her thighs were wet and her lips glistened with her ambrosia of love. He savored the sight the smell and taste. For Peter it was the very sensation of life itself.

Evelyn could scream with frustration, her body was yelling at her to let go and surrender to the orgasm that was knocking at the gates, but the control Peter had taught her kept her focused and kept her from the promised land. He withdrew again. She clenched every muscle in frustration. The emotion was too much and tears spilled from her eyes onto the bedding. It was all too much, yet she was strong and she held back the orgasm.

She was hot and hungry, yet she knew she must wait for her Master. The gap could have only been a matter of seconds, yet it felt an eternity. She stemmed the flow of tears and wiped her cheeks on the sheets. The beads of perspiration cooled her as she waited.

Her next sensation was Peter's thighs pressed against hers. She felt the head of his penis touch her slit, wet with her dripping nectar. She felt the velvet tip of his cock circled the entrance. Right then without warning he took her. She moaned with passion. She loved the feeling of his rock hard cock and the way he filled her. She exhaled, as she took the single slow, yet persistent stroke. She knew he was buried to the hilt because she felt his balls pressed against her labia.

"I wish you to squeeze my cock my pet. Use your muscles, milk my cock." His voice came in gritty sighs. "You have my permission to cum, but you must do it solely with your muscles' grip."

"Yes Sir. Thank you, Sir."

She set to her task. She worked her pelvic floor muscle and felt his phallus buried deep within her. The speed at which she squeezed and released brought her close. The world began to blur, as her body and her need took over. The spasms filled her body and the sweet and sour pins and needles raked her body. Her knees gave way and she collapsed onto the bed, Peter still mounted deep within her. They lay still.

After a time to recover, Peter withdrew his penis. He still had not cum and his penis was hard and standing proud. He untied her hands and massaged her aching limbs. She started to turn, but he kept her on her stomach.

She looked over her shoulder at her Master, grateful for her orgasm. She was tired yet wanting more, wanting to serve him in any way he wanted.

He stood before her now. It was obvious, by his position, what he wanted next form her and she opened her mouth to accommodate his penis. She could taste her own juice on him and she licked and sucked him clean.

"My pet, I want you to think again of my size. You know where I will take you next?" He withdrew his cock from her mouth, to allow her to talk.

"Yes Sir, I know where you will use me next."

"I wish you to ask me to use you in that way."

She had always had problems in vocalizing these most intimate of things. Despite her embarrassment, she did as her Master had requested, "Sir, it would give me great pleasure, if you would use my bottom for your pleasure."

"And you give this freely?"

"Sir, I give myself to you. My service to you is unreserved. My body is yours to use for your pleasure."

"Thank you my pet. Your service honors me."

Peter moved behind Evelyn once more and positioned her back on all fours. He kissed her rose bud as a prelude to opening her. He took time and applied his lubricated finger to the tight puckered skin. Slowly he opened her firstly with a finger then two.

He'd had the pleasure of taking her second virginity and had always savored the delight in taking her there. He had always thought it was one of the ultimate ways of expressing dominance and submission. So submissive to be penetrated there, so dominant to be the one penetrating. It was also a true expression of trust, maybe the ultimate intimate expression of trust. Her anus ready, he offered his phallus to her delicate opening. He heard her sigh, as slowly he took her. Her pleasing tightness gripped him. He loved her, and never wanted to be parted from her. He felt his own crisis drawing near and as it did, his rhythm increased.

Unable to hold back, he sunk his phallus to the very depths and pulsed deep inside her, anointing her with his very life essence. It was Peters turn to collapse over Evelyn's back. He was spent. He pinned her to the mattress and for a time, still inside her yet relaxed, while he recovered the energy to move.

Evelyn was comforted by his weight. She enjoyed this period of closeness. The tender embrace. Although a little tender, she was at peace feeling complete, whole, and at one with her Master and the world. At that moment time had no meaning. They lay there for what seemed like hours. Her first sensation of reality was the feel of Peter's penis slowly and carefully withdrawing from her.

He moved around the bed and bundled her up into his arms. "Time for us to shower my pet."

With heavy limbs, he guided her to the bathroom. He ran the shower and tested the temperature. They entered the shower together and it was Peter who washed his disciple.

Evelyn felt his hand caress every inch of her. The pleasantly warm spray eased away all the aches of tired arms and shoulders. It took the tension out of her still unsteady legs.

She watched as Peter bent and kissed the amulet that hung at her throat. He bent further and kissed each of the four crop marks on her breasts, followed by the two amulets that hung from her nipple rings. She watched as water streaked through his hair, as he sunk to his knees and kissed the raised welts on her pubis one by one and then the amulet that hung from her clit ring. She knew she would carry the marks for over a week, but her Master's tender kiss removed any discomfort. She loved her Master beyond life itself.

He rose and they embraced, melting into a kiss. Their lips parted and their tongues danced. Finally parting from the spell of the kiss, she tenderly washed his body, finally sinking to her knees to pay homage to her Master's phallus. Having bathed it, she kissed the tip. She would have gladly brought him to another climax with her mouth, but Peter gestured for her to stand and he led her from the shower. She wondered for a moment, why he had not wanted to go further. Then she looked as his body, he looked frailer than he had done even moments ago. Although he did not look older, there was something about his countenance that made him look physically weak. His arms looked thinner and although his eyes sparkled, his face looked somehow gaunt.

Dried and dressed they sat together on the bed. Evelyn could smell his aftershave as she snuggled into his chest.

"Now my pet. I wish you to tell me about your year, I have missed you and I want to hear all about your life."

She loved his concern for her wellbeing. It felt so safe being with her Master once again. It was now as it had always been, Peter was involved with each part of her life.

Slowly and in detail, she told her Master how she had spent her year. This ranged from her life and love with James, the attentions on her home and her promotion at work, to her clothing purchases and a new recipe for the new turkey stuffing for Thanksgiving.

Peter sat listening, drinking in her words, as if he was taking in her very life's essence. "You sound happy my pet."

"I am, Sir," she paused wondering whether to add the words in her heart, "but I would be happier with you."

"I know my pet, and I would truly love that too, but you know we are lucky to have this time."

"I know Sir. But..."

Peter silenced her, with a look and she became passive, "What of your tasks I wished you to perform, since our last meeting?"

Evelyn smiled again at his control over her and she prepared in her mind the list of personal self-improvements. She remembered he had asked her to work on her second language, German. In the great scheme of things not the most practical for all, but as the company she worked for was part of a German conglomerate it seemed prudent to learn it. They chatted in fluent German for a while.

Peter smiled approvingly, "I am pleased my pet."

"Sir, I think it played a part in my recent promotion."

"I am pleased for you."

She knew he was sincere in his comment by the warmth in his eyes.

Peter stroked her cheek softly. He knew how difficult the next part of the conversation would be for both of them, yet the subject must be broached. "My pet, I need to talk to you about your home life."

Evelyn flinched, as if a raw wound had been probed, and with hesitation in her voice she said, "Yes Sir?"

"How are things going between you and James?"

"He is not my Master, Sir."

"I know that, but we have discussed this before," his words were steady, clear. "I have asked you to strengthen your bond with your husband. I know this is not easy for you."

"No, Sir it isn't easy, but I have tried," there was a tremble in her voice, an uncertainty. She wanted to please Peter, but there was an irony. To please Peter he wanted her to move closer emotionally to another man. "It feels unnatural to live with a man as an equal. I would be much happier in service, serving you."

"I know my pet, but it is not possible to serve me now, as you once did. We may only meet once a year. And as glorious as this annual meeting is, I want to rest in the knowledge you have a new life, a happy life..." there was a sorrow in Peter's voice.

He was torn with conflict too, she knew. He wanted her as much now as he ever had, but he loved her enough to want her to find a more permanent happiness. "I need to know your life with him is healthy and happy."

Tears welled in her eyes. "Sir, I love you."

"I know my pet. We can't always have what we want. I need you to be strong and give some of the love you have for me to James." Peter stoked away the tear as it rolled down her cheek.

They cuddled. Evelyn felt his warmth through his shirt. She clung to him never wanting to let go. She knew that all she wanted was to be here with her Master. Yet, she knew how hopeless that was. Her tears moistened his shirt. She felt as if her heart was already breaking.

She stifled a sob as she said, "Yes Sir, but it is not easy." She paused and sniffed. "I do love him too, Sir, but it is different."

"I know how hard it is, and of course it is different my pet." His hand never left her cheek, as it stroked her silky smooth skin. "James is a good man?"

"Yes Sir."

"And he treats you well?" She could hear the concern in his voice.

"Yes Sir." She thought of what a caring man James was, and smiled up at Peter. "He is a good man, he deserves someone better than me, I love you both and yet I betray both of you. I can't give either of you up. If it was possible I would be with you forever."

"I know my pet... The time we have is special, but we must always look to the future." He paused searching for the right words, "I need to know you will be happy with him. You will need to make your life with him."

In the way it often happens in the mist of sorrow, Evelyn's mind flicked to a funny time that made her laugh aloud.

Peter smiled and questioned, "What?"

Evelyn tried to put the moment into words, "It's nothing really. I was just thinking back to something that happened a few months ago."

"I'd love to hear," Peter said, holding her close.

"Well, it just tickled me. It was when I suggested to James that we try something a little new... I asked if he had ever thought of trying a little bondage. Really, it was the funniest thing. I mean he did his best, but really, it was hopeless. I bought him a book on basic seamanship and put a book mark in on the section with all the knots." She laughed again.

Peter laughed with her and kissed her tear stained cheek.

Evelyn held him even closer and cried softly. She needed the feel of her Master and she never wanted to part from him. "I do love him, Sir." She paused and sniffed. "And I need you... I need you so much."

Peter held her tightly, "I know my pet, I feel your need, but there may come a time when it is not possible for you to visit me."

"Not even once a year?" She was stunned. "Oh, my god! Does that...? That doesn't mean you are going to leave me? Are you?"

Peter comforted her as best he could. "Like all things end, this will too, but not yet. At this time next year, you will come to me again, and you will serve me again. But there may come a time..." His voice was calm and measured.

"Now my pet, dry your eyes. The time has come to part. You have served me wonderfully well, as you have always done. I wish it could be for longer, but sadly we have had our allotted time." His eyes were moist and warm with affection. "You see how weak I am becoming? It takes a year for me to recover my energy."

"Master could we not have just a little while longer?" pleaded Evelyn. Right now she would say anything for another minute, another second.

"My pet, you know we have had all the time we have. Believe me, if I had the power to give you more, I would, but sadly we have used our time and we have used it wonderfully well."

"Can't I just stay the night, or just a little while?" she pleaded tears of desperation in her eyes.

"My pet, if there were any way, but you know there isn't. We are lucky to have the time we have, few are so fortunate."

"I know but..."

Peter silenced her and stood. Evelyn reluctantly stood too and held onto Peter's hand for dear life, not wanting to let go. He slowly led her to the door. She knew she had to be strong. It was like that big long goodbye she'd had to give him four years ago. It had cut like a knife then and on every anniversary since. She swallowed hard, holding the lump in her throat tight. She did not want to break down in front of the man she loved. She watched as Peter opened the door. Their eyes were fixed, as their lips connected in a parting bittersweet kiss. A kiss she wanted to last an eternity.

Waves of emotion rolled over her as she made her way back to the car. Evelyn felt her emotions bubbling up, the joy of seeing her Master and the despair of saying goodbye for another year. Why had he abandoned her? She felt like a small boat adrift on the ocean, the waves of emotion rocking the craft.

She caught her breath as a wave of emotion washed over the deck swamping her. She sobbed back the tears, as she got to the car and fumbled with the lock. Once she was inside the sanctuary of the Jaguar, the dam burst and her emotions washed over her. She leaned over the steering wheel as floods of tears fell from her. It was like the sorrows of the world draining from her in her tears. She was inconsolable as she wept. Emotion rolled over her like breakers on the shore, one after the other, each bringing another devastating feeling of grief and despair.

Grief like love has its own time zone. When the here and now returned to Evelyn she realized it had only been minutes that had passed, and not the hours that she had felt. Drying her eyes and blowing her nose, she gathered her composure and put the key in the car's ignition. She felt mildly irritated with her own loss of control. This had been the fourth time she had parted from Peter like this; surely, she could control these emotions by now? Of course, she couldn't. Yet, she also knew life goes on.

She drove slowly from the grounds of the Manor. Her journey home was cold and dark in contrast to the joy she had felt earlier. Her somber mood made her more introspective, thinking on past joy and sorrow, a bittersweet kaleidoscope of memories. It was always the silly little things.

Even the tie he wore tonight, such a small detail, but it was enough to provoke a sob, she had bought him that tie and it had been the tie she had selected with the clothes he was to be buried in. She was again aware of the four amulets. It was their power that kept them connected.

She retraced her journey until she got to a shrine situated on a rather sharp bend. The shrine was a simple cross with the collection of floral tributes. She pulled the car over to the side of the road and got out, taking with her the single red rose that lay on the passenger seat. She walked over to the cross and with a loving smile on her face; she touched the timber that had weathered there for the past four years. Before laying the rose at the base, her voice cracked as she read aloud the words written on the card:

"My eternal love, to you, my friend, husband and Master. E"

Evelyn cried again. It had been four long years since the crash had parted them, taking Peter from their earthly life together. Why had he not taken more care of his precious life? That night it had been raining and the car had lost its grip of the road. He had been so anxious not to be late for their anniversary meal.

Waves of emotion flooded over her again. How she missed him. How she wanted to be with him again. Many times, she had thought of taking her own life, at this very spot, just to be reunited with her Master for all eternity.

She probably would have succumbed to those dark thoughts too, if it had not been for James. It had been James that had brought her from the edge. All she wanted now was to be held; held by James who would bring her back to life again.

She loved him too. He was a good man. It was his love that would fill the void, to cushion and comfort her, as it had just after Peter's tragic death.

Evelyn's car pulled into her driveway. She let out a sigh. Home and sanctuary. The tangle of emotions still swirled around in her head. She felt physically drained and mentally exhausted.

As she stepped from the car, James appeared at the door to greet her. She ran to his arms and clung to him desperately, as if they had not seen each other for years, rather than at breakfast just that morning.

"God, I am so happy to see you," Evelyn whispered in his ear.

"I've missed you too darling."

Evelyn could hear the warmth in his voice and felt the warmth of his embrace. She felt truly home again.

James held her close, "I know it is a difficult day for you." He paused and kissed her softly on the cheek. "I know you miss Peter terribly," he kissed her again, "and I know it must be worse today," he paused again and ran his fingers through her hair. "I do understand you know… you needing to be with him on your wedding anniversary… I don't know how it works, but if it helps to see him, I understand."

"God, James, I don't deserve you. You are so good. You deserve so much more. You deserve someone better."

"But it is you I want, you that makes my life complete. How could I not give you back to Peter this one day a year? When that person Zachariah contacted us and said it was possible, how could I deny you this chance to see him again?

Tears welled up in Evelyn's eyes again, as she clung to James. His warmth revived her. She loved him, she truly did. She could not and would not think of her life without him. She gripped him tighter. He had given her so much, and she loved him even more for giving her back to her Master Peter, if only once a year.

The One

Robert Cloud

Zachariah paused and looked into Melanie's eyes. His heart was growing closer to her every moment they spent together and he knew was doomed. Even though he maintained peace with Lilith by telling her he loved her, his heart had long stopped having any feelings for her. He could not care for someone that had betrayed him with so many lies even if she were not the monster he knew she was.

As he looked at Melanie he knew that he could not be with her at his age. He was too old for someone her age and after he was young again she would not even recognize him.

Even if Melanie stuck around and fell in love once he was young again it would be far too dangerous for him to ever allow her to be alone. Lilith was still very much with him and was a very active spirit. Worse still he suspected that that Lilith was able to return to her bodily form even beyond the times that the magic of the commissioning allowed.

If that were true then Melanie's life could be in danger every single moment. A relationship with her could mean her death. That was the primary reason he had remained alone all these centuries. He could not risk anyone being hurt by the rage and jealousy of Lilith. Still he yearned to hold a woman close to him again and in his heart he knew that Melanie was right for him.

There was still more to the story so he continued, "For many years Peter and Evelyn continued to meet and the anniversary of the tragedy was one of great reward for both of them.

"About a month before I closed the doors of my last shop I had a very weary and special visitor." Zach sighed and wiped a single tear from his eye, "He asked if we might sit and talk for a while, and I agreed.

"I offered him a drink, and he asked if I had any cognac.

"It is rare that I partake of alcohol, but I had a feeling that this meeting was one that I should share a drink with him so I brought out a bottle of Napoleon Cognac and two snifters and filled them half full.

"He talked through the next several hours and told me of Peter and Evelyn's last anniversary.

"Evelyn had been diagnosed with cancer about six months before the night of the anniversary and the doctors had told her that it was inoperable. They gave her only a few weeks to live. Yet she was determined to make it to the anniversary. However, just in case it was not fate's design she prepared a package and wrote and rewrote a letter for Peter.

"Every night she would sit down and go over that letter again, rewriting it, perfecting it. If it was going to be her last words to him she wanted it to be absolutely perfect and every night she would go to sleep curled in James's arms crying because she knew that no matter how hard she willed it she would not live to see Peter again and that her words would not be the perfection he deserved. James would hold her until her tears carried her off to sleep.

"Two weeks before the anniversary as she sat trying to plan something special for Peter she called James into her and asked him to hold her. Then she told James that he was very special to have understood her need for Peter, and to not have condemned her for it. She wanted him to know that her heart was big enough for two loves and that she loved him as deeply as she loved Peter. That night she asked James to make love to her. He was reluctant because of her pain, but she told him that he could be gentle she still wanted to have him inside her again, that it had been too long and she loved him.

"Gently and with tender passion they made love and then fell asleep with her spooned tight against him. In the morning she did not awaken.

"James was not the only one at the graveside when she was laid to rest but he felt like he was alone in the world. The mourners had not known the depth of love he and she had had, nor would they have understood the love she'd had for a love that had long gone.

"On the night of the anniversary James carried the package and the letter to the room where Evelyn and Peter always met. When the eyes of the two men met Peter knew without a single word having been exchanged what had happened. 'Did she suffer?' Peter asked.

"James answered 'The cancer caused her a great deal of pain, but in the end she went in peace and in her sleep.'

"Peter's voice broke as he responded, 'I am sorry you had to deal with it alone.' His voice was solemn and filled with pain. James could tell that Peter would have done anything he could to have been able to give his respect to the woman they both had loved.

"James added, 'I loved her, Peter; if you were there you would have done no less.'

"The two men nodded. James handed the package and the letter to Peter. As Peter read the letter James could see the tears well up so he turned away to let him have a moment of privacy. Then Peter opened the package. Within it were the pendants that Evelyn had worn, the ones that had kept Peter and her bound even beyond death. James watched as his face grew even more mournful. He could see from the look upon Peter's face that he was remembering moments that Evelyn and he had shared. Peter's eyes glistened and a thin smile crossed his lips as he said, "Thank you."

"Then he lifted his hands to the pendant about his own neck and removed it, laying it alongside the ones within the box. With one last mourn filled look he covered the pendants with the tissue paper and replaced the lid.

"Peter lifted the box and handed it to James. 'I know you have done a great deal for me and Evelyn. I have one more favor to ask of you. Would you carry this package to a shop called *The Crimson Z*? These items are what held Evelyn and my love together all these years. It is time they are returned to the man that made them for no other can truly know the value they hold.'

"James nodded and as he took them he was surprised to see the wrinkles upon the back of Peter's hand. He was sure they had not been there when he had shaken hands with Peter upon entering. As he raised his eyes to bid him farewell he noticed the wisp of grey hair at Peter's temples. It was so distinguished a characteristic, surely it was not something he would have missed. He was positive that when he had met Peter at the door that Peter's hair had been solid chestnut brown and that of a young man.

"Peter stood, and he did not stand as tall and straight as he had before. As he walked James to the door he thanked him, and James turned one more time to see a man that was easily in his seventies, his hair fully white, his face creviced, and his spine bent. As the door shut James knew that Peter had gone to join Evelyn.

"My visitor finished his sifter of cognac and offered me the box of pendants.

"I offered to pay him for them but he lifted his hand and replied, 'I had been friends with Evelyn at work. We used to share lunch together, but then darkness entered her life and she became distant. No longer did I see her smile or laugh and she separated herself from everyone. I tried everything I could to breathe life into her; to reach out and touch her heart, but nothing I did seemed to work.' James paused a moment and looked at me and said, 'Then I received your phone call. After I told Evelyn what you said it was like a miracle, like something had suddenly grasped her and pulled her back from the edge of despair. I had hoped that a huge part of what pulled her back from the edge was me and for years I allowed myself to live with that delusion.'

"James wiped a tear from his eye as he looked at the box before he continued and said, 'However, when I saw Peter and those pendants I knew it was more than just me. It was the magic within those pieces in that box. I now believe what pulled her back was that the pieces reunited them and she saw hope.'

"He looked at me and added, 'But, I know that she needed more than their one night a year for peace. It was in me that she found that solace. Yes, the pendants gave her hope but when she came back from those nights with Peter she would come back to my arms and I would pick up the pieces. She needed me as much as she needed him. Those pendants gave her the chance to see that she needed us both.'

"James lowered his head and I could see a tear in the corner of his eyes as he continued, 'If it had not been for them I would not have had a chance to get to know her and win her heart. They gave me a chance to find a place in her life as well. Now they have come full circle and are being returned to the one that made all that possible. There is nothing you could give me that is more valuable than what you have already given me. You gave me a lifetime with the woman I loved for without those pendants I have no doubt that Evelyn would have gone to join Peter long before I ever had the chance to know her love.'

"He stood and offered me his hand and I accepted it. As we shook he added, 'Thank you, you gave Peter, Evelyn and I all something worth more than all the gold in the world.' Then he turned and walked out of the store.

"There is one little epithet to this story that James is unaware of. The magic of the jewelry sometimes tells me more than what occurred during the time it was held. Sometimes it tells me what will be the fate of the last to have held it. James will live for many years longer and he will live with his memory of Evelyn in his mind. He will not remarry, though he will have a lover enter his life. When he passes he will go to join Peter and Evelyn. They are both waiting for him. The pendants created more than a union between Peter and Evelyn it created a bond with James as well and he is the last link in their circle."

Zachariah coughed as he held back his tears. Many of the stories of his jewelry told tales of love so deep that it touched him. At those times he would often remember the love he had felt for his own Lilith the first time he had actually seen her smile and knew God had answered his prayers and she would live. He looked at Melanie and smiled but as he did so Melanie faded from his sight and he drifted to memories of the past, his mind caught upon those first moments when he was truly happy. In silence he flitted from one happy memory to the next.

He saw his mother trying to hand Lilith a bowl of broth and Lilith looking at it like it was poison. She had even said that if she ate that she would be sick. His mother had laughed and told her that she had already eaten two bowls, that while she had been unconscious she had been spoon fed two large bowls of it. Lilith's eyes had grown huge. Zachariah could not remember ever seeing anyone's eyes so large, nor so dark and beautiful. Had he not already fallen for the woman he would have then. As it was his heart melted more as he drowned within their depths. He watched as Lilith tentatively took a spoonful of the soup and tried it. She waited, then after a moment she threw away the spoon and drank it from the edge of the bowl like someone who had never tasted anything so good in her entire life. Lilith's reaction was precious and it endeared her more to him and his family.

It was only moments later that she suddenly pulled the blanket up and screamed, backing into the corner and asking if it was daytime. His mother had said yes. Lilith responded that she was allergic to the sun. Rachel, his mother said she had never heard of such a thing. Then his father had asked Lilith how her allergy affected her. Lilith said it caused her extreme pain. He asked her if she was in any pain right them. She said no. He asked her if she would look at her foot. When Lilith did she saw that a slither of light had penetrated through a hole in the thatch of the roof and was shining upon her foot. She wiggled her toes. Then she waved her hand in front of the light. Slowly she climbed out from under the cover and walked outside the door. She looked up at the sun and stared at it like it was the first time she had ever seen it. She pulled Zachariah out into the sun and began dancing, then Rachel and Zakarias, so that all the family was dancing in a circle. Lilith laughed like a child, free and happy. Dancing about and swirling the new white shift that Rachel had given her to wear, Zachariah's heart was dancing along with her every step.

In those days normally courtships from the time of the marriage proposal to the wedding were required to last at the very least a year. Because Zachariah was well past the normal marrying age, and due to other special conditions the village elders allowed a much shorter than normal courtship. They were married only six months after she had entered into his life.

It was also very important for the people of that time that men and women remained virgins until they were married, and the wedding sheets were displayed as proof of a woman's virginity. A woman that was not a virgin would be scorned, run out of the town, and possibly even killed in the village of new her husband. Yet when he had seen her on the road he had suspected that she might have been raped by some brigands and when there was no virgin's blood he took a knife and cut across his foot to cover the sheet and protect the woman he loved.

He was surprised and somehow pleased when Lilith had carefully, even passionately licked the wound upon his foot and sworn her love to him.

***

"Papa Zach, are you alright?" Melanie's voice broke the trance that the past had brought upon him. He shook his head and looked at her.

"Yes, sweet child. It is just these stories; they remind me so much of my own loss."

Melanie nodded and placed a hand upon his shoulder, "You miss your wife don't you, Papa Zach?"

"Yes, Melanie, there are times I miss her more than I thought possible. There are others that I barely remember her at all." He knew as those last words left his lips that they were a mistake. He could already hear the rattle of the mirror and knew Lilith was not happy with him. She would blame his lack of memory upon his daydreaming of Melanie. Yet in some ways it was not entirely false. Melanie reminded him so much of the sweet side of Lilith that he had fallen so deeply in love with.

Melanie leaned down and kissed his cheek, "Papa Zach, I have got to be going, it is getting late and tomorrow is a school day.

"I will be here about an hour after I get out of school. I have to go home first and do a couple of quick chores and then will race right over."

Zachariah looked up at her and smiled, "But you have already done all the unpacking."

"Yes, but there is still the cleaning, and if the Grand Opening is Halloween night then we need to decorate." She smiled so innocently his heart ached to hold her close to him like he used to hold Lilith.

"Then I will see you around four in the afternoon."

Melanie leaned down and kissed his lips again. He knew it was like a granddaughter kissing her grandfather yet she seemed to hold the kiss a little longer than a granddaughter would. As she stood up and turned to run out the door he laughed at himself for being foolish. It was just his old heart wishing that there could be more between him and her. He was nearly a hundred, and yes soon he would be young again, but she would not know him then and he would have to act entirely different towards her or Lilith would come out seeking Melanie's blood.

No sooner than the door had closed behind Melanie than the mirror began rattling violently. Zachariah stood and walked to it quickly, "Lilith, settle down. You do not want to break the mirror now, do you?"

You lecherous old man, if that girl had not commissioned a piece I would make you swear to bar her from this building. I know your heart and I can tell you want her.

"Come now, Lilith, be serious. You know I can do nothing. She thinks I am over 100, and after the change she will think I died. The younger me will have to treat her differently. I will not be able to get close to her or she will see that I am the same person and know our secret."

Then you had better remember that, old man, or on the night when I walk, I will visit her.

"Lilith, leave her be. You know I love you."

Do you? If you do, then why have I had to feed the last few times I have risen?

"Perhaps it is the magic has grown old? Or the children have not been as pure? That one child that was nearly a devil could have had something to do with it."

Maybe? But I wonder if your love for me is as strong as it used to be Zachariah.

"Lilith, if it was not, I would not still be here. When I became young I would have left you and sought another. I would have risked that the magic would have worked with another love as well. But no, Lilith, it is you that I love," he said as he tenderly stroked the mirror.

And I love you, my Zachary. I am sorry to have doubted you. Now it is time to begin to make the piece, or it will not be ready in time for the commission.

"Yes, I know. All is ready."

Zachariah walked by the counter and gathered all the tools he had used to measure Melanie's crown for the tiara. Especially the tool that still held the hair and flesh from her scalp and the cloth that had been soaked with her blood but now lay dried. Then with a spry step that did not match the age of his body he went to the chest of treasures and pushed the hidden latch. Soon he was within his little workshop and the table was ready once again for his new offering of blood.

Zachariah stood looking at the table, the table that had been so much a part of his life since the day he had knelt upon it and prayed to God to save the life of Lilith.

It was almost eighteen months later that the carving that it now had upon it had been completed and by his own hand but even now he could not remember doing the work. He had been in some kind of trance. The prophetess had said it was a trance invoked by God. That he did believe. The fact that the he and the stone were connected there was no doubt in his mind. He also believed that the magic he used came directly from God, however he was told by the prophetess that the stone could be used to summon dark magic too so he should never let anyone else use it.

Centuries had passed and he had noticed changes in Lilith. He had begun to suspect that she had lied to him about some of the things she had claimed to be facts that she had told him before her death. There were also suspicions about things she had told him upon the first night she had risen about what the magic of the commission would allow her to do.

Then one day he had stumbled upon proof that there was nothing that Lilith had ever told him that he could believe was true. He found out that when she came forth upon the night of the magic she would feed.

He had lain awake for months in torment wondering how many people he had helped her to kill, how many innocent souls were upon his head and believing he was as guilty as she was for their bloodless bones lying perhaps never found. He made up his mind to walk away from the stone and never return.

Three days later he had heard the chimes and bells of the churches, an announcement was being read at the Papal Palace. Pope Lucius III had made a discovery of a device of greatest heresy.

Zachariah had pushed his way through the throng of people and upon a wagon being pulled toward the palace was his table. He knew immediately that for the Pope to get his hands upon it would be disastrous. The carving upon the stone was not something that the Pope would see as Holy but as vile and obscene. To him it would have been seen as a remnant of some form of pagan worship and would be judged as unholy in the eyes of God. Zachariah feared that if the Pope tried to destroy the stone some catastrophe would occur. His mind returned to the scene of Pompeii and the tremendous loss of life there.

He followed the wagon and when it stopped along the road still about twelve miles outside of the city of Rome Zachariah took a chance and jumped into the seat. Whether it was the magic of the stone, or his luck or some other divine guide watching him he was far away from the small tavern and no one had seen him. However, his sin of leaving the stone did not go unpunished. Pope Lucius III started blaming a witch for having secreted the stone away from his couriers. He began a massive search for witches to try to find the stone. It was that one night that led to the instigation of the Spanish Inquisition.

He sighed, no matter what he wanted to do his fate was tied to that stone, he could not leave it, nor could he stop the magic once it had begun. Whether the magic was truly of God, which he believed with all his heart and soul; he was bound to it as a slave was to their master.

He walked to the stone and sat the tray down upon the table. From the dresser under the table he took a glass jar and set it on a tray. Then from the basin he ladled out two cups full of rain water. Carefully lifting the measuring instrument he took a small wooden rod and pushed the flesh and hair out of the scoop so that it fell into the jar, and lastly he dropped the cloth that was soaked with Melanie's blood into the jar as well.

Slowly he stirred the contents of the jar until the water began to take on a pink hue, then he placed a screened lid upon it and screwed it down. As he poured the blood water mixture onto the table and it filled the etching of the tree of Life the engraving began to glow brilliantly. The crimson gold hue filled the room as the blood flowed into the last lines of the etching. Zachariah nearly stumbled as he fell back into the chair behind him for the glow did not dissipate but grew even brighter until above the stone table stood a three dimensional image of the tree as if it were alive and living growing out of the stone. The branches swayed as if caught within the wind, and the roots drank deeply of the blood.

Slowly the tree turned into a webbing of silken golden fiber. In the hundreds of times that Zachariah had performed this ritual only once had the webbing been more than a two dimensional form just an inch above the stone table. Even then it was nothing compared to this, this was far beyond anything he had even imagined was possible. His heart pounded like thunder reverberating within his chest. He could hear Lilith calling to him from the other room, wanting to know what had happened. She had to have seen the flash of light, it was so brilliant it had to have shown through thin openings around the hidden door to the room but he did not dare answer her. How would he explain this? Zachariah shuddered. He couldn't bear to imagine what Lilith would do with this much power.

What are you trying to hide from me? By the Light and Dark! Is that the Tree of Life?

Zachariah shook, "Lilith, I thought you could only speak and see from the mirror in the main room?"

That was all I could do, but something happened. Suddenly I found myself here.

"How? If you are bound to that mirror, how could you get here?"

I do not know. Are you questioning my honesty, Zachariah?

"No, my Love," but something told him that she was lying, and he began to wonder how many other things she had lied about. Yes this was extraordinary, but she had told him that she was bound to that one mirror and he had to protect it with his life for if it ever broke she would perish. Now here she was in another mirror. Perhaps it was this magic, but somehow he suspected it was not.

Is that the Tree of Life, Zachariah?

"I think so. It happened as soon as I put Melanie's blood on the stone." Oh!

Zachariah could almost feel her thoughts; he could sense her mind weaving together the import of this monumental moment. This much magic must mean something so powerful that it would change things forever between him and Lilith, his only prayer was that it would leave Melanie unharmed.

Do you know what this means, Zachariah?

"No, Lilith. I have not a clue, yet I can tell you do so inform me."

It means that the girl is the One! She is the One that will allow me to live again, to walk on the Earth again and to finally leave this mirror realm I have been bound to.

"How? The body that is created from the magic is only a shadow; it fades in but one day."

No! Zachariah, it means Melanie and I can share the same body. She is pure, untainted. She has caused no one any harm, and she has never been touched by passion. She is a virgin.

"There have been other virgins, Lilith."

Zachariah! Yes, but not one that has never had an impure thought. This girl has not even thought of impure sex, but she has also never even thought of causing someone to be hurt. She has never hated someone, never thought ill of someone. She has always done her best to do the right thing. This girl in every sense of the word would be considered a saint.

Zachariah looked at the mirror oddly, "First what do you mean about impure sex? Kinky sex? I know there is no way that this girl has thought about that. She is too traditional."

He could feel her laughter in his head, No you old fool. Impure sex is sex without love. Even if she thinks of sex with love she must still think of it as happening only after they have committed to being together forever.

He nodded, that was something he could understand and it definitely fit with what he knew about Melanie. She was that type. He looked into the mist of the mirror and asked, "And until now we have never met another like her?"

No never.

Zachariah did not like the idea of Lilith sharing Melanie's body. He knew that Lilith would taint her. Lilith would turn that saintliness into a demonic and diabolical monster in a very short time. There was no blinding light of insight just a deep painful acceptance that what he had known since shortly after Lilith's death was indeed true. The woman he had fallen in love with had never truly existed. From the very day Lilith had entered into his life she had been hiding her true nature from him. She was a liar and a monster and now she wanted him to trust her with Melanie?

How could he trust her when the last several times she had formed she'd had to feed and she had been very cruel and evil about it? She had even made him watch, delighting in his revulsion of her hunger. If she were to share Melanie's body would Melanie become the Wampyr that Lilith was.

"How would you share her body? How would it affect her?"

She could have the body during the day, since your love can no longer protect me from the sun, and I will take it at night.

"But won't your nature affect her? Won't she become an undead like you were?"

Zachariah! I know you care for her! Once you are young, maybe you will love her enough to protect her. Besides, we do not know she will become as I am.

"We do not know she will not either!"

You are correct! We do not! However you have no choice! You know the contract of the commission and the ritual. Once you begin it you must follow it through. The stone is the one that decides what happens. The fact that the full Tree of Life is there is the sign that she is the One! You must offer her the option. Only she can decide to accept or deny it.

"And if she denies it?"

We both die.

"Then I pray for death."

I knew you had lied to me. You do love her, you old fool.

With a scream the mirror in the room shattered and Lilith screeched out of the room back to the mirror in the main room. Zachariah knew she was right. He had no option he had to complete the commissioned piece. The distant smoke of Vesuvius rose into his memory as with a trembling hand he reached toward the Tree of Life and pulled a fine wire of golden filament from the tree. Slowly he began to weave it into the form of the tiara. As he worked the tree unraveled and the tiara took its shape.

***

The mirror trembled as Lilith broiled in fury. Yet she waited. She waited until she was certain that Zachariah was deep in his trance and weaving the gold for once he had started he would not awaken from his trance until the framework of the piece was finished. As she waited her hatred for Melanie grew deeper.

She thought back to the days before her death, when she had learned that Zachariah's love had protected her from the sun and ended her need for blood. For a long while she basked in the new found freedom his love had given her, but then something else had begun to eat at her.

Over the centuries of feeding upon humans she had come to enjoy the hunt. To watch their eyes when they knew they had come face to face with a monster of legend and were about to die had filled her with such wondrous power that she had felt invincible. Soon the bloodlust had come back, not because she had the need to feed, but because she had the need to kill, to taste again the power she could hold over someone's life.

She began to sneak out at night. Many of her powers had dimmed but not all, she could still transform. She could still command the creatures of the night, and she could still hypnotize with a single thought. Yet she was careful. She did not kill too many. She did not want Zachariah to know. She relished in the fact that she had taken the lives of twenty two people before she found out she was with child. Her only regret was that she had not taken more, but then she found out that that number twenty two had an important effect on the rest of her existence.

She found out that every twenty two days she was able to rise out of her prison in the form of a mist and hunt. She had often wondered if she had killed fewer people if the number of days would have been less, she did not understand the connection but knew there was one. It was only after her death that she began to be thankful she had not taken more lives because she thought if she had killed fifty then she may have been stuck in her prison for fifty days before being released to kill. Her hell would have been even a greater torment.

This had remained her secret. In the nearly six thousand years since she had died she had never told Zachariah about this ability, and she had left hundreds of thousands dead without him ever suspecting. How fortunate for her that tonight was the 22nd night for if it had not been she would have brewed until the 22nd night and she might have spilled her secret to Zachariah. Of course soon it would not matter. Once she was reborn as a Wampyr she would turn him into her slave and he would regret ever having betrayed his love with that little girl. It was only a shame she could not take her anger out on the girl.

As soon as she was certain that Zachariah was lost in his trance the red mist began to seep from the edges of the mirror. It floated quietly to the center of the room and began swirling about like a cyclone of blood. There was no sound, yet it seemed like a silent thunder filled the room and the form of a woman stood where the cyclone had been. She was little more than a vapor but she was startlingly beautiful. As she gazed at her own blood colored reflection in the mirror she smiled at herself vainly. She had known that Zachariah had no choice but to fall in love with her the moment he had seen her. There was no woman that had ever walked the earth as lovely as she was.

She took one last glance at herself and then screamed in rage. How could he not still love her? Then she shot straight upward and the mist exploded through the little cracks and crevices that were invisible to the eye and came out through the roof. She reformed above the roof as a large red hawk and flew in circles to get her bearings.

Her ears picked up sounds of laughter and screams of terror many miles away, yet the screams were not true terror. It was more like those screams that are then turned into fun. She flew towards them. Soon her eyes saw all the lights of a larger commercial area and a mall but what was pulling her was a little further to the north. Yes. A park. An amusement park, it was open and there were a lot of people in costume but it was too much out in the open. Yet the idea of feeding on someone on the roller coaster while the person sitting next to them watched tempted her. It was an amusing thought but she had to be careful, she needed that bitch, Melanie's body and if she were to kill someone openly like that then it would be more difficult for her to kill later.

There was a building next to the park that had a lot of activity. She remembered now, the amusement park had opened an all year around indoor water park, but that would also have no privacy, no place where she could find someone alone that would not be discovered quickly. However she recalled that Zachariah had told her that they were near a tourist resort. Even further north of the amusement park there was a village called Lake George. He had laughed about them having a Haunted House that was open all summer long. Actually two, one called the House of Frankenstein and the other Dr. Macabre's Haunted Mansion, and with Halloween just around the corner she bet both of them were packed with visitors.

Perfect! She flew in that direction and finally saw Dr. Macabre's. Slowly she spiraled down and entered into a window that was open in the back. Once inside she allowed herself to become a cloud of red mist and drift along the ceiling.

From one room to the next she drifted looking for a suitable victim. Then she spied a young man, about seventeen, the same age as Melanie. He was dressed in an outfit like a prisoner from a penitentiary. There were fake holes that looked like bullet wounds and he had a chainsaw in his hands to scare people as they walked by. The chainsaw was a fake. It roared but there was no chain on it.

Slowly Lilith drifted down behind the kid and as he stepped out and took a deep breath to scream at two girls that were walking past the spot where he was hiding, Lilith allowed him to breathe her into his lungs. Immediately she began to feed upon him from the inside out.

Lilith watched through the eyes of her victim as the girls saw him stumble forward. Her victim struggled against her but there was nothing he could do. He dropped the chainsaw and grasped at his neck. There was a large mirror on the far wall and Lilith was particularly enjoying seeing his eyes begin to protrude from his face, one even popped out of its socket and hung from the nerve. The girls screamed and ran.

Oh how sad, Lilith thought, they are going to miss the best part. Then she laughed and the hideous laugh came strangled from the mouth of her victim.

She continued to look through the one remaining eye of her victim as his face began to turn ashen. He dropped to his knees reaching out toward the fleeing girls but they never saw him. From his finger tips his flesh began to fall away as ash and the outer layers fell away leaving muscle tissue then it too began to become ash. Finally the skeleton fell into a heap and the last thing to dissolve was the eye that Lilith had used to watch.

Slowly the red mist rose to the ceiling as the next couple entered into the room and found a prisoner suit filled with nothing but a skeleton. She had read the boy's mind while she fed upon him and knew that Billy was prone to days of drinking and drugs. As he had died he himself had thought no one would miss him until he did not show to pick up his paycheck. Lilith laughed to herself for the one thing she always loved was when she picked a real winner for a victim and this one was a real peach. Before he had left for work he had punched his girlfriend in the face. As far as Lilith was concerned this boy deserved to die.

When Lilith had finished watching a few more couples enter and noticed that none of them even paid any attention to Billy's bones. She headed back to the window. Her hunger was satisfied but her anger was not. She had to kill again, she had to kill a female, someone that reminded her of Melanie, but she had also learned not to commit two murders too close together, and not to make them too similar in nature. She had almost gotten her only hope of release, Zachariah, killed by making that mistake.

She flew south, following the highway that ran alongside of Lake George. She decided she would follow it for as far as she dared so that she would still have time to get back before the sun rose. In her form when she stayed high she could fly at a pretty good speed. So in about thirty minutes she was upon a really large city. Her eyes caught the signs above the highway just before going into the city. Albany.

She followed a main road that was labeled Central into the city and there she found a large arena like structure. Some event was going on and there were people on the streets. There were some alleys too and she continued to circle about. Looking in the alleys, Lilith was hoping to spot someone that reminded her of Melanie. She had no idea how much time had passed in her journey but she was certain that the sun would not be waiting too much longer before it rose above the horizon. If she were not in the mirror before it did then she would die, yet she was having no luck in finding anyone that paid even the slightest resemblance to Melanie. Finally she saw a blond haired girl covered in tattoos walk into an alley on the tottering heels of stilettos. She was followed closely by a man with a red Mohawk. He was covered in even more tattoos, so many in fact that Lilith had trouble seeing skin that was not marked with a tattoo. The girl stopped and leaned against the wall. The man looked around him furtively making certain they were alone, then he looked at the woman and Lilith could see the smile cross his face as he reached into his back pocket and pulled out his wallet. After fishing out some bills he handed them to her and watched while she stuffed them into her bra.

Lilith did not want to watch her kill get fucked. But before she moved the man did something that sent Lilith into a blinding fury, he slapped the woman across the face and screamed, "Bitch," at her. Lilith decided she would take them both, but she had a special treatment for him. Like lightning she struck. The mist of blood formed into two blades of red crystal and she struck downwards. One caught the man just under the sternum and she lifted him dangling him above the ground. He tried to scream, but she knew he could not pull in the air to do so. She did not want him dead just yet.

The girl screamed, only to be silenced by the blade as it cut upwards between her spread thighs, stopping at her heart. Lilith then made second stroke across the woman's breast and left the body lying in three pieces. As she looked down she smiled.

Then she turned back to the man and formed a mouth in her mist form whispering, "So you like being rough with women?"

He shook his head no, and as he did so her free arm shifted from the blade form into an arm with a hand whose fingers ended in five blades sharper than any surgeons' scalpels. The fingers sliced through fabric and flesh as she deftly severed his cock and scrotum and lifted it up to his face. "Open wide!" She commanded with her Wampyr ability and against his own will his mouth opened. His eyes grew wide as she stuffed his mouth full.

Then she turned her arm that was still a blade in a perfect circle and pulled out a cylinder of his flesh that contained his heart. She watched his face go slack as he died. Now she was satiated. She looked up at the big clock upon a building nearby and saw that it was only a little past two in the morning. She would be back in plenty of time. So back to the shop she flew, returning to her prison until the night that the commission was completed and the time was right for Melanie's decision.

***

The sun had risen and the clock had struck nine when Zachariah's trance finally broke. Lying within his hands was the complete gold-work of the tiara, gone was the Tree of Life. He rose and laid the tiara on a table to the side and lowered the heavy glass plate to the top of the stone table.

If this had been a normal commission, he would have covered the table with a cloth, then left the room and locked the door of the cabinet making any chance of an accidental discovery impossible, but this was not a normal commission. He still had one chance to return to this room with this commission. If Melanie said yes.

He turned back to the tiara and lifted it. Looking at it carefully he was amazed at the intricacies within it. All that was left was the placing of the gemstones and for that he usually did not have to enter a trance. As he turned the tiara around his eyes caught upon the jeweler's mark on the backside of the tiara, the mark of the Z. It resembled the one upon both the cabinet and the table. Each time he looked at the figure of the tree the sensual woman within the trunk enticed him to stare longer upon her. Zachariah had often wondered if the woman was supposed to be anyone in particular. She seemed to be familiar and at one time he thought she sort of resembled Lilith but it was not Lilith of that he was certain. As he turned the piece a beam of light hit the mark and it just for a brief moment appeared as if it filled with blood. It was for this unique trait of the mark that the shop had been named *The Crimson Z*.

He carried the tiara out into the main room and shut the cabinet behind him hiding the entry to the mystical room once again. For some reason he did not feel it safe to leave the tiara out of his sight so he carried it up to his apartment and laid it on the dresser beside his bed.

Melanie would be there in just a little over seven hours and he had not slept at all the entire night. He also knew from the silence that had met him when he had left the ritual room that Lilith was not in a good mood. As he walked past the mirror he did not even feel her icy fingers reach out to touch his mind and sense his thoughts and that was not a good sign at all. He knew it was best not to press the issue. For his own peace of mind and sanity it would be best to try to get what sleep he could for when he did finally have to deal with Lilith there would be hell to pay. Slowly he climbed the stairs for once he did feel every bit of the one hundred and ten years of his body's age. Working the magic drained a great deal from him. Sitting down on the edge of the bed was the last thing he remembered.

***

"Papa Zach, Papa Zach!" He felt a nudge at his shoulder. He opened his eyes and saw Melanie holding the tiara in her hands; her eyes were wide and filled with tears.

"Papa Zach! Is this? Is? It can't be? You only showed me the design yesterday. Even had you been up all night no one could have made this in one night."

She leaned down and helped him up and then hugged him tight. This time when she kissed his lips he was not mistaken they definitely stayed there longer than was appropriate for a granddaughter and grandfather. His heart thundered tightly in his chest.

"Yes Melanie, that is it, and I told you that some of my items are magic."

"Papa Zach! I thought that magic stuff you have been telling me was just stories." She danced about and then sat down beside him, hugging him tightly, "But for you to have made this in only one day the magic has to be real!"

"Sweetie, I was up all night. I did not get to bed until nine this morning."

Melanie frowned. "Well then, Papa Zach, you lay back down, and I am going to go make you a late breakfast and after you have eaten it then you can take it easy while I clean."

He smiled and then said, "I still have the gemstones to set."

"If you did the gold in one night, there are still four nights before the dance, you have plenty of time. So you can rest tonight. In fact, after you eat your meal just go back to sleep. No story tonight. You can tell me one tomorrow night."

"Okay, sweetheart, I definitely could use the sleep."

Melanie was true to her word. She made Papa Zach a hearty breakfast, but a healthy one, only one piece of bacon, toast, one egg, a slice of cantaloupe, and some orange juice, and then she tucked him in, kissed his forehead, and told him to go to sleep. He did not take much urging and quickly went to sleep.

While he slept she cleaned the place. Lilith watched her, memorizing her every move. When she took over her body she would have to fool Zach so she watched her every move and listened to every sound she made committing each movement and sound to her memory so that she would be able to draw upon them to fool Zachariah when the time came. Her only worry was that he would become wise to her plan beforehand and then she might have to kill him. That would be a shame for without him that stone was worthless. He was the only one that could use it. Of course without the stone he was nothing but food.

Melanie closed up and locked the shop at nine and went home. When she returned the next day Zachariah was still asleep and she knew the old man had to have worn himself out. She also knew it was not healthy to sleep the clock around so she went to wake him.

Carefully she nudged him, "Papa Zach!"

"Is it time for you to go home now? Do you need me to lock the door?"

Melanie almost giggled, "No Papa Zach that was yesterday. It is now four in the afternoon on Tuesday."

Zachariah sat up quickly for a man his age and looked at her with a look of wonder in his eyes. "Are you telling me I slept for over twenty four hours?"

"You sure did! I told you, you over did it, making that tiara in one night. Now you need to get up and stretch and then when you are done shaving and cleaning up I will fix you a meal. So come downstairs when you are done." She leaned over and kissed his lips again, "Thank you again, my Papa Zach."

Zachariah smiled at her words and watched as she nearly danced out of his room. He heard her as she skipped down the stairs. Thirty minutes later he was sitting beside her enjoying the light dinner she had fixed them. Cucumber sandwiches, she had said. He had never eaten a sandwich without meat on it, but it was not bad.

After the meal she cleaned up and then began to put up the decorations as he began to set the stones. For the main stone he chose a sapphire the same color as her eyes. It was an offset diamond cut, so it formed a cross with the way the facets were cut. It was also large, nearly as large as his thumb. To each side of it and on the lower base was a ruby, round cut and a little larger than a standard dress shirt button. The remainder of the stones were twenty eight diamonds, ranging from one quarter carat to one carat in size for a total weight of twelve carats. Zachariah knew that there could not be a price set on the piece. If it were appraised it would bring a value of well over a million dollars. However all the kids at her school would think the stones were fake or rhinestones. Only Melanie and he would know the truth. He would not finish setting the stones in one night, but it would be done in plenty of time for her dance.

At about eight Melanie came in and sat down beside him as he was finishing setting the two rubies. She smiled at him and he returned her smile and for many moments they stared at each other in silence before she finally broke the silence by saying, "Well Papa Zach, I do not regret missing my story yesterday, but I do have to say I have been dying all day to hear one today. So can I go pick a piece from the cabinet?"

"Sure, sweetheart."

With the exuberance that only youth has she leapt from her seat and bounded to the cabinet. Opening the doors she looked at all the pieces and her hand started toward one piece and then another and then shifted to another then suddenly darted and she chose one. She carried it over to him and in his hands laid a pendant with three interwoven triangles upon the face of it.

The old man smiled, "This is an amazing tale. Not only in the story but in how it came to return to me."

"Let me tell you a true ghost story, but not your ordinary ghost story. For this is one ghost that had a lust for life, and that lust did not pass away when she did, she was able to find a way to fulfill her lust even after death."

Incorrigible
Abby Blythe
Chapter One

"Can you believe this place? It's amazing, and it's all yours."

Anne Kemper nodded in agreement then sank onto one end of the sofa. She surveyed the handful of boxes scattered on the hardwood floor of the bare living room. Dust-coated windows diffused the sunlight spilling into the room and softened the grime years had layered on every surface.

"I'm still waiting for the other shoe to drop." She ran her fingers through her loose sable curls then rested her elbow on the threadbare arm of the sofa. If it was possible, things were going too well. "There has to be some reason this place was so cheap."

"Don't look a gift horse in the mouth. You were lucky. Period. End of story." Debra Armstrong, her best friend, sat on the arm of the sofa and brushed her corkscrew, dark brown curls away from her face.

"Lucky." The word slid slowly through her lips as if she was testing the sound of it. A distant relative leaving her a small fortune was lucky, finding this lovely home, a Victorian cottage in an upscale neighborhood, just seemed too good to be true.

"And if I'm going to get lucky, I have to head out right now." Deb grinned and stood up. She picked up her purse from the top of one of the piles of boxes and started toward the door. "Are you sure you don't want to come? We're going to the Chrysalis."

"Not tonight." Anne only knew the member's only club via its reputation for being the hottest spot in the city, but she didn't feel like venturing into a world where culinary delights weren't the only offerings on the menu.

Deb crossed her arms, impaling her with a look that could only mean well-intentioned advice was about to be delivered. "Look, Mark's been out of your life for almost three months. It's time to plunge back into the singles' scene."

"You're right... but not tonight. I have too much to do." That was her defense, and she was sticking to it. Anne pushed off the couch, hoping to signal an end to the conversation. She walked beside her closest friend toward a wide archway leading to a spacious tiled foyer. The soft pat of her sneakers echoed off the bare walls. "This place might have been a steal, but it still needs a lot of elbow grease to make it habitable. There's no way I'm celebrating until the kitchen has been disinfected."

"If a little dirt is the only thing keeping you at home, then I'll be over tomorrow morning to help you clean." Deb laughed softly. "Make that the afternoon. Trust me, a few good lays, and Mark will be a hiccup in your past."

In spite of the knot twisting in her stomach, Anne smiled. Deb's answer to most of life's problems was sex – the hotter and the more frequent the better.

"Girlfriend, you're far too young to be celibate," Deb said as she grasped the ridged glass doorknob. "He did you a favor moving on."

It hadn't felt like a favor at the time. Hell, it still didn't, but at least the sound of his name didn't hit her in the gut like a sucker punch any more. Like clichéd dialogue in a two-bit movie, he'd said he still cared for her and wanted to be friends, but sex with her was too tame, and he needed more. He explained that he'd been patient at first because she was a virgin, but he'd thought things would heat up after they moved in together, and it hadn't. So, for the sake of their friendship, he felt it would be better if they moved on. Anne cringed mentally. She might have believed him if he hadn't move right into the bed of a hot little number who had recently joined his firm.

"Anne, if you change your mind... give me a ring on my cell. I'll meet you at the door."

"Thanks, but don't hold your breath." Anne gave her a tight hug, warmed by her friend's unfailing loyalty and friendship.

"Ciao, sweetie!" Deb strode across the threshold and onto the covered veranda, lifting her hand in a farewell salute.

Anne stood in the doorway and watched her friend's silver, imported sedan, back out of the driveway and start down the quiet, tree-lined street. She grasped the edge of the door, about to close it, when a prickle across the nape of her neck brought her gaze around. Following the uneasy feeling, she looked into the narrow-eyed stare of a woman peering at her from an Adirondack chair on a wide covered veranda like her own. Wings of white encroached on the auburn waves framing her scowling face.

With a tentative smile on her lips, Anne lifted her hand and offered a silent greeting. The scowling woman lifted her chin, pushed herself out of her chair and stomped toward her front door. A shiver slid down Anne's spine at the unexpected display of hostility.

"What's her problem?" Anne muttered as she shut the door. "I only moved in this morning... hardly long enough to offend someone."

Shrugging off thoughts about her prickly neighbor, Anne walked down the short corridor to the kitchen. Her home was a puzzling assortment of old and new. The layers of dust on every flat surface confirmed the fact that the home had been vacant for decades. Yet, according to the real estate agent, it had been maintained with regular upgrades to electrical, plumbing and other structural features as if the previous owner, a globetrotting spinster, would arrive at any time. But, she never had. Instead, she put the lovely Victorian cottage on the market.

Anne walked over to the sink where she'd left the bucket and several bottles of cleanser. Nothing was going in those cupboards until she'd scrubbed them.

***

Four hours later, she stepped out of the shower and toweled down. Every muscle complained about the cleaning marathon, but she didn't care. The kitchen shone, and the empty dining room, her future workshop, glowed from amply applied elbow grease.

Tomorrow, she would start setting up her workshop in the spacious dining room. Large windows in the spacious room supplied ample natural light for her to work on her sculptures. As she hung her towel over the rack, she once again thanked the childless, great-aunt who had left her enough money so that she could quit her day job at the art shop and focus on her own art.

Though tired when she emerged from the bathroom, a growing sense of restlessness drew her across the room. She followed a luminescent ribbon of moonlight that trailed across the hardwood floor. Anne pulled the belt of her terry robe tight around her waist and stopped in front of the window to draw the curtains. Her mules scuffed softly against the polished surface, the sound eerily loud in the silent room. For all the physical exertion, going to bed would be a waste of time because she certainly wouldn't sleep for quite some time.

As she reached up to catch the curtain in her hand, she glanced toward the house next door, hoping to catch a peek of her hunky neighbor, Sam Decker. He was a masterpiece created by the tempter's own hand – tall, blond, and muscular.

From a brief exchange over the fence earlier that day, she knew his eyes were just the color of the sky on a summer morning. Unlike the disapproving, older neighbor, she and Sam had chatted amicably over the fence for a few minutes until the moving truck had arrived with her meager collection of boxes and furniture and ending their conversation.

Captured by the sight of Sam's silhouette in his bedroom window, she let her hand drop to her side. Anne sank onto the deep window seat and watched as a woman joined him, their forms framed by the window, their outlines softened by a sheer curtain.

Anne peeked over the pillows covering the back of the deep window seat. The last thing she wanted was to get caught in her role as voyeur. Intrigued, she watched as Sam placed his hands on the woman's waist. In a leisurely gesture, he drew her against his body. His lady friend tilted her head to one side, and he nuzzled her neck.

Anne placed her hand on the same spot on her neck, wondering what it would be like to feel his lips against her skin. The thought took her by surprise. After her experience with Mark, she'd assumed she had a void where a sex drive should have been.

Sam pulled his companion's top over her head then tossed it aside. The lucky lady turned in his arms and started unbuttoning his shirt. Anne held her breath as his partner slid her hands up his chest then pushed the garment off his shoulders in a deliberately sensual movement. Her hands slid down his arms, pushing his shirt ahead of them until it dropped to the floor. Then, the woman drew his head down, and they kissed. Anne drew a fingertip across her lips, wondering what it must have felt like to feel his lips against her and his bare, muscled chest pressed against her body.

She watched as they shed their jeans. He grasped her waist and spun her around, tugging her against his body. Every movement was predatory and controlled.

Anne's pulse accelerated when his hands cupped the woman's breasts from behind. Hers swelled in response to the seductive stroke. Impatiently, she loosened the belt of her robe then pulled it open. Mimicking his movements, her hands curled under her breasts, her thumbs circling the dusty rose areolas. Needy buds pinched under the light touch. Her breasts swelled, reacting to the gentle friction of skin against skin.

When his hands drifted lower, moisture seeped between swollen labial lips, and the barrel of her vagina clenched. Her robe fell to her elbows, but she didn't care. She continued to imitate his hands' erotic safari, skimming over her abdomen, then raking through her pubic curls until he swept the woman off her feet and carried her away from the window.

"Damn!" The word burst through her lips at the bite of disappointment and frustration she experienced as they disappeared from view.

"What the hell?" Anne shook her head then glanced down at her near naked body. She couldn't believe the view. She was sprawled across the overstuffed pillows of the window seat, her legs parted with her hand cupping her pubis. She'd never done anything like this. It almost felt as if another person had possessed her.

"Enough!" she muttered as she bolted out of the window seat and started toward her bed. "I might not be stellar in bed, but I'm not this desperate." Anne shook off her rob and pulled a tee shirt and boxers from a dresser drawer. She slipped between the cool, cotton sheets, and as she slipped into slumber, wondered what had happened to her tonight.

"We've only just begun, Anne," the spirit standing beside the bed thought with smug satisfaction. Virginia Marshall watched the sleeping woman, cursing the selfish lover who had fuelled her inhibitions and self-doubt.

After almost thirty years of chasing people out of her beloved home, something about Anne's curious blend of innocence and insecurity had touched her. Instead of ejecting her, as she had all the other people who had toured her home, she'd wanted to help her sample all the marvelous delights sex could provide. Virginia grinned or would have if she'd had a body. This could be a fun as well as a mutually beneficial relationship. She could help Anne explore a sensual new world, and Anne could help her find the person who murdered her.

"Now, let's begin..."

***

Anne woke with a start, her heart pounding in her chest. Vaginal muscles rippled around her finger in a heated and moist climax. With a soft exclamation of disbelief, she yanked her hand from between her legs.

"I can't believe this." Anne tossed aside the bedcovers then jumped out of bed. She looked down at her half-naked body, her boxers a silky pile on the carpet beside her bed.

"That's what I get for being a peeping Tom," she muttered as she pulled on panties and jeans. She avoided looking toward the window and went straight downstairs.

"Coffee," she said as she crossed the kitchen. "The stronger the better."

With shaky hands, she scooped coffee into the paper-lined hopper then filled the reservoir with water. She watched the first drops of dark elixir drop, then bounce across the bottom of the glass carafe, hissing in protest. With a sharp sigh, she folded her arms across her chest, belatedly realizing that she had forgotten to put on a bra. She looked down at the soft curves of her breasts. Why not just be relaxed and comfortable for the day, an impish voice in her head suggested.

"Why not?" Anne echoed the thought aloud.

She pulled a mug from the cupboard then filled it with the rich brew mellowing it with healthy helpings of cream and sugar. Taking a sip of the steaming beverage, she strolled into her new workshop. Boxes containing shelves, supplies and a table were piled in one corner. Today, she would focus on setting up her workspace and savoring ownership of her new home.

Anne spent the morning assembling shelves and arranging supplies until the doorbell chiming stopped her. She glanced at her watch. "One o'clock."

That seemed early for Deb, but then, she seemed pretty determined to take her out for a hot night on the town. She stood up, brushed her palms over the seat of her pants and headed for the door.

"Ready to clean?" she said as she pulled opened the door, then gasped.

"Sure." Sam, her neighbor, stood on the veranda. His brilliantly white tee shirt clung to sculpted pecs, and snug blue jeans molded to muscular thighs. "If you'd like me to." Deep dimples bracketed a brilliant smile.

"I'm sorry... I thought you were someone else." Anne flushed. Shoot me now she silently begged any guardian angel within earshot. Why did she turn into such a babbling idiot when guys were around?

He grinned then held up a brown bag with the logo of her favorite coffee shop. "I brought some donuts over to welcome you to the neighborhood, but if you need help cleaning, I can do that too."

"Not really, Deb, my friend, said she'd be over later to help." Of its own accord, her hand pushed the door open wider. "I was just about to take a break from unpacking. Would you like to join me for a coffee to go with those donuts?"

Anne blinked in surprise at the ease with which the invitation slid through her lips. For a few seconds, it was as if her words had taken on a life of their own.

"Love some." His grin, brilliant white, sparked a knee jerk reaction of feminine appreciation. Perhaps she wasn't as bedroom deficient as Mark had accused her of being.

"Come on in," she said and moved back, watching as he stepped over the threshold.

Anne's pulse accelerated as he followed her into the kitchen. She fought down images of Sam and his lover replaying in her head. She tossed a glance over her shoulder. He was standing in the archway that separated the kitchen from her workshop in what had been the dining room.

"Wow, you've got quite a set up," he offered. "Are you some kind of artist?"

"A sculptor. And you?"

"I'm a contractor, and I restore old homes in my spare time. I buy them cheap, live in them while I fix them up, then sell them."

"Why didn't you buy this place? It was a steal"

"It would have been too hard to sell," he said, offering a wry grin. "It has a reputation for being haunted."

"But you braved the ghost and came over," she challenged.

He laughed. His sapphire eyes lighting up with humor. "I had to meet the person who could stay in the place overnight."

"It really wasn't any great feat of courage. It felt like home." Even more than that, it felt as if the house liked her and wanted her there. She gave herself a mental shake. Perhaps it was the fact that she'd grown up in small apartments in poor neighborhoods that made the house so welcoming.

His blue-eyed gaze slid lower and touched her pert nipples pushing against the soft fabric of her tee shirt. At the flare of male interest in his eyes, a moist heat started to pool between her legs.

He looked up and warmth swept across her cheeks.

"Cream and sugar?" Her voice sounded breathless, but thankfully, she got the words out without stammering. After last night, her body craved fulfillment, and Sam with bulging pecs and snug jeans would be the perfect appetizer.

"Love some."

In that instant, the lights flickered then went out. The coffee maker sputtered to a stop.

"That's odd. The electrical was just overhauled." He moved forward. "If you have a flashlight, I'll check out the power panel."

She nodded. His male scent mingled with a musky cologne and drifted toward her. It was a primal scent and heady with promise. Without a word, she reached in a drawer and pulled out a brand new flashlight.

Anne followed him down the stairs to the basement. Her foot slid off the step, and a strong arm caught her by the waist, pulling her against a solid chest, sandwiching something equally hard between their bodies. His forearm supported her breasts.

"Careful now," he said.

At his husky, whispered words, a quiver of need rippled through her sex, and her crotch grew slick with anticipation. Remembering the way he had held the woman last night her head fell back until it came to rest on his shoulder.

She moistened her lips, caught in the heady, sensual silence closing in on them. With his free hand, Sam brushed her hair away from the side of her neck, and she let her head tip to the side in a silent invitation. He touched his lips to the spot below her earlobe, then nipped and kissed a path lower until he reached the crook of her neck. The soft touch shot through her straight to the apex of her thighs. If this was foreplay, then she wanted to dive into the game.

He relaxed his hold long enough for her to turn to face him. Her gaze moved to the fly closure of his jeans, now straining over his arousal. The sight awoke a primal force that guided her hands under his tee shirt. She circled his nipples, exploring every dip and rise on his chest, savoring the soft texture of the whorls of hair covering his chest. His skin felt like sun warmed silk against her palms, and she wanted to explore more intimate curves. She followed the silky trail to his waist and lower, sliding a finger under his waistband, surprised by her boldness, and yet unwilling to stop.

His hand caught her wrist but didn't pull her away, just impeded her progress.

"You don't have a girlfriend or significant other who might object, do you?" The question slid between her dry lips on a whisper.

"No, but I didn't plan to hit on you this soon no matter how much I wanted to." He offered a lopsided grin. "At least, not on our first meeting."

She grasped the hem of her tee shirt. This might be insane, but she couldn't stop. Lust held her prisoner and guided her hands. She wanted more and was ready to make it happen. With an impatient gesture, she pulled her shirt upward, over her head, then let it fall beside her. Though startled by her uncharacteristic boldness the blatantly provocative action had empowered her as well. "Well, what better way to welcome a neighbor to the area?"

Sam sucked in a sharp gasp, then put his hand over hers. "Are you sure?"

He set the flashlight on the step then as he straightened he cupped her breasts. She arched, pressing the taut nipples against his palms.

He leaned forward and circled each areola with the tip of his tongue.

"More," she whispered.

"My pleasure." His voice was a low growl.

She felt him grin against the sensitized skin of her breast. He took a nipple into his mouth, sucking and tugging at the hungry bud. Anne looked down at the top of his head, at his sun-kissed waves and felt like two women, one observing the scene with disbelief, the other impatient to open her legs and feel him plough his swollen penis deep inside her.

She raked her fingers through his closely cropped hair. The erotic pulse between her legs accelerated, and her labial lips started to swell in anticipation. He moved to the other breast, and she closed her eyes, enjoying each lick and tug from his talented lips and tongue.

He lifted his head, then stroked his hand across her cheek. A sexy, lopsided grin turned up the corners of his mouth. "When I came over, I was hoping to get to know you better." He laughed softly, a quiet rumble echoing in his chest. "Though this wasn't quite the welcome I was expecting."

"Are you disappointed?" she teased, lifting the hem of his shirt. He lifted his arms over his head then leaned over so Anne could pull it off.

"Hell, no," he said, smoothing his hands under the curves of her breasts. "This beats any welcome to the neighborhood visit I've ever had before."

Anne smiled, then reached for the snap on his jeans and then tugged it apart. She slid the zipper slowly down his bulging erection. He sucked in a breath, his body tensing. At the soft sound, smug satisfaction spread as fast as the lust spreading in her belly.

She slipped her hands down the sides of his pants and then pushed them over his hips, her palms skimming over the soft fabric of his briefs, then down the sides of his muscled thighs, and lower to tight calves. He kicked off his jeans, then pulled the snap of her jeans apart. He pushed both her panties and jeans down in one smooth stroke and then tugged them off.

"I want to feel you inside me." The words came out on a ragged whisper from somewhere deep inside her, from a different woman, who was wanton and bold. Her body ached, craving fulfillment so badly it hurt. She'd never felt anything like this before.

"Your wish is my command." He nudged her legs apart then leaned forward, grazing his nose across her pubic hair, before separating the lips of her sex with his fingertips. "But I want to taste you first."

"Taste me?" The first moment of hesitation filtered through the wild abandon leading her forward in this sensual adventure. "But."

"But what?" he murmured. The heat of his breath skimmed over inflamed flesh.

"No one's..." The words failed to come.

"No one's ever touched you like this?" His tongue slid between the slippery folds.

Anne sucked in a breath.

"Or like this?" His lips closed around her clit, and he suckled the sensitized nub.

"Oh, God." She arched again, letting her legs fall further apart. Embarrassment succumbed to breathtaking awe. She rocked with him, gasping out mews of pleasure, then a growl of frustration when he pulled away.

She rested on her elbows on the step behind her and watched as he disposed of his briefs. The dim light filtering through the small windows softened his features. Perhaps it was best this way. She'd never been able to make love in the daylight, something Mark had grumbled about. Now, she was half-naked with a man she'd just met, thrilled and alarmed at how easy it had been to yield to the demands of the lust welling up inside her.

Sam's erection stood out from his body. A bead of moisture formed on the helmet-shaped tip of his penis. Curious, she slid her finger over the tip, collecting the sticky drop, then smiled when he sucked in a quick breath.

She licked it off her finger, surprised by the salty taste. She slid her hands down his rigid erection, to the nest of golden curls circling the base, then lower to the soft but uneven skin covering his genitals. She dragged a fingertip lightly over the textured skin of his scrotum. Perhaps it was the darkness or the fact he was almost a stranger that made her feel like an adventurous stranger in her own body.

He pulled back.

"Is something wrong?"

"Wrong? This is perfect," he said. "But I'm about ready to cum."

Anne savored the sight of the tanned, rippling muscles of his legs and butt, content to enjoy the view as he leaned over and dug his wallet out of his jeans pocket, then pulled out a small foil packet.

"Here, hold this." He passed her the condom package then grasped her by the waist, lifting her off the step. He turned around and sat down, settling her between the v of his legs.

"Let me put it on," she offered. Another first. She'd always insisted that Mark put on the condom. The quick rip of a condom package seemed loud in the silence. She took it, then smoothed the latex sheath over the bulging head, then slowly over the rod and the veins standing out along its length. *God he was large, she thought. A lot larger than Mark who was excessively proud of his manhood.*

"I thought you were in a hurry," he growled. He put his hand over hers, smoothing the plastic sheath the rest of the way along his shaft.

Sam grasped her waist again, lifting her and sliding his legs between hers, spreading her legs wide and drawing her close until his penis rested against her pubic hair. Unable to look away from his sex, Anne felt his hands at her waist move her until the tip of his arousal slid along her moist sex. He was so large; she couldn't imagine him fitting the whole length of it inside her. Mark's smaller member had at times been uncomfortable.

He eased her down over the quivering pole until their bodies met. She sucked in a gasp of air, dizzy with the ripple of sensation, warming her insides. A murmur of pure pleasure rose in her throat.

He lifted her then lowered her, each time rising to meet her, setting a primitive rhythm. Anne rested her knees on the step on either side of his hips to participate in the primal dance he'd begun. She started to rock, using her hips to grind against his body. She arched backward, his hands supporting her while she rose and rocked, gulping for breath until her vaginal walls finally clenched around him in an explosive burst of sensation.

"Oh, God," she gasped as she fell against his chest and his arms closed around her.

"Double ditto on that," he murmured against her neck.

Anne wasn't sure what to say or do. Nothing in past experience could compare. This sampling of sex had sated her and left her hungry for more all at the same time.

"Lady, you can come and borrow sugar at my place anytime," he said, then kissed her shoulder.

A soft laugh bubbled up from deep inside her as aftershocks rippled through her sex. "I just might take you up on it." She wasn't sure she'd ever be able to do this again, to fall into a glorious sexual union, but she wasn't about to close a door on a place she might want to revisit.

She straightened, looking down at the base of the v where their bodies were still joined. His crisp blond curls mingled with Anne's golden brown pubic hair. His tanned skin contrasted against her pale limbs. Her gaze climbed higher over a tight rippled abdomen and rounded pecs with dusty brown, dime-sized nipples. Male beauty swept away embarrassment.

"Hello! Anybody home?" Deb's voice came from somewhere above them.

Anne straightened; a fiery blush burned her cheeks. Once again, she was caught in that eerie, what-have-I-just-done sensation.

"Downstairs," she returned. "Just checking out the power panel. Hold on, we'll be right up."

Sam grinned as he lifted her quickly off his body. She picked her tee shirt from the step where it had fallen, then pulled it quickly over her head. Sam pressed her jeans into her hands. She pulled them on with trembling hands, still a prisoner of the feeling of disbelief.

She didn't look at Sam but heard the rustle of clothes, then a zip. He picked up the flashlight before he walked over to a metal box in one corner, then immediately after a click the bare light bulb suspended on a wire overhead came on.

Deb stepped into view at the top of the stairs. "Anne?"

"Hi, Deb. The power went out, and my neighbor, Sam, arrived just in time to help out."

Deb started down the steps, then paused about half way down. Anne flushed, aware of the musky scent of sex still suspended in the air. Speculation lit her eyes, and her lips twitched, promising a ribbing later.

"Sam," Anne said as she turned toward Deb who had reached the bottom of the stairs. "This is Debra Armstrong, my friend."

"The one who was coming to clean?" He extended his hand toward her friend.

"One in the same. Although, it looks as if Anne has most of it finished."

"I can still find a floor or two that needs scrubbing," Anne returned, starting to feel like her world was returning to normal. "But first why don't we have a mug of coffee and some of the donuts Sam brought over?"

"That would be great," Deb replied, squinting as she looked past Anne. "Why is that section bricked in?"

Anne turned. "I'm not sure. The real estate agent said that it used to be a cold room, but he wasn't sure why the previous owner had sealed it off."

"Maybe there's a dead body." Deb's eyes shone with mischief.

"More likely a crack in the foundation," Sam said. "You should probably take a look just in case it is and so you can have it seen to."

Virginia leaned against the wall and watched as Anne's tawny-skinned friend came down the stairs. She felt stronger than she had in year. Not since randy teens had made love several times in one night on the bare living room a decade ago had she felt this powerful. The force of their explosive climax had fed energy to her, just as Anne's coupling with her sexy neighbor had.

She moved toward the trio, willing them to look toward her resting place, where her murderer had buried her alive. The real fun could only begin once her body, or at least when what was left of her body was found and Anne took possession of the necklace that held her here on the mortal plane.

Instead, the mortals climbed the stairs, their laughter trailing behind them. Frustration nipping at her hopes, Virginia watched them go but didn't go after them.

Soon, she promised, soon....

Chapter Two

"How about if I order pizza for our demolition party," Deb offered as Anne put their three coffee mugs in the dishwasher a few minutes later.

"Demolition party?" Anne asked as she straightened.

"The brick wall in the basement," Deb responded. "Don't you want to know what someone hid behind that wall?"

Anne suppressed a smile, suspecting her friend's interest in the basement had a lot more to do with Sam than curiosity about what might have been hidden downstairs.

"There could be a crack in the foundation," Sam added. "If that's the case, it should be seen to right away."

A tingling slid over Anne's skin. She had an uneasy feeling something important was behind that brick wall, but she wasn't sure what. "Okay, let's get to it."

"I'll get a sledge hammer," Sam said. "Be right back." He grinned then strode out the back door with a long legged stride.

Anne watched him disappear, a slow flush creeping along her cheeks. Less than an hour ago, she'd seen them in their muscled glory, had felt the impact of each primitive thrust as he buried himself deep inside her. He was Belgium chocolate for the body, sweet, satisfying and highly addictive.

"Lord, girl, when I came in, you could smell the marvelous, musky scent of sex in the cellar. Girl, I'm proud of you."

Anne looked at Deb, wishing she could suppress the heat spreading across her cheeks. "I can't describe what happened. It was like another woman woke up inside me. One minute we were going downstairs to check the electrical panel, then I tripped, he caught me, and the next thing I knew we were naked and having the best sex I've ever had in my entire life."

"Remind me to take a tumble when we're headed down the stairs. He's such a hottie. I wouldn't mind taking him out for a test ride." Deb winked. "That is if you don't have any plans for him."

"You are incorrigible!" Anne laughed softly. "And no, I don't mind."

Strange as the thought might seem, what they'd shared had been gratuitous and glorious physical satisfaction – no strings attached – at least for her. For the first time, she understood the difference between having great sex and making love, and she hadn't had either with Mark.

The sound of Sam's footsteps on the back porch brought an end to their conversation. The door swung open, and he strode in. "Ready?"

"For anything," Anne responded, and she realized that she was. "Let's go and see what's behind that wall."

The trio trooped down the bare wood stairs and within minutes, Sam's sledgehammer had made a small hole in the red brick wall. Muscles bulged with each swing and impact. Her eyes met Deb's, and her friend flashed a grin and waggled her eyebrows. Meanwhile, chunks of the wall crumbled under his assault. Anne and Deb made a pile in the corner while Sam chipped away at the uneven edges of the opening. Once it started to fall apart, it took only minutes before he'd created a hole large enough to look through.

"Where's the flashlight we used this morning?" he asked, placing his hand beside the hole, peering into the darkness.

Anne passed it to him, wondering what they would find. For some reason, she didn't think it would be a crack in the foundation, but where the thought had come from, she wasn't sure.

"Holy shit!" At Sam's vehement exclamation, both women looked at each other.

Anne moved closer. "What is it?"

"A body... or rather... what's left of a body."

Anne snatched the flashlight from him and peered through the opening. The pale beam of light traveled down a skeleton curled in a semi-fetal position on the concrete floor. She sucked in a sharp breath, then moved the beam along the length of the remains. Reeling from the sight, she didn't resist when Deb pulled the flashlight from her hand.

"Shit is right!" Deb turned. "I've heard of skeletons in the closet, but walled up in the basement... that's twisted."

"Whoever it is, they've been here for quite some time judging from the decomposition," Sam said. He placed his palm on one side of the opening, his gaze fixed on the remains.

At his deep voiced observation, a shudder bumped down Anne's spine as if a cool finger had traced a line down her spine. "I guess we'd better call the police."

Though she couldn't explain why, a part of her hadn't been surprised at the first sight of the skeleton. Instead, an eerie sense of confirmation had claimed her. Inexplicably, a part of her had been expecting to see a body with scraps of fabric and long strands of hair still clinging to the bones, but she wasn't sure where the thought had come from.

She climbed the stairs then gulped in several deep breaths when she reached the top. She moved into the kitchen, picked up the phone, but didn't dial. She sagged against the wall and closed her eyes, the weight of today's events pounding her like a storm-driven tide. She'd thought having sex with Sam would have been hard to top, but it seemed fate was out to prove her wrong.

While they waited for the police to arrive, the trio continued to chip away at the wall. As soon as the hole was large enough, Anne stepped over the small ridge of bricks and into what must have been a storage room. Rough wooden shelves lined three walls, canned goods coated in dust still stood in rows like squat sentinels. There was just enough space for her to walk around the skeletal remains. The white beam of light from the flashlight traveled the length of the body, then snagged on a gold chain on the floor. The gilt, serpentine trail led to a circular gold disc resting on a boney palm. Nausea rose in her stomach at the thought that this person might have been buried alive and endured a lingering and gruesome death. Who could have been so cold and sick?

"I'm no forensics expert," Anne answered as she bent down. "But judging from what is left, this person must have been buried decades ago. Probably as long as the place has been vacant."

Almost of its own accord, the flashlight pointed toward the delicately interwoven triangles, a triquetra, engraved on the gold medallion. Anne strained against the impulse to snatch it off the bed of bones but failed. It was as if her hand belonged to someone else. She could only watch as her fingers lifted it from the skeletal hand, then slid it into her pocket. Beads of perspiration formed across her forehead. Removing evidence was wrong, yet the irresistible urge to possess it hadn't given her a choice. She knew that she couldn't let the police take it away, but she didn't know why.

Disturbed by what had happened and the strange compulsion that had gripped her, Anne stood quickly and moved out of the room.

"Are you okay?" Sam curled his hand over her shoulder.

"Not really." She shook her head, the necklace in her pocket prodding her conscience. "It isn't everyday a person literally finds a skeleton in the closet."

The doorbell rang, and together they went up the stairs. Anne slid her hand in her pocket and pushed the necklace further in, a wave of protectiveness washing over her.

After taking a deep, steadying breath, she opened the front door and welcomed a uniformed officer and his partner. This was going to be a long day.

Chapter Three

Anne leaned against the wall in her foyer and watched the officer open the door. He led the coroner and the forensics team through the house to the basement. Her heart beat double time. What had possessed her? She'd committed a crime – tampering with evidence at a crime scene. The weight of the necklace in her pocket accused her of her deception. Once again, she'd acted out of character, unable to resist a compulsion to act.

She decided to move to the living room to watch the parade of uniformed people troop through her home to the basement. Nearby, Sam and Deb followed into the room, chatting easily. But then Debra usually did when she had a man she wanted in her sites. Sam was definitely worth the effort.

"If you don't need me any longer, officer, I'm going to head out. I have a date," Sam said when the officer with his stomach dipping slightly over his belt strode into the room.

The police officer paused and looked at him for a couple of seconds before he nodded. "I have your number if I need to ask anything more."

Sam glanced over at Anne and winked. "This certainly has been the most eventful welcome-to-the-neighborhood visit I've ever experienced."

"That's for sure." At his broad grin, heat swept across Anne's cheeks. Spontaneous, steamy sex with a near stranger and a body behind a bricked wall in her basement – definitely topped the meter for strange. Anne looked at the officer. "I only moved in yesterday."

Unexpectedly, his lips twitched in a half smile. Perhaps there was a sense of humor lurking under his serious look. "After this, unpacking boxes will seem pretty tame."

Anne felt the weight of male appreciation in the detective's gaze and an answering hollow ache deep inside her. What the heck was going on with her? If a chubby man in blue could switch on her libido, she needed to take her temperature. Heck. She probably needed a whole psych evaluation.

"Right now, tame is perfectly fine by me." She needed time to reflect on everything that had happened today to her and to what they had found.

She stepped back as the mystery victim enclosed in a body bag and riding on a stretcher rolled through the foyer.

"Cause of death?" the detective asked the stocky fellow with coroner stamped in bold letters across his back.

"Best guess... blunt force trauma... with lethal force. The skull was fractured and compressed."

Bludgeoned to death. At the thought, Anne shuddered. The blow might have been lethal, but from the way the body was curled on the floor, she had a feeling death hadn't been instantaneous.

Within the hour, the detective and his associates were gone. Anne dropped on the couch.

"What a day!" Anne scrubbed her hand across the back of her neck, easing kinks in her knotted muscles.

"I'm heading out to a friend's cottage tonight for a beach party. Why don't you tag along? After today, you could probably use the distraction." Deb grinned. "We can even go skinny dipping if you'd like."

Yesterday, heck, even this morning, she probably would have passed, but now, the invitation tempted her. "When?"

Perfectly sculpted brows arched in surprise, then Deb grinned. "Now. Go put on your swimsuit. We'll grab a bite to eat on the way."

The journey to their destination lasted only thirty minutes, but it had felt much longer to Anne who was caught in a twilight zone of disbelief as much from her own uncharacteristic behavior as from finding the body in her home.

Anne slid the gold charm back and forth on the chain as Deb pulled to a spot behind a trio of vehicles on the side of a wooded lane.

"Time to party!" Deb twisted in her seat and pulled a canvas bag from the back seat.

Caught in a jumble of conflicting emotions, Anne grasped the handle of her own bag and then opened the car door. She climbed out of the car, then followed Deb down the hard-packed dirt lane beside the line of cars.

Deb turned and said, "Mike and his significant other built this place about a year ago. I've been down a couple of times this summer. It's amazing."

Anne had heard about their parties – food, fun, and sex – no drugs allowed. Still, second thoughts dogged her steps. "Deb, I..."

Curls bounced as her friend stopped and swung around to face her. "Second thoughts?"

"Third, fourth and fifth." She hitched the straps of her bag higher on her shoulder. "Sometimes it feels as if..." How could she describe the uncharacteristic lack of inhibitions that welled up inside her? "I'm starting to feel like two women. This morning with Sam, a part of me couldn't believe what was happening, and yet, I didn't want to... I couldn't stop."

"Hallelujah!" Deb looped her arm around Anne's. "Sometimes you think too hard. Maybe it's a sexual awakening... you just needed a kiss from the right prince or several princes to let go and live a bit."

"Ditto to that thought," Virginia added, liking Anne's friend more and more. Between the two of them, they should be able to help Anne loosen up and sample some of life's best delicacies – men.

The burst of energy generated by her steamy union with the Viking wannabe had given off enough energy so that she'd been able to force Anne to take the necklace before it was confiscated by the hunky police officer. She couldn't allow the necklace to fall into his possession. It was her anchor to this dimension, and if it had been locked away in a box in an evidence locker, any chance of bringing her murderer to justice would have vanished along with her chance of passing over.

Another good lay should generate enough energy for me to make an appearance. Inside, she grinned. "Let's find a nice, delicious hunk to expand your horizons, Annie, my girl," she murmured. "And help me make an appearance."

As Anne emerged from the bedroom where she'd taken off her street clothes to reveal a one-piece swimsuit. She scanned the people milling about the large gathering room. She felt over-dressed, even prudish. Most of the women wore triangular pieces of spandex that barely covered their pointed nipples and pubic triangles.

"Anne? This is a surprise."

"Jason," she replied without turning around. Her heart sank to the hardwood floor beneath her bare feet as she turned slowly to face the man who'd offered the familiar deep-voiced greeting. She came face to face with Jason MacIsaac who was a friend of Mark's. Why did he have to be here? His distance and unnerving stares had always made her uncomfortable.

"And to think I almost didn't come," he said.

Wishing he hadn't, Anne lifted her gaze to meet his. Instead of the scorn or derision she'd expected to find, frank and totally male admiration warmed his deep brown eyes. "Aren't you glad you changed your mind?"

The flirtatious words had slipped through her lips as if someone else had placed them on the tip of her tongue. Heat burned its way across her face as she watched as his dark, straight eyebrows lifted in surprise, and dimples creased his cheeks at the corners of his mouth.

"I certainly am," he returned, laugh lines fanning out from the corners of his eyes. "I always regretted that Mark saw you first."

"What?" She pulled in a sharp breath, stunned as much by his warm smile as his statement. Never had she suspected anything lurked behind his neutral gaze other than a calculator planning his next financial venture. "I never knew."

"You weren't supposed to. Mark was one of my best friends. I wasn't about to poach in his territory, but I wanted to pump air and pound the shit out of him all at the same time for being such a jerk and then ending it with you."

Surprise startled a soft laughter through her lips. The knots of tension his appearance prompted started to ease. This man was both foreign and familiar all at the same time. Assumptions she'd made about him started to melt under the heat simmering in his gaze.

He stepped closer and cupped her elbow with his hand. "Let's get a drink and catch up."

"That would be nice," she returned, actually meaning the words and not just offering a platitude. The dismay she'd felt at his appearance was quickly dissipating. Though she still wasn't used to a Jason who openly expressed his desire for her, he was familiar enough so that his presence felt like an anchor in a sea of uncertainty. The events of the day had turned her life upside down, and she was still off balance and not quite comfortable in her new skin, but at least Jason was familiar even though it was the first time she'd seen behind his reserve.

She snuck a glance at her companion as they moved between chatting couples in the great room as they made their way toward the kitchen. Her gaze drifted from his lips to his chest. Whorls of light brown hair followed the muscular definition of his pecs then narrowed as it followed a tempting trail to the waist of his very brief swimsuit. She'd always admired Jason's classic good looks. Admired them? She nearly snorted aloud. Jason surpassed good looking by miles. If sex appeal could become incarnate, it would be him. Only his chilly demeanor had made her keep her distance.

Even in sweats after a run, he'd always managed to look as if he'd stepped off a GQ page. His looks combined with his Adonis physic were a lethal combination, and the reason she'd been surprised when she'd learned he was a successful banker. In her mind, the word banker had brought to mind images of a grizzle-haired man with a paunch not an athletic, drop-dead gorgeous man.

She took a soda from the tin washbasin filled with ice and cans.

"A beer?" she asked, automatically reaching for the brand she knew he preferred. Strange the things people remembered. How you could know so much about a person without really knowing them.

He nodded, his gaze drifting toward the v in her swimsuit. "Thanks."

He popped the tab then took a drink.

"So, I heard you bought a house," he said as they strolled through the kitchen door onto the broad covered veranda overlooking a sloping lawn and sandy beach.

"I moved in yesterday and found a skeleton in my basement this afternoon," she said, with a wry grin, her gaze following a thin band of orange resting on the horizon.

"Seriously?"

"Really." Their gazes met, and Anne didn't have any trouble reading the male hunger in his eyes. At one time it would have unsettled her, perhaps even sent her scurrying for cover, but this time it made her feel attractive and desirable.

Muted melodies from speakers hidden in the foliage drifted around them. "Would you like to dance?" He offered her his hand, then looked toward the couples on the lawn swaying to the soft, sensual melodies. Some completely out of sync with the music, their hips creating a sensual rhythm of their own.

"That would be nice." Anne placed her palm against his, glad she had come. She had taken a new road, destination unknown, and she was happy to see where it took her.

Virginia circled the couple moving with the music, anticipation humming through her. The virile hunger in the fellow's eyes could singe and satisfy all at the same time.

"Annie, let's have some fun with this one. I have a feeling he knows how to take his time and savor the moment, and the fact that he's totally smitten with you doesn't hurt."

All she had to do was to keep whispering suggestive remarks to help the cause. Anne seemed to be very receptive to her suggestions even though she was unaware of her presence.

Virginia paused and studied Anne. She was looking at her partner with wide eyes full of lust and uncertainty. What had happened to make Annie-girl so insecure, so unwilling to take risks? The fact that she cared about Anne surprised Virginia. When she was alive, she probably wouldn't have given the retiring young woman a second look, writing her off as a prude, but spending decades with only her own thoughts as company had sobered her, softened her self-centered outlook on life. She sensed there was a lot more to Annie Kemper than met the eye. She suspected she was a woman worthy of a special man.

Jason's hand slid to the small of Annie's back, drawing Virginia's attention back to the couple moving in time to the sensual tune. Invisible lips twitched at the sight of his arousal stretching the spandex of his scrap of a swimsuit. If he was any bigger the tip of his arousal would be peeking out of his suit. She drifted closer to them, leaning over Annie's shoulder. "He's hot to trot, girl. Give him a reason to hope."

Annie closed the distance between them, sandwiching his arousal between their bodies.

"That's it, Annie. Relax, have fun, let your hair down."

Virginia floated on her back toward Jason until her head was level with his shoulder. "Treat her right," she murmured in his ear. "And if you don't, you'll have me to answer to."

Chapter Four

Anne watched the slender fingers of the bonfire stretch into the inky black sky. Music drifted on the breeze, mingling with the sound of the water slapping against the dock. Couples had long since given up on dancing and had gathered around the fire on the beach. Some to kiss, others to stroke their bodies. Anne marveled at their lack of inhibitions. In spite of her actions this afternoon, some of her reserve still remained.

The evening had played out pretty much as Anne had expected it would. Couples danced, touching, and teasing. Now, as midnight approached, couples wandered to secluded spots just beyond the reach of the light of the flames. What she hadn't expected was that she would have enjoyed the evening so much. Jason had proved to be a perfectly entertaining and provocative partner.

Anne surveyed the scene, sliding the delicate pendant hanging from the chain around her neck back and forth. Debra was in the water with a new conquest. Their swimsuits dangled from the branch of a tree over hanging the water. Anne grinned, amazed at her friend's insatiable appetite where men were concerned. Perhaps it was catching if today was any indication.

Anne snuck a glance at Jason who sat on the blanket beside her. His forearm rested on his knee, and his gaze was focused on the slender orange flames dancing along the huge logs of the bonfire. He'd teased and flirted all evening, delivering a subtle foreplay that had managed to both arouse and relax her at the same time.

"Would you like to dance again?" he offered.

"Not really." Pushing aside doubt, Anne leaned forward, sliding her hand around the nape of his neck. Then, she leaned forward until she could touch her lips to the corner of his mouth. Her boldness surprised her. She wasn't sure what had happened today, but she was willing to ride the tide for a time and see where it carried her. She was changing and, surprisingly, she was enjoying the learning curve.

She kissed him again, this time full on the lips. His lips parted slightly, and she touched the tip of her tongue along his lower lip. He opened, and she slid her tongue into his mouth, circling his tongue, then drawing back, hoping he would follow. He cupped her head with his hands, dipping and tasting, a full partner in a provocative and primitive dance, but not taking a lead.

Anne placed her hands against his chest. His nipples, taught buds, pushed into her palms. The uneven plain of his chest intrigued her. The warmth radiating off his skin, the silky texture, and the silky abrasion of the soft whorls of hair, fascinated her. Her hands slid lower following the trail of curls leading to his groin. With the back of her first knuckle, she followed the outline of his arousal straining against the scrap of spandex covering his privates.

Jason sucked in a sharp ragged breath, his hips twitched at the deliberately arousing touch.

He pulled back just enough so that he could look into her eyes. "I really don't expect sex, regardless of the mood of the crowd."

"But I want sex." Anne recognized her voice and acknowledged the truth in her words. But still, it was still a surprise to hear the sentiment slide so frankly through her own lips.

His expression sobered. "I'd rather make love, but I'm too horny to debate terminology," he said, offering his hand. "Let's find some privacy."

She took his hand. He brought her up with him as he stood. He cupped her face, then kissed her, a light brush across her lips, yet not tentative, but rather an invitation and a promise. She leaned toward him, aware of the heat and tension radiating from his body.

His arm around her waist, they strolled along the beach. The muffled moan of pleasure rose from behind a granite boulder. Jason looked down at her then grinned. "Just a little further," he whispered. He led her around a rocky point, to a small crescent beach with a granite pebble beach.

He drew her toward a small private enclosure formed by the root of a fallen tree. Private, yet with a view of the cove. Moonlight danced on the rippling surface of the water. She placed her palms on the trunk of the tree, hoping he would make the next move. Her uncharacteristic boldness was starting to falter.

"It's beautiful here," she murmured, ill at ease with the silence swelling between them.

"Not half as beautiful as you," he whispered as he curled his hands around her shoulders, then dropped a kiss at the crook of her neck. The light caress shivered across her skin in lazy, yet exhilarating, ripples.

Her breath hitched as each heartbeat seemed to explode in her chest, and her heart responded to the sincerity in the softly spoken words. "Are you sure you haven't been taken over by an alien?" she teased. "The Jason I knew was so cold I thought I'd get frost bite if I got too close."

She felt the warm puffs of his breath against the nape of her neck as he laughed. "I didn't have a choice. I knew if I touched you or you touched me, I wouldn't be able to stop from making you mine."

At his predatory and provocative words, her breasts started to swell. She looked down. Needy nipples pushed against the fabric stretched across her chest, the taut points clearly visible through the spandex of her suit. They felt heavy and anxious to be free of their thin restraint.

His hands slid across her shoulders, dragging the shoulder straps slowly over her shoulders and down her upper arms, peeling the suit over her breasts until they hung free. His hands slid around her ribs, then under her needy breasts. Anne sucked in a soft breath as his palms circled the soft, curved flesh, and she arched, letting her head ease back onto his shoulder. A wonderful lethargy spread through her limbs while the pulse between her legs throbbed, moisture leaking out with each beat.

"What I want to do right now is peel that suit off you and bury myself as deep, hard, and fast as I can... but." He paused, then exhaled slowly before he continued, "I've waited too long for this moment to blow it now."

"Don't take it too slowly," she murmured, moving her legs apart to ease the throbbing ache blossoming at the apex of her thighs. The cautious woman inside of Anne lost the war with her waking wanton side. The heat of his body fueled the hunger taking root deep in her sex. She slid her hands inside her suit, pushing it over her hips until it slid easily down her legs to her ankles.

Jason sucked in a sharp breath. The large hands sliding down her ribs paused at her waist, then turned her around.

Instinctively, her hands grasped the elastic of his suit and eased it over the bulge in his groin and down his legs. In the moonlight, Anne could see the helmet shaped head jerk upward as if delighting in its freedom.

With a fingertip she slid her finger over the swollen organ, fascinated by the silky warmth of the smooth skin of the tip.

"Please tell me I'm not dreaming, and you will not disappear," he growled and caught her wrists.

"You aren't dreaming, and I'm definitely not going to disappear," she whispered, curling her hand around his rod. He closed his eyes, his breath catching. He'd hidden his feelings and desires well. Perhaps that had been for the best. Visible desire would have only made her more uncomfortable with him than the distance he'd held between them. "I can't believe you wanted me so badly."

"I fell for you from the first moment you strolled into Mark's life," he murmured, backing up, then sitting on a granite boulder, drawing her along with him.

His frank declaration washed over her. Anne smiled with pure feminine satisfaction as she raked her fingers through his hair and straddled his legs, then lowered herself until her moist crotch pressed against his arousal.

Jason leaned forward then took a peaked nipple into his mouth. Anne arched backward, his hands supporting her.

"God, that's amazing," she moaned as he sucked and laved her breast. "Please, don't stop."

Though Sam had caressed her breasts, Jason's touch opened a whole new world of sensations, touching places and sparking sensations she'd only read about. She'd thought the authors had grossly exaggerated their reactions.

When he released the nipple, she mewed a protest. She raked her fingers through his short wavy hair and drew his head to her other breast, the nub hard and hungry for his touch. She shifted her hips, enclosing his erection in her labial lips now slick from her pre-cum juices then lifting her hips slightly to stroke him with the moist core, almost laughing aloud at his groaned gasp of pleasure.

"I want you inside me," she said. Impatient vaginal muscles quivered in anticipation. She wanted him filling her, stroking her intimately, carrying her to a climax.

Jason lifted his head, his thoughtful gaze meeting hers. He leaned over and kissed the tip of her taut nipple. "Your wish is my command, but not like this." With a sweeping glance, he scanned the beach then muttered under his breath. "Damn."

"What's wrong?"

"Not a soft spot in sight. And I don't intend on taking you on a rocky beach."

Anne followed his gaze. "I don't care."

"I do," he returned. "I don't want your first memory of sex with me being stones sticking in your back." He met her gaze. "But I have an idea. If you're game, that is?"

Anne wasn't sure what he had in mind, but she was more than willing to give it a try if it satisfied the ache between her legs. "What did you have in mind?"

"Better yet." He lifted her off his lap. "I'll show you." He picked up her suit and draped it over the fallen log. "Turn around." His hands slid down her arms, then eased her forward until her forearms rested on the thin fabric. His swollen cock rested in the crack of her butt cheeks.

He was going to take her from behind. Another first. A shiver of anticipation tingled through her body and she parted her legs and pressed back against his groin. His hands skimmed over her hips to her pubis, then into the already slick labial lips. He found her clit, sensitized and screaming for more.

He shifted his pole until it burrowed between her legs. He stroked the length of her sex with the tip of his penis. Each time the smooth, warm skin grazed her clit, she arched, pushing back, rocking until she felt the tip at the entrance of her sex. He slipped into the well-lubricated canal, thrusting his hands and her hips. "God, I wanted to take this slow, but..."

A breath-stealing climax rolled through her body, strangled cries of pleasure bursting through her lips and mated with Jason's deep-voiced growl of satisfaction. Her legs went weak as aftershocks rolled through her body. She and was glad that he was holding her hips because her legs wouldn't have supported her.

Jason sucked in a ragged breath, his chest heaving. In the wake of passion, he laid his forehead against her back. Her intimate muscles tightened and relaxed around his shaft. Anne closed her eyes sinking into disbelief. Jason MacIsaac was probably the last person she'd ever expected to have sex with, but never had anything felt more perfect or fulfilling.

"Yes!" Virginia's silent exclamation filled her thoughts. Sensual energy flooded her essence, and she'd barely stopped herself from materializing when Annie and her partner reached the explosive apex of release. She floated on her back, drinking in the last of the sexual energy radiating from them. She watched the couple exchange lazy caresses, then Anne picked up her swimsuit, Jason grinned and took her hand pulling her toward the water before she could put it on. She floated behind them as they strolled across the pebbly beach then dove into the water.

Virginia turned away, fighting both envy and sadness. She'd had many lovers, but only one true love. Only one man had looked at her the same way this man looked at Annie. She'd never had the chance to tell him just how much she loved him before a faceless murderer had stolen her life from her. Annie had to help her set things right, to find her murderer and let her speak to Clay one more time.

"Annie, my girl, this one is definitely a keeper." It was more than just the raw emotion in his eyes when he looked at her. When their energies blended together, it was sweet and powerful. Whether she knew it yet or not, Annie had found her soul mate.

Chapter Five

Several hours later, Anne returned home, exhausted but completely sated. Without turning on any lights, she went straight to her room, then stripped, dropping her clothes on the floor beside her bed. She thought about pulling on a tee shirt, but instead tossed back the puffy comforter and slid her legs between the smooth sheets. All she wanted right now was to sleep.

She glanced at the red digital letters of her alarm clock. "Four thirty-two!" she exclaimed softly.

Anne laid her head on the pillow, her thoughts spinning in spite of her body's fatigue. Could the events of the last twenty-four hours have actually have happened? With a long sigh, she pressed the back of her forearm across her eyes.

"Can this day get any stranger?" she muttered.

"Well, yes, actually, it could, and it's just about to, Annie my girl."

At the sound of a feminine voice responding to her rhetorical question, Anne flung her arm away from her face and bolted upright in the bed. She sucked in a sharp breath at the sight of a semi-transparent figure of a woman with long brown hair who was perched on the footboard of the bed.

"Great," she muttered, closing her eyes and pressing her fingertips to her temples. "Now, I'm seeing things." Anne dropped back on the bed, then whispered, "This is a figment of my over-sexed, over-stressed imagination."

"I'm nothing of the sort! I'm Virginia Marshall... or at least I was thirty years ago."

"Was?" Anne whispered. She peeked through slitted eyes. She could see right through the luminescent figure to the wall and window opposite the foot of her bed. Goose bumps rose over her bare skin.

"I thought about breaking the idea to you that you're sharing a house with a spook gradually, but that just isn't my style." Humor tinted the words. "Sometimes it's better to take the plunge and get the shock over with right at the get go."

Her heart thundering in her ears, Anne shut her eyes then said, "I don't believe in ghosts, spirits or apparitions." The mantra slipped through her lips again. "I don't believe in ghosts. I don't-"

"Then, it's time you did because I'm not leaving here until you help me find my murderer."

Anne opened one eye and then the other. The transparent, luminous form of the woman seated on the end of her bed grinned. Then, the specter's gaze dropped to Anne's bare chest. Realization that she was bare from the waist up prompted her to grab a handful of bedding and pull it up to her armpits. The action earned a hearty chuckle from the specter now floating above the foot of the bed.

"A little late for modesty, don't you think? Besides, we're both women... so there's nothing new in this view."

Denial hung on the tip of Anne's tongue. Surely, there had to be an explanation for the blurry figure facing her.

"Is that lingering skepticism I see in your eyes?" The shimmering figure sighed then folded her arms across her chest. "I guess you need a little more convincing."

"Convincing me that I'm not losing my mind," Anne responded more to herself to the ghost or whatever it was.

"I heard that," the spirit chided. "I might not have a body, but I'm not deaf."

Transparent hands reached forward then snatched the bedding away from her body. It hung in the air in front of her. Anne made a grab for it, only to have it jump out of her reach.

"Parlor tricks," she accused, still clinging to denial, but more convinced than she was willing to admit.

"You didn't complain about my parlor tricks when you were getting laid by the muscle-bound blond." A smug grin formed on her lips. "Or the hunky banker. Who really is a keeper by the way."

"What?" Anne went still. She swallowed hard.

"You heard me." The woman drifted closer, then floated to a spot on the edge of the bed facing her. She extended a ghostly hand toward the necklace. "I was so weak all I could do was turn up the heat a bit. But, that seemed to be enough."

The necklace rose from her chest, suspended between a ghostly forefinger and thumb.

"So, did you take possession of my body or something?" Perhaps that would explain her uncharacteristically wanton behavior.

"Girl, I planted a few lusty thoughts, then backed off. You were a pretty quick study in that department." She grinned. "But then, with the primed Viking wannabe, you had plenty of inspiration, and the delicious banker-boy was the perfect ending to the day."

The spirit withdrew her hand and the charm fell to Anne's breastbone with a light tap. Anne sucked in a breath, her head spinning.

"I know you are having trouble accepting the fact that you are talking to a ghost, but the sooner you do the better – for both of us." Virginia *sat* on the side of the bed facing her and hugged her knees to her chest in a very human gesture. "I was never one to beat around the bush when I was alive, and I'm certainly not going to start now. Thirty years ago, I was murdered, and I need you to help me find my killer, so that I can pass over to the spirit realm." The specter shook her head. "I can't believe I'm saying this. For so long I didn't want to let go, but it's time. But I can't as long as I have an anchor here. I think it has something to do with the necklace, but I'm not exactly sure how."

Anne felt like she'd just been transported into a scene from a movie, a two-bit thriller. "Okay, for the moment, let's say I believe you really are a ghost and I'm not delusional. Why would you need me to help you find a killer? Don't you know who killed you?"

"The coward hit me from behind, so I never saw them. I drifted in and out of consciousness a couple of times, but by then I was in the dark and couldn't see anything at all. The next thing I knew, I was a ghost."

A shudder rippled down Anne's spine at the image of the body in the storage room of her basement. Her words confirmed what the coroner had said.

"What did you say your name was?"

"Virginia Marshall."

Why did the name sound so familiar? "Wait a minute. I bought the house from someone named Virginia Marshall. Is she a relation of yours?"

The specter shook her head. "Not a chance. I'm the only child of older, only children. My parents were both gone by the time I turned twenty-seven, and I didn't have any children of my own."

Anne exhaled a long slow breath, rubbing the tips of her thumb and first finger over her gritty eyes. In spite of the initial adrenalin rush at the first sight of the spirit, the day and event-filled night were catching up with her. "So, someone bumped you off and stole your identity?"

The ghost nodded. "That's it in a nutshell."

Anne leaned back against the headboard, bringing the comforter with her. "Who would want to kill you?"

Virginia rolled her eyes and shrugged. "If I knew, then I wouldn't need your help. I led a rather hedonistic, self-centered life, but I didn't knowingly hurt anyone. I didn't have any enemies."

"That you know of," Anne inserted.

"True," Virginia conceded. "But I had more than my fair share of friends... especially the male variety."

"Then, why would anyone kill you?"

"Greed."

"Greed?"

"When my parents died, I inherited an indecent amount of money. My father was always taking out patents on his inventions. One of them ended up being worth a lot of money."

Anne covered her mouth and tried to stifle a yawn, but failed. "So, maybe the person who killed you might have been a stranger who simply broke into your house."

"Unlikely. I'm almost positive it had to be someone who knew me, who knew my habits and had something to gain." The ghost pursed her lips, a crevice forming between slender, arched brows. "Besides, having the supplies and time to brick me into the closet in the cellar certainly suggests premeditation."

Sobered by the images taking form in her mind, Anne nodded, unsure of what to say when it was obvious this ghost, Virginia, thought that someone close to her might have been the one responsible for her death. Anne's eyelids drooped, and she blinked them open.

"Look, why don't you catch a few z's, and we'll start to work in the morning," Virginia said, moving to the end of the bed again.

"Sounds like a plan," Anne responded, fatigue making her voice husky. She closed her eyes. "Please let this all be a figment of my imagination," she murmured under her breath, hoping the morning wouldn't bring any more surprises or hallucinations.

"Not a chance, Annie, my girl. Not a chance. You're stuck with me."

Chapter Six

"Wake up sleepy head!"

"Deb, go away." Anne groaned, pulled the covers over her head. Her first thought was that she should never have given Deb a spare key. Her second was that she could smell bacon cooking.

She pushed the covers off her face and came face to face with a luminescent face of a woman. She squawked out her surprise, sleep falling away and the bizarre events of last night flashed in instant replay in her mind. Instead of her incorrigible friend, she looked up into the shimmering features of the specter she'd thought she imagined last night.

"Good morning," Virginia said with a grin. "Hunky banker boy will be here in half an hour for the brunch you promised him. It was right after you had the sex in the water and before he—." Virginia grinned.

Anne gulped in a deep gasp of air. "Oh, God. I should have set my alarm..."

The covers rolled away from her body without the aid of visible hands. "Virginia!"

"That's my name," the laughing luminous figure quipped. "And if you don't want your stud to catch you in the shower, you'd better get your butt out of bed." She floated to a prone position three feet off the ground, then grinned. "Perhaps that isn't such a bad idea. Water sliding over those delicious pecs does have a certain appeal. He could make Adonis weep from envy."

"You're as bad as Deb," Anne chided, but without censure. The sense of the bizarre was fading. And she was starting to enjoy the exchange.

"You bet!"

Anne swung her legs over the side of the bed and headed for the ensuite. She paused at the threshold and turned back. "If you've been haunting the place for so long, why didn't you appear when I first moved in?"

"I couldn't. I know this is going to sound strange, but I was too weak."

"So, how does a ghost recharge their spooking batteries?"

Virginia rolled her eyes, but didn't comment. "It depends on the ghost. For me, it was sexual energy."

Anne blinked. "But you don't have a body to have sex."

"Not me, silly." Virginia floated toward her, then by her into the bathroom. "You."

"Me? Specifically me, or just anyone?"

Transparent fingers lifted the pendant from around her neck. "I think it's whoever is wearing the necklace." Virginia dropped the pendant and grasped Anne's shoulders.

A pleasant tingling sensation skimmed across her skin where Virginia had placed her hands.

"This necklace binds us together. As long as you wear it, you can see me, and your energy gives me strength."

Anne looked into Virginia's eyes and knew that she had to help her. For all her brash talk and over appreciation for sex, there was something in her eyes, a sadness, which touched Anne. "My energy? Are you some kind of personal energy vampire?"

"Nothing like that. From what I've been able to tell. There is a tremendous burst of energy generated when people climax. The more often you and hunky banker boy climax, the stronger I get. At the rate you're going, I'll soon be invincible." Laughter danced in dark eyes.

Anne could feel an answering grin tug at the corners of her lips. If her house had to be haunted, at least it was a lusty ghost with a sense of humor and not one trying to drive her out of the house.

"I've got to scoot," Virginia said. "Or breakfast will be ruined."

The shimmering specter vanished, and Anne shook her head. Before she bought this house, her life had been mundane and downright boring.

"It certainly isn't any more," she whispered, then twisted the faucets. If she thought yesterday was remarkable, she had a feeling today would be as well. She washed quickly. "You deserve to be sore after yesterday," she murmured when she rubbed the cloth across her pubis, but she was glad that she wasn't.

By the time she'd finished her shower, Anne had decided against a bra. Virginia might be making breakfast, but she had a feeling Jason would be providing dessert. Her blouse allowed a hint of a shadow of her nipples to show through, and she put on a silky summer skirt that rippled around her calves. She looked in the mirror and was startle by the vibrant woman looking back at her. Her green eyes sparkled, and a smile played on her lips. Even her hair seemed to have a new luster.

"Everything's ready," Virginia said from behind her.

Anne jumped and swung around.

"Sorry, I didn't mean to startle you, but this has been fun. I didn't realize how much I..." Her words faltered and her expression sobered. "I didn't realize how much I missed entertaining until you moved in. For so long, I vented my anger and frustration at being killed before I'd had a chance to live. I terrorized anyone who dared venture into my home. Now, it's starting to feel like our home."

Anne's heart contracted in sympathy. "We'll find out who killed you and set things right." The promise surprised Anne. Her life had rested solidly in the mundane until just two days ago. Taking up residence here had shown her Virginia wasn't the only person missing out on life, but at least she had the chance to change her life while she could still do something about it.

"Hustle, hustle, girl." Virginia said with a grin, there's a sporty little vehicle pulling into the driveway.

"What are you a psychic as well as a spook?" Anne teased.

She shook her head and pointed to the window.

Anne made it to the foot of the stairs before the doorbell rang. She saw Jason's silhouette in the frosted glass window of the door. Her heart skipped a beat in anticipation. Why couldn't she have met him first instead of Mark? But then, if she had, she might not truly appreciate him or the feelings he shared. His openness had surprised, even disconcerted, her at first, but now his declarations of love enveloped her like a warm blanket.

Her own feelings were a little jumbled. As a sexual partner, he sated her completely. She was already in lust with him. Anne grinned. Could she fall in love with him as well? It was a definite possibility. For now, however, she would take this blossoming relationship day by day and not worry about a future, only savor each moment. She grinned. "Deb, you would be proud of me."

She gripped the antique glass doorknob and opened the door, her heart racing and her breath quick. No matter how undecided she was about her feelings for Jason, the thought of seeing him again made her very happy and a little shy even though he'd seen, touched, and tasted parts of her body in ways no one else had.

"Hi," she said, opening the door wide and stepping back. "Everything's almost ready."

His slow smile and the affection in his eyes melted any lingering reservations she had about seeing him again. He cupped her face and leaned forward, brushing his lips across hers, lightly at first, then more deliberately.

"You know, I have a confession to make," he said with a grin. "After you broke up with Mark, I was planning a not so accidental meeting, but I like the way things worked out better."

"I do, too." Anne reached up and slid her hand along his jaw, smooth, and freshly shaven. In less than twenty-four hours, he'd slipped into her life and body in ways Mark never had in all the weeks they'd been together. She was glad Mark hadn't touched her like that. Perhaps Virginia had helped or perhaps her experience with Sam contributed, but whatever the reason, sex with Jason felt as normal, and as necessary, as breathing.

"Stop making gah-gah eyes at lover body or my lovely breakfast will burn," Virginia exclaimed as she appeared at her elbow.

Anne started, startled by Virginia's protest.

Jason quirked an eyebrow. "Are you all right?"

"Fine." Anne gave a soft laugh. "I almost forgot about brunch."

"That's good," he said with a grin. "I'd like to think I can distract you."

"He's a delicious distraction," Virginia interjected, now lying on her side, her ghostly head resting on her hand, level with Jason's shoulder. "I could turn up the heat." She turned and started to blow in his ear.

"No!" Anne exclaimed. At a quizzical look from Jason, she added, "I know exactly what you mean." She looped her arm though his and led him from the foyer to the kitchen. "I mean, I hope I can be a distraction as well."

Jason stopped abruptly on the threshold of the kitchen doorway. "Wow!" he said. "When you said you were going to make brunch, I wasn't expecting a feast."

Anne's jaw dropped at the elegantly set table. Cinnamon buns and muffins were piled in pyramids on delicate china. Orange juice filled a crystal pitcher. Matching goblets sat at each perfectly appointed place setting. Where on earth did all the beautiful dishes and silverware come from? Could spirits conjure as well as create havoc? "I wanted to surprise you."

Hopefully, Virginia didn't have any more surprises in store for her, but she expected she might. Anne glanced at the grinning ghost now standing by the stove, raised her eyebrows, then glanced toward the table silently asking where she'd found all this.

"Sex toys aren't the only thing I stored in the attic. This was my grandmother's stuff." The specter's expression sobered. "I was a gourmet chef by training, though I didn't have to work for a living. Grammy always expected me to put all her fancy dishes to good use when I married."

A familiar ache squeezed her heart. Virginia lost so much when the faceless murderer stole her life from her. Anne vowed to live every day to the fullest and to take risks she never would have before, including those with her heart.

"Earth to Annie," Jason said. "Is everything okay? That's the second time you drifted away."

"Sorry, I'm a little sleepy."

"Did you sleep at all?" He looked toward the table. "This must have taken hours."

"Like a log. You wore me out," she teased.

He laughed. Anne marveled how much she loved the sound, the deep rumbling in his chest, so completely male. Her father had left when she was a toddler, so she grew up with her mother and grandmother that had soured on the male race.

"Girl, brunch is going to burn if you don't rescue it."

"I'd better get breakfast out of the oven," Anne said, reaching for the oven mitts. She lowered the door then leaned over. There was a rectangular, glass casserole on the middle rack filled with an egg mixture, dotted with slivers of green onion, and bits of bacon, and splashes of orange from the cheese. "This looks delicious!"

"You sound surprised," Jason observed.

Virginia laughed. "Get out of that one."

"It's the first time I've… made it."

"It's a baked bacon-cheese frittata."

"It's a baked bacon-cheese frittata," Anne echoed, then lifted the glass pan from the oven carrying it to the table.

"Aren't you going to offer the poor man coffee?" Virginia waved a hand toward the coffee maker on the counter with a full carafe. "Or perhaps you want to start with a piece of that delicious bod."

"Coffee?" Color creeping along her cheeks, Anne pulled two mugs from the cupboard. "Cream and sugar?"

"Black and sweet," Jason said, standing beside her. From behind, he put his hands on her waist then dropped a light kiss on her neck on the sensitive spot below her earlobe.

Anne let go of the handle of the glass carafe, then turned. "If you keep doing that I'm going to pour the coffee all over the counter." She inhaled the earthy scent of his soap encircling her and felt the heat of his body. Never had she been more aware of pure male virility. Her nipples pinched, poking against the fine fabric of her blouse. The soft cotton of her blouse rubbing against the tight nubs of flesh made her breasts ache for the touch of his hands.

"If you keep looking at me like that I won't care about coffee, or anything but burying myself in you."

She followed his gaze to the needy peaks. It was as if her breasts were reaching out, begging for his touch. She raked her teeth over her lower lip. Why couldn't she control her reaction to him? Was it because of Virginia? Or had she really unearthed a new, sensual side of her personality.

"But it would be a shame to waste this lovely breakfast." He slid his hands under her blouse, cupping her breasts with his hands. He circled the wrinkled areolas with the pad of his thumb. "Besides, anticipation will only add to the pleasure later."

"If you keep doing that," she murmured, pressing her breasts into his hands. "I won't care about breakfast or anything but having wild sex on the nearest flat service."

"Over my dead... er... vaporous body!" Virginia protested. "I spent hours preparing this meal." She started to pull the carafe from the coffee maker.

Anne grasped the handle and straightened. The mood momentarily shattered. "How about some coffee?"

Jason blinked. "Ah... sure." The confusion reflected in his eyes.

Taking a couple of breaths, Anne filled two mugs. "There you go." She handed them to him. "Would you put these on the table?" As soon as his back was turned, she mouthed the words 'go away' to the shimmering specter floating in the middle of the kitchen.

Anne slipped on the mitts, then picked up the casserole and turned. The heat from the casserole seeped through a thin spot in the oven mitts, searing her hand. In a knee jerk reaction, she released the dish, and it slipped through her hands. At her soft cry of alarm, Jason turned.

"No," Virginia cried and dove for the casserole, diving for it like a runner for the home plate. Transparent hands caught it and righted it before it tipped the contents on to the ceramic tile floor.

The casserole drifted over to the table.

"What the hell?" Jason exclaimed, a deep crevice between his brows as it settled on the trivet.

How was she going to explain this? Nothing she could think of could explain the casseroles near plunge and then flight to the table. Perhaps the truth was the best, even though she wasn't sure how he would react. This certainly would be the acid test of their relationship. They'd had amazing sex, sizzling chemistry, but would it be too much to thrust Virginia's tale on him as well?

"Anne, did that casserole just stop mid-air and then float over to the table?"

She nodded. "When I dropped it Virginia... she's a ghost who lives here... caught it and took it to the table."

"A ghost?" He scrubbed his hand across his face. "Are you trying to tell me this place is haunted?"

"You remember I told you that we found a body in the basement yesterday."

He nodded.

"Well, it belonged to Virginia Marshall, the previous owner of the house. She was murdered, and her body was walled up in the cold room. She can't cross over to wherever spirits go until she finds out who killed her." The words rushed out before she lost her courage.

Skepticism glinted in hazel eyes. Anne swallowed hard. Why couldn't she have at least had some time together before she shared Virginia's existence?

"Let me show him," Virginia said, gliding toward him.

"Virginia!" Anne watched her pick up a cinnamon bun, then another, and waved in front of his nose.

Jason jerked back, the surprise in his expression turning darker. "What kind of parlor trick is this? Some kind of hypnosis?"

"Hypnosis!" Virginia snorted, then picked up a muffin, juggling the three items in the air in front of his nose. "What I wouldn't give for a few chains to rattle! But then I'd probably wrap it around his unbelieving throat."

His gaze moved from the food floating in front of him to Anne. Uncertainty replaced the irritation.

"No tricks, Jason. I wouldn't have believed it myself if I hadn't seen her."

"You've seen her?" Skepticism laced every carefully enunciated word.

In that instant, Anne knew she'd lost him. "Virginia please put the food down. It's hard to concentrate with you waving those things around."

The transparent figure dropped them on the table then drifted toward Jason.

"Give me a few minutes, and I'll make a believer of him."

"Leave him alone!" Anne warned. She didn't think Virginia would hurt him, but she didn't want him scared or traumatized.

"I suppose you are talking to the ghost." Jason folded muscular arms across his chest. "Okay, let's just suppose for a minute that the house really is haunted, and she's here. Get her to show herself to me."

"Only the person in possession of the necklace can see her." Inspiration struck. She lifted the chain of the necklace from around her neck and pressed it against his palm and then curled his fingers around it.

"Hi, Jason." Virginia lifted her hand and wiggled her fingers at Jason glad that Annie had tried letting him hold the necklace. He was perfect for her, and she didn't want to be the reason he bolted. "I'm Virginia Marshall."

He sucked in a deep breath, his eyes wide as they focused on her.

"Actually, I think Anne would have preferred to wait for a bit to tell you about me, if ever, but now it's done, why don't we get to know each other?

Jason blinked, then looked around the room. "This is a joke, right? Where are the mirrors?"

"I can see you are going to be as hard to convince as Annie." She drew a transparent finger from his crotch to his waistband. He gasped at the bold caress and jerked back. "Need more proof?" She undid the button and pulled the zipper down over his semi-aroused penis. "Nice package! Loads of potential."

"Virginia!" Anne protested as she took a step toward him.

Virginia slipped her hand into his boxers and curled her hand around his half-aroused cock and stroked, drawing it out through the slit in his boxers as it began to swell. "Very nice indeed."

"What the hell?" he gasped his voice raspy. He looked down, shaking his head. "This can't be."

"Jason, I'm sorry. Virginia, stop this instant." Anne didn't need to be able to see her to know what Virginia was doing as she watched Jason's penis emerge from his pants.

"Hold out your hand," Jason said. "Virginia has an idea."

"Virginia has too many ideas if you ask me," Anne muttered, then held out her hand in spite of her misgivings. "They aren't all good ones."

He looped the chain around her wrist while he held onto the pendant. Instantly, Virginia was visible.

"Can you see her?" he asked.

She nodded. "So, you a believer now?

"I guess so." He looked down at his aroused penis sticking upright from his body, a clear drop of pre-cum forming at the slit of the helmet-shaped head. "It's hard to deny the evidence."

Relief flowed through her.

"How about breakfast before it gets cold?" Virginia interjected.

"How can you think about food at a time like this?" Anne asked.

"I invested too much time in it to let it go to waste."

"Virginia made all this? How?" Jason enquired. "It's one thing to feel a person up, but to grasp solid objects..." His voice trailed away.

"I'm not one hundred percent sure, but I'd bet it has something to do with sex." The words slipped out before she could stop them.

"I beg your pardon?"

Anne repeated what Virginia had said about gaining energy from sexual climaxes.

"And you two were better than a nuclear generator," she said with a grin. "Potent or what!"

Anne watched ruddy color wash across Jason's cheeks, mentally chiding the irrepressible spirit. "Virginia, do you have to be so blunt?"

"It was a compliment"

Jason shook his head, a lop-sided smile playing on his lips. "I take it death hasn't dulled your appetite for sex."

"Maybe my appetite, but not my interest. If you eat up, I'll show you how to get to the playroom. You might enjoy some of the toys. I'll go tidy the attic up a bit while you eat. It's collected a bit of dust in the last thirty years."

She vanished, and Jason released the pendant. He exhaled slowly, shaking his head from side to side. "I'm still trying to wrap my head around the fact that ghosts exist. She's a spirited spirit."

"That's for sure."

Anne looked at his arousal still standing out from his body, moisture pooling along the crack of her sex.

He followed her gaze and offered a rueful grin. "I guess he'll have to wait for a bit." He pushed his cock back inside his pants, wincing as he tugged up the zipper. "I don't want to see what she'd do if we didn't eat this breakfast."

"Probably something that we would enjoy," Anne replied, feeling more relaxed, almost light-hearted. It had to be a reaction to the tension of the last few minutes.

He pulled out a chair, and Anne sat, then he took the seat beside her. "You said Virginia was murdered? Who killed her and what does she expect you to do about it?"

She took the cloth napkin and spread it across her knee. "She doesn't know. The killer hit her from behind. That's why she needs me to help her find her killer, then she can pass over to wherever spirits go."

"That sounds dangerous. If he or she has killed once, what's to stop her from killing you?" he said.

"I hadn't really thought about the logistics. I've just been trying to get used to the idea that I'm sharing my home with a precocious spirit." Anne cut a square of the breakfast casserole, put it on Jason's plate, then cut another and put it on a plate for her, hungry for food as well as for him.

Jason gave a soft laugh. "That she is."

They were just finishing up their meal when Virginia materialized.

"Okay, people, time to play!"

Chapter Seven

"Follow me!"

"Virginia says to follow her." Anne looked at Jason, wondering what Virginia had in store for them. Whatever it was, it would probably be lewd, and laced with awesome sex. Their eyes met and a mischievous spark danced in his eyes. He looped his baby finger around the chain and glanced in Virginia's direction.

"Lead the way!" With his other hand, he drew Anne away from the table. "Time to play," he murmured. "I think I'm really beginning to like your ghost."

Anne's body tingled with anticipation as they climbed the stairs and followed the flowing specter to her bedroom, then into the large walk in closet.

Virginia pointed to a panel with a triquetra engraved into the wood. "Push this one, it will unlatch the door."

Jason reached over Anne's shoulder and gave the square of wood a push, and they heard a click, then it swung open. He glanced over his shoulder before he stepped forward.

"The light switch is over here. I took the liberty of turning it on for you." She drifted up the stairs. "Most of the time we used candles, but every once in a while this was more convenient."

Anne stepped through the doorway and found herself at the bottom of a polished, wood staircase. The banister and railings were carved and gleaming. Not the normal bare, rough wood staircase she'd expected.

"After you," Jason said, then pressed his palm against the small of her back.

She climbed the stairs, not knowing what to expect, but judging from the mischievous look in Virginia's eyes, it wouldn't be tame. At the top, she paused, allowing her eyes to adjust to the subtle lighting. Stained glass windows muted the midday sunlight.

Instead of bare rafters, wood polished to a satiny shine covered the ceiling and walls. Anne turned on her heel, scanning the elegant space. Alcoves lined the walls. She squinted trying to figure out what the strange tables and other contraptions residing in each inset area were for.

"My God," Jason murmured. "This is exactly like the Inner Sanctum at the Chrysalis on a smaller scale."

The Chrysalis. The Inner Sanctum was for privileged members only – an ability to pay was only a part of the admission. There was an interview as well. Mark hadn't passed muster. Anne wasn't a surprise that Jason was a member of such an exclusive club. He had an inner finesse that Mark lacked. Only she hadn't experienced or understood it until now.

"The Chrysalis? Clay Montgomery's club is still in business?" Virginia swung around in a sparkling lavender mist.

"Still in business? It's thriving," Jason answered. "He owns clubs in several cities now."

"Clay always was determined to make a success of his club. I'm happy for him." Virginia skimmed over the floor and pointed to the first alcove, in a not-so-subtle move to change the topic.

The shimmering lavender haze dissolved and returned to Virginia's normal opalescent glow. The resident ghost might be transparent, but she wasn't good at hiding her emotions. The mention of the Chrysalis and Clay Montgomery had affected her. Anne made a mental note to ask Virginia about Clay later.

Anne turned and looked at the first alcove, closest to the top of the stairs, which resembled a super-sized closet with an organizer.

Virginia grinned, but there was a melancholy in her eyes that hinted she wasn't quite over the emotions the mention of Clay's name had evoked. "We called this the Attic Club. Members left their clothes here, before going any further." With a sweeping gesture, she indicated toward the floor. An inlaid strip of mahogany in the hardwood interrupted the honey colored wood. "No clothes were allowed beyond this point."

She crossed her arms and tapped her foot.

"You don't actually expect us to undress," Anne protested, suddenly feeling shy, which seemed hypocritical after yesterday. Yes, with the dawn of a new day, some of her shyness had returned.

"It's not like you haven't seen each other naked."

"True," Anne replied. "But stripping in the heat of the moment is different than... this." In the daylight, when she wasn't burning up with lust, it was harder to peel away her clothes and toss aside inhibitions.

"It's easier than you think, Anne. I'll start," Jason said, as he peeled his tee shirt over his head, baring a muscular plane shadowed by brown whorls of hair.

"Virginia," she whispered, then scanned the area, but her ghostly companion was nowhere to be seen.

Jason cupped her face. "Forget her. I can. Let me give you a tour."

"You've done this before." Anne grasped the top button of her blouse, her fingers fumbling as she watched him open his jeans and slip them over his hips, exposing revealing skimpy briefs

"A time or two," Jason said with a smile. "Let me help." He undid the top button of her blouse, then traced the small v opening with a fingertip before he slid his hands along the fabric to the next one. It popped open, exposing the pale curve of her breasts. He did the last three buttons one right after the other, then drew a line with his fingertip from the flat plain of her breastbone, in the valley between her breasts, then over the soft curve of her stomach. Her skin seemed to come alive, sending tingles along every nerve ending in her body. Her areolas tightened as need weighted her breasts, heat and pressure pooled at the apex of her thighs.

He smiled then slid his hands under the cotton fabric, pushing it aside, exposing the aroused mounds of flesh. His hands drifted upward and pushed the garment off her shoulders. As the shirt slid down her arms, his hands followed, skimming over her arms. Instead of feeling awkward, his touch freed her from her inhibitions and the tenderness warming his eyes melted any remaining reservations. She looked up and smiled.

"See," he murmured, drawing his fingertips down the side of her face. "Now, wasn't that easy?" He looked at his briefs pulled tight over his swollen organ. "Why don't you give me a hand?"

"I guess I should return the favor." Anne slipped her fingers inside the elastic of his underwear, and then tugged it down. His penis bounced, standing away from his body and rising from a nest of brown curls.

On his groin, just above the coarse pubic hair, was a tattoo in the shape of a triquetra - the same sign that was on Virginia's necklace and on the wood panel of the door to the attic. He took her finger and traced the design, his swollen shaft twitched. "This provides your admittance to the Inner Sanctum."

He picked up their clothes and folded them, then slid them onto a shelf in the closet alcove. He laced his fingers in hers, then drew her forward to the next alcove.

"The first and only time you stop at this alcove is during your first visit."

The rounded, wood-paneled walls rose to a dome ceiling. In the centre was a low table, and beside it a chair on wheels. "Let's pretend it's your first night. Lay down."

"Okay."

He sat in the chair and pulled open a drawer under the narrow upholstered bed. "Amazing."

"What?"

"Everything is an exact replica of the Inner Sanctum suite, just scaled down a bit."

"So you do you think that Virginia based her Attic Club on the Inner Sanctum."

"Or vice versa. IS has been around for about three decades."

Anne couldn't believe she was lying naked on a table, having a conversation about the history of the most notorious members' only club in the city. "So, what happened here that you could do only once?"

"This is where a tattoo artist would give you the Chrysalis mark. A mark given to only a favored few."

Anne's gaze dropped to his groin. "It must have hurt."

"A bit." He leaned over and traced the symbol on the side of her breast. "A woman would have her mark placed here."

The light touch started heated hunger simmering deep inside her. She looked into his eyes and heat flared in their deep brown depths.

He stood up, and extended his hand toward her. "From here, you can go anywhere you want to."

She grasped his hand and got off the table. Her gaze traveled from the tanned skin stretched over his thigh muscles, to the smooth plain of his abdomen, and then to the rippling muscles of his chest – each a testament to hours spent in the gym. But most intriguing to her, were the whorls of hair on his chest. She stroked the small curls with her fingertips. Dime sized, dark brown nipples puckered.

He didn't attempt to stop her but allowed her to explore the dips and planes of his chest. This slow exploration was so different than her experiences the day before. Then, a heady, wanton hunger had been the driving force behind her actions. This time, a newly awakening passion drew from a deeper well, stealing her breath as she lifted her gaze and met his. From the first time her body had rippled around his in climax, she'd felt a connection. A connection that was growing stronger with each look and every touch.

"In the Chrysalis, each club member can reserve an alcove, sometimes

two. I'm not sure if that's what they did here, but the toys are the same."
This alcove had leather cuffs hung from a metal bar suspended on a thick
wire. Below, in the floor large metal rings different widths apart were
imbedded into the floor. On the walls and shelves were a variety of whips,
chains, wooden paddles and several items Anne couldn't identify, and
probably didn't want to.

"I usually skip this one. I'm not into pain; pleasure is my aim for
both me and my partner."

"Have you had many partners?" Insecurity reared an ugly head. Was
she only a passing infatuation, wooed by words of love?

"My fair share, and enough to know when I found the real thing." He
cupped her face and kissed her, touching and teasing with his lips until
tension eased. "And I'm not going to let you go easily now that I've found
you." There was a predatory note in his voice she'd never heard before.
Behind the tender foreplay, she sensed and an iron will.

"Jason..." She held up her hand, and he pressed his fingertips against
her lips, stalling any more words.

"I know I'm pushing, probably harder than is wise, but I'll try to
give you some space if you really need it." His grin was rueful. "But
probably not a lot."

"You are pushing, but I think I can push back if I need to," Anne said
and realized the words were true. The last few days had changed her. She
felt like a blossom reacting to the warm of the spring sun.

He placed his fingertips against her lower back directed her to the
next alcove. "Now, this is a favorite of mine."

Anne looked at the semi-circular space. In the center of the room,
below the domed ceiling a poster bed stood in the middle of a plush,
Persian carpet. "Okay, I'll bite. This looks like an ordinary bed."

"Appearances can be deceiving." His slow sexy smile made promises
she wasn't sure he could keep. "This is probably one of the most versatile
and comfortable alcoves," he said quietly as he grasped her waist and
lowered her into the center of the bed. "Lay back and relax."

Relax. Her pulse was skipping beats and a demanding pressure was
building in her sex. She rested on her elbows, her legs bent at the knees,
her torso turned toward him. Jason took two small leather cuffs from a
large collection on one wall. As he approached, she rolled to her back.

"Do you trust me?" he asked.

Did she? Yes. But that didn't mean she didn't feel a little apprehensive about what was going to happen.

Anne nodded. He took the cuffs lined with sheep's wool and buckled them around her wrists.

"Up just a bit," he said, she looked over her shoulder as he flipped open a small door on one side of the headboard then pulled out a large metal eye on a short chain.

She inched upward, her breath accelerated, from both nerves and anticipation. "I take it this isn't your average bed."

"Not really," he said with a laugh, then leaned over and popped open another little door with a matching chain.

He lifted her arms above her head and hooked them to large metal eyes on either side of the headboard. Anne tugged at the restraints. They didn't hurt her, but they held her fast.

He returned to the wall and took two more leather straps. Anne wondered if they were intended for her ankles. His eyes held her gaze prisoner as he separated her legs creating a sensual v. He clipped the ankle cuffs to chains attached to the footboard.

"Still trusting me?" He leaned one knee on the bed. His liquid chocolate gaze captured hers.

Anne nodded. The air seemed to thin as she drew in a tremulous breath.

"Even though you're completely at my mercy?" As if to prove the point, he traced one of his fingertips along her collarbones to the base of her throat, then through the valley between her breasts, drawing a figure eight around the soft, eager globes before continuing downward. The fine line he was drawing with his finger sent shivers of anticipation all over her body.

He circled her belly button, then took a twisting path through the sable curls of her pubis. If her legs hadn't already been spread-eagle, she would have definitely moved them apart so he could have access to intimate parts.

Anne tipped her hips, hoping to encourage him to explore further.

"Impatient are we?" he murmured as he climbed onto the bed to kneel between her legs.

"I thought guys liked to hurry," Anne whispered, her voice husky.

"Sometimes." He leaned over and drew his hands down the length of her arms, around the curves of her breasts and lower until they trailed through the soft curls covering her mound. When they skimmed over the sensitive skin of her inner thighs, she dug her teeth into her lower lip.

Her skin felt alive, rippling with reaction. "I can't believe how amazing that feels." Inwardly, Anne winced. Her words sounded so trite, so adolescent. If he thought so, nothing reflected in his gaze.

Anne she tested the leather straps holding her legs apart as she had the wrist restraints. For the first time in her life, she was bound and helpless.

Without a word, he leaned over, taking a screamingly sensitive nipple in his mouth and sucked. She arched, gasping, bombarded by sensations, and the ache between her legs grew more demanding. His tongue circled then laved her nipple. Anne closed her eyes and pressed her head into the pillow, each sensual tug felt as if it was connected to the primal core of her desire deep inside her.

Jason's shaft rested against the folds of her sex. Unconsciously, she lifted her hips, the soft moist folds separating and stroking the base of his pole, spreading her own juices on his body.

"Hmm, impatient are we?" He licked the nipple still shiny and moist. "Didn't you know that anticipation heightens the pleasure?"

"It's frustrating the heck out of me," she growled.

He laughed and then took the other nipple in his mouth, and a mew of satisfaction slid through her lips.

"Not much longer my impatient little minx," he said, sitting back between her legs.

He looked at her sex, then separated the labial lips. Instinctively Anne tried to draw her legs together. No one had ever inspected her there so openly. With her hands and feet bound, she felt exposed and vulnerable – afraid and excited all at the same time.

He leaned over and inhaled, his face only inches from her pubis. "You smell divine and you taste…" He licked the length of her crack. "…even better."

His tongue circled her clit then he teased the sensitive nub. Her hips lifted, and she strained to open her legs as wide as the restrains allowed.

Anne could feel her heartbeat pulsing in her crotch, building the aching pressure that demanded satisfaction. A needy ache screamed for him to push himself deep inside her. "I'm not sure I like being tied up like this," she whimpered. "You're driving me crazy."

"You can think about your revenge when we switch places." He offered a lopsided smile before he lowered his head to tease her intimately with his talented mouth.

"If you keep that up, I'm going to come," Annie warned, wondering what it would be like to tie him up like this. What would she do? She still had a lot to learn about real foreplay and satisfying a partner.

He lifted his head. "We can't have that. At least... not yet."

"What?" she gasped, blinking in disbelief. "Don't stop now."

"When you come, I want to be inside," he murmured, positioning the head of his penis against her opening, gently nudging it into the folds, sliding slowly inside her. Anne strained against the restraints, lifting her hips as high as she could when he pulled back. She tightened intimate muscles around him.

He sucked in a quick breath covered her with his body as he thrust deeper. "Playing dirty?"

"Playing to win," she quipped.

"Annie, you'll always win," he murmured, then kissed her. Muscles bunched as he thrust into her.

Their bodies met and Anne gasped from the wave of pleasure stealing her breath. She strained against her bonds, wishing she could wrap her legs around him. He plunged, faster and deeper, until she cried out with each stroke.

Like fireworks, exploding inside her, the climax hit. Anne arched, her arms pulling hard on the restraints, her whole body shuddering with the release. "Oh, God, Jason!" she sobbed as she sank into the mattress, dizzy and gasping for breath.

When she could finally catch her breath, she kissed his shoulder awed by the intensity of the aftershocks squeezing his shaft. "I've never experienced anything like that before."

"Annie, you are just entering a whole new world of experiences. Today barely scratched the surface."

"Maybe next time I won't be so impatient," she said. "This is so new. There are times when I look at you and can't believe what is happening between us."

"I can't believe it happened so soon." He rolled to one side then undid her hands and feet. "But I planned to do everything in my power to make it happen."

Without hesitation, she turned snuggling up against the length of his body, a post-climactic lethargy weighting her limbs. She closed her eyes and murmured, "When will it be my turn to tie you up?"

"Soon," he said in a sleepy whisper.

Chapter Eight

Anne woke up, only then realizing she'd fallen asleep. Under her ear, she could hear the slow and steady beat of Jason's heart. His chest rose and fell in a regular, sleepy rhythm.

"It's about time you woke up!" Virginia growled, then offered a rueful grin. "But then again, I'd probably need to sleep off a climax like that too."

"Virginia!" Anne chided in a whisper. "Couldn't have given us a little privacy?"

"Girl, I wasn't anywhere near you. The energy you and wonder boy created shot through me like a bolt of lightning. That's not a complaint. Every contribution is gratefully received."

It was Anne's turn to grin. Her life was in dramatic metamorphosis. She wasn't exactly sure where she'd end up, but she had a feeling she was going to enjoy the ride.

"Annie, why not give Jason a taste of his own medicine or just taste him. I'm sure there are some cuffs that would fit him on the wall." She grinned. "I'll see you later."

"Why not?" Anne eased away from his relaxed body. Even in his sleep, he protested her moving out of his embrace. She collected the fleece-lined cuffs Virginia had pointed to before she disappeared and then Anne quietly returned to the bed. She fastened the cuffs around his wrists, gently lifting each arm until she could hook them to the headboard.

She worked faster buckling them around his ankles as he muttered in his sleep. She knew the minute he regained consciousness, his eyes flew open and he jerked against the restraints.

Anne sat beside him, grinning.

"I guess I underestimated you."

"I'm a quick learner, and Virginia gave me a few pointers."

"Now, I'm getting worried," he teased, the humor in his voice contradicting his words.

Anne swung her leg over his body, straddling his abdomen, not exactly sure what she was going to do with him. For the most part, the male body was uncharted territory. Although it was true she'd lived with Mark for several weeks, and she'd had sex with him, she'd never been able to relax enough with his nudity or her own to explore his body at her leisure, to really learn the ins and outs of what a man enjoyed. Not that he'd ever encouraged her. Once they were naked, all he'd ever wanted was sex.

"I don't really know much about a man's body," Anne said honestly. "I think I'd just like to figure out what you like and what turns you on."

Jason's smile and the light warming his eyes were both tender and encouraging. "Be my guest."

Anne let her gaze wander over his body before she leaned over and placed her hands on his pecs, the flat of her hand exploring every inch of the gentle, yet firm, slope. His body heat seeped into palm. "You're so warm."

"I'd rather be hot." His lop-sided grin was both boyish and sexy at the same time.

She laughed softly, a little envious of his comfort with his own body. Too often, insecurity eroded her self-confidence. She drew a circle on her palm with his nipple. She loved the way it puckered under her light touch. "You like?"

"Very much, but then I love it when you touch me, it doesn't matter where."

"Are you always this agreeable?"

Jason shook his head. "No, it depends on who's doing the touching."

"So you like this, too?" Her fingertips slalomed down his ribs and then traced a line down his sides. He jerked.

"Ticklish?" Drawing a line with her fingernail, down his side again and was rewarded with another twitch.

"You could say that. It sends an amazing sensation straight to my groin."

Sobered by his openness, she paused. Her gaze traveled up his chest until she looked into his eyes. She might not be in love with him, but she was seriously in like with him. He was a man she could admire, someone she could call friend.

"What's wrong?" Jason asked, a slight frown lining his brow.

"You are so open, so… good to me and for me. I just wish…" Her words trailed off. "I just wish I'd met you first." She wished he'd been her first. It would have been such a different experience.

"But if you had..." His voice trailed off. A playful smile turned up the corners of his delicious lips. "Then, we wouldn't appreciate what we've found now as much, would we?"

"You're right." Her appreciation for his consideration, tenderness, and frankness would never have been so intense if she had met him first. She might have even taken it all for granted.

Anne moved, settling in the v created by his legs, fascinated by the sight of his partially aroused penis and scrotum. Once again she marveled at the experience. With her hands she cupped his scrotal sack, awed by the soft, yet knobby texture, of his skin. When she traveled across its curves with her fingertips, it started to swell.

As she explored his genitals, Anne's body responded. Her nipples tightened, and moisture seeped through the lips of her sex. Had she simply turned into a nymphomaniac? Or, perhaps she was finally proving what Deb had always said. That she just needed to relax, toss aside the inhibitions her mother and grandmother had drilled into her, and then find the right partner.

Her gaze lifted to his semi-aroused penis, and she grinned. "I guess we'll have to do something about this."

"You won't hear any complaints from me."

Anne smiled, happiness welling up from a private spot deep inside her. With a fingertip she traced the vein trailing up the side of his rod, then circled the helmet shaped head, finally drawing a line across the slit.

Jason inhaled sharply. "Now that's incredible."

Her fingers curled around his shaft, which was quickly filling her hand and rising from the coarse pubic hair. With her palm wrapped around him, she drew her hand up and down his rod, watching every reaction – his ragged breaths, his shoulders pressing back into the cushions, his eyes closed.

Anne watched the drop of pre-cum forming at the tip. Her hand still hugging him, she dipped the tip of her tongue into the slit, catching the clear, salty drop on her tongue.

His torso arched. "God, now that's amazing."

His penis twitched against her palm as if it was begging for attention. She dipped her head, and with her tongue traced the outline of the head, inhaling the musky scent of him, ending once again by collecting another clear drop forming at the tip.

Once again, he arched, then sucked in a ragged breath. Before his body relaxed, she took the head into her mouth, exploring the shape and savoring the taste of him, gratified by his strangled exclamation of pleasure. He lifted his hips off the bed, but his movement was restricted by the leather cuffs. She took more of him into her mouth, then drew back, imitating the intimate act, stroking his sack and losing herself to the myriad of sensations building in her body.

"I need to be inside you," he growled, straining against his bonds.

"In a minute," she returned.

"In a minute, I'll probably come in your mouth if you keep this up."

Anne paused, unsure if she was ready for that. She'd come a long way in a short time, but there were limits to her learning curve. Besides, this erotic exploration had fueled her own hungry ache, so why deprive either of them of satisfaction?

She straddled him, impaling herself on his thick shaft in a single swift stroke. Their bodies met, and her breath hitched at the first wave of pleasure rising from her feminine core. With her hands on his chest for support, she lifted her body, traveling up and down his rod, squeezing him with the barrel of her vagina. She pumped him, squeezing him with intimate muscles. His hips met her as much as his bonds allowed, matching the mating rhythm until he cried out in release.

In that instant, a shattering climax shot up through her body, erupting like a geyser from the point where their bodies touched to the very top of her head, flooding ever part of her. As the heady tide receded, she collapsed on his chest, sated and sleepy. "I don't think I'll ever get enough of you," she whispered against the side of his neck.

"I know I'll never get enough of you," he returned, then pressed his lips to her forehead.

His tender words and the chaste kissed warmed her spirit. Anne moved off him, and quickly undid the cuffs. She wanted to curl up against him and feel his arms around her, realizing and savoring the knowledge there was so much more to this relationship than sex. The thought both awed and frightened her. Every moment they were together forged another link, bonding them together. Anne stretched out beside him, and he hugged her close to his body.

"Don't you dare go back to sleep!"

"Virginia!" Anne exclaimed, startled by the spirit's abrupt appearance. A bright, opalescence sheen radiated from her transparent form.

Jason slipped his first two fingers and grasped the chain. "Hello, Virginia."

"As I was telling Annie," she said, looking at Jason. "Don't go back to sleep. You've had fun with my toys, but now it's time to get down to work."

"Finding your murderer," Jason supplied.

"This one is bright, Annie, my girl. Definitely a keeper."

"Thanks," he said with a laugh.

Anne breathed a sigh of relief. He seemed to be taking the resident spirit and her unusual personality with good humor.

"I suggest we have a shower and get dressed," he proposed, cupping Annie's breast with his hand, gently massaging the soft flesh. "Annie's luscious body is just too distracting."

Their hands linked, Anne and Jason moved off the bed. Reluctantly, Anne led him toward the alcove with their clothes, promising to bring him back soon. This had been the best afternoon she'd ever had.

"I really don't want to leave," Anne said as they took their clothes from the shelf. "But I want to help Virginia if I can."

"Soon, I'll take you to the Inner Sanctum and we can play with their toys," he promised, cupping her face with his hand. He leaned over and kissed her.

"Come on," Anne said when he lifted his head. "Or Virginia will be up here to drag us down to the shower."

"True, but I'd rather spend the afternoon after our shower napping in bed with you."

"Me, too, but I'd rather not risk Virginia's vengeance." Anne laughed feeling happier and more alive than she ever had before. They returned to her bedroom then hurried to the en suite where Virginia had already started the shower.

"I'll do your back if you do mine," Jason offered his smile, a splash of white against his tanned cheeks. He climbed into the shower and drew her along with him.

Anne picked up a facecloth hanging over the shower doors and lathered it up with soap. "I was thinking of starting lower."

"And I'm thinking you might get something started you'll have to finish."

"If I could only be so lucky," Anne quipped then laughed, knowing she would get lucky from the glint in Jason's dark eyes.

Half an hour later, when they came down the stairs, the kitchen was spotless.

Jason turned, surveying the room. "Wow, would you like to rent Virginia out? I could use someone to go through my place."

"I heard that!" Virginia said as she appeared. "I had to do something while you two were busy playing with my toys."

"Virginia would love to," Anne said with a grin, still feeling playful and light.

"Very funny," she drawled. With ghostly fingers, she lifted the chain and dangled it toward Jason who slid his first two fingers around the chain. "Why don't we make a three way connection and try and figure out where to start looking for my killer?"

The trio sat at the table.

"Why couldn't we just take what we know to the police and let them figure out who killed you?" Jason asked. "I don't like putting Anne in danger."

Virginia grinned. "I don't either. That's why you're here."

"Thanks," he returned.

"I've already talked to the detective on the case," Anne interjected. "I mentioned that the body could be Virginia Marshall's. He investigated then told me in no uncertain terms that she's still alive and I should have realized that since I bought the house from her."

"I guess, first, we should track down Virginia Marshall, the impostor." Jason exhaled thoughtfully. "I know a fellow who could nose around – discretely. We don't want to tip off the impostor, possibly the murderer, we are onto her."

"In the meantime, we should talk to the people who were closest to Virginia at that time," Anne added. "To be able to take over her life so completely, they had to know a lot about her."

"Who were you closest to Virginia?" Jason looked at the spirit's glistening form. "Who knew you well enough to step into your life?"

Her forehead puckered, and she pinched her lips together, then she named a half a dozen people.

"What about Clay Montgomery?" Jason mentioned, watching her intently.

"What about him?" Lavender spread through the sparkling mist surrounding her.

"It's too much of a coincidence that your Attic Club and his Inner

Sanctum are identical."

She shrugged. "We were lovers. He proposed. I accepted, and before the day ended. I was dead. End of story."

"Wait a minute," Jason said. "You accepted his proposal, then disappeared, and Clay didn't file a missing person's report? Didn't look for you? That doesn't sound like the Clay Montgomery I know."

"You know him?" Anne sat forward in her seat.

"Very well, and he's not the type to just sit back and do nothing if his fiancée disappeared."

"That's what I thought too, but obviously I was mistaken." The purple hue of her aura deepened.

Bands of compassion closed painfully around Anne's chest. Perhaps finding the murderer wasn't the only reason Virginia's spirit couldn't rest. Perhaps it had as much to do with a broken heart.

Chapter Nine

"I'll see you tomorrow," Jason said an hour later when he prepared to leave her home. He cupped her face in his hands and kissed her deeply, dipping and tasting, stroking her tongue. "Though I'd much rather stay and make love to you again… and again… and again." Each pause was filled with a kiss. "I have a teleconference to attend."

Her breasts growing hard with need, Anne leaned against him. "When?" she murmured.

"An hour," he returned. "The executive is having a supper meeting then we'll be going to the teleconference, which will probably run late."

"Then, you have just enough time to have a snack before you leave." Fluid from her sex soaked the crotch of her underwear. She reached behind her, under her shirt and released the hooks of her bra. She grasped the hem of her top and pulled it quickly over her head, dropping it on the ceramic tile floor of the foyer before she shrugged off her bra.

A sensual chuckle rumbled in his chest and his eyebrows arched.

"If there's one thing I learned today," Anne said as she reached for his belt buckle and started undoing it. "It's that what we have today could be gone tomorrow. Look at Virginia and Clay. They were in love and going to get married. The next minute, she was gone. From now on, I'm going to live every day and not just go through the motions. If I want to make love to you, then I'm going to do it."

"You won't hear me complaining." Jason curled his hands around her breasts, massaging them in a sensual, circular motion, grazing the nipples until they wrinkled invitingly.

Anne undid his pants and quickly pushed them over his hips. They slid down his hips to his ankles. While she pushed her skirt and panties off, he stepped out of his pants. She reached for his thick erection, drawing her hand along the rigid shaft, loving the softness of the skin. Gripping his organ, she drew him into the living room, her sex aching and empty. "I want you in me now."

"Yes, ma'am. Your wish is my command." He eased her onto the couch, covering her body with his. His mouth closed on her nipple, sucking and laving while his hand traveled to her clit, teasing the bud until it stood erect.

Her legs fell open wider and her hips lifted, pushing herself against him until the tip slid inside. In a quick thrust, he was inside her, pumping in and out. A breathtaking satisfaction gripped her body. Anne dug her nails into his back, and closed her legs around him holding him tight as an orgasm burst through her body. There weren't any lingering caresses. It was just tumultuous sex.

His cry of satisfaction came at a powerful thrust, then he slowly relaxed, raining kisses over her breasts, licking the still taut nipples. "I hate to bang and run, but this is a meeting I can't miss."

Anne combed her fingers through his hair, sated. "I know. Go."

He withdrew his semi-flaccid penis, then dressed. Anne watched his efficient movements, making no attempt to cover her nakedness. Instead of embarrassment, she relished the feelings his hungry gaze traveling over her body evoked. He dropped a kiss on her lips, then nipped each breast. She followed him to the door, then stepped back, watching him through a crack in the curtains.

He strode toward his sporty vehicle – sleek and powerful – like him, then climbed in. Even before his car disappeared from view, she missed him. A part of her wanted to deny this feeling could be love blossoming. A cautious part of her that argued this was too soon to call whatever she was feeling love. It was probably just a mix of infatuation and lust. That was proving to be a heady combination.

The phone rang rescuing her from the internal tug of war.

"Am I interrupting anything?" Deb asked.

"Not a thing." Anne grinned. "But if you'd call five minutes earlier..." She let her voice trail away heavy with suggestion. "Well, let's just say, I would have let the answering machine pick up.

"Tall, wavy brown hair, and a body to die for?"

"One in the same." She wondered what Deb would think of the adult playroom in her attic. One day, she might tell her, but not today. She wanted a chance to investigate all of the nooks and crannies with Jason before she invited anyone else.

"Okay, I want all the details. How about coffee?"

"Sounds like a great idea," Virginia said, appearing at her elbow. "Can I come? I haven't been downtown in thirty years. I imagine it's changed a lot."

Anne put a fingertip to her lips. "The Coffee Stop?"

"In twenty?"

"I think I can manage it. I need to get dressed."

"Please tell me you're naked and dripping."

Anne laughed at Deb's lewd comment. "Yes, to both," she said with a laugh.

"You know I'll expect details."

Anne laughed feeling more light-hearted that she had felt in years. "See you soon."

"Ciao."

Returning the receiver to its cradle, Anne turned to Virginia. "You can come, but you have to behave or next time I'll leave the necklace here."

Transparent fingertips traced a cross over an equally see-through chest.

A grin surfaced and stayed there while she snatched her clothes from the floor and dressed. She brushed her hair then headed for the door.

Anne picked up her purse from the semi-circular table in the foyer, then dug her keys out. "Let's go."

As she walked along the stone path toward her car, Anne noticed the stern, middle-aged woman watching her over the fence. The same woman who had been watching her house yesterday. She turned and walked toward the hedge separating their homes.

"Sandra Steers won't help you," Virginia said.

"You can't know that," Anne whispered under her breath, then stepped up to the hedge.

"She used to be one of my closest friends, but we… we had a falling out just before I was murdered."

"Hi!" Anne offered, unsettled by the woman's cool grey stare. Maybe Virginia was right. Maybe she wouldn't help.

"Hello." The tone was neutral, offering neither welcome nor rebuke.

"I'm Anne Kemper. You're new neighbor." She extended her hand across the hedge. The lady paused before she took it, her gaze piercing. "I guess you noticed the police cars were here on the weekend..." Anne left the sentence hanging, hoping to start a dialogue with her prickly neighbor.

Regardless of what Virginia said. If she'd lived here thirty years ago and had watched her house as diligently then as she did now, perhaps she had seen the murderer leave the house without even knowing it. "I found a body in the basement. It had been there quite a while... decades. I... they think it was the previous owner. Did you know her?"

The lady touched her fingertips to the gold cross hanging against the lace of her blouse. Her lips pulled together in a tight line. "No, and I didn't want to. She was evil – a demon." Color stained the wrinkled cheeks. "They had orgies and worshipped the devil."

"Orgies," Virginia snorted and rolled her eyes. "Devil worship. If that's the case, then she was his number one disciple. Her cunt was insatiable."

Fighting to keep her expression neutral, Anne tossed a quick glance in Virginia's direction at the spirited spirit's choice of words, then she looked back at the wizened woman, unable to imagine her doing anything but watching neighbors, disapproval wrinkling her face. "How did you know this?"

"I wouldn't step foot in there, and you should leave while you still have your soul."

Anne withheld a sigh. The woman was obviously a religious fanatic. "Then, how do you know they had... orgies?"

"Because she used to be the first one to strip, Virginia interjected. "And the last one to leave. At least, she was until she got religion and wanted to sermonize more that she wanted to get screwed. She's used every toy in the attic and brought a few of her own to share."

Anne pressed her lips together to fight the grin trying to emerge. It really was difficult to imagine this nosy, sanctimonious shrew visiting the attic playroom.

The woman pointed a wrinkled hand toward the windows in the attic. "Bold as brass she strutted around naked, having rutting with any male who'd have her."

"She's describing herself. I was a little more discerning. I actually had to like the man I screwed. Quantity was all she cared about. The more men the better, usually two at a time." Virginia floated around behind the woman, ghostly arms reached around; her hands skimming over the front of the woman's chest until they cupped her breasts, then sank beneath her clothing.

"Enjoying sex doesn't make them demonic." Anne pulled her gaze away from the woman's chest. If that's the case, then she would soon be sprouting horns and a tail. She definitely enjoyed sex.

"There we go," Virginia said with a grin. "Tight little tits."

The woman shifted, then tugged on the hem of her shirt, and Anne pressed her lips together to stop from scolding Virginia at the woman's obvious discomfort. Ghostly hands moved lower, and Anne gave an imperceptible shake of her head.

Virginia grinned. "I'm enjoying this too much to stop now."

"Think what you like," the woman said, a rosy flush rising to her cheeks. The older woman pressed her thighs together, her face pinching. "Virginia Marshall was evil incarnate."

"Hypocrite!" Virginia snorted. "The man she set her sights on loved me, and she couldn't handle it. The day after he rejected her, she got religion and condemned us all to hell."

"I can't believe that." Even if only half of what Virginia said was true, Anne had had enough of this woman and her moralizing. Anne took a step back from the hedge.

"That's because you never met her. If you want proof, just check out the attic."

At the sight of Virginia's forehead puckered in a frown with pinpricks of light exploding around her, Anne decided it would be a good idea to retreat before Virginia did something they'd all regret. "If you remember anything about that time period that might help the police figure out who the body is or who might have killed her?"

Anne turned away, not waiting for or expecting an answer or information that would help her solve the mystery of Virginia's murder, and walked quickly toward her car. It was probably best not to tell her that she'd visited the playroom and intended to drag Jason up there again at the first opportunity.

As she slid behind the wheel, Virginia slid through the passenger side. Anne let her mutter about her hypocritical neighbor during the ten-minute drive to the Coffee Stop. She had just sat down when Deb strolled into the shop.

"Wow!" Virginia exclaimed. "Has this place ever changed? I came here all the time when I was in high school. Lost my virginity here, you know."

"Here?" Anne whispered behind her hand, looking at the menu. "In this shop"

"Yes, siree." Virginia floated into a chair. "In fact, the stud is serving up drinks as we speak."

Anne looked at the stocky owner of the café, Greg Mason, trying to imagine the balding, middle-aged, family man as a stud. His love for his wife and family was common knowledge.

"Okay, spill!" Deb demanded, dropping into the seat across the table. "I couldn't believe it when I saw you were hanging out with Mark's bud at the party."

"I couldn't either at first. Let's just say, he's not like Mark." He wasn't even the Jason MacIsaac she thought she had known.

"As good as, Sam?"

"Better," Anne quipped. Sex with Sam had been great. But it had only been sex. With Jason it was so much more.

"Hmm… maybe… I should sample. He sounds delish."

"No." Anne wasn't ready to share him, now or ever. The immediate and predatory response surprised her.

Deb laughed. "That good?"

"Amazing."

"Sam's nothing to sneeze at."

Anne blinked, then laughed softly. "You've laid him already?"

"You bet," Deb returned. "Now, there is amazing."

"A girl after my own heart. Sampling is great." Virginia inserted with a grin.

"In fact," she continued. "I'll be heading over to Sam's from here. He's having a few friends over for drinks and whatever strikes their fancy. Why don't you come over? Be neighborly?"

"Go on, Annie. Sample a bit, if only to be sure Jason is the one for you."

"Maybe another time." She and Jason might not officially be a couple, but she didn't feel like sampling. She just wanted to figure out how she felt about him without confusing the issue with gratuitous sexual encounters.

Greg strolled over to the table. "Are you ladies ready to order?"

"One quickie," Virginia said with a laugh. "He's got the most amazing dick. His wife is a lucky lady. I hope she truly appreciates him."

Anne battled the urge to look at his crotch. "Peppermint Mocha."

"The same," Deb answered.

"I didn't love him, but he was good at popping cherries." Virginia grinned. "Highly recommended. And he definitely lived up to the rave reviews."

Anne tried to ignore Virginia, but her comments echoed in her head, and her gaze dropped to his crotch.

"Look, there's Jen and Leigh." Deb waved them over.

They pulled over more chairs and sat down. Anne was more than glad to let the conversation flow around her. Virginia was a distraction, and after her comments, she would be hard pressed not to inspect his family jewels each time she visited this cafe.

"I chose the night to lose my virginity... exactly one month after my sixteenth birthday. I'd been on the pill long enough not to get knocked up. He helped his father out then. I'm sure his pop knew what was going on. No one could help but notice the number of gals who wanted to help him clean up the shop at the end of the day. His old man probably would have done the same at that age. They both sowed a load of wild oats before they settled down... but once they did, they didn't stray. A shame really."

Anne looked at Virginia and gave a slight shake of her head. As provocative as her tale might be, she couldn't keep up with both conversations. As soon as she could escape, she made her excuses.

"If you change your mind, drop over." Deb waved good-bye.

"Thanks," Anne answered. As soon as she climbed in the car, she turned to Virginia. "Look, if you want to go out with me again, you'll have to be quiet. I can't carry on two conversations at once."

"Party pooper." Virginia pouted, then grinned. "I bet you still want to know more about Greg and his talents."

"Maybe a bit... it's pretty hard to imagine Mr-family-man Greg as a stud."

"Well, to help you with that, I want to try something when we get home."

"I just hope I won't regret it," Anne muttered under her breath.

"You won't. I promise."

Anne parked the car wondering what Virginia had in mind. As she climbed out of her car, Anne looked at her home. For so long she'd loved the place, walking by it on her way to school, never imagining it would one day be hers. Now, she couldn't imagine living anywhere else.

Virginia floated to the middle of the living room. "Lay down on the couch and relax."

Anne sat down, kicked off her shoes then laid back, resting her head on a plump cushion. "I hope you know what you're doing."

"Take the medallion in one hand, and then put your hand against mine." Virginia lifted her hand with her palm facing Anne. "Nothing ventured, nothing gained," she added when Anne hesitated.

Anne turned her head on the cushion, looked at Virginia, then followed her instructions. Where their hands met, her palm tingled.

"Close your eyes."

She closed her eyes, suspecting whatever Virginia had in mind would probably have an orgasmic ending.

"Okay... travel back with me."

Even though she knew she wasn't moving, she felt as if the room was spinning. Images flashed in Anne's head: Her house was new, the elms circling the house saplings. The Coffee Stop, like her house, was fresh and new. Vintage cars parked in front of the building. In her mind's eye, she looked around. The trees on the boulevard in front of the shop were small compared to the mature trees surrounding the building today.

The sun had almost disappeared below the horizon. Golden fingers of color streaked the sky. She knew she was looking through Virginia's eyes, moving in Virginia's body, feeling through Virginia senses, yet not in control of her body. It was following a course of actions already set in time.

Together, they strode up the steps. Anne could feel Virginia's heart racing in anticipation and the pulse pounding between her legs. She could hear her thoughts, her wonderings if this would be anything like when she'd masturbated. In a few minutes, the Coffee Shop would be closing for the night. Anne knew because the youthful Virginia knew. She wasn't sure how this worked, but somehow it did.

Greg, a much younger leaner Greg with riotous black curls, was occupied bussing tables, clearing the dishes and wiping the circular tops with a damp rag. Virginia was right. He was definitely a stud muffin. His new jeans stretched taut over a trim butt and emphasized his slim hips. He turned and grinned as she moved closer a rich green apron covering his package.

"Hi, Virginia," he said quietly. "You're a bit late, we're closing, but I could probably rustle up a cup of coffee for you."

"I'm not interested in anything on the menu," she answered directly. Anne marveled that she could feel Virginia's heart throbbing so hard it seemed to tap against her ribs. It was like it was happening to her.

"Really?" He might have asked the question, but the lusty look in his eyes was rife with expectation. "What did you have in mind?"

She leaned closer, inhaling the mix of his cologne and coffee, then said in a low voice, "I was hoping to you'd pop my cherry tonight."

He blinked in surprise and laughed, shaking his head. "God, Virginia, don't hold anything back. Tell me what you really want."

Inwardly, Anne smiled. Years, even death, hadn't changed her much. Her lusty love of life and sex were constants.

"If I'm going to have my cherry popped, I want it done by the best," Virginia said. For all her bold words, Anne felt the tremor of nervousness and the chill of apprehension washing slowly over Virginia's body. "And you come highly recommended."

"I do?" He gave a soft laugh of surprise. Ruddy color stained his cheeks. "Give me a few minutes to close up and then we'll discuss it."

Thoughts of awe tripped through their joined minds – Virginia's thoughts – youthful anticipation that in a few minutes she would no longer be a virgin, and questions about what it would be like. Sure she'd masturbated, but would it hurt much? Jen had said it had been excruciating, but then an impatient jock had impaled her on the beach. Greg had been Leigh's first, and she had talked about the experience for days.

"Hey, Pop," he called over his shoulder to his father, a man who looked very much like he did today. "I'll close up if you want to turn in. Virginia will give me a hand with the chores."

The older man's lips twitched. Anne felt chagrin even though Virginia didn't. The twinkle in his eye and the suppressed smile signaled he had a pretty could idea what he'd be doing as part of the closing routine.

Virginia swept while he counted the cash and made up the deposit.

"Are you sure you want to have sex?" he asked. "I mean we're friends. And, we're not even going steady. Don't you want to have special feelings for the man who you make love to for the first time?"

Virginia paused then leaned the broom against the wall. "I don't want to wait until I fall in love to have sex. That's a long way in the future – if ever. Who better to have the first experience with than a friend who's good at it?" She grinned, and Anne grinned with her. The young Virginia's logic was flawless.

"You're certainly good for my ego. I just hope you won't be disappointed. The first time can be uncomfortable for some girls, and the digs are pretty simple." He untied his apron and dropped it over the back of a chair, then leaned over and brushed his lips over hers. "Come on." He slid his arm around her waist and guided her to a back room with a cot. "Sometimes when I have to get up early to do the baking, I sleep here."

An initial wash of arousal, washed through Virginia's body. Anne felt it even though it was happening to the youthful Virginia.

"Well, first," he said. "Let's just kiss a bit, and if you change your mind, then we can stop. No harm done."

He slid his hand around the nape of her neck, then brushed his lips over hers. Anne recognized his experience behind the light, but not tentative, touch of his lips against the young Virginia's. He slid his other hand around her waist, drawing her body against his, just enough so she could feel his growing arousal without pressing it into her abdomen.

Virginia linked her hands behind his neck. She'd kissed before and opened, so he could dip deeper. He didn't hesitate, slipping his tongue into her mouth, stroking hers. Slowly, she became aware that his large hands bracketing her waist were under her blouse. He hands were warm against her eager flesh. When had they moved? She didn't care. Now she'd started on this path, she just wanted to move forward.

His hands inched higher until they reached her bra. Somehow, Anne heard Virginia's thoughts. She heard her wishing she'd remembered to take her bra off in the car and that his hands creeping to the closure of the lacy undergarment. With an ease that bespoke practice, he unhooked the lacy garment and it relaxed.

"Do you mind if I touch your breasts? I'll stop if you're having second thoughts."

From the bulge in his pants, Anne thought with wry humor, he was probably hoping she wouldn't have second thoughts, but he was wise to offer these assurances. She could feel some of the tension in Virginia's body ease away.

"Go ahead," Virginia said, holding her arms above her head.

Greg grasped the ribbed hem of her sweatshirt, pulled it over her head, and then tossed it on a chair. He dragged the elastic straps of her bra over her shoulders and down her arms.

Anne felt Virginia fight the urge to cover herself. Sure, she'd necked before and a few fellows had touched her breasts, but he was the first to see her naked breasts.

"They are so beautiful," he murmured then circled them with his fingertip.

Virginia's breath trembled, but she didn't tell him to stop. "Did you want me to take your shirt off?" she offered.

"Not tonight. I'll do that. Tonight will be totally for you and your pleasure. You won't get this night back."

Admiration grew for the randy, but wise, youth Greg had been. He pulled off his shirt and shucked off his jeans, only briefs covered his swollen shaft. He helped her out of her jeans, and led her to the cot. The wool blanket felt rough and warm under her skin. Anne marveled at how the thoughts and sensations Virginia had experienced, echoed in her body.

For the first time, Anne felt Virginia's determination waver, yet she didn't bolt when he sat beside her. He leaned over and took a youthful nipple into his mouth, circling his tongue around the taut bud.

"This feels odd." Virginia looked at Greg's loose curls tumbling over his forehead. So many firsts were happening within a few minutes. It was the first time she'd felt a man's mouth on her tits, and she loved the sensations blossoming between her legs.

He lifted his head, then grinned. "Let me try something else." This time when he took her nipple into his mouth, he sucked, tugging on her breast. Awe spread through her as fast as the swelling of her labial lips. Of their own accord, her legs relaxed.

"This is amazing," she murmured, raking her fingers through his hair. Then, she guided his head to the other breast. She protested when he lifted his head.

"If you think this is amazing, I'll show you something else in a bit that will blow you away." He pushed her legs apart then crawled into the v.

Anne felt her mouth go dry as Virginia realized she was only minutes away from losing her cherry. No one, no male, had ever seen her like this. Granted, Stan had shoved his hands inside her pants at a party, cupping her pubis, but she'd pushed him away. She hadn't been ready then, now she was and any apprehension was normal.

He grazed her clit with his fingertip then circled the little nub, and she exhaled slowly. Having him touch her between her legs felt so different than when she had brought herself to climax. He separated the folds, then bent over. He slid his tongue in between the slick folds.

"God, you taste good," he murmured against the swollen lips of her sex.

If having him suck her breasts had felt strange, then his mouth against her crack, and his head between her legs was embarrassing. Instinctively, she tried to bring her legs together, but his shoulders held them apart.

He continued to tease her clit, circling and rubbing until she felt her hips rise off the bed of their own accord, and primitive hunger rose. He slipped a finger inside her. The penetration felt strange and good at the same time as he inserted another finger, stretching untried muscles.

Anne frowned. If only Mark had been so thoughtful. He'd taken very little time to prepare her for the moment he drove his cock inside her. A few kisses were followed by some heavy petting.

He worked her clit until a climax rocked her body, her hips arched and vaginal muscles closed around his fingers.

"Aren't you? Didn't you?" Virginia's voice was husky in the aftermath of her climax.

"Oh, yes, but first I wanted to give you an idea of what is to come."

He rose onto his knees then slid his briefs down, giving Virginia a moment of pause. The pictures she'd seen never really did a man's penis justice. How on earth would he fit all of that in her? The helmet shaped head, purplish pink, fascinated her. He moved forward, then took her hand and curled it around the shaft. "Touch it, get used to it."

"It's soft and hard all at the same time." The skin stretched over his erection was soft, yet in places bumpy. A clear liquid leaked from the top. Curiosity momentarily displaced her nerves. She touched the drop, then rubbed it between her thumb and first finger. It was warm and sticky.

"So that's pre-cum," she said.

Anne was awed by the young Greg's control as a youthful and curious Virginia, stroked him, exploring his swollen sac and rigid shaft with her fingers and her eyes. "Will that really fit inside me?"

He grinned. "One size fits all." He covered her body with his, returning to her breasts. This time, however, Virginia felt the length of his shaft between her legs, each slight stroke separated the lips a bit more until they wrapped around him, and her juices covered the length of him. Anne moved with Virginia, following his strokes, her body acting from an age-old instinct. Her body arched with Virginia's, passion lifting her hips.

Then, his hand traveled to his shaft, and he slid the head into her tight opening. It stretched her. How could she take more of him into her body? She stilled, and so did he.

"It would be hard to stop now, but I can." His voice was ragged as he made the offer. Anne couldn't believe his offer. Admiration grew for both the youth and the man.

"Don't stop," Virginia returned.

"This is the point of no return," he warned.

She nodded. He inched in giving her time to adjust as he pushed further and further into her body, pausing when their bodies met. Virginia thought about Greg and knew she would never be able to look at him in quite the same way again. Granted, a typical horny youth, he'd snatched an opportunity to get laid but not without some concern for Virginia.

When he hit resistance, he pushed by the virginal barrier with a slight thrust of his hips. The pain was brief, and the discomfort made Virginia wonder why everyone was so hyped about sex. He started to pull back, and Virginia was relieved that he would soon be out of her body. Empathy washed through Anne. Her first experience had left her impaled and in pain.

Instead of leaving, he thrust again, their pubis met and a wash of pleasure ebbed out from her clit. Slowly at first, and then gaining momentum, he thrust and retreated, the discomfort eased and waves of pleasure shot through her body. Then, it burst over her, her second climax of the day, but the first was pale in comparison. This exploded over her body like fireworks. She arched upward, pressing into him as he gave his final thrust and cried out as he reached release.

Anne landed back in her body abruptly, her hips arched and gently rocking, her body throbbing. The climax had broken her connection with Virginia. Her ragged breaths were loud in the silent room.

"So, what did you think?"

"I wish that my first lover had been as considerate and good," Anne said honestly, her breathing ragged and her body pulsing with aftershocks of climax. "But perhaps if Mark had been, I wouldn't appreciate Jason as much."

"And there's plenty about your stud muffin to appreciate." Virginia floated to the horizontal position. "Definitely a keeper."

The phone rang, and Anne slid to one end of the couch, then picked up the receiver.

Virginia pressed her ear to the other side of the receiver, an unabashed eavesdropper.

"Hello?" Anne tried to shoo her away with her hand, but Virginia just grinned. Having an irrepressible spirit as a roommate meant a profound lack of privacy, but she couldn't work up any real resentment. Deep down inside, she really liked the spirited ghost and enjoyed her company.

"Hi, Beautiful."

A smile touched her lips at the sound of Jason's voice. "Hello yourself."

"We're going to be here for a while. It's an international teleconference, and we're trying to span several time zones, so I was wondering if I could pick you up and take you out for breakfast. I cleared my schedule for tomorrow morning."

"I'd love it." As much as she liked Virginia, she was wondering how her resident spirit would take it if she left the necklace behind, but then she'd always made herself scarce when they made love, so perhaps she would bring her along.

"Oh, yes. You can tell Virginia that I have a call in for Clay to set up a meeting. It might take a couple days. He's a busy man."

Virginia's expression sobered and a lavender hue washed through her luminescent form.

"She heard." Her heart went out to Virginia. Anne mentally crossed her fingers that they not only found her murderer, but that she would have a chance to resolve things with Clay Montgomery.

"Coffee break's over," Jason said. "I have to get back, but I'd rather be there with you." He paused, and when he spoke again his voice was barely more than a whisper, "and in you."

"I wish you were here, too." Anne winced at her trite response. Why couldn't she think of something witty? The words, no matter how corny, were true. When he was gone, it felt like a piece was missing from her life.

"See you at ten," he added.

"See you then."

Her life was changing faster than she'd ever thought it could, and she was enjoying every second. She dropped the receiver in its cradle and yawned. No matter how much excitement having a lusty ghost in her house injected into her life, her lack of sleep and mega doses of sex had worn her out.

"Come on, Virginia. It's time for bed." And how she wished Jason was there to share it with her, and not just because he provided mind-bending sex. He'd stormed into her life and provided a missing piece that she hadn't even known was missing.

"You go on ahead," the luminescent figure said. "I'm going to hang out upstairs for a bit."

"See you in the morning."

After a lengthy, hot shower, Anne crawled into bed, relaxed and warm from the shower. "What will tomorrow bring?" she murmured.

"More hot sex with your hunky banker, I hope." Virginia's voice popped into her head in response. "G'night!"

"Goodnight." Anne grinned, suspecting and hoping that Virginia was right. Never had she looked forward to a Monday morning more.

Chapter Ten

When Anne woke up golden fingers of light streaked across the sky. It would be at least three hours before Jason would be making his appearance. She pulled on some sweats and strolled downstairs to the kitchen and put on the coffee pot.

"Virginia?" Anne said softly as she pulled a mug from the cupboard.

"Good morning!" she answered, then appeared seated at the table. "I thought you were going to sleep forever."

"One of the disadvantages of being flesh and blood," Anne rejoined. "I do need some sleep." She smiled and pulled the carafe from the base and filled the mug. "And some hot coffee."

"I miss that lovely elixir almost as much as sex. And speaking of sex, you have a few hours before the amazing Jason arrives. What are you going to do with yourself? Masturbate?"

"Honestly, Virginia, did you ever think about anything other than sex when you were alive?"

"Food." She shrugged and offered a mischievous grin. "One appetite or another."

Anne just grinned and shook her head. "Well, I'm going to do a little work until he arrives. In fact, I have an idea. Come on, I could use your help."

"My help? Work? You are talking to the wrong ghost."

Anne walked into her room, anxious to put her thought into action. "I want to sculpt you."

"Me?"

"I make art dolls... mixed media figures. Well, I've dabbled in it in the past. But when my aunt died and left me the insurance, I knew it was a chance to try something that I really enjoyed doing." Anne sat on the stool and pulled out the of spool aluminum wire she used to build the armature, her thoughts leaping ahead.

"Do I get to pose nude?"

Anne laughed. "If you can take off your clothes... sure." Ever since she'd appeared Virginia had worn the same clothes they'd found decomposing on her skeleton. "I wasn't sure if you had to keep the clothes on that you... that you..."

"That I died in?"

Anne nodded.

"Honestly, I don't know either, but let's give it a whirl."

Virginia lifted her arms and linked her fingers and then spun around, her clothes vanished. She stood in front of Anne nude. Like a Greek statue, her body was curved, bordering on plump but perfectly proportioned. In a deliberately sensual movement, Virginia cupped her ample breasts then slid her hands down her ribs to her waist until they stopped at a mound of dark brown, curly pubic hair. If this image was a true reflection of Virginia, she had been a beautiful woman.

"Okay, let's get started!" Her fingers itching to get at the clay, Anne picked up pliers and started manipulating the wire.

"Whatcha' doing with the wire? I thought you were going to sculpt me? Doesn't that involve clay?"

"Eventually, but first, I have to build an armature, or a skeleton to support the clay before I start applying it." Her thoughts moving ahead, she twisted the wire into a stick person. "I don't suppose one of your talents is shrinking to about this size?" She held up the armature.

"I don't know. Let's see." She puckered her forehead in concentration. "Nope, sorry."

"That's okay." Anne pointed to a spot by the window. "Stand over there."

Virginia floated to a spot a few feet away. "Okay, what do you want?"

Anne paused. She wanted her to take a pose that reflected her sensual nature, but also her vivacious personality. After a lively debate, they agreed on one hand resting between her breasts the other on her abdomen between her hip and her pubis. With a mischievous smile, Virginia assumed the pose.

Anne picked up a ball of clay and to begin putting the first layer on the armature, pressing cylinders around the wire. This would be the base for the detailed work.

"This is pretty scrawny."

"This is only the base for the outer layers of clay. I'll bake it and then add more levels." Anne walked over to the oven in one corner of the workroom by the French doors.

"How about giving me bigger boobs and a smaller hips and waist?" Virginia asked.

"How about you let me work? You're beautiful just the way you are... or were."

A sad smile spread slowly across her lips. "Clay used to say that, too."

She took the scrawny figure to the oven in the solarium.

"An oven?" Virginia floated beside her. "I thought you needed a kiln."

"If I was working in porcelain, but this is made from a polymer clay."

Once the basic body was hard, Anne added the layers that would bring the figure to life. Losing track of the time, her hands worked at the figure, bringing small limbs to life. Then, she worked on the face, praying she could capture the life in her features. Anne drew her teeth over her lower lip. She was trying to capture the irrepressible love of life in the face of the spirit of a dead woman. Why did this happen to her? Virginia didn't deserve to die young.

"Hey, Stud Muffin will be here any minute. Shouldn't you be getting ready for his arrival?" Clothes instantly covered her nude body. "Time to play!"

"Yikes! You're right!" Anne exclaimed then made a dash for the stairs. In her room, she grabbed a simple, loose flowing dress from the closet, then walked to her dresser and pulled open her underwear drawer.

Virginia pushed it shut. "No way. Underwear is not an option. Let him suffer. There's nothing that drives a man crazier than knowing you're naked under your clothes and there's nothing he can do about it." She grinned, then leaned against the drawer.

"You are a wicked woman, Virginia Marshall!" Anne chided with a laugh.

"Why thank you, Annie my girl."

***

She watched Jason climb out of his car. His simple outfit of white tee-shirt and jeans accentuated every muscled line of his muscular physique. He moved with a signature, male grace that could make her feel feminine even at this distance. She pushed away from the window then hurried down the stairs.

She opened the door before he reached the top of the steps. Her smile started somewhere deep inside her and spread through her whole body.

Could this be love?

"Hi, Beautiful," he murmured, then took her in his arms, bringing her tight against his body, sandwiching his thick arousal between them.

Her breasts felt weighted, and a steady pulse grew stronger between her legs.

"Hello, yourself," she responded then lifted her face for a kiss, arching her body into his to increase the pressure on his already swollen penis.

"Has Virginia been coaching you?" he murmured against the sensitive spot on her neck just below her earlobe.

"Actually, she's off doing whatever ghosts do when they aren't haunting." Anne closed her eyes, tipping her head to one side to allow him more access to the sensitive spots on her neck. When had her body become so sensitive? Perhaps he was the key unlocking the sensual mysteries of her body.

She slid her hands lower toward his groin. Before she could reach the prize, Jason caught her hands and pinned them behind her back.

"What?" she exclaimed softly. "Don't you want a little appetizer before breakfast?"

"God, I'm tempted, but I think I'd rather have you as dessert."

"But I thought…" Doubt demons nipped at her new-found self-confidence. "I thought you wanted me."

He shook his head as he offered a rueful laugh. "Want you? I want you so badly that my groin thinks I must have had a head injury because I'm not stripping you and taking you here against the wall."

"Then, why aren't you?"

"Because anticipation can be as stimulating as foreplay."

"Maybe for a masochist." Through the soft well-washed fabric of his jeans, Anne massaged his rigid shaft with her abdomen. Pounding need blossomed in her sex. Impatient moisture seeped through the slit between her legs. She cupped his tight scrotum. "And I'd say you've been anticipating plenty already."

With her soft laugh, he raked his fingers through her hair. He curled his fingers around the sandy waves and tipped her head back. His other hand slid to her behind, cupping the soft mound as he claimed a branding kiss. This one was different than anything she'd experienced with him before. It was as if he was placing his mark, invisibly yet indelibly on her spirit. Deep inside something primitive responded to the primal gesture.

"No underwear?" His whisper was raspy.

"Not a scrap," Anne returned with a saucy grin.

"What the hell? We can play the anticipation game some other time." Before the sentence finished his hands slid under the silky material of her dress to her waist. Anne relished the weighty pressure swelling her breasts, an ache and a pleasure all that the same time.

"Now, that's sounds more the Jason I've come to know." Anne laughed then gave him an open-mouthed kiss, relishing his capitulation. Could this be the same man who had restrained himself for months, not hinting at the depths of his feelings for her? Sometimes it was hard to reconcile the differences of the two different men – one whose touch could make her belt or the Jason from the past who used to make her cringe under his inscrutable looks. Looking back, the clues had been there, and a part of her had probably even noted them, but it was only in hindsight and her recent experiences that unveiled them to her.

All those months ago, his penetrating gaze had followed her around the room whenever they had been together. She'd been aware of his observation, but unaware of its source. All she'd known was that it had unsettled her. He'd kept his distance. Considering how quickly he could be aroused, she knew that physical proximity would have been true torture.

Anne unsnapped his jeans and opened his zipper, slipping her hand inside with a confidence that surprised her. She slid her hand inside his briefs, curling her hand around his shaft, stroking the length of it with her palm, finally reaching the coarse hair at the base of his rod. The ache in her sex demanded satisfaction.

"You know," he murmured, then drew a soft breath of satisfaction. "If you keep meeting me at the door like this, I might think you might enjoy having me around."

Anne paused momentarily sobering. "How much I want you and want you here keeps surprising me."

Jason cupped her face, and her skirt slid down her hips. With tenderness in his gaze, he smiled. "It's what I'd hoped would happen between us if given a chance. It just happened faster than I expected."

His open expression of his feelings knocked her off balance, drawing out an expression of her own state of mind. "I don't know if this is love… but I do know that I've never felt like this before and it's more than stellar sex." Her climatic union with Sam hadn't touched the deepest parts of her that had responded to Jason. Her response to Jason was imbued with the sense of ease and comfort. Granted she had boldly seduced Sam, but their union hadn't created a deeper connection.

"It's a great starting point, and I won't force myself on you if you discover you can't love me, but I won't walk away without a fight."

Determination glinted in his eyes, confirming his statement. The unconcealed iron will should have unsettled her, but his words wrapped around her and she hugged them to her heart.

Their gazes locked. He undid the buttons to her waist, then slid his hands inside her dress, pushing aside the garment, exposing her breasts. Her heart raced and she could feel her pulse in the swollen lips of her sex.

He cupped her breasts, holding the soft mounds against his palms, massaging them gently. Mesmerized, Anne watched her nipples pinch. Such a light touch, and yet, the flush of arousal spreading through her body needed to be sated – now. Instinctively, she curled her fingers around his shaft relishing the heat and rigid length of him.

He sucked in a gasp of air. "Come along," he murmured, leading her to the living room. "I want you now, and I don't think I could make it much farther than the living room."

"Are you a mind reader?"

He laughed, then stepped behind her, sliding his hands down her arms, applying just enough pressure so she bent over, placing her hands on the arm of the couch. Anne closed her eyes, savoring the sensation of his hands sliding her skirt upward until it exposed her legs and buttocks. Her breath accelerated when she heard the soft sound of his jeans sliding down his legs. His hands slid under her dress to her breasts as he brought his body against hers. His cock slid between her legs, into the heated slick folds of her labia, then back, then with a thrust he was inside. A raspy gasp escaped from her lips and her body arched. Wet and ready, her body welcomed him, intimate muscles clenched, hugging him, holding him tight. Before he could move, she moved along his shaft, impaling herself on the rigid length of him then pulling away. Only to have strong hands bring her tight against his body, then relax so that she could stroke him with her body.

She squeezed him with intimate muscles. At his gasp of pleasure, a smile turned up the corners of her lips. Immediately, he plunged into her faster, driving her toward ultimate satisfaction.

Now, it was her turn. Gasps of pleasure burst through her lips as the climax hit. A pinnacle of sensation that turned muscle and bone to jelly.

He pushed her dress up and kissed her back. "Why don't we skip breakfast and have dessert again?"

"And try out some more toys in the playroom?"

"I think I'll clear my afternoon schedule as well," he said with a laugh. "There's no way I can leave."

He slid out his semi-flaccid rod from inside her and reached for his jeans. His cell rang as he pulled it from his pocket. With a flick of the wrist, he opened the phone and put it to his ear. Anne sank onto the couch, slipping into a post-sex lethargy.

He snapped it shut. "That was Clay. We can meet with him tomorrow evening."

Anne's heart skipped a beat, and her hand flew to her locket. In the heat of the moment, she'd forgotten about Virginia, her murderer, and her ghostly friend's relationship with Clay. She prayed they would find the answers to the three-decade-old questions, and she didn't just mean who Virginia's murder was. Why had Clay given up on her and their relationship so easily?

Chapter Eleven

"I've arranged this meeting for you with Clay," Jason said as they climbed the stairs to private office of the owner of the Chrysalis.

Anne loved the pressure of his hand at the small of her back. The protective gesture warmed her heart.

"But convincing him Virginia was murdered isn't going to be easy. He's a tough nut to crack. If he trusts you, he'll talk to you. Otherwise, he'll never let on what he's thinking, and he'll kick you out so fast you won't know you're standing in the hall until the door is slammed shut behind you."

"Sounds like someone else I know."

"Only because I couldn't tread on Marks territory. Otherwise, I wouldn't have left you alone," he said. "Come on. Clay is waiting."

Virginia materialized in front of Clay's door. "Could we have a few minutes with him first?"

Anne turned to Jason. "Virginia wants us to have a few minutes with him first."

He didn't say anything, but the conflicting emotions flitting across his face spoke volumes. He nodded. "Fifteen minutes. That's it."

The shimmering ghost shot over to Jason and then dropped a kiss on his cheek.

Jason put his hand to his cheek. "That was Virginia, wasn't it?"

Smiling, Anne nodded, then leaned over and kissed the other cheek. "We both thank you."

A few minutes later, Anne walked into Clay Montgomery's office then sank slowly onto the upholstered chair opposite his oak desk. She looked at the Armani suited owner of the most notorious club in the city. Silver streaked deep wings in his closely cropped hair. Though trim, his body had lost the definition of a man in his prime – softening his profile.

Even so, it was obvious he still worked out from the smooth stomach and athletic grace. She tried to imagine what he had looked like thirty years ago. His black Irish coloring with striking blue eyes would have been a lethal combination at any age.

Virginia floated toward his desk, sitting cross-legged on one end. Ripples of lavender moved through her transparent form. Hungry eyes studied Clay.

"So, Miss Kemper, Jason said you wanted to speak to me about Virginia Marshall." He let the statement dangle between them, then he rocked back in his seat, his blue eyes cool and assessing, revealing none of the curiosity she was sure he must be feeling.

"Don't let him pull that stare on you. He's dying with curiosity but he'd dance on red-hot coals before he'd admit it," Virginia advised. "Clay was never one to let you know what he was thinking." She grinned. "Unless he wanted sex."

Anne wondered if all Virginia had thought about when she was alive was sex. But then, if she had been independently wealthy, the only child of indulgent parents, who knows how different she would have been.

"Three days ago, I moved into Virginia's home." Anne pulled the necklace from under her sweater. "I believe this was her necklace."

Not so much as a blink betrayed his thoughts, yet Anne felt the tension radiating in gigantic waves off his body the moment his eyes locked on the round gold disk with the engraved triquetra dangling from the glittering chain. She turned it over, showing the jeweler's mark an intricately woven z.

His gaze narrowed. "Where did you get that?"

"He gave it to me," Virginia interjected. "But he's not going to admit it. At least, not yet."

"I found it on Virginia's body. She'd been killed by a blow to the back of her head, and then her body was bricked into the cold room in the basement of her home. Judging from the decomposition, the coroner thought her body had been there for about thirty years."

"Her body? It can't be Virginia's body. She left the city thirty years ago to see the world, and, other than a brief Dear John letter, I haven't heard from her since then."

A fine thread of tension laced with pain twined around his words. Anne paused, guessing that Virginia's departure had wounded him and was probably still a raw and open wound.

"Someone else must have written the letter," Virginia declared.

"She didn't write the letter," Anne echoed Virginia's words. "And you gave her the locket."

Ruddy color spread across his cheeks. "Look, you couldn't possibly know that. You weren't even born when she left. If you are trying to somehow capitalize on the fact that you've moved into her home and found the locket, you'll be very sorry."

"Let me talk to him, Annie."

Everything she'd said and done until now hadn't helped convince Clay Montgomery that it was Virginia's body in the basement and she hadn't jilted him thirty years ago. Anne turned toward Virginia feeling desperate. "How?"

"Give him the necklace."

"I beg your pardon?" Clay asked.

"I was talking to Virginia. She wants to speak to you directly. Just take a hold of the chain and you'll be able to see her." Anne held the necklace out toward him.

"I don't know what sick game you're playing, but it stops now. It's time for you to leave." Beautifully sculpted lips pressed together in a straight, unyielding line.

"No way!" Virginia answered even though he couldn't here hear. "Annie you have to let me talk to him through you. Just relax, let me slip inside you, and I'll do the rest."

Anne looked at Virginia's glistening outline, tiny dots of light bursting all over her vaporous body, indicating her agitated state of mind. She nodded, not sure how Virginia would accomplish this, but willing to let her try.

Virginia slid into Anne's body. She lifted Annie's hands and wiggled her fingers. It was strange to be back in a body. It wasn't quite as comfortable as being in her own, but it felt good just the same. She scowled, or tried to. It had been a while since she'd had to manipulate so many muscles at once. "Clay Zachariah Montgomery, you are going to listen to me."

"Young woman, that's enough." His finger hovered over the button of the intercom on his desk. "If you don't leave right now, I'll have my security remove you."

"I'm not leaving until you listen to me, Clay. It's really me, Virginia." She knew if he called his security, they might not get another chance to talk to him. "Annie has let me borrow her body for a few minutes, so I can speak with you directly."

He punched the button and told his security to come in.

"You have a tattoo on your penis."

He paused. The door swung open. She had caught his interest she just had to keep it – to prove that she, not Annie, was talking to him before he had his man throw her out.

"That's common knowledge." He looked at the man entering the room. "Miss Kemper is ready to leave. See her to her car."

"Maybe it is common knowledge, but I doubt the reason they are there is." Virginia leaned forward in the chair. "It was a dare. You won." Her challenge to have entwined hearts on his organ had been her response to his marriage proposal. "I agreed to marry you if you had two hearts tattooed on your cock... on the right hand side."

His head snapped around, and his gaze narrowed on her. "Philip, give me a few minutes and make sure that we're not interrupted."

The suited muscular man nodded and then moved toward the door. He cast a glance in her direction before he left the room.

As soon as the door closed, Clay rose out of his chair and moved around his desk. "Miss Kemper, I don't know how you found that out, but I'm going to."

"Clay, you won the challenge. In fact, I was humbled when I saw the hearts." She grinned. "And it took a lot to humble me back then."

Clay studied her. Then, as if he couldn't stay still, he pushed out of his chair and walked around the desk, his eyes boring into hers. A deep crease formed between his dark, straight brows. He hitched onto the desk. "My gut is telling me I'm talking to Virginia, but my eyes are seeing Anne Kemper."

"Trust your gut. You did win that night, Clay." At the guarded look spreading across his face, her heart contracted in pain. The more he controlled his expression, the more deeply he was affected. "I left the club and drove straight home that night... the night you showed me your tattoo... all I wanted to do was pack a few clothes, then drag you to the justice of the peace. I didn't know it at the time, but someone was waiting for me. They hit me with something hard, crushing my skull, then they buried my body in the basement."

"Then, how was it, a week after you walked out on me, I received a letter from London telling me that you'd changed your mind?"

"I didn't write it." Virginia got out of the chair, immediately reaching for the desk to steady herself. This body might fit like a glove, but it would take a little getting used to balancing again. She hadn't moved in physical form in thirty years. "I loved you. I still do, and I always will." She could see the struggle sliding into his gaze. Part of him believed her, but he was still looking into Anne's eyes. "You still aren't sure it's me, are you?"

He shook his head.

"I was always better with actions than with words. Let me show you what I did the day you showed me the tattoo." She dropped to her knees in front of him. "The furniture wasn't as fancy that night. You'd just opened the club." Mentally apologizing to Anne for what she was about to do, she pushed open his suit jacket, reached for the fly of his pants, then slid the zipper down. She didn't have a choice. Making sure he learned the truth was just as important, perhaps even more important, to her as finding out who murdered her. "You tried to look casual when you said that I'd have to marry you and you had the license. I said you'd have to prove it, and I took matters into my own hands... literally." Virginia smiled slowly remembering those precious moments. That night, she'd actually fractured Clay's formidable self-control.

"Look, Miss Kemper, I don't know how you know this, but I think it's best if you leave." Clay was retreating. Strong emotion was about the only thing that made him truly afraid enough to bolt. If he accepted she was Virginia, he would also have to accept the woman he'd loved, then no doubt hated, hadn't betrayed him, but had been brutally murdered.

"Like I said, Annie has stepped out for a few minutes, so that we could talk. Let me show you what I did that night." She parted the fly opening and drew his partially aroused penis out of his silky, black boxers. She felt Annie's body respond. Clay had aged well. His body had lost the leanness of the late twenties, but he was still a virile, attractive man. The wings of silver in his wavy hair only made him more striking.

The moisture collecting at her labial lips, and the ache of need blossoming in her pussy was real, and she savored the sensual sensations. Time had dulled the memory of how an arousal moved through a body, the hunger weighing her breast, and her heart beat thrumming out an accelerated beat in the swollen lips of her sex. Thirty years was a long time to wait for satisfaction, but she would have Clay one last time.

He sucked in a sharp breath. "Miss Kemper... Virginia... stop." Tension tightened his voice. "Now!"

"Not on your life, Clay. Not until you're convinced, it's really me." She curled her hand around his organ. "No one else would know that the last time we would be together, I pumped you until you were hard." She grinned. "So hard, in fact, that I could easily see the hearts on the side of your rod."

She slid her hand up and down his penis. It grew rigid under the firm strokes, the little hearts became visible. She bit her lip. This moment by moment recounting of the evening was bringing back memories and feelings that were ripping her apart, but she had to continue. "I kissed both hearts, licked a drop of pre-cum from the tip of your cock." As if on cue, a clear bead of pre-cum formed at the slit of his swollen organ. Virginia slid the top of her tongue across the purplish head, catching the salty drop, and earning a smothered groan. "I pushed you backward on the desk. You didn't put up much of a struggle if I remember correctly." She remembered how in that moment his guard dropped, and he had grinned, his sky blue eyes sparkling with merriment. For the first time, he had allowed himself to believe that someone loved him and to let her know that he loved her. His vulnerability had only made her love him more.

"Virginia?" he whispered. He gasped when she ran her fingertip along the slit, dipping into the opening.

"Yes, in spirit, if not in my own flesh." Another clear drop of fluid leaked from the slit, and she curled her hands around the rigid pole that was warm and soft, and yet still hard. Virginia flicked her tongue across the top and he twitched in her hand. I milked you with my mouth until you begged for mercy, then rode you until you came. It was the best…" Virginia swallowed the knot of emotion caught in her throat. Hot tears blurred her vision. "And the last sex I ever had."

Her hands went to his belt buckle. Impatiently, she undid it then pushed his trousers off his hips. He lifted his body enough so that she could push them the rest of the way down his legs. "This can't be happening," he murmured.

"Clay, just trust your instincts and close your eyes." Virginia curled her hands around his shoulders and pushed him backward until he rested on his elbows. She climbed onto the desk, straddling him, stroking his shaft with her body, slick, wet folds curling about him. "I tormented you for a while," she said, then took the head into the, lubricated vaginal opening, enclosing the head in her warmth. "Taking you an inch at a time, until you got impatient." She edged a little further down his shaft, barely able to stop from sliding over him until their bodies met.

"And I grasped your waist and ended the torment." Just as he had three decades ago, he grasped her waist, forcing her down, impaling her on his pole until their bodies met and his shaft was completely hidden inside her. Anne's golden pubic hair blended with his dark curls.

She gasped at the wave of sensation that rippled through her sex. She had forgotten how incredible the waves of reaction coursing through her body could be. She lifted her hips then dropped, gripping him with intimate muscles.

He gasped. "God Virginia, are you trying to kill me?"

At his strangled exclamation, tears slid off her lashes. "Just trying to show you how much I love you."

The same dialogue they had exchanged that night thirty years ago. The sob that burst through her lips was a mixture of pain and ecstasy. Her heart was breaking while the barrel of her vagina rippled in response to his thrusts. The tables had turned, and she was tumbling under his control.

Tears streaming from her eyes, she rode the wave each thrust sent rushing through her body. Each one carried her higher until a climax exploded through her body, and she felt herself being expelled from Anne's body.

"No!" she wailed, but it was too late. The powerful climax had shattered the fragile link anchoring her in Anne's body.

Anne returned to consciousness with a jolt. She was straddling Clay, impaled on his shaft with her face wet from tears. Aftershocks of pleasure from a shattering climax rippled through her feminine core. His eyes were closed as he thrust and a cry of release burst from his lips.

Anne couldn't believe what had happened in the brief time she'd been out of touch with her body. She'd been in her body, and yet unaware of what Virginia had said and done. "Virginia, I said you could use my body to talk to him, not let him use my body," she growled.

"Sometimes actions speak louder than words. Besides, I was using his body."

"A technicality."

"She's gone, isn't she?" Clay murmured, his voice husky, tinged by the sex they'd shared.

"She's in the room, just not in residence." Anne looked into Clay Montgomery's incredible blue eyes then bit the inside of her lip. There wasn't any graceful way to dismount or to diffuse the uncomfortable silence filling the air between them. "I... I..."

Large hands closed around her waist and lifted her off his body. "There's a bathroom through there." He pointed to a door. "Why don't you freshen up, then we'll talk."

"Thanks, I think I will," she said then walked straight toward the door. She stalled in the doorway. It was the most luxurious bathroom she'd ever seen. Gold trim, ceramic tile, and crystal clear glass doors on a large shower stall.

Anne slipped inside then closed the door. She sagged back against the door, and when Virginia took form in front of her, she muttered. "Virginia, you owe me big time!"

Shimmering hands lifted in a gesture of surrender. "I do... I do... and I promise I'll make it up to you, but there wasn't any other way to convince him."

"Yeah, right, and I'm Bugs Bunny." Anne filled the sink with warm water, then splashed some warm water on her face before she used a plush facecloth to remove the sticky residue left from their sex she'd, no Virginia'd, had with Clay. Mentally, she apologized to Jason. They might not officially be a couple yet, but her heart had already started to bond with him in ways it never had with Mark.

"Okay, so I might have taken advantage of the situation a teensy bit, but..." The mist enclosing her turned lavender. "Annie, I love Clay more than I thought I could ever love another living being. I think you might have done the same thing if our positions were reversed."

Anne folded the facecloth and placed it on the edge of the sink then pulled the plug. "I might have." She thought about Jason. The feelings she had for him were jumbled, but one thing she knew for sure was that if he left, he'd leave an even bigger wound in her heart and life than Mark had or ever could - a wound that would take a lifetime to heal. "But that's a moot point. What we have to do is see if Clay can think of anything that might help us."

Facing Clay again was easier than Anne expected it to be. With his suit straightened and seated behind his desk, she could almost believe what had happened was only a dream, but the faint musky scent of sex lingering in the room declared that it wasn't a dream.

"So, Virginia is here?"

Anne nodded, looking toward the corner of the desk where Virginia was sitting cross-legged. "She appeared once I put on the necklace." She deliberately omitted the part about having sex to help make her appear.

Virginia leaned forward, then reached out and raked her fingers through his hair. He started, then smoothed his hands over his head.

"You might not be able to see her, but she's letting you know she's still here." Anne offered a half smile.

When Virginia's hand drifted lower, toward his crotch, Anne scolded, "Not now, Virginia, we have to figure out who might have wanted to hurt you, and that's not going to happen if you distract him."

"Party pooper." A ghostly hand skimmed over his crotch then she pulled back.

A ruddy flush stained his cheeks, then a wry grin turned up the corners of his lips. "She hasn't changed much."

"Mr. Montgomery—"

"Clay, please. I think we're way beyond formalities."

"True." Now, it was Anne's turn to feel color wash across her face. She cleared her throat. She lifted the chain over her head and held it out toward him. "If you link your hand in the chain of the necklace you should be able to see her. It's worked before."

Clay didn't hesitate. He hooked his first two fingers into the chain.

Virginia lifted one of her hands and wiggled her fingers, glowing lavender for a few seconds. "Hi, Clay."

His gaze sobered. "Virginia."

The husky, murmured word brought tears to Anne's eyes. His love and pain was wrapped up in a few short syllables. The look in his eyes was the same one Jason had when he looked at her. The revelation stole her breath.

"We've been trying to figure out who might have wanted to kill me, Virginia said. "I know I had my share of friends and enemies, but I can't imagine anyone who would want to kill me."

He rocked back in his seat. "You're right."

Virginia turned toward Anne with a smug grin on her face. "Told you so."

There was a knock on the door.

Clay got up from his seat and opened the door. "Jason, come in."

Anne looked at Jason as he strode into the office, his square stubborn jaw and the love in his eyes, and suddenly she knew exactly how Virginia must have felt given the opportunity to have sex again with Clay... even to touch him again. In a short march of days, her heart had wrapped itself around him without a hope of ever returning to her.

Jason curled his hand around the side of her neck and pressed his lips to her temple before he eased into the chair beside hers. She curled her hand over his. Every time they were together, he surprised her. His open gestures of affection still conflicted with the controlled man she'd first met. His gaze met hers and he smiled.

A guilty flush crept up her cheeks even though logically she knew she had nothing to feel guilty about. The intimacy her body had shared with Clay had nothing to do with her.

"Is something wrong?"

"Let's just say Virginia created a bit of a distraction," Clay answered for her, the humor in his eyes the only hint of emotion in his otherwise neutral expression.

Virginia waved her hand in front of Anne's face. "Hello! How about seeing if we can do a three way connection?"

"Virginia wants us to see if we can all see her."

Jason leaned forward and hooked a couple fingers in the chain of the necklace.

"Well?" Virginia demanded.

In unison, the trio turned toward her.

She grinned. "Guess it worked."

"Guess it did, though if someone had told me I'd be talking to a specter today, I'd have banned them from the club – forever."

Anne straightened in her chair. "I guess the next question would be: who could have gained from her death?"

A crevice formed between straight, dark brows as Clay shook his head. "I think the question should be who would gain from her disappearance. Whoever killed her deliberately covered up her death."

Virginia settled on the corner of the desk, her forehead wrinkling in a frown. "I can't imagine who could benefit from my disappearance."

"I can," Clay said quietly.

The icy menace in his voice and hard glint in his eyes sent a chill down Anne's spine.

"Who?" Anne asked.

"Michael Williams."

"Mikey? He's harmless." Virginia whipped her head around toward Clay. "You can't be serious."

"Deadly." Clay looked from Anne and Jason to Virginia. "Who has control of your trust fund?"

"Mike."

"In the event of your death, who would inherit your trust fund?"

"You would."

"What?" Clay bolted upright in his seat.

"I changed my will a couple of days before I died. The day you proposed."

The chain slipped through his fingers, then he grasped it again. "Who knew about the change in your will?"

"Only Mike. He drew up the will." Virginia slid off the desk and started to pace. "Clay, I just can't believe he'd hurt me. We'd been lovers off and on for years... until I met you."

Anne mentally sided with Clay but decided to withhold comment until she'd met the man. Greed was a powerful motivator. "Perhaps I should pay him a visit."

"Not on your life."

"No way."

Two male voices declared in unison.

Jason gave her an implacable look. "If Clay is right, he's killed once. He probably wouldn't hesitate to kill again."

"But he might be more willing to talk to me. Besides, Virginia will be with me."

"She's a ghost," Jason returned.

"But not without a few tricks," Virginia quipped.

"No," Jason and Clay said in unison.

Chapter Twelve

Anne sat on the upholstered chair in the waiting room of Michael Williams' law office. She glanced at Virginia who was leaning against one wall tapping her foot. A twinge of guilt pinched her conscience. She'd come here without Jason and Clay and without their knowledge. They'd growled every time she'd suggested visiting his office. Men. Their smothering protectiveness might have been attractive in another situation, but not this time. She would have bet her inheritance that Michael Williams would be the key to figuring out who killed Virginia.

Jason's detective had located the Virginia impostor in France. They wanted to confront her before they spoke with Mike Williams.

"Mr Williams will see you now," his secretary said.

"I'll bet her credentials weren't the only thing good old Mikey was checking out when he hired her," Virginia commented as she floated by the woman's desk.

Anne tried to smother a grin as she cast a glance at the buxom, blonde bombshell. From what Virginia had shared about Mike Williams, he'd been a founding and very active member of the Attic Club. He'd been one of Virginia's lovers, but not exclusively so, though Virginia suspected he wanted to be. Though he was a talented and creative lover from the tidbits Virginia had shared, he'd never been able to capture her heart.

Anne walked into his office, a shiver of apprehension rippling through her body. It reeked of money. As lawyers go, he must be pretty successful.

"Good morning, Miss Kemper," he said rising from his leather swivel seat. He extended his hand toward her.

"Good morning," Anne replied. Mike Williams equaled Clay and Jason in height, but he'd allowed the years to add weight to his abdomen and a roll under his chin. His hair was almost completely silver.

"What can I do for you?" he asked. Curiosity flashed in his light blue eyes.

"I can't believe how he's let himself go," Virginia observed moving to his side behind the desk.

He scanned the sheet on his desk. "You said you wanted to talk to me about the Marshall house. You recently purchased Virginia's home."

"Yes," Anne said, wishing her thoughts would slow down enough for her to snag a few of them so that she wouldn't sound like an idiot. "By now you might have heard on the news that they found a body in my home."

"A body?" He bolted upright in his chair. His surprise appeared to be genuine. "In the cold room. That must have been quite a shock."

"If he's the murderer, he probably didn't expect you to find my body so soon... if ever."

"A woman's body. It was hard to identify the body because it was in such an advanced state of decay. Possibly decades." Anne watched for a reaction. He paled slightly before a light blush stained his cheeks. He wasn't giving much away, but enough for Anne to keep prodding him. "The police think she might even be Virginia Marshall," Anne lied, hoping to apply a little pressure and rattle him a bit.

"That isn't possible," he returned, easing back into his seat. This time when he studied her chips of ice had formed in eyes.

"It isn't?"

"It isn't?"

Anne and Virginia spoke in unison.

"How can you be so sure?" Anne asked.

"Because I have been in communication with Virginia for the last thirty years." He rested his elbows on the arms of his chair and steepled his fingers in front of him. His gaze never wavered from her face, but it revealed none of his thoughts. "In fact, I spoke with her just last week."

"You did?" Anne responded. "The police seemed so sure the woman was Virginia Marshall." She fought the guilty flush rising to her cheeks at her repeated lie. Though she wasn't sure why, the more time she spent with him, the harder her instincts twitched.

"Then, they are mistaken." Mike Williams rocked back in his seat, looking completely at ease.

Anne had nothing to go on but her gut, but his poise was too perfectly executed to be natural. If that was the case and he was Virginia's murderer, he was too consummate a liar for her to take him on single-handedly. Though it would mean confessing to Jason and Clay that she had come here on her own, she couldn't prove if he was telling the truth or not without help. She gripped the top of her leather purse and slid to the front of her seat, preparing to rise out of her seat.

"Let me talk to the lying bastard," Virginia growled. "He has to know the person wasn't me. He'd known me for years and would know my voice."

"I understand that it must have been a shock to find the body in the basement, Miss Kemper, but the police are mistaken. It can't be Virginia Marshall. I will, however, pass along the information to Virginia. I'm sure she wouldn't know anything about any body. She left the city thirty years ago and hasn't returned. In all likelihood, someone killed the person then stashed the body in Virginia's home because it was empty."

"Yes, you're probably right. Thank you for seeing me." Anne stood and made her way to the door. She pulled open the door, but a scowling Virginia slammed it shut.

Anne closed her eyes and gripped the doorknob, then gave it a tug. It wouldn't budge.

"Annie, you aren't going to just walk out of here. He knows more than he's letting on."

"Miss Kemper?"

"I seem to be having trouble opening the door." She sent a warning frown toward Virginia, but it bounced off the anger radiating from her sparkling form.

"Let me talk to the slimy weasel, or I'll do more than slam doors."

"Virginia, please." The plea was through her lips before she could stop it. She wanted to get out of here and create a plan before she talked to him again. Either he was telling the truth and someone else had killed Virginia and stolen her identity, or he was lying and she was standing a few feet away from a calculating, cold-blooded killer.

"Did you just say Virginia?" he said.

Anne exhaled slowly and nodded.

"Tell him, Annie, before I do something you'll really get upset about."

"Yes," she replied. "I did. Virginia Marshall is here as a spirit. I know she was the person killed thirty years ago because she's haunting my house."

Mike Williams impaled her with an artic stare. "If this is a joke, it isn't a very funny one, Miss Kemper."

"Murder is never a joke. Virginia was killed by a blow to the back of her head, and she can't pass over to wherever ghosts go until her murderer has been caught and justice is served."

"Annie, let me talk to him."

"You said that Virginia is here. Did you mean in this room? Are you some kind of psychic?"

"No, I'm not a psychic. Anyone who wears her necklace can see and hear her." Anne pulled the necklace from under her blouse. His eyes narrowed on the pendent dangling from the chain. "I found it in the house."

Even though Virginia could probably stop him from hurting her, a shudder of fear rocked her body. "If you loop your fingers through the chain you'll be able to see her, too." She'd made the suggestion, but she hated the thought of him getting that close to her.

"Really Miss Kemper, you don't expect me to believe this nonsense."

Virginia grabbed his tie and started lifting the tip. "I should strangle the louse," she muttered.

His eyes widened as the silky piece of fabric rose in the air before him. Without another word, he slid his fingers under the chain, and Anne held her breath.

"Hello, Mikey," Virginia said.

His head whipped around. His eyes widened as the blood drained from his face. "Virginia?"

"In the spirit."

"It's you?" His chest rose and fell in deep breaths. He shook head as if he was trying to clear his thoughts.

"No, it's the Easter bunny! Yes, it's me."

Anne put her hand up. "Virginia, sarcasm isn't going to help. We came here to see if he could help us figure out who killed you."

He stared wide-eyed at the shimmering specter. "You're a ghost." He said the words as if he needed to hear them to believe what he was seeing.

"I'm not sure of the logistics behind my inability to cross over. But I think it has something to do with the necklace and the fact that some scumbag got away with murder, my murder."

"We were hoping you might be able to help us figure out who killed her." Anne was glad that her voice didn't reflect the fear twisting her tummy into a painful knot.

"You mean she doesn't know who killed her?"

"The coward hit me from behind. I never saw them. And there doesn't seem to be any cosmic exchange of information to help me find out." Virginia scowled. "Though no one from higher up has communicated with me directly, I just sort of know that I have to figure this one out... with your help of course."

"Why did you think I could help? As I said to Miss Kemper, until today I believed you were still alive."

Anne studied him. Some color had returned to his face, but his expression gave nothing away. Could he really have been duped by the murderer, or was he trying to convince them? She wasn't sure.

"Mike, you knew me better than most, in the Biblical sense and as a friend," Virginia said. "I'd like to know how someone fooled you into believing I would really leave town. I told you how I felt about Clay when I changed my will."

"You were always impetuous and a bit hot-headed. I assumed you and Clay had had some kind of lovers' spat."

"An argument wouldn't have stopped me from marrying him."

He shrugged.

"You said that you were in constant communication with Virginia, but obviously that was impossible," Anne interjected. "How can you explain that?"

"The morning after she left there was a letter in my mailbox, saying she'd left and she'd contact me when she got settled in her new place. A few days later I received a letter from her from a villa in Italy, and with instructions to forward her spending allowance to a bank in Venice."

"And you didn't think it was strange that she would just pick up and leave the country?" Anne persisted.

He shrugged. "Like I said, Virginia was impulsive."

"Do you have the letters?"

He nodded, looked over at Virginia one more time, then slid his fingers from under the slender chain. Anne breathed a sigh of relief. Even if he wasn't the murderer, he still gave her the creeps. She couldn't imagine ever letting him push any part of his body into hers. Though she doubted Virginia would, she made a mental note to warn her never to use his body with hers like she had with Clay.

He went to a filing cabinet, drew a key chain from his pocket, and slid it into the oval lock. Anne sucked in a breath as he drew the drawer open. A vision of him taking out a gun paralyzed her. Virginia wasn't bullet proof, so she prayed what she lacked in substance, she could make up for in speed to deflect his aim.

When he drew a couple of files from the drawer, Anne exhaled slowly, nearly dizzy with relief.

"Here are copies of our correspondence and financial records for the first couple of years." Mike pointed to the drawer. "There's a file for each year."

Anne flipped through some of the letters. All were typewritten and signed with a bold Virginia. "Have you only communicated by letters?"

"No, in fact, I chatted with her just last week."

"What?" Virginia started pulling files from the drawer and stacking them on the top of the filing cabinet. "Do you mean to tell me you couldn't tell the voice was different?"

"It's been a long time since I heard your voice, and the phone can distort, especially an overseas call." Mike made a grab for the files when the pile started to slide to one side. "Whoa!"

"Annie, can you believe him?" Virginia exclaimed, throwing her hands up in the air.

"Virginia, slow down." Annie didn't believe him, but she wanted to find out as much as she could without arousing his suspicions. "If he said he was talking to you, then he probably thought that he was. There must be an explanation."

"Annie, are you blind? He's hiding something." She placed her elbow on the top of the filing cabinet. "Probably the murder weapon."

"Maybe," she answered trying to calm her down without giving her true thoughts away to Mike Williams. She didn't need Virginia to do something they'd both regret later. "Mr. Williams, the Virginia you've been communicating with has never returned to the city in thirty years? She grew up here. Didn't that strike you as strange?"

"Not really." He dropped the files in his hand in the middle of the desk then turned, folding his arms across his chest. His expression shuttered. "Virginia didn't have any close family members here in the city."

"So what happened to my money?" Virginia asked. "Did he give it to the impostor or pocket it himself. And don't think about not asking him. I want to know."

"Virginia was wondering if the impostor has been collecting her allowance."

"Yes, I continued to manage her investments, rather successfully if I say so myself, and she's collected the monthly allowance."

"So out there somewhere is an identity thief and murderer who has been living off Virginia's money for thirty years."

He nodded. "Of course, this can't go on."

His concerned words were delivered perfectly. Too perfectly. Anne didn't need Virginia's prodding to push him, to put the squeeze on him. His controlled veneer was really starting to irritate her. "Could you give me the information on the impostor's last known whereabouts?"

"Of course, but I don't have her current address. When we spoke last week, she said she would be leaving for France the next day, so I'll have to wait a week or so before I'll have her new address."

Virginia leaned over and whispered into her ear, "He's stalling."

"If you could call me then, I'd appreciate it." She wrote her number down on a card and passed it to him. Virginia might have powers enough to stop him from doing her harm, but she wouldn't feel safe until she was out of here. "I think we should go home and think about what our next move should be. Until we hear from the fake Virginia, there isn't much more we can do here."

"Okay," the shimmering spirit said and crossed her arms in front of her see through body.

Mike Williams looked at her, his eyes so cold it made her skin crawl. Then, the look was gone as quickly as it had come.

"Well," Anne said as she moved toward the door, praying Virginia would follow without giving her any trouble. "We'll head home and wait for your call."

"Certainly, and I'll help you in any way that I can," he said. "I want Virginia's murderer apprehended as much as you do."

Anne held her breath until she was out of the room and in her car with the door locked. She put the key in the ignition but didn't start the car immediately. Her hand shook, and her knees felt weak from reaction. Michael Williams was convincing, and she had no reason to doubt his word other than a gut instinct that twisted her stomach into an uncomfortable knot. The only time she'd seen an honest reaction on his face was when he'd seen Virginia. Then, for a few seconds, she'd seen a flash of fear.

When she pulled into the driveway of her home, Jason was sitting on the steps of the veranda. He lifted a hand in greeting when she pulled into the yard.

"Great," she muttered through her teeth while she smiled and waved back. She'd hope to snag a few minutes to herself to regain her equilibrium before she told him about the visit to William's office. Not telling him was out of the question. She just hadn't been prepared to tell him so soon.

"Hi," she said. She climbed out of the car and shut the door.

Jason looking every inch a banker in a tailor-made, navy suit and crisp white shirt walked along the flagstone path toward her. When his arms closed around her, she burrowed into his chest. The security of his embrace managed to chase away some of the uneasy feelings that has taken root inside her from her meeting with Mike Williams. With his arm looped around her waist, they walked toward her front door.

"How would you like to go out for supper?" he grinned. "And then come home for dessert?"

"That sounds great," she slipped the key in the lock and cringed. Her voice was tight. "Or perhaps dessert, then supper."

"What's wrong?" He curled his hands around her upper arms, his eyes mining for answers. "Has Virginia been giving you a hard time?" He hooked a finger in the chain and scanned the area, then let it drop.

Anne smothered a groan. Was she really that transparent? "Let's go inside, so we can talk."

"This sounds serious."

"It is." She walked into the foyer then dropped her purse on the semi-circular table beside the door before she faced him. "This afternoon, I... Virginia and I visited Mike Williams."

"You did what?" Jason's voice was quiet. Without shouting he'd managed infuse a quiet anger into his voice to make her realize that behind the man who treated her with such tenderness was a lion protective of his own. "After we told you not to?"

"We had to go," Anne said, wishing she could evict the timid note slipping into her voice.

"Annie girl, don't let him talk to you like that." Virginia slid between her and Jason, planting her fists on her hips. "You can put a cave man in a suit, but you can't take the cave man out of the suit. They go all primitive once they start thinking about you as their woman. Though there are times when that smothering protectiveness has an appeal, they have to learn when to rein it in."

Anne grinned in spite of Jason scowling at her.

"It's not funny," he growled. "You could have been hurt, possibly even killed. He's the only person who could gain from Virginia's death and non-disappearance."

"Look, even with the strong silent types distraction works every time." Virginia grinned. "They growl, but they are a push over. Some things always work. Pout. Give him the eyes...a tear or two, and he's putty in your hands."

Anne's smile grew a little wider. "Virginia, you're shameless!"

"Will you listen to me please?" Jason stepped forward, right through Virginia, then jerked back in reaction. "Did Virginia do something?"

"No, you did. You walked right through her."

He shivered. "Remind me not to do that again. It felt like someone plunged me in icy water."

Anne placed her palms on his chest, his warmth radiated through his shirt. She massaged the uneven plane of muscle. She closed her eyes, wanting to strip away the thin layer of fabric and skim her hands over his skin. "Virginia, give us a few minutes of privacy."

"Your wish is my command." She winked and disappeared.

"I know what you're doing." Jason grasped her wrists but didn't move them away from his chest. "And it's not going to work."

"It's not?" Anne grinned. The fact that he held her wrists without trying to stop her as she drew circles on her palms with his tight nipples contradicted his statement.

"You're trying to distract me, but it won't work. You shouldn't have gone to Williams' office without me."

Anne skimmed her hands down his ribs, then cupped his crotch. The fine fabric strained over the bulging arousal of his pants. "No? You could have fooled me."

He huffed out a sigh. "I want you, but I'm still upset that you took such a risk with your life. I don't want to lose you."

Anne slid her arms around his waist, pulling him tight against her body. Right now, she didn't need or want a lecture. What she needed was his arms around her, to hear his heart beating against her ear, to have him make love to her and chase away the uneasy feelings that had taken root since her meeting with Mike Williams.

"Be upset in my bedroom while I'm undressing you," she murmured, tugging him toward the stairs.

"We're going to talk about this later," he promised then slid his hand around the nape of her neck, burying his fingers in her hair. He brought his head down and kissed her, touching his tongue to her lips.

Anne opened to him, teasing his tongue with hers, inviting him to begin the primitive dance.

"You really were succeeding in distracting me," he said with a laugh.

Anne laughed softly. "I figured out that much." She pressed her hips into his groin, sandwiching his stiff penis between their bodies. "You aren't exactly subtle."

He swung her up in his arms and started up the stairs. Anne looped her arms around his neck, impatient to drag him to her bed and sate the wet ache growing between her legs. He wasn't the only one who could be distracted by the promise of sex.

When he lowered her legs to the floor, she cupped him once again, anxious to feel the soft skin of his rigid shaft sliding between her legs and deep inside her. No one had ever fit into her body or her life as well as Jason.

She slid her hands under his suit coat and pushed it off his shoulders. He shrugged it off and tossed it over a chair, then peeled off his tie. Anne started to unbutton his shirt. Tempted by the sight of his tanned skin dusted with whorls of soft curls exposed as she undid his shirt, she pushed the fabric aside and circled an already wrinkled nipple with the tip of her tongue.

"Distract me any time you want," he murmured, grasping the hem of her shirt then pulling it over her head.

Anne unhooked her bra and tossed it to one side, then reached for his belt buckle, while he cradled her breasts in his hands, stroking the soft curves. She pushed his trousers and briefs down together, anxious to see him naked. His stiff shaft stood out from his body, rising from a dark circle of pubic hair. She curled her fingers around his warm flesh, drawing her hand along his rod. "I love touching you."

"And I love being touched by you. Anywhere and everywhere."

He hooked his finger inside the elastic of her underwear then pushed them over her hips. They slid down her legs, and Anne stepped out of them. Still holding onto him, she led him to the bed, marveling at how quickly intimacy with him had felt right.

She pushed him back onto the bed then crawled toward him. She licked a glistening drop of precum from the slit in his shaft. She traced the outline of the helmet shaped head with her tongue. She took the head into her mouth, circling him with her tongue, while her hands stroked his scrotal sack, the rough but soft skin was pulled tight over his testicles.

She loved the salty taste on her tongue. If someone had told her a week ago, she would drag Jason 'Ice Man' MacIsaac' to her bed, tasting him and exploring his body inch by delicious inch she would have signed the papers to have them committed and yet here she was.

Broad shoulders pressed into the mattress, his eyes closed. Anne climbed higher, nipping and licking, then suckling his nipples. She centered his penis at the top of her sex then stroked the tip with her body. Each pass teased her clit, and she arched, stroking him again and again. Basic instincts moved her body. She resisted the feral urge to impale herself on his rod, no matter how badly she wanted him inside her. Slowly she slid along the length of him, up and down until he was arching under her.

"Woman, have you been taking lessons from Virginia on how to drive men out of their minds?" he growled.

"Maybe one or two," she admitted, accelerating the pace of her strokes. Suddenly, she was on her back with Jason's body pressing her into the mattress.

He shackled her wrists above her head. The head of his engorged shaft slid easily into her lubricated vagina.

She sucked in a ragged gasp of air. The touch of him, sliding into her body, stole her breath. Of their own accord, her hips lifted off the bed and her body swallowed up the length of him.

He withdrew and thrust, and she matched him in the mating dance.

"Oh, God," she murmured. A gasp of pleasure slid through her lips on a raspy breath.

He ground his pubis against hers. The climax was building, rising like a rocket toward an explosive climax. His shout of release came at the same moment her body clenched in primal satisfaction.

For a few moments, he didn't move except to drop feather light kisses on her shoulder. "Every time I think it couldn't possibly get better, it proves me wrong," he whispered, then rolled to the spot beside her on the bed.

"Let's forget supper," Anne murmured. "And just have dessert again."

"How about a nap first," he suggested, drawing her snug against his body.

"Sounds like a plan," she said, drifting in the languorous wake of sex.

By the morning, she'd had sex as much as she'd slept. She smiled as she thought of their shared shower and his lingering good bye before he left for work. If every day could be like that, she'd be a very happy woman. Heck, she already was a very happy woman. She'd be deliriously happy.

"Good morning, you sexy thing you!" Virginia appeared at her side as she strolled into her workroom. "If I wasn't so happy for you, I'd be green with envy."

Anne curled her hands around her mug of steaming coffee and smiled. "I'm definitely going to keep him. It's happened fast, but I know that I love him, and the next time we're together I'm going to tell him."

"Don't wait," Virginia said, her expression thoughtful. "I toyed with Clay for weeks, hinting about my feelings. If I could do it over, I'd have told him from the get go."

"He knows now. It's not the same, but I think it's helped him." Anne put her coffee on the table. "How about we finish the sculpture?"

"Let's," Virginia replied, then held her hands in the air, twirling around shedding her clothes.

By the middle of the afternoon, the figure was finished, only the wig was left to make. Anne glanced at the clock. It was almost suppertime, and she hadn't heard from Jason. Ever since they'd started having sex he'd called her every lunch hour. Almost as if in response to her thoughts, the phone rang.

"Hello?" Anne said, a smile playing on her face.

"Miss Kemper? Mike Williams."

Her stomach knotted. "Hello, Mr. Williams."

Flashes of color, like miniature fireworks, burst over Virginia's shimmering image at the mention of his name.

"I understand that you've grown close to Jason MacIsaac and Clay Montgomery."

A cold chill shivered through her body at the cool tone he used when he said their names.

"Yes." Anne's grip on the phone tightened.

Virginia pressed her ear to the receiver.

"Close enough that you wouldn't want anything to happen to them."

Her breath left her lungs in a single, painful gasp, suspecting what was coming next.

"If you want to see them again be at my estate on Greenwich Drive within the hour. Otherwise they'll be keeping Virginia company."

Her hand shook when she replaced the receiver in the cradle. Tears blurred her vision, but she wouldn't let them fall. Tears wouldn't help Jason or Clay. She swallowed hard then turned to Virginia.

"I think we need a plan," she said, glad to hear that her voice didn't shake like her insides.

Chapter Thirteen

Anne parked her car in front of Mike Williams' mansion overlooking the bay. Her heart beating so fast and hard it made her breath shake. Her hands, still gripping the wheel, were icy cold, and yet sweat slicked her palms.

"Gorgeous place," Virginia observed. "And he probably used my money to pay for it."

"Probably." Anne turned to the shimmering figure at her side. "Can you find Clay and Jason and make sure they're all right?" When Williams had said he had them and would kill them if she didn't come, she couldn't help but wonder if they were already dead, but she still came. She couldn't risk not coming if they were alive.

Virginia shook her head. "I'm not sure... I just don't like the idea of leaving you alone any sooner than I have to with that creep. Besides, I'm pretty sure if anything happened to them, I'd know."

"I hope you're right." Hot tears blurred her vision. Anne blinked them away. This wasn't the time to give into tears. If they were still alive, she had to rescue them. If not, she'd make damn sure that Michael Williams paid for his actions.

She climbed out of her car.

"Good evening, Anne."

At the sound of Williams' voice, Anne started and swung around and watched him walk down the stone steps from the front door of his home. "I want to see Jason and Clay."

He smiled, baring his teeth in a gesture that had nothing to do with welcome. "That is exactly where I intended to take you."

He grasped her upper arm in a cruel grip. "You and your male friends are going to go for a little boat ride. Straight to Davy Jones' locker."

"You don't really believe that you can get away with killing three more people?"

"Four, actually," he said pushing her ahead of him along the flagstone path leading to the private dock. "Once the bitch I'd hired to impersonate Virginia got wind that someone was investigating, she threatened to turn state's evidence if I didn't pay her several million dollars."

"And now she's dead."

"And speaking of the dead, where is Virginia?" He looped his fingers in the chain, then scanned the area around them, then dropped the chain.

"She couldn't leave the city," she said. "Loads of rules for ghosts."

From the penetrating glance he sent her way she wasn't sure if he believed her or not. She held his gaze hoping she could deceive the master liar.

"How unfortunate for you," he said, then dragged her down the dock toward a gleaming white yacht.

"This must have swallowed up a tidy chunk of Virginia's money."

"Not really." He pushed her ahead of him onto the boat. "She's worth a couple billion. Early on, one of the investments I made with her trust fund turned a huge profit. I kept investing, and for some reason, anything her money touched succeeded. I just kept collecting my ten percent. She was one lucky bitch."

"Not really. She had the misfortune of trusting you, and now she's dead," Anne contested as realization struck. "When she willed everything to Clay, you knew you'd never be able to convince her to marry you and that it wouldn't be long before she would get him to help her invest her money instead of you, which would mean losing control over her money and your inflated fees."

He shoved her forward. "You're right, but it's not going to do you any good because in a few minutes, you'll be joining her in the spirit world."

***

Virginia felt anger boil up inside her. She wanted to toss the louse overboard and perhaps she would, but she'd promised Annie that she'd try and find Clay and Jason if she could move that far away from the locket. Reluctantly she left Anne with Mike. She drifted down the stairs, and through a palatial sitting room, testing the limits bonds to the locket.

"Damn you to hell, Mikey!" she muttered under her breath as she moved toward the bedrooms. She leaned through one door, cursing the luxury and the empty room then she pushed through another.

"Clay!" she exclaimed and pushed into the room. He was alive, bound and gagged on a large bed. His arms strained as he tried to work at the ropes holding his hands prisoner. She shot over to the bed then started working on the knots. He stilled.

"Virginia?"

She slid her hands inside his jeans and cupped him.

He drew a sharp breath. "Damn it. If you're here, then Anne's here. That woman is as stubborn as you are."

"All the more reason to quit gabbing and get you out of here," she muttered even though she knew he couldn't hear her.

He grinned. "You're probably cursing me, aren't you, Ginny?"

An ache seized her chest. Virginia's movement faltered. It had been thirty years since he'd used her nickname, and usually then he'd only used it when he wanted to annoy her. She tugged the last knot free then ruffled his hair. The silver mingling with the dark brown waves only made him more attractive.

"God, Virginia, I've missed you," he growled. "For so long, I hated you because I was hurting so badly." He leaned over and untied his ankles while he spoke. "Damn it, if I'd only been less of a coward, I would have tried to find you. But then, the 'Dear Clay' letter brought me to my knees, I wasn't about to get a rejection face to face."

Virginia cursed every deity she could think of because she couldn't talk to him. Moments when Clay opened up like this were rare, she hated the fact that she couldn't communicate with him.

He stood up, rubbing his wrists. "If I'd gone after you, instead of feeding my wounded pride," he continued. "I couldn't have saved you, but Mike wouldn't have gotten away with murder or lived off your money for the past three decades."

Clay crossed the room and grabbed the doorknob. Dark brows with flecks of grey arched as he looked over his shoulder. "I don't suppose that you can unlock doors."

"Being a spirit does have its advantages," she quipped and slid her fingers into the lock, manipulating the tumblers. "There! Try again."

Clay turned the knob and opened the door a crack. "I think Jason is in the next room," he whispered and moved quietly into the hall.

Virginia peaked into the next room. "Bingo!"

She slid her hand in the lock, clicking tumblers in place, unlocking it just before Clay grasped the handle.

"Thank you, Ginny!" he whispered, then opened the door.

With a speed that surprised her, he slipped into the room, shut the door, and untied Jason.

"The girls are here," Clay said quietly. "Virginia untied me. She has a way with locks."

"Annie?"

"She must be here."

The yacht shuddered as large engines sprang to life. The large ship rocked.

"Damn it! He's probably planning to dump us all out in the bay." Jason sprang off the bed. We've got to stop him."

Virginia moved away. Clay and Jason could take care of themselves. She'd left Annie alone with the maniac far too long.

***

Anne sat in the overstuffed, leather pilot's seat on the bridge of the yacht, while Mike Williams stood at the helm. His gaze was trained on the ocean. Where was Virginia? Had she found Clay and Jason?

As if privy to her thoughts, Virginia appeared beside her. "The troops are rescued and on their way. And in the meantime I'm going to provide a little distraction." She stretched out on the control panel and played with a few knobs.

"What the hell?" Mike muttered, quickly readjusting levers with one hand and holding the small wooden wheel with the other. The vessel's engines shuddered then fell silent.

"Virginia!" Williams growled.

Anne swallowed hard as he turned and pinned her to her seat with a searing look. "Loads of rules for ghosts, are there?"

Virginia moved forward, placing her hands on his chest forcing him backward.

Anne held her breath as he staggered backward, fighting for his balance.

"Bitch," he growled, his hands flailing as she lifted him off the floor and started carrying him toward the door.

Clay and Jason burst onto the bridge. Anne sprang out of her chair and into Jason's arms. Tears filled her eyes. "I was so worried about you."

He smoothed her hair away from her face and wiped her tears with the pads of his thumbs. "God, I love you. And if you ever do anything this risky again, I'm going to kill you."

"Hey, lovebirds," Clay interrupted. "Virginia seems to have Mike well in hand, but we'd better do our part."

Anne turned to see Mike Williams dangling mid-air over the water. As she watched, he slid his hand into his pocket and pulled out a plastic square that looked like an electronic car lock.

"Should I drop him here or a little further out?"

Anne shook her head. "Virginia was wondering if we should drop him here or take him a little further out."

Williams held up the little plastic square pressed against his palm.

"Drop me, bitch, and you'll be doing me a favor. This is the trigger for a detonation device. The yacht is loaded with C-four. One touch and your friends will be joining you in the hereafter, and I'll be safe and sound in the water."

Anne watched anger and frustration play across Virginia's glistening features then she saw something else. Alarm sparkled in her ghostly eyes.

"Annie, I can't hold him much longer," Virginia said. "I think I overdid it a bit."

"Bring him to the deck," Anne said. "We'll take care of him."

Virginia lowered him to the deck, her shimmering form a little more transparent than when she first arrived.

"I don't suppose you could have a quickie with Jason?

Anne looked at Virginia. For the first time since she'd burst into her life, Virginia seemed to be struggling to remain visible.

Clay took a step toward Mike, then froze as he lifted the trigger.

"I think we've reached a stalemate," he murmured. "If you rush me, I'll blow this ship and your buddies to bits."

Jason straightened. "I don't think so. It would be suicide."

"And the alternative is life imprisonment or lethal injection," he countered. "Do you really think I care?"

Anne looked at Jason and then Clay. They were both physically in better shape than Williams, but still, neither could reach him and wrench the detonator away before he set it off. Her hand curled around the pendant, wishing she could come up with something.

"Here, give me that," Williams said yanking on the chain.

Anne felt it give, then watched in horror as he fixed his gaze on the last spot she'd seen Virginia. "I wanted to see your face, bitch, when you watched your friends die." He lifted his hand as if he was about to squeeze the device with a little flourish, then he jerked.

"Okay, guys, I don't know how much time I have. I'm weakening fast and Mike is fighting me for this body." It was Williams' voice, but Virginia's words. Williams' face twisted then he dropped to his knees. "Jump! Now! I'll hold him here as long as I can and then detonate the explosives. This bastard is not going to get away with murder again."

"Virginia!" Anne exclaimed.

"Jason, toss her over board! Get Annie as far away from the ship as you can." Williams' body twitched.

"But what will happen to you?" Anne burst as strong hands gripped her waist and lifted off the deck.

"I'll be fine. Go!"

"Jason, stop! The necklace…"

Jason tossed her over the railing then followed, Clay right behind him. Anne took a gulp of air just before she hit the water and sank. The salt water closed over her head. She struggled to the surface, turning toward the ship; she looked up and saw Virginia in Williams' body struggling to stand.

"Anne," Jason called to her from a few feet away. "Swim! And don't look back."

In a few clean strokes, he was at her side, Clay only a few feet behind him.

Flanked between the two men, she started to swim. She struggled to keep up, her lungs burning from the effort. Just as she started to slow down, the yacht exploded. The thunderous explosion pounded against her ears. Instinctively, she reached for Jason, holding onto him as she turned to look back as flames seemed to burst from every level of the vessel.

"He wasn't kidding when he said that it was packed with explosives," Clay said, treading water a few feet away. "Let's get out of here. I don't want to be around when the coast guard comes to investigate."

Chapter Fourteen

Anne staggered out of the water, Jason supporting her, Clay an arm's length away. The trio dropped onto the sandy beach. She rolled over and, resting on her elbows, looked out at the flaming yacht. Black smoke billowed from the flames enveloping the sleek vessel now half submerged.

"Virginia..." she whispered. What had happened to her dear friend? A true kindred spirit in every sense of the word. Tears filled her eyes at the sense of loss pressing on her chest like a weight. What would happen to the necklace? Would it melt in the heat of the flames? What would happen to Virginia then? Would she be able to pass over to wherever spirits go? If it sank with the ship, Virginia would be chained to it on the bottom of the bay, unable to communicate.

Jason turned toward her then pressed his lips against her temple. "She saved our lives."

Anne laid her head on his shoulder. "Williams had the necklace. It's probably at the bottom of the bay or melted. What's going to happen to Virginia?"

Jason cupped her cheek, turned her face to him and kissed away her tears. "I don't know. But if justice for her murder was her anchor here, then perhaps she's already passed over."

Clay's voice was husky when he said the words. "She's here."

Anne turned to him. "How do you know that?"

His lopsided smile didn't match the somber look in his eyes. "Let's just say she has a one track mind."

Knowing Virginia too well, Anne looked down at his crotch and saw his arousal straining against his pants. Her lips twitched. "Virginia, don't you think about anything but sex?"

"Look!" Jason said. "I think she's writing a message."

Letters formed in the sand. "Crossing over... see you in a few decades... love... bye."

Anne grinned when two hearts, intertwined, appeared beneath the words. Then, *"PS he's a keeper."*

The trio laughed in spite of the mixed emotions each were feeling.

"Goodbye, Virginia. I'm really going to miss you." A gentle breeze skimmed over her face. Anne knew it was the last time Virginia would touch her life, but she would carry a piece of her ghostly friend with her forever.

Jason wrapped his arms around her, holding her close against his body. She looked at Clay over his shoulder. His gaze was focused on the yacht, his expression relaxed. In only a few days, years of anger and hurt had been righted. More than justice had been served. Decades of misunderstanding and pain had been resolved.

"You're definitely a keeper," she murmured. "I'm never going to let you go Jason MacIsaac. I love you way too much."

"Remember who said it first," he said then grinned. "And I'm going to make you pay for taking so long to realize it."

Anne smiled. "Promises, promises." He put his arm around her waist, pulling her close to his side. She knew they'd have their ups and downs, but this was where she belonged, and she would savor every moment they had together.

Anne laid her head on Jason's shoulder, silently thanking Virginia for being a part of her life. From this day forward she would live, grasping each moment, never letting a moment pass that she could tell Jason she loved him.

Off to the Dance
Robert Cloud

"Before I began telling you this tale I mentioned that how the pendant returned to me was almost as intriguing as the story itself." Papa Zach added.

"A few months back, I was walking down the street in Boston where my old shop was located when I looked in a pawn shop and there in the window of the shop was the pendant. Normally I do not even gaze into windows as I walk but felt a sudden impulse to turn my head.

"As I walked in a man reeking of fish was counting a wad of money and telling his story to the pawn broker. So I listened.

"Jeb used to have a lucrative fishing business, but as the number of fish had dwindled he became one of those boats that hired out to weekend fishermen who were looking for their chance to catch a big one.

"On this particular trip the man was a loner and talked Jeb into fishing along beside him. Normally Jeb just ran the boat and paid little attention to his clients, other than to make certain they found a good spot to fish, but he actually found himself having a good time with this client and helped him haul in a good size salmon out of the bay.

"As soon as his client's fish was on deck the client pointed back to his pole, and Jeb turned to see it bent over straining against a real fighter. Had the pole not been in its anchor stand it would have been lost. Jeb grabbed the pole and they began to wrestle with another salmon this one even larger than the first.

"When they pulled it onto the deck it thrashed about and knocked both the men off their feet. Jeb landed so he was staring right into the eyes of the fish. When the fish's mouth opened to gulp he noticed something shining, something that should not have been there.

"Together the client and he wrestled with the fish and Jeb took a pair of long needle nose pliers, usually used to pry hooks out of the jaws of the fish and reached into the mouth to grab the end of a golden chain. It turned out to be this pendant." Zachariah held up the pendant and looked at it. He could almost feel the connection that it still held with Virginia and knew that it was another piece he would never sell. "In all the years he had been fishing he had never seen a salmon swallow a piece of jewelry before.

"Well, I just smiled, for I understood the magic of the jewelry I make. It always finds its way back.

"I waited until the fisherman had left and then approached the broker.

"That was sure an interesting story, I said. I wonder if there is any truth in it.

"The broker replied that Jeb was one to make up fish tales so he doubted it, but the piece was definitely worth some money.

"I agreed, and offered to pay him what he was asking for it without even trying to haggle. He was surprised but did not reject my offer."

Melanie laughed, "I can see, and now that I have seen how quickly you made that piece I do believe there is magic in your pieces. I have no doubt his story was true."

"Neither do I, sweetheart." Zachariah patted Melanie on the shoulder and added, "Now that was a long story and it is getting really late. You have school tomorrow so you should be going."

She lowered her eyes and he could see a small pout upon her lips, "I know, Papa Zach, but I feel so much more comfortable here. I wish I could just stay here instead of going home."

"Oh sweetheart, you do not mean that. I am an old man, and you would worry your mother."

"Maybe, but I do mean it." She stood and kissed his lips, each of her kisses had lingered a little longer, this time her hand had slid to the back of his head. Though Zachariah wanted her love and to love her he began to feel uncomfortable. The age difference was tremendous. How could she be falling for a man of his years?

As her lips separated from his he looked at her bewildered but he had no doubt that the look in her eyes was one of love. She lowered her eyes trying to hide her feelings. Maybe she also realized that there was something wrong with a love between two people so far apart in years. Softly and sadly she spoke, "I guess I should go. I will see you tomorrow, Papa Zach."

"I look forward to seeing you too, Melanie." He smiled at her, and her face suddenly beamed with a brilliant light. She went towards the door to leave but kept turning back to look at him several times as she headed that way. She was hesitant to leave him, but finally she stepped through the door, turning the lock before closing the door behind her.

Zachariah waited. He was expecting the rattle of the mirror but it never came. He stood and walked to the mirror and asked, "What? No jealous remark?"

If I am going to be sharing her body it is good that you love her you old fool. Then your love of her will protect me too.

"So it does not bother you that I am fond of her?"

Well, you finally admit it. No, it does not bother me anymore. Now that I know she is the one, I know I need her, and I know the reason you are attracted to her is so that when she and I are one then you will be pleased.

"I am still not happy about this. I am worried that the demon inside you will corrupt her."

You do not love the dark side of me, Zachariah. So I do not see that happening. I believe your love for her good side will protect her. The magic in the stone is from you after all.

"From me? You always told me it was from you!"

How could it be from me? I am dead, a vapor, a mist. The magic you create is living, vibrant, real.

"Well I have three days and two nights to set the diamonds, so I should retire.

"Lilith, if she says yes, you swear you will do her no harm?"

I swear, Zachariah!

***

The next few days went by rather quickly for Zachariah and he was amazed at how quiet Lilith remained the entire time. From the time he awoke he would begin setting the diamonds. It was delicate work because he had to match the stones. The stones on opposite sides of the tiara had to match perfectly. Sifting through the stones to find two perfect emerald cut diamonds that were identical matches was what took the most time. He would only take time to nod his head when Melanie entered, though she would come over and stare in wonder at all the diamonds laid out before her. She would then turn his head sweetly and kiss his lips. No longer would she just settle for kissing his cheek, and though Zachariah still tried to make his mind believe it was nothing but a grand-daughterly kiss he knew better. Her heart did not see his age, she saw only that he had treated her with the respect and kindness that few others had shown her and she was responding to that as a young woman to a man.

While he would set the stones his mind would drift and he would remember how even during the early days of his love for Lilith there seemed to be a shadow hanging over her. He never could place it, yet he did not let it interfere with how he felt for her. He now realized that the feeling he was developing for this young girl was deeper than any he'd had for Lilith. There was no taint, no shadow of doom waiting to descend upon her heart. Yes, he knew Lilith had plans, but it was not the soul of Melanie that carried the taint.

On the night before the dance as Zachariah was setting the last of the stones he began to remember how soon after he had married Lilith his village had come to be called cursed even though no one from the village died unnaturally or was hurt. No diseases infested the animals, and nothing seemed to plague the village. It was all the villages that circled his that suffered. Reports of healthy men going into the fields at night to check the flocks or crops and did not return. In the morning all that would be found would be their bones and dust piled within their clothing. It was as if something had drained all the life fluids from them, not only the blood but the water from their tissue as well.

Rumors of a monster had begun to circulate. The only village that went untouched was his. Someone mentioned it all began about the time his wife had shown up and that soon the neighboring villages were going to come with more men and want to examine her. As suddenly as the murders had started they had ceased. The examination had been called off and he and Lilith had been apologized to.

Zachariah had thought everything between he and his wife was going to be as he had dreamed, until the night before their anniversary. That night she had been distant, cold, and had barely spoken to him at all. Then on their anniversary she had come to the shop and had confessed what she was to him. She had confessed everything except the most important thing. She had not told him she was carrying his child.

Zachariah stopped, a tear running down his creviced face. Melanie looked up as she heard him sob and ran over to him. She wrapped her arms around him and asked, "Papa Zach, what is wrong?"

For several minutes Zachariah could not control his tears, he just wrapped his arms around her as she climbed into his lap and they held each other. His tears rolled down as he buried his head against her shoulder. "Papa Zach, please tell me. What is wrong?"

"I... I..." He coughed, then took a deep breath and raised his head, "I was just remembering the night before Lilith died. It was our anniversary and she committed suicide on the night of our anniversary. I did not know she was carrying my child until several days later when my mother told me."

"Oh Papa Zach," Melanie wrapped her arms around his head as his tears came freely. "Why would she kill herself? Why would she hide that wonderful news from you?"

He whispered, "I cannot tell you yet, Melanie. I will, but give me another day or two. Maybe after the Grand Opening, I will tell you the hardest tale, that story of the ring that you wanted to know about."

"Only if you really want to Papa Zach."

"I do not think I have a choice, Melanie. I think it is a story you will have to hear."

"Okay, Papa Zach, but please stop crying. It hurts me so to see you so deeply hurt. I love you Papa Zach, and I want you to always be happy."

Zachariah looked up at her and his tears stopped immediately, his eyes wide with shock. "What did you say, Melanie?"

"That I want you always happy?" she smiled, she knew what he wanted her to repeat.

"No, before that."

"That I love you?"

"Yes." Papa Zach looked at her closely, "Melanie, you do mean that like a friend, don't you?"

"No." Melanie paused, then laid her head on his shoulder and looked down. Her fingers fidgeted on her knee and he could see that she was trying to gain the courage to repeat what she had said. Zachariah could tell that it terrified her that her words were about to change things between them for the worse. "I mean that I am in love with you."

Zachariah took a deep breath, they were words he wanted to hear, but they were also words he had dreaded hearing for he had to make her realize that the age between them was wrong, that that kind of a relationship was impossible.

Even though soon he would be almost as young as she was he was not permitted to tell her. Even if he was able to let her know he doubted she would believe him. Yet maybe there was a way. He reached up and caressed her cheek with his fingertips and looked into her eyes.

She was the One, and if Lilith could be thwarted so that Melanie was not harmed or possessed by her then once the ritual was in progress he could reveal the truth. She might even accept it. Would she still love him if he were young again?

His heart beat rapidly. Was she truly in love with him and who he was or was she in love with the image of who she thought he was? He knew this was a dangerous thought for the ritual was in progress. He could tell her nothing. She had to be pure.

Thanks to Lilith he understood better what that purity entailed, it did not mean that her kisses were making her impure. He did not have to worry that if she happened to have a sexual thought about him that it would ruin the ritual for if she were truly in love her thoughts did not matter as long as she held to the belief that sex had to wait until after marriage. Still she could not agree to the ritual just so that it would secure her his love. That would ruin the ritual as surely as if she had lost her virginity.

Yet in a way he prayed something did happen to change her purity for he was afraid that she would agree to Lilith taking her. He would rather die than have that happen, and he knew he would die if Melanie said no. Lilith had left the images in his mind that she and Melanie would share Melanie's body, that Lilith would only be able to use her body at night and even then not every night. For the most part Melanie would be in control of her body.

Zachariah knew Lilith too well and he knew that there were many things that she was not telling him. The images that she left in his mind were filled with darkness and it felt like they were covered in a red mist. Besides the last few times he had spoken with her he could tell she was blocking a part of her mind, even more than she normally did. She had always kept things from him, but now it was like she was only letting the tiniest of fragments out the hatred she felt for Melanie scared the shit out of him. He knew she would not harm Melanie because she was Lilith's only chance for freedom, yet he did not trust Lilith to tell him even the slightest bit of truth unless it benefited her.

He looked at Melanie and smiled, his heart was warmed by her confession but he had waited too long to respond to her for he could see tears beginning to form in her eyes. He reached out and took her hands and pulled her close to him and looked her directly in the eyes so she could see that his words came from his heart, "Precious girl, listen, this body before you is over a hundred years old. I may not live until tomorrow let alone any length of time after that. You should not waste your love on me, but seek out someone your own age."

Melanie lowered her eyes, "Papa Zach, please don't reject me. I know the difference in our ages, and it is not like I want sex with you. I am not ready for sex at all. Yet I love being with you, and I would rather be with you than anyone else in the whole world. If you only live the one day let me spend it with you, yet if you live twenty more years I want to spend those twenty years being with you."

"Honey, I am not rejecting you, I am just being realistic."

Melanie dropped to her knees and laid her head upon his thigh, "Yes Papa Zach, you are rejecting me. What does realism have to do with love? Love is in the heart.

"I have been thinking about this. I was surprised about my feelings for you. I too thought of the age difference and then I realized that love does not discern age. Your heart chooses who you love, and I love you." Her body began to shake as she began to cry.

"I know you may think I am a drama queen, or that I am given to emotional outburst. Papa Zach, I have never loved anyone before. I have never had a boyfriend. It was nice to be asked to the dance but I did not want the boy to be my boyfriend because I do not feel anything for him. I don't get emotionally attached to people easily. Yet there is something between you and me. I feel drawn to you. I felt it the very day I was walking by outside the store. It was why I stopped. Looking up at your sign and seeing it was backwards was only an excuse to talk to you. I felt a pull. I wanted to talk to you.

"I want to be here. I want to hold you. I want to cuddle with you. I want to kiss you. When you touch me I tingle deep inside. Your words make me quiver. Your stories fill my heart with joy." Melanie raised her face and looked to his face as he looked at her. He could see the tears rolling down her cheeks and he wanted to lift her into his arms. He could see from the frightened look in her eyes that she was worried he was going to send her home and that he would not let her come back. "The boys my age are only boys, they do not look at me for me, they look at me as someone that they can have sex with. If I gave in to them every boy in school would be asking me out. Since I don't they tease me and play tricks on me and call me names."

Melanie smiled. Zachariah offered his hand and she took it as he helped her to her feet. She leaned over him and kissed his cheek, his forehead, his nose, and his lips, then added, "Thank you for not sending me away immediately and for letting me explain at least. I know I am young and inexperienced. However, I know what I feel too.

"Papa Zach, what I feel for you is not lust, but deeper. I do not see you as a hundred year old man. I see you as a man that cares for me and that reached out to me to make me feel special when no one else has ever done that.

"Papa Zach, please do not refuse my love." Melanie held her hands together as if pleading, almost praying with him, "I would serve you in any way I can. Please do not think that my love for you is less than it is."

Zachariah looked at her. He knew there was no way he could send her away, he took her hands into his and pulled her back onto his lap. "Melanie, I feel that the age difference may not make as much difference soon as it does now. No, I will not send you away."

For a long time they held each other then Melanie returned to her decorating and Zachariah to his work of setting the last of the stones.

An hour later Melanie returned and announced that the decorations were done. She then sat down beside Zach, but on the floor, resting her head upon his knee. "Papa Zach, I can see you are shuffling through stones trying to find another set of matching stones. Since we spent some nice time in each other's arms I do not mind if we forego the story tonight if you need to work. I know tomorrow night is the dance, and I do not want you staying up all night. It is not good for you."

He paused and looked down at her, smiling. "Actually I was going to say something similar." Tenderly he ran his fingers through her hair and she lifted her head and moaned. It almost sounded like a purr, and a thought struck him now how much she reminded him of a cat. Her steps were so light that he barely heard her, and there were many times she was right beside him before he knew she had even been approaching. Slowly and gracefully she rose to her feet and leaned in to kiss him. He was surprised that she was so eager and not repulsed at kissing a man his age in such a manner but he was thankful as he savored her kiss.

***

Melanie felt warm in her heart. She had not meant to confess her feelings to him. Truth was until she had said it aloud she was not fully sure she was in love with Papa Zach, but once she had said it she knew it was true. It felt so right. When he looked at her she could feel the warmth from his heart coming from him even from the day they had first met. Maybe it was that sixth sense of hers, but it always guided her in the right direction. Even though he was much older than she was somehow she knew that she would be with him a very long time.

When he stroked her hair it had been almost like he had petted her as if she was his pet. She had suddenly felt like a cat sitting upon his lap and she had wanted to purr, for she felt so at peace and soothed when she felt his tender caress. For a moment she had even wondered what his touch would feel like when they were married but quickly she had put that thought out of her mind. Yet somehow she knew the day would come when she would be his bride and that filled her with even more joy for she knew that with Papa Zach she would be able to be the type of housewife she had always wanted to be. He would not be the type of husband that expected her to go find a job at a grocery store or convenience mart just to get a few extra dollars so he could have his beer. No, Papa Zach would want her to take care of their home.

She rose from his lap and leaned in to kiss him. It was a sweet kiss. Once again a brief thought of passion entered her mind. She wanted to love him more and deeper but it was too soon and she was not yet eighteen. Yes, it was legal in New York but even she felt odd not being eighteen. So she rose and smiled at him, savoring the moisture that was left on her lips instead. As she turned she ran her tongue over her lips and tasted his. It was nice. Maybe sometime she could share more passionate kiss with him. She turned back around and looked at the man that had so quickly entered her heart and said, "I know I should probably call you something other than Papa Zach, since you know I love you, but that just feels so right. If you really do not mind me calling you that I would like to still do it?"

He laughed out loud, nearly falling out of his chair as he did, but caught himself, "When you first began calling me Papa Zach my heart swelled because it felt right too. My mother used to call my father Papa. She did so all the days that she lived. So if you have no problem with it I do not mind."

Melanie could feel her eyes get really big at his news; she'd had no idea, "Your mother called your dad 'Papa' all the time?"

"Yes, from my earliest memories."

She smiled, "Well maybe if we are together for a long time I will someday call you just Papa in their honor."

He smiled at her, "That would be nice."

Melanie could not help but smile broadly. She leaned down and kissed him once more and then said, "Well, Papa Zach, I have to be going but I will see you tomorrow just before the dance. I will dress up for you here so you can see how I look and then head to the dance."

Melanie's eyes suddenly teared.

"What is wrong, Melanie, sweetheart?"

"Well, now I wish I was not going to the dance. I would rather be here."

"No! Dear, you need to go. Have fun, and then come back after the dance, and tell me all that happened."

She smiled. "Oh, you want me to come here after the dance? It could be late."

"Yes come back. If it is okay with your mother, come and tell me all that happened."

Melanie nearly danced about, "I am certain my mother will not mind. I will be here."

Then Melanie danced out the door she was so happy that Papa Zach wanted her to come back after the dance that she swirled about and danced all the way home.

Zachariah smiled as he watched her leave, then he went back to sorting the stones, his heart singing a song so loudly that his mind did not catch the whispering and muttering that he would have normally heard had he been paying attention.

Lilith was fuming. The glass of the mirror was blood red. She would have pretended everything was okay had Zachariah asked her, but her anger was boiling beyond anything she had ever felt before. *When I get into that body of hers I am going to eat her soul, but before I do I am going to make her suffer. I am going to make her watch me turn Zachariah into a monster just like me and then when he awakes as a beast and sees what I have done and knows that I have betrayed him I will tell him I am about to destroy her soul. Then I will let her see him struggle against the power of my mind, unable to move as I devour her. That fucking cunt, how dare she fall for my husband! How dare she kiss him in front of me! And that fucking fool of a husband... how dare he allow her to do that in front of me!*

Once I am free of here I will take him and kill her entire family. I will make Zachariah feed upon them. I will make him know what it is like to feel the hunger and to be betrayed like he has betrayed me.

***

An hour before Melanie was due to arrive; Zachariah finished setting the last of the diamonds. As he bent over the last tine that would hold the stone in place the entire piece glowed brilliantly and filled the room with a soothing warm red hue. It was complete and the magic was set and ready for Melanie. He laid the tiara on the counter and walked upstairs to his room to get the dress he had chosen for the night. It was an elegant black evening dress that plunged nearly to the waist in the back. The skirt portion was three layers of lace, the inner most dark, but all three were not dark enough to completely obscure the view of her legs. They would hint at them in a hidden glance. The front was black velvet that would come up and cup her breast, accenting them nicely but not too provocatively. Two black velvet laces would come from the outside edge of the cups and wrap over each shoulder then cross in the back and fasten to the black velvet corset just below her shoulder blades.

Melanie would look stunning in the dress, and with the tiara she would look like a queen. Zachariah had no doubt the dress would fit her too. Something had told him that this dress would be a perfect fit, and the magic was never wrong. As he walked down the stairs with the dress draped over his arm he heard the door chime. Looking at his watch he saw it was only 3:30 but he had no doubt it was Melanie, and as he rounded the corner and saw her lifting the tiara he was not surprised to see her eyes sparkling even brighter than the gemstones of the tiara.

He snuck up behind her and said, "So how do you like it?"

Quickly she sat it down and spun about, placing her arms about his neck and kissing his lips then pulling back, "It is perfect, Papa Zach."

It was only then that she saw the dress in his outstretched arm. Her jaw nearly dropped to the floor as she took it in. Slowly she lifted it. "Papa Zach!" She said her face turning beet red with embarrassment. "I cannot wear this. I would feel like I was wearing nothing."

"Melanie, you need a dress fit for a queen. This is perfect, and yes you can wear it."

Melanie looked up at him, and smiled. Then she ran back to the door and turned the latch locking the door. Then she turned the bar on the blinds closing them and hiding the shop from the outside world. Then turning back to Zachariah she said, "Papa Zach that is the most beautiful dress I have ever seen, but I have never worn anything that sensual. I am not certain I can. I will be so embarrassed."

"Sweetheart, there is nothing to be embarrassed about, you are a beautiful girl, and you are not going there to seduce anyone. You are just going in a costume. Think of it like you are going to be in a play."

Zachariah said.

Melanie smiled as she took the dress from him and held it up, "A play? I think I can do that.

"Now where can I go to put this on?"

"You can use my room upstairs," Zachariah said. "But why did you lock the door and pull the blinds?"

Melanie blushed, "When I put this on I want you to be the first one to see me. With the door locked and the blinds closed I know no one can come in or look in the window. I would be so embarrassed."

Quickly she took the dress and ran upstairs. Zachariah waited for a while then he heard her yelling down the stairs, "Papa Zach, I need your help."

Up the stairs he went. At the top of the stairs he knocked on his bedroom door. She answered, "I am not decent, Papa Zach, but I can't get this dress on. I don't know how to put on one like this."

"Okay, now this is a problem, I had not thought about that. I have other dresses you can wear," he said.

He could hear her sniffle and she said, "No, Papa Zach you chose this one special for me, I really want to wear this one."

"Well can you tell me what the problem is?"

"I don't have any idea as to how to put it on."

"Honey, what can I do to help?"

"Do you know how they go on?"

Zachariah felt like it would be better if he lied but he had already told her too many lies that he'd had no choice about. He could not tell her one now, "Yes, precious, I do."

Melanie whimpered and then said softly, "Will you help me?"

"Melanie, are you sure?"

"If you were my grandfather and I needed help to get dressed would there be a problem with you helping me?"

"No, not really."

"Then will you help me?"

Slowly Zachariah opened the door. His heart almost stopped when he saw her sitting on the side of his bed wearing only a mini slip and a bra. He was certain she wore her panties under the slip but thankfully that was hidden. Actually he breathed a sigh of relief for she was more covered than most girls he had seen on television shows that took place on the beach.

Melanie's face was blotched with tears and red with embarrassment, "Papa Zach, no man has seen this much of me since I was born. I have always had female doctors."

"It is okay Melanie; I can handle seeing you this way. Now let's get you dressed and end your embarrassment." He helped her put the dress on. Since it would require her to remove her bra he had her leave it on until the very last moment and only when he was standing behind her did he have her remove her bra so that he could help her with the straps.

Her dignity had indeed been preserved even if she felt it had been soiled. He assured her it had not and before she left the room she was smiling again.

As the last touch he had a pair of black low heeled shoes for her. Finally she was ready and as she turned about he smiled. He walked around her and took her hair out of the braid that she always wore it in. Then he took the tiara and placed it upon her head. As an added bonus from the jewelry counter of standard pieces he took a large sapphire pendent and placed it around her neck.

Slowly she turned for him and he smiled. Melanie was the most startlingly beautiful woman he had ever seen. She surpassed even Lilith, and not by a little bit but by leaps and bounds for not only her physical beauty surpassed Lilith but the beauty of her soul shown through as well. The magic of the tiara had already begun, and he could see Melanie for all that she was, the true beauty of her heart was visible for all to see.

The dance did not begin for another hour yet, and Zachariah could not resist. He walked over to his old record player and set an old waltz onto the turntable then he returned to her and said. "I may not be able to be at the dance, but if I may, I can have the first dance with you this night."

Melanie smiled. There had been one regret she'd had and that was that she would not be able to dance with the one person she cared most about. Almost as if he had read her mind he had wiped away her regret and made her night into a true dream. She reached out with both her heart and her hand and took the hand he offered as he led her into a waltz.

From the smile upon his face she could see he was surprised that someone her age knew how to waltz. If it would not have ruined the moment she would have told him that the housekeeper that had spent a lot of time with her had taken dance lessons and Melanie had been her practice partner. Melanie knew how to lead better than she did how to follow but she had always watched the housekeeper closely so when the day came that she had the chance to dance she would know what to do. Her heart sang along with the music as that day had finally come to her.

After a few moments of waltzing she looked up at the man she loved and smiled at him saying, "Papa Zach, can we just slow dance. I want you to hold me for the rest of the song."

He smiled down to her and nodded. She felt wonderful as she laid her head against his chest and they danced slowly to the rhythm of the music. She looked at his hand within hers, the wrinkled skin against her smooth skin and knew that it was going to be difficult to get past the differences in their ages when it did come to the issue of sex. It was one thing for her heart to be in love with him. She knew it was going to be another for her to lay next to him naked and make love to him. It hurt her to think that she would have problems with it so she began to try to imagine it.

At first it was something that was a little disturbing but then she remembered the look in his eyes and the love that was there. Soon the images no longer bothered her, soon she found she was even becoming aroused and that was something she had never felt before. She looked up into his face. The lines were heavy upon his face but his eyes had youth and love for her in them. As his eyes held hers she found that she did not care, as long as his eyes continued to hold that look of love for her she would be his. She would hold him in her arms and when it came time she would have no problem being his wife and lover.

Melanie realized that she had seen a movie recently about a couple that were called a May/September romance, she smiled for if they compared that movie to her and Papa Zach they would call them an Early March/Late December romance. She held onto him, not wanting the music to end and not wanting to let him go. She wished there was some way she could pass some of her years to him just so she could have him with her for a little longer. Then she heard the music end and felt a tear slide down her cheek. Quickly she wiped it away before he could see it and smiled up at him. As she did she heard a rattling sound on the wall at the back of the shop. She looked that way and the only thing there was a mirror.

Melanie looked at the mirror for a moment and wondered what could have made it rattle and then she heard a large truck pass by on the main road outside. Perhaps that had been it, but she did not remember hearing a truck a moment ago. She turned her gaze back to Papa Zach and put the rattle out of her mind.

As the dance ended Zachariah heard the mirror rattle. He looked to it and could feel the waves of fury coming from Lilith. He had begun to come up with an idea now that Melanie had told him that she loved him that may just save Melanie. He did not yet know if there was a way that it would allow him and Melanie to be together but at least Lilith would not get her.

Zachariah smiled returning the lovely smile that Melanie was giving him and then said, "There is one more thing that you need to go with that dress."

He went to the closet and pulled out a black velvet opera purse then returned and handed it to her. It was just big enough to carry her identification and a little money and a couple of emergency items. Then he made a phone call and ordered a pizza from Chef Jeff's. Melanie looked at him funny and asked, "Won't that hurt your stomach?"

"No, I have a cast iron gullet. Now, sit down and talk to me a bit before you go. You do not want to be too early." She agreed and they sat and talked for a while. Then there was a knock on the door and Zachariah went to answer it. Turning the latch he let the pizza driver in. He looked outside and saw the large station wagon the driver was using to deliver pizzas and smiled.

After paying for the pizza he looked to the driver and said, "Hey, what's your name." He had noticed that the driver could not pull his eyes from Melanie.

"Ummm, it's Philip. Why?"

"How would you like to make an extra fifty bucks tonight? Twenty now, and thirty a few hours from now, and all it takes is a five minute detour on your delivery route."

Melanie looked up and began to protest, "Papa Zach, I can walk!"

"Not in that dress you can't."

Philip looked at the twenty being offered to him, "Sure, what do I have to do?"

"Drive Melanie to the High School for the Dance, and in three hours pick her up and bring her here."

"Three hours? Papa Zach, I may not need that long."

"Or you may need longer," Zachariah thought. "Okay, Melanie, when you are ready to be picked up call here. Then I will call Chef Jeff and leave a message for Philip."

"Philip, the message will be, the pizza was very good, and your service was great. Then you will know to pick her up." Zachariah looked at Philip; upon his face was a dazed look, "Do you have it? Or do I need to write it down?"

"Nah, I got it," Philip responded. "It is just no one has ever asked me to do anything like this before."

"Well there is a first for everything," Zachariah said as he handed him the twenty, and Melanie followed Philip out the door. Zach could tell she wanted to kiss him goodbye but with Philip there thought better of it, but she did kiss his cheek and said she would see him later. Then out the door she went. After she left Zachariah turned the bar and opened the blinds again. Then he returned to the area where the gemstones were still out. He had not worried about anyone seeing them for the way the counter was set up they were hidden from the view of anyone unless they were looking right down upon them.

An hour had passed and Zachariah had finished sorting out the gemstones he needed. He set those aside and took the last drawer of containing the rest of the gemstones back to its hidden locker and closed the vault. As soon as he heard the click of the vault's locking mechanism he also heard the front door chime announce a visitor.

"Sorry, we do not open until tomorrow." He hollered out to the visitor.

A woman's voice responded in a very prim and proper manner, "Mr. Zachariah?"

He looked around the corner at a very lovely woman in her late thirties to early forties. She was dressed in a woman's business suit of a blue grey jacket and skirt with black pinstripes. Her blouse was a pale grey, and the thing that passed for a woman's tie was a deep violet. She was blonde and her eyes were a light blue. As he walked toward her he noticed that her skin tone was well tanned, but from the suit and her stance Zachariah was pretty certain it was from a tanning salon and not the beach. "May I help you?" He brushed dust from his hands off on his apron as he neared her.

"You are Mr. Zachariah then?"

"That is close enough, so how might I help you?"

"My daughter is Melanie. I am Rebecca Morgan, Representative to the State Senate from this area." She held out her hand to shake his.

He reached out and took it and was surprised that she shook it firm like a man and not wimpy or soft. At least that was something she had in her favor. He liked women that showed a strong nature when they took on such responsibility.

"It is good to finally meet you. I had expected you earlier." Zachariah smiled at her.

She did not smile, but her tone was not harsh, "I have been busy down in Albany and this is the first chance I have had to come by."

She glanced around the shop and then back at him, "You have some nice pieces here. Melanie mentioned on the phone that you had some very interesting pieces. Do you mind if I take a look at them?"

"No, not at all, but don't you wish to ask me any questions?"

She turned and took her gloves off and placed them in her purse and responded, "Not really, Melanie is really not my concern. She was adopted. My husband and I thought we could not have children so we found this girl that was about to get an abortion and paid her to live with us and have her child. It was only days after we signed the contract that we found out I was pregnant.

"My husband, who is a lawyer, was very careful to make certain the contract was unbreakable, unfortunately it was unbreakable by us as well. Our son was born two days before Melanie.

"We have pretty much let the nannies we have had raise Melanie. We knew it would be too difficult not to play favorites, so we did not try. We had two more children after our son, another boy, and a girl. Melanie was raised in the servants' quarters. We make sure she gets everything she needs. She never gets in any trouble so we pretty much let her do as she wishes. It makes it easier on us to not have to watch over her.

"We have told her that after she turns eighteen she can stay until the end of the semester but then she has to find a job and move out."

Zachariah was shocked at how coldly and bluntly the woman told him this. It was like it was common knowledge and she did not care who knew about it. Now he knew why Melanie had said many of the things she had said. She had so many things stacked against her. She had different ideals about the way a woman should be but then the way her parents treated her as well. Now he understood why she was so often the butt of the other kid's jokes.

He almost regretted having agreed to show her the jewelry but he had so he walked to the special cabinet and opened it. Her eyes opened wide as she gazed at the pieces.

"I have never seen anything like these pieces. They are amazing, such craftsmanship and detail." Her eyes were glued to the pieces of jewelry as she asked, "Are they for sale?"

"Most of the pieces are for sale, there are only a few pieces that are not." Zachariah pointed out the pendants of Peter and Evelyn, and the Ring he had made for Lilith on their anniversary and said that neither of those was for sale.

She eyed the pieces and finally her eyes settled upon a ring. It was gold with a large black onyx stone. Set in the stone was a diamond in the center, and a ruby in each corner. It was a man's ring.

"Might I ask how much for that ring?"

"That is a wonderful piece. Legend has it that it was made for a King of France. I would be able to part with it for say $15,000."

"That is a little expensive for a legend isn't it Mr. Zachariah?"

Zachariah smiled and opened the case. His fingers touched the ring and he could almost feel Mrs. Morgan's eyes on his hand as he drew the ring out. Seductively he turned the ring so she could see the inside of the ring.

"If you look at the Maker's mark, next to it you will see that the Maker has added an L and the Roman Numerals X, V, and I for sixteen.

"The legend says that when the King came to pick up the ring he looked at it and was impressed but upon seeing the Maker's mark wanted his own mark on the inside of the ring as well so he ordered the Maker to add an equally impressive mark for him."

As Mrs. Morgan reached into her purse she said, "You have made a sale, Mr. Zachariah. Do you accept credit cards?"

"I do not have the gadgets set up yet, but I will trust you as I trust Melanie. I am certain you can bring me the money tomorrow, and I will let you take the ring home tonight."

Zachariah carried the ring to the counter and placed it in a ring box. After placing the box into a small sack he handed the sack to her. Instinctively her hand shot out and he took it shaking her hand but this time he was not impressed for he realized that it was an automatic reflex with her and that there was no real thought behind her actions. Her only thoughts were on her prize within the sack in her other hand.

"This is a true piece of history." She smiled and turned, then headed for the door.

"Yes, Mrs. Morgan it is." Zachariah replied. "I will tell Melanie you were here."

"Who?" She asked absentmindedly, "Oh her, yes, do that. I will return and pay you after your Grand Opening."

"That will be fine."

She walked out the door smiling broadly. Zachariah watched her go as he smiled to himself. "Yes, it is, it was on his finger when the blade came down, and Marie Antoinette followed him shortly after."

***

Three hours passed and the phone rang. Zachariah picked it up and as expected it was Melanie. She sounded very happy, but she would not tell him why, not until she was able to see him face to face. He agreed and hung up the phone then called Philip and left his message.

Less than fifteen minutes later Melanie came bounding in the door and raced to him wrapping her arms around him and kissing him hard. Zachariah heard a coughing at the door and looked up to see Philip. He reached in his pocket to get the thirty and Philip said, "Never mind, man, after seeing that. I don't want anything. I will never get that image out of my head."

He left shaking his head muttering something about, how can an old dude like that get a chick like that when he couldn't get a date with anything that wasn't blown up with a tire pump?

Melanie laughed and said, "Oops, I forgot you were going to pay him some more money or I would have waited until he had left."

Zachariah joined her, "It is okay, I kind of think we made his life. I think he will actually have more confidence now."

Melanie jumped up and down, "Papa Zach, Papa Zach, I won!"

"What?" He sat her in a chair and told her to tell him the whole story.

"Well, when I got there, I thought I would be a wallflower all night," she smiled at him, "but that is not how it turned out.

"Every guy there wanted to dance with me, and you should have seen the looks of jealousy from their dates. Even Rebecca Straine's date danced with me, I almost laughed when I saw her eyes for they were glaring at me so vehemently that she will lose half her eyesight in this one night alone." Melanie was giggling while she told the story. "However, while all of them danced with me all I could think about was the dance I had with you. I was having fun yes, but I wanted to be here."

Slowly she slipped her hand into his. "Then it came time to count the vote, and I was going to leave but Rebecca Straine and her friends stood in front of the door. They wanted to make certain I saw her accept the crown. Only thing is as she walked toward the stage when they came out to announce the Homecoming King and Queen I was not upset. It did not bother me for I already knew I was somebody's queen. "They announced the King first, for it is custom that he put the crown on the queen's head, and as expected it was Tommy Juckett, the quarterback of the football team and Rebecca's boyfriend. Rebecca had already taken the first step leading up to the stage when they announced the queen. She took the second step before she realized it was not her name they had called. It was mine."

Melanie beamed, "I won. I cannot believe it. They voted for me as Homecoming Queen, Papa Zach!"

Zachariah hugged her, "I am so happy for you, Melanie, you deserved it."

"So I walked from the door where I had been waiting to leave all the way to the stage and climbed up on the stage. Tommy stood there waiting; even after I stopped he still waited like he was expecting something. I asked him what he was waiting for, and he said I would have to remove the tiara to put the Homecoming Queen's crown on, but when I put my hands on the tiara I could not remove it. I did not want to."

"It meant more to me to be your Queen than it did to be the Homecoming Queen, so I looked at him and said, 'No.' He said, 'What?' and I said, 'No. I do not want to be the Homecoming Queen,' and I turned and walked away.

"Everybody looked at me, and I heard Tommy ask the Dean what to do. The Dean said he was not certain because nobody had ever refused the position before, he guessed that they should take the runner up. So then Rebecca Straine's name was called.

"I was told as I left that she was runner up yes, but that is because she was the only other person to be voted for and there were only five votes for her, which means that if you count her and her four friends and her boyfriend one of them did not vote for her."

Zachariah smiled at her, "In other words you won by unanimous vote."

She wrapped her arms around him tightly and whispered in his ear, "I do not know how you did it Papa Zach, but thank you."

"Melanie, there is magic in the jewelry yes, but often that magic only reveals what is already there. This magic I think just made people see what is already within you. So I do not think I did anything. I really think it was you." She brightened at his words, and then kissed his lips, "I know you had something to do with it, but thank you."

"Now, let's get comfortable, and I will tell you your story for the night. I am going to pull the recliner over to the cabinet and you can pick out the piece and then if you wish we can cuddle while I tell you the story."

Zachariah could almost see a scolding coming from the look in Melanie's eyes. Suddenly her voice got very strong and she became very protective as she said, "You listen here, Papa Zach, you are too old to be pulling furniture around the store like it was nothing. Now you go stand over by that cabinet and I will pull the recliner over there."

He tried to stifle the laugh but had to cover his mouth to do so. As he walked over to the cabinet he watched the little Melanie that did not weigh much more than the recliner did struggling to move it across the room. First she tried to pull it; finally she kicked off the low heeled shoes and got behind it and with all her weight pushed it over to a spot near the cabinet. She then worked on positioning it and finally announced it was right and he could come and sit.

As she stood breathing hard Zachariah noticed that one of the straps was hanging off her shoulder and that she had not realize that part of the gown had slipped and most of her breast was exposed. He was thankful that her nipple was still covered or when she discovered it she would probably have burst into hysterics. The thought of telling her about it dominated his mind and he was about to do so when she noticed it herself and quickly lifted the strap. As she turned her head to see if he had noticed he glanced toward the cabinet.

After a moment he turned back and saw that she was waiting for him and her dress was on correctly again. He walked by her and sat down in the chair and then looked at her and repeated, "Why don't you pick out your piece and then come and sit on my lap, then I will put the recliner back and we will cuddle while I tell that story."

Melanie smiled at him, then she walked to the door of the shop and locked the door and pulled the blinds before returning to the cabinet and opening the door. Zachariah could see her eyes scanning the variety of jewels within and then he saw her gaze fix upon something. She reached inside and chose a piece and closed her hand tightly about it. Slowly she walked to him then paused, "Should I go change back into my other clothing first?"

"That dress gave you a special night, are you ready to let that night end or do you want to keep it going a while longer?"

Melanie did not say a word, she just climbed upon his lap and Zachariah reclined the chair. After the chair was sat back, Melanie wiggled to get comfortable. Zachariah gritted his teeth for her bottom wiggling about in his lap was highly arousing and he had to focus his mind on thoughts that would keep his arousal from becoming obvious to her.

"Papa Zach, is something wrong." Melanie asked as she looked at him with a quizzical look upon her face.

"Ummm, precious, next time warn me before you wiggle. I need to distract myself first. That was just a little disturbing," he said as he let out a deep breath.

Melanie looked at him strangely then it dawned on her what he meant and she blushed brightly. Her heart raced as she could feel every muscle in her body quivering as if she was ready to leap from him his lap like a startled rabbit surprised by a wolf on the prowl. Just as her embarrassment was reaching its peak his loving arms wrapped around her and soothed her. There were tears in her eyes as she looked up at him. She heard his gentle voice say, "It is okay now, sweetie, I know you did not mean to do that. Perhaps one day you will want to know that wiggling like that causes that reaction."

Still blushing she looked at him, a smile crossed her lips and then she kissed him gently. Her hand caressed his cheek as she chided, "Well then at least I know that even at your age there is nothing wrong with that part of your body." A giggle burst from her lips and she wrapped her arms around his neck and kissed him sweetly.

When she reluctantly ended the kiss their eyes met and Zachariah knew that her confession of love was not a child's wish but was indeed from her heart. He could feel the waves coming off of her and there was no doubt in his mind that Melanie did indeed love him. The warmth he felt within was something that had gone unfelt in so long he had forgotten how wonderful it could be.

He opened his hand and Melanie laid a ring that was a slender golden band with strange fan-like markings etched softly into it. Upon the band was a single oval jewel the color of the deepest ocean that held the shadow of the crescent moon within its depths. "Tell me about this piece, Papa Zach."

Zachariah looked at the ring. He remembered it well. The images of the events surrounding the ring flooded his mind. He looked at Melanie and began, "Now this piece helped a woman named Terran pass a test that she did not even know she was taking…

On the Wings of a Dream
Kara Elsberry
Chapter One

A tinkling of laughter, like the bells of fairies, rang out across the dewy spring air.

She was racing through the forest, her tiny slippered feet scarcely touching the forest bed as leaves floated up around her to join in the merry race. Beside her, his hand clamped tightly in her own, was her dearest friend. Oddly, she couldn't seem to quite recall his name, but she knew that she was safe with him and that all would be well.

With another peal of laughter, she pulled him along, her hair floating behind her in wild, coppery wisps. She snuck a quick peek at her friend, only to find his head turned and bathed in the shadows. Her only glimpse was of his beautiful wavy hair… billowing behind him in a golden halo.

The forest abruptly gave way to a meadow of colorful wildflowers as they stumbled to the ground in a tangle of arms and legs. Their breath came in gasps and giggles. They lay on their backs for a few moments to rest, pointing out fantastical creatures in the marshmallow clouds and making up even more fantastical stories about them.

She caught sight of a very beautiful and unusual flower from the corner of her eye and went to investigate, leaving her friend to his own devices for a few moments. With a triumphant squeal, she rose quickly and turned to show her friend the lovely prize she had discovered. Instead, she ended up bumping foreheads with him, as he was coming up directly behind her.

She was drowning…

…in two deep pools of aquamarine… his gaze was mesmerizing and innocent… calm and absolutely peaceful. He was so close that she could smell the blade of sweet grass he had just been chewing on. For a moment that seemed to stretch on into eternity, they held each other's gazes, each of them afraid to speak and break the spell. The flower dropped from her hand unnoticed. His pupils expanded and deepened in color as he took a deep breath, he moved in closer. He pressed his warm lips to her earlobe, sending a pleasant tingle all the way down to her toes.

"I want you to have this'… he whispered softly into her ear.

She felt a small cool object being pressed into her palm. She started to look down but he squeezed her hand tightly and she gasped, startled by his sudden aggressiveness. Curious, she unlocked his fingers and began to open her hand.

Suddenly, the air around her began to shimmer and become misty. He kissed her softly as he whispered three powerful words against her lips…

"You are mine."

Chapter Two

Terran awoke very suddenly, sitting straight up, her hands clutching the cushy sleeping bag to her breast.

"What the heck was that all about? She wondered as the shards of the dream began to break away. She reached up irritably to swipe an errant piece of hair from her eyes.

Well, she might as well greet the day; she had a lot of unpacking to do. It was time to 'rise and shine' as her dad always used to say.

She sighed deeply and threw back the covers, sitting up to stretch her stiff and aching body. Well, that settled it, she was definitely too old for sleepovers. She stood up to make her way to the bathroom, still muttering under her breath and holding her lower back like a decrepit old woman.

After finishing up with her morning routine and feeling vastly refreshed from her shower, she decided to clean up her bed and get to work unpacking the seemingly endless pile of boxes. If this is what it was like to move into your dream home, someone please give her a good swift kick in the you know what if she ever voiced such ridiculous ideas again!

She rolled her sleeping bag up tightly and put it back into its duffel. Grabbing her pillow, she was just about to throw it all on the recliner when she glimpsed a shimmer of gold from the corner of her eye.

"That's odd, I remember clearing off this spot to sleep on last night, she mumbled to herself. She was absolutely certain of it.

Maybe the zipper pull came loose from the sleeping bag? She dropped the pillow and leaned forward. On the old wooden floorboards lay the most unusual and beautiful ring she had ever seen. The golden band was slender, with strange fan-like markings etched softly into it. There was a single oval jewel setting, the color of the deepest ocean, with the shadow of a crescent moon in its depths. Her breath came out in a sigh… how absolutely breathtaking. But where did it come from?

As she slipped the ring onto the middle finger of her right hand, she felt a warmth pulsing through her hand and up into her arm. Its heat reached up into her heart and finally encompassed her thoughts, so that the air around her seemed to shimmer for an instant.

Her breath caught in her throat and she reached out to steady herself.

"Whoa." She gasped. "What is *wrong* with me this morning?"

She stood there for a few moments more, leaning against the wall and allowing her breathing and heart rate to return to normal. She just didn't have time for this today! She had big plans for this house and couldn't wait to get them under way. What a wonderful omen, to find such a beautiful golden ring in her new house! She gazed down at her finger, absentmindedly tracing the markings on the band with the tip of her pinky finger. She recalled a time when things hadn't been so good for her and banished the thoughts quickly from her mind, lest she ruin the perfectly lovely day ahead of her.

"Only happy thoughts!" she admonished herself.

Terran walked to the kitchen, to search for the box of cleaning supplies that had made the move with her. An hour later, she still hadn't located the box and decided to give it up as a lost cause. She would have to make a trip to the store and it was no use putting it off. She caught a glimpse of her reflection in the hall mirror on her way out and stopped to run a quick hand through her coppery tresses, fluffing them a bit to give her hair the 'wild and untamed' look she favored. Other than that, she looked pretty darn good for being dressed down for a long, hard day of unpacking. A cute and sporty powder blue sweat suit hugged her curvy figure; the white tank top accentuated her ample breasts. She threw on her hoody and zipped it up half way.

She was proud of her womanly figure… she was certainly no size six model, but she had long come to terms with that unpleasant fact, thank you very much. It had taken her years to realize that looking like you survived on a diet of only water was just not the norm for most women. She was a healthy and vital woman in the prime of her life, with long shapely legs, a flat stomach and breasts that were more than a man's average handful. She smoothed her hands down over her body and gave herself a sly wink on the way out the door. She felt vibrant and alive!

Chapter Three

She stepped out the door to greet the morning with a spring in her step and a contented smile upon her face. It had rained the night before and the air was fresh and clean, clearing her mind as she inhaled deeply. As she walked, she mulled her dream over again. She had the strangest feeling that this wasn't the first time she had dreamt it, but it had been quite a while. The mysterious boy… who was he? Why couldn't she see his face? When she tried to bring his features into focus, there were only shadows. Two bright oval pools of aquamarine dominated her vision and got in the way of any further contemplation. She was almost to the corner now, so she pushed all thoughts of the dream aside and crossed the street to stop at the town's only hardware store. The wooden door's bell chimed pleasantly as she entered. The store was small and cluttered, but in a clean down home sort of way. The town's old-fashioned charm had been one of the deciding factors in her big move. A fresh start to a new and happy life; a life she felt was well within her reach.

She stopped daydreaming to focus on the purpose for her visit here and began to browse the shelves, looking for a hammer and some nails. She had a ton of pictures and knickknacks just screaming to be hung up in their proper places. It was a hobby she indulged herself in, collecting beautiful and unusual things. Some might even call them odd, (and in fact some had) but they each had a special meaning in her heart and she cherished each and every one of them. Most of her favorite pieces were ones given to her from her family. Those personal ones she reserved for her bedroom or den, so that she could surround herself in happy memories.

"May I help you find something, miss?" a gruff, but gentle voice behind her inquired.

Terran jumped slightly and blushed at the stocky, bearded man standing behind her. He was just about her height, maybe an inch or two taller, but he had to be twice, maybe even three times as wide as she was. He reminded her of a shorter version of Paul Bunyan. He could have been his son Paul Jr. He was even dressed the part with a pair of dark blue jeans, tan work boots, and a red flannel shirt rolled up to his elbows. He was staring at her with bushy eyebrows raised.

"Oh! Yes, I guess that would be nice. I'm afraid I'm new here and don't know my way around just yet." She smiled sheepishly at him, shrugging her shoulders slightly.

She held her hand out to introduce herself. He looked somewhat surprised, like he hadn't shaken a hand in a few turns, but he recovered quickly and reached out, if somewhat roughly, and grasped her hand in his. She had a moment to register just how absurdly hairy his knuckles were, when she was no longer standing in the hardware store, but in cool dark room, with only a single bare bulb hanging from the ceiling, its miserly glow straining to reach the shadowy corners. She heard a furtive movement from behind her and she spun around quickly, a scream building in her throat.

She had but a moment to register a hulking shadow coming towards her before it passed right through her body! She was so shocked that it was all she could do to remember how to breathe. The light fell upon the shadow and revealed it to be a man... the man in the hardware store! He was humming a little tune that sounded suspiciously like something by the Village People. What's more, he was dressed in a lacy pair of red panties, a matching red bra, and a pair of black fishnet stockings that had definitely seen better days. She took it all in slowly, watching as he waltzed around the dim room humming to himself as he headed towards an old wardrobe she had overlooked on her first glance about the room. He began searching the contents of the wardrobe and soon she heard a pleased grunt emanate from within. He seemed to have located what he had been searching for. He spun around with a flourish, fixing a hideous platinum blonde wig to his head and smiling beatifically.

"Okay, Terr, calm down." She whispered to herself. "You're just going crazy, that's all. You knew it would happen sooner or later, you just didn't know it would be because of Paul Bunyan's doppelganger decked out as a trashy cross-dresser." A crazy little giggle bubbled up from her throat as she sank to the floor and hugged her knees to her chest. She closed her eyes and rocked herself back and forth, whispering her own name over and over into the cool darkness.

"My name is Terran, my name is Terran, my name is Terran…"

She opened her eyes and found herself face to face with the store clerk, her hand still engulfed in his hairy hand shake. A sudden hot pain flared through her hand and up her arm and she jumped back, releasing his hand immediately. She was back! Gone was the dingy basement, gone was the cross-dressed lumberjack; she was back in the real world! At least, she sincerely hoped so.

"Good to meet you Terran, my name is Daryl and I'm the owner of this fine establishment." He smiled warmly at her, gesturing widely about the store. His teeth were bright white against his dark bushy beard. "I've been here 'bout oh, 20 years now. Business is slow, but steady and I couldn't ask for a nicer town to live in."

Daryl went on to regale her of the town's finer assets, but she was barely listening. All she kept thinking of was whether or not he was wearing that red bra and panties under his jeans and flannel shirt. She shivered imperceptibly.

Terran exited the hardware store not long after, carrying her paper sack of hammer and nails. She hardly remembered her conversation with Daryl. Surely it had been quite one-sided, as she felt as if she were thinking through a wall of water. Shaking her head, she wondered just what was going on with her. Was she really going crazy? She had to be, didn't she? No one in their right mind would daydream about a lingerie wearing, cross-dressing lumberjack that sang and pranced merrily around his basement.

Chapter Four

Crazy... such a harsh and final word. Was she really losing her mind? Terran certainly didn't feel as if she were. She contemplated a future of wearing faded house robes, munching on cookie dough ice cream (which she loved) and talking to her 2 dozen cats all while watching her daily 'stories' on daytime television. Yikes. The funny thing was she didn't have any trouble envisioning this horrific future.

Well, not while she was in charge! She giggled to herself at the silly thought and continued on to the town's only grocery store, the 'Bag 'n Go'.

The cool air of the store's air conditioner blasted her in the face as she pushed open the doors. She grabbed one of the shopping carts and headed for the cleaning supply isle.

Three minutes later, she found it and was scanning the multiple bottles of soap when a woman, fuzzy dark brown hair escaping her long braid, pushed her cart into the narrow isle. She was actually kind of pretty if you overlooked the beginnings of dark circles under her eyes and the frazzled look of a mom who definitely needed a vacation.

A cute freckled tot wearing a cherry red jumper sat screaming bloody murder at her two older brothers, who were paying her no attention at all. They were too busy pulling on their mother's flannel shirt and arguing loudly over whose turn it was to sit in the front seat of the car on the way home. One of the boys reached over, quick as a whip and yanked on his brother's shaggy brown hair, then darted behind his mother before his brother could retaliate in kind. The woman smiled apologetically at Terran and she returned the smile a bit distractedly as she continued her search for the perfect power cleaner. Terran tried to block out the racket and concentrate on her choices, but her ears were suddenly assaulted with the scream of a banshee. She flinched as the small girl's screams grew to octaves likely to break glass.

The boys, not to be outdone by their kid sister, raised their voices as if in competition and Terran could feel a severe headache approaching like a storm. Maybe a visit to the pharmacy counter wouldn't be a bad idea after this. Making her decision the split second the mother's patience hit its boiling point; she reached out and grabbed the nearest familiar cleaner just to get the heck outta dodge. She also quickly grabbed some sponges and window cleaner on her way by, nearly knocking a display case of Mr. Tidy's kitchen floor cleaner to the floor in her haste.

She could hear the mother speaking low and fiercely as she attempted to make her escape. "If you don't all be quiet this instant, there will be no treats for you tonight!"

Terran had a feeling that no amount of treats would calm these children. She felt a pang of sympathy for the mother and briefly wondered where her husband was. No doubt he was at home; 'getting ready' for a long hard day of six packs and sports shows. She smirked to herself.

"Excuse me," Terran said as she tried to maneuver around the noisy bunch. The isle was so narrow; their carts bumped and squeaked against another as they passed.

The woman was still lecturing her children in low tones as she nodded to Terran and tried to move her boys far enough to the side so she could get by.

Terran got all of two steps forward when the two boys, still arguing, jostled into her from behind, causing the woman to bump into Terran. The woman reached out to her to apologize and Terran cut her off with a wave of her hand.

"Please, don't worry; kids will be ki..." her remark died on her lips as the woman's hand brushed her own and a wave of electric heat shot up her arm. She yanked her hand back to cradle it against her chest, her ring flashing and causing lights to dance behind her eyes. When the spots behind her eyes cleared, she began to realize that she was no longer speaking with the woman in the grocery store. In fact, she could no longer see the woman *or* her children at all. What's more, she wasn't even in the grocery store.

"Oh god, it's happening again." She thought to herself frantically as she surveyed her surroundings. She was in a place that looked... well... like a romance novel set for lack of a better explanation. There were exotic flowers and trees as far as the eye could see. The air was permeated with their spicy fragrance. In the background, the ocean lapped lazily at the shore as the sun was just setting over the horizon. A picture perfect scene if she ever did see one.

"Well, at least I'm not in a cold, dark basement this time." She smiled wryly to herself as she turned around to see the view behind her. She gasped as her mind adjusted to what she was seeing. It was the woman from the grocery store, only she didn't look unkempt and harried any longer. She looked… stunning… and totally relaxed. As well she should with a line of men surrounding her, seemingly at her beck and call!

They were in a semi-circle around her, all bare-chested and delicious, in an assortment of delectable flavors.

For cripe sakes, she didn't think she was in a romance novel anymore, she *was in one*! She watched, utterly spellbound, as one of the young men who suspiciously resembled a certain muscular blond who couldn't believe his butter was not really butter, lounged beside her and fed her plump purple grapes, one at a time. Another hottie fanned her from behind and still yet another, this one with straight raven hair down to his waist and the tightest ass she'd ever seen massaged her dainty little feet. Terran noticed that her toenails were painted a juicy red apple color as they glinted in the light. The other men just stood around her, gazing with rapt adoration, as they waited their turn to please her highness.

Terran could tell that the woman was absolutely in heaven. Her dark hair hung loose around her bare shoulders, blowing lightly in the breeze.

Wait a minute, breeze? Terran looked around her, noticing that none of the trees were blowing. It was as if the wind was blowing only for the other woman and her harem, as if a fan was strategically placed somewhere out of sight to produce just the right effect. In fact, it all looked a little too perfect. It was as if she had been pulled right into one of those cheesy daytime soap operas, or 'stories' as her grandmother used to call them. She was in this woman's own personal version of a romance novel and it was almost like she was in her dreams or maybe even…

She felt as if a light had just gone off above her head. That's it! She was seeing other people's fantasies… but how could this be? She had never experienced anything like this before, she thought as images began to race through her mind. The lumberjack reaching out to introduce himself and the feel of his hairy knuckles against her palm, the woman in the grocery store brushing against her hand and the… the RING!

It had to be the ring. It was the only explanation, the only thing that had changed since she had awakened early this morning. She looked down at her finger, but the ring didn't appear any different to her than it had when she had found it.

It looked like a normal ring, albeit a very beautiful and unusual one. Her mind began to spin and she just couldn't seem to focus on one thought or another. They spun around in her mind like a rampant meteor shower.

A magic ring?

Impossible! How could this be? And why here, why now, why...her? This had to be some sort of mistake. Maybe she was just going crazy? Yeah, right, that was all, *just* going crazy. Or maybe...

A high pitched giggle cut off her train of thought and she looked up to see one of the men leaning over to nibble on grocery woman's ear, no doubt whispering something delectably naughty. Terran turned around again to look out at the sunset, her head feeling a little dizzy. She reached out to steady herself on a nearby palm tree and found herself back in the grocery store, staring into the eyes of the woman. Terran shook her head as if to clear it and the woman, now back in her ill-fitting clothes and disheveled hair, looked at her with growing concern.

"Are you sure you're okay?" the other woman raised an eyebrow at her.

"I'm fine... probably just a little overwhelmed with all I have to do today." Terran brushed some non-existent dust from her pants and smiled back at the woman. "Really, I'm fine; you have a wonderful day... and good luck with the rest of your shopping." Terran smiled absently and made a bee line for the checkout counter.

***

She left the grocery store without any further incidents and began her trek home. As she walked, she studied the ring on her finger, turning it this way and that. The sun caught in its depths, making the color glow. The crescent shape inside remained dark however and she turned it again, hoping to see what caused the strange effect.

She sighed as she lowered her hand and began to take notice of her surroundings. She admired the town's impressive array of plant life. There were trees that appeared to be eons old, their trunks wider than she was, their arms twisting and reaching for the sun. Unique flowers in every color of the rainbow filled her senses with a mixture of musk and spices. She spotted some beautiful red roses and hydrangeas in a multitude of colors. Some weeping wisteria draped a breathtaking Victorian house across the street, and... ahhh, a lavender bush! Heavenly! She walked up next to it and picked a sprig, inhaling deeply. Mmmm, she was in a small town paradise! She absently tucked the flowers behind her ear and started humming a little tune.

As she continued on her way home, children played in the streets, rode bikes, giggled around every corner. She smiled as she heard a little girl and boy bickering over whose turn it was to play their video game system as they went inside. The sound of their little voices hit home with her, making her feel a twinge of long-buried sadness.

The little boy, with grass stained blue jeans and shaggy hair hanging in his eyes reminded her of her brother Liam when he was that age. Her eyes filled with tears as she thought of him. He had been not only her brother, but her closest friend and she missed him terribly.

What she wouldn't do to have him with her now. She closed her eyes briefly at the horrible memory that always crushed her when she thought of him...

***

The phone rang shrilly throughout the dark house.

Terran crammed the pillow down onto her head and tried to ignore the shrill ringing. She rolled over and pulled the covers to her chin, doing her best to block it out. Finally, the sound died and she sighed in relief, sleep overcoming her quickly.

It wasn't much later that she heard the creaking of someone walking down the stairs and she lifted her head to see who it was, bleary eyed.

"Terran, Terran are you awake?" her father said softly. Something was wrong. She could tell it in his voice. She was definitely awake now.

"Yes, what's going on?" she asked as she glanced at the clock. It was 4:30 in the morning. She was staying overnight at her dad's house and was sleeping on the couch. A chill had begun to creep up her back and into her neck, making her feel cold and clammy all at the same time.

"Terran, come here." Her father said from the archway in the dining room. Terran fought with the covers a moment, stumbling in her haste to escape them. She walked towards her father and he rushed to her, no longer able to wait. He grabbed her to him and squeezed tightly, his breath coming out in ragged gasps.

"Liam's dead, he was killed in a drunk driving accident late last night." His arms tightened around her as if he would never let go. She went limp in his arms as his words began to sink in.

Dead? Liam dead?

It wasn't possible. He was only 18! No way, no freaking way!

They stood that way for a while, his arms so tight they were almost crushing her. She could feel him trembling softly. He finally let go of her and she sank to the floor.

"Are you okay honey?" he said with despair deeply etched into his face.

Okay? Was she okay? How could she be okay? How could she ever be okay? He seemed to understand that she couldn't talk and shambled away with glossy eyes into the kitchen to make some coffee. She knew he was just doing that to calm his nerves. She also knew it wouldn't work.

She was going numb. She couldn't talk, she couldn't move, she couldn't feel… she couldn't even think. What was wrong with her?

Her brother had just died and she couldn't even cry! She rose to her feet and stumbled into the bathroom, where she looked at her face in the mirror.

"Okay Terran, this is a very, very bad dream and you're going to wake up any second," she whispered to her ghostly image in the mirror. Her face, white and emotionless, stared back at her. Her blue eyes shone out at her feverishly. She looked around her, everything looking surreal and strange, as if it were happening in a movie or a dream, cloudy grayness kept trying to creep in around the edges. She took a deep breath. Why can't I cry? She was trembling harshly and she clasped her hands in front of her to steady them as she slid limply down the dryer to land on the floor again.

Her mind scrambled to make sense of her surroundings. She pulled herself to her feet with the aid of the bathroom sink and stared at her image in the mirror. Somehow, the ghostly vision her face had become brought her to the harsh reality and the tears seared her face as they fell. Great sobs wracked her body. It wasn't fair!

Oh sweet Jesus, Liam!

How could this have happened? It's impossible… she had just talked to her brother last week over the phone and they had made plans to meet and have a night of fun together.

Her brain seemed to be working a thousand miles a minute, flashing over all the good times she'd had with him. She remembered giggling under the covers as their parents told them to be quiet for the hundredth time, she remembered them creeping around in the dark pretending to be animals when everyone was asleep… she and Liam against the world, through the tough and the happy times.

As tears cascaded down her face, she recalled the first time Liam had visited her after she'd left home to go to college. They'd never been a real touchy feely brother and sister. Giving hugs was something they reserved for mom and dad. When the day came for Liam to go back home though, he stood there with tears swimming in his eyes and when she stood before him he rushed forward to give her one of the sweetest hugs ever. When he finally released her his voice cracked as he said goodbye. She'd watched him look, back at her as he walked to his vehicle, tears still shining in his eyes. That moment would always be burned into her memory. It was one of the last times she saw him.

***

Terran jerked back to the present as a ball whizzed past her head.

"Heads up!" a little voice shouted.

Terran bent down to retrieve the ball for them and threw it back.

"Thanks!" they shouted to her as they went back to their game.

She wiped the tears from her eyes and rounded the corner to her new home.

Chapter Five

That night she dreamed again….

She was back in the forest. She was standing in a clearing of the tallest evergreen and birch trees she had ever seen. The sunlight was filtered here, dappling the leaves of the trees and her skin with bright spots and shadows. She looked down to find herself dressed in shades of green and lavender. The material was iridescent, layered with the appearance of leaves as the skirt ended in points that came just below her knees. She blended into her surroundings, almost seeming to be a part of them.

She smiled and looked around her again. The breeze was light and moist, as if it had just rained, bringing the scent of fresh pine and rich earth. She breathed deeply of it, thinking it just had to be the most delectable smell she had ever experienced. She lifted her arms and danced in a circle, her face raised to the sky, eyes closed and her skirt billowing out around her. She felt so alive… so free.

Suddenly she felt she was no longer alone and she spun around, expecting there to be someone or worse, some*thing* directly behind her. However, no one was there.

She froze, her hands clasped in front of her, listening to all the sounds of the forest. She heard the breeze through the trees, a bird singing in the distance, and… there! She heard something! She turned around again, peering into the trees.

It was darker further in, as the trees grew together in a tightly knit group. As she squinted her eyes and opened her ears, her finger began to tingle.

She looked down to find her ring glowing… not just from the sunlight hitting it, but actually glowing. Rays of aquamarine light shone out around the edges. The crescent moon within seemed to be the source of it all, filling the jewel with a white hot light.

She heard soft giggling and she looked up, her eyes wide and searching. She saw a small shadow, about the size of a hawk, flit from behind a tree off to her left. To her right, a twig snapped and leaves floated to the ground. She looked up as she heard more of the eerie giggles as yet another small shadow darted up into a nearby tree. The breeze picked up gusting the leaves up from the ground, making them spiral around her and catch in her hair.

"Terran."

She drew in her breath to scream as she began to turn and a hand covered her mouth. A hard body pressed against hers from behind. Her scream came out muffled and short. She caught her breath, inhaling the scent of the hand covering her mouth.

The hand was so warm…almost hot, a curious combination of rough yet soft and smelling of rich earth and all things green and alive. Her heart pounded furiously within, trying to escape to no avail.

"I've waited so long for you to come to me." A low masculine voice whispered seductively into her ear. A shiver went through her, causing her body to tremble. "Do not be afraid my love. Well… maybe a little if you will, I love the way your body feels, trembling against me…" his voice seemed to touch every part of her at once, traveling from her toes to the top of her head, seeming to touch her very core.

The ring glowed brighter with each shiver of emotion coursing through her. He ran his hands down her arms and back up, cupping her chin and turning her face towards his own. Inhaling deeply, he ran his lips lightly from her shoulder to just underneath her chin. She moaned softly as his tongue flicked out and slid across her lower lip.

"*You smell of sweet, spicy cinnamon, taste of wild, sensual musk and…*" his voice trailed off for a moment as he pondered wickedly before he roughly pulled her back against him, growling his words across her lips. "*You feel like… **mine**.*"

He ran his hands down her sides, leaving a searing trail of heat in their wake. She could feel his need pounding through her, primal in its ferocity. Her body jerked against him, molding to him in perfect fusion and they gasped out in unison, her neck bending back as she found the soft lobe of his ear and took it gently between her teeth.

"*Terran…*" he moaned breathlessly into the soft arch of her ivory neck. She could feel his control slipping and just the thought of it caused her knees to go weak as liquid heat flared between her legs. She turned to him as he wrapped her tightly in his arms and she lifted her face to his. The sun shone from behind him, creating an aura of golden light and cloaking his face in shadows.

She leaned into him, "*Who are you?*"

He began to lower his face to hers. "*Look for me…I am near…*" and he kissed her eyelids tenderly as the dream spiraled into long wispy clouds, accepting her into the deepest realm of sleep where dreams are abandoned and true rest is found.

***

Terran awoke to find her body tingling with anticipation, which quickly turned to irritation as she realized she was not in the dream anymore. Nope, she was on a hard wooden floor, tangled in a sleeping bag that was just a bit too hot to be truly comfortable. Great, juuuust great. Today she was going to work on her bedroom and she knew just the place to start... the bed! She'd had enough of the hard wooden floor.

She pushed her hair out of her eyes with a huff and kicked the offending sleeping bag across the floor so that it landed in a heap by the wall. It didn't make a near satisfying enough thump.

She grumbled under her breath, stomping off to the bathroom. It was bad enough that she had a hard time getting to know guys, let alone dating them, but now her dreams were going to start torturing her too?

Fan-freakin-tastic!

Chapter Six

Terran spent the entire day unpacking boxes and hanging up her knickknacks, the bed taking up her entire morning as she struggled with the stubborn frame. She stepped back to admire her fantasy art.

Dragon sculptures over here, fairies statues over there, numerous paintings hung meticulously and with care… she pursed her lips, squinting her eyes and turning her head this way and that, until finally a slow smile spread across her face, making her eyes twinkle. Perfect! The place was finally starting to feel like home. She smiled again and dusted her hands off on her jeans as if to say 'that's that!'

She was tired and sore and she held her lower back as she shuffled her way to the kitchen for an early dinner. She'd earned it by golly and she intended to enjoy every minute of her meal. She began rummaging through her cupboards, sliding cans around and pushing boxes back. Yeck! Everything looked positively grotesque to her right now. She needed some real food…. Something with substance!

She smiled to herself as she said those words to herself. Her older brother Eugene used to say that all the time. "Mom, I don't want soup for dinner, I want something with substance!"

Terran giggled to herself as she imagined the look on her brother's face, all scrunched up with teeny pinched eyes. Ahhh, brothers. She knew them well. She grew up with three of them after all… and *no* sisters.

So why did she have so much trouble finding a man?? She was comfortable with them, friendly… just one of the guys so to speak.

When it came down to it though, intimacy scared the hell out of her. There always came a time when her guy friends wanted more from her than she was willing to give. She became closed, scared and…dare she say it, *cold.* She couldn't help it; there must be something wrong with her.

She sighed as she shut the last cupboard, giving it up as a lost cause. She would just have to get ready and go out for a bite. She headed for the shower, grabbing some clothes from her closet as she went by. She'd seen a lovely café in town earlier and wondered if they had her favorite dish... spaghetti with garlic bread!

***

It was such a mild evening that Terran decided to walk again. Her spirits felt high as she walked through the town again, seeing it in a new perspective. The moon was full and the sky was full of stars... so different from life in a big city, where the pollution and lights fog out most of the sky's beauty. She promised herself that she would stop on her way home to admire them properly... after she'd calmed the raging tiger inside of her stomach!

Terran secured the light blue shawl around her shoulders as she opened the door to the café. The shawl had been her great-grandmothers and it was so soft and beautiful. It matched her sky blue sundress perfectly.

Wonderful smells of roast beef, French fries, and even pumpkin pie wafted to her nose and she inhaled deeply, her stomach grumbling expectantly. She would just have to have some of that pumpkin pie for dessert! With lots of whipped cream on top of course.

She made her way to a booth in the back, not wanting to disturb anyone. It was not lost on her that all the talking had died away as she walked in and all eyes were watching her, curious. Most of the café's patrons were older and looked quite at home here. There was even a game of cards going on between a group of old farmers, still in their denim overalls. She smiled at the sight and received six friendly smiles in return.

Terran took her seat and was only there moments before the waitress, Doris her name tag read, brought her a glass of water and a menu. She smiled brightly at Terran, her lips painted a garish red.

"You must be our new neighbor! Aren't you just the sweetest thing!" she squealed a little too loudly. Terran slouched a bit as all eyes turned to them.

"Earl and I live right across the street from you, in the little yellow Cape Cod?" She touched Terran's shoulder.

"We've been just dying to come over and say hello, but have been trying to wait until you're more settled in." She cracked the gum in her mouth and fluffed her orange poofy hair. No redhead Terran had ever met (herself included) had ever been able to boast that pumpkin color.

"Well, it's lovely to meet you Mrs…"

"Oh, Doris Dear! Just Doris…. Doris Fieldley. My husband's name is Earl and our two kitty cats are Lucy and Ethel. I sure do love my kitty cats to pieces… I'm sure you'll see them around the yard, they just adore slinking about my flower garden and lazing in the sun." She smiled again. She had the most unusually white teeth… so straight and perfect. Must be dentures.

"It's nice to meet you Doris. My name is Terran, Terran Morgan. I hope I get to meet the rest of your family soon and I love animals too." She smiled at her and then glanced down at her menu to indicate to Doris that she would like to order now.

Doris took the hint and flipped open her tablet, removing the pencil from behind her ear. Terran hadn't even noticed the pencil there before. Huh.

"Well, we'll just have to drop by then someday soon, won't we? I have the most delectable recipe for oatmeal cookies… I'll make sure to bring some with us! So, what can I get for you, dearie? We have Broccoli and Cheese soup for our Soup of the Day if you would care to try some. I made it myself." She winked conspiratorially.

"Oh, that does sound delicious. I will try some of that. I would also like a small plate of spaghetti with marinara sauce and a slice of garlic bread. Oh, and do you have chocolate malts?" She smiled hopefully at Doris. She was absolutely ravenous!

"You're in luck! We happen to have some of the most popular malts and shakes in town! I'll whip one up for you straight away and see if you don't come back for more next time!"

She scribbled furiously on her little notepad and Terran found herself wondering if that poor little tablet would hold up under the pressure. "I'll be back in a jiff with your drink sweetie pie." She grabbed the menu and took off for the kitchen window, little white tennis shoes squeaking the entire way.

Terran sighed in relief as she slumped in the booth. She liked Doris well enough, but she was kind of overwhelming when right in front of you.

She gazed around the café while she waited for her drinks and took in all the people. The conversational volume was back up to normal now and Terran was no longer the center of attention. There was the occasional whisper and glance her way, but nothing big.

There was prairie art on the walls featuring beautiful scenes of barns, pheasants, and deer. There was a cute little counter to check out at with a small display of candy and an old fashioned cash register.

She just loved it here. She felt so safe and secure… nothing like when she had lived in the city, where she always had to lock her doors and watch over her shoulder when she walked late in the evening.

Terran sat up as she saw Doris sashaying back to her table with her chocolate malt, complete with cherry on top. Mmm mm good. Her mouth began to water as Doris finally made it to her table.

"Extra thick and extra malt, the best malt you'll ever taste." She smiled broadly at Terran as she sat down a cute little doily napkin, with lacy edges. How cute.

Terran smiled back at Doris and reached out for her malt as Doris handed it to her. She was really looking forward to that malt, she could already taste it! Her hand slid around the frosty cup and met with Doris'. All of a sudden, Terran got a brief flash of what had to have been Earl Fieldley himself. He was on his hands and knees with Doris standing in front of him, tickling him on the nose with a… well; it was a stick with a feather hanging on the end of a string. Yep, that's what it was. He was dressed in a tight black leotard, with a set of cat ears upon his head. He even had a little tail safety pinned to his plump behind! As Terran watched, strangely transfixed by the sight, Mr. Fieldley wiggled his round bottom and made the tail sway, causing Doris to giggle shamelessly as she reached around to pat his ass playfully.

He turned around with a Cheshire grin and by the gods he had a little pink nose and whiskers painted on his plump cheeks. His long walrus-like mustache only added to the effect. Earl reached out a 'paw' and batted at the feather, causing Doris to shriek and run for the couch, her husband in hot pursuit… on his hands and knees. Doris was wearing a red, Asian print house coat that matched nicely with her ruby red lipstick. Her hair was done up high, hair sprayed to perfection, her eyes outlined in the deepest blue of the ocean.

She turned around and sat down on the sofa, her house coat gaping at the legs, clearly revealing that she did not have on anything beneath. She leaned back in an overly dramatic pose, pouting out her red lips and crooking a finger.

"Come to mama you sweet little kitty cat. Mama's got some cream all warmed up for you…"

Terran gasped and spun away, to find herself facing present day Doris, who looked a little flushed herself as she pulled her hand away rather shortly. She quickly excused herself and shimmied away, pulling out her little notepad to fan herself as she disappeared into the back somewhere.

Terran sat back at the table, malt temporarily forgotten. She felt as if she was in a state of mild shock. All that information conveyed to her in just a few seconds. What had changed from before? Doris had barely brushed fingers with her, yet when she became alarmed, the 'vision' had ended abruptly, almost as if she had caused it to end.

Doris soon brought out her meal, a steaming plate of delicious looking spaghetti with garlic bread. Terran quickly devoured it, never minding that Doris was still too flustered to look her in the eye. And was that a blush she had seen grace her features as she had scurried away from her table?

Terran couldn't help it, she laughed out loud as she took another bite of spaghetti, causing a few people to look at her strangely. Well, she did say she liked cats. Terran almost choked on her dinner as she attempted to swallow with that thought. This time, a young farmhand that had been sitting in the booth behind her, came up to her table.

He reached behind her and patted her briskly on the back, causing Terran's breath to catch.

"Are you okay ma'am?" He asked with concern in his dark green eyes. He was quite attractive, Terran noticed, but a little on the young side. He had strong hands and arms, with shoulders just beginning to broaden with maturity and hard honest work. She made an instant decision. On the spot. No questions asked. No thoughts required.

She reached for his hand.

"Yes, I'm fine thank you so much for your help."

"My name is Terran, what's yours?" He reached for her hand, engulfing hers with a strong, warm grip and he opened his mouth to tell her his name.

Terran felt a cool breeze lift the strands of hair around her face and she closed her eyes at the luscious feeling. It smelled of fall… rich and spicy, laced with undertones of spring. Fall was her favorite season and she relished it in her senses for the moment. She opened her eyes when she heard a soft sigh from behind a nearby haystack. She was in a field scattered with haystacks. She tiptoed to look behind one of them, where she thought she had heard the sound.

She peered around and caught sight of a smooth creamy leg, wrapped around the young man Terran had just met in the café. His upper torso was bare, allowing her a view of rock hard muscles and skin darkened to perfection. She watched as he ran a hand down the girl's leg and back up, to cup a firm young breast in his palm. Another sigh followed the touch and the girl's body arched against her lover's. Terran smiled and closed her eyes, leaving the two young lovers to their own devices. She opened her eyes and blinked in the bright light as the young man just finished telling her his name.

"Luke" he trailed off dazedly. Terran could tell he was flustered as she watched his eyes flick about. He licked his lips nervously and stuttered, "Well, if you're quite sure you are all right, I had better be going. Ma'am." He nodded to her as he scurried out of the café, a blush creeping up his cheeks as he fled.

Oh, this was just too much fun! Terran giggled to herself as she finished up her meal. She hadn't had this much fun in a long time and intended to enjoy it for a little while before she returned home tonight.

She slurped up the last of her malt and dug out a tip for Doris. She started to walk away and added another dollar, just for brightening her mood so much.

She headed for the cash register, with a purposeful gleam in her eye. Playful, yet wicked all at once. Playfully wicked, yes now there's a term for the mood she was in. She fairly pranced the last few steps to the register; she was in such high spirits. She looked up from her purse and giggled, startling the cashier, a pretty woman with long black hair. She handed the woman the receipt that Doris had graciously left for her with a cinnamon candy that Terran had stuffed in her purse for later.

The ring brushed up against the cashier's palm as Terran turned her hand craftily at the last moment. A quick flash and...

She was relaxing in a bathtub full to the brim with bubbles; the light around her was soft with candlelight.

"Well, this is certainly different." She thought to herself as she looked around. She was in a light airy bathroom, painted in shades of pale yellow and blue, with a lighthouse motif. There were fluffy blue towels on a white shelf in the corner and small, yellow votives lit strategically around the room in place of artificial light.

This was all very nice and all, but that still didn't explain why she was in a stranger's bathtub and not watching someone else's fantasies from a distance. She sighed deeply and reached up to push her dark hair back from her shoulders.

She sat up abruptly, bubbles and water flying off of her body. *Dark* hair?

Curious now, she looked down to see small firm breasts with large pink nipples, hell the nipples were the main attraction! Because let's face it, this body didn't have much for breasts. She hesitated only a moment before running her hands down and over the nipples, watching in fascination as they beaded into two perfect buds. She ran her hands down the rest of the way to feel a nicely flat stomach and firm thighs and legs. She realized who she must be: the cashier from the café.

She'd never actually *been* the person in these fantasies though, only the spectator. Why had things changed… again? Well, she didn't know for sure, but she intended to fully enjoy the fantasy while she could. No sense panicking and acting like a loon.

She eased back into the hot water again and sighed with pure pleasure. Running her hands over her 'new' body, she realized one thing: This woman was outrageously horny and practically burned to be touched. She reached lower, intending to find out just how turned on she was and maybe relieve some pressure for her. She gasped guiltily when the bathroom door opened suddenly. A stunningly beautiful man filled the doorway, his manhood jutting proudly before him.

She ducked below the bubbles, intending to hide behind them as he stopped in front of the tub and started to get in with her. She began to protest but he silenced her by leaning over her and kissing her passionately.

Her breathing was ragged and she grabbed for him frantically as he started to pull away. Her hands left soapy trails as they slid helplessly down the muscles of his chest. She wasn't finished yet! No, no no!

His swollen tip brushed against her breasts as he slid into the tub facing her. She looked up at him to find him smiling mischievously down at her… the fiend was doing it on purpose! Well, she would show him who would be doing the teasing. She dipped her head and her tongue darted out, flicking over the tip of him. He jerked against her, moaning in surprise. She grinned and licked out again, this time running her tongue delicately around the edges of the head and his hands reached out to tangle in her hair, roughly pulling her against him.

The sudden movement jarred her out of the fantasy and she found herself back in the café, gasping for air. She was staring into the cashier's eyes and the woman wouldn't release her hand. They both were left breathless in the wake of the fantasy and Terran trembled a bit as the after effects of it fell away reluctantly. The other woman seemed about to speak, but Terran shook herself back to reality and left the café in a hurry, not even bothering to wait for her change.

The doorbell clanged loudly behind her.

Her face was burning hotly and her lower body clenched tightly. She hugged her shawl to her and walked brusquely down the sidewalk, lost to thought. After walking a little ways, she began to calm down, but her body still hummed with desire and her cheeks still felt warm.

That last vision was *intense*. It was so real, so emotional and physical at once, so… *unlike* her. She fretted about what that could possibly mean as she walked along, her steps slowing as her thoughts ran a mile a minute. Well, she was just going to forget about any more playing tonight, she was ashamed of herself for peeking into other people's personal fantasies like that. But…..it had been so long since she had enjoyed herself like that and it had felt… well it had felt damn *good*, she admitted and smiled to herself.

She raised her head up to the stars and hugged her arms around herself. It was so bright out tonight; she could see her way perfectly. The puppy calendar hanging in her kitchen had informed her it was a full moon. Lots of strange things have been reported to happen on nights such as this and she giggled to herself as she walked along, knowing all too well how strange things could get.

She walked a bit further before realizing she was no longer headed for home. In fact, she was nowhere near her house. She came to a stop, her shoes scraping on the sidewalk. She must have taken a wrong turn while she had been so distracted. She turned around full circle, not recognizing the neighborhood at all. Well, this was just crazy. She had just decided to head back the way she'd come when she noticed a large grove of trees off to her left.

"Now, where did they come from?" She whispered to herself with an eyebrow raised. She had a strong feeling it was time to call it a night. She fully intended to go straight home to bed… she really did. So why now, heaven tell, was she heading straight for a small clearing in the edge of the trees??

Her feet seemingly moved of their own volition and she was but a passenger to their flight. She slipped in past a large dead bush, briefly snagging her shawl on a limb as she pushed her way into the trees. Strange, it was just as light in here as it was outside of the grove. Okay, well not as bright, but she could still see clearly enough to walk without stumbling. An owl hooted off to her right and she jumped, her breath catching in her throat.

"What am I doing here? I must indeed be going crazy... frolicking off into the forest in the middle of the night..." her voice trailed off as she realized what she had just spoken. Forest? There were no forests in these parts, only small groves of trees at best. She gazed about, seeing no end to the mass of wilderness and she started to panic. Spinning around, she tried desperately to locate the opening she had just entered through. Nothing, nothing at all. No opening and in fact she could not even see the town's lights anymore.

This was madness! She began to dart among the trees, searching for any break in the trees, but to no avail. Jogging now, she tried to go back the way she had come from. She burst through a patch of bushes and small trees to find herself...

...in the forest clearing from her dreams.

"Oh My God," she said slowly. This was absolutely impossible, but hell... with what she had been experiencing the past few days, anything was possible now.

The only thing that was different was that there was a giant oak tree in the very center of the clearing.

"Okay, I must be dreaming again," she said matter-of-factly. I made it home from the café and I'm soundly asleep in my big comfy bed with the giant fluffy comforter bundled about me.' She closed her eyes, hoping when she opened them that she would indeed be in her bed at home. She cracked one eye and moaning, she opened them the rest of the way. Nope, no such luck. She was still in the clearing.

Her breathing began to speed up and her heart was pounding within her chest. Against her better judgment, she entered the clearing, whereupon everything she had ever known to be reality was shattered into a million pieces.

Chapter Seven

Small, colorful lights spun around her, darting back and forth, up and down, causing the ends of her hair to lift in the slight breeze they were causing. She smelled cinnamon and spices, apples and even lavender. The little lights spun faster and faster, starting to make her dizzy.

Terran's mind was reeling. She couldn't nail down one solid thought. Through the mist of spinning colors, she could see that the clearing was full of the lights, darting this way and that. She was moving now and she wasn't even sure if she were walking herself, or if she was merely floating along with the movement of the lights. They were so beautiful, so mesmerizing, she thought as her eyelids and limbs grew heavy. She felt as if she could sleep for an entire year she was suddenly so exhausted.

"Enough." a deep voice said softly. Just the one word and nothing more and all of a sudden the lights were no longer there, all that was left of them were the tracers behind her eyes and a soft giggle as they disappeared up into the Oak's branches.

Terran was in a daze and she had somehow ended up on her knees. Her eyes were still heavily lidded and her body pulsed with all the energy the little orbs of light had infused her with. It seemed contradictory that she be in such a dream-like state and also so full of energy, but that is how she felt.

Her hand began to tingle and she lifted it to her face, already knowing that it would be softly glowing.

She was wrong. It wasn't glowing, it was blazing. And it was sucking her into its depths as she gazed at it, mesmerized.

"So, you have finally come home to me, my love."

It was *him,* the man from her dreams. He had snuck up behind her while she wasn't paying attention... *again*. Well, not this time by the gods, this time she would be in control!

She spun around to face him, beginning to rise to her feet and gasped at what she saw. He was absolutely the most beautiful man she had ever seen. Oh, she had seen her fill of beautiful men, but this one... this one was... well *damn!* That one word just said it all. She ran her eyes up his body, drinking in every drop of him. His feet were covered in soft brown leather boots that came up almost to his knees. Her breath caught in her throat as her face came level with his muscular thighs, which were covered tightly by his pants. Oh, so very tightly.

She gulped loudly. Oh lord, she didn't have the strength of will not to touch him, if she didn't back away from him, she was going to lose all self-control. As she rose to her full height, now fully standing on her own two feet, she took in the rest of his body... broad muscular chest and shoulders, covered in some strange shimmering material that seemed to change color as he shifted, blending him into his surroundings. His hair fell in a golden wave just past his shoulders and his eyes...

She was drowning...

...in two deep pools of aquamarine... his gaze was mesmerizing and innocent... calm and absolutely peaceful...

At the very moment her gaze touched his, those two pools of aqua were no longer calm and peaceful. They were quickly filling with liquid heat and desire as he reached for her with large, strong hands. She began to back away, afraid of the emotions coursing through her body so quickly, she felt she would choke on them if she didn't calm herself down and get away from this god-like creature... right *now.*

"Terran, come here." He demanded softly, holding her gaze to his.

Her body betrayed her and began to shuffle towards him, her hands clenched at her sides, and her body trembling.

She was terrified. Not that he would harm her, but that she wouldn't be able to control herself once she ventured too close to him.

Terran had spent her entire life learning and mastering her self-control... and for what? To see it shattered at her feet the moment a good-looking guy showed some speck of interest in her?? Gods, she was so weak.

She stopped just short of touching him and he grasped her chin lightly with his fingers, raising her face to meet his gaze.

"You are mine, Terran. You always have been and you always will be, no matter where you go or who you pretend to be. Mine." He growled this softly against her lips, the vibrations traveling over her lips and

through her body, to touch her in the most intimate of places, causing her to moan softly. He captured her moan with his lips, drinking in her restrained passion, swallowing her self-control and making it disappear as if it never existed.

She lost herself then, though maybe she had been lost from the moment he had first whispered her name inside of her dreams. She raised her arms around his neck and he gripped her against him tightly, deepening their kiss.

The ring was now blazing so brightly it was almost surrounding their bodies, enveloping them in its power.

"*I want you NOW.*" He said urgently. "*I can't wait any longer…*" he pushed her roughly against the trunk of the enormous oak, lifting her legs around his waist as he did so. The bark bit sharply into her back, but she hardly noticed the sensations as she was swept away in desire.

She didn't respond to his words… how could she? She felt safe with this man, safer than she had felt in many years and she *wanted* him. *Needed* him. And he needed her. She knew that now.

They kissed passionately, their tongues dancing, tasting… devouring each other. He broke the kiss only to trail a string of kisses down her neck to her shoulders, where his tongue flicked out and ran over the hollow in her throat, causing her to throw her head back with a gasp. It felt so damn *good.*

His hands roamed her body and found the buttons on the front of her dress, ripping them apart to expose her white lacy bra. He growled low in his throat as his gaze melted her, causing her to go limp around his body. He tightened his hold and lowered his head to her breast, taking a swollen nipple into his mouth, right through the material of her bra. Her breath caught in her throat, the sweet ecstasy of friction on her nipple combined with the hot wetness of his mouth tugging and pulling… caused her to come undone.

She tangled her fingers into his silken hair and pressed him harder against her. He broke contact and looked up into her eyes, smiling wickedly.

"Do you want this, my love?"

She nodded at him frantically, not able to find her voice.

"Then, say my name. Tell me who I am and who you know me to be; who you've always known me to be." He said softly as he gently licked her nipple again.

"I… I don't know your name! You haven't told me!" she shouted in a whisper.

He raised his mouth to her ear and kissed her there, his tongue entering inside, causing her body to arch against his.

"*Say it Terran, say my name or I will stop right now and leave you wanting…*" he said the last word as his tongue entered her ear again, causing her to cry out.

"I don't know! I swear I don't, please tell it to me, please… *please…*" she said desperately, in a small voice.

"*Say it now, Terran.*" She moaned helplessly against him. "*NOW!*" he growled into her neck as he bit down firmly on her shoulder.

A flash of blinding white flared behind her eyes…

She was racing through the forest, her tiny slippered feet scarcely touching the forest bed as leaves floated up around her to join in the merry race. Beside her, his hand clamped tightly in her own, was her dearest friend…

"*ROLAND!* Roland, please Roland, take me now, *NOW!* I need you Roland, I've always needed you!" and then she knew. He was her life mate, her consort, her lover… her savior.

He smiled with triumph as he released his teeth from her shoulder, licking the marks he had left on her and relishing in her moan. She was his again.

He took her then, right there, against the tree, tearing her clothes from her body in his passion and slamming into her in one long stroke. She was ready for him, as he knew she would be. She screamed his name into the branches and the glow surrounding them closed in tighter, pulsing with their energy.

They came together in an explosion of aquamarine and copper light that bathed the forest in its glow. White hot fire burst up her back and she screamed Roland's name again as she lost all conscious thought…

***

The lights were back, flitting around them and tickling their skin, playing in their hair as she opened her eyes, still in Roland's arms. He looked down at her with love in his eyes and just a bit of amusement.

What the hell? She had just had the most amazing experience of her life and he was sitting there and laughing at her? Oh, hell no! She became angry and started pushing away from him.

"'Terran, don't," he laughed.

She growled at him and pushed him away, ready to have it out with him, right there and now, right here in the nude. Right here in the… *sky*?

She screamed as she began to fall and found herself in Roland's arms again. She was too terrified for words.

"Oh Roland, Roland I almost died! Thank goodness you were here to catch me before I fell." She sobbed into his shoulder.

"Terran, look." He whispered tenderly.

She opened her eyes and looked up at him questioningly.

"Omigod, Omigod! Roland, you have wings!" she shouted loudly.

"You mean, WE have wings, love." He laughed as she looked down to discover they were still in the air, floating in place above the old Oak tree.

She screeched and hugged Roland tightly, burying her face in his chest.

"What is going on Roland? Why are we in the air, why are we flying, why do we have WINGS?" She was babbling now and didn't care.

All of a sudden the little balls of light were surrounding them again, but this time, she could see that they weren't just light, but beautiful tiny beings… with wings just like Roland's! Fairies! They were fairies! Roland was a fairy… *she* was a fairy! She must be…

"No, you are not dreaming my love. It will all come back to you soon. We have always been mated to each other. Meant to be together forever.

"You were taken away from me when we were very young and I have been searching for you ever since. I knew that you had to leave and be a part of the human world so you could come back and rule our race with a kind and generous heart.

"I sent the ring to you to keep you safe and to bring you back to me when the time was right. Only after you had been through all that human beings go through, could you be the best ruler you could be.

"You now know what it is to feel innocence and kindness, what it is to feel the happiness of your hard earned accomplishments without the aid of magic and servants at your beck and call… but most importantly, you learned what it is to suffer the loss of someone you love and still make it through with your spirit intact. You've made it Terran. You're home now."

His speech ended with a sweet kiss on her lips and it all flooded back to her then, on the wings of a dream. She was with her prince again, and she was a princess, daughter to the King and Queen of the Fae.

Her head was reeling from all the recovered memories. This had all been one big test. Her life as a human… a *test*… and she had passed with flying colors.

A flash of light and they were no longer surrounded by tiny orbs of light, but were part of them. She looked over her shoulder to see her wings pumping... her beautiful, beautiful wings! She never knew how much she had missed them. Copper and cream, with lacings of black, they shone in the moonlight, flashing as she danced in the air with her soul mate.

Everyone that she knew and loved was here, even her...

"Liam! Oh my god, it's really you!" Terran screamed with tears running down her cheeks as she and her brother, whom she thought she had lost forever, met in the air for the biggest, longest hug of her life.

She was sobbing openly now, so happy to be home, so happy to have all of her family here together.

"I thought I had lost you little brother. I've missed you so much. You have no idea what excruciating pain I have been through." She cried as she hugged him closer.

"I love you too Sis." He laughed and cried with her, doing twists and turns in the air, playfully swatting at each other.

Her family surrounded her then, welcoming her home and congratulating her on her accomplishments.

They had the biggest party that night, her family and friends all attending. They celebrated far into the wee hours of morning and she fell asleep in her lover's arms, feeling completely content for the first time in her entire life.

As she slept... and dreamed... the ring on her finger faded and returned to its rightful place, waiting for the time when it would be needed again...

The Grand Opening
Robert Cloud

"I remember the day the ring reappeared in the cabinet." Zachariah said as he took a short pause and kissed Melanie upon the forehead. "I saw a flash behind the closed doors of the cabinet and when I opened them it took me a moment before I noticed that the once empty spot had been filled."

"No piece of jewelry I had ever made had returned upon its own like that. I reached in and the moment I touched it all the images of what it had been through since it had left the shop entered my mind."

Melanie sat snuggled close to Zachariah. She was so at peace as he spoke that her heart nearly sang. She could not remember ever feeling this much like she belonged. Slowly she sighed as she realized the story was over, and with sad eyes looked up at him and nuzzled against his cheek.

She smirked as his rough evening beard rasped against her cheek. It was the first time she had felt it and though it was scratchy against the soft skin of her cheek, something about it was wonderful. His stories were so full of magic. Even though she knew how fast the tiara had been completed and knew that had to have been done with magic she still had disbelief in many of the stories. Dragons, Androfoxes, Fae, ghosts that could seek revenge, people being reunited in life after one had died, it all made wonderful tales of mystical love and magic but it was more than she could believe.

She looked at his eyes. They were the color of the deepest ocean, and bright and full of life. They did not look like the eyes of a man over a hundred years old and yet they looked like they had seen more than their share of years. She could see from his eyes that he believed the stories he told her. Perhaps his mind had turned the stories real with time. She had heard that happened sometimes with people that had grown very old. She sighed, it did not matter, she loved him dearly and even if his mind was slowly going she would love him still.

She slowly ran her hand across his face and turned his lips towards hers. Kissing them softly she whispered, "I guess I should get dressed and head home. It is late, and mother will be looking for me soon."

Zachariah looked at her and his eyes clouded with tears. She laid her head against his shoulder as if she really did not want to go, and he was glad for the moment for he did not want her to see the tears in his eyes. He could feel her gentle breath flowing under his chin and his heart melted for the pain she'd carried by herself for so long. He knew her mother would not be looking for her. The sad part was he believed she believed she would because she wanted to believe there was at least a little goodness in her mother. The truth was that the woman that Melanie called a mother did not care whether Melanie ever came home. Looking outside he realized it was late, and dark. It seemed even darker than normal like all light had vanished from the sky. Zachariah knew that was not the case, that it was it was another sign pushing him to make a choice. He knew he was making the right one. "Sweetheart, your mother was in here this night."

Melanie sat up quickly! "She was?"

"Yes. She came by and spoke to me."

"Oh." Melanie lowered her head. Zachariah's heart melted, the poor girl was trembling. He knew from the waves of emotion emanating from her and flooding his mind that she was terrified her mother had told him something horrible. Then like a sudden blast as she looked up into his eyes he was hit directly with a solid thought of hers. *She told you I was not allowed to come here anymore! Oh god, I can't lose you!*

He had to recover from his shock quickly and not let her know what had just happened, not yet. His hand went to her cheek and he kissed her lips, "She did not say anything bad about you, only that she trusted you to make your own decisions. That if you wanted to work here and stay here that it was up to you."

Tears filled Melanie's eyes. Zachariah could feel the relief washing over her as she wrapped her arms around him and asked, "What are you trying to tell me, Papa Zach?"

"I am saying that I think it is too dark for you to try to walk home by yourself. So if you want to stay the night you can."

Suddenly her arms squeezed him even tighter as she hugged. "Thank you, Papa Zach, thank you." Then her tears flowed freely as she wept. Zachariah would have been worried if he could not feel the waves of happiness that were engulfing them both.

This girl was far more special than Lilith knew and he now knew he had to do whatever it took to protect her from Lilith even if it meant he had to sacrifice his own life to do it. He hated the idea that such an act would hurt Melanie, but she was young and had a long life ahead of her. The gifts he felt coming from her had to have a purpose in serving God, not in being the host of a monster like Lilith.

Abruptly she sat up and waved her finger close to his face and he could see by the look upon her face that she was teasing him as she said, "But you know, it still means no sex." Then she smiled at him as she wrapped her arms around him and held him close.

Zachariah stroked her hair lovingly, "Hun, I would not want it any other way. There are two bedrooms upstairs or we can pull out the folding bed in the Master bedroom, whichever you prefer."

He could feel the smile on her face broaden even through the fabric of his shirt, "I would like to be in the same room, so the folding bed sounds nice."

Zachariah turned his eyes to the ring that he still held in the palm of his hand. Deftly he lifted it between his thumb and index finger and looked at it a moment and was struck with an idea. He took his other hand and lifted Melanie's face so he could kiss her lips gently and then said, "Sweetheart, I know you believe in a touch of the magic that lies within this shop but something tells me you have strong doubts about the real magic that is here."

Melanie pulled away and looked at him. He could see from the look in her eyes that she was wondering if he had read her mind. "Papa Zach, it just seems too unreal. There are so many things. I mean Vampires are legends, myths and so are Dragons they never really existed. It is the same thing with Elves and I had never even heard of an Anthrofox.

"I know many people believe in ghosts but a necklace that allowed one to seek its revenge and to experience the feelings of eroticism through the body of the living again? All these stories are romantic and beautiful but they are too hard to believe. Your jewelry is almost magical in the very fact that it exists. It is incredibly beautiful and the artistry is beyond anything I could imagine. It belongs in the most famous of museums but to think it is enchanted just stretches my belief too far." She lowered her eyes.

"Yet I know you believe it. I know you truly believe that there is magic in these pieces you are telling the stories of."

Zachariah smiled to her and held up the ring before her eyes. He rolled it between his fingers. "What if there was a way to prove to you the magic?"

"Papa Zach! I do not want to see your fantasies! I don't want to wear that ring!" Melanie nixed with a look that bordered on fright.

His smile deepened and a small laugh escaped, "No, sweetheart, I was not thinking of that.

"There is a second magic within this ring. This ring will not allow itself to leave this shop unless it is locked within the cabinet. That is the only way I can move it from one shop to another.

"I once made the mistake of trying to sell it to another. No sooner than they stepped out the door than there was a flash within the cabinet and it had reappeared inside. The customer accused me of trying to swindle him. I wound up giving him his money back and giving him a diamond necklace for his wife to keep him from calling the authorities."

Melanie looked at the ring as he placed it in her hand and said, "Go unlock the door. Keep your hand open and on the ring and step outside. See if what I say is not true."

He saw her look at the ring and then up into his eyes, "Papa Zach, you do not need to prove anything to me."

"Melanie, precious, yes, this is important. If you are going to become a major part of my life you need to know that the magic is real as it will become as essential to you as it is to me. Yet even more imperative is that you must decide whether you can live with it in your life because if you cannot then we cannot be together either."

He hated to say that for he saw that those last words stung her deep, even more he was now feeling the pain in her growing as it replaced the happiness that she had felt only moments before. Melanie looked down at the ring and back up into his eyes. He saw a look of determination cross her face as her jaw set and her eyes became focused on him. "Papa Zach," she said, "whether this is really magical or not, you are not going to get rid of me that easily."

She placed her free hand over his heart and added, "There is a strong heart beating here, and there are times I can almost swear I can feel it beat faster when you look at me. I have seen your eyes shine when we look at each other and I know the feelings I have for you are returned."

Slowly she climbed out of his lap and looked at him then held out her hand and said, "Whether I return with this ring still in my hand or not I will still love you. No matter how shaken I am by the surprise that magic exists or how hurt you are by the knowledge that it does not I am not going to let that come between us. I want to find out for ourselves if there is a chance and not let this change that."

Zachariah could not believe his ears as he stared at the young woman before him. This woman may have been only a few hours shy of being eighteen but she had just shown maturity and wisdom far exceeding that of the one that had adopted her. His heart thundered with pride at the strength of Melanie's courage and fortitude. Her conviction that the love she felt for him was the genuine thing and not something imagined or just hoped for because she had not experienced it before.

Her eyes shone with the fire that he had only seen before in the eyes of his mother when she was helping to save a life. Melanie was determined to prove one way or another that she was going to be by his side. He knew she was going to be stunned when the ring vanished from her hand but he believed her when she said she would not leave him. To have that much trust in someone in this short of a time was a miracle. As her hand closed on the ring, he smiled. He knew in his heart he had found his *One*.

Melanie turned and walked to the door. Zachariah watched as she slowly turned the lock. He could see her hesitate and take a deep breath at the threshold and then like she was jumping from a plane without a parachute she stepped over the sill.

He did not have to see her face to know what her eyes were like. He could see the sudden glow that highlighted her and then the glow within the cabinet as the ring reappeared in the place where it belonged.

She whirled about and ran to the cabinet, looking within then she turned to him. Her eyes were wider than he had ever seen them and they were liquid pools that he wanted to fall into, letting his soul swim into their deepest depths. Her mouth moved but nothing came out. He reached a hand out to her and she slowly lifted a hand and took his. Guiding her to him he eased her back onto his lap and held her until her shock began to fade.

"Pa... Pa... Papa Zach... I... I... believe you."

He kissed her forehead and as he did she bolted upright in his arms and made him bite his lip. Her eyes were bright as she looked at him, she obviously did not realize what she had done. "That means those stories were true!"

"Yes," he said as he wiped blood from the corner of his lip. When she saw it tears came to her eyes.

"Papa Zach," she held her hand to her mouth, "I am sorry, I did not mean to hurt you." She began to wipe his blood with her hand and then kissed his lip to make it better. "I am so sorry."

He pulled her tight, "It is okay, precious. You were just excited."

Melanie snuggled against him, "Yes, you were afraid I would want to leave you, but the idea of those stories being true and me becoming a part of the enchantment makes me feel like Cinderella. I feel like I have fallen into a fairy tale."

"Papa Zach, that means you are my Prince Charming."

He laughed. "I might be charming, but I am far from a prince.

"Now sweetheart, it is time we begin to get ready for bed."

She hugged him tight again, then paused and looked at him, eyeing him carefully.

"What is it, sweetheart?"

She cocked her head and a quizzical look crossed her face, "Papa Zach, if you were widowed so young why didn't you ever remarry?"

As he stroked her hair and smiled at the curious look upon her face his mind drifted to the mirrors. Lilith had been too quiet. Even though she had encouraged him to embrace the relationship with Melanie he knew Lilith well enough to know that he should have still heard the occasional grumble of jealousy.

Zachariah knew it was Lilith's plan to share Melanie's body, but he suspected there was more to it than that. With the fact she was hiding every single emotion from him he knew she had to be planning something far more sinister than what she was letting on. Over the years, as things she had told him were true were proved to be false, he had learned not to trust her. The love he felt for her was more for the memory of the woman he had thought she was than for who she had truly been.

At one time he had thought that the monster within her could be separated from her and that if he could find a way to make her human again, that he could have his wife and live a normal life with her. It did not take long after her death to find out how deep her betrayal had gone. Even then he still had hope because the true prophetess had told him the table could heal all. He had hoped one day to have the opportunity to heal Lilith. It had taken him time to learn that the table could heal all but only if they truly sought to be healed. Over time he had learned that Lilith never truly wanted to be anything other than what she was.

The monster that resided within Lilith was Lilith herself. He knew that the table was not responsible for Lilith's actions but that somehow he had been condemned to this torment. Centuries had passed as he tried to find a way to be rid of Lilith and the curse that she brought with her. He had sought out one prophet after another, journeying from every port and city he could find. He spoke to the Oracle at Delphi with little success. There were many times his faith in God would begin to waiver but then he would meet a prophet of God and they would tell him something that only one of God could truly know.

They would tell him something about the creation of the stone, or about Lilith and his life. Sometimes they would even look at him and tell him his age. These were the ones he would listen to. It was from one of these that he learned that the Ritual of Commissioning was not supposed to have anything to do with Lilith. That a spell had been placed upon him binding him and the stone together in such a way that it could not be broken until *The One* came into his life. From that moment on he had dreamed of meeting *The One.*

Another prophet told him that *The One* would be the way Lilith would be reborn. That one bothered him but he also knew that if she was reborn that he could find a way to kill her. At least he would have the curse lifted. Now to find his heart so wrapped up with the girl that had that designation was tearing him apart. She would be the one to free him from the curse of Lilith, but he could not let her do it if it meant she would be taking Lilith into herself.

He had to find a way around it. His mind kept returning to the night of the suicide and he kept trying to figure out why. What had happened that night that was so significant that it could solve his predicament?

Zachariah could see that Melanie was waiting for an answer so he nodded toward the mirror, "You see that mirror back in the corner, the one with all the gemstones and gold inlay?"

Melanie lifted herself and looked over his shoulder. Zachariah shifted his head to the side to avoid getting a mouthful of her breast. Even though she was still covered by the black velvet of the evening dress, the dress did not leave much to the imagination. For a moment he could feel his mouth water as his mind began to drift and the idea of sucking her nipple between his lips to savor its sweetness filled his every thought. It took him a moment to push the thought aside. He truly did believe in the idea that there was magic within the power of sex and because of that he believed it was best to reserve the release of that energy until after marriage. If he were not a practitioner of his craft and if it were not a stricture of the things he had learned of his magic he did not know if he would have had the restraint that he did. Maybe, yet maybe not.

As she sat back down, he could see that she realized what had happened for she turned red and giggled then she could not meet his gaze. He could tell she was very embarrassed. She folded her arms over her breasts to cover herself as if to hide from his view even further. Her voice jittered nervously as she responded, "Yes, it is a lovely mirror."

"That is the main reason I never remarried."

"A mirror?" Melanie tried to look at it again. Her arms were still crossed over her breasts so that she could not make the same mistake twice. Zachariah could see from her eyes when she sat back down that she was confused.

Zachariah lowered his head, "I told you that Lilith committed suicide the day of our anniversary, killing herself and my unborn child. She was looking into a mirror when she did it. It was almost like she was watching the mirror so she could see her last breath."

He remembered running into the bedroom full of excitement because he had something wonderful to tell her and finding her in the pool of blood. One hand still clenched around the hilt of the dagger embedded in her heart, the other clenched around the mirror. He began to tremble and tears ran down his cheeks.

"At first I wanted to throw the mirror away. I even tried to destroy it, but I could not so I took it into my shop and sat it near the table. I fashioned a new frame for it, one that I could hang upon the wall because when I had tried to destroy it the handle had been damaged.

"There is something very strange about that mirror. One day it rattled upon the wall and when I went to investigate I saw a face within it."

Melanie gasped. Zachariah turned and he could see a look of fright in her eyes. He could also feel her emotions reaching out to him grasping him as if she was seeking him for protection. He knew she had guessed the secret to the mirror.

"Yes, Melanie, the mirror holds the soul of Lilith, and yes, she talks to me from time to time."

A look of horror slowly transformed Melanie's face. She wrapped her arms around Zachariah and buried her head against his chest saying, "You mean she can see us now? She knows about us?"

"Calm down, sweetheart. She not only knows about us, she is

encouraging me to fall for you." Zachariah looked toward the mirror himself half expecting to see a red mist rising from it and coming to seek revenge. "I do not fully trust her, but I know when something is to her benefit she goes along with it. She sees me falling for you to her benefit."

Melanie stopped and stared aghast at Zachariah. Her arms at her side, her jaw open. Slowly her mouth began to move but no words came out. It tore him apart that she was so frightened. He had to calm her down and try to explain better, "Melanie, it is okay.

"It has to do with the commission of your piece of jewelry and how special you are. Somehow she feels you are going to help her be free from her prison," he kissed her forehead and then whispered in her ear, "and if I can have any say in the matter it will be to send her straight to where she truly belongs.

"Precious, please trust me, I will not let her hurt you."

Finally the silence broke through Melanie's vocal chords and her words were cold. "I do trust you Papa Zach."

Zachariah held her very tight against him and said, "As far as Lilith is concerned. I am not certain of her plans. I just know that the magic has led you here. And I know that in all this time the magic has never been wrong. So whatever Lilith has planned, good or bad, I will protect you."

Melanie wrapped her arms around him and whispered, "Thank you, Papa Zach."

Softly Melanie whispered, "I am tired. Can we go to bed?"

Without a thought, and in defiance of his age, Zachariah picked up Melanie like she weighed nothing, "Yes, sweetheart, we can." It did not matter anymore whether she knew he was stronger than he should be for his age, she already knew about the magic of the shop. She had seen it with her own eyes.

The young girl laughed, "Papa Zach, there is no way you are over a hundred years old."

He laughed as he kissed her lips then he whispered to her, "According to the birth certificate on file I will be one hundred and ten very soon."

Melanie gulped, "No way!"

"Yes, way!" Zachariah smiled as he carried her up the stairs and told her, "in fact, I share your birth date. Only I was born at midnight in what is now called Jordan. So I will turn one hundred and ten about seven hours before you turn eighteen."

Melanie laughed as they neared the top of the steps. "Eight."

"What?" Zachariah asked.

"I was born in Illinois not New York so I actually do not turn eighteen until one in the morning." She kissed his lips, "We will have to remember that."

A light flashed in his head before he opened the door to the bedroom and said, "Yes we will."

He pushed open the door and carried her over to the bed where he set her down. Then he went to a double doored closet and pulled out the hidden bed and laid it down and began to make it but Melanie interrupted him.

"Papa Zach, I trust you. I know you will not take advantage of me.

"I look at your eyes and I have never felt so loved." Melanie looked at Zachariah and he saw her gulp then lower her eyes. She clasped her hands in her lap and her voice was soft and sullen. Like before her emotions began to come off of her in waves and when they hit him he could feel his own tears begin to rise, she was in so much pain and despair he wanted to run and pull her into his arms but he could also tell she needed to tell him what was bothering her. If he interrupted her now she would not be able to get it out of her system and he wouldn't be able to help her to voice it. It was now or never.

"You said my mother was here tonight. Then I know you know I am adopted. She tells everyone. She also tells them that she does not love me and never even tried.

"Papa Zach, my entire life, I have not felt loved, and maybe that is why your kindness touched me so much. Others around here have been kind to me, but most have tried to use me. The boys wanted in my pants. The older men wanted there too. The few that did not want something and that were truly kind I have been thankful for. Yet there was something truly different with you.

"I have never had a boyfriend, and yet I know I love you. I know I do not want to sleep alone tonight, and I also know that even if we share a bed you will not force yourself on me. You will honor my wish to remain a virgin until I am married. So please, put that bed back up and lay down with me." Melanie patted the bed and looked at Zachariah with eyes so pleading that he could not refuse.

He began to feel the waves of her emotions hitting him but he knew he had to make his mind up without her emotions persuading him. Over the years he had learned how to close off portions of his mind from Lilith when he had needed to. Though he did not want to close off his mind and heart from Melanie, right now he had to think with his own mind and not with her emotions so he imagined himself sitting upon the stone table and a dome of golden light sealing him off from all intrusions.

The waves ceased. Suddenly he felt empty and he hated it. He immediately wanted to tear down the wall but he had to think on his own and clear headed. Was this right? He knew he did love Melanie. He could tell that, it was not just her emotions. He could feel his need for her as well as her need for him. As he looked at her pleading eyes he wanted to sit beside her and pull her into his arms and love her, and show her what real love was.

How could anyone have let this child grow up and not have loved her? How could that woman have called herself a mother even to her own biological children and looked at this child and not felt something? His heart collapsed, he needed her in his life and he would find a way to have her even if for only a few more hours.

Zachariah let the wall crumble and felt the waves hit him. They hit him so hard they almost sent him to his knees but he stood tall and smiled at her. Slowly he turned around and lifted the bed putting it back into the closet and closing the doors behind it. Then he took the blanket that he had planned for the bed and covered the big mirror. Melanie looked at him with a question in her eyes and he answered it before she could voice it. "The other day Lilith spoke from a different mirror than the one she had told me she was confined to. She said it was the special magic of the day but something inside me tells me she has been able to do that for a long time. By covering the mirror I am hoping to not only hide what she can see but what she can hear. Even though nothing will happen between us, I want her silenced to our time together.

Melanie smiled, "Thank you, Papa Zach."

He then went to his wardrobe. There were a few things there from when Lilith had aged him with the evil little kid. Even after she had found an innocent child he had been sick and had had to have a live-in nurse for a short time. The nurse had left a few items behind one was a knee-length nightgown. "Well you cannot sleep in that evening dress, I think it would be better if you wore this."

She took it and looked at it. It was heavy cotton and the polyester underwear she had on would cause friction. "Papa Zach, if I wear this it would be best if I take off my underwear."

"Oh!" Suddenly Zachariah felt his own cheeks blush, Melanie burst out in laughter. Quickly he turned around while she slipped out of her underwear and slid the gown over her head.

"All done, Papa Zach," she announced. However when he turned around she was leaning over with her bottom exposed, mooning him.

"Melanie!"

"What?" She said as innocently as she could muster before she burst into laughter. Then they both laughed. He was glad to see she had a little of a mischievous side to her as well as the serious side he had seen. He could tell from the things he was feeling it had been nothing but a jest and that she was teasing him. She had really enjoyed seeing him turn bright red and she'd had to do it again. He smiled, for he knew that she truly was comfortable with him. If she had not been she would not have done that for that would have been to tempt the devil.

Zachariah began to unbutton his shirt.

"Papa Zach, wait!" Melanie said then she quickly got up and walked over to him. "Please do not take this wrong, I am not trying to be sensual. I just want to do some of this for you, besides I am curious."

She finished unbuttoning his shirt and looked at him. "You said as you carried me up the stairs you will soon be one hundred and ten, but Papa Zach, I could feel your muscles ripple beneath your shirt. You lifted me like I was a pillow not a girl that weighs a hundred pounds."

She ran her hand over the hair of his chest and added, "Except that your hair is white, and the lines on your face your body looks like a young man's. I would guess your chest to be the chest of a man in his thirties or younger not over a hundred?"

Zachariah held her head between his hands, "I know, the only thing that really gives away my age is the lines of my face, but think Melanie. You have already seen the magic of this shop. It works through me; it keeps me young as well so I can work on more pieces."

She looked up into his eyes and smiled, "But when you are outside you look old. Your hands are almost claws, and your back is stooped?"

"Again that is the magic at work," Zachariah said, "and when that window is open and the light from outside enters no matter how little or how much I will look older than I do right now too. People know me to be an old man and that is what they will see."

A deep smile crossed Melanie's face, "And since I know the truth of the magic I am beginning to see the real you."

"That is right, precious."

Zachariah did not think it was possible but her smile broadened even more, "Then I do not have to worry that you will not be around for me as I grow older?"

Zachariah kissed her lips, "That might not be a worry you will have to have, sweetie. The magic may keep me around a long time, but for now, let's get ready for bed."

She smiled wickedly. "Do you sleep in pajamas, Papa Zach?"

Slowly he blushed, "Umm, no, normally, I sleep as I came into this world, but tonight I think I should at least sleep in pajama bottoms."

Melanie's lower lip stuck out in a pout and Zachariah laughed as he leaned over and kissed it, then he added. "It is best that we tempt each other no further than we have. For like you I believe sex is something best saved for marriage."

She pushed the shirt over his shoulders and off his arms and carried it over to a chair and laid it down. As he rummaged through the top drawer looking for a pair of pajama bottoms she turned and said, "Eww! I had not thought about your back being covered with hair."

Zachariah laughed. "Well there is not a lot I can do about that."

"Oh yes there is," Melanie said adamantly. "We can go get your back waxed."

As he pulled out the pajama bottoms he turned around and looked at her and just as adamantly said, "Not in this lifetime and this has been a hell of a long lifetime."

Melanie laughed as she ran over to him and hugged him tight. She kissed his lips and said, "I am teasing, I like you as you are, even if you are a grizzly bear."

He hugged her close and suddenly released her as he felt her hardened nipples through the nightgown against his chest. Tempting the devil was going to be difficult to handle if he kept teasing fate.

She looked at him with a little disappointment in her eyes and he had her sit on the edge of the bed and said, "Melanie, how do you feel right now?"

"Happy! I want to be held by you. To kiss you and have you kiss me." She said smiling at him.

He nodded at her. "And how does your body feel when I hold you?"

"Wonderful. I feel warm, and tingly. I feel excited to have you near me."

"Melanie, precious, think on that word excited a moment," Zachariah said. "When you just hugged me, your breasts were pressed hard against me. How did that feel?"

"Like heaven!" Suddenly he saw by Melanie's face that she had caught on to where he was leading. "Oh!" She turned red again, and lowered her head, but then raised her eyes to look at his, and said, "But I do love you, and I know we are not going to do anything unless we get married. You have not even proposed. So I know nothing is going to happen.

"Is it bad to feel that way?" She asked.

He looked her in the eyes and said, "No, precious, if you can control it. Sometimes people let it go too far and lose control. The problem is you need to be aware of it."

She smiled, "So now I am aware of it, and I will not let it go any further."

"Sweetie, some things you may not be able to control whether they happen or not, but you can control whether sex happens or whether touching happens. So you keep your gown on and your body covered. I will go into the bathroom and put these bottoms on and then come back to join you." He smiled at her and as he stood he kissed her forehead.

Before he got to the door Melanie called after him, "Papa Zach, I just remembered something. You said your birth certificate said you were one hundred and ten. It was sort of like that was a piece of paper saying something but I got the feeling that it was not the truth of your age. You are older than a hundred and ten aren't you?"

Zachariah stopped at the door and without turning said, "Yes."

"How old are you, Papa Zach?" She asked.

"Truth is Melanie. I am far older than you may believe even with you believing in the magic. I will tell you tomorrow night when I tell you the most important story of them all."

"Oh?" He could feel Melanie's eyes drilling holes into his back.

"Remember the ring, the one that I refused to tell you the story of?"

"Yes."

"Tomorrow night that will be your birthday gift, or part of it."

Melanie clapped her hands, "I cannot wait, Papa Zach."

He stepped into the bathroom and put on the bottoms. He knew that that story had to be told to her but he dreaded it all the same. It was going to bring up a lot of painful memories for him and it was going to possibly put both of their lives at risk.

As he returned to the room Melanie patted the bed beside her and added, "Please come to bed now, and hold me."

Zachariah paused a moment and looked at her, "Sweetheart, you are so precious, but it bothers me because sometimes you act almost as if I have already proposed to you."

"I know Papa Zach, but I also believe it is going to happen. It is only a matter of time, and," she paused as she smiled at him, "I have a feeling it is going to be rather soon. These feelings I get usually are not wrong."

"Oh you do, do you?" He said as he climbed in beside her and pulled the blankets up over them.

"Yes I do," she replied as she snuggled into his arms with her back pressed against his chest. Zachariah could feel his groin stir, but he would do nothing about it. This girl was too precious and yes, he did indeed want to marry her, after the ritual was complete, but only if he could find a way that both of them could walk away from the ritual alive. If they couldn't both live he planned to be certain she did, he would protect her from Lilith at any cost.

However the memories of the night of Lilith's suicide were finally leading him to a potential answer; and Melanie had indeed been a key in guiding him there. The answer lay with the ring.

***

Melanie awoke first and for the first time in her memory she awoke feeling as if she belonged. She lay on her side looking into the face of the man she loved. It did not matter to her that their ages were so disparate yet she tried to imagine what he had looked like in his younger days. How she wished it had been her that had been with him in his youth and not Lilith for though she could see he loved Lilith whenever he spoke of her she could also see that there was something that he feared and even hated about her as well.

Maybe it was just that her spirit had been overseeing him all these years and had not allowed him the freedom to love again until now, but Melanie's senses told her it was something deeper and darker than that. She thought back to how the fear had overwhelmed her when Papa Zach had told her about the mirror. At first as she had looked at it there had been no feeling at all, even the second glance. Then when he had told her about Lilith's soul being trapped within the mirror it was like suddenly a door had opened and behind that door was an opening directly to Hell. The hatred and evil that had flowed forth from the mirror had been directed at her and it had been filled with jealousy and vengeance. Melanie had begun to wonder who was going to be protecting whom when the time came to face the evil within that mirror for if Papa Zach had ever felt the dark force she had felt he would never have even come close to that woman. Still, she knew he would protect her to the best of his ability, and something told her that even though he doubted himself that there was a way that he could indeed protect her. Now she had to figure out how she was going to save him.

Slowly, so that she did not wake her love, she rolled off his arm and climbed out of bed. She was a little embarrassed by the fact that her nightgown had hiked up to her midriff and exposed her sex to him and she was thankful he had worn his pajama bottoms for as she looked toward him she could see that his manhood was betraying his age. It was hard and firm as if he were a man well in his prime and not a man in the years of his decline. She covered her eyes. She would not think of sex, yet she knew she had turned such a deep shade of red that had he seen her he would have teased her about it for most of the day.

Quickly she pulled the cover up over him hiding what she dared not think about and also making certain her gown went back down to her knees. Then she turned toward the mirror. There was something she needed to do before the day began. She needed to see Lilith.

Slowly walking over to the blanket covered mirror she felt her heart racing, thundering within her chest. Every fiber in her was telling her that this was a mistake that she should leave the blanket where it was and just get dressed. However something inside her was also telling her that she needed to see for herself. She needed to know that the evil she felt was real and not just a figment of her imagination.

She crept closer, pausing at the edge of the large dresser that the mirror rested upon. As her fingers touched the edge of the blanket she felt a small static shock, a whisper, an omen telling her to leave well enough alone. Yet she had to know, with a sudden pull the blanket fell and Melanie froze.

The scream started in the pit of her stomach growing, swelling, gaining force and yet nothing came from her open mouth. She could not move. Her eyes were locked to the horrendous image before her. The mirror was filled with two large flaming eyes filled with hatred that were the center of a demonic face so monstrous that Melanie knew what the men must have felt like when they faced Medusa for she had become like stone.

Her limbs would not obey her. She tried to turn to flee from the eyes that tore into her but it was as if the very air about her had turned into solid stone. She could feel her heart beating, racing, her pulse slamming into every vein of her body.

Hours passed, days, weeks, years, a lifetime and still she could not utter a sound, but she heard someone singing in the distance and a child crying for the mother she never knew to come rescue her. The singing voice was the voice of a man in search of a long lost love. Slowly it pulled her to awareness and she realized that the crying child was her own voice and the singing was Zachariah trying to sooth her. She was no longer in front of the mirror but was lying on her back in Zachariah's arms. He had found her and rescued her.

She wrapped her arms around him and looked up at the mirror. Once again it was just a mirror with a blanket covering it and gone was the image of the demon she had seen.

Melanie wept bitterly into his chest as she wondered if it had all been a dream. She looked up at the man she loved, "Papa Zach, tell me, what happened?"

"I don't know sweetheart," he said soothingly, "I awoke to your screaming and I tried to wake you but it was as if you were in some kind of trance so I began to sing to you. It is how I used to sing to my sister long ago, when she had nightmares."

"So it was all a nightmare?" She hugged him tight.

"What? What was it about?" Concern filled his eyes.

"Maybe I will tell you later, Papa Zach, but your big day is here, and I do not want to relive it right now." She held him tight and then kissed his lips, "Thank you for rescuing me."

"You are welcome, sweetheart."

Quickly she sat up and looked at him, "Now go and start getting ready for your day. I will make you breakfast while you clean up and after we are done eating and I have done the dishes then I will get ready. By then it will be time for you to open the doors."

Zachariah laughed and jokingly said, "Now you are acting like a wife already. Giving orders and I have not even proposed yet."

"Oh, Papa Zach, I did not mean to give you an order, I want to serve you as your wife, but it is your big day, and a helpful reminder and encouragement is not really an order. Is it?"

He wrapped her in his arms and fell back upon the bed laughing like he had not laughed in centuries, "I guess not, my love. Okay then, I will get ready, and you can go make breakfast."

***

The day of the Grand Opening went wonderfully. From the moment the doors opened the store was filled with customers. Even Melanie made a few sales and she was so excited for she had never done anything like that in her life. She truly felt like she had found the place she belonged, not only because of the man that she loved and who loved her back but because she could truly help him in his business and not be in his way.

Several times during the day people would stop and ask about the big ornamental case that was closed and locked and Zachariah would explain that the pieces within were extra special and were shown by appointment only. When a few tried to make appointments he would explain that he was waiting for his nephew to arrive but if they would come back in a few days his nephew would be glad to make an appointment with them. No one argued and everyone seemed satisfied with his explanations.

Late in the afternoon Philip the pizza driver made an appearance. He told Zachariah in a whisper that after seeing him with the young lady that he had gotten the courage to ask out a girl he'd had a crush on for over a year. She had said yes, and now he wanted to get her something special.

Zachariah took him over to a case and said he had just the thing. It was a thin gold chain that held a pendant. The pendant was a golden triskele with a perfect pearl set in the heart of it. Philip smiled but then frowned when he saw the price. Zachariah laughed and said, "I owe you thirty dollars still, and I will knock another fifty off the price because of your kindness, so does that make it more affordable."

Philip nodded and dug out the money but before he left Zachariah took him by the shoulder and pulled him to the side, "Listen to me, young man. I can see in your eyes that you see something special in this girl so take some advice.

"Don't pressure her. If she says she wants to wait to be intimate then let her. Do not be worried that she will not wait for you. Think of it this way. If she does wait for you then you will be her first."

The pizza driver smiled at that and said, "If an old dude like you can get a pretty young girl like her," Philip turned and looked toward Melanie and nodded his head in her direction, "then believe me I will listen, and yes, I like the idea of me being her first."

"Good," Zachariah said and patted him on the back. They shook hands and Philip left. As the old man watched him leave the magic that flowed through him told him he would be seeing Philip and his lady friend again in six months, give or take a week or two, as they bought a wedding and engagement set together. Of course Philip would not recognize him then, but Zachariah would be more than happy to give him a bargain anyway.

There was something about the magic within the man that seeped into all his work, not just the very special pieces. He smiled as he thought that he was probably the only jeweler in the world that could boast that he had never sold a wedding set where the marriage had failed. There were a few sets he had sold that the wedding was called off before it took place, but he had known those couples were not right for each other when they had entered his store.

After the store had been closed for the day and Melanie and he had taken inventory they had sold twenty three pieces of jewelry for over ten thousand dollars.

Zach put together some sandwiches while Melanie cleaned the store and then they sat down and ate. The entire meal Melanie could not help but smile at Zachariah. He almost felt as if he were on display. Finally he could not take it any longer and he asked, "What is it, why are you smiling so much?"

"Well, three reasons. The first is the most important really.

"I spent the whole night here. I knew my mother had said she did not care what I did, but I truly thought she would show up looking for me if I did not return home and yet there has not been a peep from her."

Zachariah smiled back, "Well that could have a lot to do with the fact that as of midnight tonight you are eighteen, and as you said, seventeen is the age of consent in New York.

"Besides, we did nothing so there is nothing she could say anyway."

"True! Yet, with her being a politician I expected she would make some sort of uproar, then again maybe that is why she did not. No bad publicity, not in an election year."

"Could be you are right there," Zach laughed, "and the second reason?"

"I feel like I am worth something. I was able to help you by selling six pieces, and Papa Zach. I sold the most expensive piece of the day!" Zachariah loved seeing her so proud of her accomplishment.

"Yes, sweetheart, you did. I am proud of my little employee." She beamed brightly.

"However the most important reason of all is…" She left it hanging, waiting for him to say something.

For a moment he ignored her, so she asked, "Well aren't you going to ask me what it is?"

"Oh? Was I supposed to? I thought you would tell me when you were ready." He teased.

"Papa Zach?" Melanie huffed and stomped her foot.

"Oh okay, what is the most important reason?"

"You promised me the story of the ring."

Zachariah did his best to put on a look of confusion, "I did? When did I do that?"

"Papa Zach!" Melanie whined, "You promised!"

"I don't remember making any such promise. Maybe it is senility. I am an old man you know. Besides, I am not certain I remember any story about a ring."

Melanie jumped out of her chair and went over to him. She placed a hand on each of his cheeks and kissed him deeply. For the first time she slipped her tongue between his lips and its velvety texture played teasingly with his. She had never French kissed anyone but suddenly she found she really enjoyed it, and the look within his eyes made her enjoy it even more. "Do you remember the story now?"

He blinked his eyes and looked at her, "Ummm, uh, ummm, hunh! Story?"

"Papa Zach!?" Melanie stomped her foot and her hands went to her sides, if he did not tell her that story she was going to act like a two year old and throw a tantrum. Well she would not really, but she would make him think she would.

Zachariah laughed heartily, his laughter filled her heart with warmth, "Yes sweetheart, I remember the story, but I think there are some other things that need to be done before I tell you this story."

She smiled, but was confused at what he meant. What things could possibly need to be done? He had never had to do anything special before telling her any other story.

He stood and put his finger to his lips making the motion for her to be silent. Then he took her hand and led her into the main room in front of the large cabinet.

She watched as he reached beneath the edge and his fingers found something that she heard make a very delicate click. Perhaps it was a button or a lever. Suddenly the cabinet began to pivot without making any sound at all. She took a deep breath and watched in amazement. This whole week she had been here and the cabinet had seemed too solid to be moved by ten men and now it was gliding along on its own with no noise. When he had shown her the magic somewhere in the back of her mind she had pictured him in a workshop like some wizard with a secret laboratory, but she did not truly believe it.

He took her hand and led her inside, then turned and touched his lips with his finger again to indicate for her to remain silent. Melanie had no problem with that, she was in awe. She had no idea what to say even if he had not asked for her silence. He guided her so that she was next to a large table covered in a tablecloth and then reaching under the tablecloth to some hidden drawer he pulled out a jar of reddish-white powder. He also pulled out a bag that looked like it was made of some kind of animal hide. He carefully poured some of the powder into the bag and then walked until he was just inside the entrance to the room. He touched the back of the cabinet and it began to swing closed sealing them inside. Once the door was shut they were only in darkness for a single second. Suddenly beginning at one side of the door a candle lit. Melanie thought Zachariah had lit it but she saw from the light of the candle that he was nowhere near it. Then another lit and another, they continued around the room one after another until the all four walls were lined with burning white candles.

She turned her eyes back to Zachariah and saw that he had begun to pour the powder out onto the floor. He had actually begun the moment the first candle had lit and had completed a quarter of a circle by the time all of the candles were done and her eyes were turned to him. He continued the circle in a counterclockwise direction, until it was complete. Then he laid the bag onto the floor and looked at her, "Now we can talk."

Melanie looked at him. She stood with her hands at her side and her mouth open. Yes, he had shown her magic, but now she was thrust into the middle of something so significant she knew that both their lives were going to change this night. She also knew that one or both of them might die.

"Papa Zach, I do trust you. I do love you," Melanie said. "But what have you gotten me into." Her heart was racing, yet still she could feel the love of this man for her and she still felt safe.

"Sweetheart, it is going to be difficult for you to understand if I do not tell you the story from the beginning." Papa Zach told her, "I will tell you a few things. To the best of my knowledge I did not choose you for this. I do not know if you were chosen before you came into my shop or not. I know the moment you handed me the wet wipe with that child's blood upon it the first day we met was when things began."

He lowered his head and looked at the ground, she could feel his pain, "There have been many times I wish you had not stopped that day, and yet just as many I have been thankful you did. All I can say is I know that Lilith intends to do something and you are the center of her plan. If there is any way I can stop her even if it means I die to protect you I will."

Melanie threw her arms around him and pleaded, "Please don't say that Papa Zach, I can't lose you."

He lifted her face to his and kissed her lips and said, "And you are too young to lose your soul. I cannot allow that."

"This room once held a mirror, and it was in this room that Lilith made her mistake and revealed to me that she could speak and see out of other mirrors than the one in the main showroom." He pointed to the powder on the floor. "That is a mixture of items from the holy land. Items that can bind and hold Lilith, so she cannot enter here in spirit nor can she hear what we are saying."

Zachariah went to the table cloth and pulled it off the table. Melanie's eyes grew big as she looked at the stone table. The table had the exact same image as the wooden cabinet did.

"This table is the true source of much of the magic. It was carved long ago. I think if you look at the underside edge you can tell it is far older than you had imagined. I have protected the topside with cover after cover so it has worn very little since it was made."

Slowly Melanie looked at the table and ran her fingers along the lower edge, "Papa Zach, the edge of this is worn with time. I am not a geologist, but I know stone wears slowly and this table has to be over a thousand years old. I have seen stones like this in museums."

She turned to look at him, "I have no idea how the top of this table has remained so untouched by age but the bottom of it shows it is very old."

Melanie looked at Zachariah face, the lines were etched deep into his brow and the corners of his eyes, but his eyes showed a youth that told her that even if he was the one hundred and ten he claimed to be there was no way he was as old as this table. Her eyes clouded with confusion. No one lives that long. Yet, he had no reason to lie to her about something like this. There had to be some other explanation, maybe the table had been aged by being under a waterfall.

"Is this table artificially aged?" She knew the answer before she had said it, and saw him shake his head no.

"Papa Zach, you cannot have possibly made this table. There is no way you can be that old. You would have to be over a thousand years old." Melanie looked at him hoping for some simple explanation.

Zachariah looked at her, his gaze locking with hers and he said, "Melanie, because of things I have had to do to protect you and to protect some secrets I have had to tell you a few lies. Each one of them has torn into my heart more deeply than if I had twisted a dagger into it myself, but I swear to you that I am not lying now. I did indeed make this table, and though I was in a trance and barely remember doing it, I carved the image upon that stone when that table was first made."

She looked to him, her eyes wide, "You are telling me that all the aging of this table has occurred since you made it. Not that you made the table upon an aged stone aren't you?"

"Yes."

She then added, "And you are you telling me you are as old as this table?"

"I am older than the table. Not by much, but I am older. This table was carved over a period of a month just prior to the first anniversary of mine and Lilith's marriage at the direction of a prophetess that Lilith had brought to our house. The prophetess said it was the only way to insure that Lilith and I would have a long and happy marriage and that once it was carved a decision would be made that would lead to happiness or tragedy." Tears formed in the corner of Zachariah's eyes and slid down his cheeks to disappear into the crevices that were etched there.

Melanie could feel a deep sadness within him. She suddenly wished that she had not asked for the story of the ring but knew it would not have mattered for even if she had not she suspected that she would still be hearing the tale that was tearing the heart of the man she loved. He looked up at her and she could see in his eyes that he was grasping for her, holding onto the love he had for her as he gathered strength to be able to tell this story.

"The table itself is not evil. It and I are connected and I believe it is as good as I am as long as it stays within my possession and is not used by someone with an evil intent. Its purpose was to help heal Lilith and to give her a normal life."

Melanie could not believe this. Her love had to be far older than she had ever thought possible. Papa Zach must have seen the question within her eyes for as he looked at her he said, "Go ahead, precious, ask the question, I believe I know what it is."

"Papa Zach, how old are you?"

"I was born about a hundred years before Samson."

"Samson?" Melanie looked at him quizzically. "Are you saying the Samson of the Bible, Samson of Samson and Delilah?"

"Yes. That was roughly twelve hundred years after the flood of Noah, or a hundred and fifty years after Moses led his people into the land of Israel."

Melanie was thankful for the chair that was behind her. She did not even realize it was there as her knees gave way and she sank into the seat.

"Melanie, I was born three hundred and fifty years before David who became the king of Israel. So now you know that the magic of this table has kept me alive for longer than you could have imagined. I am not a one hundred and ten year old man. I am over three thousand years old and I think it is time I tell you the story of Lilith, myself, and of that ring, because soon it will affect us all."

The Awakening
Robert Cloud
Part One
Lilith
Chapter One

"Melanie, as far whether there are Lost or Secreted Books to the Bible, many of them I have seen when they were not considered lost or secreted, and some were considered canon and law. Others were considered false from the moment they began to circulate." Zachariah shook his head sorrowfully, "Even as to whether the Bible is complete or not has always been in controversy, even with the Torah.

"It seems as if it was almost the very nature of man that from the very time that Moses began to write down the words of God others began to write false stories about God. Some contradicted Moses, others told fantastical tales that no one could believe and yet people did.

"From the very day that there was a true prophet of God, there was also a false prophet and it has been that way throughout time.

"But I have drifted from the story. Now where was I…? Yes, the days of creation!"

***

During the period that God spent on His creation some of the angels came to Him and tried to alter His plans. They felt that God would be better served if He did this or that, yet God remained firm in His resolve to His course and His creation continued according to His plan and not their persuasions.

At the end of the last of the six eras God created what Moses called the "Sons of Man" in the book of Genesis. Scientists would refer to these "Sons of Man" as Neanderthal and Homo-Erectus. Then God rested. Yet, the seventh era was a short era, not as long as the first six for the angels were busy, and some were already making plans for these "Sons of Man" that God had created. God overheard these plans and was not pleased.

It was then that He decided on His true masterpiece, in the very center of the earth, in a lush area far from the realms that had cropped up God set up His Garden and named it Eden. From the dust in the center of the Garden He formed a man and breathed life into the man and named him Adam.

Adam was different than the others, he was perfection. He was like unto God in that he had a soul. So God called Adam a "Son of God" and for many years God and Adam walked about the Garden and spoke.

Within the Garden God had placed two of every animal He had created upon the earth. Where the Garden touched the waters He had placed the Behemoth and the Leviathan and many more of the creatures that scientists would call dinosaurs.

One day God set a task for Adam to name all the creatures of the Garden. Adam was thrilled with this task and went about it with a passion. Yet only a few hours later as God was walking through the Garden He found Adam sitting beneath a tree staring up into the sky, Adam looked as if he was lost in deep thought.

God looked to Adam and asked him what was troubling him.

Adam looked up and answered, "My Lord, as I went about to do Thy command I saw that each beast I would stop to name had a partner. I would look about and realize I was alone."

***

Zachariah paused and looked at Melanie and said, "Up to this point these are my beliefs based off what I have read in the Torah and some of those lost books as well as what I have seen of science. However from here on things do not follow what I knew as I was growing up. The rest of this is what Lilith told me when she told me of her life. How much of it is true I cannot say. It may all be a lie, or it could all be true. If it is true it would explain some of the reasons she is the way she is, if it is a lie it just further aids in understanding her betrayal.

***

Adam stood and then knelt before God, "My Lord, please do not get my words wrong, Thou hath been a marvelous friend to me, and Thou art my Lord, but I cannot help but wonder what it would be like to have a partner."

God nodded, and kneeling down to the earth He gathered a mound of dust and from the mound of dust He created Lilith.

Lilith looked about and saw Adam and God and she knew she had just been created. She knew she was the second to be created and as she looked at herself and then Adam she noticed the differences though she did not understand them. She decided that they were because Adam had been God's first attempt and that she was His perfect creation. She then knelt down and kissed God's feet and thanked Him for creating her. It would be the last time she ever knelt to a male of any kind.

After God introduced Lilith to Adam and then Adam to Lilith He told Adam, "Adam here is the partner you wished for, I hope that she is the companion you sought and that she is the friend you need."

Adam thanked God and watched as the Lord ascended into the Heavens. During this Lilith said nothing. She had heard what God had said but she had not truly paid attention. She was lost in her thought that she was perfection and Adam was inferior. As the Lord disappeared she walked about looking at the Garden and the beasts of the Garden, marveling that everything in the Garden had been made for her.

Then she noticed two beasts, one was over the back of the other and the smaller one which she thought was the female was making a low growling and rumbling sound. As she watched she realized that the male was doing something that pleasured the female. Then suddenly the male was gone and about his business. Lilith looked over to Adam and wondered if that was why God had made him. She wondered if Adam was supposed to do something to pleasure her.

Lilith looked down at her body and noticed it was very different from Adam's. She had swelling upon her chest where Adam had none but as she touched the swellings, a sensation shivered through her body and a low moan escaped her lips. Upon each swelling a hard nub grew. Her fingers caressed the nub and again those sensations spread through her. She took each nub between her fingers and squeezed them, then tried different things, savoring each new sensation. When she rolled the nubs between her thumb and finger, twisting them she let out a soft scream and she felt a quivering between her thighs she had not felt before.

As she stood in the middle of the Garden Lilith felt no shame, for she did not know that what she was doing was anything to be ashamed of. She was in complete innocence yet there was a hunger in her that was not so innocent and a fire burning that was full of self-pride and selfish desire. She felt no shame not only because she did not know what sex was but she would not have cared even if she had.

Her hands traveled hungrily over her body, delivering pleasure to every location where she felt any sensation or tingle of excitement. Though the juncture between her legs was calling to her hands she denied it for she also enjoyed the building hunger that was growing there. Soon she knew she would have to feed the flames or be consumed by them, yet once more she paused to tweak the nubs of the swellings and make that tingle between her legs grow even more intense.

A moan escaped from her lips as she closed her eyes and teasingly slid one hand along the muscles of her taut belly past her navel and to the mound of hair just above the juncture of her legs. She twirled her fingers within the course hair and then pushed them further down discovering the beginning of the folds of flesh there and a moisture that she had thought she had noticed but her fingers now confirmed. Pushing apart the folds her fingers probed and found a hard nub at the very top. As she gently touched that new hardened nub she could not hold back the scream that began deep within her and exploded out of her lungs.

She bent over and rocked, her hand rubbing that nub harder. Then she began doing to the nub the same things she had done to the hard nubs upon the swellings of her chest. Her breathing became rapid, her heartbeat sped and she moaned. She grew hungry for more of this pleasure. The memory of the male beast upon the back of the female resurfaced and she raised her eyes toward Adam. It was time that he did what he had been made to do. It was time for him to give her pleasure.

She raised her eyes in search of Adam and saw him standing not far from her. It was quickly apparent that he was watching her and that what she was doing was having some effect upon him. For at the juncture of his legs, where she had the sweet and wonderful folds that were beckoning more attention, he had grown a rod that was standing out from his mound of hair. Adam looked confused as his gaze traveled from her down to his rod and his hand that was sliding back and forth along that rod of flesh.

Lilith knew he had been in the Garden longer than she had and she was sure that he had seen the male beast with the female beast. She had no doubt that Adam knew what to do with that rod of his, so she lifted a hand beckoning him toward her.

Little persuasion was needed for as soon as her hand began to rise in his direction the look of confusion in Adam's eyes was replaced with one of determination. With four large strides he was beside her. He quickly guided her to her knees and like the beast she had seen in the field he climbed behind her and she could feel the tip of his rod as it touched her folds of flesh.

Adam thrust hard, and his rod slid under her along her folds. It caressed her very sensitive nub and caused her to moan but it was not where the hunger was calling from. She slid her hand under her and pushed his rod back and upward and the next time he pushed she felt him slide into some mysterious opening that she had not known existed. She gasped and her breath caught as his rod filled the opening. Muscles that she was unaware that she possessed clenched about the rod as if they did not want to let it go and then she felt him sliding back out. She nearly screamed out as she was afraid he would pull the rod out of her but once again he thrust it into her. Yes, she thought, he had watched the beasts. She began to push her hips back against him as he thrust into her.

His thrusts were slow at first, but she began to grind against him more urgently and he responded in kind, building speed, faster and harder he thrust. She heard him moan but she did not care if he was getting pleasure from what he was doing, he had been made to pleasure her.

She bucked her hips against him driving his rod into her even harder and faster. She tightened her muscles about the shaft to savor its presence every fraction of a second it was within her and sliding along her inner flesh.

Then she felt an amazing feeling as his rod pulsed and grew even larger within her as he slammed into her hard. Then his rod spasmed and a warm spray of fluid erupted from his shaft and filled her. Adam relaxed and let his rod slide out of her.

Lilith was furious, she was at the height of her need, what he had just done had only inflamed her more, he could not stop now. She looked down at him as he lay upon his back and watched as the hard rod began to lose its firmness and fall to the side. This man-thing was not perfect and she would have to speak to its maker about fixing it, but for now she needed more. She had to make the man-thing's rod solid again.

She knelt on the ground beside him and looked at it. She remembered how he had run his hand along it before he had come to her so she put her hand upon it. It was covered in a sticky slime. She wondered if that was the way it always was, though maybe it was because of the fluids from within her and those he had sprayed into her. Either way she needed him hard. So she began to slide her hand along the now limp rod.

Adam just looked up at her and then laid his head back down. She was not getting the rod to come back to life and she was getting angrier by the moment. In frustration she looked at him and absent mindedly raised her hand to her lips to lick the stickiness away. At first she turned her lips away in disgust, the smell was not pleasant, but then there was something about the taste that excited her even more. Before long she was hungrily licking it off her hand and had cleaned every drop of it away. Yet the scent of it was still heavy in the air.

She looked down at Adam's rod. The rod was still coated in the sticky fluid. Lilith lowered her head and began licking the fluid away from the rod. To her surprise and delight the rod soon began to come back to life. Within only a few moments it was as hard as it had ever been as she licked and kissed all the fluids off of it. There was still a little of the fluid at the tip so she slid her mouth over the tip of the rod and found she liked the sensation of having it there because Adam moaned when she did it and it brought her pleasure to tease him. He had teased her, now it was her turn. She would get revenge.

She pushed her mouth down upon the rod until his rod was almost all the way in her mouth. Adam raised his head up and looked at her. His eyes were wide with shock, he started to say something but she sucked upon his shaft and slid her mouth back up to its tip and all he could do was drop his head back and moan. Lilith was in complete control and she was relishing the power she had over him. However it was time for him to fulfill her need as once again she felt the fires within her begin to ignite. She lifted her head from his shaft and Adam started to rise but she pushed him back to the ground. He tried to protest that this was not the way he had seen the beasts do it as she lifted her leg to straddle him. Her response was blunt and cold. She told him that they were not beasts but were better and therefore could think of better ways to fulfill her pleasure. Then she looked at him and said; "Besides you failed to please me, as you were made to do. So now I am going to make certain that you do not fail a second time."

She took his rod in her hand and guided it to the opening he had penetrated before and rammed her hips down upon him. Adam lowered his head back to the ground; the words she had said had already slipped from his mind as she began to grind her hips against his. This time she guided the pace, she controlled everything, and when Adam sprayed his fluid into her she tightened those inner muscles and worked him inside her until he had gone from the slightly loosened state to the hard as a rock state again.

Lilith took Adam's hands and placed them to her breasts, "You watched me as I was rubbing these swellings. Do as I did to them."

Without a thought Adam obeyed her. He even smiled and she realized as she looked at him that he was finding pleasure in touching her. Her mind soared with the power she had over him. The idea that what she was doing turned him into a mindless beast filled her and she realized that with that power she could make him do almost anything. She would have to test her theory at a future time but for now something was beginning to happen and she could not concentrate very easily. Deep within her it was as if the ocean had receded and a massive wave was about to hit the shore and transverse over her every nerve and fiber. It had been building, this fire within her, but it was reaching a peak and now the walls were about to give way, she could feel something new was about to happen.

Then it did. It erupted. Her mind exploded. Her body ignited. The wave coursed over her. Every fiber became alive. She screamed out loud, wailing unto the heavens. Her back arched, and her muscles tightened as her body quivered from the very crown of her head to the tip of her toes. Then she leaned forward over Adam as a second wave crashed down on her and another scream burst from her lungs. At that moment Adam's shaft sprayed its fluid within her and ignited yet a third wave. She rocked against him as the waves receded and withdrew slowly.

Whatever had just happened to her she now knew that that was truly why Adam had been made and that there really was no other purpose for his creation than to bring her that pleasure. Slowly she climbed off of Adam and let his shrinking rod slide out of her. She knelt down and licked the fluids away from the rod for she truly did love the taste of them but she was also glad to see that he was weakened and that his rod did not grow hard again for she did not desire to please him, she wanted only the taste of their mingled fluids.

Once he was clean of the fluids she went walking about the Garden and left him lying there asleep. Lilith thought about what they had just done and wondered why it was that Adam got pleasure from it as well if he had been created to give her pleasure. She decided it had to be a way that she could manipulate him and get him to do other things for her.

That evening she returned to Adam and again she made him do to her what the beasts did, and this time she tried something new. Before she would let him enter her she asked Adam if she could help him name the beasts as it had been given to him to do and not to her. At first he was reluctant, but when he saw that she was not going to allow him to penetrate her he agreed and she smiled for she had proven her theory. Indeed she could manipulate Adam and get what she wanted. Together the two howled into the night as they coupled like the beasts several times and only finished when Lilith was satisfied and Adam lay panting and exhausted.

When the sun rose Adam and Lilith again did as the beasts and afterwards went into the fields to begin naming the beasts of the Garden. As Adam began to name the first beast he called the one with the large mane a Lion, but Lilith looked at him and frowned. He asked her what was wrong and she said that she did not like that name. It sounded as if someone was lying. She wanted to think of another name. Adam was not happy. He told her that God had given him the responsibility to name the beasts and creatures of the Garden not her.

Lilith bursts into tears; it was something new she was going to try. She did not really feel like crying, but the moment the tears began she saw how Adam reacted and she let them flow even faster. Adam put his arm around her and asked her what she had in mind to name the beast. Lilith started to say something and then held off and said no she wanted to think of an even better name so she sat down and began to think. When the sun was high in the sky and half the day had gone by Lilith still had not decided upon a name. Adam looked at her, and she looked up at him, she could see the total frustration upon his face.

"Lilith, at this rate we will never get all the beasts named."

She stood up and leaned close to him, her hand reaching down to his rod. She began to stroke it softly but Adam turned from her suddenly and then looked back at her. "Listen, Lilith, this game you play is fun, and I enjoy it, but I was commanded to name the beasts, and I cannot play the game all the time neither can I wait an entire day for you to make up your mind on the name of one beast.

"This beast is named. We will call it a Lion. I know you can think of many names better." Lilith looked at him in fury. How dare he deny her pleasure and then change his mind and name the beast after saying she could. She started to say something but Adam held up his hand and she held her tongue, something inside her told her that his anger with her was dangerous at this moment. "Now as far as you helping me name the beasts. You can stay here and name the rests of the beasts around this area. I have seen the beasts here so I will go to the other side of the Garden and name the beasts that I have not seen here."

Lilith watched as Adam turned and walked away from her. However she had not had her say so she decided to follow him but stay hidden so she could see what he was doing. She followed, keeping a good distance behind as he crossed half the Garden. When he came to a clearing he paused and rested beneath a tree. She decided it would be best to stay under the cover of the tree line and wait for him to move on. However while he waited, God came down from the Heavens and stood in front of him. The first thing that God did was ask Adam where Lilith was. When Lilith heard this she ducked down behind some bushes and pulled some brush over her. As angry as Adam was she surely did not want the wrath of God upon her as well.

Lilith heard Adam explaining to God about the problems he was having with her. She was getting more furious by the second. She had thought God had made Adam for her, now she was learning that she had been wrong, that she had been made for Adam. That was something she just did not care for at all. Then when God asked Adam how the naming of the animals was going Adam responded.

"My Lord," Adam said reverently, "the woman that Thou made for me has no respect of me. She doth ridicule the names that I come up with, saying that they are but foolish names and that she doth have better names. Then she spent half the day trying to decide upon one name for an animal I had already named. Finally I told her she could name the animals on that side of the Garden and I came this way to name the animals on this side.

"My Lord, in earnest, I suspect that when I name all the animals on this side she will still not have decided on a name for more than one or two."

Then Adam looked about the Garden and pointed to the Lion and said to God, "My Lord, the female of that beast, the one I named the Lion, she doth submit to the male. She seeks the male for protection and guidance. Why doth not the woman that Thou hath created for me treat me as such?"

God looked at Adam and answered, "When I created the Lion I knew there would be times that the male would have to fight other males for the right to keep his female so I made her to submit to him. To make her that way I made her from one of his ribs.

"When I made Lilith, I did not wish that thou would have to fight to keep thy female so I made her stronger and more like thee. I made her as I made thee, from the very same dust as I made thee."

Lilith overheard every word, and she needed to hear no more. She knew that Adam would ask God to create for him another female and if God did that then there would be no place for her in the Garden.

Yet she was afraid to move, afraid that if God heard her he would call her out. She did not believe God would unmake her, but wondered what he would he do? Would he force her to be subservient to Adam? Why had she not paid attention to the fact that Adam was God's favored? Instead she had taken pride in herself that she was God's perfection and Adam had been only a flawed first attempt.

God looked upon Adam and said that He would speak with Lilith, but just in case Adam saw her before He did He wanted Adam to let her know that He had placed two trees in the middle of the Garden that day, they were the Trees of Knowledge and of Life, and that neither Adam nor Lilith were to eat of their fruit.

Adam shook his head and said, "My Lord, if I tell that to Lilith, that is as sure as guaranteeing that she will eat from those trees."

"Then I will tell her, Adam," the Lord said, and He turned and vanished from sight.

Lilith did not want the Lord to find her before she got to those trees. Maybe if she got to the trees they would give her the knowledge of how to make Adam happy and still maintain her control and self-respect. She could not see herself being a servant to Adam. Maybe the Tree of Knowledge would give her the knowledge to solve her dilemma. Since she was going to eat from one tree she might as well eat from both. If she got to the trees before the Lord told her she was not to eat from them then she was not disobeying Him.

She was not that far from the center of the Garden, so quickly she rose and darted out from under the trees. She saw Adam waving at her but she ignored him and ran straight toward the center of the Garden.

She did not have any time to waste. There in front of her, surrounded by a shallow mote of crystal blue water, were two trees in full bloom and bearing fruit. The mote's waters were narrow and at her speed she was easily able to leap across the waters and she grabbed a single fruit from each tree and then dashed back off the island and toward another tree line not very far from the other side of the mote. No sooner had she gotten under the trees than she began to hear the melodic voice of God calling for her. She knew her time was limited. So as fast as she possibly could she devoured both fruit and then buried their cores in the dust at her feet. Just as she was standing and wiping the dust from her hands God was before her.

"Lilith, what are thou doing?"

"I am planting some seeds so that they will grow," she responded quickly.

God looked at her, "But Lilith, I have not yet taught thou about seeds, how doth thou know about seeds?"

Lilith looked about and saw a bird fly overhead and she thought quickly, "I saw a bird drop some after eating a piece of fruit and I figured out what they must be."

"No, Lilith, I know what thou hath done. Thou hath eaten from the Tree of knowledge, and hath gained the knowledge and yet thou stand before me with no shame. Thou doth not care that thou are naked before me?"

"Why should I care? Thou made me. If Thou wanted to use me Thou could at any time."

"Lilith, did thou not know that I commanded thou not to eat of those Trees?"

"No one told me, Lord."

Thunder clapped in the sky, and lightning struck down to the ground around Lilith but did not strike her. God's fury with her for her vile thoughts and lies was beyond compare.

"That is not what I asked. Thou knew I had commanded it?"

"Yes, I knew, but no one had told me, so I did not disobey Thy command."

Again the lightning struck the ground before Lilith and she was thrown into the air. Her hair smoked, and crackled. She landed on her hands and knees before God. "You did disobey, for you knew what my command was." The ground shook with the booming resonance of the anger in the voice of God. His eyes were filled with fire as he looked down upon her and said, "Thou vile creature, and you have not only eaten of the fruit of the Tree of Knowledge so you know of all the things that I wanted to keep you innocent of but you have also eaten of the Tree of Life.

"You thought to hide this from me.

"Lilith, you were created for Adam. Not he, for you. Yet from the moment I breathed life into you it has been in your mind that you were the one that I favored. You have done nothing but be a hindrance to Adam. You have tormented him. You have taught him things I did not want him to know yet, and you have disobeyed my commands. Your pride has been your undoing." God looked down at Lilith as she tried to raise her eyes to look at him, but the power of the lightning bolt that had scorched through her had weakened her too greatly and she fell to the ground.

God lifted His hand and pointed it at Lilith. "Therefore I give thou what thou sought, life! I curse thou with life. Thou will feed upon the life of man, upon the very fluids that give him life thou will depend. I curse thou with an enemy, the very Sun. It shall burn thine flesh, and devour thy bones. I curse thou with life, for thou will not die neither shall thou see sunlight again until thou finds one that will love thee even though they hath seen the monster that thou art."

With those words God lifted His hand and Lilith was lifted into the air and flung out of the Garden and into the world of man. She landed hard, breaking every bone in her body, but within a matter of only a few moments wracked with great and horrendous pain, her bones knitted themselves together and mended. Her split and broken flesh healed, and she was whole. With tear filled eyes she took one last look toward the Garden and saw that an army of angels had surrounded it with blazing swords lifted.

Slowly she turned and walked away from the Garden, never to return.

Chapter Two

With the Garden to her back Lilith walked toward some unknown future. Hours passed and she began to grow weary, yet she continued along her path knowing only that the Garden lie behind to her. It began to enter into her mind that it was her pride that had been her undoing and she wondered if it was truly worth all the marvels she had lost. For a moment she turned around and thought that perhaps if she were to return to the Garden upon her knees that God would forgive her of her sins but as soon as she turned thinking to return she stopped. She knew that she could never kneel before God.

So she returned again to her path and began her long trudge along trails that some large beasts must have made for they were worn smooth. When the trail turned she would follow a different path for she wanted to continue in as straight a line away from the Garden as it was possible to take.

As she continued to walk it struck her that she would be alone on the earth. She would have no one to talk to and only animals for company. Was life really worth this emptiness that she felt growing inside her? Slowly she sunk to her knees and wept. Her tears were full of anger and she screamed up at the heavens and at God, cursing Him for what He had done to her. Looking down at the ground her eyes caught a glint as the moon's light reflected off the edge of a black crystal formation. Within it was a long sharp rock, which when she touched its edge it bit into her fingers and drew blood. Lilith lifted her fingers and watched as the wounds upon her fingers closed and the blood flow ceased. Rage and emptiness tore into her making her feel all that she had lost.

Suddenly she realized that she had indeed felt something for Adam. She did not think it was love, but it was something. Lilith could not live a life like this, with no one, no person to share her life with, no one to talk to, nothing but herself in this world.

She reached to the long black blade like rock and lifted it with her hands. The pain she felt was worse between the mounds that swelled from her chest, it had to stop so with one quick motion she plunged the blade between the swellings and into the beating, pulsing part that hurt so deeply.

With a crack Lilith was thrown from the spot she was kneeling. She flew through the air and crashed hard against a tree that had been more than ten strides from where she had been. Slowly she slid to the ground, her flesh grating against the bark of the tree. She could see the remnants of the black crystal as it lay on the ground where it had been shattered into fragments that were all bathed in a crimson hue that was so brilliant it hurt her eyes to look upon it. Each one slowly winked out of existence as they burned away to nothing.

Lilith could feel her shattered bones already knitting and her flesh growing. She screamed in agony as the pain cut through her like a million razor shards. When her healing was complete she stood and looked to the stars and screamed out again. Tears rolled down her cheeks as she wept. Her curse was life. Her knees folded beneath her and she cried bitterly, her sobs carrying across the empty night.

When the moon had traveled half way across the sky she finally rose and began walking again. She now knew that she would not be allowed to take her own life, at least not by that method. Tears still flowed down her cheeks as she walked.

Time passed but it had no meaning to her. Slowly her senses began to notice that the nights chill was turning to a sweet warmth and about her a gentle mist was rising, but it was peculiar it was not rising from the earth or stones around her. She lifted her hand and from her fingers the mist danced and swirled into the air. She smiled for it was beautiful to see this veil of vapor surrounding her, but as those pleasant thoughts entered her head they were quickly dashed to bitter and harsh fragments. Like the bolt of lightning that God had struck her with, searing pain erupted over her entire body. She watched in horror as first small blisters began to appear upon her hands and then larger ones. It was as if her skin was turning to fluid and she was beginning to boil.

With a frantic start she looked over her shoulder and on the distant horizon she saw the orange glow that was the precursor of the coming sunrise. Her gaze darted about her wildly from right to left and back again looking for anything that might provide her some form of shelter from the coming blaze of the sun. In the back of her mind it did strike her as ironic that only hours before she had wanted to die, but the thought of bursting into flames, and the pain that was intensifying with each passing second had suddenly increased the instinct of survival within her. Her eyes caught site of a stand of trees that were the outcrop that led to a deeper woods, they were about forty running strides from her. She looked back at the horizon. The bright yellow orb was beginning to crest the horizon. Her eyes felt as if they had been struck by fire.

Turning toward the trees she dashed toward them, hoping she still had time to make the distance, but afraid she had already taken too much time. As she ran she noticed that she was moving faster than her legs had carried her before, it was like she had moved in slow motion before, even when she ran. Still the distance seemed to close maddeningly slow, and though she knew God would not listen to her she prayed that the trees would shade her until she could find a better shelter from the sun.

As she ran the pain in her hands and arms grew even more intense, she could see flames beginning to shoot from the ends of her fingers. From behind her she heard a wailing scream but she did not dare look to see who it was. Then it dawned on her that it was her own howl of pain. The sun crested the horizon and she was engulfed in flames. With all that she had in her she dove for the trees and landed hard, rolling through wet muck and moss that quickly and thankfully extinguished the flames.

Slowly Lilith rose to her hands and knees and looked down at the charred flesh. The pain was already diminishing and as she watched the charred black shell began to flake away and new skin appeared beneath the black soot. She heard it from somewhere, a laugh, coming from somewhere close by. It sounded like it was a female laugh but from a very small female. She looked about but there was no one. As she turned her head the sound shifted with her. Then as it had been with the scream she realized the laugh was coming from her. She slammed her fist into the ground and her fist sunk far deeper than it should have, but she barely noticed as she lifted her head and screamed out every vile curse she could think of at God for what he had done to her. Yes, she knew she had done wrong, but she did not deserve this.

She pulled her hand up out of the dirt and scooping a handful of the wet green moss she began cleaning herself as best she could of the black scales and soot. She lifted her long ash coated black hair and laid it upon her lap as she began to divest it of the ash and bits of leaves and twigs.

She took a great deal of time in preening herself even though there was no one else that would see her. As she stood and looked down at her body, satisfied that she was clean she noticed a light shining upon the ground not far from her.

She turned her eyes to the canopy of the trees and realized she had spent too much time. The sun was high in the sky and the trees would soon offer her no protection for the sun's fingers would penetrate the canopy like spears of fire. She might be able to survive but each time one of the fiery fingers hit her it would cause that horrendous pain and she had no desire to repeat the experience of being a living fire. She needed to find some other form of shelter.

As she stood looking about the small canopy that covered what was the beginning of a much deeper wooded land she turned toward the darker hidden environs of the forest and began to push her way through the undergrowth. The branches that scratched and tore at her were an annoyance but she healed almost as quickly as they cut through her flesh so she just kept pushing through and tried her best to ignore the pain. Lilith screamed piercingly when she brought her foot down on a three inch long briar whose barb pierced through the top of her foot just behind her large toe. She tore the branch from her foot and pulled the barb out. Once she found shelter she would have to figure a way to protect herself from the environment.

The deeper into the gloom and dark of the woods she walked the more she noticed her senses were becoming more alert. She began to hear sounds that were much farther away than she had been able to hear before. Small creatures would dart into hiding places and her eyes would catch sight of them, except now they seemed to glow with a reddish hue, like they were a warm fire. Her nose could pick up scents that she had never been aware of, the smell of the moss, and leaves, even the musk of the animals. It was from that musk that she was able to tell that a large animal had recently been traveling along the very path that she was now following.

Lilith set her mind to following the scent of that beast and she soon found she could pick up every single place it had set its large paws down upon the earth even though the moss and brush had risen and hidden the prints. She could follow its scent markings as easily as she could have followed it had she seen it before her. From the smell of the beast she could also tell that this beast made its home beneath the earth in some form of large shelter. There was a damp dirt smell that surrounded it, but not enough to tell her that it dug its way into the earth. Though she had never seen a cave, from the scents that penetrated into her inner mind an image of one took up residence in her mind. It was a perfect place for her to be hidden from the sun and sheltered from all that the environment threw at her.

The beast she followed had stopped once and Lilith noticed that high above her head on a tree were four large claw marks that had been dug deep into the bark of the tree. The scent of the beast was also strong here, as if it had urinated upon the tree after gouging out its markings to prove who owned the territory. Deep within her chest Lilith's heart raced. A beast of that size would surely protest her trying to enter its home, but she had little choice for as she looked upward she could already see the fingers of the sun beginning to break through the canopy. They were at an angle but within a short time they would penetrate to the ground and then she would be in trouble. Maybe, Lilith thought, she might be able to sneak in undetected and find a corner small enough to keep her out of reach of the beast.

Then a lance of light struck her shoulder and the searing pain erupted in her mind as her shoulder turned black and charred. She shrieked out with the pain as she jerked her arm out of the ray of God's wrath. All around her the beams were beginning to pierce through the canopy. She was running out of time, but whatever was guiding her was on her side for her gaze lit upon the entrance to the cave. It was hidden behind some branches and had she not pulled out of the light suddenly the way she had she may not have seen it. Yes, her sense of smell would have guided her to it, but she needed haste, and that may have taken too much time.

She had already learned she could run faster than had been possible for her before. Now she needed to avoid a myriad of beams that could cut her to ribbons. Lilith gathered all the strength she had in her legs and leapt, and found herself gliding through the air. She landed on her feet like some feline and then leapt again, bounding from one surface to another. She would spin in the air and avoid the beams and catch a limb only to reflect herself to a safe surface and then bound off again to another. Like an ape, a monkey, and a feline all combined her agility was unmatched and she found herself standing outside of the cave untouched by even one of the beams. Even more surprising to her was that she was not even the least tired for her exertion. It was as if she had merely walked from where she had been to where she was now. Lilith looked up to the sky and wondered, *are there gifts with this curse that are equal to the curse?*

Lilith lowered her gaze to the foreboding and dark entrance to the cave. Deep within her stomach she felt a churning as fear of what might happen to her if the beast were to discover her sent her heart thundering against her chest. She slid next to the edge of the wall and as slowly and silently as she could she began to inch into the cave. Even though no light penetrated into the shadows that concealed its inner depths Lilith's eyes could make out every detail. Several tiny mammals scurried along the ground and she watched as their glowing red shapes crossed the caverns rough floor and then vanished into smaller holes or crevices deeper inside.

This new attribute to her sight fascinated her, especially as she watched a larger creature, still small, but larger than the tiny ones she had seen. She could see the red better and with the red she could actually see a pulsing object within the creature and something almost fluid like coursing through the creature's body. Lilith did not know how she knew it but the knowledge suddenly came to her that she was seeing the life of the creature, the fluids that kept it alive and the pulsing thing was what made the fluids flow. This was the very thing that the Lord had told her she would feed upon, but not the life of beasts. He had said the life of men. With that thought of feeding Lilith felt suddenly very hungry, a hunger so deep it made her nearly double over in pain and a moan escaped unbidden from her lips.

That moan was a mistake, for no sooner had it come to life than it reverberated off the walls of the cavern and echoed deeper into its depths. Lilith stood up straight pressing her back against the wall but she knew it was too late, she could smell the spore of the beast as it approached.

From the depth it came on all fours, and still it was nearly as tall as she was. Even in the red hued form she could see that its head was large enough that a single bite of its jaw could bite her into two. It paused in the center of the chamber and stood on its hind legs, rising to a height that nearly touched the ceiling of the cavern. The beast towered over her by more than twice her height and it very obviously could either smell or see her for its massive paws clawed menacingly at the air in front of her.

There was no hope for escape. Lilith knew that her death had come, and if she were going to face death she should at least do it with some courage. She took a deep breath and took a step forward. The beast lunged and its paw struck her hurling her against the far wall of the cave and smashing her hard against it. Slowly Lilith slid to the ground. It felt like every bone in her body had been broken, but she could feel the horrendous pain as they began to mend. She could see the beast charging toward her and thought that this would be a curse indeed, to be beaten and healed over and over for eternity.

However something in the healing process was different, there was a shift in the nature and intensity of the pain. It was sharper, no longer grinding, but piercing and felt like it was coming from deep within her outward, not from the healing of her flesh and bones. Then in a single instant her breath was ripped out of her lungs. The scale of pain was so intense that it was beyond pain and her mind could not comprehend it any longer.

In shock she stared at her hands. They felt as if they were being shredded from within by millions of tiny sharp teeth as her flesh tore open and then literally erupted and flew off her fingers and palms. Long black fingers slowly unfurled. From their ends protruded talons of pure ebony that were as long as her fingers had been. Her new avian-like hands were twice the size of her old hands. As she flexed the five razor sharp talons the pain tore into her arms and her skin began to peel away revealing a black scale covered skin beneath her old skin that now floated off of her like the dead skin of a reptile. Her new skin pulsed and expanded as the muscles beneath it grew and took shape.

Lilith was gaining in size and mass. Whatever she was becoming she was much larger than she had been. She looked down and the flesh all over her body was ripping and tearing away. The new body while remaining female was rippled with muscles. She stood up tall and flexed those muscles and reveled in her new form, and as she did she felt a rush of wind as the muscles in her shoulders flexed with the others. Lilith turned her gaze to look over her shoulder and there upon her back were wings of black leather. They were similar to those she had seen on some of the creatures that hung upside down in the trees in the Garden, but they were also covered in small scales, and from the joints were long barbed spikes. As she lifted the wing to take a closer look at it she was pleased to see that they ended in spikes as well. Not only were the wings useful for transportation but they would be formidable weapons.

She had no more time to think upon her miraculous transformation for the cave beast's body suddenly slammed into hers and they rolled across the floor of the cave together. The beast was still larger than she was, but not by as much, and Lilith had the strange feeling that it was soon to find that it did not match her in strength.

The beast tried to wrap its front limbs around her, but Lilith grabbed the paws and easily pried them apart. She then turned to the beast and roared. The hair upon the beast flew backwards in the force of her breath yet it showed no fear. It was fighting for territory as well as its life. It tried to strike at Lilith and Lilith let it, but the claws did nothing to the new scaled skin that covered her. She lifted her head and laughed, but the laugh sounded more like a bellowing roar. Her taloned hand moved so swiftly that it was a blur as it tore through the chest of the great beast and out the other side. Slowly Lilith closed her fingers around the still beating heart of the beast as it hung on her arm. Then just as quickly she retracted her arm from its living sheath and let the beast fall to the ground.

A pool of blood began to cover the floor and her hunger cried out to her. She was not even aware of what she did next. The beast that she had become knelt before the creature and placed its mouth over the wound in the chest, its jaws spread impossibly wide and she began to drink, draining the blood from the beast.

As she drank her mind floated. She was drifting through blackness and space. Somewhere in the distance she heard music though she did not know that that was what it was called. It was lovely and she allowed herself to float toward it. Then a soft voice sang to her, *My sweet child, greetings.*

"Do I know you?" Lilith's dream self-asked.

"We have never met, but we are of one mold, you and I."

"I do not know what you mean? Who are you?" She asked the singing voice.

"In time I will have many names, so my name is not important. I have come to tell you but one thing. When you kill, drink all the fluids. Do not let the body remain, and never allow the body to have any of your fluids. You must be the only one like you."

"The only one like me? Yes! I must be the only one like me!" Lilith did not know who the voice was or if what it had said was true but she had too much pride to allow another like herself to exist. With a hunger like nothing she had ever felt she sucked even harder upon the beast as she returned from her dark journey. Soon the beast began to crumble beneath her, and still she drained the fluids. She could feel there were some left so she continued to drink.

Finally there were no fluids left and as she opened her eyes and looked down she looked upon nothing but a fur hide filled with bones and dust. She took one taloned nail and ran it from under the chin of the beast to its groin and emptied the hide of the remnants of the beast. As she did this she felt sleepy and strange. She could tell her hunger was not abated. The fluids of the beast did not satisfy her completely but they took the edge off of her need, yet still they had also made her drowsy. She pulled the hide toward a corner of the cave but as she did so it grew heavier and she was having a difficult time dragging it across the ground. She looked back at it had it grown in size? *No!* She was wrong. She looked at her hands, she had returned to what she was before her transformation, and there had been no pain, nothing to even tell her she had been changing except the drowsiness and the weight of the hide.

Lilith struggled to get the hide to the corner of the cave. She had planned to pull it over her but now was thankful that she had thought to cut it open. Instead she climbed inside it and curled up in the warmth to try to sleep the rest of the hours of the day away. When night came she wanted to explore her new home and maybe see what lay about it. The last thing she remembered was closing her eyes. From that moment until the sun set she did not dream and nothing at all entered her mind.

Shortly after the sun had set Lilith's eyes sprung open. There was a sound in the cavern. Some other presence had intruded upon what was now her home. She lay quietly hidden within the hide of the large cave beast as she listened to the sounds of the other creature slowly making its way around the cave. No, she was wrong. She could make out the sounds of three of the beasts. They were nowhere near the size of the one she had killed, but they were a pack. She heard one head back toward the entrance and then she heard a low howl into the night.

Lilith was worried it may be summoning more of its kind. She had to act quickly. Her speed amazed her as she slid from the cover of her hiding place and was upon the back of the nearest creature. Her arms wrapped around its neck and it rolled upon the ground as if it was trying to knock her loose. The one at the entrance came charging back in. It and the other circled her and the one she was fighting. She had chosen the largest, and the battle was short. Her hands went to its jaws and with one quick pull she heard the snap as the bones in the jaw broke and she tore the lower jaw away.

The two other beasts dove in but they did not attack her. They immediately began to attack and disembowel the one that had been the largest. She felt the hunger hitting her and she buried her mouth to the wound at the throat and began to drink.

No! The voice in her head yelled, Do not drain it of all its fluids!

But Lilith was already into her bloodlust and she drank deep. She heard the cries and yelps of the other two beasts as they ran out of the cavern and when she looked down nothing remained of her kill but hide and bones. Then dizziness overtook her, she tried to stand but her legs would not support her and she fell. Darkness swam in upon her and before long she was floating through a massive sea of black.

Chapter Three

She landed hard on a solid black surface and slowly rose to her feet. Around her was nothing. It was black in all directions. She screamed but no sound came from her throat. She stomped her foot upon the hard surface and there was no sound from the concussion of her foot hitting the surface. There was only complete and utter silence. Slowly she turned around and now, where before there had been nothing, she could see the outline of what looked like some kind of surface to sit upon but again it was black, except upon it was a man so white that it hurt her eyes to look upon him.

Everything about him was white, his hair, his clothing, his skin, his lips, but his eyes were closed. She wondered if he were asleep and as that thought entered her mind she got her answer for his eyes opened and they were as black as everything else around her was. There was not even a white to his eyes. They were solid black from eyelid to eyelid.

Though his mouth did not move his voice boomed within her head, *I warned you not to drink of all of its fluids.*

"Why?" Her word echoed forever in the stillness of the void but at least there was sound and it gave her some semblance of comfort, though she could not fathom why. She should be terrified, but she was not. For some strange reason she knew that this being would not harm her.

Slowly he stood and as he did two large white feathered wings rose behind him. From tip to tip they were easily four times as wide as he was tall. They beat one time and lifted him off the ground and then he glided and stood directly before her. He towered over her. Her eyes were about the level of where his navel should have been but he had no navel.

His black eyes glared down upon her, *the most important reason is I told you not to.*

Lilith looked back up at him and said, "I do not know who or what you are, but do you think if I would disobey God, I would obey you?"

The beings eyes darted around quickly, do not say His name here, we do not want to draw His attention.

"So! That you are also disobeying Him is aiding me." Lilith threw back her head and laughed. Suddenly she found the beings hand over her mouth.

Listen you fool! The reason you should not drain the life of every creature you feed upon is each time you drain all the fluids from them you will become weaker. Stop at the blood. Just drink their blood.

"But He said I would hunger for all the life fluids of man."

Yes, MAN! The fluids of man will not drain you, but only if they are descendants of Adam. Be careful there are men that walk the earth that have no blood ties with Adam.

"If it is so dangerous to drink all the fluids, why did you tell me to do it that first time?"

Because gifts come with drinking all the fluids as well. You can change your form into their exact form. Now you can become as the cave beast, what Adam has named a cave bear, and this new one is a wolf. You will even be able to take the likenesses of the men and women you kill. You will be able to disguise yourself as them for a time, but only until the sun rises. Then you must take your true form again. When the sun sets you can return to the other form, but you must also be warned, the longer you hold another's form the greater the hunger will be and the more you will need to feed.

Lilith looked at the being and then suddenly she realized that it was not wearing pants but where Adam had had a rod that had become hard this being had nothing. There was only smooth flesh. There was nothing to tell Lilith if this being was male or female. She started to reach out to run her hand over the smoothness but held back her impulse, whatever this being was she knew it was powerful and she had insulted it enough.

"I have one more question."

I have put up enough with you! I should destroy you!

"But I do not think you will because you will not want Him knowing you have talked to me. So answer this last question. You told me not to let anything taste my blood, why?"

If you drink the blood of a being and bring it near death and then it drinks of your blood you will make it similar to you. However, there is a penalty for making one like you. You will lose the ability to drain all the fluids. You will only be able to drink the blood from that moment on. Each one you make will have your same abilities, and they will be able to make more as well.

Lilith looked at him, "Well you have nothing to worry about there. I don't want there to be anyone like me. I am the only one like me and will always be the only one."

Of that I am glad to hear You are Wampyr. Now return to your body Wampyr, you have the night to conquer.

Chapter Four

The last word still resounded in her ears as her eyes opened. She also heard the soft whimpering of the other two wolves and felt their muzzles nudging her. She looked up at them and one came to her and began to lick her face. Something about it felt odd but she was still a little dazed from her visitation with the stranger. She tried to rise but found that it was not quite right. As she looked at her hands she howled, but it was supposed to have been a scream. Her mind leapt out and touched those of the wolves and she felt them respond with a feeling of submission, that she was their leader, except it was not she. They responded to he.

Lilith turned her muzzle and looked between her furred legs, the beast she had killed was male and now she was male too. Again she howled. Lilith was confused. She did not understand how she would handle being in the body of a wolf let alone the body of a male. She rose to her four paws and dashed out into the night. The two female wolves followed closely behind her and soon she found that it was exhilarating to run like the wolf. Under branches and through the woods she traversed as fast as her four legs could carry her. It was not as fast as she could have traveled as Lilith for as a wolf she was limited to the abilities of her new form but still it filled her with a joy like nothing she had ever felt before.

Then suddenly she pulled to a quick stop. Her sense of smell was even stronger than it had been as Lilith. There was a new smell that she didn't recognize. It was foul and yet alluring, a mixture of filth and yet appetizing. She turned her little pack toward the scent and began to head towards it. She had not traveled very far before the two wolves behind her began to whimper in protest. Like in the cave she suddenly thrust out her mind and picked up an image. It was an image of something similar to Adam, but not quite. It stood slightly bent and the forehead was sloped. It was also covered with a great deal more hair than Adam's body had been covered with. The images in the wolves' minds also showed her what made the foul stench. These beings kept a place near their caves where they would leave their bodily waste and the other rotten things they came across. They also threw the bodies of their dead into these piles like trash.

Lilith pushed with her mind that the two females could stay where they were and then she went closer. She had to see for herself. She lowered herself onto the male haunches of the wolf and crawled closer to the place where the beings had made camp. As she crawled over a rise in the ground she saw them. They were hideous. To her they almost looked like monsters in their own way. She could see the males using the women like the beasts in the garden had but it was the males that sought their pleasure and openly, without regards to privacy or to the females at all. She even watched as one female was used by one male and then another and another and yet another, then when they were done with her they gave her a small handful of food and she ran off to eat it in as hidden a place as she could.

What Lilith saw began to cause the blood in her veins to boil. Yet she continued to watch the tribe of cavemen.

She noticed that the men all wore some form of garment but not one female wore even the slightest hint of clothing. Even the male children were given something to cover their manhood, but the female children ran around as the day they were born.

There was a disturbance at one end of the encampment as a large group of men drug in a carcass of a beast and one of the men ran over and chased the others away. He growled at all of them waving a club like weapon and after all had backed away he began ripping the carcass apart. He gave large chunks to the men that had brought the beast into the camp first, then smaller to the other men of the camp that were still young, then to the male children he gave yet smaller pieces. To the women that were fat with child he gave pieces about the same size as he had the male children. While he was doing this a little female child ran up with her hands up begging a piece.

The man that was tearing apart the beast growled at her but she just stood there with her hands up. Suddenly he jumped down, grabbed her and lifted her high above his head. Then as if she weighed almost nothing he hurled her across the field and into an area littered with rocks and boulders. Lilith heard her body hit and from the sound knew that many of her bones had been broken. She could hear the little child's whimpers and cries but the man ignored them and went back to separating the beast.

Lilith crawled over and stared down at the little body. She watched as the chest of the child struggled to breathe and Lilith felt her own heart pleading to let the girl not suffer any more. Then the breathing stopped. Deep within her, Lilith felt something snap; she had not felt true outrage before but now she did. She stood on the four legs of the male wolf and a howl escaped from its lungs. The male that was cutting up the beast turned and all the eyes of the males of the camp followed his toward the howl she had made. Suddenly spears were flying through the air but it did not matter for her transformation had already begun. The skin of the wolf split, and the pain that Lilith felt this time was welcomed.

She spread her massive black wings and lifted herself into the air. Then lowering her head toward the encampment below like some vengeful wraith she descended upon the men of the camp. With talon and wing she tore them limb from limb, flinging their pieces across the fields as if they were nothing and leaving them to the beasts of the fields. All save one. She saved one for last. The man that had killed the girl held a spear to defend himself as she approached.

He thrust it at her but the blade broke upon the scales of her hide. She thrust her wings around from behind her and drove the spikes on each end into his shoulders and brought him close to her face. She smelled his fear. She looked down at his manhood as he urinated upon the ground and with her taloned hand she reached down and with one swift gouge of her talons tore his manhood, sack and rod from his body and held it up to his face. With her other talon she forced his mouth open and placed his own manhood into his mouth. Then she leaned in and sunk her fanged mouth into his neck. She drank deeply. She knew he was not of Adam's line but she did not care, she drank of all his fluids until the only thing that remained of him was his skeleton and his manhood within the mouth of his skull.

Lilith knew that not one of the women or children stood a chance at survival without the men. So she intended to watch over them. She would have the wolves and the cave bears take care of them and protect them from the other beast as well. Then she turned and flew to the dead child's body. She had not seen children before this night, but she knew what they were, the Tree of Knowledge had taken care of supplying her with that knowledge. She lifted the child and held it out to the women, but not one of them even acted like it was theirs. Tears flowed from her eyes as she looked to the sky and rose into the night.

Zachariah paused; there were tears in his eyes. "Melanie, that night changed Lilith in many ways. In some ways it made her even harder than she was. In others it brought some compassion into her that she had never felt before. You see Lilith knew that with her curse she would never have a child of her own, so for many hours she flew across the skies cradling that child to her chest. Wishing it could nurse from the blackened breast upon her scaled hide.

"It was a dead child that no mother had claimed and had it been living Lilith would have claimed it as her own. Had it been living Lilith may have repented and been a very different woman as she watched that child grow. However as she stood upon the ground wiping the soil from her hands and looking down upon the little grave she began to hate all men. Not mankind, just men.

"It was on that night that Lilith swore to never have a male lover, and whether she was in male form or female form until she met me she kept that oath. It was also on that night that Lilith swore to never kill a female, and until she felt jealousy over a woman's attention to me that oath too she never broke.

Zachariah wiped away the tears and added, "Yet there is still one more major event in Lilith's history that must be told before I tell you of our meeting."

***

For many years Lilith watched the encampment and took care of the women. If any male so much as looked like he might cause harm to a woman Lilith would fly over the camp at night and shriek out her warning. She did not attack the men of that camp as she wanted the camp to gain men so she could stop watching it, but if a man did harm a woman they would find his blood drained body lying near the camp the next day as a warning to the next man that might think he could get away with it.

As far as feeding upon men, Lilith found the blood of this species of men far more filling and satisfying than anything else she had tried so when she flew she would hunt far and wide searching for other camps of men. She even came across another race of men that were closer to the race of Adam but still were not of Adam's line. This species had less hair than the cavemen did and they walked more erect and Lilith liked their blood better. Like she had done with the cavemen she drained all the Life's fluids from one of the males just in case she ever needed to enter into their numbers and pretend to be one of them, but she could also tell it weakened her so she did not drain more than the one. Each time she was weakened her speed and strength when she was Lilith was less and she was afraid that someday she may be as she was in the Garden with no added strength or dexterity.

After about thirty passings of the seasons the encampment had completely recovered from the devastation she had done upon the male portion of the camp and she was able to leave them to themselves. She however stayed in her cavern and began to build upon it. Digging tunnels deeper into the earth in portions and adding stone huts above ground at others. This gave her additional places to sit and watch as time passed.

Lilith studied her gifts and the abilities that they had given her. She learned that there were other things she could do as well. She learned that with the right concentration she could call upon some of those that she had drained all the fluids of. She could call upon the wolves, and cave bears, and she could call upon the Neanderthals at will. The hairless men as she called them were harder, some she could call and control, others she could not even touch their minds.

She also learned that when she shifted from one form to the other all wounds she took in her animal form would heal completely, and in no form could she be killed. In a battle with a different species of bear that occurred while she was a wolf, the bear had actually torn her head off. She was certain she was going to die. Instead she felt tendrils form of her own blood and they became like iron bond and pulled her head back to her body. She switched forms to Lilith immediately and was healed.

In her Lilith body she had killed the bear. She had not even bothered changing to her monstrous self for her strength was that great and she healed quicker as Lilith. In anger at having her head torn off she had not even thought of switching to the monster form. She just charged the bear and with fangs that suddenly grew within her mouth she bit into its throat and drank its blood.

It was the first time she had drank the blood of any creature while still in her Lilith form. As she sat up she felt the sharp fangs in her mouth and laughed. What a marvel she was, even to herself. This curse was to her more a blessing than a curse. She did miss the sun, and she missed talking, but the life she had was a miracle.

Chapter Five

Over seven hundred years passed and Lilith learned more about the creature she had become with each passing year. Then one night while she was out with her two wolfen companions strolling along in her Lilith form she happened to hear something new. A voice. Someone was singing.

Lilith was clothed but only because she had gotten tired of the little barbs and thorns tearing at her. Yes she healed quickly but each thorn and barb still hurt. Yet even had she not been Lilith had no shame, she would have walked up to the man naked or clothed. To her it did not matter. However, her being clothed was a good thing for had she been naked this man would have turned and not spoken to her out of embarrassment.

As she approached him she saw he was pulling behind him a strange contraption, it was some kind of wood item upon two round items that were revolving as he pulled it and on the wood item sat a little boy and a little girl. They were listening to him sing.

He saw her coming close and saw the two wolves beside her and Lilith heard him say softly to the two little children, "Quiet, Seth and Tabitha, they seem to be with her, so they should not hurt you."

The two children acted afraid and wrapped their arms around each other. Then he turned towards Lilith and said, "My children have only seen wild wolves, or the damage the wolves have done to livestock. They are afraid your wolves will attack us."

Lilith looked down and with her hand motioned to the wolves and they bounded off back into the woods.

The man smiled at her and said, "Thank you." Then he turned to the children and added, "See children, they are tamed, they are like her pets. So you do not need to be afraid."

Lilith interjected, "No, not my pets, more like my friends."

He turned and smiled, "Well that is even better."

He sat the long poles of the wooden thing onto the ground and helped his children out of it, then turned to her before looking up at the sky, "I have traveled late this night and should be resting, would you care to join us for our evening meal and drink."

"I will sit with you, if you do not mind, but I have fed."

Something about the man's smile kept touching Lilith, it was very genuine and it looked very familiar. He also had a scent about him that was familiar and it did not take her long to place it. She could smell Adam upon him. As he sat down and turned to her he said, "My name is Adam, I am descended from Cain, son of Adam."

It took everything Lilith had to keep from reaching out and ripping the man's throat out. Adam, the very name of the man that had caused her to be cursed filled her with such vehemence that she barely controlled her rage. She had to turn her head while the fire in her eyes dissipated for she had already learned her eyes glowed red when she was angry.

The only thing that staved off her anger was that she remembered the little girl long ago and she had seen the faces of the two children as they sat beside their father. She would not make that little girl fear her or see her father killed before her eyes no matter how much his name ripped into her soul.

Once she regained her temper she asked, "Do you speak of the Adam from the Garden?"

"Yes, of course," he said, as if she should have known that already then he added, "oh wait, you are dark-haired and your skin is dark. You are probably further away from the bloodline than I am. Maybe you do not know the whole story."

She wanted to tell him who she was, that she was not further away, that she was not descended of anyone, that God had made her Himself. Instead she held that within her and said, "No, I do not know the story, would you mind telling me what happened?"

He began telling the story. There was no mention of Lilith in his tale of the Garden, only of Adam and his second wife Eve, and how Eve had been tempted by a serpent and how Adam and Eve had both been cast out of the Garden after eating of the Tree of Knowledge.

Lilith had stopped him and asked him about the Tree of Life. He was surprised to see she knew some things but he added that no, God had banished them before they could eat of that tree. Lilith had had to force the smile from her lips so as to not give her delight in that part of the tale away.

Then he had gone on about how Cain had slain Abel and that his family was of the descendants of Cain. He told Cain's side from that point and said he was sorry but knew nothing more of Adam other than he and Eve did have more children.

Through the night he talked, about an hour before the sun was to rise Lilith thanked him for his time and asked him where he was headed. He informed her that he and his entire band was headed this way for new farmland. He had just broken ahead of the rest to get a good spot for he had lost his wife and wanted to make certain he had a good spot for a dowry for his daughter and a place for his son to inherit.

She then asked about the rest of his people. He told her that there were well over twelve score more of his kind. She looked at him funny when he said the word "score" and he explained by showing all the fingers of his hands twice. Lilith smiled and then bid him farewell.

If it had not been for those two children that man would not have survived the night, but Lilith had a weak spot and that was young children. She let him and his little ones travel on safely, even sending a mental message on ahead to the wolves and cave bears to guard their path.

However when the main band came through they were not so lucky.

Lilith sat in the hills along the side of the moonlit road and watched as the wagons rolled by. One by one they passed. It was unusual for a caravan to travel past the setting of the sun, yet this one had not found a good place to make camp. She watched as men walked by, some leading mules with women on them, some pulling carts and some guiding wagons. The entire time Lilith kept her eyes open for the men that were alone. When she spied one she would wait until they passed a stand of trees and there she would be luring them with her body and promises of the delights that she would give them.

Often when she went hunting it would take her a while to find someone out at night alone or a caravan traveling at night. However when she did she would try a different strategy to lure her victim.

Sometimes she would play the demure girl bathing in a pond and pretend that she did not know she was being seen but let them glimpse just enough of her nakedness to entice them to want to see more.

Some of the men that saw her ignored her, then finally one saw her and he was enraptured by what he saw. She could see the lust in his eyes. As he watched she began to rub her hands over her body, teasing him even more. Slowly the man turned his mule away from the caravan and toward the woods. He dropped off the back of his mule and tied it to a branch on a tree, then he looked about and made certain he was unseen. As he did so he also slipped a knife out from his belt. Lilith saw the blade and knew that in his mind his intent was that he would have her even if she changed her mind. She had already made up her mind a long time ago, no man was going to enter her ever again, but him lifting his blade had sealed him to a deeper fate. She would drain him of all his life. There would be nothing left of him for anyone to recognize.

He slipped into the woods and Lilith stood there with open arms, as if she awaited him as her lover. He did not even bother to undress, it was like he was going to let her do everything, well she would, just not the way he wanted her to. He slipped into her arms and she wrapped her arms around him. Her lips met his, her eyes met his, then she lowered her lips to his neck and as her mouth opened and her teeth sank in she expected him to scream out but he did not. Her mind entered his and she knew that the moment her lips had touched his that he had become hers. Lilith drank, and while she drank she read his thoughts, she read everything he had ever done. Every evil deed, and what few good, she learned the language of his people and then as she drained the final fluids of his life she felt a new surge. It was like nothing she had ever felt before.

Similar in many ways to the orgasm that had swept over her when Adam had been within her, yet greater; she did indeed orgasm, as one wave after another swept over her. As the final fluids of the descendent of Adam filled her she knew what it meant to truly feed upon the life fluids of the sons of God. She felt stronger, renewed, refreshed. She had not regained all the strength she had lost after draining the Life's fluids from the beings that were not sons of God but she was no longer hungry, and she felt alive.

She looked down at the pile of bones at her feet and as she did she also noticed that her thighs were drenched with her own cum. She lifted her head to the heavens and laughed then with an instantaneous shift that was completely painless she shifted to the winged beast and lifted into the air.

Lilith had learned that drinking the Life's Fluids from the sons of god was the best thing for her to do, however, the next night she also learned that she could not do it on a daily basis for she was wakened by the sounds of dogs running through the woods and men following them. There was a hunt for a monster that could turn a man to bones. Unlike the other species that did not pay attention to their dead, the sons of God paid a great deal of attention to those that died around them.

The home that had been Lilith's for over seven hundred years was no longer safe and she had to move for she had killed too close to her home. She was outraged, but she had also learned a valuable lesson. They did not know whose bones it was that were found only that it was one of theirs so with her abilities she took his place and hid amongst his people for a few days, but she had to be careful for she could only be with them at night. During the day she had to seek shelter far away from the group so she would tell them that she was going to look for the monster. Sometimes they would want to send others but she would refuse and say it was best she did it alone. Then she would hide for the day and return at night. In this way she was able to stay hidden and follow the group for several months. The feeding she'd had satisfied her well enough that she did not hunger during that time though there were many times that her rage towards men had almost risen up to the point it had almost gotten the better of her. Had she not needed to find a new permanent home she would have ripped many men's throats out.

When the band Lilith was with met with another band it was time Lilith switched groups and her hunger was rising again. So she fed.

***

Zachariah smiled to Melanie and then sighed, "For hundreds of years Lilith managed to keep hidden this way. She became wise, feeding on the wealthier and greediest of those she traveled with, and in doing so began to accumulate a vast fortune. She played two roles, by taking on the persona of the man she killed, and then pretending that she Lilith was that man's mistress, lover or wife and in this way for well over a thousand years she stayed well fed and well hidden. At least until the Flood, but that part of the story is not significant to our tale, so I am going to jump forward now to what is important to our tale. That is the time when Lilith and I met."

***

After the flood things were much harder. For one she had to return to feeding off of beasts and even these were scarce. There were long periods that she would have to enter a state similar to hibernation to give the animals a chance to repopulate the world. It was a great struggle for her, and during this time she again drained the life from another beast, for her hunger was so great and her mind was in a state of delirium that she was unable to stop herself. She drained the life's fluids from a large bat that had happened to fly close enough to her sleeping form that her body's own instincts reached out and plucked it from the air as it flew by her.

Lilith wavered in and out of her near coma state for over twelve hundred years then one night she awoke. She was so weak she could barely move at all. Her mind told her that if she did not eat soon that she would die. She pushed her way through the layers of branches and leaves that had covered the entrance to the hole she had once crawled into. Lilith even tried to reach out with her mind to the animals that she knew she could talk to but she could not touch their minds, she was too close to being truly dead. Something told her that she would not die, but she did not want to lie for eternity beneath the ground waiting for something to get close enough to her that she could feed and gain enough strength to climb out.

She tried to stand but only fell back onto her face. With what little strength she had she managed to get to her hands and knees and forced herself to crawl, but she did not get far before blackness overtook her and she knew nothing.

Part Two
Zachariah
Chapter Six

The moon was bright in the night sky and though it lit Zachariah's way it also threatened to reveal his chosen hiding places as he skirted from one to the next. As he had done for over three weeks he had snuck out of his father's house and followed this path, but it was not his father he was trying to hide from. Neither was it a secret clandestine affair that he was running off to. Zachariah was simply trying to get his chores done before being spied by his peers within the camp. For if they spotted him they would challenge him to some silly form of competition to prove that one of them was stronger, faster, or braver than he was.

It had been that way since the first day he had walked out of his father's door and met them. It was as if he had been glowing and suddenly he became the center of attention. The ones that had been there before him decided they had to beat him in order to win back their rightful spot. He had only been a toddler then and did not even seek anything but to have fun and be friends with all the children he was meeting for the first time.

His mother had kept him away from them before. She had lost her first child in a miscarriage and was overly careful of Zachariah but she had finally decided she had to let him be a child and discover the world. Still she had kept a close eye on him through the entire celebration.

No sooner than she had set him down than he had seen the other children about his size and had toddled over to play with them. From that very moment the girls and boys began to play with him and laugh. Then one of them pushed through them and began pulling upon the toy that Zachariah was holding. He screamed, "Mine!"

Zachariah let go and the boy fell. The boy looked like he was going to cry but when he looked at the others he climbed back to his feet and tried to push Zachariah down, but even though Zachariah was about the same size his feet were planted and the other toddler could not move him at all.

Another boy began helping the first, and still Zachariah remained firm. Then a third, and though Zachariah's feet began to slide along the ground they were not knocking him down. It was then that Zachariah's mother showed up and picked him up and carried him back over to where she and his father were.

It was nearly eighteen years later and the challenges between he and that boy had never stopped. That boy, now a young man, had galvanized most of the young men of the town around him because Zachariah preferred not to cause problems and would not resort to name calling or other slander tactics.

Yet the thing that made things even worse was when he tried to lose. The others were so much outclassed by him that it was impossible for him to lose without it being obvious that he was trying to throw the competition. He had finally realized he could not do that, he had to either compete honestly or do what he was doing now and avoid the competitions entirely.

He was out of bed long before them and got his chores done then went to his father's shop where he was apprenticing, all before they even opened their eyes. For three weeks he had managed to succeed in avoiding them, but tonight the moon was full and every one of his hiding places was within its brilliant light.

They had become wise to his tricks and he could hear them searching for him. If he could just get past them and on the road to the river he would be fine. Today was a light day for chores. He only had two. Haul water to the livestock and feed them; then he could go and begin smelting the silver for today his father was going to begin teaching him to be a silversmith. It was the first of the many levels he would go through on his way to becoming a master jeweler like his father.

Zachariah rounded a corner behind the hut of the camp's leader and could see the road to the river clearly. The moon shone down upon Samuel and Judiah who were standing at the gate to the village and blocking his path to the river. He could jump over the fence and cut through the briars but his legs would be torn to shreds. He backed around the corner and cursed himself, trying to second guess their actions. He knew he should have tried to stay in the shadows away from the moon, but he had taken the path that had been loyal to him for three weeks. Tonight however, his path had betrayed him into the hands of his peers.

Suddenly he heard Tobiah's voice, and lifting his eyes he saw his arch-rival walking straight toward him. There was nothing to do but stand and accept their challenge. He might as well face one challenge and get it over with for the day.

"Well, well," Tobiah said tauntingly, "I see we have finally managed to catch the rat who has been trying to avoid us."

Zachariah rose up and looked Tobiah square in the eyes. He easily stood two hands taller than Tobiah. Even so his rival had always tried to make Zachariah angry, but he held his temper. Not only was it not a good thing to lose your temper when you were strong enough to hurt someone without even thinking about it, but to hurt the grandson of the village leader would have been very bad for his father as well. "Tobiah, you have found me, make your challenge and be done with it."

As the others in Tobiah's gang gathered around Tobiah sneered and laughed, "So now you want the challenge. Hasn't it been you that has been avoiding a challenge for these last three or four weeks?"

"It has been twenty days to be exact Tobiah. Had I gotten past you today it would have been three weeks, but your cohorts barred my path." Zachariah took a step forward and every one of Tobiah's crew including Tobiah took a step backwards, even in their numbers they knew his strength. "Now you have caught your rat, as you have called me, so make your challenge."

Tobiah whistled and a large young man that was about four hands taller than Zachariah came walking out of the shadows. He lumbered forward and stopped several feet away from the group. Zach looked at him and then at Tobiah, "You could not find someone of the camp to beat me so you went elsewhere?"

"Shut your mouth, Zachariah, son of Zakarias the jeweler. This is Kobas, my cousin from two villages to the south of us. He is blood to me so he is eligible to compete." Tobiah crossed his arms and smiled.

"Fine by me, I care not if you change the rules to suit your needs," Zach said. He saw Tobiah stiffen at the accusation and knew it was true, "Now go ahead and make your challenge, I have chores to do, as do all of you."

The other young men nodded to one another, many of them had more than once gotten in trouble because of Tobiah's vendetta with Zachariah. Yet they continued to stay at Tobiah's side and risk additional punishments in their vain hopes to also see Zachariah fail.

Tobiah lifted his hand and motioned for his cousin to come forward.

"Kobas here is strong, stronger than any man I have ever seen, and I think he is stronger than you Zachariah, son of Zakarias."

Zachariah just looked at the new arrival, it was indeed possible. He definitely had the build for it, and Zachariah did not really try to build his strength it just came from working hard and doing his chores like his father had told him to do. There were no other children in his household so if Zachariah wanted to learn his father's craft he had to do all the chores and do them fast and efficiently. He'd had to learn to do them at a very young age. When he was as young three he was carrying the baby goats by himself, at four he was carrying the adults, at five he was carrying two. It was a matter of need not choice, yet he never really grew much in bulk like many did, he just did what had to be done. Sometimes he would pay for it with aches and pains that night, but his mother would rub a liniment into his muscles and sing him a soothing song to help him relax.

Sadly he often had to return the favor. Many times he would hold his mother after she had lost another child before it was born. She would cry bitterly for it was her deepest wish to give her husband, his father, another child. Yet for some reason it was God's plan that Zachariah would be their only child.

Now this only child of Zakarias looked at Kobas and actually prayed that indeed he would be strong enough to win the competition for maybe then this silly game of Tobiah's would stop. Yet something inside Zachariah also told him that he could not let Kobas win if it was not a true win. He had to give it his all for it would be less than honorable for his father if he lost willingly. He turned to Tobiah and asked, "What is the challenge?"

"We go to the blacksmith shop. He has just made a large amount of iron spikes to be shipped to the coast. We will place a yoke across Kobas' shoulders and then a basket on each end. Jacob and Michael will load the baskets with a spike at the same time until Kobas cannot stand. Then if you can lift the yoke you win," Tobiah pushed his finger into Zachariah's chest and added, "but if not you lose."

"Well," Zachariah said, "to me that does not seem quite fair."

Tobiah laughed and turned to his buddies and said, "See I told you he was a coward."

However Zachariah ignored him and continued his train of thought, "Kobas will have been standing there with that weight getting heavier and heavier, draining his strength. By the time he collapses I will be fresh and have not been tired at all, I will be able to lift more than he was able to hold up even were he and I equally matched to start out with, or even if I were a little weaker."

Tobiah stood with his mouth agape. Zachariah looked at him and added, "After all, we do want the competition to be fair, don't we?"

For a few moments Tobiah stood still as if he did not know what to say then he said, "Okay, then what do you suggest."

"Kobas and I both get yokes with baskets. You have enough friends to load the baskets for both of us and besides it will help the blacksmith get his delivery ready, so we are doing him a favor too. Then there will be no counting, they keep loading until both of us go to our knees. Once to our knees, they count into the shipping crates the number of spikes. The winner of course is the one who has the most spikes."

Tobiah looked at Zachariah and said, "Agreed." Then he waved to his buddies and they headed towards the blacksmith shop but before he could take a step Zachariah grabbed him by the shoulder and pulled him up short.

"There is one more thing, Tobiah."

Tobiah turned angrily brushing Zachariah's hand off of him like Zach had some form of disease. "What is that?"

"This is the last competition. We are getting too old for this childishness."

"Who are you to decide this?" Tobiah glared at him.

"Then I make you a wager."

"Wagers are a sin, you know that Zachariah." Tobiah sneered. "Perhaps I should tell the priest of your attempt to get me to sin."

"Pride is a sin too, Tobiah, and your constant attempt to beat me at a competition is nothing more than something to appease your pride."

Tobiah growled under his breath, "What is your wager?"

"If I lose, I will take every bit of profit I make above what is needed for me to survive under the basest of means and give it to you for the rest of my life, if you stop the competitions."

"And if you win?"

"You simply stop the competitions."

Tobiah looked at him, "You mean you don't want anything else?"

"Nothing."

Zachariah held out his hand and waited for Tobiah. From the look in Tobiah's eyes Zachariah could tell that he did not have to think long.

After all, ending the competitions really was not that big a deal, and the prospect of having all of his money for the rest of his life was easily enough to tempt Tobiah into accepting the deal. Tobiah's hand grasped Zachariah's firmly. To Zachariah, even if he did lose the end of the competitions would really be worth him living on the edge of poverty for his entire life.

Tobiah turned and headed toward the blacksmith's shop and Zachariah followed. By the time they had arrived Kobas already had the yoke over his shoulders with the two empty baskets dangling from the ends. Jacob and Michael were ready to begin loading the baskets for him. Samuel and Judiah, the two that had blocked the path to the river were holding the yoke for Zachariah. He suspected that they would also be loading two spikes at a time to make him stumble to his knees sooner even though it would come to a count and not who actually fell first.

He walked up and let the two position the yoke, and immediately felt a pain in the back of his neck. The yoke had been tampered with but if he complained it would look like he was trying to back out. So he kept his mouth shut. If they wanted to cheat and he lost, at least he did the best he could, and their dishonor would be on them, not him.

Tobiah walked to stand between the two young men and gave the command to begin. With a clank the spikes hit the bottom of Zachariah's basket. He had been right they were tossing in two at a time. The first ones into Kobas' basket had hit quietly.

As more spikes hit the sound of the spikes reverberated throughout the camp. It sounded as if the blacksmith had opened his shop well before dawn. People lit torches and candles in their homes and some came out to inspect what was going on. A crowd began to build around the two young men with the yokes upon their necks as they continued to take more and more weight into the baskets.

One man shouted out that there was blood running down the back of Zachariah's neck, and a woman pushed her way through the crowd. It was his mother; she came to him and wiped the blood. "Zachariah, what is going on?"

He whispered to her, "They put something on the yoke, but they will not leave me alone. They always challenge me, but I made a wager with Tobiah and win or lose the challenges will stop."

"Then why not give up, you are hurt, my son," she said as she wiped away more of the blood, "and they are cheating."

"Something deep inside me will not let me dishonor my father by giving less than my all, mother," Zachariah said, "besides if I lose, which if I can keep from doing it I will not, I will live in poverty the rest of my life."

She frowned at him, "You gave so much in your wager? What do you gain if you win?"

"Just an end to these childish games."

She wiped his brow, "Oh my Zachariah, always the noble boy, never have you done a thing for yourself. Neither do you think ill of anyone. Do you not see that not all people carry truth the way that you do? When will you learn they will not honor their bet to you, but they will be sure you honor yours?"

"In truth mother, I know. I also know that at least for a while they will cease. It may not be long, but it will be for a while, and when they come to me I can for a short time ask Tobiah why he reneges on his wager. I know he will pretend he never made a wager but some of the young men who know me will know I do not lie and they will stop following him. He will lose his control over many of them, and for someone that hopes to be the leader of the camp someday that will not be a good thing. I may indeed be able to make him keep his part of the wager."

She stood on her tiptoes and could barely reach his chin to kiss him then she added, "You are wise beyond your years, my boy, perhaps you will win this time indeed, either way. I should let you do what you must." Before she left she wrapped her kerchief around his neck and then returned to the crowd where she joined his father. Zachariah could see her talking to his father and then saw him nodding. The look upon his father's face told him that he was proud. Even if he lost today nothing that could happen would take away that moment of comfort that filled his heart.

He turned and focused his energies again upon the weight that was building within the baskets, they had switched tactics now. Samuel was loading two spikes but Judiah was only loading one, so one basket was getting heavier a lot quicker than the other. Whatever it was that was cutting into the back of his neck had begun to slide along his neck as the weight shifted. He turned his gaze to Judiah and whispered to him, "If you do not play this fair, I will let the girl you are courting know about the time you fell in the ditch and cried like a baby. It was I that found you and rescued you, Judiah. When we came back, what did Tobiah do? For a week he pretended you did not exist, and yet you are cheating for him now."

Judiah's eyes widened, he did remember the time. He began to throw three spikes in for a while until Zachariah nodded and let him know the weight was even again. Then he returned to two. He whispered to Zachariah, "I am sorry, and I should never have befriended Tobiah again. When this is over can you forgive me, and once again we be friends?"

"Judiah, there is nothing to forgive. I never saw you as anything but a friend. You are always welcome at my door and my table." Zachariah smiled at him then he heard a whisper from Samuel.

"I too am sorry about all of this Zachariah. I hope I too can be forgiven."

"Samuel, as with Judiah, I see no sin, you too are welcome wherever I may be."

On that day the three became friends, and their friendship would last until Samuel and Judiah were laid to rest. Those two would be the two that would stand firmest against the wrongs that Tobiah would from time to time try to inflict upon Zachariah, and even though Zachariah needed no support they would rally around him still, confirming their bond once again.

Even though it was obvious that Tobiah was routing for Kobas, his cousin was a stranger to the rest of the villagers except for his direct family. So all the villagers were shouting out Zachariah's name, even Tobiah's own father, Tobyas was cheering on the favored contender. Then suddenly Zachariah began to stumble under the weight, it was obvious he could not handle much more. The crowd cheered him on stronger yet for all they did he could not hold up more and he went to his knees.

Another ten minutes of silence except for the clank of spikes hitting steel continued before Kobas could not handle his weight and he too fell to his knees. It was then that the counting began, but two of the men of the village who had watched it decided they had seen too many things that made them think the counting would not be fair so they stepped in and told the young men that they would be the judges.

Shipping crates were brought out, and as the stakes were counted they were loaded into the shipping boxes as Zachariah had suggested be done. The crowd remained silent, and those doing the counting did so silently and without talking to each other so that a full count would be taken. It was only fair that both young men be given full credit for what they accomplished, for it was obvious that no matter who won or lost both had accomplished an amazing display of strength.

While the counting continued Kobas walked over to Zachariah and for the first time saw the blood. He then looked at the yoke and pointed it out to his uncle. There was no doubt in any of the villager's minds that Tobiah would be in severe trouble for his deed. Then Kobas told everyone about the wager and that all Zachariah had requested win or lose was the end of the competitions that Tobiah kept insisting upon. He told them how Zachariah he had offered all his earnings if he lost, just to get Tobiah to agree.

Tobyas was furious as he looked at the spike that had been driven through the yoke so that just the point stuck out. It was not enough to cause severe damage, but it was enough to cause severe pain. He grabbed his son by the ear and led him before the entire village and announced to the listeners, "My son, the greedy ingrate that I have the shame to have to call my offspring, tried to rig this contest so that he would win.

"The yoke that Zachariah used was tampered with to cause him pain and make him give up early.

"We have all seen how hard of a worker Zachariah is. There are times he has gone out of his way to aid others when they have needed help and he gets his own work done as well. Yet it seems that my offspring has harassed him and hounded him to compete in one form or another for years." Tobyas looked at his son and then smacked him across the back of the head.

"There was a wager made on this competition, and since my son cheated, I call it in favor of Zachariah no matter the outcome of the count."

Zachariah stood and walked forward, his legs could barely support him as he came to Tobyas, "High Elder, I made the wager, I also felt the sting of the spike. I could have called foul. I did not. I chose to continue the competition. I ask you let the count decide the winner."

With a look that could only be shock Tobyas stared at him, "But son, you have nothing to gain if you win, and everything to lose if you don't."

"That is not true, High Elder. Whether I lose or win, if it is by the count I gain my self-respect. If you declare the winner by fault because of cheating it will always be that I won because Tobiah cheated. If I lose I lose fairly, and respectfully. I held up as long as I could, and Tobiah will have to live with the knowledge that he aided in my loss. His self-respect will be damaged, but mine will be intact."

Tobyas took Zachariah's hand and said, "So be it." Then he turned to his son and added, "From this young man you could learn a lot. If he loses, I know he will keep his debt to you, but I will disown you as mine and your younger brother will be the next leader of this camp. If he wins, you will go to his home every day and thank him that I have not disowned you, for it will be because he stood up against your treachery and won that I will keep you so you can learn something from him." Then he turned his back on his son and walked back into the crowd of the villagers to await the count.

Both counts ended within moments of each other fueling speculation that the contest was going to be close, perhaps even a tie. Tobiah yelled out to hear Kobas' count first and since no one disagreed the man who did the count stepped up and announced, "Kobas' baskets held 233 spikes."

The crowd cheered for that was a tremendous amount of weight indeed, the yoke and baskets alone weighed a lot and then to have that much added weight. Kobas was a strong young man. However then the crowd began to chant out Zachariah's name, they wanted to hear his count. The man that had counted them had called some people back and they were counting his again. So the chant went louder yet, the man came forward and said to the crowd that he was sorry but he had to have made a mistake in his calculations he wanted to make sure and have another count made.

The crowd would not be quiet. They continued to chant Zachariah's name. There were three men together handling the count this second time and they all shook their heads as they came forward and spoke to the man. He looked at them and his eyes got large then he turned to the crowd and announced, "Zachariah's count is 352 spikes."

The cheers were wild; Zachariah's parents ran to him and hugged him hard. Then Tobyas shook his hand and said "Well done." All the villagers filed past him and congratulated him and told him they knew he was a strong lad but not that strong.

***

Zachariah paused in his tale and looked again to Melanie, "I know you are probably wondering how much weight that was, but remember it was all in the legs. A man can lift a lot more with his legs than he can with his arms.

"The yokes weighed about 40 pounds by today's weights, and the baskets were sturdy leather and reinforced to hold a lot of weight, they each weighed about 15 pounds.

"Each spike weighed a little over five pounds but for this we will say five pounds, so Kobas was holding 1235 pounds before his legs could not hold anymore."

Melanie waited but it seemed like Zachariah was not going to tell her so she asked, "And you, Papa Zach?"

"Do you really need to know?" he questioned.

"My love, I do not need to know, and if you do not wish to tell me you can go on with the rest of the tale. However, I would like to know." She smiled at him, and waited for his decision.

"Before my knees buckled I was holding 1830 pounds."

Melanie's hands clasped together in delight. "I just knew you were a strong man, Papa Zach, but it is not your physical strength that delights me. In your tale it is the strength of your character that shows me that I have chosen wisely in falling in love."

He leaned over and kissed her lips tenderly and added, "There is still much of this tale to tell, and the time is running short. So I need to get back to it, precious."

She smiled brightly when he called her precious, it was the first time he had used that word as a pet-name for her. "Please continue my love," her heart sang as she spoke the words.

Zachariah slowly closed his eyes and in his mind he returned again to that night so very long ago.

***

After they were all done congratulating Zachariah they began heading back to their homes. There was one person that Zachariah sought out. He had to speak to Tobiah and settle things as best he could. He walked up to Tobiah and said to him, "I do not agree with your father belittling you in front of everyone, but it was wrong of you to put that spike in the yoke."

Tobiah turned and nodded, "Yeah, I know, I just have this urge to beat you at something."

"Why Tobiah? You already have."

He looked at Zachariah with a look of bewilderment in his eyes, "What do you mean? I have tried to beat you since we were little kids at everything I could think of. You are smarter than me, faster than me, stronger than me; even when I get other people that I think can beat you, you beat them too. I have never beaten you in anything."

Zachariah smiled. "You did when you were born in two ways. You are one day older than me, so you beat me out of your mother's womb."

Both young men began laughing at that.

When they stopped Zachariah added, "But more importantly, you will lead this village someday. That is something I will never do. You have a future ahead of you that means you will govern our people. I will be a jeweler, and make the jewels for your coronation, that is the greatest achievement in life I can hope to achieve. You can guide our people to new lands, new dreams, and even new prosperity."

Their eyes locked for a moment and then Tobiah raised his hand and took Zachariah's. "The competitions are over. I had never thought about my life like that. You are right. I should not have wasted our time in this silly competition."

They parted, and went their separate ways. They never did become friends; the punishment of Tobyas guaranteed that. Even after Tobyas passed over, Tobiah would from time to time make life hard on Zachariah until he finally had no choice but to move away from the village. When he did he continued to write letters to his friends Samuel and Judiah until they passed away. His move however had had more to do with other things than Tobiah.

After he had watched Tobiah walk away Zachariah looked up at the moon. There were still a few hours before the sun would be up and if he hurried he could still get the water and feed the livestock before the sun rose. He grabbed the kerchief his mother had left with him and placed it around his neck to protect the sore that the spike had caused. He grabbed a yoke at the gate and two large oaken buckets and placed the yoke on one shoulder. He tied the handles of the buckets off. If he ran at just the correct pace the buckets would bounce in time to his step and he could jog there and gain much of the time he had lost during the competition.

Chapter Seven

The muscles in his legs were sore, but that was from the strain of the weights. Running actually helped to stretch his muscles and he felt better for it. Normally he would have taken his time and enjoyed the air and beauty of the night but not this morning, too much time had been wasted. There was one point about halfway where he slowed briefly for he thought he had heard a wild animal struggling in the brush and had expected an attack but nothing had come so he continued on.

It did not take long to fill the barrels at the river, but he did waste just a little time to jump in and cool himself off. The run, and the exertion from the contest had drained him, and he needed the coolness as well as a good cold drink to revive him. Carrying the water back would be slower for the buckets were near full and he wanted to spill as little as possible. He did not think today that his father would give him hell if he split a lot of the water but there was still that chance. There were times his father was hard to read.

He still walked at a good pace but it was nowhere near a jog. He was coming to the top of a rise and remembered that this was the spot that he had thought he had heard the wild animal rustling about in the brush. He slowed, his gaze alert. His eyes followed the line of bushes watching for the animal in case he had to defend against it. As he topped the rise he saw something that at first he thought was a fallen limb from a nearby tree lying partially into the road.

As his pace carried him nearer his heart quickened. It was the slender hand of a young woman. Almost too suddenly he stopped. The buckets swayed upon the yoke and threatened to pull him off his feet as he stopped. As quickly as he dared he knelt and laid the yoke and buckets upon the path and then approached the woman. His heart was racing for he was certain she had been preyed upon by a band of brigands and left to die. What clothing she had on was tattered, it even looked like it had rotted away in places but that would be impossible, unless she had found it in the woods after having her own stripped from her.

He was afraid to touch her; afraid she would be cold as death. Then he saw her back raise and lower slowly as she took in a breath and he nearly fell onto his ass in shock. She was alive! He slowly turned her over onto her back.

Slowly his lungs filled to the point he thought they would burst. Before him lay the most beautiful woman he had ever seen. The garments she wore barely covered her but it was not her nakedness or her body that attracted him it was her face. The lines of her face were almost feline in nature, her eyes, though closed, would be large and symmetrical. Her lips were red and full and looked like they were begging to be kissed. He shook his head for in the twenty years since his birth he had never once thought of kissing a girl and here he was thinking of kissing one that was unconscious and unable to say yes or no.

Her hair was black, the deepest black he had ever seen and even though it was filled with twigs and leaves it was the fullest and most luscious head of hair he had ever imagined a woman could have. His heart was pounding so hard from just the first few moments of gazing upon her that Zachariah knew that if this woman did not already have a husband that one day he would ask her to be his wife.

Quickly and carefully he cradled her in his arms and out of the brush. Then as he looked at the yoke he tried to decide how he could carry the yoke and at the same time get the woman back safely. A solution came to him.

As tenderly as he could he lifted her up and placed her over his shoulder. Wrapping his arm around her legs he held her in place. Then he knelt down and lifted the yoke to his other shoulder and stood. If he held all those spikes then this should be an easy task for him. Only thing now was he had to make haste and spill as little as possible on his journey. He dared not jog for he did not want to jostle and take a risk at further injuring the woman, but he walked as quickly and smoothly as he could.

Zachariah had not had much time to think about sex during his almost twenty years. His mind now drifted to the few times that it had crossed his thoughts. His village had rules that kept the bodies of women covered from the sight of men in public. It was not as strict as may villages in that they did not require veils nor that their hair be bound or covered, but even so he had not seen many girls and sex had not entered his thoughts, until one day a little over a year ago when he had gone out to hunt rabbits for his mother. While out he had heard some laughter and thought he would see what all the fun was about. He had not intended to intrude upon the young women of the camp while they were bathing at a hidden pool that he had not even known existed.

For the first time in his life he had been frozen in his steps. His eyes were locked upon their bodies for he had no idea how beautiful they could be beneath the garments that they had worn. Zachariah had only stood there for a few moments and none of them had noticed him but that next morning when he woke his manhood was hard and there was a wet spot upon his bed. Quickly he had gotten up and taken his bedclothes to the river and cleaned them himself. When his mother had asked about it he had simply said that he had an accident and had spilt something on his bed and did not want her to have to clean up his mess. He was thankful that she did not press him further for to that point it was not a lie. If she had pressed him further he would either have had to bear his shame to her or lie and he did not know which would have been worse.

Each day for the next two weeks he had prayed for his sin and asked for forgiveness, but the biggest problem was he was not sure what his sin was. How could he be guilty of a sin when he was not aware he had committed one? Stumbling upon the girls was embarrassing but not a sin. Spilling his seed upon the mattress, if he had done it on his own would have been a sin, but was it a sin if he had done it in his sleep? Still he did not want to risk that it was.

It had taken months before he could face any of the young women of the camp without turning brilliantly red. Rumors had even gone up that he had a crush on one of them and would be asking to speak to their father soon, but when it did not happen the rumors died down. Rumors that he was not interested in women started, for he was past the age that most of his peers had already married. Zachariah did nothing to affect the rumors in either way. The truth was not that he was not interested in women but that he was more interested in learning his father's craft. He did not have time to court, and since he was an only child his parents were not eager to see him spending his time seeking a girl's hand either. There was too much work to do.

There had been one other reason Zachariah had never sought to court any of the girls of the village. It may have been distantly, but even so, every one of them was related to him in one way or another. Most were distant cousins, some not so distant. When he looked into the faces of any of them he saw either his mother or his father or one of his friends. It just did not seem right to him. He had planned that once he had finished his apprenticeship with his father he would go into a distant village to look for a bride.

He had never expected to have a woman come to him.

Now as he sped along with the nearly naked woman over his shoulder he could not keep his mind off of her body. All the feelings that he had kept under control for these many years were raging within him. He knew it was wrong to think of her in that way, for she could be seriously hurt. He had to get her back to the village and let his mother tend to her. Yet he found he was having trouble controlling his hand and it kept sliding up and resting upon the roundness of her bottom. He had never imagined how wonderful it would feel to touch a woman there and then suddenly he would struggle with his conscience and pull his hand back down to her legs. Yet even there it sent a thrill into his loins.

Zachariah was very thankful that the moon had gone behind some clouds and the night was as dark as it could be as he entered into the village and headed toward the house of his father for anyone that would have seen him would have also seen that his manhood was pushing his loincloth out from his hips. Quickly he wove through the huts of the village to the farthest hut to the south. The home his father had chosen was secluded behind a small stand of trees. He had preferred his privacy and this time Zachariah was very grateful for his father's decision.

The candles and lamps were burning so he was certain his parents had not returned to bed after the competition yet he hoped that they would not be in the main room as he entered. He pushed the door open and was relieved to see the room was empty. He hurried across the room and laid the woman on some sitting pillows upon the floor and then shouted for his mother.

The tone of his voice must have alerted her that something was wrong for she came running out of the storage cellar with an anxious look upon her face. When her eyes saw the woman she gasped and ran over to her. Quickly she pulled a cloth over the woman covering her and for the first time since Zachariah had laid her down he took a breath.

He had not realized that her beauty had so entranced him that he had almost completely stopped breathing until he could no longer see her near naked body.

His mother looked up at him and he heard her cough then she said, "Zachariah, will you stop looking like you have gotten your tongue caught on a spinning wheel and tell me what you know about this girl?" She turned her attention back to the girl; taking a wet rag she began to clean the dirt from her face. "Who is she, do you know? Where did you find her? Do you know why she is like this?"

His mother rattled off several more questions before Zachariah interrupted, "Mother, please, excuse me, but let me answer the best I can.

"I know not much more than you do.

"I was on my way back from the river with the water for the livestock when I saw her hand sticking out onto the road.

"At first I thought that maybe she was dead, or had been waylaid by brigands, but I could not see any bruises or harm to her, yet she was unconscious. I did not know what else to do so I brought her here."

His mother's eyes turned toward him and he could see a look of rebuke in them. She was about to scold him for something, and he knew even before her words came out what it would be. "You did not bother to take your shirt off and cover her before you touched her, Zachariah. You shameful man! You know it is wrong for a man to touch a naked woman that he is not married to."

Zachariah lowered his head, "Yes, mother, I know, but I did not stop to think of the laws, I thought only of her wellbeing and knew she needed assistance. If she were truly hurt, it could have been that my taking the time to cover her could have endangered her life."

"Zachariah! That is only an excuse so that you could touch her." His mother stood up and handed him a scrub brush and a bar of lye, "Now go out and scrub the skin from your hands for your sin, and be thankful I do not have you scrub it from your eyes too."

He took the bar of lye and brush and turned to head out but heard his mother say, "My son, the law is the law and I must uphold it, but in my heart I feel you did the right thing."

When Zachariah returned his hands were red and sore from the scrubbing but his heart was filled with pride at the words his mother had spoken. As he walked in and his hands touched the door he winced at the pain. He was not one to take his mother's punishments lightly and he had indeed scrubbed at least the outer layer of skin from his hands, there were even places from which they bled.

Yet his mind was not on his pain long as he saw his mother pull the blanket back over the young woman he had seen that she had been cleaned and her mother had dressed her in one of the white shift dresses that she sometimes wore to rituals. When the blanket fell about the woman's neck, Zachariah's eyes were once again locked upon a face so beautiful he was forgetting to breathe. His head began to get light and his world spun when a massive shocking blow to his back forced him to inhale.

His father had patted him hard in the back as he walked by and said, "So, Zachariah goes out for water and brings home a woman. I tell you, Rachel, that boy of ours is something special. He is the strongest boy around, wins a competition, still goes to do his chores, and not only does his chores but carries a woman at the same time."

His father sat down on the rugs as his mother brought out a loaf of bread and a jug of water for the morning meal. Zakarias turned to his son and added, "I bet he already has in his mind to marry this woman too, considering he has not found a bride amongst the village." Then suddenly he burst into a merry laughter.

Zachariah felt like he wanted to crawl in a hole. He knew that the merriment was at his expense. His parents had not pushed him to get married, but like any father and mother they had occasionally asked him if he had plans to. After Rachel had given Zakarias the bread and water she looked to her son's hands and frowned, "My son, sometimes you take me too literally. I did not mean for you to actually scrub the skin off your hands. You need these to help your father and do your chores."

"They will heal mother, besides, it is best that if anyone in the village saw me carry her in that they see I carried out a punishment fully with no slacking."

Rachel shook her head and went to get some clean cloth, as she turned she added, "Sometimes our son is too wise for his own good. His hands may be permanently scarred from this scrubbing but he is right as well. If a villager saw this woman and him touching her if he did not get punished they could demand he or she be stoned."

Zakarias nodded, "Rachel, he is right, they will heal, and with your balm and care I am certain they will not scar." After she had left the room he turned to his son, "Zachariah, your mother worries about you, and when you take her punishments so deeply it hurts her. Sometimes she cries herself to sleep after you have punished yourself like this. Please lighten them a little for her sake."

Zachariah looked to his father and then to the door his mother had vanished through. He'd had had no idea that he was hurting her by obeying her, "Yes father. I will."

No more than a moment or two passed but they passed in silence as both men waited for Rachel's return. She quickly entered carrying a bucket and basket that she sat down in front of Zachariah. She pulled a small stool over beside him and sat on the stool. From the basket she took out a jar covered with a leather lid that she untied. Then she took some of the balm from within and generously coated Zachariah's hands with it.

He tried not to grimace as she worked on his hands but even with the salve the damage he had done was severe. Slowly the healing salve did its work and the pain diminished. Even if it would be several days before his hands were healed at least they would not hurt as badly. Then she took some clean cloth and tore it into strips, wrapping his fingers and then his hands, so that he could use his hands and continue to do the work and chores that he had to do.

Even though his hands were hurt, the chores could not be left undone and it was his job to do them. He also was still an apprentice to his father so that work too would need to be done. He had no time to rest and let them heal. He would have to work while they healed. Besides it was his own fault they were damaged. He had sinned, and he had carried his mother's punishment further than she had intended. In both cases the damage was because of him, so he would deal with the pain.

When his mother had finished administering to his hands he joined his father on the rugs and his father tore him a piece from the loaf of bread. Rachel returned from the storage area with a large wedge of cheese and though it was not customary that women sat and ate with the men in the village Zakarias preferred that his wife eat with them so she sat down and took a knife and cut chunks of the cheese and passed first to her husband and then to her son before cutting herself a piece.

"So, Rachel, what is with our mysterious guest?"

"Papa," Rachel said, "I cannot see anything wrong with her. There are no wounds, no bruises, no broken bones, and no lumps upon her head.

"She seems fine except for her stomach is a little shallow like she has had too little to eat, and her skin a little pale like too little time in the sun.

"Her heart beats as it should, and her skin is warm to the touch like to should be, not too warm. I still need to wash the grime from her hair, but otherwise she is clean and healthy as best I can tell." Rachel looked at his father and smiled. Her eyes glistened and Zachariah could see how much she adored his father.

"It is not a plague? Is it?"

"No, Papa. There are no signs of any plague I have heard of. Her breathing is normal. It is like she is simply asleep."

He turned to Zachariah and asked, "And you say you found her lying beside the road?"

"Yes, father. I thought she was dead at first, but then I saw her breathing. I did not know what else to do but bring her here. I know mother is the best with herbs and medicine and if anyone could help her she could."

***

"Papa Zach," Melanie interrupted his story, "please excuse me, but I have a question."

"Go ahead, precious." Zachariah said then he leaned over and kissed her cheek to let her know it was okay that she had interrupted.

"It is just that in all the legends of Vampires I have ever heard they were like they were dead. They had no heartbeat, they were cold. Sometimes they would even sleep in coffins so that people would think they were dead and leave them alone." Melanie's eyes were glistening, Zachariah could not tell if it was from the tale or from her love for him but he let her continue her question. "Why is Lilith's condition so different?"

He smiled at her, "Very perceptive of you, sweetheart. Maybe it would be a good idea for me to cover a few vampire facts to the best of my discoveries anyway. However, before I begin let me say that there are many myths and legends and though some have truth at their foundations some are nothing more than falsehoods. Holy Water does not affect a vampire of any kind. Icons like crosses do not work to protect a person from a vampire if the person does not have true faith in their God, and even then it is not the icon as much as it is the faith. A Christian whose faith is not Cross centered will get no protection from a cross at all, the words of the Bible and their own faith are more protection to them. Yet a Catholic who is not true to his faith will also get no help from the Cross. So many of the myths are just that; myths.

"Now, including Lilith, and she is a lone specimen in her species, there are several species of Vampire. Lilith prefers to call herself by the

Hebrew term Wampyr, so we will use it to define her species as separate and distinct from the other two. When Lilith was cursed she was very much alive. She had eaten from the tree of Life, and she had never died. God did not kill her. So I think her curse kept her in this living state. She still was not able to see the sun, and she still had to drink blood or life's fluids as the other vampires but she had some advantages in that she was indistinguishable from a living person.

"As far as the other species of vampires, they all have one very important thing in common. They were all dead before they became vampires. They are animated corpses, the undead.

"Lilith never died, she was the undying. Had it not been for the love I had for her she could not have killed her flesh form, but even then it did not kill her spirit or release it to go to the next realm. She is still trapped here."

Melanie looked at him. He could see something like pride in her eyes and yet bewilderment, then she asked one more question. "Papa Zach, how do you know all this? How would you know for certainty the way you do that this is true?"

"I don't know if everything Lilith has told me is true or not. I do know about the species of the vampires. That has to do with the magic in the stone and it is one of the reasons I know it is good."

Melanie sat forward and placed her chin on her hands. Zachariah could see that she was very interested in hearing all he had to tell her about vampires. He smiled at her, halfway suspecting that if she had a library at home it was filled mostly with fictional stories of vampires and maybe a few non-fiction books upon the myths of them as well. He sensed she was excited to get some information from someone that had firsthand knowledge. He knew she would not like his response, "Sweetie, that is part of another story for another time. There are too many things I have to tell you about Lilith and I could get lost telling you all the side details. So for that answer you will have to wait." He was right. He saw her lips curl in a pout, a pout he could not resist as he leaned forward and kissed her lips. She returned the sweet kiss and then sat up and waited patiently for him to continue.

He looked at her a moment, his heart enraptured by her. "Oh!" he interjected, "I remembered there is something I wanted to tell you about my mother and father.

Melanie brightened, he did not think it was possible for a person to glow but she truly seemed to be glowing she was so happy.

"Rachel had called Zakarias Papa from the day they were married.

"He was ten years older than her but it was not because of their differences in age that she called him that. She had felt the need to show him a profound respect and the only way she could was to call him the same thing she had called the only other man in her life she had respected, her father.

"When she had asked if it was okay to call him Papa he had told her it would be an honor for her father was a great man. They were always happy, and there were even times late at night I would hear my father slip and call her Mama." Zachariah smiled at the memory of the sound of his parents' lovemaking when he was young. It no longer embarrassed him but brought a warm feeling to his heart that his house had been so filled with love.

He turned to Melanie and added, "That was why I was so honored when you asked to call me Papa. It was in a way like you were showing the same respect for me that my mother showed to my father."

Melanie rose up, wrapped her arms around Zachariah's neck and whispered, "I love you, Papa" then she kissed him hard. When she released her hold Zachariah had to think to begin breathing again. He smiled at her.

After a moment of them both smiling at each other he said, "Now where was I, oh yes, I had just told my father I had brought Lilith to our house because if anyone could help her I knew my mother could."

***

Zakarias nodded, "You did right, my son.

"Now if she will wake up, maybe we can find out more about her." He turned to Rachel, "Any idea when she might awake?"

"No, Papa," she said. "It could be today, it could be tomorrow, it could be days from now.

"I know she has not eaten so I am boiling a stock of some meat and vegetables now. I will strain off the broth, let it cool and then spoon it to her. Hopefully her body is hungry enough that it will take it even in her sleep. This way I can keep her alive until she awakes. If not, then without food and water she could die, even tonight."

Zachariah felt his heart sink. There was no way that the Creator could allow this woman to come into his life and then be taken away so quickly. She had to be able to eat. He stood and felt the eyes of his father upon him. Zakarias said, "Son, you have not finished your meal."

"Father, I have chores that still need to be done. Besides I am not hungry. May I be about my chores?" He was praying inside that his father would not deny him the chance to step away, he could not bear to remain inside right then and he fought to hold the sigh when he saw his father's head nod and permission was granted. Quickly he knelt and kissed the top of his mother's head and then went outside.

Chapter Eight

He paused outside the door only long enough to kneel and lift the yoke to his shoulder. Then he carried it around back and began his chores. Watering the livestock and then making certain that grain was spread in the bins for them to eat. Once that was done he turned and walked to the stand of trees that separated his father's property from the rest of the village and entered the woods. The woods extended into a much deeper forest that ran to the west and south of the village and Zachariah soon found the path that he had been following since he had turned twelve.

On that day he had decided to run away from home. His father had punished him and told him he could not begin studying the basics of being a jeweler for another year because he had not gotten his chores done on time. It had not been his fault. It had been one of those competitions that Tobiah had demanded he do. So Zachariah had put some of his things upon a cloth and tied the corner of the cloth together and then threw it over his shoulder and into the woods he had trudged. He had been lost in less than a half hour, but had come across this path that some animal had made. So he had followed it in hopes that it would take him out of the woods but instead it had taken him even deeper.

Eventually it led him to a small spring where he had gotten a fresh drink of water and some fresh red berries to eat. Then he saw it. It was like nothing he had seen. It was a large flat rock, nearly round, and almost completely flat. He had christened it table rock, and set his pack down and went to sleep on the rock. While asleep he'd had a dream of a lady with long black hair coming to him and singing him a song, but he never saw her face. From that day on whenever he had any spare time Zachariah would come to the stone bearing tools. He began to work on the stone to make it smoother, and rounder, so that when the lady came it would be ready for her. For three years he had kept it up, but when he turned fifteen it suddenly seemed like a childish thing to do so he had stopped.

Now Zachariah headed straight to that stone. Was this the woman of his dream? He was not certain if she was or not but when he got to the stone he looked at it. Then he stripped off all his clothing and laid them on the ground and climbed onto the rock. Kneeling upon the cold stone he looked up into the sky and prayed, "Lord, I pray to you, do not take this woman. I have never felt love before and I now know what love is. I truly love this woman. Please, Lord. Let her live."

Then Zachariah wept. He wept well past the rising of the sun. Thunder sounded in the distance and he felt the cold splash of rain land gently at first upon his skin, then within moments it was a downpour drenching him. Zachariah rose and gathered his clothing, they too were soaked but it would not do to return naked so he dressed before turning toward his father's house.

As he walked into his father's house he saw his father had left but his mother was seated beside the woman and was just about to stand. She turned and looked at him. Her eyes filled with worry. His heart sank and then her words came, "Zachariah, you are going to get sick. Get out of those wet clothes and get dried. Then once you are warm join your father in the shop. He is expecting you."

His eyes darted past her to the woman, and he heard his mother add, "Don't you worry about her. She has a healthy appetite. She drank two full bowls of the broth. Even if she does not wake for days she will not starve or die of thirst. All we have to worry about now is whether or not her mind will be healthy when she wakes." Then he felt her hands pushing him toward his room. "Now get out of those wet clothes, you foolish boy. I do not need to be tending to two patients."

He turned, and his heart was already lighter. God had heard his prayers. Zachariah was out of the wet clothes dried and out to join his father in a matter of only a few moments. His hair was still wet, but he wrapped a cloth around his head to keep any water from dripping into the smelting pot while he helped to melt down the silver for the lesson his father was going to teach that day.

As with every lesson his father taught, Zachariah got so wrapped up in it that he did not notice the time pass. His hands did not feel the heat; his body did not notice the strain. It was as if this was what he had been born to do and by the end of the day he had actually forged his first pieces of silver jewelry. They were not elaborate, not much more than simple bands that he had taken a small tool and added a little decorative scrollwork with while they were still warm. His father looked at them and smiled, "My boy, you will make a fine jeweler someday. For today I think you deserve a promotion. I promote you to apprentice second grade. Tomorrow we will begin teaching you how to make settings for gemstones upon your pieces."

Zachariah smiled. He did not feel he was ready for the raise in rank but he had learned never to argue with his father so he accepted his father's praise. Together they carried his first two rings into the house for his mother to see.

He was disappointed to see that the woman was still asleep but her breathing was steadier and that filled his heart with peace for now he had hope she would live. As they ate he could hear his parents talking but his mind was not upon their words and more times than not his eyes were upon their sleeping guest. He had no idea how long the room had been quiet but he suddenly looked at his parents and they were both staring at him. As he tried to say something they burst into laughter. Rachel said, "I think our son has found someone his heart belongs to even before he has seen her eyes or heard her voice."

Then his father added as best he could between his laughs, "Careful, boy, you need to know a woman before you love her. There could be a viper in that woman's spirit and she might have venom in her words."

Rachel's eyes turned to Zakarias and she said with a hint of playful hurt in her voice, "Papa!"

He laughed and pulled her into his arms and hugged her tight, "Not you, my wife, but you know it is true. Some women can think of nothing better to do than to find a nastier or meaner way to sting someone with the words they speak."

"But Papa, men do it too."

Zakarias threw back his head and laughed harder, "No, my love, men do not. We just punch each other instead." That sent all three into a laughing fit so hard that none of them noticed that the strange woman had sat up on the mats she was resting on and was looking at the three rather strangely.

Softly a strange yet melodious voice interrupted their laughter, "Excuse me."

All three of their heads turned towards her and the room was silent again as she added, "How did I get here?"

Zachariah's heart stopped. Her eyes were so dark blue that he was lost within them and could not speak at all. Rachel rose up from her husband's lap and went to kneel beside her and took her hand, "My son," she indicated Zachariah with a nod of her head, "found you on the side of the road. He thought you might be hurt and brought you here.

"I am a midwife and an herbalist, what most people around here would say passes for a doctor. I can set a bone, or stitch a wound if need be and if you were hurt it was best he brought you here, but there was nothing wrong with you that a little food did not help."

The woman looked at Rachel strangely, "Food?"

Rachel stood and went to the cook pot and brought another bowl of broth over to her. "Here you go. I don't know how long it has been since you have eaten, but it may be a little soon for solid food."

Lilith took the bowl and looked into it then handed it back and said, "I am sorry, I cannot eat this it will make me sick."

Rachel almost laughed before she said, "Sweetie, you have already eaten three full bowls of it today and all three stayed down.

"Is your stomach bothering you?"

The look on woman's face made Zachariah think of someone that had just been told they were going to have a baby. It was a complete look of shock. Then she said, "No, in fact, I do not feel hungry at all. I feel very full."

She lowered her eyes and closed them and shook her head. Zachariah could hear her whispering, "How can this be? How can this be?" Then she looked up and took the bowl of broth back and took a tentative sip from the bowl. She was acting almost as if the liquid inside it was poison, but after a moment she took another sip, then a smile crossed her face and she looked at everyone in the room and drank deeply of the broth. When she was done she wiped her mouth with her arm and a laugh that touched Zachariah's soul exploded from her lips as she fell backwards on the mat and let the laughter loose from her lungs. It seemed as if she had not eaten in so long that the very thought of eating was a miracle to her.

As beautiful and lovely as the laughter was it was shockingly disturbing when it abruptly ended and the woman bolted upright and backed into the corner pulling the blanket about her. "I do not see any candles or lanterns burning," she said.

"It is too early for that, sweetie," Rachel answered her. "The sun is still out and there are no clouds today."

"The sun!" The woman said with more than a little terror in her voice,

"I am allergic to the sun."

Rachel looked at her oddly, "I have heard of allergies to plants but not the sun, are you sure? What happens when you get in the sunlight?"

The woman looked at her frantically and pulled the blanket up over her head, "It burns me. It hurts. It feels like I am on fire."

"Do you feel like you are on fire now?" Rachel asked her.

"No."

Then Zakarias asked, "Are you in any pain at all?"

The woman lowered the blanket and looked at him and answered, "No."

"Honey, will you look at your foot?" Rachel asked.

The woman did and for a moment it looked like she was about to scream. For upon her foot was a small spot of sunlight that was coming through a hole in the roof thatch. It was not much bigger than a person's thumb but it was definitely the light of the sun. The woman wiggled her toes and looked at it. Her eyes grew bigger as she did. She reached forward and waved her hand under the ray of light and as she did a smile crossed her face.

Like a rabbit leaping out of its hole she threw aside the blanket and bounded to her feet and out the front door. Zachariah was right behind her, followed closely by Rachel and Zakarias. The three stared at her in amazement as she looked up at the sun as if she had never seen it. She began swirling about in the sun and dancing. She looked at them and then said to Zachariah, "You are the one that found me, right?"

"Yes."

"Dance with me." She did not wait for his answer but grabbed him by the hands and began swinging him about in a circle. Before long all four were dancing in a circle together laughing and singing. Although Zachariah was supposed to fix the roof the chore did not get done that night.

Through the afternoon and early evening they asked her many questions but she did not remember much of her past beyond her name. They laughed about her name and its tie to the legend of Lilith and the Garden of Eden. It also seemed to Zachariah that she was more interested in learning about them anyway.

Late in the night she sampled some cheese and bread and a little meat and laughed with each bite she took like she had never had them before. Zachariah was thrilled for it was like he was introducing her to life and with each moment his heart grew closer to her.

Over the next few months Lilith became like part of the family. She took on chores and helped wherever she could. She even joined Zachariah and his father in the shop and began to learn the craft herself. Everyone was amazed at how quickly she picked it up. She had almost as much natural talent as Zachariah did.

The two young adults became inseparable but they also were never alone. Zachariah would not allow it, and it often seemed to him that that sometimes frustrated Lilith. It was as if she did want to be alone with him but he just did not feel it was proper. They were not even engaged, and definitely not married. So he made certain that wherever they were there was always another adult with them.

Three months passed and one day he had made a decision. That morning when Lilith stepped outside and took his hand she asked him where their escort was. "Today I have something special I want to show you, so I do not think we need an escort. Besides I think we are adult enough we can be trusted to behave."

The smile on her face made him doubt that he was going to have the willpower to behave if she truly wanted to misbehave. He took her hand and led her into the woods and to the path that he had followed many years before and on that night when she had first come to the house.

"Ah, a hidden secret place," she laughed. Zachariah could feel the heat in his loins rise just hearing her sensual laughter, but he would not allow that to happen, not yet. He had to have things right. He tried to ignore his building hunger as he pulled her deeper into the woods.

Finally he came to the large stone table and stopped. Then turned to her and said, "On the night I brought you into the house my mother did not think you would live. I came out here and stripped down and knelt upon that stone table and prayed with all my heart and soul to God to let you live."

Lilith's eyes looked at him strangely then at the stone. "Why would you do that? You did not know me at all."

"The moment I saw you on the road my heart stopped. I knew that very second that I loved you and that if you were not already married or betrothed I would one day ask you to marry me."

She took a step away from him and looked into his eyes, the look on her face was very serious. "Did you say you loved me? From the very moment you saw me?"

"Yes! From the first time I saw your face. Your clothing was in tatters but I did not look at your body, my eyes were locked to your face. I knew I loved you then."

Lilith looked to the ground and then up at the sun, and whispered, "That explains everything."

It was Zachariah's turn to be confused, "What? What explains what?"

"Don't worry about it, Zach. Go on with what you were saying." She said as she put her hands upon his shoulders.

"Lilith, I want you to marry me. Since this stone is where I prayed for God to spare your life, I wanted to ask you here. Will you be my wife?" Zachariah's heart was beating so hard in his chest that he thought Lilith had to hear it.

She did not wait anytime at all to respond, "Yes. I will marry you!"

Then she wrapped her arms around his neck and kissed him like he had never been kissed. In fact he had never been kissed beyond the kiss of his mother. Lilith's tongue invaded his mouth and he was surprised but he loved the sensation and before long he was reveling in the passion that was burning between them. Then Lilith stepped back and with a quick pull of a couple of knotted ties her shift fell to the ground and she stood before him naked. "Zachariah I have wanted you to make love to me since the day I first saw you."

This was something he could not do. Quickly he turned and covered his eyes.

"Is there something wrong with me, Zach?"

"No, Lilith. On the contrary, you are beautiful, and were we married I would not hesitate to make love to you here and now, but I cannot. It is not in me to make love to you before our wedding night. Please understand, I want to, I just can't. It is against everything I believe." Zachariah was turning redder with each second and he was trying to keep from turning around. He wanted to look at the woman he was now engaged to, for she was indeed the most beautiful woman he could have imagined, but he could not.

After a moment he heard Lilith say, "It is okay, Zach, you can turn around."

When he did she was again covered. She wrapped her arms around him and said, "My gallant fiancé, at least I know you have never been with another woman and I know you will never cheat upon me." Then she kissed him again and when the kiss ended asked, "How soon can we be married?"

"Normally the minimum engagement period the village elders allow is a year. I can approach them and maybe get it reduced to six months."

Lilith frowned, "Even six months seems such a long time to wait to be married to you, but if I must wait the year I will do that as well." Lilith pulled Zachariah tight to her and they hugged and kissed each other again before walking arm in arm back to the house of Zakarias.

Zachariah held back the furred hide that acted as a door to let Lilith in and no sooner than they entered than Rachel, whose back was to them asked, "Where have you two been?"

Zakarias was seated and Rachel was handing him a bowl of something for the evening meal but he immediately set the bowl aside and stood up. Rachel was almost bowled over as he stepped forward and took his son in his arms and said, "It is about time."

"How? How?" Zachariah could not even form the sentence.

His father put his hands on his shoulders and held him at arm's length, "I could see it in your eyes." Then he turned and hugged Lilith and said, "I guess I should begin calling you daughter."

Rachel dropped the second bowl she was holding and her jaw dropped with it. Tears came to her eyes, "Why am I the last to know?" Then she leapt across the room and jumped up and hugged her son with all her strength and added, "I knew the day you brought her here and you could not keep your eyes off her that you loved her but I had only dreamt that she would return the love. Since she has no family we could not go to her father and arrange a marriage so it had to be her choice."

She kissed his cheek, "I am so happy for you." Then she turned to her husband, "Now if you will let go of my future daughter-in-law I would like to hug her myself."

Zakarias laughed and said, "But Rachel, it has been so long since I have hugged such a young and lovely thing as she."

Rachel pulled her arm back and hit him as hard as she could in the shoulder and added, "And it may be a long time before you get to hug any woman ever again if you do not let go of her now."

He rubbed his shoulder but stepped back laughing merrily. There was no doubt that he loved his wife with all his heart and the occasional tease and spat that he had with her only reignited the passions that they felt for each other. Zachariah prayed that he and Lilith would have even half the joy that his parents had had in their life for even then they would truly be blessed.

As soon as Zakarias had let loose of Lilith Rachel had wrapped her arms around her and kissed her cheeks, "Welcome to the family, my daughter.

"I have so badly wanted to call you that for weeks. You have become a part of this family even before now and to know you and my son are to be married makes my heart sing." Again she kissed her cheek and added, "Well, there will be much to do before the wedding. Have you two decided when that will be?"

Zachariah looked at both of them and looked down, "I told her about the tradition, and truth is neither of us wish to wait that long."

"And I do not think you should have to," popped in Zakarias. "I will speak to the village elders and see when is the soonest that they will allow the two of you to be married. As far as I am concerned you began courting the day she came here so that time should count for something."

Rachel added, "And Zachariah is beyond the normal marrying age that too should count for something. They should reduce the amount of time even further." She turned to Zakarias, "See what you can do, Papa. Personally, I think tomorrow is not too soon, but I know they will not allow that."

Zakarias laughed, "Rachel you just want another baby in this house."

Zachariah could feel the flush come to his face, he turned quickly before anyone could notice, however as he turned to look at Lilith he was surprised not to see a blush upon his betrothed's face. It amazed him that she could hide her embarrassment so well. "Father, the village elders do not meet for two more weeks."

"I am one of the elders and I can call a meeting. Besides I think I heard something today about someone wanting an early meeting about Bereth, the village to the west of us. I will go to the elders in the early morning and see if I can get a meeting for tomorrow afternoon." Then he patted his son's shoulder. "Son, I will do all I can to help you and your bride have an early wedding. I feel you deserve it."

Then he whispered in Zachariah's ear, "Besides if Rachel does not have a grandbaby in this house soon I think she is going to drive me insane. Just knowing you are engaged and not making babies is going to make her nearly mad." Then he stood back and laughed.

Rachel looked at him and crossed her arms, "Are you laughing at my expense?"

Quickly Zakarias said, "No, my wife, not at all." Then he and Zachariah nearly doubled over in laughter and had to step outside.

Normally the house of Zakarias was a house that did not drink wine or alcohol of any kind but that night Zakarias took his son into the village and to the house of Tobyas. Though Tobiah and Zachariah had not been good friends, Tobyas and Zakarias had been the best of friends since early childhood. When Tobyas was told about the engagement he welcomed the two in and pulled out a flask of his finest wine. Even his son was asked to join and the four drank not just that one flask but three more as well.

Zachariah did not remember getting home but he did remember the sudden splash of cold water hitting him and looking up at two very angry women standing over him and his sputtering father as they both tried to sit up and shake off the effects of the wine.

Chapter Nine

To Zachariah the day went very slowly. His father had vanished immediately after breakfast, while he had done his chores. He had even done things around the house that had not been a part of the list of things he was supposed to do because he had finished his chores early. Normally he would have been in the shop with his father but he could not concentrate on making jewelry while his father was out trying to gather a meeting of the elders. He felt his stomach roiling and knew that the meeting would have been rejected.

He looked up into the sky and the sun was at its apex, so he turned toward the house and walked home for the midday meal. As he walked in he saw his father already seated and his mother and Lilith getting ready to serve the meal.

In silence he sat down beside his father and let the women serve them and then take their seats. It was too quiet, so he bowed his head and thanked God for his father for trying to arrange an early wedding. It was then he felt the heavy slap of his father upon his back. Laughter rung out, "Why so glum? You have a meeting to prepare for after the meal."

Zachariah looked up almost choking. "They are calling a meeting?"

"Well, your business was not the only reason, but they all said even if it was the only one your reason was good enough to call a meeting on its own." He smiled at Zachariah, "I told you, my son, the elders here are good people."

Zachariah could feel his lips pulling into a smile so broad he tried to hide it behind his bread but it was too late. Rachel said, "Now, if you can just get that grin off your face long enough to eat maybe you can get cleaned up and go to that meeting as a proper young man."

"Should I go with him?" Lilith asked.

Rachel put her hand on her shoulder and said, "No, my daughter, I do not know the ways of your village, but in ours, women are not allowed at the meeting of the elders."

Zachariah saw Lilith lower her head. He could almost swear he saw her eyes turn a brilliant red but she kept quiet and whatever had glowed red for a moment disappeared. It had to have been an illusion. No one's eyes glowed like that.

About an hour later Zachariah followed his father into his first elders' meeting. Normally he would not have even been allowed to observe the meeting, for only married men of the village were allowed to witness the meetings. However since part of the meeting was going to be about him he was allowed to enter for the entire meeting.

Tobyas stood and announced that the meeting was an emergency meeting called for two reasons. The first order of business was to deal with an incident that occurred at the village of Bereth. There were two men of Bereth that had come to the village to speak about a serious matter. The second was to deal with a matter concerning Zachariah.

All the elders looked to Zachariah and several of the men began in hushed whispers to mutter amongst themselves wondering what it might be. Many had seen the woman Lilith, and more than a few suspected it had to do with setting a date for a wedding but it was unusual to come before the elders for that.

Tobyas motioned to the two men of Bereth to stand and come forward.

They rose and carried a heavy wooden box between them. They sat the box upon a table at the front of the gathered villagers. The two men opened it and spilled its contents upon the table. Out tumbled some clothing filled with the bones of a human, but the clothing looked almost new. It definitely had not been long enough for the body in the clothing to have turned to dust, for the clothing would have in that length of time become rags.

"This is how we found Macob. We know this is Macob because of this." One of the men raised the skeletal hand and showed a ring upon the finger bone. "Macob was my brother. He was only one year older than me."

One of the elders stood and asked, "So why do you dress his bones in new clothing and bring him to us."

"No." Macob's brother said, "You do not understand. These were the clothes he was wearing last week when he disappeared."

There was a gasp from the group and then another elder stood and said, "Are you telling us that those bones are the bones of a man that was alive last week?"

"Yes," the other man said. A cacophony of whispers arose amongst the elders as they tried to ponder the possibility of such an event.

"I am his father, Coboth is my name," the man continued. "Macob broke his leg when he was but six summers old. It was not set properly and he hath walked with a limp since. The leg bone of this here skeleton was broken and not set properly." The man held the bone up to show how the bone was misaligned and then added, "I know this is the thigh bone of my son. This is all the proof I need."

One of the elders asked, "How is this possible?"

Again a cacophony of whispers erupted and it spread from the elders to the villagers that were gathered to witness the meeting. The volume rose as each struggled to be heard above the other whisperers. Soon shouts were being thrown as one would say that it was not possible that only God could cause such a thing to happen and another would say he had heard of legends. Finally, Tobyas had to strike the floor with his staff to get the group to settle.

When the crowd had silenced he addressed them, "We have come here to let these men present their case. They have come here to warn us of a potential danger. Now let them finish." He turned and nodded to the older man to continue.

Coboth said, "There are legends of a monster of long ago, that can kill a man and steal his soul. That monster can then walk about as if it is that man. Yacob here thought he spied Macob in Saldoth at a fair, he tried to chase him down yet when he caught him and turned him about it was someone else. Yacob swears that it was Macob only a moment before, that even the color of the hair changed.

"I think the monster doth exist. What else is there that could turn a man to bones except a judgment from God himself? Macob was a good man. He followed the law."

Tobyas stood and said, "Coboth, I am not disagreeing with you, but who can say we know the mind of God?"

Coboth huffed, and began to put the bones back into the box, "When it is one of your own whose bones you find then maybe you too will believe."

"Coboth, I said I was not disagreeing with you. It could be a monster. Or it could be someone is playing some hoax on you and your family for some reason. If Macob has been missing for two weeks then I think he has met foul play or an accident, but I have a difficult time believing these bones are his." Tobyas looked about the elders, "Has anyone here heard of the legend that Coboth mentioned?"

One lone hand rose. Slowly the man stood. His spine would not straighten as age had bent him to where he had lost nearly a foot of his height. He shook a he held onto his cane and another man helped to steady him on his feet. He was Zapeth, the oldest man of the village and when he stood everyone else was quiet with respect.

His voice sounded as if it was filled with gravel yet it was firm, "I have heard of the legend, but it was told to me by my parents to keep me out of the woods at night when I was a young child and prone to wandering. It was said that any man that gave into his lust and sought a woman that he should not have could fall prey to the Wampyr."

"Wampyr? I have not even heard that word," Tobyas pondered aloud, "but why would it be told you to scare you as a child? It seems a tale to scare men to make them control their lust."

"They also said that the Wampyr would steal children to suckle them as her own because she was barren. It is an old legend," the old man added. "I believe my father's father told me that it was from even before the flood and that he had not heard of any stories of Wampyr since."

Tobyas turned to Coboth, "If there was such a monster before the flood, surely it died during the flood. Only Noah and his family survived."

Coboth nodded. "Maybe, or maybe it found a way to survive and stay hidden until now.

"I swear these are the bones of my son, and I will find the monster that slew my son if it takes my entire life to do so." Then Coboth and Yacob lifted the chest and left the building. They had come for assistance in their hunt for a monster and had found only disbelief. Something inside Zachariah told him that they were not wrong, but how he knew he had no idea, and he was a lone voice within his village.

Tobyas waited until the two men had left and then stood again before the elders. "I want us to put those thoughts from our minds. Whether true or not, they are thoughts we can dwell on at another time.

"We have one in our village that deserves our attention and all of our thoughts should be directed toward him.

"Zachariah approach and address the elders," commanded Tobyas motioning Zachariah forward. From the day he could first walk and until now Zachariah could not remember his knees ever feeling so wobbly, neither could he remember his stomach feeling so tied in knots. As he began the walk he felt more like he was walking toward his death than to a new life with the woman he loved. Each step felt like his legs had gained another twenty pounds and it was harder to make that next step and yet somehow he found himself on the platform and turned facing the elders and the villagers.

He opened his mouth and at first nothing came out. His voice had gone, then suddenly the words miraculously came into the air, "As many of you know three months ago I found a woman on the road who I had thought was injured or harmed in an attack.

"I brought her to my parent's house for my mother is the one whom all of you seek when you are ill or hurt and it was the best place to take her if indeed she was hurt.

"When she recovered she was healthy, but remembered nothing of her past. There are no signs that she was married before. There were no marks, no jewelry.

"She has none of the signs she was ever married. She has none of the piercings that some do as part of the wedding ceremony, nor does she show the marks where she has worn a ring. In the three months she has been with us no one has come to the village looking for her.

"For three months she has stayed with my family and has become a part of our household. I do not know if she is of the twelve tribes. Her characteristics look like she could be, but I could not swear to it. Yet in my heart it does not matter.

"Last night I asked her to be my wife." The room filled with yells and cheers. Zachariah could not continue talking as several of the men, elders and villagers alike jumped up and began to congratulate him. They hugged him and kissed his cheeks, several said that it was well past the time he should have been married and they were very happy for him.

Tobyas finally got them to quiet down and said, "That is not the reason the boy is here. He is not here just to announce his engagement. Please sit and listen."

It took a few more minutes but everyone returned to their seats and Zachariah was able to continue, "As you know, normally a man marries when he is eighteen. On my next birthday I will be twenty one. We have no idea of Lilith's age; my mother says that from her health and body she guesses she is between seventeen and twenty which means she too is beyond the normal marrying age.

"Lilith and I wish to be married as soon as the elders will allow us to be. Custom dictates a minimum of a year engagement, but I know that custom has been overruled by the elders in the past for special reasons. I ask the elders to consider my condition and allow Lilith and me to marry sooner than that one year's time." Zachariah lowered his head and added, "If it pleases you."

Then Zakarias stood and added, "I know this boy is my son, but on the day the girl entered our home I could see in his eyes that he loved her. My wife and I feel he was betrothed to her from that very moment. So I feel that the elders should consider that."

Tobyas stood, "I also want each of you to consider how much this young man has done for this village and for you.

"Zachariah once mended a portion of the village fence without being asked and with no assistance. He also fixed my sheep pen and rounded up the stray sheep, also without being asked and without recompense. In all the work he has done for us he has not once asked anything for himself.

"This is the first time he has come to any of us either singularly or as a group and asked anything. Even during that competition my son forced him into three months ago he refused to accept my awarding him the win because my son had cheated. This boy is a good man and deserves the best we can offer to him." Tobyas then took his seat.

Judyas stood and said, "I am normally one to stick to the customs but this is a time that I agree that the custom can be altered. I say we cut the time in half and we count it backwards to the day Lilith entered into their home.

"Does anyone disagree with me?"

Zachariah could not believe his ears. What Judyas had just proposed meant Lilith and he could be married in three months. He waited and all he heard was one voice after another say "Not I."

Then Tobyas stood and said, "So a vote of the elders goes, three months from today, we will allow Zachariah to marry Lilith. All those in favor say, Ye!"

It was unanimous, every elder and the village men even though they technically could not vote all stood and said, "Ye!" Even Tobiah joined in with his vote.

That night the entire village turned out for an engagement celebration. It lasted for three days. No one got any of their work done during that time, but no one cared. It was rare that such respect was found for one young man as was found for Zachariah, and the whole village joined in celebration to show how much they loved him and how happy they were for him.

The next three months went by very quickly as Rachel and Lilith were lost in the preparations for the wedding and Zachariah and Zakarias along with several other men built another house upon Zakarias' land for the soon to be married couple. Zakarias gave all his land to his son and just asked that he and his wife be allowed to live out their days there. Zachariah looked at him and hugged his father and said, "That was something you should have known you needed not to ask permission for. This is your land as well as mine and we will share it. It will only become mine when you and mother have gone to meet God."

They built a new shop between the two houses and made it quite a bit larger so that Lilith could work with them for her talent was amazing. With the three of them together they had already begun to sell quite a few pieces to outside villages and were beginning to become one of the wealthiest families in the village.

During that three months there would occasionally come news from one of the outside villages that another pile of bones had been found. Yet the village of Tobith paid little attention to it because no one from their village was directly affected by it. Not even one of the many cousins of the villagers had been harmed. So instead the village continued to prepare for the biggest wedding celebration in its history.

Part Three
The 'Z'
Chapter Ten

The day of the wedding arrived and for Zachariah it felt surreal, almost as if he was in a dream and nothing that was happening was real. The first thing that was different that day was that he was not allowed to see Lilith when he got up and ate his meal. During the night she and Rachel had been secreted away to some other house in the village and he was not allowed to even know which house it was.

He and his father served themselves their meal and to his surprise his father could cook. He had never had a meal that his mother did not prepare but his father did the meal justice. He wanted to question him about it but let it go. He was too anxious about the rest of the day.

No sooner had they finished their meal than the door flap lifted and Tobyas entered and sat down on the mats beside Zachariah. He put his hand on the young man's shoulder and said, "Well today the boy is about to become a man. Are you ready to begin, Zachariah?"

Zach turned and looked at him, his heart thundered in his chest. This was the day he had been waiting three months for but it felt like he had been waiting for it his entire life, "Yes, Elder Tobyas, I could not be more ready were it already done."

Tobyas and Zakarias laughed merrily and both stood and pulled Zachariah to his feet and guided him out the door where all the men of the village had gathered awaiting the groom. Sudden apprehension filled Zachariah. He had not been allowed to participate in this ritual before because he was not a married man and only those who were married were a part of it. From the looks on their faces he was not certain he wanted to participate, yet he would go through anything for Lilith.

Then two of the larger men snaked their arms around his and slid a yoke under his forearms and behind his back. They tied his wrist to a rope that wrapped around his waist making it impossible for him to move his arms at all. The two men then held the yoke and he heard Tobyas call for the Priest.

Soon a man from the tribe of Levi came forward. He walked up and nodded to two other men standing near Zachariah. Without any hesitancy the two men grabbed Zachariah's loincloth and breech and removed them so that from the waist down he was naked before the congregation of men. Then the Priest began to say, "It is a custom of the Tobith village that since a woman who is a virgin must shed her blood upon her wedding day so must a man. As you are already circumcised, we do a ceremonial circumcision to mark this occasion."

Zachariah's jaw dropped. He felt a man pull his manhood forward and place it upon a cutting block. He watched as the priest took a rather large and wicked looking cutting instrument from a bag he had set upon the cutting block. Then Zachariah saw only black as his knees went limp.

Cold water splashed in his face and all the men gathered about were laughing, even the Priest was on his knees he was laughing so hard. Zakarias knelt down beside his son and said, "My boy, it was a joke. No one is going to cut you."

Zachariah jumped to his feet. His arms were unbound and he was glad to see that his garments were back on but his face was red with both embarrassment and anger. He looked at his father and asked, "Does every male go through the same joke?"

"Sometimes they do not make it as far as you did before they pass out. They hear the word circumcision and down they go." The laughter started again, then his father added, "However one time one stood there long enough that the Priest was caught off guard. The man was ready to actually receive the second circumcision. So the Priest actually did knick his manhood, rather than tell him it was a joke."

He looked at his father and asked, "Who might that have been?"

Zakarias laughed, "Son, I would like to say it was me, but I did not make it as far as you did, almost, but not quite. However he was of your blood line. Your mother's father was the man. A braver man I have never met."

"What did he do when he found out it was a joke?"

"Well, the story has it that no one told him until it was the next young lad's turn to get married. After the kid passed out, your grandfather picked him up and held his manhood upon the block for the Priest and waited. That was when they remembered that he did not know it was a joke so the Priest informed him.

"Your grandfather let go of the lad's manhood and then dropped him. In silence he went to the river with a bar of lye and washed his hands until the bar of lye was gone. He never mentioned it again to anyone, nor did anyone ever mention it to anyone else. From that day on he also never went to any of the pre-marriage jokes but sat them out and waited until the groom was ready for the wedding."

Zachariah looked about and said, "I think I will follow my grandfather's example. Let's finish what needs to be done but I do not think I will join in these in the future."

"Ah son," Zakarias said, "it is just in good fun and has been done for over a hundred years."

"Maybe so, but father you know me well, and of all people you should know that this is not the kind of thing I would enjoy."

Zakarias nodded, "You are right, and perhaps I should join you as well."

Zach shook his head, "No father, this is something you enjoy and have done for many years. If you enjoy it, continue."

His father put his arms around his son and hugged him tight, "No, my boy, there are times that the elder can learn from the younger. I think it is time I stop."

Then he turned to the others that had been too busy laughing to hear the two talking softly between themselves and said loudly enough, "Let's get on with this wedding, I have a son that is eager to meet his bride."

All the men cheered and the four largest ran forward and lifted Zachariah off the ground and onto their shoulders then carried him toward the center of the village where a large platform had been erected so that all the village could witness the marriage. They sat Zachariah on the lowest step then he climbed four more and looked out across the villagers. From his view he could see the entire village and was amazed that everyone was there except for a handful of the women.

He knew they must be helping Lilith get ready for her part of the wedding.

Then the waiting began. To Zachariah it seemed like each moment lasted an hour. Every time he looked up at the sun he would have sworn it should have moved a lot further than it had and yet the shadows showed him that not even a half an hour had passed, but it felt like an entire day.

The Priest walked up onto the platform with him and handed him a length of yellow rope. It was for part of the ceremony, he had seen it used, though he did not agree with what it symbolized. It was a symbol that he was enslaving his bride. Zachariah's father never treated his mother like the servant that most men of the time did. To Zakarias Rachel was a treasure.

Zakarias had lost his first wife and child to a problem during the birth and an inexperienced midwife. He had mourned her for many years and had said he would never marry. Then one season he had taken ill and a good friend of his had sent his daughter to care for him. Had it not been for her gift of healing Zakarias would have died. After he was well she continued to come by and check on him, saying he was keeping himself too lonely in his little shop and before long a love grew. Rachel and he were married shortly after that. She had become his friend before becoming his wife and that friendship was always a key element in their marriage. It made their love far more special than anything Zachariah had ever seen and that was what Zachariah wanted for him and Lilith.

He would follow the tradition for the sake of the ceremony, but he would follow his father's example when it came to his life with the woman he loved.

In the back of his mind an image rose, he remembered finding Lilith on the side of the road and thinking she had been waylaid by brigands. What if indeed she had? What if she had been raped? Her mother had never checked her maidenhood, and when she said she had never been married they took her to be a virgin. The entire village thought she was a virgin. If she had been raped and he took her to bed and there was no virgin's blood to show her virginity to the village they would demand that she be stoned for lying to the village and to him.

He could not allow that to happen. His eyes began to dart around the platform and he tried to think. There would be nothing in the marriage bed he could use to cut himself or her to fake the virginal blood. Then his eyes caught upon the bag on the Priest's hip. It held that wicked looking blade that they had used to play the joke upon him. He hated the idea of lying more than almost anything else, but he could not let them kill the woman he loved. If he could get the blade then after he had shown the virginal blood he could sneak out and drop the blade in front of his father's house near that block that they had used for the joke. Maybe then someone would find it and tell the Priest where and the Priest would assume he had dropped it or left it after the joke.

That way Zachariah would only be telling one lie and a lie to save a life was worth it.

Zachariah coughed and stumbled bumping into the Priest.

"Are you okay, Zachariah?" The Priest asked.

"I need something to drink," which was not a lie at all for he had not had anything to drink since breakfast and the thought of what he was trying to do had caused his mouth to go completely dry. As the Priest turned, Zachariah's hand was on the cord that tied the bag closed and it untied. He could see the handle of the blade and he slipped two fingers in and deftly lifted it out while the Priest was asking someone to hand him a cup of water. It surprised Zachariah that the Priest did not notice, but surprised him even more that no one noticed. With a quick toss of one of the cords, a knot was redone and the bag looked sealed again. The blade was small, not like a large knife, so it was easy to conceal. He placed it at the top edge of his breechcloth and with a little roll of the cloth tucked it under and it looked like he was doing no more than adjusting his clothing. Just then the Priest turned and handed him an earthen ware cup filled with wine.

"I asked for water, but all the flasks around are filled with wine for the celebration." The Priest apologized.

"That will do, Teacher." Zachariah took the cup and quickly drained it.

The Priest looked at him with wide eyes, "Are you sure you were thirsty or did you need something to enhance your courage for your next few moments?"

Both men laughed and Zachariah said, "I was thirsty, but the added courage will not hurt."

As Zachariah handed the cup back down to one of the men around the platform the sound of a bell was heard, then another, twelve chimes in all rung out across the village, once for each of the twelve tribes of Israel. Zachariah rose and turned before the resonance of the first bell had ceased. He looked about the village for he still had no idea to what house Lilith had been taken.

It was not until after the third bell that he saw them coming from the south and he realized that they had taken her to what was going to be their new home. He laughed. How sneaky of them. Of all the places he might have thought to look had he had the chance that would have been the last place he would have looked. Two of the village women were in front and they held the front edges of a white cloth that was covered with some kind of yellow substance. The cloth was then draped over Lilith and he could make out the mound of her head in its center. Then behind her four more women came, two holding the trailing cloth and two holding baskets filled with flowers.

The villagers parted for the women and let them pass unimpeded as they led Lilith to the platform. Zachariah tried his best to see through the cloth but he could not. For all he knew it could be any woman in the village beneath that cloth but when he saw his mother was one of the women holding the cloth in the back he had no doubt that it was Lilith.

Curiously he looked at the yellow substance as they got closer and he realized it was a fine powder. He heard a few people sneeze as they passed and it dawned on him what it was. He was late in getting married according to the village's tradition so they had borrowed from a local custom of the native people and covered the cloth in pollen. Supposedly it was to guarantee fertility and virility. Zachariah smiled at his mother. He had no doubt that she was responsible for this idea. He knew she wanted a grandchild very badly.

He hoped that he and Lilith could deliver one for her as soon as God would allow it, but he also knew that sometimes God kept a woman barren or made a man's seed wither. Judiah and his wife had been married five years, and even though she had given him her servant to try to bring a child into the house they still had no child.

When the women came to the bottom of the platform they dropped the cloth and took Lilith by the hands to guide her up the steps. The cloth trailed the yellow pollen behind her as she climbed leaving a golden ribbon where she had walked. Zachariah smiled for he felt it was almost like God had smiled upon him and given him a true treasure for his bride.

She was led to Zachariah and her hands were placed into his. The moment her hands touched his hands he knew it was her and his doubts vanished. He wanted to throw off the cloth but he knew he could not. That was not for him to do in public. He had heard that the bride was naked under her wedding blanket and he had to wait to remove it until they were within the wedding chamber itself or others would gaze upon what was to be his alone.

The Priest began to say the words that would bind them as man and wife, before all present and before God. Then as he finished his long liturgy he motioned to Zachariah and Zach took the cord and wrapped it around Lilith's wrists. He could feel Lilith tense like she was going to turn and run but she stayed, and then the Priest added a few more words. Zachariah had the feeling deep in his stomach that if Lilith had not seen how his father had treated his mother that she would have indeed turned and fled. He hoped she knew his heart well enough to know that the old custom was not the way he wanted it either. That to him a wife was not a slave. Yes, she would cook and clean the house, but she also could share in many of the things of the husband and not be separated from him and the family.

There were some houses where the women were not even allowed to eat with the men or even talk to them. Some young men had never even seen the faces of their own mothers. Zachariah was thankful his home had not been one of those for he had grown up happy and with the love of both parents. He wanted Lilith to experience that if they ever had children.

Finally the Priest finished his words and the two ladies carrying the baskets of flowers tossed them into the air so that they fell onto the newly married couple. Zachariah lifted his bride into his arms, careful to make certain that the blanket was well wrapped around her because it was also a tradition that all the unmarried boys would come and try to pull the blanket off while he made a mad dash to his house.

What they did not expect was that Zachariah was prepared for them. He took two steps back and then with a running jump leapt over the boys and landed a good fifteen feet on the other side of them. He dropped to his knees but did not fall and the added momentum allowed him to push to a good run. The chase was on but even with him carrying Lilith in his arms none came even close to touching his bride's wedding blanket.

Quickly he dashed through the village and down the path that led to his new house. He pushed the flap aside and once inside he held Lilith tight for a moment while he caught his breath and she laughed for the sheer joy of the moment.

From beneath the blanket he heard her sweet voice say, "I cannot see a thing, but I would love to have seen the crowds face when you leapt like that. I could feel your muscles tighten. My husband must have been a sight to behold."

She paused for a moment and then said, "My husband! In truth I never thought I would want to hear my voice say those words but they feel good to come rolling off my lips, my husband." She wrapped her arms around his neck and added, "Now carry me to our bed, my husband."

Zachariah did not have to be told twice he carried his blanket wrapped wife over near the bed and stood her up in front of it. Slowly he lifted the large pollen coated blanket and was more than a little disappointed to see that the stories that she was completely naked under that one blanket were false. She was wrapped in several more veils that he had to remove from her as well. Yet each veil revealed a little more of her body, and aroused his desire for her just a bit more. It was maddeningly frustrating that it took so long and yet deliciously enticing. Each layer of the veiling revealed hints and subtle curves that lured him further until one layer revealed a single nipple. He gasped at how wonderfully the silks framed the luscious diamond and he had to pause and just look upon it a moment. Then he leaned forward and lovingly teased with his tongue and was delighted by her sweet musical moans.

The next layer allowed her other breast to be completely free and he could not resist the urge to fondle and caress it; kneading it and suckling it like a baby hungry for its mother's milk. He could feel Lilith's body trembling as he made love to just her single breast before removing the next wrapping of silken veil.

Zachariah gasped as this one revealed to him the mound of luscious black fur above the juncture of her thighs. His hand slid down and he softly ran his fingers through the fur and between her thighs. He had no idea what to expect, he had only seen a woman naked from afar that one time and then when he had brought Lilith home but he had never seen her close and the moisture there was very pleasant to his touch. Lilith moaned as his fingers caressed her. She slid her hand over his and pushed his fingers against a hard spot at the front near the fur and near where a slit in her flesh occurred. He pushed with his fingers and separated the two halves finding a treasure of warmth. He was rewarded by a deep guttural moan from his wife. She took his face in her hands and placed her lips to his kissing him hard and deeply. Then she whispered, "My husband, remove the rest of the veils and take your wife, I hunger to have you inside me."

He needed no more prompting. As quickly as he could he tore the rest of the veils from her body. Then she climbed onto the bed and lay with her thighs spread as he undressed himself. He knelt before her and kissed her thigh and looked at her saying, "Lilith, my wife, I love you with all my heart. Today we are one."

She reached out her hand to his and he took it, climbing between her thighs. With her free hand she took his manhood and guided it to her opening and whispered to him, "Do not worry about being gentle, just enter your wife and make me yours."

With one hard thrust he drove his cock deep inside her burying himself fully, but he also felt his heart sink for what he had feared was true. She was not a virgin. It did not matter to him, he loved her with all his heart, but now he would have to lie to the village to protect her and that saddened him for he had never lied before.

Lilith wrapped her legs around his hips and began to grind her hips against his and soon the thoughts of what he had to do vanished from his mind. Zachariah was lost in making love to his wife. Their bodies became as one as they danced with each other. Faster she thrust against him, and harder, for him it was the first time he had ever made love, for her he later learned, it was the first time in almost three thousand years since she had been with a man. She screamed as she neared an orgasm and as the wave overtook her she bucked wildly against him. Zachariah could not hold back his seed with her wild dance of passion and he exploded within her.

He rolled onto his back and looked up at the ceiling, the world had changed for him, he was now a man but as he was beginning to think about how wonderful it was to have Lilith as his wife he suddenly felt something he had never expected. Lilith had slid down and her tongue was sliding along his shaft. He looked down his belly at her and started to say something and she held up her hand as she slid her mouth over the head of his cock and began to suckle his cock.

She cleaned all their joint fluids from him but she continued to slide her mouth up and down upon his shaft and her tongue teased the underside of the head of his cock. It did not take long before he was fully hard again, yet she did not stop. She continued to suckle him. Faster her head bobbed up and down. Her mouth sucking, hard and then she would stop and run her tongue over the head and without warning plunge her mouth over his cock again. Zachariah had never even heard of this. If she had heard of it the act must have come from wherever she had come from. He only hoped it was told to her by the women of her village and not taught to her by some man, but he could not help but enjoy what she was doing and was soon thanking whoever it was that had taught her.

He could not hold back his seed much longer and he tried to warn Lilith but she pushed his chest down and he sprayed his seed into her mouth. He did not believe his ears as he heard her hungrily lap and slurp up his seed, drinking it. Then she sat up and looked at him smiling and said, "I hope my husband liked that, because his wife definitely did."

All Zachariah could do was nod his head yes as Lilith laughed a little. Then she climbed on top of him and guided his cock to her opening again. "Lilith, you are going to drain me dry."

She smiled, "Oh no, my love. Yet you are still hard, so one more time should not hurt you."

Another hour passed before Lilith rolled to her side and lay in the crook of his arm, snuggling with him and whispered to him, "I am so happy with you, my husband."

Zachariah looked at her and smiled then he said, "There is one thing I must do."

"What, my husband?" Lilith said with a little fear in her eyes.

"Lilith, you are not a virgin. The villagers are waiting outside this house right now for me to come out with the bloodied blanket to prove to them that you were indeed a virgin."

For the first time since Zachariah had known Lilith he saw true fear fill her eyes. "What will happen if you do not show them that blanket?"

"They will demand your death, for letting them think you were a virgin and lying to them," Zachariah said. As he saw her lower her eyes and tears come to them he ran his fingers across her face and wiped them away, "Do not worry. I had already devised a plan.

"I remembered the day I found you I thought you might have been waylaid by brigands. Since you do not remember what happened, that is still possible. If that were so it is not your fault you are not a virgin.

"Normally they search the wedding bed and area to make certain that there are no sharp objects so that what I am about to do cannot be done." Zachariah went to his clothing and pulled out the Priest's blade.

"They had also made certain that I had no knives before I went to the platform for the marriage, but the Priest had this. He had used it as a joke on me earlier in the day. Once I use it I am going to take it to the place where they played the joke and drop it on the ground. Then perhaps someone will find it and take it to him, telling him where they found it. We will be fine." Zachariah then took the blade and after taking off his shoe cut the sole of his foot and let the blood drip onto the bed.

Lilith's eyes grew wide; Zachariah had never seen them so large. Then she did something unexpected again. She licked his wound until it had stopped bleeding. "If my husband can cut himself to save my life, I can help his wound heal," she said.

Zachariah smiled at her then slid his shoe on. Then he stood on the bed and slipped the knife into the thatch of the roof just in case someone came in to search the wedding chamber. Once he was done he lifted the sheet from the bed and wrapped Lilith in the pollen coated blanket. After he put his loincloth on he placed the blood coated sheet over his forearm and guided Lilith to the door and outside where all the villagers were waiting for the news.

With one hand he threw the blood coated sheet down to his parents and said. "She is true, and she is my wife, true and just."

His father held the sheet up for all to see, and a cheer resounded throughout the crowd.

Zachariah and Lilith returned inside and lie down upon their bed cuddled together as they slept for the first night as man and wife.

Chapter Eleven

The first few months of their marriage were blissful. The couple could not have been happier. They were lost in their own little world. Zachariah still helped with the shop and the chores at his parents but the two were so much into each other's love that they spent all their time together in their house. Even though Zachariah was then eligible to attend the elders' meetings as a member of the audience he was too busy making love to his wife at every chance he got to waste what little time he had there.

After three months Zakarias asked his son to bring Lilith to dinner. Rachel was missing them and wanted to see how the newlyweds were doing. Zachariah suddenly felt a deep pang of guilt; he had not meant to shut out his mother. It had just not occurred to him that he saw his father every day at the shop, but unless he stopped by their house he did not see his mother. So he agreed and that night Lilith and he were at their door a good hour before the normal meal time so that they could spend some real time with his parents.

Lilith helped Rachel prepare the meal and they were talking together when a small accident occurred. Lilith was using a knife and for a moment was distracted in her thoughts. She cut the tip of her finger. It was not a bad cut, but it bled.

She ran out of the kitchen area and jumped into Zachariah's arms weeping like a little child. Rachel was right behind her with her basket of bandages.

"What is wrong?" Zachariah asked.

Lilith looked at him and cried, "It won't stop bleeding." She held up her finger and he saw a small drop of blood form at the tip.

Zachariah wanted to laugh, it was such a small cut and for Lilith to be reacting this way was so overblown it was almost ludicrous but he knew better for there was something in Lilith that had changed greatly since he had first met her. Her emotions had become very intense and poignant. It was like she did not know how to handle having emotions at all.

Rachel sat down beside them and began to bandage the finger, "Sweetie, it will stop. It is a small cut. It will just take a moment to clot."

Lilith looked at it and said, "But it should have stopped already."

Zachariah hugged her tight, "It will be okay, Lilith. It will be okay."

Burying her head in Zachariah's shoulder Lilith wept and said, "Nothing is okay."

Rachel looked at Zachariah and shook her head, "It could be that some of her memories are fighting to come back. Dinner is almost done. We were just slicing some cheese, so I will bring everything out. Lilith can stay with you."

As Rachel served the meal Lilith climbed out of Zachariah's lap and sat beside him. The four laughed and joked together. Yet every once in a while when Zachariah looked over at Lilith he would see her staring at the bandage upon her finger like it was some kind of plague. He truly did not know what to make of her reaction but he tried his best to keep her happy and get her mind off of it by talking about things around the shop.

"Lilith," he suddenly said, "you know how the shop needs a new table for smelting and forging?"

She nodded.

"Well of course, wood is out of the question, it would burn from the heat. So, I was wondering if you might know of a special round stone that was almost flat that with just a little work could be made into a good table."

The smile on her face was so bright he knew that she had immediately forgotten about the bandage upon her finger, "Yes, the stone that you proposed to me by."

"Do you really think it is good enough?" He said jokingly.

She placed her hands on her hips and looked at him, "Good enough, why let me tell you Zachariah, if it was good enough for you to propose to me at it is definitely good enough for you to use as a table in your shop."

Neither man could hold back their laughter as both of them burst out and began rolling. Lilith began to get red in the face and said, "Zachariah!"

"Lilith, my wife, it is already in the back of the shop," he said. "I am only teasing you. Of course it is perfect."

She leapt from her kneeling position and wrapped her arms around him hugging him and kissing his face. After a moment Rachel chimed in, "Now you two, save that for when you are back at your house."

Zakarias added, "I don't know, Rachel, they are kind of giving me a few ideas."

"Oh Papa!" Rachel blushed indignantly then she too was in her husband's arms hugging him.

After another moment Zakarias called a halt to the affection however, then said, "Zachariah, there is a second reason I invited you here tonight."

He turned and looked at his father, "Yes?"

"You have not been to any of the elders' meetings so you do not know the news about what has been happening.

"There have been more attacks and more of those bone remains found. In each case they have been from villages near us but not in any way connected to us. Not one cousin or relative of anyone from Tobith has been killed.

"The other villages are beginning to suspect that the Monster does exist and is somehow connected to our village. They want to come and do a search. They also want the elders to let them know of any new people that have come to the camp within the last year. Since Lilith is the only new person in this camp the elders have asked me to talk to you. They will not tell them about Lilith because she is now of the camp and she is protected by the camp, but they want you to know in case someone else in the village tells them."

Lilith and Zachariah looked at each other, then Zachariah said, "How could they suspect Lilith of being a monster. She is the gentlest of people I know. Besides, did not the legends say that the Wampyr cannot go out in the sun?"

Zakarias nodded, "That is correct, but they say there are other ways to tell if someone is a Wampyr. That maybe that part of the legend was not true."

"Father, if one part of the legend is not true then how do they know which parts to believe and which not?" Zachariah queried.

"That is a good question, my son, and the next time they come before the elders I will ask them that. Better yet, it would be good if you were there."

"I will be." Zachariah pulled Lilith into his arms and looked at her, "There is no way that my wife is a monster, and I will protect her with my very life if I have to."

"My son, it will not come to that, I am certain."

It was two weeks until the next elders meeting and when it came

Zachariah was there waiting for the people from the other villages to show up. He was not surprised to see Coboth amongst the group of ten men that came to the meeting to address the elders. He remembered him from the day he had stood before the elders to ask for permission to marry Lilith earlier than was customary. However, his other son was not with him and he wondered about that.

It was not Coboth that stood to talk to the assembly. The man who rose was younger. He stood and turned to the villagers. "Since the first set of bones were found it has become almost a regular event that just shy of four weeks another body is found. Based upon that another body should have been found ten days ago but it has not been, and no one in any of the surrounding villages has gone missing."

Coboth grumbled and the two men sitting beside him held him down in his seat and tried to get him to quiet down. Zachariah could tell it was grudging but eventually he did quiet and the younger man continued.

"We have come to the decision to wait on continuing with our request of this village to see if the murders start back up. Some of the elders in the other villages believe that the Monster has either moved on or has been killed. Others think it has gotten word of our plan to flush it out and is just hiding, but eventually it will reveal itself again."

Coboth jumped up and pulled his sword and slammed the point into the floor at the front of the room, "I lost two sons, my only sons to that Monster. If it shows up, I know it will be in this village. This village refused to believe and it is cursed. I will be watching and when it comes back I will be here to take revenge."

The two men that had held him back came up and guided him away. The younger man added, "As you can see, some have lost a lot and their emotions are high.

"I do not blame Coboth. I lost a brother. If I was certain that monster existed and was here I would hunt it down too, but I am still not certain what it is. One Priest told me he thinks it is the wrath of God upon the sins of those men and their lust. I know my brother, and I do know he was full of lust. I know he would seek out a whore from time to time, so perhaps the Priest is right." The man turned and walked out with the nine men following him.

Tobyas stood and addressed the village saying, "We were spared whatever it was that harmed those other villages. Let each of us give thanks to the Lord this night for our fortune."

Then the meeting was concluded and everyone went back to their homes, Zachariah nearly ran to his house and to the arms of Lilith to let her know that the other villages had called off their demands. They held each other long after they had finished their love making, falling to sleep in each other's arms.

The next morning Zachariah began construction on the table. He first paid a visit to the blacksmith who brought out a heavy hide and shaped it to the top, which was the side that Zachariah had prayed upon, and the side that was visible when he had proposed to Lilith. Zach did not want to do anything at all to that side so he was going to protect it. When the blacksmith was done with the hide, he took the hide back to his shop and began to fashion a plate that was molded to match the underside of the hide perfectly.

There was nothing more that Zachariah could do to the table until the base was done so he worked on setting up the other major items of the shop. The furnaces, the bellows, the smelting pots, but while he was doing this he kept wondering how he was going to get a perfectly smooth top on the other side of the stone. His mind was so involved on the shop and the stone table that he did not notice what Lilith was doing with her day, but when he came home at night she always seemed to be happy and they were very comfortable and loving in each other's arms. To him, nothing seemed to have changed at all.

One day while he was using a jeweler's saw to cut a gemstone an idea struck him. He was not certain how he would go about doing it but if he could somehow rig a saw blade that would rotate on a pulley system and do so continually, then use its own weight on a pivot he would get a perfectly smooth surface. The idea would not leave his mind so he went and spoke to his father and then a few other villagers about it. Some thought he was crazy, but a couple thought the idea could work. A thin wire coated with an adhesive dipped in gem dust could cut through the stone, which meant he needed to make the wire continuous, a single loop. He realized the blacksmith could do that.

Two wheels that were grooved and lined with fur could guide the wire. If they were pulled tight apart the wire would be strong and a good cutting tool. The only problem would be how to make it move constantly. That was solved easily because the baker had already dug a canal from the river to his mill and it ran right by the shop as well. A wheel like at the baker's mill could keep the wire turning, and after the cutting was done the wheel could be used to power other things like the bellows in the shop.

The stone would have to be turned on its edge and steadied for the cutting. So several of the villagers came and helped. Logs were set in place to lock the stone into place and the saw was set to begin cutting. Zachariah did not want to risk breaking the blade so he let the weight of the device itself do the cutting and did not add any weight to it.

At first everyone thought it was not working but after an hour the blade had cut into the stone about a half inch. As the stone got wider, the cutting would get even slower so it was going to be a long and slow process. Yet Zachariah was pleased to see that the cut was not much thicker than a finger nail. That meant that even when the cut was all the way through, if no one was present the stone would not collapse and shatter. There would be too little room for it to move.

Zachariah thanked his friends for their help and paid them all for their contributions with a ring of gold that he had made, each one had a circular disk upon it to represent the stone and a 'Z' upon the disk to remind them that they had helped him and his father at this time in building this shop. The villagers all tried to refuse but Zachariah insisted and said, "It is true I have helped you in the past but I want you to know how much I appreciated the fact you were each willing to stand up and protect Lilith and me from the other villages when they came to seek a monster. Keep this ring as a reminder of my gratitude for the time you may have saved my wife's life."

Each nodded and shook his hand as they left. In turn as they left they fingered their rings and admired the craftsmanship of the piece. Zakarias came to his son and said, "My boy, that was more gold than most of them will see in a year."

"I know father, but I also know that each of them will brag about that ring wherever they go and the business it will bring us will more than make up for the amount of gold that I gave away this day."

Zakarias smiled and patted his son on the back, "Not only are you a man with a good heart, but you have a good sense of business too. My boy will go very far and be a very rich man."

They both turned to the saw and the stone and his father asked, "How long do you think we will have to listen to this screech of the blade as it cuts through the stone?"

He turned to his father with a smile, "It is ear piercing, isn't it? In truth I have no idea. I can only hazard a guess, but my best guess would be a week."

"I hope that is all it is. For in a week that noise is likely to drive me insane." Zakarias said, then he patted his son on the shoulder again and added, "I knew you had talent to be a jeweler, I did not know you would be an inventor too. This saw of yours could come in handy in other trades."

"Perhaps, but I doubt anyone will want to put up with the noise."

"That is true," Zakarias added. "Maybe once the table is cut then we should dismantle it."

"I think that would be best."

The two men looked at it a little longer and then they parted each heading to his own home. The sound faded behind him as Zachariah walked to his house but he could still faintly hear it as he stepped under the hide at his door. Inside he was greeted by his wife running toward him and throwing herself into his arms. She wrapped her arms around him tightly and embraced him. It all happened so quickly that it shocked him and nearly knocked him off his feet.

"OOOFF," the air gushed from his lungs as he caught her and returned her hug, then when he regained his breath he asked, "What is up, my wife?"

Lilith let go of his neck and slid to the floor where she took his hands and led him to the pillows upon the floor and said, "Sit my husband, let us eat our meal and then I will tell you my news."

Zachariah sat but he pulled her down into his lap and both rolled laughing, "No, my love, you can share your news now. Our meal can wait. I am more anxious to hear what has you so happy."

Lilith sat up, and then rose to kneel upon her knees, lowering her head she laid her head upon his lap and said, "I pray you will not be angry with me, but I have been leaving the house during the day."

Zachariah's intake of air startled her and she rose to look at him with frightened eyes, "No, my husband! I am not cheating on you. I have been seeking information only."

As he exhaled he could see her relax as well, then she continued, "A woman in the camp told me of a prophetess that lives in the hills beneath Mount Zaboath. Even when I heard the name of the mountain it seemed like an omen to me, the very initial of my husband upon the name of the mountain. So I knew I had to seek her out."

Lilith paused and looked at her husband. Zachariah saw that she was trying to see how he was taking her story but so far there was nothing for him to be upset or happy about so he listened. "It took me a few days to learn the proper path to her home, especially since I wanted to be here each night when you got back. Then last night you said you would not be in because setting up the saw would keep you up all night and if you made a mistake it might damage the stone.

"So I took the chance and went to see her. I found her right where they said she would be."

Zachariah stopped her, "Lilith that is impossible, the trip to Mount Zaboath is a three day journey with a wagon in just one direction. You could not have made it in one day there and back."

"Husband, please believe me. There are things about me you do not know, and I cannot yet tell you. I told the prophetess you would not believe I was there so she gave me this," Lilith reached behind her and pulled a feather from under the pillow. It was a large colored feather of a bird that only dwelled within the region of the Mountain. She handed it to Zachariah, "The prophetess said that this feather would help you believe until the time that I could reveal all to you."

His eyes got hard as he looked at her, "When you could reveal all to me? Do you mean to tell me that some of your past memories have returned and you have not told me about them?"

Lilith lowered her eyes, "Husband, please forgive my lie, but I never lost my memories."

Zachariah leapt to his feet and looked down at Lilith, "Woman, how dare you lie to me all this time! How do I know you even love me enough to be my wife?"

"Zachariah, my husband, please listen. Please forgive me." For the first time since Lilith had been made she truly felt shame. The emotions welling up inside her were like nothing she had ever felt before. She realized she was about to lose the man that loved her and her heart was ripping apart. There was no hesitancy upon her part as she knelt and crawled to his feet and wrapped her arms around his ankles saying, "My husband, if I told you all you would never have loved me. I am not worthy of your love. Please forgive me. Even the prophetess said it is not time to reveal my past to you."

As he looked down at her and felt her tears upon his calves he could not stay mad at the woman he loved. Slowly he lowered himself beside her and lifted her lips to his. He kissed them softly and said, "All the elders have said that this prophetess is a woman of God and I have no reason to doubt them. If she says there is a reason for you not to tell me your past yet then who am I to second guess a prophet of God?"

"There was one thing she asked of us." Lilith then added.

"A payment?"

"No.

"She asked me to tell her all about you and me. She wanted to know everything. When I told her about the stone you had prayed on, and then proposed to me beside she was very interested in it.

"Later I told her how you had brought it to the shop to use as a table for your work, and that the side that the prayer had been done on you were protecting. She then asked if the stone was good and thick.

"I showed her roughly how thick.

"She asked that when you are done cutting the piece away, that you cut a second piece about the thickness of the end of your middle finger to the first joint. She said she would need the stone for the magic that would heal me."

Zachariah looked at her. *Heal her how?* He knew that there were times that Lilith had acted like things were wrong. Maybe the magic would simply be to help restore her full memory and if it would help his wife he would do anything. He smiled at the woman he loved and said, "It is a small price to pay but an odd request. It will be done though."

Lilith threw her arms around him and hugged him tight, "Thank you, my husband, but did you hear what I said, Zachariah? The prophetess said she can heal me."

He looked at her and smiled, "Sweetheart, I did not know that you were hurt."

"It is something about my past. She said she can fix it. She said in two months that I am to come for her and she will come here and stay here for one month. When she leaves she will leave with us the means for me to be cured." Lilith smiled at him, "In a little over three months I can truly be the wife you deserve."

Zachariah smiled and laughed, as he tried to hide his confusion. Lilith was the wife he wanted, what could possibly change? But if this would make her that much happier and lift this cloud that seemed to be over her then he would do all he could. He kissed her lips lightly and said, "Well then it will be about time because in just a little over three months we will have been married for one year and I think it is about time I have my wife." Then he rolled Lilith onto her back and began kissing her deeply, his hand sliding along her thigh and pushing her dress away from her.

"Zachariah, we have not even eaten."

"I am hungry for something else, my wife." He smiled at her and she returned his grin.

"Then that makes two of us," she added as her arms wrapped behind his head and pulled him into an even deeper kiss.

Chapter Twelve

Though Zachariah had guessed it would only take a week to cut through the stone it took one month to the day to complete the first cut. He set the saw immediately to begin the second cut and it dawned on him that the piece would be finished almost at the exact time that the prophetess arrived. It was like she knew that if she had come any earlier the stone would not be ready for her.

Three weeks later, Zakarias, Rachel and Lilith climbed onto a wagon that had three oxen harnessed to it. Zachariah had another one of his ideas and he had taken long pieces of metal and fastened them to the wagon and then had fastened hides to the metal. It formed a shelter from the weather for the women and a place for them to sleep at night. He had even added a board in the wagon making a separate place for Rachel and Zakarias to sleep so all could sleep inside and safe. The last thing he did was tie bells around the outside rings of the steel so that when the flaps were closed if anyone moved the flaps the bells would ring. It would warn his parents and Lilith if someone tried to enter the wagon while they were asleep.

Once again Zakarias was amazed at the mind of his son and said he ought to take his idea to the blacksmith, but Zachariah did not think anyone else would appreciate it. They were set in their ways of doing things and few wanted to change to new ways. Before they left Lilith leaned out and kissed Zachariah and whispered to him.

"Husband, remember the rings you gave to the men for helping you? So many have come asking about the maker that marked his rings with the 'Z', I was thinking, maybe you should create a fancy 'Z' and put it on the back of all the jewelry you make. Not where it is easily visible, but where when people see a piece and are examining it they can see the maker's mark on the inside and say, 'Whose mark is this?' Maybe it would bring my husband even more business."

Zachariah smiled at her and kissed her cheek, "And my father thought

I was the one with a mind for business, my wife. That is an excellent idea. While you are away, I will try to think of a design for that mark." Then he kissed her fully on the lips and reluctantly let her go as his father took the reins and got the oxen moving. Watching them leave he waved to Lilith and his mother.

He did not know exactly how long they would be gone. The prophetess had said to come and get her in two months, but did that mean she wanted them to arrive at her place in two months or she wanted to arrive at Zachariah's place in two months? The family had discussed it and decided it would be best to plan on the latter but expect the prior. So they would go there with one extra day to spare in case of bad weather. That way they could arrive back in exactly two months. Then if the prophetess did not want to leave yet, they took enough food to wait an additional three days for her.

To Zachariah it did not matter. It was still the loneliest time of his life. From the moment he had been born he had always had his parents and then Lilith around. He had never had a day when someone was not there to talk to and as they pulled away he could already feel the silence enveloping him and he did not like it one iota.

Quickly he entered his house and sat down with some vellum and began tracing various designs for the symbol that Lilith had suggested. However in no time he had gone through his supply of vellum and had to go into the village to see if he could find some more. As it turned out vellum and parchment were items that were in rare supply because few people had any use for them. He began to head back home without any but as he passed the potter's hut he got another idea. He walked in and asked the potter for a pail of raw clay and a rectangular form.

The potter had no problem giving them to him and even refused payment pointing to the ring on his finger and saying it was already paid for. Zachariah thanked him and carried the items back to the house. He then sat the form on a flat stone and filled it with clay. Taking a wire he dragged it across the form and gave himself a smooth surface. Then with a quill he carved his next idea for the mark.

He still did not like it so he added a little water and clay, erasing his mark and dragging the wire across again. In this manner he had an endless writing surface and he continued to try one new idea after another. Late into the night he tried, his mind so absorbed with the idea that he forgot to eat and fell asleep lying on the floor next to the clay and the mold.

When he awoke the clay in the mold had hardened but he broke it up and mixed it in with the clay in the bucket and soon it was viable again. Then he cleaned the mud from his hands and found some bread to eat before again trying to discover the perfect design for the mark that would represent him and his father.

Day after day passed and nothing struck him as right. He needed it to be perfect. Everything he tried was too simple, too plain, and he needed it to be profound. Not just a 'Z' but a mark that told people that this was the 'Z' of the Zakarias family. He wanted to make his father proud with the symbol, to make it bold and daring, to make it speak to whoever looked at it and have them say "I have got to have a piece of jewelry made by the hands of the one whose mark this is." Yet try as he might nothing said that to him.

Then one day the flap opened and Lilith rushed in and stopped short looking at him. He looked up and saw her hand rise to her face as she tried to hide the smirk on her face. "Why are you smiling at me like that?"

"I leave for a week, and I come home and my husband has reverted to a little boy playing in the mud." Just then Rachel walked in, there was no doubt she had heard what Lilith had said and as her eyes looked at him both women began to laugh near hysterically.

As they were laughing a woman that was so old that time itself must have not started ticking before she was born stepped in. She was bent over a walking stick and she looked at the man on the floor. Her eyes shown of life and fire, "Zachariah the symbol you seek is not in clay, but will be found in stone. Get cleaned up and then come join an old woman for a meal. You have not eaten in three days and you look like you are about ready to waste away."

Lilith looked again at Zachariah, "Husband, why have you not taken care of yourself? Have you at least drunk fluids?"

He lifted a flask and poured out about a mouthful of water, "Yeah that is the last of that flask. I think I filled it two days ago."

The old woman blurted out, "Three. He needs food and water and rest. He has been in a trance with this idea in his mind, but the idea he has is close but it will not come in mud but in stone."

Zakarias helped the women carry him to his bed and then Lilith undressed him and cleaned him of the mud. Once he was in a night shirt she called to Rachel and together they fed and nursed him through the night.

In the morning he awoke and was surprised to see anyone was around him at all, he did not remember them coming in, but the moment he saw the old woman he bowed to her and welcomed her to his home. She answered, "We have already met. The mud man awakens hungry and with no memory but tomorrow you will begin to find your symbol."

Zachariah looked up at the old woman. Suddenly it was like he was brought out of a dream and the woman he was looking at was one of the oldest and most hideous looking women he had ever laid his eyes on. He could not help but stare at her. It felt like his eyes would fall out of their sockets if they were to get any wider. Her hair was white but frazzled and looked as if it had never seen a comb. Most of her teeth were gone, upon her nose were several warts, and some of the warts looked like they had warts. The bags beneath her eyes sunk to the middle of her cheeks. She looked like she was composed of skin stretched tautly over a skeleton she was so devastatingly thin.

While he looked at her she told him everything he had been doing, how he had gone into a trance while seeking the symbol and that the symbol was not to be found the way he had been searching for it but now he was ready for the next step. Now he could enter the trance to find the true symbol of his family. Even though she knew all he had done the true shock was still in her appearance and not in her knowledge for he already knew she was supposed to be a great seer.

All of them sat around and listened to her as she spoke, "Lilith came to me seeking to be healed. Her healing lies within the path of this family. Within the symbol that Zachariah will discover.

"It began when Rachel's father took a joke as serious and accepted a cut that was not supposed to happen. That marked your family to be healers. From the moment Rachel was born she could find the herbs that healed without even being told what they were, she needed no teacher. She knew how to set bones, and those she touched healed faster than when they sought others for their aid.

"Even Zakarias when he married Rachel changed. His hands became more talented. He could mold metal like he had only dreamed of before. It was almost as if he was finding the shape within the metal that it wanted to be. Then once he had seen it he would work on pulling it out to become something even more beautiful than it had dreamed of.

"And Lilith, her very nature began to change. There is still a war within her but her heart has softened too and she truly knows love for the first time in her life.

"Zachariah was born special. He could not think ill of anyone. He was strong like no one could imagine, and fast like the wind. His hands were like his father's when it came to metals and he also has a gift for healing but it has not yet manifested for it lies in a different path than his mother's. He is also a dreamer. Ideas come to him and he creates things that others cannot even begin to think of. In a thousand years the things he has created now will become common place, but today they will be his and his alone then turn to dust for no one will see their value but he and his family.

She turned to Zachariah and said, "Lilith came to me seeking healing, and only you can heal her. However it must come after you have found your symbol. Only then will the power within you begin to manifest.

"There is something you must know though. I see two paths to her healing. In one path she will be healed and you and she will have many children and grandchildren. All her sins will be forgiven and you two will live to a very old age and die within a single breath of each other.

"The other path is not so kind, and I dare not speak of it. I will say she is healed, but it is not a path either of you wish to take."

Zachariah looked at her and said, "How will I know to choose the right path?"

The old woman lowered her head and said, "That I am forbidden to say, for it steps over the line of free will. If I tell you which path to choose then when it comes time to choose you will not choose freely but will choose what I have told you. I can say this; the choice is not yours alone. In the second path Lilith has a choice that can return it to the first path."

Lilith wrapped her arms around Zachariah and said, "Husband, I am certain you will choose wisely when the time comes and if not I will then choose to be with the man I love so we will be on the right path no matter what."

Zachariah hugged her tightly, "I pray you are right my love."

There was a sudden stillness in the air, the ambience changed and for a moment everyone looked at each other with a look of confusion upon their faces then the old woman blurted out, "It is the saw, you young fools. It has stopped. The stone is done."

For two months there had been the constant whine of the saw cutting through the stone and the sudden silence of it had been startling but Zakarias was the first to lean back and look up at the ceiling and say,

"Praise be, I can finally hear the crickets again when I lay down to sleep. I never thought I would miss their song so much."

Rachel laughed and added, "And in two months you will be yelling at them to go find someplace else to play their tune."

"Yes, but for now, I will sure enjoy their music." Zakarias fluffed the pillows on the floor beside him and pulled Rachel down to them. Then he hugged his wife tight and said, "If anyone needs anything they know where it is at, you can lay here with me for a while, baby."

The old woman looked at them and then at the younger couple and asked, "Are you sure that you two are the newlyweds and not them?" She then let out a cackle that was her form of laugh and Rachel turned a brilliant red.

Zachariah said, "All my life my parents have never hidden their love for each other, and I for one am glad that they have not."

"Good!" added the old woman then she turned to them and said, "Never forget to remain young in your hearts and remain newlyweds all the days of your marriage for when you forget that is when your marriage grows stale."

Zakarias nodded and said, "With this woman that will never happen, Prophetess, for I love her as much as the day I first laid eyes on her."

The woman looked at Rachel and said, "Then you are truly blessed among women."

Rachel found an even darker shade of red to turn.

The old woman smiled at Rachel and then turned to Zachariah and asked, "How long before you can have the table ready?"

"What do you mean?"

"Well the top part, the first part you cut off, that part can go out front of the shop. Eventually you should have a hole dug and it placed like a welcoming stone to the shop. Do not smooth it out. The roughness will keep it from getting slick when it rains.

"The slab I had you cut off, that is going to be your work surface, your table top."

Zachariah looked at her strangely, "I thought that was for you?"

"Well in a way it was, it was so I could get inside the stone and give you the work surface you wanted." He continued to look at the woman like she was more than human. How could she have known that he had wanted to use that surface as his work surface for a reason?

"Now, the base, you had the blacksmith make a stand to hold it. Once it is set up, place the slab someplace safe where it will not be broken and then call me. You and I will go into that room alone and I will help you enter the trance to find your symbol."

"Are you saying I am going to carve it in that stone?" He looked at her filled with bewilderment.

"Yes."

"But I have never been a stone carver or touched their tools in my life. I do not even have any tools to do the carving."

She smiled and said, "Don't worry, I had Zakarias stop and we purchased three complete sets on the way back here."

"Three sets? Why would you do that?"

"Because you are going to break most of the pieces in the first two sets while you are doing the carving," she said. Upon her face was a soft smile that simply said that she had no doubt he could do it and that what she said would happen.

Zachariah sat back and stared at her. After all he had already heard from her he also had no doubt she was right. He just could not imagine it happening.

The woman looked at him and said, "Now go lie with your wife. Make love to her, for when we enter that room at sunset tomorrow night it will be a long time before we come back out."

It was almost as if he was in a trance as he stood, he turned from her and walked to his room and found Lilith standing beside the bed putting some items away. He was no longer in his trance but he also felt the need to follow the woman's advice. He turned his wife around and kissed her hard and deeply.

"Zachariah, we have guests in the house." She said.

"I know, and to be honest, my mother and father made love while I lived under their roof so they can hear us tonight. As far as the old woman, if she is ashamed at the sound of our love making she can step outside. You are my wife and there is nothing wrong with what I am about to do to you." With those words he placed his hands at the throat of her shift and with all his strength ripped her shift off of her in one motion leaving her standing naked before him. Then he lifted her and laid her on the bed, but he did not climb on top of her.

He whispered, "From the first day you tasted me I have been curious and tonight I will satisfy that curiosity." He pulled her legs toward him and spread her thighs wide as he knelt on the floor. Slowly he kissed along her inner thigh, first one, then the other, his mouth and kisses inching closer to the folds of flesh where her thighs met. He could hear her breathing become more rapid as his mouth got even closer to that spot he was ravenous to taste.

Her scent was driving him insane with desire to plunge his tongue between those folds of flesh but he wanted to savor every second of this new experience. He rose onto his elbows and blew lightly upon the patch of fur just above the folds and then where they began he could see a small swelling. With his fingers he pushed the folds apart and for the first time looked upon the little jewel that her fingers had often guided his too. He had no idea what it was called, as he blew upon it he whispered loud enough for her to hear, "I name this your jewel."

"My jewel," she responded. "Please play with my jewel."

He blew one more time upon on it then he licked it with his tongue. It tasted like a mixture of tastes and yet like nothing he had ever tasted before. It was sweet and yet bitter, tangy, and yet had a slight smell and taste that he thought urine might have but it did not bother him. It was wonderful to watch his wife squirm as he licked it again as her moans beckoned even more attention.

He knew how much she loved it when he suckled upon her nipples, and in some ways this jewel was hardened like them but very different too. He decided to see how she would react, so he lowered his lips over it and sucked hard upon it. Lilith bucked her hips up, and wrapped her fingers into his hair pushing his head against her even harder. The moan that escaped from her lips was loud enough that even had his parents been in their own house they would have heard her. He nibbled lightly upon it and Lilith bucked again, her scream of ecstasy filling the whole house. He could hear his parents laughing in the front room but he was lost in the moment. This was something that was too precious and wonderful to stop.

As he suckled on her jewel again he slid a finger into the hole where his manhood would penetrate and began sliding it in and out. Lilith squirmed against him and rolled her head to the side biting a pillow to try to muffle anymore screams. Her hips bucked and ground against his face and hand. Soon he could feel a fluid running around his finger and he pulled away to see a heavy white cream running from the canal that was the sheath his cock usually filled. He could not resist and lowering his head he began to lap at it, his tongue running along the folds and occasionally entering into her opening. Lilith continued to squirm each time his tongue touched her then she finally spit the pillow out and sat up.

She pulled him into her arms and kissed his lips, tasting her own fluids upon his and pulled him on top of her. Her hands were already unfastening his straps and pushing aside his breach cloth. She did not care that he was still mostly clothed. She had to have him inside her. When he was freed from his loin cloth she guided his cock to her opening and pushed her hips upward impaling herself upon his shaft. Even though Zachariah was on top of her, Lilith was grinding and rocking her hips against him so fast he barely had to move, her hunger for him was so great. Yet his hunger was as great for her and he began to meet her moves. They began to thrust against each other, pounding hard. Their lips locked to each other's, their tongues locked in a grinding fuck of their own.

They were two people so in love that they did not care that the world watched them as they rode each other to that pinnacle of pleasure. Lilith threw her head back as the wave hit her and she clamped her mouth shut holding in the scream but the moan was deep and her body shivered. Zachariah felt the muscles inside her clamp onto his shaft and that was all it took he had reached his peak and his seed burst within her, pumping and spasming as it filled her. She buried her head into his shoulder and held onto him. Together they cried in their bliss, then they rolled over and held onto each other.

After a few minutes a voice came from the front room. It was his father. "Son, I don't know what you did to her, but you are going to have to tell me because I have never gotten a reaction like that from your mother and I sure would like to try."

"Papa!" Then there was the sound of a slap as Rachel hit Zakarias on the shoulder.

Lilith and Zachariah looked at each other and burst into laughter. He did not know if he could tell his father, or even if he could explain how the idea had come to him, but the worst part was he knew his father well enough to know he would not let it go and Zachariah would be hounded until he finally broke down and told him.

The two lovers fell asleep in each other's arms.

Chapter Thirteen

"Ahem!" Then there was a sharp crack as wood slammed against wood.

Quickly Zachariah sat up and stared at the old woman standing at the end of his bed.

"If you do not mind covering up, I have seen enough of those in my life I really do not care to see anymore." she said.

He looked down and he was completely uncovered. He grabbed a blanket and threw one over Lilith as she began to wake and try to cover herself and he pulled a pillow to cover his groin.

The old woman sat down on a stool and said, "It is getting late, the sun will be up soon and there is a lot to do."

Zachariah looked at her and said, "You mean the sun is not even up yet and you say it is getting late?"

"Of course!" She said matter-of-factly, "There is a lot to do today. You have two large stones to move out of the shop and another to get onto its pedestal before nightfall.

"So we need to get to it. I have already woken your parents, they are getting breakfast ready so the two of you should get dressed and come join us." Then she turned then walked out of the bedroom.

Lilith looked at Zachariah and said, "I should have warned you. She has been bossy ever since we picked her up. I do not know if it is her age, or the fact she has God's ear, but she seems to really take control."

He turned and kissed her, "Well truth is, I do not mind too much. It was her idea that I go to bed early and make love to you. Though she did not tell me what to do, that was my own idea." He smiled wickedly.

"And it was a deliciously sweet idea, my husband," Lilith said before wrapping her arms around him and kissing him with a passion so deep it threatened to reignite the fires of the night before.

Zachariah took a deep breath and looked at her when she released him, "I do not think the prophetess will give us time to do that again." He gave her a quick kiss, "I sure wish she would though," he added with a laugh then he rose and gathered his clothing and got dressed.

Lilith found herself another dress and put it on then whispered to Zachariah, "You need to give me more money for clothing if you are going to rip them off of me like that."

They both were laughing as they entered the main room but the looks and smiles that met them from his parents made them both blush brilliantly. Zachariah knew even before his father opened his mouth what he was going to say, "So when are you going to tell me what you did to Lilith. Those screams from her were absolutely amazing."

"Papa!" Rachel smacked his shoulder again and he rubbed it.

"Rachel, you are going to bruise that arm if you keep that up. Besides last night you asked me to ask." Suddenly Rachel was turning brilliant red as she hid her face against Zakarias' shoulder while he let out a guffaw that almost shook the thatch of the roof.

After breakfast the two men and the prophetess left to go work on the table.

***

Zachariah paused for a moment and looked at Melanie. "I know this is a long story precious, but we are getting near the end."

"You really did love her, didn't you?" Melanie asked.

"I loved what I thought she was, and what I thought she was going to be, but in a little bit you will see I found out more than I could handle.

"I stopped for a moment though to tell you that as you may have guessed some of the things I have told you were told to me later, but this next part that happened was told to me by my mother a little more than a month after it happened." Zachariah wiped away a tear, "It is hard for me to tell this, but I think it is best it is told in the timeline properly now."

***

Rachel and Lilith began to clean the house after they had left but it was not more than a few moments after the men had left that Lilith ran to the back door and began vomiting. Rachel was right beside her, holding her. Then she went inside and got a cloth and wet it with water and came to Lilith and wiped her brow.

Rachel asked Lilith, "How long since you last had your moon cycle, sweetie?"

Rachel was surprised to see the strange look upon Lilith's face, "You know the monthly visit when a woman bleeds from her female parts."

Lilith shook her head and said, "I have never had one."

"Never?" Rachel could not believe her ears.

"No, not once. I have heard of other woman having them but I have never had one and did not know what they were for or why."

Rachel looked at her and said, "Normally a woman begins to have them when she is somewhere between eleven and fourteen years old, sometimes younger, sometimes older. It is a cleansing in a way. Every month the woman's body prepares a place for a baby, but if a man's seed does not plant itself then the place needs to be cleansed and that is what the monthly flow does. It cleanses the place of the baby.

"That flow usually only stops at one of two times. When a woman has grown too old to bear children, or when a woman is with child. I have no clue why you have never had one. You are well past the age you should have started." Then Rachel took her hand and looked at her.

"But there are other signs that a woman may be with child. One of them is what you just did, morning vomiting. Also I have noticed your breasts have grown a little larger. It is usually not this early that a woman's breasts grow larger but it can happen.

"And last night, did Zachariah do something new or were you more sensitive?"

Lilith blushed, "He did something new, but to be honest I was more sensitive too."

Rachel smiled and hugged Lilith tight, "Then Lilith, my daughter, I would say from all my years of experience that you are with child."

Lilith's eyes grew very wide as she looked at Rachel. She shook her head and said, "That is impossible, that just cannot be!"

"Sweetie, you have been married for almost a year and you and my son have a healthy sex life it most certainly could happen."

Lilith stood and shook her head, "You do not understand! I can't have children!"

She turned and ran out the door. Rachel ran after her but by the time she got to the door Lilith was nowhere to be seen. Rachel went to the shop and tried to speak to Zachariah but the prophetess only told her through the door that Lilith was fine and would return in a few days.

For several days Rachel frantically paced the house of her daughter-in-law, waiting. At night she would cry to Zakarias saying that she had not meant to upset Lilith so badly and truly did not know what she had done. All her husband could do was hold his wife and comfort her for he too was worried about the wife of his son. If she did not return he did not know how he would tell his son what had happened.

Then on the fifth day Lilith entered the house. She was carrying a basket of flowers and singing a song that sounded something like a lullaby. Rachel started to ask her where she had been and Lilith replied, "I remembered a part of my past, a child I had seen long ago who was killed unjustly.

"I had to go visit her grave.

"Once I did, I realized that maybe having a child of my own was not a bad thing." She smiled at Rachel, "Maybe it is a sign I am being forgiven."

Rachel hugged her tight, "You could not have done anything so horrid that you needed a sign this great to prove you were forgiven. My daughter, you are a blessing to this house."

Lilith hugged her back, "Time will tell." Then she turned to Zakarias and asked, "Did the prophetess say how long she and my husband would be in the shop?"

He came up behind the two women and held both of them, "She only said it would be a very long time. I am afraid that since she told you she would be here for a month that that is how long they will be in there."

Lilith's face darkened and she looked towards the shop, "So I have almost a month to think of a way to tell my husband about his child and everything else he should know."

The parents of Zachariah looked at each other and then at Lilith, "Everything else he should know?"

"It is something the prophetess told me, and only for his ears." Lilith looked at them and then hugged them both, "Please trust me. It is for him alone."

They returned her hug and together they said, "We trust you."

Chapter Fourteen

It took most of the day to get what had been the bottom of the stone outside and lying on the ground. The men set the round edge on the ground and the flat surface up for they decided that would be the best and safest place to lay the slab. It was Zachariah that pointed out that laying the slab upon the ground or leaning it against something could cause a stress fracture to form and cause it to crack or shatter. Most of the men did not believe him but it was better to listen to him than argue with him, besides these men had not been there the first time and they wanted to get rings like the first crew had gotten so it was best to listen to the boss.

They laid the slab on top of the other piece and Zachariah felt secure that it would not be broken. He then gave each of them a ring similar to the ones he had given out before. Zachariah's name was being spread around as a generous boss but also that his work was exceptional and with each ring he passed out he knew that it would bring in ten customers or even more.

The final thing was to lift the last stone up and set it on the pedestal that the blacksmith had made and all the men stayed to help with that. It was heavy work but with more than twenty men circling the stone it was not as difficult as it had been when the stone had been larger. The pedestal was slid under it and positioned where Zachariah wanted the table to be for once it was set there was no way his father and he would be able to move it by themselves.

With the moving of the slabs completed and the table set the sun was on the horizon and beginning to slip beneath it just as the prophetess had said it would be. She pushed in a wheelbarrow of bread then she shooed everyone out except Zachariah. The shop was the only building on the property that had doors made of wood. The prophetess closed the door and tied each one shut. Then turned to Zachariah and said, "We will be in here for a long time, my boy. There is plenty of bread and water." Then she threw down a sack, "and I have plenty of dried meat so we will not go hungry, but the truth is, I will have to nearly force you to eat.

"Once the trance takes you it will be hard to get you to stop to eat and drink anything, it will be a real effort on my part to keep you alive but I have seen that I will and you will get the work done."

Zachariah looked at her and asked, "Just how will I go into a trance that deep. I don't drink wine and I cannot imagine it happening."

The prophetess took out one of the sets of carving tools and handed them to Zachariah then said, "Climb on the stone and just scratch at it. Think of your symbol, imagine it and try to recapture the feelings you had when you were working with the clay."

He took the set from her and followed her instructions. Once on top, the stone was hard and rough. The saw blade had cut it level but not smooth; he would need to polish it. He took out one of the tools and began to scrape a small 'Z' shape into the stone.

"No!" The woman said, "Bigger, fill the stone. The stone is the 'Z' it is the foundation of your family."

Zachariah reached out and took the tool and first drew a rough circle around the edge of the stone.

"That is it, fill the stone."

"Listen," Zachariah said, "if you want me to do this be quiet and let me think. Your talking is only breaking my concentration and I am getting nowhere."

She quieted down and went to sit on a stool while he began to try to imagine the 'Z' filling the entire stone. He wanted to make his father proud, he wanted a symbol that would let people know that this was from the hands of someone that truly cared about the work that they did. Slowly he began to trace out a giant 'Z' upon the stone and as he worked his mind filled with images of his father and all the love of his family.

He saw his grandfather coming to visit and how he showed so much love to his mother, Rachel. It was unlike other fathers showed their daughters. Then he was saddened because he had never gotten to meet his grandmother. She had died three years after Rachel was born in an accident by a river. A branch had suddenly fallen out of a tree and knocked her into the river, she was a good swimmer but the branch had knocked her unconscious. Rachel had seen everything but she was too small to save her mother and by the time she had gotten her father to the river it was too late.

They pulled her mother's body out of the river about a mile further down and had buried her that night. The village had mourned for a long time because she was so well loved, and because a man should not have to raise a daughter alone. But his grandfather could love no other and had never married again, he had also done a wonderful job in raising his mother.

"Zachariah, it is done. You can wake now."

"What?"

The old woman was standing above him. He was lying on the floor of the shop. "It is done, you have finished and you have done wonderfully, my boy."

He looked up at her. There was no way he could be done. Even if he had gone into a trance all he remembered was a very short dream, it was not possible enough time had passed during that dream for him to have completed the stone. But as he tried to move pain tore through his arms and legs. It was like they had been in a bent position for too long and now did not want to straighten out.

It took every ounce of his willpower to force his muscles to obey but slowly he got to his feet. He rose with his back to the table finding that he was more than a little afraid to look at it. All he could remember was the dream of his grandfather, and that dream did not seem to take long enough to allow him to do all the work the prophetess had told him he would do.

He turned and his eyes could not believe what he saw.

The table was polished smooth as glass, and carved into it in relief was what looked like a tree but it was shaped like a 'Z'. The roots were twisted and gnarled from the right to the left and then the trunk began.

The trunk was the form of a woman, naked, her legs crossed at the knees, one arm lay along her side and the other held up beside her head. The limbs that were the upper part of her arm and her hair twisted around each other.

Around the outer edge of the stone was a circle that one of the roots tapped into and along the circle at twelve equidistant points a different character of his language was inscribed. He had no idea why they were in the order they were in, there was no saying that he knew of and they did not match the twelve tribes.

However the work as a whole was amazing, even a master stonemason could not have done the work as well. Then something else drew his attention and he looked into the carved lines. Within each line were thousands of letters of his language strung together in an endless series of words. This was more than just an amazing piece of work, this was a miracle. He turned to the prophetess and said, "I could not have made this."

"But you did, my son."

"There is no way, I could have. Those words, those are incantations, I could not have known those." Zachariah looked at her. He could feel terror rising in his heart.

"Calm, my boy, what you have done you have done as an instrument. Whether it was God himself that worked through you, or an angel or one of the prophets returning to guide your hand, whoever it was the work is done. Now, whether it is used for good or evil depends upon you and Lilith."

Zachariah looked around, "Lilith, I need to see her."

Part Four
The Ring
Chapter Fifteen

Zachariah struggled on his own for several moments before the prophetess caught up to him. Even at her advanced age the little support she could offer him was a help for he had been on his hands and knees on top of the stone for a month. His legs would not straighten fully and his arms were sore and crooked. Yet he limped forward with determination to reach his home. He tried to yell but his voice was weak and hoarse from having done no talking. He had only been barely able to whisper to the old woman when she had woken him and he had seen the 'Z'. Suddenly he heard the old woman intake a deep lung full of air. It reminded him of the way the bellows by the smelting furnace took in air. Then she yelled out across the field with such force that he half expected to see the thatch of his roof go flying off and into the distance.

It was only a brief moment after the release of her verbal assault that the door to his house opened and Lilith appeared. She was the first one through the door but was followed closely by his father and mother. His father passed Lilith and ran to help the old woman support him. Lilith and Rachel also came to his side. When Lilith was near enough Zachariah let go of the prophetess and wrapped his arms around Lilith. He hugged her with what little strength he had. "To me it seems I was only in there a short time but my body tells me it was much longer, how long has it been?"

Zakarias answered, "The doors closed on you thirty days ago."

He turned and looked at the old woman, "A full month. You kept me from my family a full month?"

She looked at him and in a voice as cold as ice said, "It was not I that kept you there. It was the calling of the one that put you in the trance. You saw the work, and you know it was by the design of a powerful and good being so do not question the time.

"As far as your pains, they will heal. Before your parents return from taking me home you will be your old self again."

Zachariah looked at her and asked, "When do you leave?"

"I figured I would give you at least tonight and one more day with your parents before separating you again, then I will leave." She then looked to Lilith, "There will be no payment for this, what was done had to be done. It is His will.

"However, for the time that I am to remain here, I will stay in the shop and sleep there. So that the family can be a family and not have to worry about a strange old woman being around."

"No," Rachel interjected, "you can sleep in Zakarias' and my house."

"It is not necessary. I have made myself a spot in the shop where I have slept for nearly a month. I am quite comfortable there." Then she turned and headed toward the shop. Zakarias watched as she closed the door behind her.

The three helped Zachariah into his home and to his bed where they all sat about him and talked. He wanted his father to see the symbol so badly, but decided it could wait until just before they were ready to leave so that they did not disturb the prophetess.

Rachel and Zakarias decided to let Lilith and their son have some time alone so they stepped into the front room and went to the corner where they had slept while their son was sequestered within the shop.

Once his parents had stepped out Zachariah looked at Lilith and said, "I cannot believe how good you look to my eyes. I still cannot believe it has been a month, but you look like you are glowing. Come lay with me my wife."

"But Zachariah you are in too much pain for us to do anything." She said as she lowered her eyes.

"My love, I just want to feel you next to me."

Lilith climbed onto the bed and helped him sit up. Slowly she undressed him, doing her best that his stiff joints and muscles would not be hurt even more. Then she stood and removed her own clothing as he watched. Looking at him she smiled and said, "I do not think your body realizes you are in pain."

He looked down and saw that his cock was as hard as it could be and laughed, "I guess it has a mind of its own. If I were not in so much pain I would let it guide me tonight."

Lilith smiled as she climbed in beside him and then slid her hand down to his manhood and began to stroke him slowly. "Perhaps letting it have a mind of its own will ease a little of your pain." Then she slid her head under the blanket and he soon felt her lips upon his cock.

He bit his lip. It was one thing for his parents to hear Lilith moan and scream and quite another for them to hear him, but Lilith was doing everything she could to get even with him for embarrassing her that night. Her tongue ran up and down his shaft, teasing the head, and then down again. Then suddenly without warning she sucked one of his balls into her mouth. He could taste blood where he had bitten his lip hard to keep from moaning out loud. When she released his ball she flicked it with her tongue and then slid her tongue up his shaft again before taking his cock into her mouth.

She plunged her head down his shaft all the way. He could feel the back of her throat open as she swallowed and took all of his cock into her mouth. There was nothing he could do, a low guttural moan escaped then he grabbed a pillow and held it to his mouth, his arms screaming in protest from the sudden movement but the pleasure was too great and he did not care. Up and down on his shaft her head bobbed, faster and faster. Her mouth sucking harder, her cheeks pulled tight against his shaft from the suction. He began to lift his hips and piston into her mouth as she ground down upon him. Then he felt the surge building and with both hands he held the pillow to his mouth as he screamed out and his seed erupted into Lilith's mouth.

Slowly she bobbed her head a few more times then, with her hand, she milked the last of his seed from him, licking it from the tip as it came out. Lilith climbed up beside her husband and kissed his lips. He did not even mind the taste of his seed upon her lips. He actually liked it for it was a blend of her lips and him. She whispered, "Now tomorrow you can tell your mother what I did." Then she laughed and hugged him tight.

When they awoke the warmth from her body alone had eased much of the pain of his muscles and Zachariah found he could move easier. He was still stiff so his mother took some liniment that had mint and cactus juice blended into it and worked it into the muscles of his arms and legs.

That day they were a family, spending time together, laughing, and joking. Zachariah was glad his mother mentioned nothing about any sound she had heard the night before but Lilith seemed a little disappointed. There were a few times she even hinted but if the two had heard anything they were being discreet and not giving into her attempts to rouse their curiosity.

The day passed and their evening meal went quietly. They knew that the old woman would be waking them up before dawn to get started so they decided to get to bed early. As Lilith and Zachariah turned to head to bed Zakarias spoke up and said, "Lilith, before you go to bed. Can you tell Rachel what it was you were doing to my son last night that made him moan like that?"

Lilith turned a bright red and quickly turned and ran for the bedroom. Zakarias rolled back onto the pillows and laughed loudly. As Zachariah looked at his parents Rachel was pounding on his chest and he heard her saying, "Papa, you are just awful! You told me you would not embarrass the girl!"

Zachariah turned to follow Lilith but heard his father say, "Baby, it is so much fun to see you women turn as red as you do."

"Oh Papa!" Zachariah heard a thud and he knew Rachel's fist had connected with his father's chest again.

That night Lilith and Zachariah just slept cuddling, holding onto each other. It was not embarrassment that kept them from their lovemaking, but that Zachariah wanted to just hold her close and feel her warmth. "Lovemaking is wonderful," he had told her, "but sometimes just being close to the one you love is more precious than all the lovemaking combined."

She had smiled at him and nestled under his arm, resting her head upon his chest. He kissed the top of her head and went to sleep with the sweet scent of hyacinth from the soap she used to wash her hair.

The next morning as the old prophetess barged in under the flap and smacked her cane down to awaken everyone; there was a surprise in store for her. For everyone was up and ready for her. In fact they were shocked that she was not already aware that they were awake for it seemed that she had known everything else. She just laughed and said that she was not connected with the Lord all the time, just on important things. Sometimes she just went about her life like everyone else did. They all nodded for that was easy to accept, for surely God had other prophets that needed His time as well.

After their morning meal Zachariah and his father loaded the wagon and then helped the prophetess and Rachel up into it. They said their farewells then Lilith and Zachariah stood arm in arm as they watched the wagon pull away.

From the moment the wagon disappeared from their sight Zachariah could feel a change sweep over Lilith. She suddenly felt cold. She did not say a word as she disengaged from his arm and went back into the house. He followed her in and watched in silence as she cleaned up after the morning meal.

Whenever he would try to start a conversation she would look at him and he could see tears in the corners of her eyes but if he tried to approach to comfort her she would abruptly turn her back to him and continue with what she was doing. Even as they lay in bed she had her back to him and was as far from him as she could be. When he attempted to scoot closer she started to rise from the bed so he said, "Lilith, stay. I will slide back over." Then he moved to the other side of the bed and lay watching her trying to figure out what had gone wrong. Had he done something? Did his father's comment upset her so badly? If so why did she not react at all until after he was gone and why was she not telling him now when he was gone and she had Zachariah all to herself?

All night he lay there and could not sleep as he watched her. After a while he could tell from her breathing that she had drifted to sleep so he rose and dressed then went out and stood just outside the door and looked up into the sky watching the stars.

A star streaked across the sky, bright and sparkling. Shortly after it had vanished another shot across the sky. It was not as bright and it lived shorter upon the night. Something told Zachariah that he had witnessed an omen but of what he had no clue. He gazed a while longer at the night sky before striding across the field to his shop.

As he entered and looked at the stone he suddenly remembered he had wanted to show his father the symbol before he had left but the prophetess had been in such a rush that it had slipped his mind. Now as he looked upon the stone again he still felt like he had not done the carving. It could not have been his hand that had carved that image; he had not the skill or talent within him. He might have been the tool that had been used but some other being had been the craftsman. Maybe even the prophetess herself had possessed him and guided his hand.

The light of the sun began to pry its way through the gaps within the thatch of the roof and trace its delicate fingers along the stone. Zachariah watched as they drifted across the 'Z' and he almost fell into another trance when he heard a soft tap at the door behind him. He turned and saw Lilith standing in the open doorway.

"Zachariah, may I please approach you and talk to you." She said with her head lowered. He could see wetness upon her cheeks and knew she had been crying.

He lifted his hands to her and beckoned her in, "I was wondering when you would tell me what was wrong. Please come and talk to me."

Lilith shook her head 'no' and said, "I cannot take your hands yet, Zachariah, for I fear what I have to tell you more than I fear death. Please just let me come close and kneel upon the floor while I confess my past and my sins to you."

Zachariah suddenly felt very ill, yet he nodded and agreed to let her do as she wished. Lilith entered and stopped about two paces from him then before she knelt she stripped off her clothing and set it in a heap on the ground. She took from the dirt on the floor and rubbed it on her and then knelt on the floor and said, "I come to you naked, to reveal all that I am to you and hide nothing. I am filth, vile since the beginning of time, created from the dust of the earth and cursed by God."

For more than three hours Lilith poured out everything. She told her entire history from her creation by God to her discovery of her curse to the vile things she had done. She told of how she had crawled out of the earth so weak from starvation that she did not think she could live. That was the day he had found her.

She told of her shock at being able to eat regular foods and of not being hurt by the sun. She had not understood why until three months later when he had proposed to her. She still could not fully comprehend until he had told her of his prayer and that he had loved her from the moment he had seen her.

She also told him that she was the one that had killed the others in the other villages. She told him that she had a hunger within her that she had not yet learned to control but when she had felt that her husband's life could be in danger she had come to control it to protect him. Zachariah could see that she was laying herself bare before his eyes so that he could see and hear everything that she had done. Yet it did not stop the feelings that had risen within him.

While she spoke he saw before him a woman that had lied to him from the day they had met. Finally she stopped and laid her arms out before her and placed her forehead upon the ground in a symbol of subjugation.

Zachariah stood and looked down upon her. His heart was beating rapidly with anger. He did not know how he could still feel love for this monster at his feet and yet he did. "Lilith, all I can see before me is a liar."

She raised her head to look up at him, tears streaking down her cheeks. "Husband, please."

"Do not call me that," he hissed from between his clenched teeth. "From the day you met me you have lied to me. You said you did not know your past and you knew everything. You hid a monster in the house of my parents. You could have killed us in our sleep. I do not know why you did not.

"Maybe you had to find out why you could eat and be in the sun, so you kept us alive for information." He turned and looked at the stone, then while staring at the stone asked, "From the day you entered my life how many men did you slay and reduce to nothing but bones and dust before you stopped?"

"Fifteen."

Zachariah spun around and stared at her, "Fifteen, is that all?"

"Yes."

"And to you it is just a number. You do not even see all the lives of the people you ruined by killing those fifteen men." He spat on the ground in front of her. He remembered the man emptying the bones of his son upon the table in front of the village elders and now he knew it was his wife who had been responsible for the loss of both of his sons.

That filled him with deep seated anger, but what surprised him was that rising above even that anger was the jealousy he felt knowing that she had stood naked and lured the men to their deaths with promises of sexual pleasures. Just having them look upon her was a sin. She was supposed to be his.

"Your body was supposed to be mine and mine alone from the day we got engaged."

Lilith looked at him and raised her arms to him and said, "It has been, Zachariah."

"You lie! You used your nakedness to tempt some of those men to their death after we were engaged, and some even after we were already married and sharing our bed." He stood and lifted his hand but stopped himself. He had never hit a woman. He could not hit Lilith even if she were a monster.

Sitting back down he looked at her and said, "Show me!"

Lilith looked at him perplexed, "Show you what, Zachariah?"

"You said you could change form. I want to see them all, show me."

"Please, Zachariah, don't make me do this!"

He gritted his teeth and said once more, "Show me!"

Lilith stood and first she shifted into the form of the cave bear. The bear was wounded. A large gash was across its right forearm. Then she shifted into the wolf and it too showed injury as it held one paw up and limped about. Next she shifted into the large bat, who was badly hurt; one of its wings had been completely ripped off. She followed that by the rat, which was missing its tail. The last she shifted into was an asp; it had been another creature she had drained while she was in the cave after the flood. It was the only one that showed no injury.

Then she stood before him as Lilith again.

"Did you not say you could become a monstrous form, as well as the shape of every man you had drained, and what about the hairy man?" Zachariah asked.

Lilith held her hands together and pleaded with him but he stood adamant. So she shifted into the Neanderthal first, then several of the men she had killed and finally into the monster she had first found she could be. Not once during her changes did Zachariah make even the slightest of sounds, not even when she turned into the monstrous form. When she was done he looked at her and said, "I know you did not show me all the men because I counted five, but that is okay. It was enough. Now tell me, you said that when you shifted you would heal. Why were so many of your forms injured then?"

"That is why I went to see the prophetess. The first time I noticed it was the time I cut my finger while cooking with your mother. It healed but at a normal human pace, not the way I used to heal which was almost as fast as the cut would occur. In the other forms I would have to shift to a different form and then back but then I would be healed." She looked at him the tears in her eyes still falling. He could see she wanted him to forgive her and see that she was trying but instead he was growing colder to her with each moment. The myriad reasons to hate her swirled through his mind, yet he could not bring himself to hate her but he could not forgive her either. She had lied to him. She had killed numerous men and damaged the lives of their innocent families, and she could not even see that she had cheated on her marriage by allowing other men to look upon her naked. He tried to keep his heart open to her explanations but it was growing more difficult as he listened and wondered how much of what she was telling was truth and how much was lies.

"The asp had also been hurt, but I spent a lot of time in the asp form and found out it took the normal amount of time to heal. The bat form will never regain its wing. The wolf's bones will not set properly. The cave bear will heal in time but I have not had the time to be in his form because they no longer exist and being in his form attracts too much attention. The rat will not regain his tail. None of these will heal without help."

She lowered her eyes again; he believed she had finally seen that she was not getting into his heart for she sat back onto her heels and her once proud shoulders drooped and her head that had always been held high hung low as she stared at the floor. Zachariah could see that Lilith had given up. She did not believe that anything she said would break through his cold shell. She was just going through the motions of finishing out the tale.

"The old woman told me you had the gift to heal me but you needed a focus and that you would soon begin to look for one. When we went to get her she asked if you had done what she asked about the stone and I told her yes. She said 'Good, for the stone will be his focus.' I had no idea what she meant, but then when she said you would not find your symbol in the mud but in stone I had some idea." Lilith raised her head again and looked at him.

"Zachariah I do not know how the stone works, or how you will use it to focus, but that stone can heal me. It can do more than heal me. It can make me human again. It can take away the curse and restore me to being just human so I can be your wife."

He stood and looked at her then in a hiss said, "Get out of here woman, who do you think I am to remove a curse placed upon you by God.

"You are a harlot that used the body you swore to be mine to lure men to their death. I am willing to bet my life had I been lured to your temptation upon the night of my proposal I would have been a pile of bones too."

Lilith rose to her knees and wrapped her arms around his legs and said, "Oh no, Zachariah, I loved you, I could never have harmed you."

"Love? Love? Harlot from hell, you know nothing of love! Get out of my sight!" Then Zachariah kicked his legs loose of her grip and turned his back on her.

Lilith wrapped her arms around his legs again but he ignored her. She pleaded but he said nothing. After several more attempts to get him to listen she ran from the shop in tears.

Slowly Zachariah melted into his chair. Tears came to his own eyes as he recalled all the dreams and love he had for Lilith. How could he have been so wrong about her? He laid his head upon the stone and wept bitterly, his tears running down and onto the stone.

It could not have been more than a half hour before he heard the weeping of a child outside the front door of the shop. Zachariah made his way through the shop and saw two young boys helping a little girl along the path. She was hopping on one leg and her other leg was covered in blood.

"Come here," Zachariah said, as he turned and reached just inside the door and grabbed an old apron, but it was a clean one and then tore it into several strips. With one he wiped the blood away and saw a rather large gash on the girl's leg, but it was not serious, only a surface cut. His mother, unfortunately, was away for several more days but there was some of her healing balms inside the shop in case of an accident so he went back inside and got one for cuts.

He returned in only a couple of moments and opened the jar.

"Will it hurt?" asked the crying little girl.

He smiled at her and said, "Not to a brave little girl it won't."

Then he put on a generous amount and took another piece of the apron and wrapped it around her leg.

The girl looked up and smiled at him and said, "It did not hurt at all."

"See, I knew you were brave, but you should go home and rest the leg for a day."

"All right," she said and then she giggled and added to her friends, "He said I was brave."

Then the three went running off toward whatever house in the village they belonged to.

Zachariah carried the bloodied rag inside looking at it he decided it would be a good rag to clean and use for other purposes so he got a clay pot and filled it with water, but there really were no surfaces on which to place the pot inside the shop. All the surfaces were covered with jewelry or jewelry making equipment. He hated to do it but the only flat surface was the stone table. He carried the pot back to the table and set it down. Then put the rag inside it and began to try to wash the blood out of the rag.

He decided he needed some lye and turned to go get some but when he turned he did not remember touching the clay pot yet it tilted and spilled out anyway, the water and blood running out and filling the carved groove. Instantly, there was a flash of golden light and a thought entered

Zachariah's head. He saw an image of a ring, one that would bind him and his true love together in a way no other ring ever would.

He took another piece of the apron and began to sketch out the ring's design upon the apron using a quill and ink. As he set the quill to the apron it was like his hand began to sketch the piece with no aid from him. There were no misplaced lines; each mark went exactly where it was meant to be. His hand would dart across the apron as four distinct views of the ring slowly took form. The ring of two coiled serpents tightly woven about each other in a loving embrace, their heads snuggled against each other took form upon the paper. He watched in awe as his hand finished the top, side, front and three dimensional views of the ring. He had never put so much detail into sketching out a piece of work before but he wondered if it had been him at all for he truly did not feel like his hand had followed his mind, and yet the images had indeed been in his mind as quickly as they were appearing on the apron.

When he was done he held the sketch up and marveled at the miracle before him as the glow faded. He then realized that the anger in his heart had vanished and he wanted to make this ring for Lilith. He looked up at the ceiling and thanked God for he knew the softening of his heart toward Lilith was a true miracle, maybe more of one than the sketch of the ring. He started to turn and placed his hand upon the table to push himself up but his hand caught on the groove of the carving and it sliced his palm.

He wavered and fell back onto his chair as a flash of golden light lifted out of the groove. From the groove rose a three dimensional representation of the groove itself in gold wire. It was as if someone had taken two identical stones and made a casting of the carving. Suddenly he was watching as his hands moved of their own accord. He had no control over them as they reached for the wire and began to weave it together.

More than three hours passed as the weaving continued and when it was completed within the palm of Zachariah's hand lay the ring that had just been designed. He did not know if he had made it or if, like the carving in the stone, he had only been the tool however whatever had happened, the ring was real and was in his hands. As he looked at it closely he could even see on the inside of the ring not one but two tiny representations of the carving.

When he looked at the marks closely and the sun hit them the symbols looked like they filled with blood. They were crimson Z's upon the ring of gold.

Zachariah could not wait any longer he had to go to Lilith and give her the ring. He had to let her know that her past did not matter to him that he loved her and he would forgive her sins. He leapt from the chair and ran from the shop. The distance to the house was nearly fifty yards but Zachariah made the run in only a couple of moments. Under the sheep's skin door he dashed.

He yelled out Lilith's name, but there was no answer.

His only thought was she must be mad and in the bedroom crying. So quickly he ran to the bedroom and stopped frozen at the door.

His hands fell to his side and he heard a clink as the ring slipped from his fingers and landed upon the floor. Slowly he walked forward. He did not want to believe his eyes. Everything within him told him to turn and walk out and come back that it was all just a nightmare and when he came back it would be different. He knew what he was seeing would not change.

Lying upon their bed was Lilith. Her cold unblinking eyes stared upward at the ceiling, in one hand she held a mirror that had fallen close to her face, as if she had stared into the mirror to watch herself take her last breath. Over her heart was her other hand and it held the hilt of a hunting dagger that she had buried in her chest.

Lilith lay upon a pool of her blood.

Zachariah inched forward and fell to his knees beside the bed. He lifted his head and screamed out, "NO! Lilith, I forgive you, why?"

A voice behind him said, "I know you forgave me, husband."

Zachariah felt ice grip his soul. Slowly he stood and turned and looked behind him. Yet there was nothing there. As he watched a thin red mist began to swirl about, slowly it took on the shape and form of a woman. Then he could tell it was Lilith. After what he had seen he was frightened but not terrified, he did not think anything would ever truly surprise him again.

The form began to change color and solidify until Lilith stood before him as if she were living and alive.

"What are you?" Zachariah asked.

Lilith responded, "I am not exactly sure, but I know some things I should not know. I know this is because of the magic of the stone.

"It seems the prophetess put a spell on it so that if this happened I would be filled with the knowledge that we needed," She said.

"How? Lilith?" Zachariah fell to his knees as he looked up to her,

"When you told me your story you said you could not commit suicide."

She walked over to him and began to stroke his hair, holding his head close against her belly. "When you fell in love with me you made my body mortal. That is why I could be hurt and my healing was like that of a normal human. That is why I could go into the sun again, and eat food. Your love gave me gifts but made me mortal with all the frailties of being human as well.

"But it did not release my soul from the curse."

Lilith went on to tell him everything the prophetess had put in the spell and that they had the one night together before she would be trapped within the mirror and held there until someone commissioned him to make a piece of jewelry but it had to follow an exact pattern.

The person who commissioned the piece had to first come in contact with accidentally spilled innocent blood that they had to bring to Zachariah. They could in no way be aware at any time that anything was going on with the blood. Once the piece was commissioned and the design was complete then Zachariah would have to collect a little blood from his client without them knowing he did it on purpose. Only then would the stone give him the webbing to create the piece.

Zachariah pulled himself away from her and crawled to the bed and took the hand of the dead body of his mortal wife. He could hear the other Lilith step toward him and said that she did not want to wait until the next time someone commissioned a piece before she could be with her husband but Zachariah said, "Lilith I do love you but please." He looked upon her dead body and then turned his eyes to her. "This is more than I can take. My wife is dead. You may be her, but after tonight you will be dead to me again for only God knows how long and here your body lies in your blood.

"I cannot even think of making love to you." Slowly he stood. He felt pain, then betrayal. He turned and grabbed the living form of Lilith by the shoulders and looked into her eyes, tears streaming down his face, "Why did you do this?"

"I thought you would not have me."

"But it was only a half hour after you left that the magic started."

"That is the worst part of it Zachariah, I felt the magic begin with the last breath I took, but it was too late by then. My life was already gone."

The Confrontation

Robert Cloud

Chapter One

His eyes were closed and tears rolled down the wrinkles of his cheeks. Even after all the years and all the things he had learned since then remembering her body upon their wedding bed still tore into his heart like the dagger she had buried in her own. Unexpectedly Melanie's tiny arms slid around his neck as she climbed up into his lap and held onto him. She laid her head upon his shoulder and whispered, "Papa Zach, I know you loved her, and that hurt you very badly. I cannot begin to imagine what it must have felt like to find her like that and then to see her in a way still alive too."

She kissed his cheek and nuzzled against his neck, "Please know I will never leave you like that. I love you and could never hurt you that way."

Zachariah lifted her chin and looked into her eyes and said, "It was less her death that hurt me than her lies, and that is one thing I know you will never do."

He hugged her tight and then continued with a few more details of the past. "In those days we did not wait several days to bury our dead like we do today. We did so quickly for flies and rot would take the body. So I walked into the village to get the elders so that they could witness the body and know what had happened.

"Tobyas, even though he was over twice my age pulled me along in his hurry to make certain that there was nothing that could be done to help Lilith live, but once he saw her he knew that what I had said was the truth. He tried to pull her fingers away from the handle but her grip was so firm upon the hilt that he had no doubt that she had plunged the blade in herself.

"No one would have accused me but Tobyas had to be sure and make record so that none could come back later to make claim that I was guilty of her death." Zachariah paused and held Melanie for a moment and he took a breath to continue, "No one knew that in my own heart I would feel for many years that I was to blame.

"Tobyas directed the village men to use the bed clothes as her shroud. As they wrapped her not one pulled the blade out for they felt that since it was suicide if they removed the blade her ghost would come back and haunt the village. Little did they know that the blade had nothing to do with her ability to haunt the village.

"Three men carried Lilith's body out of the house. Tobyas stood beside me and handed me something small, I looked down into my hand and it was the ring. Then he offered me the mirror she had been holding. I took it and looked into the glass and for a brief moment saw a red haze reflection of Lilith's face and knew that she was there exactly as she had said she would be.

"The men carried Lilith's body to the center of the village where other men had already erected a wooded platform. However suicide was such a serious sin amongst my people that the word had spread ahead of us and as we walked the other villagers had emptied the streets and closed their doors. No one would look upon the body of one that had taken their own life. Even the men that were helping me would perform a ritual or purification before returning to their own homes.

"It was custom to bury our dead, but when one committed suicide no one wanted the body to be around so that it could rise again if it were cursed so they would burn it. I watched in tears as the flames consumed Lilith's body. I remained until I was the last one there and only embers remained. Then I turned and returned to the house."

Zachariah looked up at the clock. It read twenty minutes until midnight and there was still a little to tell Melanie before the stroke of midnight. He kissed her forehead and said, "I am going to have to rush through a lot of this, time is running low and there is still a lot to tell.

"Four days passed before I heard the wagon carrying my parents returning. I walked outside to meet them. My mother immediately noticed something was wrong with my stance and asked me where Lilith was. I fell to the ground at her feet and wept like a child. Finally I calmed down enough to tell them that she had taken her life. I could not tell them of her confession, the suicide was bad enough. That alone would haunt them forever but the images in her confession were almost too much for me to handle. I just could not destroy the happy images they had of her.

"My parents helped me into the house and another two days passed while my mother did all she could to soothe my sorrows. On the third morning I awoke and deep down knew it was time that I tried to face life. I had to move on. I got up and began to prepare to join my father at the shop but as I sat down to eat my morning meal my mother sat beside me and pulled me tight to her. She said that she had not wanted to keep something from me but she did not want to add to my pain. Her face was filled with grief and tears began to roll down her face, I held my mother tight and told her that I had lost my wife, and that there were few things that could be worse so she could tell me anything. She looked up at me and said it had been wrong of her to keep it a secret. She had wanted so badly to tell me before she and my father had left to take the prophetess back to the mountain but Lilith had made her promise not to say a word. Then she broke down and wept bitterly, burying her face in her hands.

"It took me a long time to get my mother to calm down enough that she could even speak. When I had I asked her to tell me what had made her so distraught that was when she informed me that Lilith had been carrying my child.

"The look on my face must have been horrendous because my mother sat up and backed away from me. I felt like the dagger that Lilith had driven into her heart she had driven into mine as well. I could not have imagined feeling worse than I had at the loss of my wife and then suddenly I knew a pain that was far greater and it was not pain for me alone. I had seen my mother joyful, she had wanted a grandchild in the household and Lilith had torn that from her. I had seen my father laughing and full of pride and now his name would end with me. I had been cursed by marrying a monster that knew not what love was and who had no respect for life, not even the life she carried within her.

"I have no idea how long I sat there in my stunned silence but when I looked up my mother had gained her feet and was looking down at me. She asked me if she needed for me to go get my father. I told her I was okay but that it would be best if she went on to the shop with my father.

"My mother's face filled with worry. More tears began to run down her face as she coaxed from me a promise that I would not hurt myself. I told her that I knew suicide was a sin and I had already felt its bitter sting. It was not something I would ever put her and my father through. Thus assured she went to join my father. Once she was gone I went to the hearth and grabbed an iron used to stir the embers. I took a cloth and wrapped it around the iron and then placed the cloth into the fire until the flames had leapt from the embers onto the cloth. Then I went about the house and set the burning torch to everything that would burn. Before I left I held the mirror high and looked into it telling Lilith she had lied to me once too often then I placed it on the table and left it to burn with the rest of the house.

"As I stepped through the door of the house I threw the torch back inside and walked about twenty yards away and watched the house burn. While I watched sparks from the house shoot up into the sky I remembered the omen. I remembered the night I had seen the two shooting stars, the larger one followed closely by a smaller and shorter lived one and I knew one had been for Lilith and her long life coming to an end, the other weaker one for the short life of the child in her belly.

"I was furious. I wanted nothing to remind me of Lilith. She had purposefully failed to tell me of my child and had she told me of it my reactions would have been very different. She probably would not have committed suicide. Or so I thought." Zachariah paused and held Melanie close for a moment, his head lying against hers.

"My parents came running to my side and I told them I had done it on purpose. That I could build a new house, but I needed to erase Lilith. When the fire had died I went to search the ashes and to my amazement the mirror remained unharmed. Even now I do not know why I did not try another way to destroy it. Instead I took it to the shop and placed it near the table. It stayed there until I had built my new home and then I kept it in the bedroom of the house with me. I found that I could talk to Lilith and she to me in our thoughts."

Again Zachariah gazed up at the clock and five more minutes had passed, his time was narrowing even more.

"That very week an elders' meeting was called. During that meeting I learned that Lilith had lied to me. She had not stopped at fifteen men like she had said. There had now been twenty two bodies that had been found. The last seven had been in villages further away than those where the previous deaths had occurred.

"Lilith had lied to me and to everyone and this brought up another question. Suddenly it seemed that some of the things that the prophetess had said also did not make sense for she had said that Lilith would confess all, but Lilith had not. If the prophetess were a true seer she would have known Lilith would lie and that there was no chance that the good path she had mentioned could have happened.

"I had to go see her again and ask her for myself how she could have made such a mistake. So I got the directions from my parents and went to the Mountain. When I entered the hut of the prophetess I was in for a shock for the woman sitting upon the pillows on the floor before me was not the woman that had come to my house. I asked her when the prophetess would return and she informed me she was the prophetess and that she had just returned from being away on a pilgrimage. She had been away for six months.

"My knees grew weak and I fell to the floor. She told me many things about what had happened and that there were some things that were even hidden from her.

"I asked her about the stone and what should I do with it? She told me that the stone was a neutral thing and that it was the person that used it that was good or evil. She said that my heart was good and that I would do a lot of good with it. She also warned me that there was evil connected with it but said that the good I would do would outweigh the evil and in the end either the good would win or the stone would be destroyed and neither would win.

"So I did not destroy the stone. I found that if someone came to me that was ill or hurt I could use the stone to speed their recovery. I could even cure them of illnesses that others said they could not be cured of but the person had to be someone with a good and decent heart or it would not work."

Zachariah sighed and lowered his head and said, "Yet there have been many times I have been tempted to destroy the stone too.

"In the beginning when the first commission happened and Lilith returned in body something amazing happened to me too. My age was restored to the very age I was on the day that I first used the stone. The first time was a major shock. Then when Lilith appeared I felt something happen and it happened swiftly, almost instantly. I had been nearly seventy years old that first time. I had been hurt in an accident when I was fifty and my back had been damaged so I had a bowed back and needed two walking sticks to get around. Suddenly there was no pain in my back and I was standing straight. I looked into the mirror that normally held Lilith and I was looking at the young man that had looked at me the day Lilith had died. I was the exact same age as I was the first day I had used the stone and I was completely healed."

Melanie looked at him, "Papa Zach, if you could use the stone to heal others why did you not use it to heal yourself."

"I had thought about that, but for some reason it seemed wrong to me. So I could not bring myself to do it. Then when the commission's magic healed me I felt that perhaps it was that magic that was supposed to heal and cure me and I thought I had done the right thing."

She smiled at him, "Maybe you did the right thing then."

"Maybe, I don't know.

"I stood feeling whole again. It felt wonderful to be young and to not be wracked with the pain I had been in for so many years but as I turned there was Lilith." The sudden surge of anger that boiled within me for all the deaths she had caused nearly overwhelmed me. With every fiber of my being I wanted to kill her for all she had done but one lone chord within me knew I could not.

"Then a second thought hit me that was even worse. If I let her know how much I hated her and she left and went out into the night then she would probably kill someone else just to spite me. I despised what I had to do but I opened my arms and welcomed her into them. When I awoke in the morning she was gone and I spent the next hour beside a bucket emptying my stomach for the foulness I felt. Yet I knew I had saved someone's life."

Zachariah paused and looked at Melanie. Upon her face was a look that he had felt within his heart the next morning when he had awoken. He had known he had done what had to be done but he was filled with self-disgust nonetheless. The look in Melanie's eyes told him that she understood the self-loathing he had felt. Had she been in a similar situation?

"I began to look around the shop and while I was doing so a customer came in. They asked if Zachariah was around and I almost answered that it was me until I remembered the massive change in my age. I told them I was a relative visiting and he was not yet awake that maybe I could help them.

"After they had left I realized that with such a major change in my appearance I had no choice. I secreted everything away in the night and moved several villages away and started a new shop. I had plenty of gold so it was easy to start a new life, and back then identification papers were not like they are today. They were not needed, so I just changed my name and started fresh."

"Wait!" Melanie interrupted, "Papa Zach, if the commission's magic makes you young why are you not young now? You are still as old as the day you made the tiara and Lilith has not returned."

He smiled at her. Melanie was a very smart girl and he truly loved that about her, "That is something I still do not fully understand even after all these centuries. There does not seem to be a rhyme or reason to how that works. Sometimes Lilith returns the very moment the piece of jewelry is complete and the glow is still fading from the stone. There are other times that it may be years later. It is different with each piece. Yet there seems to be some key moment in the piece's creation or existence when something happens and Lilith is called back and the magic is complete. There is even one piece out there in the cabinet right now that I do not even remember making for it has been there that long. The magic has never happened. I know that I only remember the story of the piece after the magic has happened so until it does that piece is a mystery to me.

"In time if the magic of yours did not complete I would forget everything about yours too until it did complete but I have a strong suspicion I know when yours is going to happen."

Melanie's eyes grew wide and he could see more than a touch of fear in them. "When Papa Zach?"

He smiled at her then held her close to him like he was protecting her from the world before he said, "I am getting to that precious, and I know you are anxious to know but there are things I need to tell you in a precise order or you will not understand what is happening and what to do when the time comes."

"First thing I need to tell you is that I realized when the woman who came to the house turned out not to be the prophetess that Lilith had never intended to become human. She wanted me to heal her so she could become what she had been. I do not think she wanted to kill me because she needed my love to be able to stay in the sun. I am quite certain she was going to use my ability to heal with the stone to keep her healed in her other forms without me knowing it. For every time I used the stone to heal her it would have healed all of her forms. An even greater magic would have occurred had she aided me during a commission for as that magic healed me completely it would possibly have restored her to being invulnerable.

"Secondly, had she been alive the magic of the stone would have restored her to true humanity, for I do believe the magic is from God and it would have cured her of the curse. However, after she took her life the way the magic affected her changed.

"Exactly how it affects her I am not certain, I do know some of the things that she said were true but she has told me so many lies I have no way of knowing what other parts are true and what are fabrications.

"She said that when a piece was commissioned that she had only one day to be in her corporeal form. I suspect that that is true. She does get at least one day in her body when the magic is finally completed. Yet, I also suspect that there is more to it than she told me. I suspect that she has some other form that she can escape from the mirror in. That may have nothing to do with the stone or its magic at all. If it is not her that is escaping then there is someone that is following me, perhaps the false prophetess herself, that is committing atrocities that resemble the kinds of murders that Lilith was responsible for.

"At first it was a vague suspicion and I only heard things upon rare occasion, but in this modern age of multimedia and fast news reporting I have become more certain with every report I hear. For the last several years I have been following every news article I can find and almost like clockwork every twenty-two days there is a pile of bones found somewhere within fifty miles of where I am living.

"I think the twenty-two may actually have something to do with the number of people Lilith killed while she was with me. I am not certain. But I suspect if she had killed only one, then it would have been possible for her to be out constantly for it would have shown that she had repented and she and I could have been together even after her death.

Melanie shivered in his arms and said, "You mean she gets out every twenty-two days to kill, just because she likes it, not because she has to?"

Zachariah stroked her hair to try to ease her fears but he felt them himself and could feel them within her. "I am not positive but that is what I think. What makes me think that even more is that the last report was only two days ago in Lake George and there were two other murders in the opposite direction down in Albany that were very grisly. They were not the piles of bones, but the viciousness of the attack and the description of the bodies leads me to think it was Lilith and that she did it simply out of anger and a lust to kill.

"Another thing that leads me to suspect it may have been her is that there is no evidence that there was a weapon at all. Steel leaves a trace when it cuts flesh, but there were no fragments of steel in the wounds and these bodies were cut into pieces with something sharper than any surgical steel blade that the coroner had ever seen."

Melanie started quivering within his arms and he did all he could to hold her tight. He knew he had told her more in the description of the bodies than he would have liked but she also needed to know how dangerous Lilith was. Time was running out. She needed to know that Lilith was not the loving woman that he had thought she was when he was married to her. Instead she was a prideful manipulative monster that would stop at nothing to get what she wanted. He knew that included killing him to get to Melanie if she needed to.

"The final reason I think it is Lilith is that I think she is taunting me to discover her secret. From time to time I have found boxes of women's clothing in the attic that I did not place there. Sometimes there have even been traces of blood upon them." Suddenly he could feel Melanie tighten and she pulled away from him, her eyes searching his and he knew immediately what she wanted to know.

"No, no sweetie. The dress you wore to your Homecoming Dance was given to me as partial payment on a piece of jewelry that a woman had commissioned. One of the rules of the commission is that I have to accept payment in whatever means they can pay. When she came to the store with the innocent's blood she looked at all the jewelry and said she so badly wanted to get a necklace for her granddaughter but she did not have any money. I told her to bring what she could to pay and she thanked me and brought the dress. It had belonged to her own grandmother and I felt really bad about taking it but I had no choice. Once she had offered it I had to accept.

"Over the centuries many women offered to pay with their clothing." Melanie looked at him with a tilt of her head and Zachariah could actually feel a small wave of jealousy emanating from her. He snickered for it was nice to know she saw him as hers even though these events happened long ago. "There is only one thing that I can refuse."

Melanie's eyes widened and she rested her fists upon her hips as she glared at him. He smiled at her and added, "If they offer their bodies I can refuse and ask that they offer something else instead." Then he leaned near to Melanie and kissed her forehead and said, "I have already told you sex to me is sacred, I have never accepted the offering of someone's body no matter how tempting it may have been."

"Papa Zach!" Melanie huffed.

"I am teasing sweetie. I have never even been tempted."

"However during the ages men were far more likely to have the money to afford the jewelry than women were. Sometimes women would trade me pieces of jewelry that had been in their family for generations to get a special piece, sometimes they would be my maid for a period to pay for the jewelry, other times they would trade me their clothing. I have lots of women's clothing upstairs in closets and trunks because I am not allowed to get rid of it, and the magic keeps it from going old. It is almost as if it is waiting for someone to come and claim it." He smiled at her and added, "In fact I had never thought of it until now, but almost every piece of clothing I have is your size."

Melanie beamed brightly, "Maybe I was always meant to come into your life, Papa Zach?"

"Perhaps that is true," he said, "Lilith seemed to think so. She said you are 'the One' that she has waited for since her death."

She buried her head against his shoulder and whispered, "That sounds so ominous. What did she mean?"

He looked up at the clock and saw it was five minutes before midnight, time was almost gone. "I am getting to that part right now."

"Remember how I said that the image of the carving was like a casting of the carving when I made the ring?"

Melanie nodded and said, "Yes."

"Well, I did not know why at the time but I think I do now."

"Every time after that when a piece was made the image was like a drawing on a sheet of paper, flat and two dimensional until the image for your tiara. That image was even grander than the one for the ring. That image was like a real three dimensional tree had grown from the stone. One exactly like the image but with a full canopy of limbs and a full spread of roots, it was like nothing I had thought possible.

"I had already learned from talking to you that you were the type that thought ill of no one. That you had a good heart and were a good person."

Melanie blushed as she lowered her head to hide her red cheeks.

"I also learned you were a virgin. You are special, a virgin with a pure heart. I think that's why the image was the way it was."

"Oh Papa Zach," Melanie blushed even brighter, "I am nothing special."

"But indeed you are Melanie," he said, "not just in my heart, but in all the realms of the arcane and the spiritual. A heart that thinks ill of no one, even those that do them harm is unique especially in today's world.

"I met your mother, and for you to harbor no ill will towards her is amazing."

"Why should I? It is not her fault that she did not know she would get pregnant when she and my father signed that contract. I can understand her loving her blood children more than one she had adopted from a woman that was going to abort it."

"Yet you do not hold ill will towards your blood mother either."

"She could not have supported a child. It would have meant living on the streets, which she may have had to do anyway. I cannot see being upset with her, she did the best she could do for me."

Zachariah looked at her with pride in his heart. He had thought that this was the type of woman he had found when he had found Lilith. He had been mistaken then, but this time there was no doubt. One of the gifts from the stone had been the gift to sense truth in people and he knew that Melanie was truly everything that he had thought Lilith was. "Melanie, you see that is my point. When I made that first piece of jewelry I was just like you. I could not think ill of anyone. Yes I was mad at Lilith for lying to me but I had already forgiven her and she was the first person in my life I had ever been mad at and even today I feel my anger was justified even if she had only been lying and had not been the monster she turned out to be. Yet if she had only been lying she could have repented and we might have had a life. I did not want her harmed. I just wanted her out of my sight while I thought of what to do.

"I think that is why the image was like a casting for me. If I had been a virgin as you were it may have been the full tree like yours was." He hugged her so tight. "You are special for people like you are rare, I wish I had found someone like you when I was young."

Melanie frowned and smacked his arm, "But then you would not have found me."

For the first time the entire night Zachariah laughed and said, "You are right, I would not have found you. So it was a good thing I did not." As he rubbed his arm he remembered his mother and father and the relationship they'd had. How it had been a deep friendship as well as a marriage. He knew they would have adored Melanie.

"Yet you are special for even more reasons. You are not only a virgin, from the things you have told me and the way I have watched you eat you have kept your body pure in ways you were not even aware of. You do not drink sodas and things that are artificial. You do not pollute your body with chemicals and drugs. So you are truly pure of heart, body and soul. In many ways the stone was right in pointing out that you are the one. For you are unique in this modern time."

"But what does that mean I am the One."

At that moment the clock began to strike midnight and Zachariah said, "Our time is almost up. I will try to hurry but stand inside this circle with me."

Melanie got up and they held hands within the circle. Zachariah stood to face the back of the cabinet as it slowly began to open of its own accord.

"Lilith has one chance at living again. That is if she can share the body with one like you."

The clock chimed the second note as a thin red mist began to seep through the crack that had formed as the cabinet continued to open. It began to swirl about like a very faint dust devil.

"But it is your choice to say yes or no. There is something that she does not know and she is not fully formed so she cannot yet hear."

The third chime sounded and the mist grew thicker as the dust devil spun more rapidly and the funnel, like a tiny tornado, swirled in front of the now open doorway.

Zachariah reached into his pocket and pulled out the ring that had once been meant for Lilith. He knew now it had never truly been meant for her for it had been meant for the one he would love and he had always had some inkling of doubt that Lilith loved him. During their one year of marriage she had not once said she loved him unless she felt she was going to lose something if she did not say the words she knew he wanted to hear. He held the ring before Melanie and said, "Melanie, you are now eighteen, if we survive tonight, will you marry me?"

As the fourth chime sounded the tornado grew thicker and a body began to form within the swirling vapor. Melanie threw her arms about Zachariah's neck and said, "Yes, my love, I will." There were tears in her eyes as he slipped the ring on her finger. Then to her surprise the ring spun and the outer layer separated and curled into her hand to form a second ring. She could see a fine gold wire connecting the two, so fine it was almost as if it did not exist. She took the second ring and said, "And Zachariah will you be my husband?"

He smiled and responded, "Yes, I will." The ring slowly uncoiled and became the serpent again. It undulated along her arm and crawled under her blouse then when it was directly above her heart there was a momentary glow and Melanie felt a small sting as it pierced her skin. She could feel it crawling into her. For a brief moment she looked up to Zachariah with terror in her eyes and then suddenly her body was covered in a warm glow as she felt the serpent pass through her heart and then suddenly like an arrow from a bow it burst out of her chest and into Zachariah's where it pierced his heart and he too was consumed in the golden light.

As the light faded Melanie could see the serpent coming out of the sleeve of his shirt. Slowly it encircled his finger and reformed into a ring. It was an exact match of hers with only the difference in the size of their fingers.

Melanie was startled by a thin gold filament that she could see that connected her heart to Zachariah's. Slowly the filament faded but she knew it was still there. Then a mouth formed upon her ring and on Zachariah's and in unison they said, "Two hearts that will beat as one, two breasts that will breathe as one, these two are wed now and forever, in this world and beyond."

Melanie looked up at Zachariah and said, "Did you know that this would happen?"

But she knew the answer from the startled look upon his face. He had not known the magic of the ring any more than she had. Then she asked, "Does this mean we are married?"

"These rings were made with magic, but I do believe that the magic was a gift from God, so I would have to say that in God's eyes yes we are. Still I would prefer we make it legal."

She nodded and then wrapped her arms around his neck tight.

"Oh look at the two love birds." Came a voice filled with vehemence and hatred from the open doorway.

Zachariah turned. He had been too absorbed with the effects of the magic and had not noticed the clock had finished striking. There in the doorway stood Lilith, as stark and naked as she had been the day she had appeared after she had taken her life. She was as alive as she had been, as beautiful as she had been, but her eyes were red flames burning upon a mask of pure hatred that was her contorted face.

He held Melanie close to him, not wanting to let her go, not wanting to let her face the monster that he knew Lilith was, but Melanie looked up at him and whispered, "Papa Zach, it is okay."

"Papa? Oh isn't that cute. Did you tell her to call you that like your mother called your father or did she just do it on her own?" Lilith sneered.

Slowly Melanie disentangled herself from his arms and looked at Lilith. For the first time she was looking at the woman that the man she loved had once been married to. She had lied to him and betrayed him and had destroyed his life. Even though she had every reason in the world to hate Lilith she did not, she felt pity for her, pity that she had not let someone as wonderful as Zachariah give her the life she could have had. The tears in Melanie's eyes were for the love Lilith would never understand. Her voice was strong as she faced what she knew was truly someone void of the ability to feel love at all. As she spoke her words were filled with the love that resounded from her heart, "From the moment I met Papa I felt safe with him. It was I that asked him if I could call him Papa Zach, he had nothing to do with it."

Lilith hissed at the girl but Melanie held her place. Smiling Lilith said, "She is a brave one, Zach, maybe too brave.

"So little girl, has he told you about your decision yet?"

Melanie looked up at Zachariah and suddenly noticed he was not yet young. "No, he has not told me what I have to decide. You interrupted us."

Melanie took a deep breath and tried to be as brave as she could. She knew that somehow she was going to have to save the man she loved but she had no idea how. For now she would try to stall. "So, Lilith, is everything you told Zachariah about you being in the Garden of Eden the truth or was that just more of your lies?"

Lilith seemed to grow a foot in height before her eyes as her anger flared. Fire literally leapt from her eyes. She turned her head and looked at Zachariah and said, "The old fool told you all about me did he? Well what does it matter whether it is true or not?"

The transformation took only a few seconds and Melanie nearly fell out of the circle and would have if Zachariah had not caught her. Before them both stood the monstrous eight foot tall black winged beast of Lilith, "What matters is that I am Wampyr!"

Lilith leapt at them and a blinding flash of gold erupted before Melanie and Zachariah as she slammed into the invisible barrier formed by the circle of salt and ash Zachariah had laid about them. The form of the creature instantly vanished and Lilith was hurled back across the room and slammed into the wall hard enough that Melanie could hear several bones break.

While Lilith was struggling to regain her feet Melanie turned to Zachariah and whispered, "Why are you not young? What is wrong with the magic?"

Zachariah looked at his hands and saw they were still wrinkled then looked at Lilith as she was resetting her bones and they were beginning to knit.

"You fool! Zach, it is because of the protective circle about you. Part of the magic that heals you comes from me. Since you have kept me out it cannot get to you, but you cannot keep me out much longer. She must make a decision."

Zachariah looked at Melanie and said, "Stay here. Whatever happens do not leave the circle, please promise me that."

"Papa?"

"Please! Precious, promise me! She is still hurt, I do not know how she is healing at all, in the past she could not heal it must have something to do with you, but at least she is healing slowly. So stay here. Please."

Lilith hissed as she turned to face Zachariah, "Precious, you never used that word with me!"

Melanie looked at Lilith and said, "For you, Papa, I promise."

Zachariah took a deep breath for he knew he was about to risk more than he had ever risked before, but he was also about to make certain Melanie would live a long and full life without being cursed with Lilith inside of her.

He stepped out of the circle. Light engulfed him and in an instant he was young again, his body was once again the same biological age it had been more than three thousand five hundred years earlier. Then he looked at Lilith. The same magic that had reversed his age had healed her completely and instantly. What little advantage he thought he might have had had vanished. He faced her and announced, "Melanie does not have to make any decision."

Lilith threw back her head and laughed. The room shook. The clock that was on the wall fell to the floor with a crash and the glass plate that hung above the table began to swing, but the chains held. She lowered her head and said, "You cannot change the magic, Zach. She is the one."

"No, Lilith, she was the one, but now there are two."

Lilith's eyes narrowed and she looked at him menacingly, "How dare you play games with me, Zachariah, she is the one that gave her blood."

Zachariah looked to Melanie and said, "Hold up your hand."

Melanie lifted her hand with the ring and showed it to Lilith. Even as she did so her eyes were still fastened to Zachariah where they had been since the moment of his transformation. She had believed in the magic. He had proved its existence to her, but she had not expected his metamorphosis would be so dramatic. He barely even looked like the man she had known.

Then Zachariah asked, "Do you recognize that ring?"

As he spoke Melanie knew it was him. It was not only his accent, which she had grown to adore, but the tenderness with which he spoke to her that confirmed his identity within her heart. The love she felt for him had not changed.

She had never thought of a man as beautiful before but as her eyes studied him she saw that he was a beautiful man. He had said he would be twenty, which meant he was only two years older than her in physical age now. The crevices that had once broken his face were replaced with the firm skin of youth and the crow's feet that had been at the sides of his eyes and reached to his temples were smooth again. His hair was as black as obsidian and his eyes were a dark blue. His skin was nearly the color of bronze, and his muscles rippled as he moved. He was a living sculpture, carved in flesh expressing a beauty that Michelangelo could not have captured in stone. She gasped as she saw Lilith step towards him.

The first sight of the ring froze Lilith in place. The fire in Lilith's eyes grew brighter. Then like a striking serpent her hand struck out and seized Zachariah by the neck and pulled him near her, "That was the ring you made for me, by what right did you give it to her?" Her lips spread and fangs grew in her mouth as she snarled at him. He could feel the grip on his throat tighten as she hissed, "Did you forget you are married to me?"

"No, Lilith. You gave up that right when you killed yourself." Zachariah struggled as he held onto her hand to keep her from crushing his throat.

"That ring was made for the woman I would love heart, body and soul, and who would love me equally. You never loved me so it was never made for you." Then Zachariah released her wrist and raised his hand to show her the ring upon his finger.

"When I placed it upon her the magic of the ring divided it into two, this is the other ring. It connected our hearts, our souls, our very breaths. We are one, and by pronouncement of the ring itself we are married."

Lilith lifted her head and howled as she flung him against the wall then she turned into the cave bear and stalked over to him ready to strike at him. Melanie screamed!

"Lilith, I am as good a host as she is. What better way to get your revenge than to possess the man that made you his slave?" Zachariah had never made Lilith his slave, but he knew that to her being a wife was as good as being a slave. The word had hit home for she transformed back into Lilith.

Slowly Lilith got close to him and looked him in the eyes. "So you are offering your own life to save hers."

Melanie fell to her knees, "No! Papa!" He could tell she was struggling to keep from coming to his side but she had made a promise so she stayed within the circle.

Melanie wept. She could not lose the man she loved. She could not let that monster take him from her. Yet she did not want to disobey Papa Zach. She wanted to be perfect in his eyes and in doing that she would do as he said. She lifted her eyes and listened to his words but they really did not matter. She loved him. That was all that mattered.

"Melanie, I cannot let her take over your life. She is a monster. I have lived for three millennia; you have only begun your life." Zach's eyes were filled with tears as he looked at her, "I love you, Melanie, let me do this."

She lowered her head to the floor and wept.

"Oh how sweet. The sacrifice for the one you love." Lilith sneered, "But what will stop me from killing her once I take your body."

"Well, Lilith, that I do know. I remembered part of your story as I was weaving the ring and I know the ring will not let you kill someone of your own sex. You are female in spirit, you will not be able to kill or even harm her."

Lilith straddled his chest, placing both hands at his throat. "I ought to rip your throat out."

"You cannot do that, for if you kill me Melanie will die too. Our hearts beat as one."

In rage Lilith leapt off of him and charged toward Melanie but she again struck the invisible barrier that the sands of the circle Zachariah had drawn made. She was flung across the room as if she had been struck by the force of a lightning strike. Her hair and skin smoked and sizzled for a moment. Her skin was charred, and she knew this time it would not heal unless Zachariah used the stone for Zachariah had been transformed now and that part of the magic was complete. Now she had to wait until she was reborn. So she walked over to where he lay and sat upon his chest.

"So I will not be able to kill or feed from women. Well that still leaves men, so I accept. I will take your body," she said.

Slowly she began to merge into his body only then did she hear him say, "No, Lilith, your body will be male. You cannot attack the same sex. Your spirit is female so you cannot attack, harm or kill females. Your body will be male so you cannot attack, harm or kill males. You will have to satisfy your appetite for blood from blood banks or from animals. For you will not be able to take it from living humans ever again."

Lilith screamed and tried to pull free from his body but the magic was already melding them together. "You tricked me, Zachariah."

Then a small voice said, "I will do it."

Zachariah turned, his eyes filled with horror for he knew what had just happened, still he said, "No, Melanie!"

Lilith laughed, "Too late! Zachariah, she was the first choice of the magic, she can overrule you."

There was no slow melding of Lilith to Melanie and the circle of sand no longer protected her. Once Melanie had spoken the circle exploded outward and Lilith flew free of Zachariah. She was free only long enough to throw her taunt at him before she merged completely with Melanie.

Melanie's eyes turned red and Zachariah knew what he had feared would happen was true. Lilith had no intention of sharing the body. She had taken over and in an instant she had either destroyed Melanie's soul or buried it so deeply that Melanie might as well no longer even exist.

The new Lilith lifted her head and stretched her arms. She smiled and looked down at Zachariah. "So, we are married again are we? How pleasant of you to have informed me of that.

"Well then, let's see about that," hissed Lilith. She walked over to Zachariah and circled him looking down at him. He could see from the wicked look upon her contorted face, that her mind was hatching some evil plan. He started to rise and she put her foot on his chest and pushed him back down. "No, not yet. I think I like you on the floor for the moment."

Lilith reached down and grabbed his ankle and lifted him off the floor as if he were a rag doll. Then she swung him over her head, in an arch, crashing him into the floor again. He felt several ribs break as the wind was also forced from his lungs. Then she dragged him by his ankle toward the table. There she dropped him and ignored him momentarily.

He forced himself to roll onto his back and watched her as she caressed the table and walked about it. The smile on her face filled with evil intent as she spoke, "Soon this table will restore me to being a full Wampyr. I will have all my abilities and heal like I used to. Nothing will stand in my way, except I am going to make one little change. You, Zachariah love the soul that is buried deep within this body. So if I want to walk in the sun I need to make certain you stay around a long time."

Once she was done circling the table she came to where he lay and stood straddling him as she slowly and seductively removed the dress Melanie had put on for the Grand Opening. Then like one of those exotic dancers he had seen on a late night show on cable she stripped off the undergarments as well.

Zachariah's heart ripped in his chest as he was forced to watch as Lilith revealed the body of the woman he loved. It was Melanie's body but he knew her soul was lost and he did not know if he had a chance to retrieve it. He had thought that the loss he had felt when Lilith had taken her life was excruciating but it was nothing compared to the torment that was shredding his soul now.

At Lilith's death he had already known of her deceit and treachery and even then he had felt the pain. This time was far worse for Melanie was a complete innocent that truly loved him and she had sacrificed herself to save him. He was not worthy of that sacrifice. He had allowed Lilith to continue to exist when he should not have. He should have tried harder to find a way to destroy her even if it had meant his own death.

What tormented him most was his arousal. He knew Lilith controlled Melanie's now naked body and yet he could not control his own body's desire.

Slowly Lilith leaned down and ran her hand over his crotch, "Oh, I see, you are still a man at least."

Then like lightning her hand was around his throat and she lifted him off the floor and threw him upon the table. He knew Lilith intended to rape him with her body and he wanted to fight it but this time when she had grasped his neck he had felt something pop. He tried to move his arm, and immediately wished he had not as a bolt of searing pain shot from his finger tip to his neck and into his brain. *Okay, this is not good. One more time.*

He went to lift his knee and again the same thing, a searing streak of pain that cut into his neck and then pierced his brain.

In both cases he had not managed to move and yet the pain was so intense he was still seeing flashes within his field of vision. Zachariah was certain Lilith had broken his neck and that if he actually did manage to move his head or neck he would be paralyzed.

Slowly and sensuously she climbed up his body, brushing her breast along his thighs and then his chest. He was thankful he was dressed, but as soon as he had thought it she began ripping his shirt to shreds as she sat on top of him. He could feel her mind entering his, so he knew she was trying to make him stay perfectly still but it was not working. He knew he could move if it were not for the pain in his neck, yet he also knew it was a good idea to play along and let her think she had control.

"From the day I was cursed I have never created another like me because I wanted to remain unique, the only one like me. However, now I think it would be sweet revenge to have the man that made eighteen months of my life pure hell as my slave. I pretended to grovel to your every need, cooking for you, cleaning for you but now you will be my slave and will do my bidding. She threw his belt to the corner of the room and undid his pants, her hand reaching inside to find his cock.

"Oh, see, you are happy to see me after all."

It was not her, she should know that. It was Melanie that he loved. Right now he hated his body for betraying Melanie and letting Lilith have her fun.

She climbed off the table and pulled his pants and boxers off and threw them across the room. This time as she climbed along his body, her body rubbed seductively against his. There were no thoughts he could focus on to drive away his body's reactions and he wanted to scream, yet he also wanted Lilith to think she had control of his mind.

She climbed past his cock and sat straddle his belly.

"Before I fuck you, Zach, I am going to turn you." She smiled down at him, "Yes, I wanted you to know that first."

He wanted to push her away but he could not for his arms would not do his bidding. Then he felt her teeth sink into his neck and his mind began to drift.

Papa, do not worry, I am not gone.

Melanie? You communicated with me telepathically before but it was softly, this is so strong.

Yes, Papa, but this is not normal telepathy. She would be able to read that.

How?

She does not know I am still here, while she is drinking she is seeing your life but she cannot see the thoughts that pass between us through the rings.

The rings? You mean we are communicating through them now?

Yes, Papa. I can see parts of her mind. She is scared.

Lilith, scared? Why?

The bond to my body is not complete. It takes time to take hold. There is something that can happen that can break it.

Do you know what?

No, Papa.

Wait!

What Papa?

She moved up to my chest. She did not rape me before biting me. She was very adamant about you being pure and a virgin.

So, if I am not a virgin she cannot stay?

That could well be it.

Then Papa, take me. Take my virginity.

Precious, you did get your wish. You are eighteen, and by the rings we are married.

No Papa, I am not eighteen yet, the clock it is 12:58; I still have 2 minutes before I am eighteen.

Wait! There is something. She is waiting for something. I bet she has to have you a certain age past your birth time, if that is so she does not know your birth time here is one in the morning. She thinks it is midnight.

That could help us, Papa!

Yes, but there is only one problem. I think she broke my neck. I will have to wait until she has turned me and I have healed. I hope that that is not too late.

I hope so too Papa. I do not like that you have to be a vampire. Will driving her out return you to being human.

No, precious, but with your love I will not need to feed on blood and I can go in the sun, so in all ways I will be human.

Then it will not be bad, will it Papa.

No. Lilith was a monster even before she was cursed. I do not think I will become a monster because I am not one now.

I think you are right.

Lilith raised her head and bit into her wrist tearing into the veins then she placed her wrist to Zachariah's lips and said, "Drink!"

He acted like he was going to refuse but she pushed her wrist harder against his lips and ordered, "Drink!"

Zachariah drank, and he drank deeply. He could feel her blood entering him and before long he began to feel the pain in his neck receding. What little numbness had been in his fingers and toes went away. He continued to drink and scents grew stronger he could smell odors from the other room. His hearing became sharper; he could hear people talking as they passed in their cars on the other side of Juckett Park.

Then he stopped drinking and opened his eyes and looked up into the fiery eyes of Lilith. As he did so his hands went to her hips and he stroked her sides.

She said, "So how is my little slave."

"I am fine, Lilith."

Lilith turned her head and looked up at the clock. Then she looked back down to Zachariah and said, "Your Melanie is gone forever now, you old fool. I needed one hour past the moment of her birth and it is now ten past one. That is more than enough time.

"Now since you were so disappointed that I was not a virgin when we married the first time, let me give you your Melanie's virginity as I rape my slave." She reached down and grabbed his cock with her hand guiding it to her pussy and then with one thrust forced herself onto him.

She screamed out as his cock pierced the hymen and then smiled down at him saying, "I had no idea that the pain she would feel would be so sweet. Too bad she is not here to feel it."

She began to move up and down upon him and then suddenly she stopped. Her eyes got big and she looked down at Zachariah, "What is this? I can feel her?"

His hands gripped her hips and pushed them down with a sudden thrust, holding her onto him. "Melanie was not born in this time zone Lilith. She did not turn eighteen until one AM here. So you still had fifty minutes to go before you were safe."

Lilith's eyes grew wild and she said, "But you should still have been in my control you should have warned your Mistress."

"You made a huge mistake Lilith. You placed me upon this table and this table is the center of my magic. You have no control over me here. I was never your slave!"

Papa I am here, I can control the sex part. Her sexual drive was so strong I can manipulate it while she is fighting for control. Make love to me Papa. That is the focus, the more I can focus on that the stronger I can become and I can push her out of my body. Papa, make love to your Melanie.

Lilith screamed as Zachariah's thrusts became more rapid and Melanie gained more control. The fire in her eyes began to fade, then it reignited as Lilith fought back, "No! Let me share! Let me stay!"

"That is what you originally told me was your plan but you lied. There is no trusting you Lilith. We cannot let you stay. If we did the moment Melanie was ill or weak you would find a way to try to regain control. I will not have that. I love Melanie with all that I am and you will not have her." With that Zachariah thrust again, hard and furious, both his love for Melanie as he could see her returning and his hatred for Lilith driving him on.

The fire in Melanie's eyes faded to be replaced with the fire of passion as she fell forward and hung onto him. A red mist began to rise out of Melanie's pores and the screams of fury became moans as Melanie drove herself onto Papa and smiled. "Now I am truly yours Papa, since we are really here, let's finish making love and forget Lilith for she is no more."

Zachariah looked up and watched as the mist turned to particles of gray dust and dropped to the ground then he looked at the woman he loved.

Suddenly he saw Melanie's face turn to a pout as she looked down, "Papa?"

"Melanie, precious, tomorrow we will go see what it takes to get married as fast as we can. Tonight we had no choice it was to drive Lilith out, but let us wait and make love on a night when we can have none of this nightmare in our minds."

She smiled at him and wrapped her arms around him, "Then for just the moment stay inside me, I had no idea it would be such a wonderful feeling.

"Yet, Papa, I am glad you want to wait too."

They lay for a few minutes together and then Zachariah picked her up and carried her upstairs to his bed and laid her down. He lay down beside her and snuggled up close. Though they were both naked he knew it was right.

He had only slept for an hour before he awoke. Carefully so that he did not wake her he slid out of the bed. There was much on his mind and much he had to do. The room downstairs had particles of Lilith in it, and though they may be ashen he did not feel comfortable with them lying about. He needed to scrub the room down.

He went back to the work room and as he was cleaning he began to wash the table and when water hit Melanie's virginal blood the table shone brightly and an image entered his mind and he drew the design. He already knew it would be either him or Melanie that would be the accidental volunteer for the commission of the final amount of the blood for the item he drew was a baby's rattle.

Chapter Two

The morning after the magic had turned Zachariah young again the Harbinger had visited the shop one more time. As the shadow had passed Melanie had felt his presence. For a moment she was terrified but this time it was good news. This was not the news of a commission.

Together they had gone to the roof where they had found a large wooden chest wrapped in red cloth. Carefully they had carried it downstairs and when Zachariah had opened it Melanie was amazed that inside were all the legal documents he would need to prove he was Thomas Zachariah, born on October 31st in 1986. There was even a driver's license, a birth certificate, and a will from Jacob Zachariah, the name he had used before the magic had made him young.

"Papa, but what will happen if they try to trace any of these things. Surely this hospital won't have records of you being born there."

"Actually, not only will they have records, but if it is one of those hospitals that videotaped the births, as some began to in the 80's, they will have a video record of me there all the way through until I was released.

"There will even be school records at a local school," he said as he pulled out aged report cards from the school he had supposedly attended. "The only problem is I have to do a lot of studying of this material just in case someone from that school ever comes by but as you see it was in Florida. So it is not likely I will run into anyone that will remember me."

As soon as they were finished going through the chest they went arm in arm to the county clerk of Washington County to see what they needed to do to apply for a marriage certificate.

As they walked out of the building they both looked at each other and without a word they knew that each was thinking the same thing. The blood test, that might pose a problem, but as they were hugging one another with their hearts heavy a cloud passed over their heads and as they looked up their fears were abetted.

They took their time walking back to the shop. It was a bright and sunny day. The temperature was warm for November and a cool breeze caressed them. For the first time in over thirty-five centuries, Zachariah did not have to worry about what Lilith would do. He could enjoy being with someone that truly loved him.

It had also been a long time since he had been young. Even though he had felt young within the shop, outside of it he suffered the frailties of his apparent age. For over sixty years he had suffered the pains of arthritis every time he had stepped out the doors of the shop. This was his first chance in over sixty years to enjoy a walk without the pain.

As they neared the shop Melanie tried to pull him into Juckett Park so they could enjoy the beauty of the fountain before they covered it up for the winter. However, he noticed that there was someone waiting outside the door to the shop and he had never turned away a customer. He promised that after the store closed they would go visit the fountain.

Together they walked toward the shop. Then Melanie grew quiet and began to try to slink behind him.

"There you are," Rebecca Morgan's voice penetrated him like daggers of ice seeking to claim the heart of their intended victim, Melanie. The smile that slowly crept across her face died before it reached her eyes. Zachariah felt a bitter chill gripping his soul as the hatred of this woman for the daughter she had adopted was far more apparent now than he had thought possible. When he had first met her he had thought it was only indifference towards the girl, but now he could see that Mrs. Morgan resented Melanie's very existence in her life.

The look within her eyes was glacial ice as it froze upon Melanie and she continued her cold bitter speech, "The housekeeper has been after me to call the police about you missing but I told her you would be fine. I see I was right." Then she turned to Zachariah and asked, "Is Mr. Zachariah about?"

Zachariah turned and looked her in the eyes, "My uncle has taken ill. I am here to attend to the shop. You must be Mrs. Morgan. He informed me you would be coming by to take care of some business."

"That is right." As Zachariah held the door open for her she passed into the shop. She did not say another word to Melanie or even bother to ask how she was. Zachariah could feel his anger growing. He had cared for Melanie the first time she had visited, but the love he felt for her now was much stronger and the apathy this woman showed toward her was unforgivable.

Mrs. Morgan walked to the counter and opened her purse. "I have brought a cashier's check payable to *The Crimson Z* for the $15,000. I hope that that is sufficient."

Zachariah looked at her, as Melanie stood behind him. He could feel the waves of pain coming off of Melanie as she tried not to cry. In response to Mrs. Morgan he replied, "That will be fine, my uncle has an account set up at the bank in Glens Falls."

"Then we are all settled." Her hand raised and she offered it in the same manner she had offered it before but something in him just would not let him accept it.

He hated to lie, but this time he felt justified, "My faith prohibits me from touching the hand of a married woman. I am sorry."

She nodded and then looked around him and said to Melanie, "I take it you will not be coming home. I will have Margaret bring your things here in March when everything has settled after the holidays and the children's birthdays. I will give her and her husband time to visit you once a month if they want to. Of course, you are welcome to come and get anything you need before then."

Then she turned and left. Zachariah was fuming as he watched her leave. There had not been a single kind word. It had all been business. He turned and took Melanie in his arms and held her while she cried.

***

It was nearly a month and a half before they got the certificate from the county and the earliest date they could get with the Justice of the Peace was February 1st, two months to the day from the events with Lilith.

On the morning that Melanie and Zachariah were going to be married they were in the ritual room for Zachariah had wanted to do something special at the stone. He had them strip naked for the ritual he wanted to do but she asked him to pause before the ritual.

"Papa, I have not seen you naked since the day we almost lost each other. I remember when I first saw you young again how amazed I was but it was so fouled with what Lilith was doing that I could not enjoy the moment and even over these two months each time I look at you I still see both my old Papa, and the new Papa in you.

"This is the first time I am getting to look upon you as the young man

I am about to marry. I want to look upon you fully." She looked deep into his eyes and her fingers drifted to the side of his face. Softly she caressed his cheek and then slid her fingers into the locks of his black curls. His hair was long, past his shoulders. He had tried to cut it but it grew back to its full length in a matter of seconds. Melanie was glad. She liked the way he looked with his long, wavy black hair cascading down between his shoulder blades.

She stood on her tiptoes and kissed his lips gently then lowered herself. Her pert breasts rubbing against the forest of hair on his chest sent a shiver coursing through her that was unexpected. She still was not used to the sensual reactions of her body but she knew that every time she looked at him she could feel the moisture between her legs and the barrel of her vagina craving to have him within her again. She felt that craving building within her while she looked at him. She could feel herself beginning to turn red as she was certain he would notice her arousal.

She tried to ignore that as she looked at the rest of him. The muscles of his chest and the muscles of his abdomen enticed her to run her hands over them. The man she loved was as beautiful as she remembered the day she had first seen him young but now she was able to see more of him.

She walked behind him as he stood still for her to examine and she took a deep breath as she saw the muscles of his thighs and his ass merge as remarkably as any sculptor could have imagined. Then she walked in front of him again and let her eyes drift to the one part she had been avoiding. His manhood, his penis, his cock. Her hands went to her face as she blushed. It was rock hard as it protruded from the nest of black hair that surrounded it. She had no way of knowing how to compare its size for it was the only one she had ever seen but to her it was perfect. She let her hand wrap around it and then her other hand as well and the tip still extended beyond them.

She could hear him breathing hard and she looked up into his face and he looked down at her and said, "Are you done making me as uncomfortable as you can now?"

Melanie laughed as she let go of his cock and wrapped her arms around him. She could feel his cock pressing into her belly and knew if she were to raise only a little bit, but she had promised not until they were married. "Yes, Papa, I just had to see you, all of you.

"You are so beautiful. I could never have imagined you this way.

"Thank you."

He looked at her and kissed her lips then said, "Ummm, now if you will step back before we both get into trouble. I want us to do something that is very important to me."

He grabbed the chair and helped her climb onto the chair and then the stone, then together they knelt and prayed. As they were standing it was as one that they both slipped and both cut one of their feet upon the carving of the stone.

Even though no water had been added the magic of the stone began and the tree formed. Zachariah had never been within the gold before and Melanie had never seen it before. She was in awe but what truly amazed them both is that it was her hands first that reached toward the gold fibers. Together they began to weave and fashion the rattle that Zachariah had designed. What would have taken him three hours to do alone only took them one together.

Melanie looked at the rattle and then Zachariah and said to her soon to be husband, "Zachariah, I have been thinking."

He responded, "I know you have, and I know about what."

"You do?"

"Yes, the ring said we two were to be one, but how can we be one if you are human and I am a vampire?" He smiled at her.

She looked up at him, "You look human, you feel human, you are able to move about and go everywhere a human can. You have none of the weaknesses of a vampire and yet all the strengths. The ring said we would breathe our last breath together. I do not want to shorten your life by being human if you can live longer."

"Precious, I have lived so long already. Living a short life would be a blessing." She smiled at him and hugged him tight.

"Then it does not matter that you would die when I would in my human time."

"No, that does not matter to me."

She reached up and kissed him, "I love you, Papa."

"I love you too, Precious, but there is something that does matter to me."

Her eyes got wide with worry, "What Papa?

"I do not want you growing old when I will not for one, and for two, I may have lived a long time but your life as a human is short and I want to be with you for a lot longer than those few years would provide."

Melanie jumped up and wrapped her arms around his neck and kissed him deeply.

Slowly after the kiss he leaned down and bit her neck. He already knew that once she was bitten his teeth would inject a small amount of fluid into the wound and all the pain would vanish. It would also cause her to become euphoric. This was why many vampires of legend were able to keep humans as minions. The minions became addicted to the venom of the vampire.

He did not have to drain her near to death as Lilith had done to him, just to a point that she wavered on the edge of consciousness. Then he bit into his own wrist and placed his wrist against her lips and she began to drink. She looked up into his eyes as she did so. The love in her eyes was powerful, and he could feel her love for him as she drank his blood.

Melanie dropped his wrist and wrapped her arms around his neck. Then she kissed him deeply, passionately, his blood was upon her tongue and hers was upon his and together they held each other as her transformation completed. Then she whispered to him, "Papa, is it just me, or do all vampires feel so sensual? I feel like my loins are on fire and I want you inside me now!"

"No, I do not think it is just you. I have had a stronger sexual hunger since Lilith turned me, and she was always very sensual, much more so than any other woman I had ever heard about. Even over time when men would discuss their lovers or wives with me none would compare with the hunger Lilith had. So I think that the sensual hunger is part of being a vampire."

Melanie looked up at the clock and the image of Zachariah naked before her returned to her mind. She remembered her hands wrapped around his penis, and the feel of it, and how her breasts had felt as they had slid down the curls of hair on his chest. She wondered how close he had been. Suddenly she needed to know what it felt like to have him cum within her. It was not a craving, it was an urgency. There was no time to waste. She looked at Zachariah and said, "Our appointment with the Justice of the Peace is in an hour. Do you think if we got there early and offered him an extra bonus if he was not busy that he would do our wedding early?"

He smiled at her, "We can try."

She grabbed his hand and pulled him toward the door saying, "Then what are we standing here for."

Zachariah asked, "Your dress?"

"I am getting married in front of a Justice of the Peace. You are the only one that I care about. They are providing the witnesses. I don't want to take the time to put on that dress." She turned and pulled on him with both hands and said, "Please, come on, let's go. I am dying here."

Zachariah laughed. "Okay, but I have been going through this for two months you could wait an hour."

She got behind him and pushed him out the door, "No, I can't."

In five minutes they were outside the doors to the Justice of the Peace's office and Melanie was trying to get the court recorder to speak to the Justice and see if he would take them early.

"He normally does not move his appointments up. Besides it is his lunch time."

Suddenly Melanie's voice got low and her eyes glowed bright blue and she said, "Tell him I would like to be married earlier, please."

The recorder turned and walked into the Justice's chambers and told him what Melanie had said. While she was doing that Zachariah said, "Melanie, you need to be careful about using your powers."

Melanie gasped and looked at him startled, "Did I? I did not mean too." Then she danced and squirmed, "It is just, I need you, Papa."

Zachariah laughed, "I guess under the circumstances it can be overlooked this time."

The door to the Justice's chambers opened and the recorder said that he would see them. Five minutes later they were married and Melanie was practically running and dragging her new husband back to their home. She opened the door to the shop and as soon as he was inside locked it behind them and then pulled the curtains down and jumped into his arms. Her kisses were deep and passionate and wild.

Her hands frantically raced from one button to the next then she gave up and just pulled the two sides of the shirt and listened to the machine gun like pops as the buttons snapped off the shirt and flew across the room with such force they ricocheted off the walls. Every kiss, every move, she pushed Zach backwards towards the steps to their bedroom. She paused at the stairs only long enough to remove her own clothing and toss it aside. Then she undid his belt and with one yank sent it across the shop.

When at last she had divested him of his clothing she darted past him and smiled then ran up the stairs with him following close behind her. With one leap from the door she landed on the bed and turned to face him as he placed a hand on each side of the door frame. Zachariah was looking at the most beautiful woman he had ever seen. Even Lilith did not compare, for the woman before him was not only a beauty but her heart and soul were beyond compare too.

She raised one hand and with a single finger beckoned him to come to her. For a brief moment he had a flashback to a time thousands of years before, but then he shook his head for that woman never loved him. The woman lying on his bed loved him. He let go of the door frame and walked to her. Slowly he climbed between her thighs kissing her belly then her breasts.

Melanie threw back her head and moaned when his lips touched her belly, but when they touched her breasts at first she giggled but as his lips encircled her nipples she gasped and then a deep moan began in her belly and resonated within her.

Zachariah kissed along her neck and then to her lips, then down to the other side of her neck and as the head of his cock touched the lips of her pussy he took his cock in his hand and slid it up and down parting her lips and moistening the tip. He could feel her sudden intake of air then he did the one thing that was a unique part of the courtship of a vampire. At the exact moment that his cock penetrated and plunged deep into her moist heat he also plunged his teeth into her neck.

Melanie screamed and was on her first wave of orgasmic bliss before he even began his first full stroke.

The Wait
The Epilogue
Robert Cloud

It began when Zachariah was stumbling out of his shop after carving the stone. The prophetess had sat her bag back down inside the shop. She had intended to return even before telling anyone she was going to stay and sleep there for the time Zachariah healed. Then when she returned that night and for the next day there had been no prophetess but instead a winged man of white with eyes of solid black.

For many long hours he tried to drill a hole into the top of the stone but nothing he did worked. He broke carving tool after tool. Then he decided to try a different strategy. He found the deepest spot in the carving and tried to drill there. It was inside the outer ring at what would be the base of the tree, directly beneath where the one tap root came down and touched the ring. There he found a weak spot in the stone. The drill he used was very small, no bigger around than a thick piece of hay, yet it took him almost a full day to drill the two inch deep hole he wanted there.

When the hole was complete, he took from the bag a small clay jar. In the jar was blood he had taken from Lilith when she had been in her monstrous form. Slowly he poured that into the hole.

With a wave of his hand the stone sealed as if it had never been drilled.

Then he turned back into the prophetess and finished the deception.

***

When Zachariah had first gazed into the mirror that Lilith had held when she took her life he had seen a red mist form. In that instant a spell had been cast upon him. He had not seen the red mist swirling about behind him and then entering his pores as it settled into him, sealing a fate that he knew nothing about. Neither the dark-souled angel nor Lilith had known the true heart of Zachariah when the spell was cast. They had no idea it would take over three thousand years before the spell would be unleashed.

***

When Zachariah and Melanie made love for the first time the fate which had been sealed when the spell was cast was loosed and the guardian seal was broken. If he had not been a man of a good heart and had been the type to take another wife or to sleep with women the seal would have been broken long before and Lilith would not have had to wait for The One.

However, since he was such a good man, and had not done those things that had been expected of him something else had happened. Something neither Lilith nor Shaitan had expected.

The seal broke and the stone covering over the blood dissolved.

Slowly from the hole a slug-like creature of blood oozed out and onto the table. It left a thin trail of moisture behind that evaporated quickly hiding all evidence it had ever existed.

The slug slithered off the table and headed for the one piece of jewelry that Zachariah knew nothing about. There was a reason he could not remember it. He had not made it. Lilith had, and the innocent blood she offered was not by accident, but by sacrifice.

She had not wanted to make a ring. She had wanted a weapon. However, the magic that was summoned through the table whether good or evil ran its own course, not the course of the one using the table as their focus.

The thing continued to slither its path across the floor as the part that was its mind recalled the night of the jewelry's making.

***

It was 1891 and they had just come to America from London. On one of her recent nights of freedom she had gone to torment a particular man. She was pleased that Zachariah had taken her advice and come to the States for the man had said he was going to go there as well.

She had paid regular visits to Mr. George Chapman and only drank small amounts of blood from him. She had found his mind was fertile with thoughts of murder and it was easy to manipulate him. It was far more fun to guide him in the commission of one of his gruesome murders and then drink from the corpse than to do it all on her own.

In London they had caused quite a stir, and he'd had to slow down the number of murders or he would have been caught. They were still searching for him as Jack the Ripper but he had killed far more than the five women they had attributed to him.

In April of 1891 she paid him another visit and together they found a prostitute by the name of Carrie Brown. Carrie was not alone that night though. She was watching the infant child of another prostitute who was walking the streets. While Chapman had his fun, Lilith looked upon the child, a boy. She flew closer to the child and stared into its eyes. There in those innocent eyes she saw her reflection, the red haze of ghostly mist and the child just giggled as she floated there.

Her anger grew. Why was she condemned to be a wraith that could never walk again? Why did she have to wait until The One came when even then she would be at the mercy of Zachariah?

In silence her vaporous mouth opened to scream but not even a hushed whisper escaped from its depths. There had to be a way to get the upper hand on Zachariah, and instantly the idea occurred to her. She needed a weapon. One made from the table to be his undoing, but to do that she needed innocent blood. Once more her eyes looked upon the child. Her arms solidified as they wrapped beneath the child and she carried him away.

Yes, the table needed innocent blood, so she would give it innocent blood. Lots of it. Then she would have a weapon and she'd be able to rid herself of Zachariah once The One was found.

She carried the infant back to the table and sacrificed him upon the stone. Then she did not wait for an idea to hit her. She seeped down and mixed herself with the blood upon the table for she was blood.

A golden image of the tree leapt off the table. It was a three dimensional tubular representation of the image. She reformed solid against her will. Her hands were pulled to the gold strands. Immediately she began weaving the threads together as she had watched Zachariah do so many times from the mirror.

When she was done she had hoped there would be a knife in her hands but instead there was a ring. A ring! She was furious. She slipped it on her finger and flew out the door in a solid form. She found Chapman on the streets and did not even talk to him. Instead she pulled him into an alley and drained his Life. There would be no more Jack the Ripper, but she did not care. What goddamned use was a ring to her?

She killed six more men that night in her fury.

As she neared the shop she wondered how she would explain her solid form to Zachariah. However it was not something she would have to worry about for when she touched the door of the shop she began to return to her mist form. She had to force herself to remain solid enough to place the ring within the cabinet. She was not worried about Zachariah discovering it. She knew that the magic often caused him to forget when a piece was made and he would assume that that was the case with the ring. She returned to the table and drank the fluids of the child. Then she wiped the dust away. The bones she placed in the sewers behind their shop.

***

The fury burned within her so fiercely that it threatened to evaporate what little moisture held her fragile form together. For more than three thousand years she had waited to have her freedom and her revenge but instead of being in the body that was supposed to be hers she was trapped in the near shapeless, slimy form of a slug. Lilith's mind could sense Zachariah and Melanie above her and the love that they were sharing infuriated her even more. Up the cabinet the slug climbed and into the hiding place crafted within the ring where she began the wait for an unsuspecting customer to come and carry her off.

The end

Author's Notes

Blood Ritual of the Crimson Z

When we began to discuss putting together this anthology we ran through a few ideas but one day, in my mind's eye, I saw an old man sitting at a mystical shape. Magic controlled his fingers as he wove fibers of gold into a piece of jewelry. Zachariah was born in my mind. I knew then that whether the group accepted him as a key figure in the anthology or not I would write his story.

I did not have to worry though, the others loved the idea and the anthology was born. Originally, the concept was to be small interludes and a short story about Zachariah. However, as I worked on the story, Zachariah, Melanie and Lilith took over and became a major storyline.

Though I had known what I wanted to do with Lilith, the story of Melanie was still a little up in the air. Yet, the more I wrote, the more the story took over. There were times it wrote itself, and I was only the instrument that it passed through. The characters took on life.

I am looking forward to working on the sequel. There is still so much to tell of the stories of Zachariah, Melanie, Lilith and many more characters that have not even been introduced yet, and many more tales of the jewelry that carries the mark of *The Crimson Z*.

Robert Cloud

Love of a Pendant Heart

Some of you may know about problems on a certain computer server and the deletion of the "user" rooms. Before all of this happened, I came across a few rooms devoted to furries.

For those of you who don't know what furries are, think "Jessica Rabbit." Furries are a combination of human and an animal. In these rooms I met a variety of characters and some of them led to the stories for *The Crimson Z.* I say stories, because my story in the anthology is really two stories woven into one. Adrian and Crys and their tale of love found, lost, and reclaimed is one story. The love that Cara and Zaven find is another very different love story about the ability of true love to overcome many differences.

Though the concepts of anthro-foxes and so on might be foreign to you, remember the the fairy tales of your youth and feel young again as you read, but not TOO young, because the romances depicted are not quite appropriate for youth!

Love of a Pendant Heart is a celebration of the infinite diversities of life and a celebration of the fact that just because people or creatures are different doesn't mean they can't find love. There are infinite diversities and the way they combine to create new ones is a wonder to behold. Enjoy these stories and consider just how different we all are and embrace those differences.

Lee Rush

The Anniversary

I regard myself firstly as an artist. I have been producing fine artwork and illustrations for more than twenty years. I first became involved with Black Velvet Seductions last year, when I was asked to do the cover illustration for Robert Cloud's book *Toy's Story*. During the production of that book cover I got to know the BVS family rather well in our group discussions.

In one of the meetings I took part in, the subject of an erotic supernatural anthology which came to be known as *The Crimson Z* was discussed. I assumed and hoped I would get the commission to do the cover, which I had the great privilege of doing. In addition, I was offered the opportunity to come up with a story for the anthology. I have been an aspiring author for several years, writing for myself at first, but later with a strong desire to get into print so I leapt at the opportunity to become a published author.

We decided as a group that all the stories should be linked. Robert Cloud volunteered to write the story of the jeweler whose creations tie all the individual stories together. For my own story I wanted to go further with my writing than I had gone before.

I find the subject of Domination and submission fascinating and I wanted to show that it can exist within everyday relationships. I also wanted the supernatural element to be a suspenseful part of the story.

The outline of the story is not over complicated, but the complexity comes with the nature of a rather uneasily balanced ménage à trois within a D/s relationship. An element of the story I hope I captured is the normality of D/s as well as the love, trust and commitment.

I also wanted to explore new areas with the characters. In many romances the men are tall, dark, and handsome and the ladies are catwalk models. I wanted my heroine to be a larger lady.

Richard Savage

Incorrigible

When we started discussing *The Crimson Z* anthology, I knew it was the perfect vehicle for *Incorrigible*, the story of a spirited ghost who teaches a young woman how to savor life while they try to uncover the mystery of murderer that had been swirling around the back of my mind for some time.

Of all the stories I've written, *Incorrigible* is, and always will be, one of my favorites. Part of the reason is because it incorporates two of my favorite elements - mystery and paranormal – but, most of all, it's because the characters came alive to me, managing to evoke a wide range of emotions from a smile because of the irrepressible antics of a spirited specter, Virginia, bent on finding her murderer to heat squeezing moments over what might have been.

I have to confess there are times when I could swear Virginia is whispering ideas in my ear. So much so, that I've already started a sequel. She simply refused to pass over to the place where all 'good ghosts go' because she had one more task to complete before she can rest. Once you get to know Virginia...you'll understand how 'persuasive' she can be.

I hope that you enjoy reading this story as much as I enjoyed writing it. Happy Reading!

Abby Blythe

The Awakening

As I worked on the story of Zachariah and Lilith I became aware that the short story I had planned to do was not going to be enough because I needed to go into more depth than I had originally planned. Lilith's tale was key. Whether you take her tale as being a fabrication, another in a long string of lies she told Zachariah, or the truth of her creation, within this story world it still helps you to see the lengths to which she will go. It helps explain her treachery and deceit and why she is the way she is.

In Zachariah's tale and the rest of the Awakening I build on the character of Zachariah and show the strength of the man. His nature and the foundation of all the magic that led to the current situation that plagues him and his new found love.

Robert Cloud

www.ingramcontent.com/pod-product-compliance
Lightning Source LLC
Chambersburg PA
CBHW020245030726
47499CB00001B/60